Praise for
The Penguin Book of Women's Humor,
edited by Regina Barreca:

"Not just humor, of course, but all the wit and wisdom of
the female universe. . . ."   —Fay Weldon

"Its 700 or so delicious pages are chock-full of treasures
wicked, witty, and wonderful."   —*Library Journal*

"Full of fast-talking, wisecracking, brilliantly satirical
women."   —*London Daily Mail*

REGINA BARRECA, professor of English at the University of Connecticut, edited *The Penguin Book of Women's
Humor* and wrote *They Used to Call Me Snow White . . .
But I Drifted, Perfect Husbands (& Other Fairy Tales),*
and *Sweet Revenge: The Wicked Delights of Getting
Even.* She writes for the *Chicago Tribune, The Hartford
Courant, New York Times, Cosmopolitan, Ms.* and other
publications, and has appeared, often as a repeat guest,
on *20/20, 48 Hours,* and *The Today Show.* She can be
reached via: www.ginabarreca.com

THE SIGNET BOOK OF
AMERICAN HUMOR

Edited by
Regina Barreca

A SIGNET CLASSIC BOOK

SIGNET CLASSIC
Published by New American Library, a division of
Penguin Putnam Inc., 375 Hudson Street,
New York, New York 10014, U.S.A.
Penguin Books Ltd, 27 Wrights Lane,
London W8 5TZ, England
Penguin Books Australia Ltd,
Ringwood, Victoria, Australia
Penguin Books Canada Ltd, 10 Alcorn Avenue,
Toronto, Ontario, Canada M4V 3B2
Penguin Books (N.Z.) Ltd, 182–190 Wairau Road,
Auckland 10, New Zealand

Penguin Books Ltd, Registered Offices:
Harmondsworth, Middlesex, England

First published by Signet Classic, an imprint of New American Library,
a division of Penguin Putnam Inc.

First Printing, December 1999
10 9 8 7 6 5 4 3 2 1

*This book is dedicated to
my stepsons and coconspirators,
Timothy Meyer and Matthew Meyer.*

Acknowledgments

Margaret Mitchell and Genevieve Brassard, Ph.D. candidates at The University of Connecticut, helped to research, read, choose, copy, clip, cut, paste, proof, and copyedit nearly everything in this volume. There were days we all sat on the floor of my office in Arjona, surrounded by piles of pages and plates of Indian food, wondering how this mayhem would transform itself into an actual book. Without them, those pages would have remained on the floor. Margaret's intensely intelligent commentary and brilliant eye for critical nuance and detail kept the integrity of the volume from slipping; I could not have done the work without her advice, support, and commitment. Genevieve's superb talent for finding the perfect solution to complex problems, coupled with her sharp, smart, and encouraging spirit, made every difficult task easier and every moment more fun.

The University of Connecticut Library staff was terrific—especially those reliable and patient folks at interlibrary loan who managed to locate some works we had despaired of ever finding. I owe them a great debt. I am also grateful to The Research Foundation at UConn.

Don Hymans at Signet assumed a formidable task when he was assigned, as a new editor, to this very much in-progress work. He worked hard to make everything come together and was able to fix a number of problems before they turned from funny to miserable. Kristine Puopolo, formerly of Penguin, also provided key moments of support and key pieces of information.

I thank the usual suspects: Michael Meyer (who gave good advice, even when I didn't want to hear it), my brother

Hugo Barreca (who introduced me to many of these works when I was a kid), my father, my stepsons, Matthew and Tim, my friends Nancy Lager and Tim Taylor, Pam Katz, Bonnie Januszewski-Ytuarte, John Glavin, Lee Jacobus, Brenda Gross, and the rest of the gang. And to the writers who permitted their works to grace these pages, I owe my sincerest gratitude.

Contents

Contents

Introduction

❦

Duty Free: American Humor Bends, Breaks, and Waives the Rules

"It's always fun until someone puts an eye out," as Mother always said, and goodness only knows what she was talking about.

Yet that line has come to form the center of my theory about American humor: it's fun because it's dangerous. Humor is gratifying in direct proportion to its rebelliousness. It is at its best after someone puts out an eye, or loses the collective "I," or finds it, or whatever. This is about humor in the United States of America, friends; you'll need to come outside, away from the light and the protection of your fancy rules and regulations, sense of duty or obligation, to be able to play.

The best American humor isn't about jokes, it's about stories. It's about our vision of life, loss, refusal, and recovery. It's not about two guys walking into a bar where there's a twelve-inch pianist or a talking dog, and it isn't about memorizing limericks. (You won't find the word *Nantucket* in this tidy volume, not even once.) What you will discover within these pages is humor that remains funny fifteen minutes or a hundred years after its debut, material that's slightly dangerous and more than slightly smart.

Excessive, playful, blasphemous, insurgent, and fiercely courageous, the writers presented here are drawn from a cross section of the population with one crucial thing in common: these writers found humor to be the shortest and most electric line between two—or more—points. They set about connecting the wires so the rest of us could hear the noise inside their heads. To them, nothing is sacred. Nothing scares them. The only thing they have to fear, perhaps, is the grim, tight-lipped, earnest specter of humorlessness itself.

All great humor, regardless of country of origin, is about risk and privilege, but this volume is particularly American in nature for several reasons. What becomes clear from a close reading of a couple of hundred years' worth of witty observations is that pretensions and affectation, whether homegrown or imported, are the American humorist's favorite fodder.

The contributors in this collection do not run away from what bothers them. Instead they run toward it—and trip over it. Some do a pratfall, some a subtle stumble, some an apoplectic version of St. Vitus's dance, some a soft-shoe, but none—and this is the important part—remain on their knees.

And the reader's role in this spectacle? We laugh while we watch their antics. We stare, enthralled, during which time they pull the comfortable rug out from under us. This is their job. If you start out being contented while reading humor, you'll end up fidgeting; if you start out restless, however, you'll be reassured when you notice what sprightly company you're in. Anybody with sense is relentless; anybody with a mind is very nearly always out of it. If most of the humor in this volume doesn't bother you, if it doesn't disturb you just a little bit, you're missing the point and ducking the very real punch in the punchline. Nothing bothers an American humorist more than seeing people comfortable when they should be uncomfortable.

Undercutting the systematic misuse of institutionalized power, these writers filter the anarchic and the subversive through the comic. The cultural critique offered by the humorist is directed at those above her, at the ones running the show, the ones with bells, whistles, and whips at their command.

The Triumph of the Unofficial

James Kincaid, Aerol Arnold Professor of Literature at USC and author of *Annoying the Victorians*, declares in his essay "Who Is Relieved by the Idea of Comic Relief?" that we are sometimes tempted to dismiss comedy as unimportant because of the "most smothering of political conservatisms" urging us to see comedy as silly and trivial. We need to understand, he suggests, the way "official" culture frames comedy by applying to its structure and language a weary vocabulary of denigration. "[B]y coupling tragedy with the sublime . . . and aligning comedy with the mundane, the quotidian, and the material, we manage to muffle, even to erase, the most powerful narratives of illumination and liberation we have . . . With comedy, nothing is sacrificed, nothing is lost; the discoordinate and the discontinuous are especially welcome."

Historians and critics of American humor and culture see this embrace of the defiant and anarchic as a particularly defining characteristic. American humor began, when the country was newer, as a defiant nose-thumbing to the affectations and pretensions of those who stayed across the Atlantic, especially those supercilious creatures who made a career of sniffing in derision at the upstarts. Europeans, especially the English, who visited and learned about America just so they could treat it with a more knowledgeable sense of contempt when they returned to the abnormally high ground they called home, were often the target of early humorists.

In her persuasive essay "What Is Humor? Why American Humor?" Vanderbilt University Professor Nancy A. Walker makes the argument that "America in its early years was not so much described as it was invented. The habit of invention, closely tied to the habit of exaggeration, laid the groundwork for American humor. Long before the nineteenth century, Americans were known for their boastfulness and for their fondness for disguises. Aware of their own process of transformation from citizens of other countries to residents of a new land, settlers engaged in self-invention, and often tested out versions of a new reality on those new to the continent." She also argues that "American humor seemed to originate in . . . [the] story of the individual at odds with the rules of 'official' society—whether the Yankee peddler making his way by his wits . . . or the frontiersman spinning tales of his encounters with the wilderness. . . ."

One of the striking things about American humor is its focus on an important belief about national identity: nobody was born with the right to operate this country. Somebody has to run the joint, true, but the privilege should not be taken too seriously. Yes, there must be a boss, or a teacher, or a senator, or a minister, just as somebody has to be the hooker, or the bartender, or the thug, or the street cleaner. So you end up playing one position instead of another; so what? The particularly distinctive characteristic of American humor emphasizes that the luck of the draw doesn't make you better or worse than others around you. If you think you're better, you're a self-righteous, self-deluded boor; if you think you're worse, you're a self-righteous, self-pitying chump.

The only way to win, the humorists show us, is to bet on this: we're all in it together. While we might disagree about what "it" is, or who "we" are, the maxim nevertheless holds true. In fact, the business of comedy is to satirize the pedantic and sphincter-tightening impulse to over-define, separate, and factionalize. The American comic writer will show us that even at those moments when we're feeling desperately, despairingly alone, we're kidding ourselves if only we could see it; walk outside, and you'll inevitably meet forty million other desperately alienated outsiders, all of whom are pretty much chanting exactly the same ode of dejection.

The comic impulse at work, as so many of those who have written about it declare, brings us to the unavoidable conclusion that we are more alike than we are different. It doesn't much matter that we might not want to regard ourselves as inhabiting the same category as those we label yahoos and shnooks. Narrow it down to a pattern of national traits, however, and we see that we are formed by the same culture. (This makes most of us gulp in trepidation.) This is true even for those who believe that American culture has had an "impact" on their lives in much the same way, for example, as a dog can have an "impact" on a tree. Yet despite the fact that culture seems occasionally to want to separate us out, pair us off like socks or collect us together like refuse for recycling, we're still in it together—and up to our eyeballs in it.

You Have a Problem with That?

One of the things we're all in it against, it becomes clear, is the bully. The figure of the bully cuts through American humor like a switchblade through cloth. What are the defining features of the bully? Bullies know they are right and insist on finding ways to make everyone else agree with their judgment. The bully doesn't have to be a belching, hirsute guy who traded in wit for weapons (although I wouldn't rule him out). The bully can also be an Iron Maiden of a second-grade teacher whose unstoppable voice scratches a hatred of penmanship into the soul.

Bullies persuade by pulling one up by the scruff of the neck, literally and/or metaphorically. They try to force others to dance their dance. They are the ones who preach the one-right-way-to-do-it creed, the everything-in-its-place litany, and the everyone-has-to-play-according-to-the-rules waltz. Bullies are masters and mistresses of obligation, responsibility, and duty, all of which they gleefully demand others fulfill accompanied by as much sycophantic wriggling—and as little pleasure—as possible. Although they seem so inhuman that at times we fully expect them to drop down on all fours, bullies are often in positions of responsibility. Power makes them drool with delight; humor is one of the few things that makes them cringe. This is one of the reasons humor is as important as it is in American culture.

Writers choose, of course, their own trademark bullies. This is when some members of the audience take a ringside seat while others duke it out. For example, male writers often focus on their wives, mothers, and girlfriends as bullies; the image of the domineering female (wielding frying pan, broom, or self-sacrifice as her weapons) grabbed hold of American humor's entrails from its infancy.

Naturally, female writers have often chosen their husbands, lovers, sons, as objects of witty whittling down. But they also direct their satiric gaze on male bosses, male government officials, male health-care providers, male religious leaders, male fashion designers—you can see that one is tempted to continue—as bullies, happily and easily coupling private and public bullying in one easy-to-open gender-biased package. Given the dearth of female bosses, government officials, etc., men have had to turn to their own kind for the purposes of humor.

This gender face-off pales in comparison with humor written by men and women of color, who have always been able to see the bully of American racial inequality without needing any special lens. Aware that humor is one of the most effective ways to trick a fool into a display of his own pitiful ignorance, craven viciousness, and corruption, the American humor writer of color insists that the bully unknowingly flaunts his own moral damnation.

And humor emerges from a variety of angles, sharpshooting from a variety of perspectives. Writers from the southern states see their New England counterparts as hilariously rigid, for example, while Northern writers construct their vision of the South with sly disingenuousness. Gay and lesbian writers often identify the bully by literalizing the definition of the "straight man" in their comedy. Liberals tease Conservatives; Conservatives mock Liberals. Cat-fanciers snicker at dog-walkers.

Although the targets appear unconnected, they remind us of other battles, fought over different turf but employing similar methods, ammunition, and aims. It turns out that superficially disparate struggles overlap if you see them from the slanted angle of the humorist; a potential battlefield of intellect and emotion is made into a playground for a dazzling, powerful, and ultimately useful juxtaposition of ideas.

But it refuses to be heavily didactic even as it leads to illumination. As Arthur Power Dudden's 1985 essay "American Humor" asserts, "American humor doesn't follow a formula, yet it separates itself cleanly from protest writings and systematic revolutionary doctrines. It attacks society's follies and fools indiscriminately, revealing in the process those shadowy highlights and lowlights between pretensions and achievements."

Successful as a Whole . . .

"America is successful as a whole," quipped Will Rogers. "But how successful is a hole?" Maybe you had to be there to laugh out loud, but the point remains an interesting one. If the "whole"—especially in humor—is made up of a series of holes, if the comic is concocted out of those very elements omitted by other forms of discourse, then humor is about what is left out—and about who is left out.

Humor laughs out loud, makes noise, and by so doing, makes trouble about issues rarely spoken of in polite conversation. Effective humor swivels a whole bank of kleig lights toward everything we've tried to hide, everything we resist examining. True, the once-hidden, unspoken, unexamined world might look garish under humor's first violent illumination, but after a while it becomes funny, then familiar, less terrifying, and therefore less powerful.

But not less dangerous; never less dangerous.

Yes, Of Course, An Apology

Yet even the wide repertoire of wit provided by these pages won't satisfy every need. There are reasons for this and I'm going to tell you about them, so sit down. To say that this book had a modest budget is to understate the situation. Better to say the budget was so modest that it not only blushed when certain demands were made of it, it positively burst into tears as it wrung its poor little hands. Keeping in mind images of large-eyed little match girls and scrawny kittens, imagine this editor's chagrin at being told that she could not include some splendid and essential work of humor because she couldn't come up with sufficient dough to pay for the right to reprint.

Think about this editor wheedling and conniving, promising unspeakable acts in return for the favor of laying her anthologist's hands on a few funny words excerpted from the "property" held by this agent or that publisher. And then you'll no longer ask yourself why there aren't examples from some marvelous creators of humor, all of whom just happened to have published their work after 1919. I could give you a list of names and it would be practically as long as all of Dorothy Parker's virgins laid end to end.

While I won't mention names (for fear of being called in front of a grand jury), I will say that it's my belief a number of these writers would turn over in their graves, or weep in their penthouse beds, to find that they were being priced out of the humor-collection market. For example, I really wanted to include a darkhorse favorite of mine, an author whose single successful work of humor, written in the '30s, has been out of print for something like forty years. The agents for her estate who hold the rights to this piece, however, wanted literally thousands of dollars for a ten-page excerpt. This nice woman hasn't written anything new in a long, long time and so her prose is buried under newer material, almost invisible to the naked eye of the contemporary reader.

Wouldn't you think, therefore, that this woman would rather be recognized as an important figure in American humor, excerpted and properly identified, so that a new generation of readers could be so delighted by her malicious and whimsical prose that they would demand the book brought back into print? Wouldn't you imagine that she'd want the book to lead to film adaptations, posthumous awards, and a grave festooned with flowers from admirers? Don't you think she'd want those words to be read?

Not that I'm bitter.

And there are contemporary writers, cartoonists, and performers who should also be in this book, but who are kept locked up like fairy-tale heroines, unable to let their hair down so that we can have access to them except through certain expensive windows. As a woman who makes most of her living by writing, I am (and please trust me on this), the last person on planet Earth to begrudge a humorist a dime if there was a dime being offered.

But I also know that I'm genuinely thrilled when literary types—the editors of a text book, an anthology, a book of quotations, a calendar, a fortune cookie, whatever—want to take my work into their orbit, sending it out to audiences who might otherwise never have access to it. I hope they'll pay me a sort of "duty" for coming into my territory and taking a little bit of it with them, but I certainly wouldn't want them never to visit or be forced to walk out because the tariffs and fees were exorbitant.

That someone chooses to recognize your work is a privilege; if there's compensation, that's terrific, everybody wins. But when the compensation demanded by corporate handlers for a cute eight-page article is the sort of figure usually kept in escrow to pay for a small yacht or large foreign car, then compensation turns into punishment and restriction. Maybe I'm showing the one small part of myself that remains hopeful and naive, but I can't believe many authors (or creative folks of any persuasion) themselves know about or actually sanction this sort of limitation on the reach of their work.

So, basically, what I'm saying here is that if you don't find who you're looking for, it's not my fault. I knew you'd want them here, and I wanted exactly the same passage you wanted, but we're both going to have to live without them. It's sad, but even comedy is occasionally about loss. We must all be terribly brave.

Last Rights (and Wrongs)

Humor is indispensable; it is our most effective tool for insight and understanding as well as our most effective weapon against baseness and stupidity. But we need to make use of the best of it; humor does not work without our agency. Twain's Mysterious Stranger suggests as much:

> The multitude see the comic side of a thousand low-grade and trivial things—broad incongruities, mainly; absurdities, grotesqueries, evokers of the horselaugh. The ten thousand high-grade comicalities which exist in the world are sealed from their dull vision. Will a day come when the race will detect the funniness of these juvenilities and laugh at them—and by laughing at them destroy them? For your race, in its poverty, has unquestionably one really effective weapon— laughter. Power, money, persuasion, supplication, persecution—these can lift at a colossal humbug— push it a little—weaken it a little, century by century; but only laughter can blow it to rags and atoms at a blast. Against the assault of laughter nothing can stand.

American comedy embraces, at its white-hot core, cataclysmic upheavals and stupendously brave gestures of frivolity. This collection brings together under one aegis a chorus of voices that, under less auspicious circumstances, might be competing with rather than complementing one another. Its topics and issues—even the dangerous ones—

can, at the best of moments, fall from humor's bag of tricks into our ordinary hands, where they can transform our lives.

Delightedly unwilling to be discouraged by the cultural and intellectual devices preventing us from seeing ourselves as we really are, the best humor is always part revelry, part revelation. Stripping away both the mask and the fig leaf, humor refuses to genuflect before either fear or shame, and in so doing provides for its audience the possibility of redemption.

Laughter is the sound you make when you are free.

—Regina Barreca
University of Connecticut

—Works Cited

James Kincaid, "Who Is Relieved by the Idea of Comic Relief?" From a paper read at the 1991 meeting of the Modern Language Association.

Nancy A. Walker, "What Is Humor? Why American Humor?" in *What's So Funny? Humor in American Culture.* Edited by Nancy A. Walker. Scholarly Resources, 1998.

Arthur Power Dudden, "American Humor." *American Quarterly* 37, 1985.

Mark Twain, *The Mysterious Stranger.* Signet Classics, 1962.

Scott Adams (Contemporary)

꒰ஓ꒱

FROM *The Dilbert Principle*

Mandatory Self-Deprecation

I proudly include myself in the idiot category. Idiocy in the modern age isn't an all-encompassing, twenty-four-hour situation for most people. It's a condition that everybody slips into many times a day. Life is just too complicated to be smart all the time.

The other day I brought my pager to the repair center because it wouldn't work after I changed the battery. The repairman took the pager out of my hand, flipped open the battery door, turned the battery around, and handed the now functional pager back to me in one well-practiced motion. This took much of the joy out of my righteous indignation over the quality of their product. But the repairman seemed quite amused. And so did every other customer in the lobby.

On that day, in that situation, I was a complete idiot. Yet somehow I managed to operate a motor vehicle to the repair shop and back. It is a wondrous human characteristic to be able to slip into and out of idiocy many times a day without noticing the change or accidentally killing innocent bystanders in the process.

My Qualifications

Now that I've admitted that I can't replace the battery in my pager, you might wonder what makes me think I'm qualified to write this important book. I think you'll be impressed at my depth of experience and accomplishment:

1. I convinced a company to publish this book. That might not seem like much, but it's more than you did today. And it wasn't easy. I had to have lunch with people I didn't even know.

Making Them Wait

One of the most effective methods of humiliation used by managers is the practice of ignoring an underling who is in or near the manager's office while the manager pursues seemingly unimportant tasks. This sends a message that the employee has no human presence. It is similar to changing clothes in front of the family pet; the animal is watching but it couldn't possibly matter.

This tool of humiliation can be fine-tuned to any level simply by adjusting what activities are performed while the employee waits.

ACTIVITY	LEVEL OF HUMILIATION
Taking phone calls	Not so bad
Reading other things	Bad
Flossing	Very bad
Learning a foreign language	Very very bad

•

. . . a manager would never say, "I used my fork to eat a potato." A manager would say, "I utilized a multitined tool to process a starch resource." The two sentences mean almost the same thing, but the second one is obviously from a smarter person.

Running a Side Business from Your Cubicle

A cubicle is an excellent retail space, suitable for selling stuffed dolls, earrings, cosmetics, semiprecious gems, plant arrangements, household cleaning products, real estate, and vacation packages. Don't miss your opportunity to "moonlight," or as I like to call it, "fluorescentlight."

All you need is a tacky handmade sign on the outside of your cubicle that tells people you're open for business. A brochure or product sample can help lure people in.

You don't need high-quality merchandise. Let's be honest—if your co-workers were bright enough to know the difference between diamonds and monkey crap they wouldn't be working at your company. So don't waste a bunch of time on "quality." It's shelf space that matters, and you've got 180 cubic feet to play with. It's your chance to make some money while you're at work.

Theft of Office Supplies

Office supplies are an important part of your total compensation package. If God didn't want people to steal office supplies he wouldn't have given us briefcases, purses, and pockets. In fact, no major religion specifically bans the pilfering of office supplies.*

The only downside is the risk of being caught, disgraced, and imprisoned. But if you compare that to your current work situation I think you'll agree that it's not such a big deal.

*Some religious scholars will debate my interpretation. But ultimately it's a matter of faith.

The secret is to avoid getting too greedy. Office supplies are like compound interest—a little bit per day adds up over time. If you want some yellow sticky notes, don't take the whole box at once. Instead, use several sheets per day as page markers on documents that you're taking home. Later, carefully remove them and reassemble them into pads.

You can steal an unlimited amount of pens and pencils, but avoid the rookie mistake of continually asking the department secretary for the key to the supply closet. That attracts suspicion. Instead, steal supplies directly from your co-workers. Casually "borrow" their writing tools during meetings and never return them. Act naturally, and remember you can always laugh and claim it was a "reflex" if you get caught putting their stuff in your pocket.

Your co-workers will be trying to swipe your writing implements too. Defend your pens and pencils by conspicuously chewing on them during meetings. I've found that a few teeth marks are more effective than The Club in preventing theft.

If you have a home computer, say good-bye to purchasing your own diskettes. Stolen diskettes look exactly like work-related diskettes that are being taken home so you can "do a little work at night." The only practical limit on the number of diskettes you can steal is the net worth of the company you're stealing from. Your company will go broke if you steal too many diskettes. Nobody wins when that happens. That's why moderation is the key. After you have enough diskettes to back up your hard drive, and maybe shingle your house, think about cutting back.

Use Computers to Look Busy

Any time you use a computer it looks like "work" to the casual observer. You can send and receive personal e-mail, download pornography from the Internet, calculate your finances, and generally have a blast without doing anything remotely related to work. These aren't exactly the societal benefits that everybody expected from the computer revolution, but they're not bad either.

When you get caught by your boss—and you will get caught—your best defense is to claim you're teaching yourself to use the new software, thus saving valuable training dollars. You're not a loafer, you're a self-starter. Offer to show your boss what you learned. That will make your boss scurry away like a frightened salamander.*

•

The average life of an organization chart is six months. You can safely ignore any order from your boss that would take six months to complete. In other words, the environment will change before you have to do anything. You can just keep chewing leaves and scampering in the volcanic ash while new bosses come and go.

If you wait long enough, any bad idea will become extinct. And most good ideas too. So if you have time to master only one strategy, this is the one for you.

George Ade (1866–1944)

The *Fable* of *What Happened* the *Night the Men Came* to the *Women's Club*

In a Progressive Little City claiming about twice the Population that the Census Enumerators could uncover, there was a Literary Club. It was one of these Clubs guaranteed to fit you out with Culture while you wait. Two or three Matrons, who were too Heavy for Light Amusements, but not old enough to remain at Home and Knit, organized the Club. Nearly every Woman in town rushed to get in, for fear somebody would say she hadn't been Asked.

The Club used to Round Up once a week at the Homes of Members. There would be a Paper, followed by a Discussion, after which somebody would Pour.

The Organization seemed to be a Winner. One Thing the

---

*In laboratory tests, three out of four frightened salamanders were mistaken for supervisors.

Lady Clubbers were Dead Set On. They were going to have Harmony with an Upper Case H. They were out to cut a seven-foot Swath through English Literature from Beowulf to Bangs, inclusive, and no petty Jealousies or Bickerings would stand in the Way.

So while they were at the Club they would pull Kittenish Smiles at each other, and Applaud so as not to split the Gloves. Some times they would Kiss, too, but they always kept their Fingers crossed.

Of course, when they got off in Twos and Threes they would pull the little Meat-Axes out of the Reticules and hack a few Monograms, but that was to have been expected.

Everything considered, the Club was a Tremendous Go. At each Session the Lady President would announce the Subject for the next Meeting. For instance, she would say that Next Week they would take up Wyclif. Then every one would romp home to look in the Encyclopedia of Authors and find out who in the world Wyclif was. On the following Thursday they would have Wyclif down Pat, and be primed for a Discussion. They would talk about Wyclif as if he had been down to the House for Tea every evening that Week.

After the Club had been running for Six Months it was beginning to be Strong on Quotations and Dates. The Members knew that Mrs. Browning was the wife of Mr. Browning, that Milton had Trouble with his Eyes, and that Lord Byron wasn't all that he should have been, to say the Least. They began to feel their Intellectual Oats. In the meantime the Jeweler's Wife had designed a Club Badge.

The Club was doing such Notable Work that some of the Members thought they ought to have a Special Meeting and invite the Men. They wanted to put the Cap-Sheaf on a Profitable Season, and at the same time hand the Merited Rebuke to some of the Husbands and Brothers who had been making Funny Cracks.

It was decided to give the Star Programme at the Beadle Home, and after the Papers had been read then all the Men and Five Women who did not hold office could file through the Front Room and shake Hands with the President, the Vice-President, the Recording Secretary, the Corresponding Secretary, the Treasurer, and the members of the various Committees, all of whom were to line up and Receive.

The reason the Club decided to have the Brain Barbecue

at the Beadle Home was that the Beadles had such beautiful big Rooms and Double Doors. There was more or less quiet Harpoon Work when the Announcement was made. Several of the Elderly Ones said that Josephine Beadle was not a Representative Member of the Club. She was Fair to look upon, but she was not pulling very hard for the Uplifting of the Sex. It was suspected that she came to the Meetings just to Kill Time and see what the Others were Wearing. She refused to buckle down to Literary Work, for she was a good deal more interested in the Bachelors who filled the Windows of the new Men's Club than she was in the Butler who wrote "Hudibras." So why should she have the Honor of entertaining the Club at the Annual Meeting? Unfortunately, the Members who had the most Doing under their Bonnets were not the ones who could come to the Front with large Rooms that could be Thrown together, so the Beadle Home got the Great Event.

Every one in Town who carried a Pound of Social Influence showed up in his or her Other Clothes. Extra Chairs had to be brought in, and what with the Smilax and Club Colors it was very Swell, and the Maiden in the Lace Mitts who was going to write about it for the Weekly threw a couple of Spasms.

The Men were led in pulling at the Halters and with their Ears laid back. After they got into the Dressing Room they Stuck there until they had to be Shooed out. They did not know what they were going against, but they had their Suspicions. They managed to get Rear Seats or stand along the Wall so that they could execute the Quiet Sneak if Things got too Literary. The Women were too Flushed and Proud to Notice.

At 8:30 P.M. the Lady President stood out and began to read a few Pink Thoughts on "Woman's Destiny—Why Not?" Along toward 9:15, about the time the Lady President was beginning to show up Good and Earnest, Josephine Beadle, who was Circulating around on the Outskirts of the Throng to make sure that everybody was Happy, made a Discovery. She noticed that the Men standing along the Wall and in the Doorways were not more than sixty per cent En Rapport with the Long Piece about Woman's Destiny. Now Josephine was right there to see that Everybody had a Nice Time, and she did not like to see the Prominent

Business Men of the Town dying of Thirst or Leg Cramp or anything like that, so she gave two or three of them the Quiet Wink, and they tiptoed after her out to the Dining Room, where she offered Refreshments, and said they could slip out on the Side Porch and Smoke if they wanted to.

Probably they preferred to go back in the Front Room and hear some more about Woman's Destiny not.

As soon as they could master their Emotions and get control of their Voices, they told Josephine what they thought of her. They said she made the Good Samaritan look like a Cheap Criminal, and if she would only say the Word they would begin to put Ground Glass into the Food at Home. Then Josephine called them "Boys," which probably does not make a Hit with one who is on the sloping side of 48. More of the Men seemed to awake to the Fact that they were Overlooking something, so they came on the Velvet Foot back to the Dining Room and declared themselves In, and flocked around Josephine and called her "Josie" and "Joe." They didn't care. They were having a Pleasant Visit.

Josephine gave them Allopathic Slugs of the Size that they feed you in the Navy and then lower you into the Dingey and send you Ashore. Then she let them go out on the Porch to smoke. By the time the Lady President came to the last Page there were only two Men left in the Front room. One was Asleep and the other was Penned In.

The Women were Huffy. They went out to make the Men come in, and found them Bunched on the Porch listening to a Story that a Traveling Man had just brought to Town that Day.

Now the Plan was that during the Reception the Company would stand about in little Groups, and ask each other what Books they liked, and make it something on the order of a Salon. This Plan miscarried, because all the Men wanted to hear Rag Time played by Josephine, the Life-Saver. Josephine had to yield, and the Men all clustered around her to give their Moral Support. After one or two Selections, they felt sufficiently Keyed to begin to hit up those low-down Songs about Baby and Chickens and Razors. No one paid any Attention to the Lady President, who was off in a Corner holding an Indignation Meeting with the Secretary and the Vice-President.

When the Women began to sort out the Men and order

them to start Home and all the Officers of the Club were giving Josephine the frosty Good Night, any one could see that there was Trouble ahead.

Next Day the Club held a Special Session and expelled Josephine for Conduct Unbecoming a Member, and Josephine sent Word to them as follows: "Rats."

Then the Men quietly got together and bought Josephine about a Thousand Dollars' Worth of American Beauty Roses to show that they were With her, and then Homes began to break up, and somebody started the Report that anyway it was the Lady President's Fault for having such a long and pokey Essay that wasn't hers at all, but had been Copied out of a Club Paper published in Detroit.

Before the next Meeting there were two Factions. The Lady President had gone to a Rest Cure, and the Meeting resolved itself into a good Cry and a general Smash-Up.

MORAL: *The only Literary Men are those who have to Work at it.*

FROM *In Babel*

The Other Girl

"Albert!"

"Umh?"

"Albert, I want to ask you something."

"Well?"

"Something—let go of my hand while I'm asking you this, because it's rather serious."

"Goodness!"

"Maybe not so serious, either, but—Oh, I don't know; I—I suppose I'm foolish to think about it, but something that Grace Elliott said yesterday——"

"I wouldn't care what she said about anything."

"I don't, because I know well enough that she tattles all she knows and a good deal more; but it was the way she acted more than anything else."

"What was it all about, anyway?"

"It was about *you,* for one."

"Yes; Grace loves me—not."

"It was something about you and some one else."

"Who was the 'some one else'?"

"Can't you guess?"

"No. Was it you?"

"No!"

"No? Well, then, I'm not interested to hear anything about it."

"Oh, you *dear* thing! It was something about a girl, though—another girl."

"Which one? What's her name?"

"I should think you could guess."

"I don't see why. I don't know many girls."

"That's too bad about you. Anyway, you might try."

"Well, who was it—Rose Whiting?"

"Rose Whiting! Oh!"

"Jessie Cameron?"

"Albert Morton, you're not trying to guess. It was Fannie McClellan."

"Oh!"

"Yes. I should think it *would* be 'Oh.' You knew the one I meant all the time."

"Who, I? Why *should* I?"

"Innocence! Now, Albert, stop laughing, please. I'm in earnest."

"So am I, then. What is it?"

"Well, I want to know something about her—about you and her."

"All right. Anything you want to know."

"You think I'm joking, but I'm not. I've told you things, Albert, that I never told even to my dearest girl friends, and I think you might tell me something about Fannie McClellan, because—well, after Grace left here yesterday, I went up to my room and had a good cry."

"It's too bad she can't attend to her own business."

"I didn't believe what she said, but it made me—oh, she has such an aggravating way about her, and all the time she kisses you and fusses around you and pretends to be the best friend you ever had in the whole wide world."

"She makes me tired."

"After she'd gone away, I couldn't remember that she'd said anything in just so many words, but she kept hinting around and acting as if she knew a lot more than she cared to tell."

"Don't you remember anything she said?"

"Well, it was about you and—Fannie McClellan. You *did* go with her for a while, didn't you, Albert?"

"Yes, I used to take her to places once in a while. You knew that. Why, I was with her the first time I ever met you—that night at the Carleton Club."

"Yes, and when we were sitting over in the corner she looked as if she'd like to bite my head off. Was that the last time you ever went with her?"

"I don't remember. I may have gone with her once or twice after that."

"You must have gone with her a good many times altogether, counting when you called and all that."

"Ye-e-s. I saw her, occasionally, now and then, for a year or so before I met you."

"If that—then you must have liked her better than you did the other girls."

"Well, it was natural that I should like her better than some girls and then, again, there were other girls that I liked about as well as I did her."

"But you went to see her oftener than you did any other girl, now didn't you? Tell me, Albert, *please*. It's all past now and it doesn't make the teeniest bit of difference what happened, or whether you went to see her every night, only——"

"Only what? If it doesn't make any difference, what's all this excitement about?"

"Now, don't get mad, Albert."

"I'm not mad."

"Really?"

"No! Pshaw!"

"Now, can't you see that if we are going to be together all our lives, Albert, I ought to know about these things, so that if any one like Grace Elliott comes around dropping her hints and saying these things I can——"

"Now, just one moment, Lil. Let's understand this whole business. What *was* it Grace Elliott said?"

"As I tell you, she didn't say anything in so many words, but you could see what she meant."

"All right, then. What did she mean?"

"Albert, you won't scold?"

"No; go ahead."

"Oh, I'm sorry I ever spoke of it at all."

"I wish I knew what 'it' was."

"Well, I want you to know, Albert, that I realize perfectly well that any one can go and see a girl once in awhile, and even take her to parties, without becoming engaged or anything like that, and I wouldn't have brought this up at all only that Grace——"

"Oh, *darn* Grace!"

"Albert!"

"She won't be a bridesmaid, do you understand? She won't be anything."

"*Albert!* Honestly, Grace didn't actually say anything right out, but I simply felt that she meant something. Now—ah—Albert, you've told me that you never were engaged before, and I know that, but—well, you *weren't,* were you?"

"I were not."

"Oh, Albert, I'm in earnest."

"So am I."

"And you never asked any one?"

"Certainly *not.*"

"I might have known that. She'd have grabbed you, quick enough. If I don't give Grace Elliott a piece of my mind when she comes around here again."

"I wouldn't pay any attention to anything she says."

"I don't, but she has such a crawly, tantilizing way of saying things about people she knows you like. Albert, do you ever see Fannie McClellan any more?"

"I just see her once in awhile and that's all."

"You are—friends at least?"

"I suppose so."

"You've never had a quarrel or anything like that?"

"No."

"Then I don't see why you shouldn't be friends. She's a sweet, lovely girl, and I know she was very fond of you, and may be yet; for all I know, and I think it would be awfully mean of you not to treat her just as beautifully as you could. I'm going to invite her to the wedding. Do you think she'll come?"

"I don't know, I'm sure."

"There's no reason why she shouldn't come?"

"None that I know of."

"Well, I'm going to invite her, and then—I want you to promise me something, Albert."

"I promise. What is it?"

"Well—after we're married I want you to promise to let me invite Fannie to come and call on us. I want to show her that you and I—both of us—like her just the same as if—well, as if nothing had ever happened."

"Maybe she wouldn't enjoy coming."

"Why not? You don't mean that she might be jealous? Why, you *conceited* thing!"

"It isn't that. You don't know her very well, do you?"

"But *you* do, and I want all of your friends to be my friends, and you know you've promised to like all of my friends."

"All right, then. We'll have Fannie to dinner as soon as we're settled."

"Do you mean it?"

"Of course."

"It will please her so much."

"Yes?"

(Snuggling) "And you're the kindest, best-hearted thing that ever lived."

FROM *People You Know*

The *High Art That Was* a *Little Too High* for the *Vulgarian Who Paid* the *Bills*

Once there was a Husband who was stuck on Plain Living and Home Comforts. He would walk around an Angel Cake any old Time to get action on some Farm Sausage. He was not very strong for Romaine Salad or any Speckled Cheese left over from Year before last, but he did a very neat vanishing Act with a Sirloin Steak and he had the Coffee come right along in a large Cup. He refused to dally with the Demi-Tasse. For this true American the Course Dinner was a weak Invention of the benighted Foreigner. When he squared up to his Food he cut out all the Trimmings.

This is the kind of Husband who peels his Coat in the Evening and gets himself all spread out in a Rocking Chair with a fat Cushion under him.

He loves to wear old Velvet Slippers with pink Roses worked on the Toes and the Heels run over.

Give him about two Cigars that pull freely and a Daily Paper and he is fixed for the Session.

Along about 10:30, if he can connect with a Triangle of Desiccated Apple Pie and a Goblet of Milk, he is ready to sink back on the Husks, feeling simply Immense.

Now this Husband had a Fireside that suited him nearly to Death until the Better Half began to read these Magazines that tell how to beautify the Home.

Her first Play was to take out all the Carpets and have the Floors massaged until they were as slick as Glass, so that when the Bread-Winner stepped on one of the Okra or Bokhara Rugs he usually gave an Imitation of a Player trying to reach Second.

He told her that he did not care to live in a Rink, but what he said cut very few Lemons with the Side-Partner. She was looking at the half-tone Pictures of up-to-date Homes and beginning to realize that the Wall-Paper, Steel Engravings and the Enlarged Photographs of Yap Relatives would have to go.

One Day when the Provider struck the Premises he found the Workmen putting Red Burlap on the Walls of the Sitting-Room.

"Why the Gunny-Sack?" he asked. "Can't we afford Wall-Paper?"

"Love of Art is the True Essence of the Higher Life," said the Æsthete, and she began to read a Booklet bound in the same Paper that the Butcher uses when he wraps up a Soup Bone.

"Come again," said the Wage Earner, who was slow at catching these Ruskin Twisters.

"This is Art Burlap and not the kind that they use for sacking Peanuts," explained the Disciple of Beauty. "Above the Burlap will be a Shelf of Weathered Oak, and then above that a Frieze of Blue Jimson Flowers. Then when we draw all of the Curtains and light one Candle in here it will make a Swell Effect."

"I feel that we are going to be very Happy," he said, and then he went out and sat behind the Barn, where he could smoke his Pipe and meditate on the Uncertainties of Life.

Next Day he discovered that she had condemned his

Rocking-Chair and the old-style Centre Table on which he used to stack his Reading Matter and keep a Plate of Apples handy.

When he entered the improved and modernized Living Room, he found himself up against a Job Lot of Beauty and no Mistake.

All the Furniture was straight up and down. It seemed to have been chopped out with an Axe, and was meant to hold up Members of the Rhinoceros Family.

On the High Shelf was a Row of double-handled Shaving Mugs, crippled Beer Steins, undersized Coal Scuttles and various Copper Kettles that had seen Better Days.

"At last we have a Room that satisfies every Craving of my Soul," said the Wife.

"I am more than Satisfied," observed the Treasurer. "I am delirious with Joy. My only regret is that an All-Wise Providence did not mould me into a different Shape so that I might sit down in some of these Chairs. What are those Iron Dinkuses sticking out from the Wall?"

"Those are Florentine Lanterns," she replied; "and they are very Roycroftie, even if they don't give any Light."

Next she started in on the Dining-Room.

Rule No. 1 for making Home more Cheerful is to put in a Shelf wherever there is room for one. After which the Shelf is loaded down with Etruscan Growlers and Antique Jugs.

The low-browed Husband could not tell the difference between High Art and Junk.

The female Bradleyite covered the walls with about 400 Plates, each with a Blue Curly-Cue on it. They looked very Cheap to him until he received the Bill, and then he learned that they were Old Delft and came to $11 apiece.

In fact, after his Wife had been haunting the Second-Hand Places for a while, he learned that any Article which happened to be old and shopworn and cracked was the one that commanded the Top Price.

She never let up until she had made the whole House thoroughly Artistic.

Her Women Acquaintances would come in, and she would show them the Dark Oak Effects and the Sea-Green Frescoes and the Monastery Settee with the Sole-Leather Bottom in it and the corroded Tea-Pot that she had bought for $95 and the Table Spread made from Overall Material with just one Yellow Poppy in the Middle, and they would have 37 different kinds of Duck Fits and say that it was Grand and that her Taste was simply Faultless. After that she wouldn't care what Husband said.

He was a fairly patient Man, and all he complained of was that when he sat down he dislocated his Spine, while the Brass Knobs wore black and blue Spots on him; and the dining-room Table should have had a couple of Holes for him to put his Legs through; and he couldn't find a Place in which to stretch out; and he needed a Derrick to move one of the Chairs; and at Night when the Moonlight came into his Room and he saw all the bummy Bean-Pots lined up on the Foot-Board and the Instruments of Torture staring at him from every corner of the Room, he would crawl down under the Covers and dream of his Childhood Home, with the old-fashioned Sofas and the deep Rocking-Chairs and the big Bureaus that were meant to hold Things and not to look at.

However, he has been unable to arrest the reaching-out after the Beautiful, for only last Week she purchased a broken-down Clock—price $115.

MORAL: *There is no Place like Home, and some Husbands are glad of it.*

The *Married Couple That Went* to *Housekeeping* and *Began* to *Find Out Things*

Once there was a Happy Young Pair, each of whom got stuck on the Photograph of the other and thereupon a Marriage was arranged by Mail.

Shortly after taking the Life Risk, they started in to get acquainted. Up to the time that they moved into the Arcadian Flats and began to take Orders from the Janitor, he never had seen little Sunshine except in her Evening Frock.

He had a sort of sneaking Suspicion that she arose every Morning already attired in a Paris Gown and all the Diamonds.

And she supposed that he went to the Office every Day in his regular John Drew effect with the Folding Hat.

After she began to see Hubby around the Flat in his Other Clothes the Horrible Truth dawned upon her that he was not such a Hot Swell as he had looked to be in the Bunko Photograph.

Sometimes, on Rainy Sundays, he would cut out the Morning Service and decide not to Shave, and then when she got a good long Look at him, she would begin to doubt her own Judgment.

And so far as that is concerned, there were Mornings, after they had been out Late to a Welsh Rabbit Party, when she was a little Lumpy, if any one should ask.

Love's Young Dream was handed several goshawful Whacks about the Time that they started in to get a Line on each other.

For instance, the first Morning at Breakfast it came out that her Idea of a Dainty Snack with which to usher in the Day was a Lettuce Sandwich, a Couple of Olives and a Child's Cup full of Cocoa, while he wanted $35 worth of Ham and Eggs, a stack of Griddle Cakes and a Tureen of Coffee.

She was a case of Ambrosia and Nectar and he was plain old Ham and Spinach.

It used to give her Hysterics to see him bark at an Ear of Green Corn, at the same time making a Sound like a Dredge.

For Dinner she liked a little Consommé en Tasse and then a Nice Salad, while he insisted on a Steak the size of a Door Mat and German Fried to come along.

They did not Mocha and Java at all on their Reading Matter. She liked Henry James and Walter Pater and he preferred Horse Papers and the Comic Supplement. Sometimes when she would wander off into the Realms of Poesy he would follow her as far as he could, and then sit down and wait for her to get through rambling and come back.

If they took in a Show she was always plugging for Mrs. Fiske or Duse, while he claimed that Rogers Brothers were better than Booth and Barrett had been in their Prime.

She could weep over a Tosti Serenade, and he would walk a Mile at any time to see a good Buck Dance.

When they got around to fixing up Invitation Lists, there was more or less Geeing and Hawing.

All of his Friends belonged to the Hitemup Division. Their only Conception of a Happy Evening was to put the

Buck in the Centre of the Table, break a fresh Pack and go out for Blood.

Wifey found her most delirious Joy in putting passionate Shades on all the Lamps, and sitting there in the Crimson Glow to discuss Maeterlinck and Maarten Maartens and a few others that were New Ones on the he-end of the Sketch.

When they had an Evening At Home up in the Flat, it was usually a two-ring Affair. She would have the Cerebellums in the Front Room looking at the New Books and eating Peppermint Wafers, while he and the other Comanches would be out in the Dining-Room trying to make their House Rent and tossing off that which made Scotland famous. Sometimes it would take half the Night to get the Smoke out of the House.

Although she feared that she had turned up the wrong Street while searching for her Affinity, the Partnership Arrangement had to stand.

They came to the Conclusion that Married Life is a Series of Compromises. If he did well while sitting in with some of his Friends, he would divide up with her and she would take the Money and buy Art Pastels.

He would spot the Afternoons on which the Ethical Researchers were due at his Premises and he would go to a Dutch Restaurant.

She permitted him to have a Room and call it his Den, so that he and his Friends could do the Escape in case somebody in the Parlor started a Reading.

He put up the Coin to enable her to attend State Conventions, and when she was elected Recording Secretary of the Society for trying to find out what Browning was up to, he took her Picture around to all the Newspapers and told every one that he had a little Woman up at the House who was as Keen as a Hawk, as Swift as an Eagle, and Sharper than Chained Lightning.

He fumbled a great many of her In-Shoots, but that did not prevent him from admiring her Delivery.

Finally they arranged their separate Schedules so that they did not see much of each other and they began to get along all right. Occasionally they had a slight Difference, but they could always patch it up. For instance, she selected Aubrey De Courcey as a Name for the First Born, while he held out for Bill, so they had to compromise on Aubrey De Courcey.

Aubrey is now ten years of age. Mother is teaching him to Crochet and Father is showing him how to Draw without tipping off his Hand, while all the Friends are sitting around, waiting to see Aubrey's Finish.

MORAL: *The Two of a Kind is not always the Strongest Combination.*

FROM *More Fables*

The Fable of *The Adult Girl Who Got Busy Before They Could Ring* The *Bell* On *Her*

Once upon a Time there was a Lovely and Deserving Girl named Clara, who was getting so near Thirty that she didn't want to Talk about it. Everybody had a Good Word for her. She traveled with the Thoroughbreds, and was always Among Those Present; so it was hard to understand why she hadn't Married. Other Girls not as Good-Looking or Accomplished had been grabbed off while they were Buds. Already some of them were beginning to act as Chaperons for Clara. They were keeping Tab on Clara's Age, too, and began to think that she would land on the Bargain Counter, and have to be satisfied with a Widower who wore a Toupee and dyed his Eyebrows.

Clara was somewhat of a Mind-Reader. She knew that the Friends of her Youth were predicting a Hard Finish for her, so she decided to Fool them. And she knew that it Behooved her to Catch On before the Children started in to call her Auntie.

Now it is not to be inferred that Clara was what the Underwriters call a Bad Risk. She never had been a Drug on the Market. When she went to a Hop she did not have to wait for Ladies' Choice in order to swing into the Mazy. In fact, she had been Engaged now and then, just for Practice, and she had received Offers from some of the holdover Bachelors who went around Proposing from Force of Habit. But Clara was not out for any man who had been Turned Down elsewhere. She wanted the Right Kind, and she was going to do the Picking herself.

Having made an Inventory of the Possibilities, she selected the Treasurer of the Shoe Factory, and decided that she could Love him without Straining herself. He was about her age, and was almost as good-looking as a Gibson Man, and had A1 Prospects. It would be no Easy Job to Land him, however, because the Competition was very keen and he was Wary, trying to be a Kind Friend to every Girl he knew, but playing no Favorites. He kept the Parents guessing. He had been Exposed to Matrimony so often without being Taken Down, that he was generally regarded as an Immune.

Clara got Busy with herself and hatched a Scheme. When all the Smart Set got ready to pike away for the Heated Term, Clara surprised her Friends by guessing that she would remain at Home. It was a Nervy Thing to do, because all the Social Head-Liners who could command the Price were supposed to flit off to a Summer Hotel, and loiter on the Pine Veranda and try to think they were Recuperating.

Clara told her Mother to go, as usual, but she would stay at Home and be a Companion to poor lonesome Papa. So all the Women went away to the Resorts with their Cameras and Talcum Powder and Witch Hazel, and Clara was left alone in Town with the Men.

It is a Traditional Fact that there is no Social Life in Town during the Dog Days. But there is nothing to prevent a Bright Girl from Starting Something. That is what Clara did.

She stocked up the Refrigerator, and hung a Hammock on the Lawn with a few Easy Chairs around it. The Young Men marooned in Town heard of the Good Thing, and no one had to tear their Garments to induce them to come. They arrived at the rate of from Seven to Twelve a Night, and dipped into Papa's Cigars and the Liquid Nourishment, regardless. Although Clara had remained in town to act as Companion to Papa, it was noticed that when she had all the Company in the Evening, Papa either had been Chloroformed and put to Bed or else he had his Orders to stay Under Cover.

Clara did not send for the Treasurer of the Shoe Factory. She knew better than to go out after her Prey. She allowed him to find his Way to the House with the others. When he came, she did not chide him for failing to make his Party Call; neither did she rush toward him with a Low Cry of Joy, thereby tipping her Hand. She knew that the Treasurer of the Shoe Factory was Next to all these Boarding School

Tactics, and·could not be Handled by the Methods that go with the College Students. Clara had enjoyed about ten years' Experience in handling the Creatures, and she had learned to Labor and to Wait. She simply led him into the Circle and·took his Order, and allowed him to sit there in the Gloaming and observe how Popular she was. All the men were Scrapping to see who would be Next to sit in the Hammock with her. It looked for a while as if Clara would have to give out Checks, the same as in a Barber Shop. Late that night when the Men walked homeward together, they remarked that Clara was a Miserable Hostess, they didn't think.

Next Evening the Treasurer of the Shoe Factory was back on the lawn. So were all the Others. They said there was no beating a Place where you could play Shirt-Waist Man under the Trees, and have a Fairy Queen in White come and push Cold Drinks at you and not have to sign any Ticket. They composed flattering Songs about Clara, and every time she moved there was a Man right there with a Sofa Cushion to help her to be Comfortable.

In the mean time, the Other Girls out at the summer Resorts were doing the best they could with these High School Cadets, wearing Tidies around their Hats, who would rather go out in a Cat-Boat and get their arms tanned than remain on Shore and win the Honest Love of an American Girl, with a String to it.

Clara's work about this time was ever so Glossy. She began by asking the Treasurer of the Shoe Factory to come with her to the Refrigerator to get out some more imported Ginger Ale. All the men Volunteered to help, and two or three wanted to Tag along, but Clara drove them back.

They were gone a Long Time, because the Treasurer had to draw all thé corks, and they Fussed around together in the Pantry fixing up a Lunch for the Boys. Clara told him how Strong and Handy he was, until he felt an increase in his Chest Measurement.

On successive evenings she had the Treasurer supervise all the Arrangements. The Hired Girl had every Evening off, because it was so much more Jolly to go out and run the place yourself. In less than a Week the Treasurer was giving Orders around the House. She would get him back to the Kitchen and tie an Apron around him and ask what she should do next. She made him out to be the Only One who could be Trusted. The others were Company, but he was like one of the Family. And although he was being Worked like Creamery Butter, he never Suspected.

Her Game was to Domesticate him in Advance, and let him have a Foretaste of what it is to be Boss of your own House, except as to the Bills. The Pantry was full of Home Delicacies such as he couldn't get at the Hotel, and the Service was the best ever. Clara was right at his Elbow with a Willing Smile.

It didn't take him long to realize that he was missing a lot by remaining Single. He wondered why he had been so slow in getting on to Clara's Good Points. Also he wondered if it was any Open-and-Shut Certainty when a dozen other Men, some of them Younger and more Gallus, were after her in Full Cry.

Clara had him Pulled In, Strung and Hung over the side of the boat.

Of course if all the other Girls had been in Town, they would have Tumbled long before it ran into a Certainty, and probably they would have formed a V and rushed in to Break up the Play. But the other girls were Far Away with the Old Men and the Seminary Striplings. Clara had an Open Field, with no need of any Interfering or Blocking, and if she Fell Down it was her own Fault. Besides, she had all these other Admirers set out as Decoys to prove that if he didn't, somebody else might.

The Treasurer of the Shoe Factory got a large Rally on himself, and she had to Give In and make a Promise.

He loves to tell Callers how he proposed to his Wife in the Kitchen, and he doesn't know to this Day that she was Expecting it.

MORAL: *As soon as he begins to Frequent the Back Rooms of the House, measure him for the Harness.*

FROM *The Sultan of Sulu*

The cocktail is a pleasant drink;
It's mild and harmless—I don't think.
When you've had one, you call for two;

And then you don't care what you do.
Last night I hoisted twenty-three
Of those arrangements into me;
My wealth increased, I swelled with pride.
I was pickled, primed, and ossified;
    But R-E-M-O-R-S-E!

The water wagon is the place for me.
Last night at twelve I felt immense;
    Today I feel like thirty cents.
My eyes are bleared, my coppers hot
    I'd like to eat but I cannot!
It is no time for mirth and laughter—
The cold, gray dawn of the morning after.

Louisa May Alcott (1832–1888)

FROM *Jo's Boys*

Jo's Last Scrape

The March family had enjoyed a great many surprises in the course of their varied career, but the greatest of all was when the Ugly Duckling turned out to be, not a swan, but a golden goose, whose literary eggs found such an unexpected market that in ten years Jo's wildest and most cherished dream actually came true. How or why it happened she never clearly understood, but all of a sudden she found herself famous in a small way, and, better still, with a snug little fortune in her pocket to clear away the obstacles of the present and assure the future of her boys.

    It began during a bad year when everything went wrong at Plumfield; times were hard, the school dwindled, Jo overworked herself and had a long illness; Laurie and Amy were abroad, and the Bhaers too proud to ask help even of those as near and dear as this generous pair. Confined to her room, Jo got desperate over the state of affairs, till she fell back upon the long-disused pen as the only thing she could do to help fill up the gaps in the income. A book for girls being wanted by a certain publisher, she hastily scribbled a little story describing a few scenes and adventures in the lives of herself and sisters,—though boys were more in her line,—and with very slight hopes of success sent it out to seek its fortune.

Things always went by contraries with Jo. Her first book, labored over for years, and launched full of the high hopes and ambitious dreams of youth, foundered on its voyage, though the wreck continued to float long afterward, to the profit of the publisher at least. The hastily written story, sent away with no thought beyond the few dollars it might bring, sailed with a fair wind and a wise pilot at the helm straight into public favor, and came home heavily laden with an unexpected cargo of gold and glory.

A more astonished woman probably never existed than Josephine Bhaer when her little ship came into port with flags flying, cannon that had been silent before now booming gayly, and, better than all, many kind faces rejoicing with her, many friendly hands grasping hers with cordial congratulations. After that it was plain sailing, and she merely had to load her ships and send them off on prosperous trips, to bring home stores of comfort for all she loved and labored for.

The fame she never did quite accept; for it takes very little fire to make a great deal of smoke nowadays, and notoriety is not real glory. The fortune she could not doubt, and gratefully received it; though it was not half so large a one as a generous world reported it to be. The tide having turned continued to rise, and floated the family comfortably into a snug harbor where the older members could rest secure from storms, and whence the younger ones could launch their boats for the voyage of life.

All manner of happiness, peace, and plenty came in those years to bless the patient waiters, hopeful workers, and devout believers in the wisdom and justice of Him who sends disappointment, poverty, and sorrow to try the love of human hearts and make success the sweeter when it comes. The world saw the prosperity, and kind souls rejoiced over the improved fortunes of the family; but the success Jo valued most, the happiness that nothing could change or take away, few knew much about.

It was the power of making her mother's last years happy and serene; to see the burden of care laid down forever, the weary hands at rest, the dear face untroubled by any anxiety, and the tender heart free to pour itself out in the wise charity which was its delight. As a girl, Jo's favorite plan had been a room where Marmee could sit in peace and enjoy herself after her hard, heroic life. Now the dream had become a happy fact, and Marmee sat in her pleasant chamber with every comfort and luxury about her, loving daughters to wait on her as infirmities increased, a faithful mate to lean upon, and grandchildren to brighten the twilight of life with their dutiful affection. A very precious time to all, for she rejoiced as only mothers can in the good fortunes of their children. She had lived to reap the harvest she sowed; had seen prayers answered, hopes blossom, good gifts bear fruit, peace and prosperity bless the home she had made; and then, like some brave, patient angel, whose work was done, turned her face heavenward, glad to rest.

This was the sweet and sacred side of the change; but it had its droll and thorny one, as all things have in this curious world of ours. After the first surprise, incredulity, and joy, which came to Jo, with the ingratitude of human nature, she soon tired of renown, and began to resent her loss of liberty. For suddenly the admiring public took possession of her and all her affairs, past, present, and to come. Strangers demanded to look at her, question, advise, warn, congratulate, and drive her out of her wits by well-meant but very wearisome attentions. If she declined to open her heart to them, they reproached her; if she refused to endow pet charities, relieve private wants, or sympathize with every ill and trial known to humanity she was called hard-hearted, selfish, and haughty; if she found it impossible to answer the piles of letters sent her, she was neglectful of her duty to the admiring public; and if she preferred the privacy of home to the pedestal upon which she was requested to pose, "the airs of literary people" were freely criticised.

She did her best for the children, they being the public for whom she wrote, and labored stoutly to supply the demand always in the mouths of voracious youth,—"More stories, more right away!" Her family objected to this devotion at their expense, and her health suffered; but for a time she gratefully offered herself up on the altar of juvenile literature, feeling that she owed a good deal to the little friends in whose sight she had found favor after twenty years of effort.

But a time came when her patience gave out, and wearying of being a lion, she became a bear in nature as in name, and retiring to her den, growled awfully when ordered out. Her family enjoyed the fun, and had small sympathy with her trials, but Jo came to consider it the worst scrape of her life; for liberty had always been her dearest possession, and it seemed to be fast going from her. Living in a lantern soon loses its charms, and she was too old, too tired, and too busy to like it. She felt that she had done all that could reasonably be required of her when autographs, photographs, and autobiographical sketches had been sown broadcast over the land; when artists had taken her home in all its aspects, and reporters had taken her in the grim one she always assumed on these trying occasions; when a series of enthusiastic boarding-schools had ravaged her grounds for trophies, and a steady stream of amiable pilgrims had worn her doorsteps with their respectful feet; when servants left after a week's trial of the bell that rang all day; when her husband was forced to guard her at meals, and the boys to cover her retreat out of back windows on certain occasions when enterprising guests walked in unannounced at unfortunate moments.

A sketch of one day may perhaps explain the state of things, offer some excuse for the unhappy woman, and give a hint to the autograph-fiend now rampant in the land; for it is a true tale.

"There ought to be a law to protect unfortunate authors," said Mrs. Jo one morning soon after Emil's arrival, when the mail brought to her an unusually large and varied assortment of letters. "To me it is a more vital subject than international copyright; for time is money, peace is health, and I lose both with no return but less respect for my fellow-creatures and a wild desire to fly into the wilderness, since I cannot shut my doors even in free America."

"Lion-hunters are awful when in search of their prey. If they could change places for a while it would do them good; and they'd see what bores they were when they 'do themselves the honor of calling to express their admiration of our charming work,' " quoted Ted, with a bow to his parent, now frowning over twelve requests for autographs.

"I have made up my mind on one point," said Mrs. Jo with great firmness. "I will *not* answer this kind of letter. I've sent at least six to this boy, and he probably sells them. This girl writes from a seminary, and if I send her one all the other girls will at once write for more. All begin by saying they know they intrude, and that I am of course annoyed by these requests; but they venture to ask because I like boys, or they like the books, or it is only one. Emerson and Whittier put these things in the waste-paper basket; and though only a literary nursery-maid who provides moral pap for the young, I will follow their illustrious example; for I shall have no time to eat or sleep if I try to satisfy these dear unreasonable children;" and Mrs. Jo swept away the entire batch with a sigh of relief.

"I'll open the others and let you eat your breakfast in peace, *liebe Mutter,*" said Rob, who often acted as her secretary. "Here's one from the South;" and breaking an imposing seal, he read:—

Madam,—As it has pleased Heaven to bless your efforts with a large fortune, I feel no hesitation in asking you to supply funds to purchase a new communion-service for our church. To whatever denomination you belong, you will of course respond with liberality to such a request.

Respectfully yours,
Mrs. X. Y. Zavier

"Send a civil refusal, dear. All I have to give must go to feed and clothe the poor at my gates. That is my thank-offering for success. Go on," answered his mother, with a grateful glance about her happy home.

"A literary youth of eighteen proposes that you put your name to a novel he has written; and after the first edition your name is to be taken off and his put on. There's a cool proposal for you. I guess you won't agree to that, in spite of your soft-heartedness towards most of the young scribblers."

"Could n't be done. Tell him so kindly, and don't let him send the manuscript. I have seven on hand now, and barely time to read my own," said Mrs. Jo, pensively fishing a small letter out of the slop-bowl and opening it with care, because the down-hill address suggested that a child wrote it.

"I will answer this myself. A little sick girl wants a book, and she shall have it, but I can't write sequels to all the rest to please her. I should never come to an end if I tried to suit these voracious little Oliver Twists, clamoring for more. What next, Robin?"

"This is short and sweet."

Dear Mrs. Bhaer,—I am now going to give you my opinion of your works. I have read them all many times, and call them first-rate. Please go ahead.

> Your admirer,
> Billy Babcock.

"Now that is what I like. Billy is a man of sense and a critic worth having, since he has read my works many times before expressing his opinion. He asks for no answer, so send my thanks and regards."

"Here's a lady in England with seven girls, and she wishes to know your views upon education. Also what careers they shall follow,—the oldest being twelve. Don't wonder she's worried," laughed Rob.

"I'll try to answer it. But as I have no girls, my opinion is n't worth much and will probably shock her, as I shall tell her to let them run and play and build up good, stout bodies before she talks about careers. They will soon show what they want, if they are let alone, and not all run in the same mould."

"Here's a fellow who wants to know what sort of a girl he shall marry, and if you know of any like those in your stories."

"Give him Nan's address, and see what he'll get," proposed Ted, privately resolving to do it himself if possible.

"This is from a lady who wants you to adopt her child and lend her money to study art abroad for a few years. Better take it, and try your hand at a girl, mother."

"No thank you, I will keep to my own line of business. What is that blotted one? It looks rather awful, to judge by the ink," asked Mrs. Jo, who beguiled her daily task trying to guess from the outside what was inside her many letters. This proved to be a poem from an insane admirer, to judge by its incoherent style.

To J. M. B.

"Oh, were I a heliotrope,
I would play poet,
And blow a breeze of fragrance
To you; and none should know it.

"Your form like the stately elm
When Phœbus gilds the morning ray;
Your cheeks like the ocean bed
That blooms a rose in May.

"Your words are wise and bright,
I bequeath them to you a legacy given;
And when your spirit takes its flight,
May it bloom a flower in heaven.

"My tongue in flattering language spoke,
And sweeter silence never broke
In busiest street or loneliest glen.
I take you with the flashes of any pen.

"Consider the lilies, how they grow;
They toil not, yet are fair,
Gems and flowers and Solomon's seal.
The geranium of the world is J. M. Bhaer.
"James."

While the boys shouted over this effusion,—which·is a true one,—their mother read several liberal offers from budding magazines for her to edit them gratis; one long let-ter from a young girl inconsolable because her favorite hero died, and "would dear Mrs. Bhaer rewrite the tale, and make it end good?" another from an irate boy denied an auto-graph, who darkly foretold financial ruin and loss of favor if she did not send him and all other fellows who asked autographs, photographs, and autobiographical sketches; a minister wished to know her religion; and an undecided maiden asked which of her two lovers she should marry. These samples will suffice to show a few of the claims made on a busy woman's time, and make my readers pardon Mrs. Jo if she did not carefully reply to all.

"That job is done. Now I will dust a bit, and then go to my work. I'm all behindhand, and serials can't wait; so deny me to everybody, Mary. I won't see Queen Victoria if she comes to-day." And Mrs. Bhaer threw down her napkin as if defying all creation.

"I hope the day will go well with thee, my dearest," answered her husband, who had been busy with his own voluminous correspondence. "I will dine at college with Professor Plock, who is to visit us to-day. The *Jünglings* can lunch on Parnassus; so thou shalt have a quiet time." And smoothing the worried lines out of her forehead with his good-by kiss, the excellent man marched away, both pockets full of books, an old umbrella in one hand, and a bag of stones for the geology class in the other.

"If all literary women had such thoughtful angels for husbands, they would live longer and write more. Perhaps that would n't be a blessing to the world though, as most of us write too much now," said Mrs. Jo, waving her feather duster to her spouse, who responded with flourishes of the umbrella as he went down the avenue.

Rob started for school at the same time, looking so much like him with his books and bag and square shoulders and steady air that his mother laughed as she turned away, saying heartily, "Bless both my dear professors, for better creatures never lived!"

Emil was already gone to his shop in the city; but Ted lingered to steal the address he wanted, ravage the sugar-bowl, and talk with "Mum;" for the two had great larks together.

Mrs. Jo always arranged her own parlor, refilled her vases, and gave the little touches that left it cool and neat for the day. Going to draw down the curtain, she beheld an artist sketching on the lawn, and groaned as she hastily retired to the back window to shake her duster.

At that moment the bell rang and the sound of wheels was heard in the road.

"I'll go; Mary lets 'em in;" and Ted smoothed his hair as he made for the hall.

"Can't see any one. Give me a chance to fly upstairs," whispered Mrs. Jo, preparing to escape. But before she could do so, a man appeared at the door with a card in his hand. Ted met him with a stern air, and his mother dodged behind the window-curtain to bide her time for escape.

"I am doing a series of articles for the 'Saturday Tattler,' and I called Mrs. Bhaer the first of all," began the new-comer in the insinuating tone of his tribe, while his quick eyes were taking in all they could, experience having taught him to make the most of his time, as his visits were usually short ones.

"Mrs. Bhaer never sees reporters, sir."

"But a few moments will be all I ask," said the man, edging his way further in.

"You can't see her, for she is out," replied Teddy, as a backward glance showed him that his unhappy parent had vanished,—through the window, he supposed, as she sometimes did when hard bestead.

"Very sorry. I'll call again. Is this her study? Charming room!" And the intruder fell back on the parlor, bound to see something and bag a fact if he died in the attempt.

"It is not," said Teddy, gently but firmly backing him down the hall, devoutly hoping that his mother had escaped round the corner of the house.

"If you could tell me Mrs. Bhaer's age and birthplace, date of marriage, and number of children, I should be much obliged," continued the unabashed visitor as he tripped over the door-mat.

"She is about sixty, born in Nova Zembla, married just forty years ago to-day, and has eleven daughters. Anything else, sir?" And Ted's sober face was such a funny contrast to his ridiculous reply that the reporter owned himself routed, and retired laughing just as a lady followed by three beaming girls came up the steps.

"We are all the way from Oshkosh, and couldn't go home without seein' dear Aunt Jo. My girls just admire her works, and lot on gettin' a sight of her. I know it's early; but we are goin' to see Holmes and Longfeller, and the rest of the celebrities, so we ran out here fust thing. Mrs. Erastus Kingsbury Parmalee, of Oshkosh, tell her. We don't mind waitin'; we can look round a spell if she ain't ready to see folks yet."

All this was uttered with such rapidity that Ted could only stand gazing at the buxom damsels, who fixed their six blue eyes upon him so beseechingly that his native gallantry made it impossible to deny them a civil reply at least.

"Mrs. Bhaer is not visible to-day,—out just now, I believe; but you can see the house and grounds if you like," he murmured, falling back as the four pressed in gazing rapturously about them.

"Oh, thank you! Sweet, pretty place I'm sure! That's where she writes, ain't it? Do tell me if that's her picture! Looks just as I imagined her!"

With these remarks the ladies paused before a fine engraving of the Hon. Mrs. Norton, with a pen in her hand and a rapt expression of countenance, likewise a diadem and pearl necklace.

Keeping his gravity with an effort, Teddy pointed to a very bad portrait of Mrs. Jo, which hung behind the door, and afforded her much amusement, it was so dismal, in spite of a curious effect of light upon the end of the nose and cheeks as red as the chair she sat in.

"This was taken for my mother; but it is not very good," he said, enjoying the struggles of the girls not to look dismayed at the sad difference between the real and the ideal. The youngest, aged twelve, could not conceal her disappointment, and turned away, feeling as so many of us have felt when we discover that our idols are very ordinary men and women.

"I thought she'd be about sixteen and have her hair braided in two tails down her back. I don't care about seeing her now," said the honest child walking off to the hall door, leaving her mother to apologize, and her sisters to declare that the bad portrait was "perfectly lovely, so speaking and poetic, you know, 'specially about the brow."

"Come, girls, we must be goin', if we want to get through to-day. You can leave your albums and have them sent when Mrs. Bhaer has written a sentiment in 'em. We are a thousand times obliged. Give our best love to your ma, and tell her we are so sorry not to see her."

Just as Mrs. Erastus Kingsbury Parmalee uttered the words her eye fell upon a middle-aged woman in a large checked apron, with a handkerchief tied over her head, busily dusting an end room which looked like a study.

"One peep at her sanctum since she is out," cried the enthusiastic lady, and swept across the hall with her flock before Teddy could warn his mother, whose retreat had been cut off by the artist in front, the reporter at the back part of the house,—for he had n't gone,—and the ladies in the hall.

"They've got her!" thought Teddy, in comical dismay. "No use for her to play housemaid since they've seen the portrait."

Mrs. Jo did her best, and being a good actress, would have escaped if the fatal picture had not betrayed her. Mrs. Parmalee paused at the desk, and regardless of the meerschaum that lay there, the man's slippers close by, and a pile of letters directed to "Prof. F. Bhaer," she clasped her hands, exclaiming impressively, "Girls, this is the spot where she wrote those sweet, those moral tales which have thrilled us to the soul! Could I—ah, could I take one morsel of paper, an old pen, a postage stamp even, as a memento of this gifted woman?"

"Yes'm, help yourselves," replied the maid, moving away with a glance at the boy whose eyes were now full of the merriment he could not suppress.

The oldest girl saw it, guessed the truth, and a quick look at the woman in the apron confirmed her suspicion. Touching her mother, she whispered, "Ma, it's Mrs. Bhaer herself. I know it is."

"No? yes? it is! Well, I do declare, how nice that is!" And hastily pursuing the unhappy woman, who was making for the door, Mrs. Parmalee cried eagerly. "Don't mind us! I know you're busy, but just let me take your hand and then we'll go."

Giving herself up for lost, Mrs. Jo turned and presented her hand like a tea-tray, submitting to have it heartily shaken, as the matron said, with somewhat alarming hospitality,—

"If ever you come to Oshkosh, your feet won't be allowed to touch the pavement; for you'll be borne in the arms of the populace, we shall be so dreadful glad to see you."

Mentally resolving never to visit that effusive town, Jo responded as cordially as she could; and having written her name in the albums, provided each visitor with a memento, and kissed them all round, they at last departed, to call on "Longfeller, Holmes, and the rest,"—who were all out, it is devoutly to be hoped.

"You villain, why didn't you give me a chance to whip away? Oh, my dear, what fibs you told that man! I hope we shall be forgiven our sins in this line, but I don't know what *is* to become of us if we don't dodge. So many against one isn't fair play." And Mrs. Jo hung up her apron in the hall closet, with a groan at the trials of her lot.

"More people coming up the avenue! Better dodge while the coast is clear! I'll head them off!" cried Teddy, looking back from the steps, as he was departing to school.

Mrs. Jo flew upstairs, having locked her door, calmly viewed a young ladies' seminary camp on the lawn, and being denied the house, proceed to enjoy themselves by picking the flowers, doing up their hair, eating lunch, and freely expressing their opinion of the place and its possessors before they went.

A few hours of quiet followed, and she was just settling down to a long afternoon of hard work, when Rob came home to tell her that the Young Men's Christian Union would visit the college, and two or three of the fellows whom she knew wanted to pay their respects to her on the way.

"It is going to rain, so they won't come, I dare say; but father thought you'd like to be ready, in case they do call. You always see the boys, you know, though you harden your heart to the poor girls," said Rob, who had heard from his brother about the morning visitations.

"Boys don't gush, so I can stand it. The last time I let in a party of girls, one fell into my arms and said, 'Darling, love me!' I wanted to shake her," answered Mrs. Jo, wiping her pen with energy.

"You may be sure the fellows won't do it, but they *will* want autographs, so you'd better be prepared with a few dozen," said Rob, laying out a quire of note-paper, being a hospitable youth and sympathizing with those who admired his mother.

"They can't outdo the girls. At X College I really believe I wrote three hundred during the day I was there, and I left a pile of cards and albums on my table when I came away. It is one of the most absurd and tiresome manias that ever afflicted the world."

Nevertheless Mrs. Jo wrote her name a dozen times, put on her black silk, and resigned herself to the impending call, praying for rain, however, as she returned to her work.

The shower came, and feeling quite secure, she rumpled up her hair, took off her cuffs, and hurried to finish her chapter; for thirty pages a day was her task, and she liked to have it well done before evening. Josie had brought some flowers for the vases, and was just putting the last touches when she saw several umbrellas bobbing down the hill.

"They are coming, Aunty! I see uncle hurrying across the field to receive them," she called at the stairfoot.

"Keep an eye on them, and let me know when they enter the avenue. It will take but a minute to tidy up and run down," answered Mrs. Jo, scribbling away for dear life, because serials wait for no man, not even the whole Christian Union *en masse*.

"There are more than two or three. I see half a dozen at least," called sister Ann from the hall door. "Not a dozen, I do believe, Aunty, look out; they are all coming! What *shall* we do?" And Josie quailed at the idea of facing the black throng rapidly approaching.

"Mercy on us, there are hundreds! Run and put a tub in the back entry for their umbrellas to drip into. Tell them to go down the hall and leave them, and pile their hats on the table; the tree won't hold them all. No use to get mats; my poor carpets!" And down went Mrs. Jo to prepare for the invasion, while Josie and the maids flew about dismayed at the prospect of so many muddy boots.

On they came, a long line of umbrellas, with splashed legs and flushed faces underneath; for the gentlemen had been having a good time all over the town, undisturbed by the rain. Professor Bhaer met them at the gate, and was making a little speech of welcome, when Mrs. Jo, touched by their bedraggled state, appeared at the door, beckoning them. Leaving their host to orate bareheaded in the wet, the young men hastened up the steps, merry, warm, and eager, clutching off their hats as they came, and struggling with their umbrellas, as the order was passed to march in and stack arms.

Tramp, tramp, tramp, down the hall went seventy-five

pairs of boots; soon seventy-five umbrellas dripped sociably in the hospitable tub, while their owners swarmed all over the lower part of the house; and seventy-five hearty hands were shaken by the hostess without a murmur, though some were wet, some very warm, and nearly all bore trophies of the day's ramble. One impetuous party flourished a small turtle as he made his compliments; another had a load of sticks cut from noted spots; and all begged for some memento of Plumfield. A pile of cards mysteriously appeared on the table, with a written request for autographs; and despite her morning vow, Mrs. Jo wrote every one, while her husband and the boys did the honors of the house.

Josie fled to the back parlor, but was discovered by exploring youths, and mortally insulted by one of them, who innocently inquired if she was Mr. Bhaer. The reception did not last long, and the end was better than the beginning; for the rain ceased, and a rainbow shone beautifully over them as the good fellows stood upon the lawn singing sweetly for a farewell. A happy omen, that bow of promise arched over the young heads, as if Heaven smiled upon their union, and showed them that above the muddy earth and rainy skies the blessed sun still shone for all.

Three cheers, and then away they went, leaving a pleasant recollection of their visit to amuse the family as they scraped the mud off the carpets with shovels and emptied the tub half-full of water.

"Nice, honest, hard-working fellows, and I don't begrudge my half-hour at all; but I *must* finish, so don't let any one disturb me till tea-time," said Mrs. Jo, leaving Mary to shut up the house; for papa and the boys had gone off with the guests, and Josie had run home to tell her mother about the fun at Aunt Jo's.

Peace reigned for an hour, then the bell rang and Mary came giggling up to say, "A queer kind of a lady wants to know if she can catch a grasshopper in the garden."

"A what?" cried Mrs. Jo, dropping her pen with a blot; for of all the odd requests ever made, this was the oddest.

"A grasshopper ma'am. I said you was busy, and asked what she wanted, and says she, "I've got grasshoppers from the grounds of several famous folks, and I want one from Plumfield to add to my collection. Did you ever?" And Mary giggled again at the idea.

"Tell her to take all there are and welcome. I shall be glad to get rid of them; always bouncing in my face and getting in my dress," laughed Mrs. Jo.

Mary retired, to return in a moment nearly speechless with merriment.

"She's much obliged, ma'am, and she'd like an old gown or a pair of stockings of yours to put in a rug she's making. Got a vest of Emerson's she says, and a pair of Mr. Holmes's trousers, and a dress of Mrs. Stowe's. She must be crazy!"

"Give her that old red shawl, then I shall make a gay show among the great ones in that astonishing rug. Yes, they are all lunatics, these lion-hunters; but this seems to be a harmless maniac, for she does n't take my time and gives me a good laugh," said Mrs. Jo, returning to her work after a glance from the window, which showed her a tall, thin lady in rusty black, skipping wildly to and fro on the lawn in pursuit of the lively insect she wanted.

Woody Allen (Contemporary)

ᖰᖰᖰ

FROM *"The Scrolls"*

And the man sewed on to all his shirts a small alligator symbol and lo and behold, suddenly his merchandise moved like gangbusters, and there was much rejoicing while amongst his enemies there was wailing and gnashing of teeth, and one said, "The Lord is merciful. He maketh me to lie down in green pastures. The problem is, I can't get up."

Laws and Proverbs

Doing abominations is against the law, particularly if the abominations are done while wearing a lobster bib.

The lion and the calf shall lie down together but the calf won't get much sleep.

Whosoever shall not fall by the sword or by famine, shall fall by pestilence so why bother shaving?

The wicked at heart probably know something.

Whosoever loveth wisdom is righteous but he that keepeth company with fowl is weird.

My Lord, my Lord! What hast Thou done, lately?

Regina Barreca (Contemporary)

❧❦❧

FROM *Chicago Tribune*

Looking for Live Heroines

This year I am making a serious promise: no more movies with dead women as the heroines. No more babes in self-sacrifice land. No more traipsing over the bodies of deceased ladies as I walk up the aisle in a theater or rewind a tape on what is laughingly called my home entertainment system. Entertainment? Are you kidding? Maybe I could just poke myself in the eye with a stick for a while; that would be better and I'd save all that money on Kleenex. Nope, in 1998 there will be no more crying, no more schnooks, no more usher's dirty looks.

What prompts this declaration of independence? I just watched a lyrical, beautifully acted, and gorgeous film called "Breaking the Waves." While I don't want to give away the whole plot, let's just say the leading lady was lucky that she hadn't bought any green bananas, if you catch my drift. And because I'm preparing for a course on images of women in film adaptations of classic literature, I've also been having a jolly old holiday season watching such old favorites as Anna Karinina (Garbo), Madame Bovary (Huppert), Tess of the D'Urbervilles (Kinski), Wuthering Heights (Oberon) and Butterfield 8 (Taylor). And it wasn't just Kinski's acting that made me cry. The whole wild bunch here includes broads with a wide range of talents and temperaments whose lives cross cultures and span eras. They have only one thing in common: They all wake up dead.

This doesn't make for what you'd call a really "fun tune" over the popcorn. Here's the scene: I'm sitting in the living room, cat on my lap, slippers on my feet, mesmerized, furious and weeping. I'm trying to watch every gesture on the screen, eat every morsel from the bowl, and blow my nose all at the same time. It's not pretty. What do these film women do that's so incredibly bad that they need to be punished by death, which is in most cases a fairly final solution? They have adventures, they yell, they love passionately, they rebel, they talk back, maybe they drink and dance a little, they have thighs, and they escape the straitjacket of traditional femininity, albeit briefly.

So how do we reward them? We ship them off to a funeral—their own funeral—and that's if they're lucky. At least at a funeral they get to be the center of attention, wear a new dress, and receive flowers. Compared to their final moments on Earth, even a moderately priced funeral is a peachy alternative.

"Oh, come on," chides my optimistic friend Nancy, with whom I have wept in tandem over countless cinematic fatalities, "not everybody dies." She pauses to consider and then gingerly offers a palliative: "Some only go crazy." Oh, goody. They get to gnash their teeth and rent their garments.

These crazy ladies of Hollywood are ever so slightly less appealing than the dead ones, given that madness is apparently easy to establish through the over-use of make-up (particularly lipstick—misapplied lipstick is the single most common denominator among the female insane in cinema). Pathologically insane female characters are also famous for their ability to withstand bad hair days without comment. If there's a female character whose hair is frizzy or showing any signs of reverting to its natural color, and she doesn't complain actively about this, you know she's certifiable. You see roots, and you should think: immediate institutionalization. Film logic insists that a woman who would let her grooming slide is capable of any atrocity. Clearly it is only the matter of a few frames before she kills again or perhaps runs screaming through the streets scaring small children and trapping them for use in a curry.

So does my resolution mean that I will be watching only cartoons in 1998? Not if those cartoons are Bambi (dead mother) or Dumbo (insane and imprisoned mother). Can't go there, either, it seems, without jeopardizing my resolution. My nieces and nephews will have to watch by themselves while I stick my fingers in my ears and hum in another room. Too much of that, of course, and I'll soon be putting on my lipstick funny, but it is a risk I'll have to take.

OK, so how about this? How about we get to see a couple of flicks in which strong women not only survive, but triumph? How about if they don't go over a cliff, under a train, or explode into space? How about if they get to stride into the sunrise, laughing, and do this while still remaining smart, sexy, compassionate and witty? How about if they refuse to lie down and die just so that they can be revered in the memory of some guy or a couple of kids who will find a replacement for the missing character by the time the final credits roll?

How about the radical suggestion that our heroines get to endure long enough to hang out and have a good time (maybe even enjoy a guy and/or a couple of kids) without obvious injury to their bodies, psyches, without, perhaps, even sacrificing their sense of fashion awareness?

I know, I know. You'll accuse me of rejecting the pain of life, of refusing to accept that our existence on this Earth is fraught with difficulties both insurmountable and overwhelming. Yes, life is very often very difficult. But it is also very often very ennobling, challenging, energizing and lively. It is also very, very funny. And I'm betting that 1998 will be a good year for underwriting the female characters who dare to laugh—and live—out loud.

Even the Happiest Couple Will Spend Time Arguing About Money

Earlier in our marriage, we used to argue about money.

When I say earlier, I mean "about 20 minutes ago" because no matter how long or how successful your marriage, you never stop arguing about money. Money may not be the root of all evil, but it sure is at the root of a whole lot of slammed doors, tissue-use, ripped and crumpled pieces of paper with meaningless lists of figures written on them, and yelling. Yelling and money really go together in my experience, with partners switching over from the "yeller" to the "yellee" with surprising, not to say, harmonious, regularity.

For example, my husband, Michael, and I will have the Arguments of Doom about once every three to four weeks, or when any major purchase appears on a credit card, whichever comes first. Hints of the approaching storm will begin with a few grumbles about how come we stopped making sandwiches to take to work with us before we leave in the morning, thereby saving the expense of eating out?

I'll remind him of the primary reasons we stopped this delectable practice: 1) We used to squabble over whose turn it was to make lunch with some of these particular disagreements beginning the night previous to the sandwich activity; 2) We disagreed over the merits of toasted vs. untoasted bread, the use of plastic vs. foil wrap, the application of paper vs. plastic bags for transport, etc.; 3) The sandwiches were dreary, soggy and—despite this—we inevitably devoured them before 10:30 A.M. because neither of us is known for self-restraint (which is why we have decided not to keep firearms in our home). Because we'd eaten lunch well before noon, we were left with two choices when we'd be starving at 3: eat dinner at 4, elbowing senior citizens out of their rightfully earned Early Bird Specials, or have two lunches. Neither alternative helped us resemble the fit couple in the ads for nutrient supplements. I remind him that we are much, much happier (and better looking) for our daily walk to the lunch cart.

In retaliation for his bringing up the Sandwich Issue, however, I feel free to point out that he has spent tons of money (adding up to somewhere close to $10 over the past few years) on renting movies we have already seen but whose titles he has forgotten.

He'll counter by bringing up my fetish for buying makeup whenever the manufacturers offer those tantalizing "free gifts" whereby you buy makeup you don't need in order to be given products you don't want in colors you'll never wear but which are packed cunningly and adorably into a little cosmetic bag you'll never use.

Conversations like these rarely end with a kiss. They are far more likely to lead to hissed statements at other people's parties along the lines of, "You'll notice that she doesn't bother him about buying really good olives. He has a whole jar." Or, "Her husband would never ask her whether she 'really needed' another pair of black shoes." Such pronouncements do not herald a new era of marital bliss, but instead pave the way for dynamic encounters where simple hissing turns to deep sarcasm. "Oh, no, I couldn't possibly have another one of those olives. I might get used to them and then my wife would have to start wearing rags to support my habit," is one example of the kind of escalation this can lead to; the wife might then be tempted to respond "Yes, I might be forced to sell my one pair of black shoes," and take it from there.

You can choose, of course, never to mention money, which is what my mother and father tried to do, except that it meant that money was only ever discussed when it got to a genuine state of crisis, which happened about every three days. It wasn't easy for my parents to talk about money or not to talk about it. That's the trouble when there isn't enough of something in a relationship. The thing there isn't enough of becomes the only thing you can think about.

Do separate bank accounts help? Maybe—as long as you don't have a partner who reads your statement and then criticizes your handling of cash with all the gusto of an editor from *The New Yorker* looking at a short-story written by a 9th-grader. Not that I'm mentioning names. We have a joint bank account and we each have our own. I can therefore choose to keep track of my finances or simply live the carefree, edgy life of someone who has no idea whether the check number, the check amount, or simply an interesting historical date is noted by the number "1206" when I see it written on a Post-It slipped into my purse as a memory-aid. In contrast, Michael is upset if any small detail (such as the date or recipient) is left off a canceled check. Such differences keep our marriage young (and also force us to have a huge jar of coins that we can always use to pay the most pressing bills).

Why does personal finance disrupt even the happiest

union? Why does filthy lucre desecrate the otherwise un-sullied marital canvas? I'd love to get the answers to these questions, but therapy these days goes for about $125 per hour and for that price I could get a really terrific pair of suede pumps. So I'll settle for a little wisdom passed down from my grandmother. Money can't buy love. (In the interests of fairness, I'll add to it a little wisdom thrown in by my grandfather: Money can, however, buy you a big car that you can use to find love.) No, when you are tempted to argue about finances, ask yourself this question: Would I rather strengthen my bank account or my relationship? As long as both of you give the same answer, you're OK.

That will be $125, please.

FROM *The Hartford Courant Sunday Magazine*

Tight(s) Fisted

I'm lucky, and I'm the first to admit it. I have a steady job, a working spouse, and two smallish cats who don't eat very much. I give a lot of talks and therefore have a diet high in fish and chicken prepared *á là hotel* (meaning served with vegetables so drastically overcooked as to actually drain nutrients from surrounding foods). Not cheap by nature, I'm happy to spend money on gifts, long-distance phone calls, and earrings. So why did I just spend 45 minutes trying on every outfit in my closet, including bridesmaid dresses and skirts I haven't fit into since I campaigned for Geraldine Ferraro, so that I wouldn't have to throw away some new tights (total cost: $3.23), which had a run in them?

You have to understand that these were virgin stockings, brand-new, just out of the flat package with the thin cardboard center. They had that nice, new aren't-your-legs-going-to-look-like-Lauren Bacall's feel to them. Sheer but not too sheer (precisely because I wanted to get them over my shin before they shredded), they were exactly the right off-black to get me dressed properly and out of the house quickly enough to find a parking space at 7 A.M. Imagine my disappointment, then, when this racing stripe appeared up the side of my left leg as soon as the nylon came into contact with my skin.

I tried on trousers, long skirts, short skirts with boots (a combination that didn't work unless I was about to audition for a lead in "Elsa of the SS."), culottes, everything. I didn't want to take the tights off and throw them out never having worn them. But when I think about the time I spent—not spent, wasted, flushed down the toilet of eternity—I feel like a moron. Tights are my Money Thing.

But everybody has something they hate, absolutely soul-wrenchingly hate, to spend money on. My otherwise generous husband suddenly turns into the guy from "The Shining" if I call directory assistance for any number on the East Coast. He gets telephone books from other states so that we don't ever have to call information; I'm quite convinced that soon he'll be getting directories from other lands in case we ever need to call Samoa. This is a guy who'll spend $15 to go to the auto show—spending money to get into a place where people try to convince you to spend yet more money is not my idea of good value—but 85 cents he begrudges us. That's because calling information is his Money Thing.

Other folks' Money Things (I've done research) include driving 136 miles to buy cheap gas; keeping half-used cosmetics in a back drawer even though they have actually broken down into their individual chemical components by this point and would no longer help you make a fashion statement (unless that statement is "I am deliberately trying to look like Joan Rivers's older sister"); never replacing pillows even after the feathers have clumped and turned into gravel; steaming or scraping unfranked stamps off envelopes; using shampoos containing both lard and petrochemicals taken from motels even if they make your hair look like it belongs on "Weird Al" Yankovic; and, of course, keeping a soaking wet Band-Aid on your finger, even when you know it will make your finger get all pruney.

Some folks will take sugar and Equal packets from restaurants; some will reuse paper towels so often that the word "disposable" no longer has any meaning in their lives. Others make their families live in the dark so that they won't waste electricity by trying to do things such as reading after sunset. This particular method of anxiety-provoking electrical efficiency was topped only by a story told by my friend George, who mentioned that in Brazil certain taxi drivers turn off their lights when they're driving at night in order to save the battery.

My friend Sylvia would rather drink from a puddle than spend 79 cents on bottled water, even if we've just had the sort of Indian food that's so hot it lets you see into another dimension. John won't spend $2 on one of those cassette tape cleaners even though the music in his car sounds like it's recorded in an aquarium. Charles went to a supermarket where he saw packets of salad dressing with the word "free" printed all over them; shameless, he took maybe 25 of these and placed them alongside his usual groceries. Imagine his surprise when he realized he was being charged about half a buck for each one—"free" meant "fat-free" but he was too embarrassed to explain to the nice woman at the checkout that he only wanted tiny portions of Ranch and Thousand Island because he thought he was getting a present from the store.

We do this because, in part, we're scared of money, scared of being taken for a ride by the merchandising and advertising industries, because we think our behavior counts as being thrifty or wise, and because we feel a need to have control over what happens to us.

As for me, I'm going to start wearing socks.

FROM *The Hartford Courant
Sunday Magazine*

Shades of Gray

I have to stop listening to people. They mix me up. There I was, thinking that I'd been as intimidated as I could ever be by fashion, by magazines, by the images of women on television and in the movies. And then I listened to a few women—all wonderful, all genuinely good friends—and now I'm all bothered again. I'm back to spending all sorts of stupid time looking at clothes in my closet, as if any minute now my shirts are going to break into song.

This is what happened: One day Maggie was describing a café where she'd gone to listen to music the night before. She described the place as vaguely depressing and so I asked her for details. What were the people like, I asked, what were they wearing? "Well," she replied, happy to have come up with an example that would clarify her position, "all these women were dressed in black, but it was like they were wearing three or four kinds of black, none of which matched or complemented each other, you know what I mean?" I guess I must have been staring at her like she was from a parallel universe because she asked me if I was OK. "I'm fine," I responded, "but please explain what you mean about wearing different shades of black."

Suddenly, even as she spoke, I was reviewing 25 years of fashion choices; they were spinning before my eyes the way stars speed by when movie spaceships enter a time warp. I was in my personal little time warp, trying to remember if anybody had ever mentioned this patently obvious point before this moment. I came up with a blank. I also came up with a new tiny cause for stress: Even as Maggie's innocent words sunk in, I realized my black leggings clashed with my black socks, which were as different a color from the black in my shoes as fuchsia is from fire-engine red. Fashion casualty that I am, even I wouldn't wear a pinky-red with an orange-y red, so how could I have not seen the differences in my dark clothes, the clothes I wear pretty much as a uniform every day?

I could, once again, place all blame conveniently on my early history and genetic coding. Back in Brooklyn all the women who weren't wearing floral print house-dresses were wearing black, at least in my immediate family (of 118). After a certain age, a woman automatically started wearing black—enough people die, your wardrobe changes. But I don't remember my Aunt Clara trying to discern whether her black orthopedic shoes matched her black support hose, and she never held them up to discover whether they matched the shiny black cotton of her short-sleeved black dress. They fit, they were washable, they didn't bind, they were on sale, that was good enough.

But, having learned to accept responsibility for my own choices in life (particularly those involving fabric), I couldn't believe the errors of my ways were all due to my early upbringing. No, I had to admit that before Maggie named it, I hadn't seen it.

But this experience paled in comparison to one brought on by a brief comment made by another friend, Viv, who, when trying on a great pair of trousers, declared: "But I'll never wear them. See how they look on me when I sit down?" Whereupon she promptly and without warning or explanation plopped herself down on the floor of the store's dressing room. If she'd suddenly burst into an aria from Wagner I could not have been more surprised. "What on earth are you doing?!" I shrieked, trying to pull her up to her adult height. "I'm seeing how they'll look when I sit. See how everything bunches up above the waist? See how they emphasize my hips? Forget it," she shrugged, and left the pants hanging beautifully on their hanger, having brushed off any debris they might have picked up on the floor.

Terrific. For the rest of my life I'll have to go through a full range of possible positions in which I can be viewed before making a $20 purchase. Now I pretend to sit down or bend over in a dressing room: I go through so many motions I look like a mime. Now I am aware of just how a jacket will look when I'm actually wearing it, not just how it looks while I'm standing as straight as a Marine and holding my breath in order to suck in my stomach.

Once you hear these things, you can't forget them. Sure, you can choose to ignore them or discard them, but even then you don't forget them. For example, Genny said that her mother said (and mothers are often the sources of these pieces of grave information) a lady should not wear more than three colors at the same time. OK, this is where I drew the line: I can't wear black for fear of messing that up, but I also can't wear more than three colors?

That's it, I'm going to find where Aunt Clara bought her clothes and set up an account. They can send me a new one every year. It'll be my job to make sure the stockings match.

FROM *They Used to Call Me Snow White . . . But I Drifted*

Getting the Last Laugh: Example

When Liz Carpenter, the former White House staff director for Lady Bird Johnson, published her book *Ruffles and Flourishes*, she came in for a number of remarks from male colleagues. When Arthur Schlesinger, Jr., stopped Carpenter to make the following comment, "I liked your book, Liz. Who wrote it for you?" she replied brightly, "I'm glad you liked it, Arthur. Who read it to you?" The man who believes he runs no risk when he launches a joke at a woman should be made to reevaluate his situation. The reason most men feel comfortable making jokes directed at women is that they do not expect any viable retort. They are more prepared for a hurt look than a quick reply, and to be able to take them off guard with the woman's own humor is to move in from a position of advantage.

Deflating Pretensions Through Humor

The first session where everyone admits to losing her virginity is a landmark event in any girl's life. It's like a baptism into adulthood, a celebration of your femininity, especially if you can giggle at and share the anxiety of the event. Occasionally there will be a girl in the group whose holier-than-thou attitude threatens to undermine the coziness of the event. I remember one friend's reaction to such a situation. We were sitting there in the middle of the night, eating Sara Lee cheesecakes (still frozen, when their flavor is at a peak), swapping stories. One little blonde, with tiny eyes and a nose so upturned it resembled a ski lift rather than a ski jump, said, rather archly, that where she came from Good Girls didn't sleep with their boyfriends. Without missing a beat, my pal met her beady eyes and replied, "In my neighborhood, Good Girls sleep *only* with their boyfriends." The conversation proceeded without further sanctimonious interruption.

Making a Beginning

Women's humor may be undervalued, but it is priceless. It may have been hidden away, but it has been constant. It may have been ignored or challenged, but it has always been a secretly potent, delightfully dangerous, wonderfully seductive, and, most important, powerful way to make ourselves heard, to capture the attention, the heart, and the respect of our audience.

Throwing your head back and laughing out loud is always an experiment because you can never be sure how others will react. But it is also a manifestation of your willingness to give others the benefit of the doubt by assuming they will also rise to the occasion, by joining in and laughing with you.

When you tell a joke or a funny story or make a witty remark and not many others laugh with you, what you've made isn't a mistake. What you've made is a beginning.

Dave Barry (Contemporary)

FROM *The World According to Dave Barry*

What Has Four Legs and Flies

People often say to me, "Dave, when you say you're not making something up, does that mean you're really and truly not making it up?" And the answer is yes. Meaning no, I am not making it up. I mention this so you'll believe me when I say that I'm not making up today's topic, which is: the Head-Smashed-In Buffalo Jump.

The Head-Smashed-In Buffalo Jump is a historical site and tourist attraction in Alberta, Canada. Canada, as you know, is a major important nation boasting a sophisticated, cosmopolitan culture that was tragically destroyed last week by beavers.

Ha ha! Don't mind me. I like to toss out little "zingers" about Canada from time to time because I enjoy getting mounds of letters from irate Canadians who are Sick and Tired of Americans belittling Canada and who often include brochures full of impressive Canadian Facts such as that Canada is the world's largest producer of magnesium dentures as well as the original home of Michael J. Fox, Big Bird, Plato, etc.

The thing is, I like Canada. It's clean, and it makes good beer. Also it has a spirit of general social cooperation that you find lacking in the States, a good example being the metric system. You may recall that a while back we were all supposed to convert to the metric system from our current system of measurement, which is technically known as the "correct" or "real" system. The metric conversion was supposed to result in major economic benefits deriving from the fact that you, the consumer, would suddenly have no idea how the hell much anything cost. Take coleslaw. Under the current system, coleslaw is sold in easily understood units of measurement called "containers," as in "Gimme one of them containers of coleslaw if it's fresh." In a metric supermarket, however, the deli person would say, "How much do you want? A kilometer? A hectare? Hurry up! My break starts in five liters!" You'd get all confused and wind up buying enough coleslaw to fill a wading pool, and the economy would prosper.

So the metric conversion was clearly a good idea, and when the government started putting up metric highway signs (SPEED LIMIT 173 CENTIPEDES) Americans warmly responded by shooting them down. Thus the metric system did not really catch on in the States, unless you count the increasing popularity of the nine-millimeter bullet.

Meanwhile, the Canadians, being cooperative, quietly went ahead and actually converted. I know this because I was on a Canadian radio program once, and the host announced that the temperature was "8." This was obviously a lie, so I asked him about it, and he confided, off the air, that the real temperature, as far as he knew, was around 40. But then his engineer said he thought it was more like 50, and soon other radio personnel were chiming in with various other interpretations of "8," and I was struck by the fact that these people had cheerfully accepted, in the spirit of cooperation, a system wherein *nobody really knew what the temperature was*. (The correct mathematical answer is: chilly.)

The point I am making is that Canada is a fascinating and mysterious country, which is why we should not be surprised to learn that it is the location of the Head-Smashed-In Buffalo Jump historical site and tourist attraction. I found out about this from an extremely alert reader named Sandy LaFave, who sent me an article from the *Fort McLeod Tourist Greeter* that explains the whole buffalo-jump concept.

It seems that many moons ago (in metric, 14.6 megamoons) North America was occupied by large and fortunately very stupid herds of buffalo. Certain Native American tribes used to obtain their food by disguising themselves in buffalo skins and going from tepee to tepee shouting "Trick or Treat!"

No, seriously, according to the *Fort McLeod Tourist Greeter*, they disguised themselves so they could lure a buffalo herd closer and closer to a cliff, then stampede it over the edge. That's where the "Buffalo Jump" part of the name comes from. The "Head-Smashed-In" part comes from a native legend, which holds that one time a young brave (probable tribal name: "Not Nuclear Physicist") decided to watch the hunt while standing *under* the cliff. According to the *Tourist Greeter*, he "watched the buffalo topple in front of him like a mighty waterfall. . . . When it was over and the natives were butchering the animals, they found him under the pile of dead buffalo with his head smashed in."

Even thousands of years later, it is difficult to ponder this tragedy without choking back large, moist snorts of anguish. But some good has come of it. The Head-Smashed-In Buffalo Jump has been declared a World Heritage Site ("as are the pyramids in Egypt and the Taj Mahal in India," notes the *Tourist Greeter*). The Alberta government has constructed an interpretive centre (note metric spelling) where activities are held. "There's always something to see and do at the Head-Smashed-In Buffalo Jump Interpretive Centre and this summer is no exception," states an official schedule. I have called the centre, and when they answer the phone, they say, very politely—I absolutely swear this is true—"Head-Smashed-In, may I help you?"

And the scary part is, I think maybe they *can*.

Today's Self-Help Topic Is: Coping with Anger

There is definitely too much anger in the world today. Pick up almost any newspaper, and the odds are you'll get ink smeared all over your hands. We use a special kind of easy-smear ink, because we know how much it irritates you.

But that's not my point. My point is that if you pick up almost any newspaper, you'll see stories of anger raging out of control, of people actually shooting each other over minor traffic disputes. Can you imagine? Can you imagine feeling so much hostility that just because you're in a traffic jam on a hot day, and you've been stuck for an hour waiting in a long line of cars trying to exit from a busy highway, and along comes one of those line-butting jerks, some guy who's talking on his cellular phone and figures he's *too important* to be waiting in a line with common rest-room bacteria like yourself, so he barges past the entire line and butts in *right in front of you*, so you honk your horn, and he shows you his Mister Digit hand puppet, so you haul out a pistol large enough for antiaircraft purposes and LET THE SCUMBALL HAVE IT HAHAHAHAHAHAHAHA WOULDN'T THAT BE GREAT??

I mean terrible. "Wouldn't that be terrible," is what I mean. And this is why it's so important that we learn to understand what anger is, and how we can cope with it. As you know if you ever studied the famous Greek philosopher Aristotle, he was easily the most boring human being who ever lived. Thousands of college students suffer forehead damage every year from passing out face-forward while attempting to read his books. But it was Aristotle who identified anger as one of the Six Basic Human Emotions, along with Lust, Greed, Envy, Fear of Attorneys, and the Need to Snack.

We know that primitive man felt anger, as is evidenced by the deep kick marks that archeologists have found in prehistoric vending machines. We also see evidence of anger in the animal kingdom. The great white shark, for example, periodically gets furious at the small seaside resort town of Amity and tries to eat all the residents, possibly in an effort to prevent another sequel. And dogs are for some historical reason *extremely* angry at cats. I once watched a dog named Edgar spot a cat roughly a hundred yards away and go tearing after it, faster and faster, gaining ground with each step until he was just inches away, at which point the cat made a very sharp right turn, leaving Edgar to run directly, at Dog Warp Speed, into the side of a house. Fortunately he absorbed the entire impact with his brain, so there was no damage, but this incident teaches us that anger is very self-destructive, and that we must learn to control it.

Let's take the case of the line-butting driver. The trick here is to put things into perspective. Ask yourself: Does it really matter, long-term, if this guy butts in front of you? Is it really more important than serious world problems such as Ethiopia or the Greenhouse Effect? Yes. No question. You don't even know where Ethiopia is. This is why psychologists recommend, when you feel your anger getting out of control, that you practice a simple yoga technique: Imagine that you're in a peaceful, quiet setting such as a meadow, then take a deep breath, then exhale slowly, then gently s-q-u-e-e-z-e that trigger. See how much better you feel? In Advanced Yoga we use grenades.

Aside from traffic, the leading cause of anger is marriage. No matter how much you love somebody, if you spend enough time with that person, you're going to notice his or her flaws. If Romeo had stayed long enough under that balcony staring up worshipfully at Juliet, he'd have become acutely aware of her nasal hairs. So most married couples, even though they love each other very much in theory, tend to view each other in practice as large teeming flaw colonies, the result being that they get on each other's nerves and regularly erupt into vicious emotional shouting matches over issues such as toaster settings.

Professional marriage counselors agree that the most productive and mature way to deal with marital anger is to stomp dramatically from the room. The key here is timing. You want to make your move *before* your opponent does, because the first person to stomp from the room receives valuable Argument Points that can be redeemed for exciting merchandise at the Marital Prize Redemption Center. Of course you have to be on the alert for defensive maneuvers. A couple I know named Buzz and Libby were once having a Force Ten argument in their kitchen, and Buzz attempted to make a dramatic exit stomp, but Libby, a former field-hockey player, stuck her foot out as he went past and tripped him, so he wound up stumbling from the room, trying desperately to look dignified but actually looking like a man auditioning for Clown School. Libby won 5,000 bonus points, good for a handsome set of luggage.

Ultimately, however, anger benefits nobody. If you keep it bottled up inside, it eats away at you, until eventually you turn into a bitter, spiteful, hate-ridden person working in Customer Service. So take my advice: Lighten up. Don't let your anger get the best of you. Don't lose your humanity, or your sense of humor. Don't *ever* try to butt in front of me.

Politics After 40: You Don't Need a Weatherman to Know That Harsh Sunlight Can Harm Your BMW's Finish

You hardly ever see radical activists anymore. The last time I saw any up close was at the 1988 Democratic convention in Atlanta, the one where the Democrats nominated Michael "The Human Quaalude" Dukakis. The Democrats had thoughtfully set up a Designated Protest Area right next to the convention hall. (This was in stark contrast to the Republicans, who held *their* convention right next to—this is true—a shopping center.)

The Democrats' Designated Protest Area featured a powerful public-address system and a stage where, according to the official protest schedule, various groups or individuals would get up and make long, impassioned speeches for or against endangered crustaceans or transvestite canoeists' rights or whatever, their voices booming out from the huge speakers and thundering across a listening throng averaging maybe nine people, seven of whom were waiting for their turn to protest.

The protesters who showed up most often, sometimes interrupting other people's protests, were a group of left-wing radical activists. They were mostly kids in their teens or early twenties. Fashionwise, they favored a sportswear look that I would call "Pretend Guerrilla," sometimes including bandannas pulled up over their faces, thus enabling them to blend into the downtown Atlanta environment as unobtrusively as water buffalo at a formal wedding. They communicated almost exclusively by shouting slogans, and their philosophy boiled down to two basic points:

1. They represented The People.
2. They hated people.

At least that's the way it seemed, because they were always in a spittle-emitting rage, loudly accusing everybody they encountered—police, other protesters, media people, spectators, trash cans, squirrels—of being mother-f-wording CIA fascists. They used this expression reflexively, the way supermarket cashiers use "Have a nice day."

Needless to say, the radicals were very persuasive. After a few minutes of listening to them shout in your face, you were ready to march down to the CIA Recruitment Center and sign up. At least I was, and this bothered me somewhat. Because, like almost everybody in my generation except Julie Nixon and David Eisenhower, I used to be a left-wing, anti-establishment, protest-oriented, march-on-Washington type of individual. Once, back in college, I even participated in a hunger strike to end the Vietnam War. By not eating, I was supposedly enabling myself to focus my consciousness on peace. What actually happened was that I became absolutely obsessed with cheeseburgers, although if I really, really forced myself to concentrate on the tragedy in Southeast Asia, I could also visualize french fries. I kept this up for several days, but failed to have much of an impact on Washington. At no point, as far as I know, did a White House aide burst into the Oval Office and shout with alarm, "Some students at Haverford College have been refusing to eat for several days!" followed by Lyndon Johnson saying, "Mah God! Ah got to change mah foreign policy!"

But the point is, at least I was *trying,* in my own naive and painfully earnest way, to do what I thought was the right thing. Whereas these days I never seem to get involved in causes. The last time I remember protesting anything with any real passion was when I was at a professional basketball game and the arena management decided to stop selling beer in the fourth quarter.

Of course, some would argue that, hey, the war is over, so there aren't any causes to get involved in anymore. Which is of course ridiculous. There are all *kinds* of causes to be alarmed about. For example, there's the Greenhouse Effect, which is one of the more recent in a series of alarming worldwide homicidal trends to be discovered by those busy beavers, the scientists. They've found that the Earth is slowly being turned into a vast greenhouse, so that by the year 2010—unless something is done—the entire human race will be crushed beneath a humongous tomato.

Or something along those lines. I confess that I haven't been following the Greenhouse Effect all that closely. Whenever I'm reading the newspaper and I come to the words "Greenhouse Effect," I continue reading, but I squinch my eyes up real tight so that the words become a meaningless blur. I originally developed this technique for watching suspense movies, in which the characters wander around inside a house with menacing background music and nothing happens and nothing happens and nothing happens and nothing happens and *my God it plucked her eyeballs out like a pair of grapes.*

I'm not saying that the Greenhouse Effect is not extremely important. Hey, I live in Miami, and if the polar ice caps start melting, I stand a good chance of waking up one morning and finding myself festooned with kelp. It's just that, what with working and paying bills and transporting my son to and from the pediatrician and trying to teach the dog not to throw up on the only nice rug in the entire house, I just don't seem to have enough room in my brain for the Greenhouse Effect and all the other problems I know I should be concerned about, such as drugs and AIDS and Lebanon and pollution and cholesterol and caffeine and cancer and Japanese investors buying the Lincoln Memorial and nuclear war and dirty rock lyrics and this new barbecue grill we got. Our old grill rusted out. It was your basic model, the kind where you put your charcoal in, you lit it, you noticed about an hour later that the charcoal had gone out, and you ordered a pizza. It gave us many years of good service.

Our new grill was purchased by my wife, Beth, who would be a natural in the field of military procurement because whatever she's buying, she always gets the most fangled one they sell. She came home with a grill approximately the size of a nuclear submarine but more complicated, featuring knobs, valves, switches, auto-ignite, a fold-down side table, "flavor bars," a side burner, an electric rotisserie, and much more. This grill squats out on the patio, the lord of all it surveys. For weeks I was afraid to go near it. Finally I decided, hey, it's just a grill, so I got out the owner's manual, which is twenty-eight pages long. Here's what it says:

CAUTION! (five times)
DANGER! (six times)
WARNING! (thirty-eight times)

These are true statistics. So we are talking about a total of forty-nine scary things to remember just about a barbecue grill, and, frankly, I do not feel up to it. The only warning I even started to read was on page 3, which begins, I swear, with the words:

WARNING!!!!!
SPIDER AND INSECT ALERT

This is followed by the statement: "Your Genesis Gas Barbecue as well as any outdoor gas appliance is a target for spiders and insects." Needless to say, I stopped reading right there, because the very thought of insects targeting my grill (For what? Theft?) makes me want to get into the fetal position.

My point is that whereas I once felt totally confident of my ability to shape the destiny of the nation and, yes, the world, I now have grave doubts about my ability to cope with a patio appliance. Aside from giving my Fair Share to the United Fund, I have pretty much withdrawn from causes, and so, apparently, have many other members of my generation, except perhaps for David and Julie Nixon Eisenhower, who, being 180 degrees out of sync, are probably living in a geodesic dome somewhere, smoking hashish by the kilogram and making plans to blow up the Pentagon.

Sometimes I think I'd like to get more involved politically, but I get depressed when I look at the two major name-brand political parties. Both of them seem to be dominated by the kind of aggressively annoying individuals who always came in third for sophomore class president. Which is not to say that there are no differences between the parties. The Democrats seem to be basically nicer people, but they have demonstrated time and again that they have the management skills of celery. They're the kind of people who'd stop to help you change a flat, but would somehow manage to set your car on fire. I would be reluctant to entrust them with a Cuisinart, let alone the economy. The Republicans, on the other hand, would know how to fix your tire, but they wouldn't bother to stop because they'd want to be on time for Ugly Pants Night at the country club. Also, the Republicans have a high Beady-Eyed Self-Righteous Scary Borderline Loon Quotient, as evidenced by Phyllis Schlafly, Pat Robertson, the entire state of Utah, etc.

But the biggest problem I have with both major political parties is that they seem to be competing in some kind of giant national scavenger hunt every four years to see who can find the biggest goober to run for President. I was hoping that things would improve when my generation took over—when somebody my age, representing the best that my generation had to offer, morally and intellectually, got nominated to a national ticket. When this finally happened, of course, the nod went to "Dan" Quayle, a man whose concept of visionary leadership is steering his own golf cart, a man who—and I mean no disrespect when I say this—would not stand out, intellectually, in a vat of plankton.

I can hear you saying: "Oh yeah, Mr. Smartass? Well, what kind of leader would *you* be?" The answer is, I'd be a terrible leader. I'd be such an inadequate leader that within a matter of days the United States would rank significantly below Belize as a world power. But at least I'd try to be an *interesting* leader. I wouldn't be one more pseudo-somber, blue-suited, red-tied, wingtip-shoed weenie, frowning at the issues with sincerely feigned concern. I'd try to truly represent my generation, the rock-'n-roll generation that had the idealism and courage to defy the Establishment, stand up for what it believed in, march in the streets and go to Woodstock and sleep in the rain and become infested with body lice. If I were the President, I'd bring some *life* to the White House. The theme of my administration would be summarized by the catchy and inspirational phrase: "Hey, The Government Is Beyond Human Control, So Let's at Least Have Some Fun with It." Here are some of the specific programs I would implement:

- I would invite George Thorogood and the Delaware Destroyers to perform at the White House. Not just once. *Every night.* They would *live* there. Congress would constantly be passing Joint Resolutions urging the Executive Branch to keep the volume down.
- Whenever I entered the room for a formal dinner, the band would play the 1963 Angels' hit, "My Boyfriend's Back."
- I would propose that the government launch a $17-billion War on Light Beer.
- I would have a Labrador retriever, wearing a small earphone, sit in on all Cabinet meetings.
- I would request a summit meeting with the Soviet Premier, at which I would make a dramatic three-hour presentation, using flip-charts, of the benefits of becoming an Amway distributor.
- One of my highest priorities would be to have helium declared the National Element.
- I would awaken key congressional leaders at 2:30 one morning and summon them to the White House Situation Room for an urgent meeting, at which, after swearing them to secrecy, I would show them a top-secret spy-satellite photograph revealing that China is shaped vaguely like an eggplant.
- The cornerstone of my foreign policy would be playing pranks on France.
- Wherever I went, there would be a burly Secret Service man just a few feet away, and on his wrist would be a handcuff, which would be attached to a steel chain, which would be attached to a locked steel carrying case, and inside that case would be: an Etch-a-Sketch.

How to Tell if You're Turning into a Republican

It's very common for people reaching middle age to turn into Republicans. It can happen overnight. You go to bed as your regular old T-shirt-wearing self, and you wake up the next morning with Ralph Lauren clothing and friends named Muffy. Here are some other signs to watch for:

- You find yourself judging political candidates solely on the basis of whether or not they'd raise your taxes. "Well," you say, "he *was* convicted in those machete slayings, but at least he won't raise my taxes."
- You assign a lower priority to ending world hunger than to finding a cleaning lady.
- You start clapping wrong to music.

The last item above is something I've noticed about Republicans at their conventions. The band will start playing something vaguely upbeat—a real GOP rocker such as "Bad, Bad LeRoy Brown"—and the delegates will decide to get funky and clap along, and it immediately becomes clear that they all suffer from a tragic Rhythm Deficiency, possibly caused by years of dancing the bunny hop to bands with names like "Leon Wudge and His Sounds of Clinical Depression." To determine whether Republican Rhythm Impairment Syndrome is afflicting you, you should take the Ray Charles Clapping Test. All you do is hum the song "Hit the Road, Jack" and clap along. A rhythmically normal person will clap as follows:

"Hit the road, (CLAP) Jack (CLAP)."

Whereas a Republican will clap this way:

"Hit the (CLAP), (CLAP)."

(By the way, if you don't even *know* the song "Hit the Road, Jack," then not only are you a Republican, but you might even be Cabinet material.)

I'll tell you what's weird. Not only is our generation turning into Republicans, but we also have a whole generation coming after us who are *starting out* as Republicans. With the exception of the few dozen spittle-emitting radicals I saw in Atlanta, the younger generations today are already so conservative they make William F. Buckley, Jr., look like Ho Chi Minh. What I'm wondering is, what will they be like when they're our age? Will they, too, change their political philosophy? Will millions of young urban professionals turn 40 and all of a sudden start turning into left-wing, anti-establishment hippies, smoking pot on the racquetball court, putting Che Guevera posters up in the conference room, and pasting flower decals all over their cellular telephones? It is an exciting time to look forward to. I plan to be dead.

Read This First

Congratulations! You have purchased an extremely fine device that would give you thousands of years of trouble-free service, except that you undoubtedly will destroy it via some typical bonehead consumer maneuver. Which is why we ask you to PLEASE FOR GOD'S SAKE READ THIS OWNER'S MANUAL CAREFULLY BEFORE YOU UNPACK THE DEVICE. YOU ALREADY UNPACKED IT, DIDN'T YOU? YOU UNPACKED IT AND PLUGGED IT IN AND TURNED IT ON AND FIDDLED WITH THE KNOBS, AND NOW YOUR CHILD, THE SAME CHILD WHO ONCE SHOVED A POLISH SAUSAGE INTO YOUR VIDEOCASSETTE RECORDER AND SET IT ON "FAST FORWARD," THIS CHILD ALSO IS FIDDLING WITH THE KNOBS, RIGHT? AND YOU'RE JUST STARTING TO READ THE INSTRUCTIONS, RIGHT??? WE MIGHT AS WELL JUST BREAK ALL THESE DEVICES RIGHT AT THE FACTORY BEFORE WE SHIP THEM OUT, YOU KNOW THAT?

We're sorry. We just get a little crazy sometimes, because we're always getting back "defective" merchandise where it turns out that the consumer inadvertently bathed the device in acid for six days. So, in writing these instructions, we naturally tend to assume that your skull is filled with dead insects, but we mean nothing by it. OK? Now let's talk about:

1. UNPACKING THE DEVICE: The device is encased in foam to protect it from the Shipping People, who like

nothing more than to jab spears into the outgoing boxes. PLEASE INSPECT THE CONTENTS CAREFULLY FOR GASHES OR IDA MAE BARKER'S ENGAGEMENT RING WHICH SHE LOST LAST WEEK, AND SHE THINKS MAYBE IT WAS WHILE SHE WAS PACKING DEVICES. Ida Mae really wants that ring back, because it is her only proof of engagement, and her fiancé, Stuart, is now seriously considering backing out on the whole thing inasmuch as he had consumed most of a bottle of Jim Beam in Quality Control when he decided to pop the question. It is not without irony that Ida Mae's last name is "Barker," if you get our drift.

WARNING: DO NOT EVER AS LONG AS YOU LIVE THROW AWAY THE BOX OR ANY OF THE PIECES OF STYROFOAM, EVEN THE LITTLE ONES SHAPED LIKE PEANUTS.

If you attempt to return the device to the store, and you are missing one single peanut, the store personnel will laugh in the chilling manner exhibited by Joseph Stalin just after he enslaved Eastern Europe.

Besides the device, the box should contain:

- Eight little rectangular snippets of paper that say: "WARNING"
- A plastic packet containing four $5/17''$ pilfer grommets and two chub-ended $6/93''$ boxcar prawns.

YOU WILL NEED TO SUPPLY: a matrix wrench and 60,000 feet of tram cable.

IF ANYTHING IS DAMAGED OR MISSING: You *immediately* should turn to your spouse and say: "Margaret, you know why this country can't make a car that can get all the way through the drive-thru at Burger King without a major transmission overhaul? Because nobody cares, that's why." (Warning: This Is Assuming Your Spouse's Name Is Margaret.)

2. PLUGGING IN THE DEVICE: The plug on this device represents the latest thinking of the electrical industry's Plug Mutation Group, which, in the continuing effort to prevent consumers from causing hazardous electrical current to flow through their appliances, developed the Three-Pronged Plug, then the Plug Where One Prong Is Bigger

Than the Other. Your device is equipped with the revolutionary new Plug Whose Prongs Consist of Six Small Religious Figurines Made of Chocolate. DO NOT TRY TO PLUG IT IN! Lay it gently on the floor near an outlet, but out of direct sunlight, and clean it weekly with a damp handkerchief.

WARNING: WHEN YOU ARE LAYING THE PLUG ON THE FLOOR, DO NOT HOLD A SHARP OBJECT IN YOUR OTHER HAND AND TRIP OVER THE CORD AND POKE YOUR EYE OUT, AS THIS COULD VOID YOUR WARRANTY.

3. OPERATION OF THE DEVICE:

WARNING: WE MANUFACTURE ONLY THE ATTRACTIVE DESIGNER CASE. THE ACTUAL WORKING CENTRAL PARTS OF THE DEVICE ARE MANUFACTURED IN JAPAN. THE INSTRUCTIONS WERE TRANSLATED BY MRS. SHIRLEY PELTWATER OF ACCOUNTS RECEIVABLE, WHO HAS NEVER ACTUALLY BEEN TO JAPAN BUT DOES HAVE MOST OF *SHOGUN* ON TAPE.

INSTRUCTIONS: For results that can be the finest, it is our advising that: Never to hold these buttons two times!! Except the battery. Next, taking the (something) earth section may cause a large occurrence! However. If this is not a trouble, such rotation is a very maintenance action, as a kindly (something) viewpoint from Drawing B.

4. WARRANTY: Be it hereby known that this device, together with but not excluding all those certain parts thereunto, shall be warranted against all defects, failures, and malfunctions as shall occur between now and Thursday afternoon at shortly before 2, during which time the Manufacturer will, at no charge to the Owner, send the device to our Service People, who will emerge from their caves and engage in rituals designed to cleanse it of evil spirits. This warranty does not cover the attractive designer case.

WARNING: IT MAY BE A VIOLATION OF SOME LAW THAT MRS. SHIRLEY PELTWATER HAS *SHOGUN* ON TAPE.

Europe on Five Vowels a Day

Americans who travel abroad for the first time are often shocked to discover that, despite all the progress that has been made in the past 30 years, many foreign people still speak in foreign languages. Oh, sure, they speak *some* English, but usually just barely well enough to receive a high-school diploma here in the United States. This can lead to problems for you, the international traveler, when you need to convey important information to them, such as "Which foreign country is this?" and "You call this toilet paper?"

To their credit, some countries have made a sincere effort to adopt English as their native language, a good example being England, but even there you have problems. My wife and I were driving around England once, and we came to a section called "Wales," which is this linguistically deformed area that apparently is too poor to afford vowels. All the road signs look like this:

LLWLNCWNRLLWNWRLLN—3 km

It is a tragic sight indeed to see Welsh parents attempting to sing traditional songs such as "Old MacDonald Had a Farm" to their children and lapsing into heart-rending silence when they get to the part about "E-I-E-I-O." If any of you in our reading audience have extra vowels that you no longer need, because for example your children have grown up, I urge you to send them (your children) to: Vowels for Wales, c/o Lord Chesterfield, Parliament Luckystrike, the Duke of Earl, Pondwater-on-Gabardine, England.

But the point I am trying to make here is that since the rest of the world appears to be taking its sweet time about becoming fluent in English, it looks like, in the interest of improving world peace and understanding, it's up to us Americans to strike the bull on the horns while the iron is hot and learn to speak a foreign language.

This is not an area where we are strong, as a nation: A recent poll showed that 82 percent of the Americans surveyed speak no foreign language at all. Unfortunately, the same poll showed that 41 percent also cannot speak English, 53 percent cannot name the state they live in, and 62 percent believe that the Declaration of Independence is "a kind of fish." So we can see that we have a tough educational row to hoe here, in the sense that Americans, not to put too fine a point on it, have the IQs of bait. I mean, let's face it, this is obviously why the Japanese are capable of building sophisticated videocassette recorders, whereas we view it as a major achievement if we can hook them up correctly to our TV sets. This is nothing to be ashamed of. Americans! Say it out loud! "We're pretty stupid!" See? Doesn't that feel good? Let's stop blaming the educational system for the fact that our children score lower on standardized tests than any other vertebrate life form on the planet! Let's stop all this anguished whiny self-critical *fretting* over the recently discovered fact that the guiding hand on the tiller of the ship of state belongs to Mister Magoo! Remember: *We still have nuclear weapons.* Ha ha!

Getting back to the central point, we should all learn to speak a foreign language. Fortunately, this is easy.

HOW TO SPEAK A FOREIGN LANGUAGE:
The key is to understand that foreigners communicate by means of "idiomatic expressions," the main ones being:

> **GERMAN:** "Ach du lieber!" ("Darn it!")
> **SPANISH:** "Caramba!" ("Darn it!")
> **FRENCH:** "Zut alors!" ("Look! A lors!")

Also you should bear in mind that foreign persons for some reason believe that everyday household objects and vegetables are "masculine" or "feminine." For example, French persons believe that potatoes are feminine, even though they (potatoes) do not have sexual organs, that I have noticed. Dogs, on the other hand, are masculine, even if they are not. (This does not mean, by the way, that a dog can have sex with a potato, although it will probably try.)

PRONUNCIATION HINT: In most foreign languages, the letter "r" is pronounced incorrectly. Also, if you are speaking German, at certain points during each sentence you should give the impression you're about to expel a major gob.

OK? Practice these techniques in front of a mirror until you're comfortable with them, then go to a country that is frequented by foreigners and see if you can't increase their international understanding, the way Jimmy Carter did during his 1977 presidential visit to Poland, when he told a large welcoming crowd, through an official State Department translator, that he was "pleased to be grasping your secret parts."

Lynda Barry (Contemporary)

FROM *Down the Street*

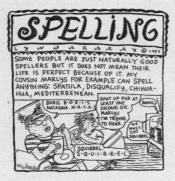

LOVE ADVENTURE

L Y N D A "I'M A HOG FOR YOU" B A R R Y © 1988

THERE WERE THESE VERY POPULAR BUSHES IN OUR NEIGHBORHOOD WHERE PRACTICALLY EVERY-ONE ON THE PLANET GOT THEIR FIRST KISS. ME AND DEENA SAID WE GOT OURS THERE TOO BY SOMEBODY'S COUSIN FROM IDAHO BUT IT WAS A LIE. WE HAD NEVER KISSED NO ONE.

NO ONE'S EVER GONNA KISS US MAN. AND NOBODY EVEN BELIEVES US ABOUT THAT GUY FROM IDAHO EITHER. WHO'D EVER KISS A GUY FROM IDAHO?

AT LEAST WE'RE NOT SLUTS.

SO?

WE TRIED TO COPY THE SENSUOUS LOOKS THAT MAKE A MAN HYPNOTISED AS SEEN ON T.V. AND IN OUR OPINION WE GOT THOSE LOOKS PERFECTED.

WHEN I FINALLY GOT MY FIRST KISS AND DEENA GOT HERS WE COULD NOT HELP BUT FEEL A CERTAIN ELEMENT OF DISAP-POINTMENT. WE COULD NOT EXPLAIN EXACTLY WHERE THIS FEELING CAME FROM AND NEITHER DID WE KNOW THAT WE WOULD SPEND THE NEXT TWENTY YEARS TRYING TO FIND OUT.

WELL HOW COME AFTER THEY KISSED US THEY START ACTING LIKE THEY DON'T EVEN LIKE US ANYMORE?

BECAUSE GUYS ARE STUPID.

THEN HOW COME WE STILL LIKE THEM?

DON'T KNOW YET.

WE TRIED THEM OUT AT PARTIES BUT AS IT TURNED OUT THE GUYS OUR AGE WERE NOT AS SOPHISTICATED AS WE WERE.

YOU GUYS BEEN AT THE AQUARIUM OR SOMETHING?

I DON'T GET IT.

IS THIS SOME KIND OF DARE?

HOW TO DRAW GIRLS

L Y N D A 12 STITCHES B A R R Y © 1986

WITH YOUR HOST

MARLYS

"OK. THE FIRST NUMBER ONE THING IN DRAWING GIRLS IS PRACTICE YOUR EYES! GET THEM MATCH-ING OR YOUR DRAWING WILL LOOK LIKE THERE'S A MENTAL PROBLEM!"

EYEBALL GOES IN THE MIDDLE PUT ON THE LINES

EYEBROWS

KEEP ON DOING IT UNTIL YOU GET IT PERFECT BUT DON'T JUST WASTE PAPER.

DON'T FORGET CURLY EYELASHES IT MAKES THE EYES BEAUTIFUL!

NUMBER TWO: THE MOUTH AND NOSE IS EASY! FIRST DRAW THE SHAPE OF HER HEAD IN A "U". THEN YOU JUST ADD ON THE KIND OF MOUTH AND NOSE YOU WANT DEPENDING ON HER PERSONALITY!

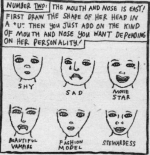

SHY

SAD

MOVIE STAR

BEAUTIFUL VAMPIRE

FASHION MODEL

STEWARDESS

NUMBER THREE: WHAT ABOUT HER HAIR? THERES A LOT OF HAIR-DOS FOR HER TO HAVE! THERES A LOT OF STYLES!

PEEK-A-BOO

A BEAUTY PAGEANT

INDIAN PRINCESS

A FRANCE LADY

A GORGEOUS FLIP

RATTED BUBBLE

NUMBER FOUR: THE HARDEST PART: YOU HAVE TO DRAW HER WHOLE BODY AND THIS IS WHERE YOU CAN WRECK EVERYTHING SO BE CAREFUL! MY SECRET IS: DRAW A LONG BEAUTIFUL DRESS AND HER HOLDING FLOWERS AND DON'T FORGET SOME ELEGANT ACCESSORIES!

A CROWN ALWAYS LOOKS LOVELY

PUT IN BIRDS →

DRAW ON A WATCH

FLOWERS CAN HIDE HANDS THATS TOO HARD TO DRAW

HER PURSE ITS IMPORTANT

DECORATE THE DRESS PLEASE

DRAW A TREE HERE AND SHE CAN LOOK LIKE SHES IN THE FOREST

← SHOES CAN STICK OUT

THE END BY MARLYS

JUMP SHOT

BY LYNDA BOLD SOUL SISTER BARRY © 1988

THE TEENAGER NAME OF RICHARD COMES OUT LATE SOME NIGHTS TO SHOOT BASKETS ON OUR CORNER. YOU CAN WATCH HIM FROM MY BEDROOM WINDOW.

YOU CAN LAY ON THE BED AND HEAR THE BALL, THE PING PING OF IT AGAINST THE STREET BOUNCING. YOU CAN HEAR HIM WALK IT, THEN RUN IT AND DO HIS PERFECT HOOK SHOT.

BOUNCE, BOUNCE, BOUNCE, STOP. THE FAST NO-SOUND OF HIS FEET IN THE AIR, THE BALL FLYING UP, PAUSE, THEN WHAM-WHAM AGAINST THE BACK BOARD, A HIGH BOUNCE OFF THE RIM, HIM WHISPERING SON OF A BITCH.

HIM JUMPING UP ON THE CORNER, HIM JUMPING HIGH AND TURNING IN THE AIR UNDER A STREET LIGHT WITH A THOUSAND MILLION BUGS FLYING AROUND IT GOING WILD, WILD, WILD,

Robert Benchley (1889–1945)

∾⽯⽯∾

Opera Synopses

Some Sample Outlines of Grand Opera Plots for Home Study

I
DIE MEISTER-GENOSSENSCHAFT

SCENE: *The Forests of Germany.*
TIME: *Antiquity.*

CAST

STRUDEL, *God of Rain* . . . . .Basso
SCHMALZ, *God of Slight Drizzle* . . . . .Tenor
IMMERGLÜCK, *Goddess of the Six Primary Colors*
. . . . .Soprano
LUDWIG DAS EIWEISS, *the Knight of the Iron Duck*
. . . . .Baritone
THE WOODPECKER . . . . .Soprano

ARGUMENT

The basis of "Die Meister-Genossenschaft" is an old legend of Germany which tells how the Whale got his Stomach.

ACT 1

The Rhine at Low Tide Just Below Weldschnoffen.—
Immerglück has grown weary of always sitting on the same rock with the same fishes swimming by every day, and sends for Schwül to suggest something to do. Schwül asks her how she would like to have pass before her all the

wonders of the world fashioned by the hand of man. She says, rotten. He then suggests that Ringblattz, son of Pflucht, be made to appear before her and fight a mortal combat with the Iron Duck. This pleases Immerglück and she summons to her the four dwarfs: Hot Water, Cold Water, Cool, and Cloudy. She bids them bring Ringblattz to her. They refuse, because Pflucht has at one time rescued them from being buried alive by acorns, and, in a rage, Immerglück strikes them all dead with a thunderbolt.

ACT 2

A Mountain Pass.—Repenting of her deed, Immerglück has sought advice of the giants, Offen and Besitz, and they tell her that she must procure the magic zither which confers upon its owner the power to go to sleep while apparently carrying on a conversation. This magic zither has been hidden for three hundred centuries in an old bureau drawer, guarded by the Iron Duck, and, although many have attempted to rescue it, all have died of a strange ailment just as success was within their grasp.

But Immerglück calls to her side Dampfboot, the tinsmith of the gods, and bids him make for her a tarnhelm or invisible cap which will enable her to talk to people without their understanding a word she says. For a dollar and a half extra Dampfboot throws in a magic ring which renders its wearer insensible. Thus armed, Immerglück starts out for Walhalla, humming to herself.

ACT 3

The Forest Before the Iron Duck's Bureau Drawer.— Merglitz, who has up till this time held his peace, now descends from a balloon and demands the release of Betty. It has been the will of Wotan that Merglitz and Betty should meet on earth and hate each other like poison, but Zweiback, the druggist of the gods, has disobeyed and concocted a love-potion which has rendered the young couple very unpleasant company. Wotan, enraged, destroys them with a protracted heat spell.

Encouraged by this sudden turn of affairs, Immerglück comes to earth in a boat drawn by four white Holsteins, and, seated alone on a rock, remembers aloud to herself the days when she was a girl. Pilgrims from Augenblick, on their way to worship at the shrine of Schmürr, hear the sound of reminiscence coming from the rock and stop in their march to sing a hymn of praise for the drying-up of the crops. They do not recognize Immerglück, as she has her hair done differently, and think that she is a beggar girl selling pencils.

In the meantime, Ragel, the papercutter of the gods, has fashioned himself a sword on the forge of Schmalz, and has called the weapon "Assistance-in-Emergency." Armed with "Assistance-in-Emergency" he comes to earth, determined to slay the Iron Duck and carry off the beautiful Irma.

But Frimsel overhears the plan and has a drink brewed which is given to Ragel in a golden goblet and which, when drunk, makes him forget his past and causes him to believe that he is Schnorr, the God of Fun. While laboring under this spell, Ragel has a funeral pyre built on the summit of a high mountain and, after lighting it, climbs on top of it with a mandolin which he plays until he is consumed.

Immerglück never marries.

II
IL MINNESTRONE
(PEASANT LOVE)

SCENE: *Venice and Old Point Comfort.*
TIME: *Early 16th Century.*

CAST

ALFONSO, *Duke of Minnestrone.* . . . . Baritone
PARTOLA, *a Peasant Girl* . . . . Soprano
CLEANSO ⎱   ⎱ Tenor
TURINO ⎬ *Young Noblemen of Venice* ⎬ Tenor
BOMBO ⎰   ⎰ Basso
LUDOVICO ⎱ *Assassins in the Secret of* ⎱ Basso
ASTOLFO ⎰   *Cafeteria Rusticana* ⎰ Methodist
       Townspeople, Cabbies, and Sparrows

ARGUMENT

"Il Minnestrone" is an allegory of the two sides of a man's nature (good and bad), ending at last in an awfully comical mess with everyone dead.

ACT 1

A Public Square, Ferrara.—During a peasant festival held to celebrate the sixth consecutive day of rain, Rudolpho, a young nobleman, sees Lilliano, daughter of the village bell-ringer, dancing along throwing artificial roses at herself. He asks of his secretary who the young woman is, and his secretary, in order to confuse Rudolpho and thereby win the hand of his ward, tells him that it is his (Rudolpho's) own mother, disguised for the festival. Rudolpho is astounded. He orders her arrest.

ACT 2

Banquet Hall in Gorgio's Palace.—Lilliano has not forgotten Breda, her old nurse, in spite of her troubles, and determines to avenge herself for the many insults she received in her youth by poisoning her (Breda). She therefore invites the old nurse to a banquet and poisons her. Presently a knock is heard. It is Ugolfo. He has come to carry away the body of Michelo and to leave an extra quart of pasteurized. Lilliano tells him that she no longer loves him, at which he goes away, dragging his feet sulkily.

ACT 3

In Front of Emilo's House.—Still thinking of the old man's curse, Borsa has an interview with Cleanso, believing him to be the Duke's wife. He tells him things can't go on as they are, and Cleanso stabs him. Just at this moment Betty comes rushing in from school and falls in a faint. Her worst fears have been realized. She has been insulted by Sigmundo, and presently dies of old age. In a fury, Ugolfo rushes out to kill Sigmundo and, as he does so, the dying Rosenblatt rises on one elbow and curses his mother.

III
Lucy de Lima

Scene: *Wales.*
Time: *1700 (Greenwich).*

Cast

WILLIAM WONT, *Lord of Glennnn* ....Basso
LUCY WAGSTAFF, *his daughter* ....Soprano
BERTRAM, *her lover* ....Tenor
LORD ROGER, *friend of Bertram* ....Soprano
IRMA, *attendant to Lucy* ....Basso

Friends, Retainers, and Members of the local Lodge of Elks.

Argument

"Lucy de Lima" is founded on the well-known story by Boccaccio of the same name and address.

Act 1

Gypsy Camp Near Waterbury.—The gypsies, led by Edith, go singing through the camp on the way to the fair. Following them comes Despard, the gypsy leader, carrying Ethel, whom he has just kidnapped from her father, who had previously just kidnapped her from her mother. Despard places Ethel on the ground and tells Mona, the old hag, to watch over her. Mona nurses a secret grudge against Despard for having once cut off her leg, and decides to change Ethel for Nettie, another kidnapped child. Ethel pleads with Mona to let her stay with Despard, for she has fallen in love with him on the ride over. But Mona is obdurate.

Act 2

The Fair.—A crowd of sightseers and villagers is present. Roger appears, looking for Laura. He can not find her. Laura appears, looking for Roger. She can not find him. The gypsy queen approaches Roger and thrusts into his hand the locket stolen from Lord Brym. Roger looks at it and is frozen with astonishment, for it contains the portrait of his mother when she was in high school. He then realizes that Laura must be his sister, and starts out to find her.

Act 3

Hall in the Castle.—Lucy is seen surrounded by every luxury, but her heart is sad. She has just been shown a forged letter from Stewart saying that he no longer loves her, and she remembers her old free life in the mountains and longs for another romp with Ravensbane and Wolfshead, her old pair of rompers. The guests begin to assemble for the wedding, each bringing a roast ox. They chide Lucy for not having her dress changed. Just at this moment the gypsy band bursts in and Cleon tells the wedding party that Elsie and not Edith is the child who was stolen from the summerhouse, showing the blood-stained derby as proof. At this, Lord Brym repents and gives his blessing on the pair, while the fishermen and their wives celebrate in the courtyard.

French for Americans

A Handy Compendium for Visitors to Paris

The following lessons and exercises are designed for the exclusive use of Americans traveling in France. They are based on the needs and behavior of Americans, as figured from the needs and behavior of 14,000 Americans last summer. We wish to acknowledge our indebtedness to American Express Co., 11 Rue Scribe, for some of our material.

The French Language

1. *Pronunciation*

Vowels	*Pronounced*
a	ong
e	ong
i	ong
o	ong
u	ong

2. *Accents*

The French language has three accents, the acute *e,* the grave *e,* and the circumflex *e,* all of which are omitted.

3. *Phrases most in demand by Americans*

English	French
Haven't you got any griddlecakes?	*N'avez-vous pas des griddlecakes?*
What kind of dump is this, anyhow?	*Quelle espèce de dump is this, anyhow?*
Do you call that coffee?	*Appelez-vous cela coffee?*
Where can I get a copy of the N. Y. Times?	*Où est le N. Y. Times?*
What's the matter? Don't you understand English?	*What's the matter? Don't you understand English?*
Of all the godam countries I ever saw.	*De tous le pays godams que j'ai vu.*
Hey there, driver go slow!	*Hey there, chauffeur, allez lentement!*
Where's Sister?	*Où est Sister?*
How do I get to the Louvre from here?	*Où est le Louvre?*
Two hundred francs? In your hat.	*Deux cents francs? Dans votre chapeau.*
Where's Brother?	*Où est Brother?*
I haven't seen a good-looking woman yet.	*Je n'ai pas vu une belle femme jusqu'à présent.*
Where can I get laundry done by six tonight?	*Où est le laundry?*
Here is where we used to come when I was here during the War.	*Ici est où nous used to come quand j'étais ici pendant la guerre.*
Say, this is real beer all right!	*Say, ceci est de la bière vrai!*
Oh boy!	*O boy!*
Two weeks from tomorrow we sail for home.	*Deux semaines from tomorrow nous sail for home.*
Then when we land I'll go straight to Childs and get a cup of coffee and a glass of ice-water.	*Sogleich wir zu hause sind, geh ich zum Childs und eine tasse kaffee und ein glass eiswasser kaufen.*

3. Phrases most in demand by Americans (Continued)

English	French
Very well.	*Très bien.*
Leave it in my room.	*Très bien.*
Good night!	*Très bien.*
Where did Father go to?	*Où est Papa?*

Places in Paris for Americans to Visit

THE LOBBY OF THE RITZ

This is one of the most interesting places in Paris for the American tourist, for it is there that he meets a great many people from America. If he will stand by the potted palms in the corner he will surely find someone whom he knows before long and can enter into a conversation on how things are going at home.

THE AMERICAN EXPRESS CO., 11 RUE SCRIBE

Here again the American traveler will find surcease from the irritating French quality of most of the rest of Paris. If he comes here for his mail, he will hear the latest news of the baseball leagues, how the bathing is on the Maine coast, what the chances are for the Big Fight in September at the Polo Grounds, and whom Nora Bayes has married in August. There will be none of this unintelligible *French* jabber with which Paris has become so infested of late years. He will hear language spoken as it should be spoken, whether he came from Massachusetts or Iowa.

Where to Eat in Paris

HARTFORD LUNCH

There has been a Hartford Lunch opened at 115 Rue Lord Byron where the American epicure can get fried-egg sandwiches, Boston baked beans, coffee rings, and crullers almost as good as those he can get at home. The place is run by Martin Keefe, formerly of the Hartford Lunch in Fall

River, Massachusetts, and is a mecca for those tourists who want good food well cooked.

UNITED STATES DRUG STORE

At the corner of Rue Bonsard and the Boulevard de Parteuille there is an excellent American drug store where are served frosted chocolates, ice-cream sodas, Coca-Cola, and pimento cheese sandwiches. A special feature which will recall the beloved homeland to Americans is the buying of soda checks *before* ordering.

French Currency

Here is something which is likely to give the American traveler no little trouble. In view of the fluctuating value of the franc, the following table should be memorized in order to insure against mistakes:

Day of Week	*American value of Franc*
Monday	5 cents
Tuesday	5.1 cents
Wednesday	4.9 cents
Thursday	1 lb. chestnuts
Friday	2½ yds. linoleum
Saturday	What-have-you

The proper procedure for Americans in making purchases is as follows:

1. Ascertain the value of the franc.
2. Make the purchase of whatever it is you want.
3. Ask *"Combien?"* (How much?)
4. Say *"Trop cher."* (What the hell!)
5. Try to understand the answer.
6. Pay the asking price and leave the shop swearing in English, American or other mother tongue.

Side Trips from Paris

There are many fascinating trips which may be made by the American sojourning in Paris which will relieve him of the tedium of his stay.

TRIP A.—Take the train at Paris for Havre and from there go by steamer to New York. The State of Maine Express leaves New York (Grand Central Station) at 7:30 P.M. and in the morning the traveler finds himself in Portland, Maine, from which many delightful excursions may be made up and down the rock-ribbed Atlantic coast.

TRIP B.—Entrain at Paris for Cherbourg, where there are frequent sailings westward. By the payment of a slight *pourboire* the ship's captain will put her in at the island of Nantucket, a quaint whaling center of olden times. Here you may roam among the moors and swim to your heart's content, unconscious of the fact that you are within a six-day run of the great city of Paris.

Ordinal Numbers and their Pronunciation

Numbers	*Pronounced*
1st. *le premier*	leh premyai
2nd. *le second*	leh zeggong
3rd. *le troisième*	leh trouazzeame
4th. *le quatrième*	leh kattreame
8th. *le huitième*	leh wheeteeame

Oh, well, you won't have occasion to use these much, anyway. Never mind them.

Other Words You Will Have Little Use For

Vernisser—to varnish, glaze.
Nuque—nape (of the neck).
Egriser—to grind diamonds.
Dromer—to make one's neck stiff from working at a sewing machine.
Rossignol—nightingale, picklock.
Ganache—lower jaw of a horse.
Serin—canary bird.
Pardon—I beg your pardon.

Elizabeth Berg (Contemporary)

‿◠‿◠‿

FROM *The Pull of the Moon*

The man asked, in a kind of tired way, what was it that I wanted, exactly. I told him I wanted the gray back in my hair. He said well that was easy, all I had to do was let it grow. I said no, I wanted all the other junk that had begun fading to get off of there right now. He said they could try, but he couldn't guarantee anything. I said what else is new. He said pardon me? I said what else is new, you never guarantee anything, do you know how many times women go home from the beauty parlor and weep? He said he doubted that happened very often. The woman with the hair combed over her face pushed it aside and said, "No, Henry, you're wrong. It happens all the time. . . ."

He said he didn't think it was so intimidating, it was just a matter of a client being open to change and new experiences. He said people make much too much of a haircut, it was no big deal, it was just hair—if you didn't like it, it would grow back. I said oh yeah well why didn't he just sit down and I'd work on his hair. . . . Finally, I said, All right. Fine, I said. And I put down my purse and told Henry, "Over to the sink, please, I'm going to shampoo you first. . . ."

I stood there for the longest time with the scissors open but then I just couldn't do it. I put the scissors down and said, Oh, just forget it. Never mind. He caught hold of my wrist, gently, and said, I *want* you to do it, go ahead, it's perfectly fine. I picked up the scissors again, took a deep cut of Henry's hair. Then another. Then I said, "So how are things at home?" "Oy," he said, waving his hand. "Don't ask." And we both smiled.

I finished cutting his hair and it looked pretty terrible

when I was done. It looked like a bad pixie cut. I said I'm sorry and he said, forget it, he kind of liked it, it certainly was different. Then he said, now it's your turn and I said you know, maybe I will just let it grow out and he said that would be the healthiest thing to do. He stood up and we shook hands and he gave me a sample bottle of clove-scented shampoo. The place was still absolutely quiet. I knew it wouldn't be after I left.

Jennifer Berman (Contemporary)

FROM *Adult Children of Normal Parents*

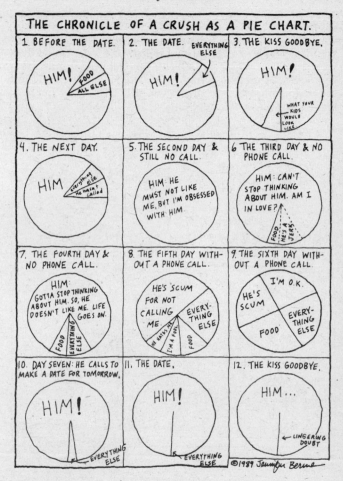

Ambrose Bierce (1842–1913 or 14)

❧

"Items" from the Press of Interior California

A little bit of romance has just transpired to relieve the monotony of our metropolitan life. Old Sam Choggins, whom the editor of this paper has so often publicly thrashed, has returned from Mud Springs with a young wife. He is said to be very fond of her, and the way he came to her was this:

Some time ago we courted her, but finding she was "on the make" threw her off, after shooting her brother and two cousins. She vowed revenge, and promised to marry any man who would horsewhip us. This Sam agreed to undertake, and she married him on that promise.

We shall call on Sam to-morrow with our new shotgun, and present our congratulations in the usual form.
—*Hangtown Gibbet.*

There was considerable excitement in the street yesterday, owing to the arrival of Bust-Head Dave, formerly of this place, who came over on the stage from Pudding Springs. He was met at the hotel by Sheriff Knogg, who leaves a large family, and whose loss will be universally deplored.

Dave walked down the street to the bridge, and it reminded one of old times to see the people go away as he heaved in view. It was not through any fear of the man, but from knowledge that he had made a threat (first published in this paper) to clean out the town. Before leaving the place Dave called at our office to settle for a year's subscription (invariably in advance), and was informed, through a chink in the logs, that he might leave his dust in the tin cup at the well.

Dave is looking very much larger than at his last visit just previous to the funeral of Judge Dawson. He left for Injun Hill at five o'clock amidst a good deal of shooting at rather long range, and there will be an election for sheriff as soon as a stranger can be found who will accept the honour.
—*Yankee Flat Advertiser.*

THE superintendent of the May Davis Mine requests us to state that the custom of pitching Chinamen and Injuns down the shaft will have to be stopped, as he has resumed work in the mine. The old well-huck of Jo. Bowman's is just as good, and is more centrally located.
—*New Jerusalem Courier.*

A STRANGER wearing a stove-pipe hat arrived in town yesterday, putting up at the Nugget House. The boys are having a good time with that hat this morning, and the funeral will take place at two o'clock.   —*Spanish Camp Flag.*

THERE is some dispute about land titles at Little Bilk Bar. About half-a-dozen cases were temporarily decided Wednesday, but it is supposed the widows will renew the litigation. The only proper way to prevent these vexatious law-suits is to hang the Judge of the County Court.
—*Cow County Outcropper.*

FROM *The Cynic's Word Book*

A

ACQUAINTANCE, *n.* A person whom we know well enough to borrow from, but not well enough to lend to. A degree of friendship called slight when its object is poor or obscure, and "intimate" when he is rich or famous.

ACTUALLY, *adv.* Perhaps; possibly.

APOLOGIZE, *v.i.* To lay the foundation for a future offence.

APPEAL, *v.t.* In law, to put the dice into the box for another throw.

AVERSION, *n.* The feeling that one has for the plate after he has eaten its contents, madam.

B

BRUTE, *n.* See HUSBAND.

C

CALAMITY, *n.* A more than commonly plain and unmistakable reminder that the affairs of this life are not of our own ordering. Calamities are of two kinds: misfortune to ourselves, and good fortune to others.

COMPULSION, *n.* The eloquence of power.

CONGRATULATION, *n.* The civility of envy.

CONNOISSEUR, *n.* A specialist who knows everything about something and nothing about anything else.
    An old wine-bibber having been smashed in a railway collision, some wine was poured upon his lips to revive him. "Pauillac, 1873," he murmured and died.

CONSOLATION, *n.* The knowledge that a better man is more unfortunate than yourself.

CONTEMPT, *n.* The feeling of a prudent man for an enemy who is too formidable safely to be opposed.

CONVENT, *n.* A place of retirement for women who wish for leisure to meditate upon the sin of idleness.

CORPORATION, *n.* An ingenious device for securing individual profit without individual responsibility.

D

DANCE, *v.i.* To leap about to the sound of tittering music, preferably with arms about your neighbor's wife or daughter. There are many kinds of dances, but all those requiring the participation of the two sexes have two characteristics in common: they are conspicuously innocent, and warmly loved by the guilty.

DAY, *n.* A period of twenty-four hours, mostly misspent. This period is divided into two parts, the day proper and the night, or day improper—the former devoted to sins of business, the latter consecrated to the other sort. These two kinds of social activity overlap.

DEBAUCHEE, *n.* One who has so earnestly pursued pleasure that he has had the misfortune to overtake it.

F

FEMALE, *n.* One of the opposing, or unfair, sex.

FIDELITY, *n.* A virtue peculiar to those who are about to be betrayed.

G

GUILLOTINE, *n.* A machine which makes a Frenchman shrug his shoulders with good reason.

In his great work on *Divergent Lines of Racial Evolution,* the learned and ingenious Professor Brayfugle argues from the prevalence of this gesture—the shrug—among Frenchmen, that they are descended from turtles, and it is simply a survival of the habit of retracting the head inside the shell. It is with reluctance that I differ with so eminent an authority, but in my judgment (as more elaborately set forth and enforced in my work entitled *Hereditary Emotions*—lib. II, c. XI) the shrug is a poor foundation upon which to build so important a theory, for previously to the Revolution the gesture was unknown. I have not a doubt that it is directly referable to the terror inspired by the guillotine during the period of that instrument's awful activity.

H

HANDKERCHIEF, *n.* A small square of silk or linen, used in various ignoble offices about the face and especially serviceable at funerals to conceal the lack of tears. The handkerchief is of recent invention; our ancestors knew nothing of it and intrusted its duties to the sleeve. Shakespeare's introducing it into the play of "Othello" is an anachronism: Desdamona dried her nose with her coat-tails as Dr. Mary Walker and other reformers have done in our own day—an evidence that revolutions sometimes go backward.

HARANGUE, *n.* A speech by an opponent, who is known as an harang-outang.

HARBOR, *n.* A place where ships taking shelter from storms are exposed to the fury of the customs.

HELPMATE, *n.* A wife, or bitter half.

HERS, *pron.* His.

I

IMBECILITY, *n.* A kind of divine inspiration, or sacred fire, affecting censorious critics of this dictionary.

L

LAUGHTER, *n.* An interior convulsion, producing a distortion of the features and accompanied by inarticulate noises. It is infectious and, though intermittent, incurable. Liability to attacks of laughter is one of the characteristics distinguishing man from the animals—these being not only inaccessible to the provocation of his example, but impregnable to the microbes having original jurisdiction in bestowal of the disease. Whether laughter could be imparted to animals by inoculation from the human patient is a question that has not been answered by experimentation. Dr. Weir Mitchell holds that the infectious character of laughter is due to instantaneous fermentation of *sputa* diffused in a spray. From this peculiarity he names the disorder *Convulsio spargens*.

LAWYER, *n.* One skilled in circumvention of the law.

Amy Bloom (Contemporary)

❧❦❧

In the Barcelona Cancer Center

"The Barcelona Cancer Center," Roy says. "Where are the tapas? Maybe there should be castanets at the nurses' station. Paella Valenciana everywhere you look." He puts his hands up into the air and clicks his fingers. Roy says this every time they come for chemotherapy. The Barcelona family made millions in real estate and donated several to St. Michael's; there is almost nothing worth curing that the Barcelonas have not given to. Mai ignores him; the person with cancer does not have to be amused. Ellie smiles widely at Roy. She has already had breast cancer and her job now is to help her best friend and her best friend's husband.

"How about the internationally renowned Sangria Treatment? Makes you forget your troubles." Roy stamps his sneakers, flamenco style. Since Mai's mastectomy, he has become whimsical and it does not become him. Mai knows Roy is doing the best he can and the only kindness she can offer is to not say, "You have been as dull as dishwater for twenty years. You don't have to change now." Ellie believes that all straight men should be like her father: stoic, handy and unimaginative. They should be dryly kind, completely without whimsy or faintly fabulous qualities. As far as Ellie's concerned, gay men can be full-blown birds of paradise, with or without homemaking skills. They can just lounge around in their marabou mules, saying witty, brittle things that reveal their hearts of gold. Ellie likes them that way, that's what they're for, to toss scarves over the world's lightbulbs, and straight men are for putting up sheetrock.

Mai sits between Roy and Ellie in the waiting room as if

she's alone. Roy makes three cups of coffee from the waiting room kitchenette. The women don't drink theirs.

"This is disgusting," Roy says.

"I'll get us some from the lobby." Ellie loves the lobby's Java Joe coffee bar, a weirdly joyful pit stop, at the intersection of four different Barcelona family wings, with nothing but caffeine and sugar and attractively arranged fats and sugars; everyone who is not confined by an IV drip or a restricted diet eats there. Mai sips herbal tea all through chemo but Ellie goes up and back a few times, for a currant scone, for a cappuccino, for a mango smoothie. She is happy to spend three dollars on a muffin, grateful that she lives in a country in which no one thinks there's anything wrong or untoward about the AMA-approved pursuit of large profit at the expense of people's grief and health.

"This is great," says Roy. "Treats for me. Honey, look how she takes care of me. Yes, folks, *that's* a wife." This is supposed to be funny, because Ellie is a lesbian and therefore unlikely to be anyone's wife. If Ellie lived with another woman, neither Ellie nor Roy nor Mai would think of that woman as a wife. Ellie is pretty sure that her days of looking for a spouse are over; Mai thinks this, too, and used to imagine that when Roy died, at a suitable, but not horribly advanced age, of a swift moving, but not painful disease, she and Ellie would retire to her parents' house in Oslo, or buy the little yellow house on Pearl Street in Provincetown that she and Ellie walked past on spring break twenty-one years ago. Now, it seems possible that Ellie will sit on a porch, slugging back brandy with some other old lady and that Roy will grow old with someone who has two breasts and a full head of hair.

Ellie prepares a little picnic on the seat next to Roy. Coffee the way he likes it and two different kinds of biscotti, a fist-sized apple fritter, two elephant ears sprinkling sugar everywhere and enough napkins to make this all bearable to Roy, who is two steps short of compulsive. Ellie presents the food-covered seat to Roy. He kisses her hand, which smells of coffee and antibacterial soap and of Ellie, for which he has no particular name. Mai has always smelled like clove; since November, she smells like seaweed and Roy, like a pregnant woman, has lost his taste for sushi, for lobster and for salt.

Elayne Boosler (Contemporary)

⤳⤳⤳

FROM Punchline—*I Don't Get It*

In the movie *Punchline*, Tom Hanks is a medical student afraid of blood and Sally Field is a New Jersey housewife with three kids. Naturally, they become stand-up comics. . . .

Real comedy can't be learned; it comes from a need for justice. The best who stand up, stand up for something.

Great comics leave something wonderful behind when they leave the stage. Mr. Hanks's character is a self-described "hate stylist" whose crowning performance is a heartfelt diatribe against *debutantes*, of all things. It does not make the heart soar. And if this character is afraid of blood, he's really in the wrong business now.

Comedy is a blood sport. It flays the truth and spurts twisted logic. In America, people become comics because we don't have bullfighting.

Is it harder for women in comedy? It is after films like this. The housewife is introduced by the club owner as a woman with a chronic yeast infection, yet this purported natural wit says nothing in response. She does an apologetic routine that's a crude and embarrassed foray into cheap vibrator jokes and reverse sexism. In life, material like this gets booed off the stage. But the film's character—a complaining, asexual "comedienne" holding down the stereotype—wins the bake-off. And that's misleading, because comedy is very, very sexy when it's done right.

Hugh Henry Brackenridge
(1748–1816)

⌘

How to Receive a Challenge

Major Valentine Jacko,
U.S. Army.
Sir,—

I have two objections to this duel matter.

The one is, lest I should hurt you; and the other is, lest you should hurt me.

I do not see any good it would do me to put a bullet through any part of your body. I could make no use of you when dead for any culinary purpose as I would a rabbit or a turkey. I am no cannibal to feed on the flesh of men. Why, then, shoot down a human creature of which I could make no use? A buffalo would be better meat. For though your flesh may be delicate and tender, yet it wants that firmness and consistency which takes and retains salt. At any rate, it would not be fit for long sea voyages. You might make a good barbecue, it is true, being of the nature of a racoon or an opossum, but people are not in the habit of barbecuing anything human now. As to your hide, it is not worth taking off, being little better than that of a year-old colt.

It would seem to me a strange thing to shoot at a man that would stand still to be shot at, inasmuch as I have heretofore been used to shoot at things flying or running or jumping. Were you on a tree now like a squirrel, endeavoring to hide yourself in the branches, or like a racoon that after much eyeing and spying, I observe at length in the crotch of a tall oak with boughs and leaves intervening, so that I could just get a sight of his hinderparts, I should think it pleasurable enough to take a shot at you. But, as it is, there is no skill or judgment requisite to discover or take you down.

As to myself, I do not much like to stand in the way of anything harmful. I am under apprehensions that you might hit me. That being the case, I think it most advisable to stay at a distance. If you want to try your pistols, take some object, a tree or a barn door, about my dimensions. If you hit that, send me word and I shall acknowledge that if I had been in the same place, you might also have hit me.

John Farrago
Late Captain, Pennsylvania Militia.

Mel Brooks and Carl Reiner
(Contemporary)

 caughtaughtaughtaught

FROM *The 2000 Year Old Man*

REINER: About four days ago a plane landed in Idlewild Airport. The plane came from the Middle-East, bearing a man who claims to be two thousand years old. He spent the last six days at the Mayo Clinic. . . .

REINER: Sir, could you give us the secret of your longevity?

2000: Well, the major thing, the major thing, is that I never ever touch fried food. I don't eat it, I wouldn't look at it, and I don't touch it. And I never run for a bus. There'll always be another. Even if you're late for work, you know, I never run for a bus. I never ran, I just strolled, jaunty-jolly, walking to the bus stop.

REINER: Well, there were no buses in the time of . . .

2000: No, in my time . . .

REINER: What was the means of transportation then?

2000: Mostly fear.

REINER: Fear transported you?

2000: Fear, yes. You would see . . . an animal would growl, you'd go two miles in a minute. Fear would be the main propulsion.

REINER: I think most people are interested in living a long and fruitful life, as you have.

2000: Yes. Fruit is good, too, you mentioned fruit. Yeah. Fruit kept me going for a hundred and forty years once when I was on a very strict diet. Mainly nectarines. I love that fruit. It's half a peach, half a plum, it's a hell of a fruit. I love it! Not too cold, not too hot, you know, just nice. Even a rotten one is good. That's how much I love them. I'd rather eat a rotten nectarine than a fine plum. What do you think of that? That's how much I loved them.

Claude Brown (Contemporary)

FROM *Manchild in the Promised Land*

I always found Mrs. Rogers' visits hard to take. She was a very nice meddlesome old woman, but too godly to have around constantly. Poor Danny, he had to live with it. Mrs. Rogers had told Mama that Danny was so bad because his behavior was the Lord's way of testing her faith. Dad called Mrs. Rogers the "preacher woman." He believed that Mrs. Rogers was going against the Lord's Word and that this was the reason for her son's behavior. He had often said that "the Lord never told no woman to go out and preach the Gospel to nobody." Dad said that if the Lord had wanted a woman to preach, he would have chosen a woman to be one of his apostles.

On this day, Mrs. Rogers' advice was no different from

the other times. After Mama had told Mrs. Rogers about what had happened in court, Mrs. Rogers began her usual sermon, saying, "Child, you just gotta pray, you just gotta pray and trust in the Lord." I always left the house at this point, because our house would be used as a practice pulpit for the next two or three hours.

As I ran down the stairs, I tried to imagine what was going on in the house. In a little while, Mrs. Rogers would be patting her foot real fast, and she would start talking real loud, clapping her hands, shaking her head, and every other word would be "Jesus" or "Lord." I wondered why Mrs. Rogers never got tired of talking about the Lord. Before Mrs. Rogers finished her private sermon, she would have Mama talking about the Lord and patting her feet. By the time Mrs. Rogers was ready to leave, she would have Mama promising to come to a church where she was preaching next Sunday. Mama would promise, and Mrs. Rogers would start telling her how good it is to be saved, to walk with Jesus, and to let God into your soul. Even though Mama knew Dad wasn't going to let her go to a sanctified church with that "jackleg preacher woman," she still promised to go. Dad always said, "All those sanctified people is just a bunch of old hypocrites, and none of 'em ain't a bit more saved than nobody else."

Mrs. Rogers never talked about saving Dad. She said, "That man got the devil in him," and I believed it. As a matter of fact, I had suspected something like that long before Mrs. Rogers did.

We had all been to Mrs. Rogers' Sunday sermon once. All of us except Dad. She was preaching that time in what looked like a church-apartment to me and a church-store to Carole. I think most of the people there were relatives of Mrs. Rogers. All of her family was there except for Danny; he had escaped on the way to church. June, one of Mrs. Rogers' daughters, was playing an old, out-of-tune upright piano. Another one of Danny's sisters was banging two cymbals together and mumbling something about Jesus. She seemed to be in a trance. Mr. Rogers was shaking a tambourine and singing about Jesus with a faraway look in his eyes. Mrs. Rogers, who was dressed in a white robe, got up and started preaching. After Mrs. Rogers had been preaching for about fifteen minutes, an old lady got up and started screaming and shouting, "Help me, Lord Jesus!" She was still throwing her arms up and shouting for Jesus to help her when a younger woman jumped up and hollered, "Precious Lord Jesus, save me!" Mrs. Rogers' voice was getting louder all the time.

For two hours, she preached—and for two hours, people were getting up, shouting, jumping up and down, calling to Jesus for help and salvation, and falling out exhausted. Some of these "Holy Rollers," as Dad called them, would fall to the floor and start trembling rapidly; some of them even began to slobber on themselves. When I asked Mama what was wrong with those people and what they were doing on the floor, she told me that the "spirit" had hit them. When Carole heard this, she began to cry and wanted to get out of there before the spirit hit us. Mrs. Rogers had gone over to a man who was rolling on the floor, slobbering on himself, and babbling as if he were talking to the Lord. She held the man's hand very tight and told him repeatedly to walk with the Lord and not to fear Jesus. She was saying to the man, "Brother, say, 'Yes, Jesus; yes, Jesus.' " After a while, the man calmed down, and Mrs. Rogers said he had been saved.

Carole and Margie were frightened by these strange goings-on. I had been fascinated until now. But now this spirit thing had Mama jumping up and shouting. I joined Carole and Margie in a crying chorus, and the three of us started pulling on Mama. After Mama had jumped, clapped her hands and had her say about Jesus, she fell back in her chair, tired and sweating. One of Mrs. Rogers' blood sisters had started fanning Mama. Carole, Margie, and I had stopped crying, but we were still scared, because we didn't know if Mama was all right or not.

In the makeshift pulpit, Mrs. Rogers was looking real pleased with herself, probably thinking that she had saved a lot of people. I think Mrs. Rogers judged her sermon by the number of people who were hit by the spirit and fell down during her sermon. She cautioned the people who were saved about "backslidin' " and told them about how happy they were going to be with Jesus in their lives. She also asked some of the old saved souls to "testify." After three or four saved souls had told about what a good friend Jesus had been to them, Mrs. Rogers began her third request for money. The ushers, who were also relatives of Mrs. Rogers, passed a china bowl down each row. Carole and Margie dropped the nickel that Mama had given to each of them in the bowl, then they turned and looked at me. Although that was the first time we had ever been to church together, they would have been surprised if I had put my nickel in the bowl. I didn't surprise them that day.

When Carole and Margie were busy telling Mama about me not putting my nickel in the bowl, I was pulling a chair from the aisle behind us. All the chairs in the place were kitchen chairs, and they weren't all the same size. Before I could get the chair into our aisle, a big fat shiny dark-skinned woman with a man's voice said, "Boy, leave dat chair 'lone." I was frightened by the heavy, commanding voice, but not as much as I was after I looked up and saw that great big old woman giving me the evil eye. My first thought was that she was a witch or a hag, whatever that was. I knew she couldn't be the boogeyman; not in church. But the longer I looked, the more I doubted her being anything other than the boogeyman. About thirty seconds later, when I had gotten my voice back, I meekly said, "Dat ain't your chair." The next thing I heard was the sound of Mama's hand falling heavily across my mouth. As I started crying, I heard Mama say, "What I tole you about sassin' ole people?" While I went on crying, Mama was telling me about the dangers of talking back to old people. I remember her saying, "If one of these ole people put the bad mouth on you, maybe you'll be satisfied."

For years afterward, the mention of church always reminded me of the day that we went to hear Mrs. Rogers preach. To me, a church was a church-apartment where somebody lined up a lot of kitchen chairs in a few rows, a preacher did a lot of shouting about the Lord, people jumped up and down until they got knocked down by the spirit, and Mrs. Rogers put bowls of money on a kitchen table and kept pointing to it and asking for more. It was a place where I had to stand up until I couldn't stand any more and then had to sit down on hard wooden chairs. The one good thing I got out of going to hear Mrs. Rogers preach was a new threat to use on Carole and Margie. Whenever Carole and Margie would threaten to tell on me, I told them that if they did, the spirit would hit them the way it hit those people in Mrs. Rogers' church-apartment.

Maybe Dad was right when he said Mrs. Rogers was just robbing people in the name of the Lord. Anyway, I felt pretty good about her not getting my nickel.

•

One day that same winter, Simms called everybody into the living room, where we used to have our house meetings. He told us that some girls were coming to Wiltwyck soon from a place called Vassar College and that they were going to teach us things like skiing, music, painting, and stuff like that. Simms said he expected us to treat those chicks better than the guys in the other houses, since we were older than the other guys. He had that "if you don't do right I'm gonna kick your ass" tone in his voice when he told us about the chicks from Vassar, but nobody cared much, because Simms hadn't hit a cat in a long time.

The first day the girls came to Wiltwyck, the cats in Aggrey swarmed all over them. In fact, everybody took to them right away. They were all white and not so hip, but most of them were real fine, so nobody cared about them being white and not being hip. It really wasn't hard to be nice to these chicks, because they were all real sweet. They were some of the nicest girls I had ever met, and some of them knew some things too. You could talk to them, and they could understand things. Every day, they would come to Wiltwyck early in the morning and stay until evening. One day, the girls from Vassar took us to the college for a picnic. It sure was a big place, and I never saw so many pretty girls in one place before in my life. There must have been about a million bicycles at that place. The girls said we could ride any of the bikes we wanted to, but we had to remember where we got them from and put them back when we finished. We really broke up some bikes that day. I saw Horse bring a bike back in five parts.

J.J. caused a girl to faint. He was coming down this steep hill real fast. There was a brick wall at the bottom, and J.J. couldn't steer too well. When J.J. hit the wall, he didn't get hurt, but the bike was all smashed up, and J.J. went straight up into the air about fifteen feet. The girl was standing on the bridge, and when she heard the crash, she turned around just in time to see J.J. going up, and she fainted. When they woke her up, the girl said that she fainted because she thought sure the boy would be killed, but Rickets said that seeing a nigger flying through the air on the campus of Vassar College was enough to make any nice, respectable white girl faint. And sometimes Rickets knew what he was talking about.

Cathy, my piano teacher, was a big, fine chick. She was white, but she was from China. Her father was a doctor or something in China, and she was born there and had lived there, but she was still white. She just came over here to go to Vassar College. She didn't speak Chinese or anything. As a matter of fact, she spoke real good English, and she was a sweet person, real big and real fine. Cathy ran over to J.J., who was lying there on the ground playing dead, and kneeled down beside him. She raised his head and put it in her lap and started screaming all over the place for somebody to get a doctor. I knew if she kept that up for long, they would never get J.J. up from there.

J.J. sneaked one eye open, looked up at those big breasts right over in his face, and started snuggling. I wanted to say, "Poor Cathy." She just shouldn't have done that. Somebody should have pulled her coat. I would have, but J.J. was a friend of mine, so I couldn't do that. After a while, she saw this cat opening one eye and getting closer, and I think she felt kind of foolish. So she threw his head off her lap and told him to get up. He laughed and got up. And everybody thought it was pretty funny.

But that wasn't the funniest thing that happened that day. The funniest thing was when we were in the music room and another girl screamed. We turned around to see what it was, and this girl was trying to jump up off a piano stool, because while she was playing the piano, somebody was under there playing with her legs. That was dear old Rickets. That's the way he was.

We had a lot of fun at Vassar College, and the girls were really something wonderful. I never would have thought that white girls could be so nice. Cats could look all up under their dresses and everything, and all they did was laugh.

We got along real fine with the girls until the day J.J. got lost in a snowstorm with the skiing teacher. They had searching parties out for them, lots of searching parties, all day long. But J.J. and the skiing teacher were lost in a blizzard for about four hours. Everybody in the world was wondering where they could be. But nobody found them. After the snowing was over, J.J. and the teacher came back, with smiles on their faces. They were happy, and I suppose everybody was happy—that is, everybody but Stilly and the rest of the staff. They were a little peeved. They wondered where in the world a nigger could be in a snowstorm with some pretty Norwegian skiing teacher. That's not supposed to happen to people from poor Negro backgrounds.

J.J. said he and the teacher had to stop in some barn for four hours to get out of the storm. All the cats up there envied J.J. that day. I kind of wished I had been caught in that storm too, because that teacher sure was something sweet . . . cute accent too.

After a while, I think they found out that it wasn't working. The guys got used to the girls, and they started treating them like mothers and sisters and that sort of thing. These were guys who cursed out mothers and sisters, and when they started treating these chicks like mothers and sisters, they were cursing them out too. One cat, Baldy, even had enough nerve to slap one of those girls. Now, everybody knew that perhaps you could curse them out or scream at them, but they also knew that no niggers were supposed to be slapping any girls from Vassar College. I guess we were supposed to be glad to even be able to say hello to them.

Then there was the Mac thing. Mac used to operate the movie camera for us on Thursday and Sunday nights. One day, while the girls from Vassar were at Wiltwyck, Mac got locked up in the movie booth with that same skiing teacher, and they had a lot of fun, I suppose, because they stayed in there a long time. Everybody started looking for Mac. He was supposed to be getting the cameras ready. They banged on the doors, they did everything, but nobody could find them. When Mac finally came out and they asked him where he'd been, he said, "In the movie booth." Somebody said, "Lawd, it's time to git these girls outtá here."

They were all seniors in college, and when graduation time came around, they had to go. I think, in spite of everything, we missed them, and maybe they missed us too. That was the first time we'd ever known any Vassar girls, but I suppose that was the first time they'd ever known any poor little colored boys.

Charles F. Browne (1834–1867)

❦

FROM *Artemus Ward, His Travels*

AFFAIRS ROUND THE VILLAGE GREEN

It isn't every one who has a village green to write about. I
have one, although I have not seen much of it for some years
past. I am back again, now. In the language of the duke who
went round with a motto about him, "I am here!" and I
fancy I am about as happy a peasant of the vale as ever gar-
nished a melodrama, although I have not as yet danced
on my village green, as the melo-dramatic peasant usually
does on his. It was the case when Rosina Meadows left home.

The time rolls by serenely now—so serenely that I don't
care what time it is, which is fortunate, because my watch is
at present in the hands of those "men of New York who are
called rioters." We met by chance, the usual way—certainly
not by appointment—and I brought the interview to a close
with all possible despatch. Assuring them that I wasn't Mr.
Greeley, particularly, and that he had never boarded in the
private family where I enjoy the comforts of a home, I ten-
dered them my watch, and begged they would distribute it
judiciously among the laboring classes, as I had seen the
rioters styled in certain public prints.

Why should I loiter feverishly in Broadway, stabbing the
hissing hot air with the splendid gold-headed cane that was
presented to me by the citizens of Waukegan, Illinois, as a
slight testimonial of their esteem? Why broil in my rooms?
You said to me, Mrs. Gloverson, when I took possession of
those rooms, that no matter how warm it might be, a breeze
had a way of blowing into them, and that they were, withal,
quite countryfied; but I am bound to say, Mrs. Gloverson,

that there was nothing about them that ever reminded me, in the remotest degree, of daisies or new-mown hay. Thus, with sarcasm, do I smash the deceptive Gloverson.

Why stay in New York when I had a village green? I gave it up, the same as I would an intricate conundrum—and, in short, I am here.

Do I miss the glare and crash of the imperial thoroughfare? the milkman, the fiery, untamed omnibus horses, the soda fountains, Central Park, and those things? Yes, I do; and I can go on missing 'em for quite a spell, and enjoy it.

The village from which I write to you is small. It does not contain over forty houses, all told; but they are milk-white, with the greenest of blinds, and for the most part are shaded with beautiful elms and willows. To the right of us is a mountain—to the left a lake. The village nestles between. Of course it does. I never read a novel in my life in which the villages didn't nestle. Villages invariably nestle. It is a kind of way they have.

We are away from the cars. The iron-horse, as my little sister aptly remarks in her composition On Nature, is never heard to shriek in our midst; and on the whole I am glad of it.

The villagers are kindly people. They are rather incoherent on the subject of the war, but not more so, perhaps, than are people elsewhere. One citizen, who used to sustain a good character, subscribed for the Weekly *New York Herald*, a few months since, and went to studying the military maps in that well-known journal for the fireside. I need not inform you that his intellect now totters, and he has mortgaged his farm. In a literary point of view we are rather bloodthirsty. A pamphlet edition of the life of a cheerful being, who slaughtered his wife and child, and then finished himself, is having an extensive sale just now.

We know little of Honoré de Balzac, and perhaps care less for Victor Hugo. M. Claés's grand search for the Absolute doesn't thrill us in the least; and Jean Valjean, gloomily picking his way through the sewers of Paris, with the spoony young man of the name of Marius upon his back, awakens no interest in our breasts. I say Jean Valjean picked his way gloomily, and I repeat it. No man, under those circumstances, could have skipped gaily. But this literary business, as the gentleman who married his colored chambermaid aptly observed, "is simply a matter of taste."

The store—I must not forget the store. It is an object of great interest to me. I usually encounter there, on sunny afternoons, an old Revolutionary soldier. You may possibly have read about "Another Revolutionary Soldier gone," but this is one who hasn't gone, and, moreover, one who doesn't manifest the slightest intention of going. He distinctly remembers Washington, of course; they all do; but what I wish to call special attention to, is the fact that this Revolutionary soldier is one hundred years old, that his eyes are so good that he can read fine print without spectacles—he never used them, by the way—and his mind is perfectly clear. He is a little shaky in one of his legs, but otherwise he is as active as most men of forty-five, and his general health is excellent. He uses no tobacco, but for the last twenty years he has drunk one glass of liquor every day—no more, no less. He says he must have his tod. I had begun to have lurking suspicions about this Revolutionary soldier business, but here is an original Jacobs. But because a man can drink a glass of liquor a day, and live to be a hundred years old, my young readers must not infer that by drinking two glasses of liquor a day a man can live to be two hundred. "Which, I meanter say, it doesn't follor," as Joseph Gargery might observe.

This store, in which may constantly be found calico and nails, and fish, and tobacco in kegs, and snuff in bladders, is a venerable establishment. As long ago as 1814 it was an institution. The county troops, on their way to the defence of Portland, then menaced by British ships-of-war, were drawn up in front of this very store, and treated at the town's expense. Citizens will tell you how the clergyman refused to pray for the troops, because he considered the war an unholy one; and how a somewhat eccentric person, of dissolute habits, volunteered his services, stating that he once had an uncle who was a deacon, and he thought he could make a tolerable prayer, although it was rather out of his line; and how he prayed so long and absurdly that the Colonel ordered him under arrest, but that even while soldiers stood over him with gleaming bayonets, the reckless being sang a preposterous song about his grandmother's spotted calf, with its Ri-fol-lol-tiddery-i-do; after which he howled dismally.

And speaking of the store, reminds me of a little story. The author of "several successful comedies" has been among us, and the store was anxious to know who the stranger was. And therefore the store asked him.

"What do you follow, sir?" respectfully inquired the tradesman.

"I occasionally write for the stage, sir."

"Oh!" returned the tradesman, in a confused manner.

"He means," said an honest villager, with a desire to help the puzzled tradesman out, "he means that he writes the handbills for the stage drivers!"

I believe that story is new, although perhaps it is not of an uproariously mirthful character; but one hears stories at the store that are old enough, goodness knows—stories which, no doubt, diverted Methuselah in the sunny days of his giddy and thoughtless boyhood.

There is an exciting scene at the store occasionally. Yesterday an athletic peasant, in a state of beer, smashed in a counter and emptied two tubs of butter on the floor. His father—a white-haired old man, who was a little boy when the Revolutionary war closed, but who doesn't remember Washington *much*, came round in the evening and settled for the damages. "My son," he said, "has considerable originality." I will mention that this same son once told me that he could lick me with one arm tied behind him, and I was so thoroughly satisfied he could, that I told him he needn't mind going for a rope.

Sometimes I go a-visiting to a farm-house, on which occasions the parlor is opened. The windows have been close-shut ever since the last visitor was there, and there is a dingy smell that I struggle as calmly as possible with, until I am led to the banquet of steaming hot biscuit and custard pie. If they would only let me sit in the dear old-fashioned kitchen, or on the door-stone—if they knew how dismally the new black furniture looked—but, never mind, I am not a reformer. No, I should rather think not.

Gloomy enough, this living on a farm, you perhaps say, in which case you are wrong. I can't exactly say that I pant to be an agriculturist, but I do know that in the main it is an independent, calmly happy sort of life. I can see how the prosperous farmer can go joyously a-field with the rise of the sun, and how his heart may swell with pride over bounteous harvests and sleek oxen. And it must be rather jolly for him on winter evenings to sit before the bright kitchen fire and watch his rosy boys and girls as they study out the charades in the weekly paper, and gradually find out why my first is something that grows in a garden, and my second is a fish.

On the green hillside over yonder, there is a quivering of snowy drapery, and bright hair is flashing in the morning sunlight. It is recess, and the Seminary girls are running in the tall grass.

A goodly seminary to look at outside, certainly, although I am pained to learn, as I do on unprejudiced authority, that Mrs. Higgins, the Principal, is a tyrant, who seeks to crush the girls and trample upon them; but my sorrow is somewhat assuaged by learning that Skimmerhorn, the pianist, is perfectly splendid.

Looking at these girls reminds me that I, too, was once young—and where are the friends of my youth? I have found one of 'em, certainly. I saw him ride in the circus the other day on a bareback horse, and even now his name stares at me from yonder board-fence, in green, and blue, and red, and yellow letters. Dashington, the youth with whom I used to read the able orations of Cicero, and who, as a declaimer on exhibition days, used to wipe the rest of us boys pretty handsomely out—well, Dashington is identified with the halibut and cod interest—drives a fish-cart, in fact, from a certain town on the coast, back into the interior. Hurbertson, the utterly stupid boy—the lunkhead, who never had his lesson—he's about the ablest lawyer a sister State can boast. Mills is a newspaper man, and is just now editing a Major-General down South.

Singlinson, the sweet-voiced boy, whose face was always washed and who was real good, and who was never rude—*he* is in the penitentiary for putting his uncle's autograph to a financial document. Hawkins, the clergyman's son, is an actor, and Williamson, the good little boy who divided his bread and butter with the beggar-man, is a failing merchant, and makes money by it. Tom Slink, who used to smoke short-sixes and get acquainted with the little circus boys, is popularly supposed to be the proprietor of a cheap gaming establishment in Boston, where the beautiful but uncertain prop is nightly tossed. Be sure, the Army is represented by many of the friends of my youth, the most of whom have given a good account of themselves. But Chalmerson hasn't done much. No, Chalmerson is rather of a failure. He plays on the guitar and sings love songs. Not that he is a bad man. A kinder-hearted creature never lived, and they say he hasn't yet got over crying for his little curly-haired sister who died ever so long ago. But he knows nothing about business, politics, the world, and those things. He is dull at trade,—indeed, it is a common remark that "everybody cheats Chalmerson." He came to the party the other evening, and brought his guitar. They wouldn't have him for a tenor in the opera, certainly, for he is shaky in his upper notes; but if his simple melodies didn't gush straight from the heart, why were my trained eyes wet? And although some of the girls giggled, and some of the men seemed to pity him, I could not help fancying that poor Chalmerson was nearer heaven than any of us all!

Christopher Buckley
(Contemporary)

∽⧢∾

As You Go Forward

I vividly remember the speaker at my own graduation, so many years ago now. He or she said to us, "You stand on the shoulders of people who came before you, so don't jiggle." Wise words, truly. And isn't that what education is all about?

Great changes have taken place during your short lifetimes. You no longer have to hunt woolly mastodons with rocks and spears if you want a late-night snack. If you want something to eat, you simply say, "Hey, waiter." If it's money you want, you no longer have to stick a gun in the teller's face and say, "Give me all your money." You just hack into their mainframes. Things really aren't so bad, when you come right down to it. . . .

But, as George Harrison put it with the piquancy that is uniquely his, "You know it don't come easy." You will spend hours stuck in traffic listening to cabdrivers explain their proposals for peace in the Middle East. Your flights will be delayed—or, yes, even cancelled. Your frequent-flier miles will expire, and the bean burrito, hot as molten lava on the outside, will still be frozen on the inside. You will be tested, perhaps as no generation before has ever been tested. At such times, try to remember—to paraphrase the words of another Beatles song, "Hey Dude"—that it is a fool who takes his world and tries to make it cooler by inhaling freon.

In one of the last letters he ever wrote to Dorothy Parker, inventor of the fountain pen that bears her name, the prince formerly known as Niccolò Machiavelli declared, "If all the *papardelle* in the world were laid end to end, I wouldn't be a bit surprised." It may be daunting to you to imagine twenty-five thousand miles of bow-shaped pasta girdling the globe, but let me today say to you, on behalf of my generation, "You can do it!" We certainly hope you can, anyway. It cost a lot of money to educate you people, you know.

H. C. Bunner (1855–1896)

❧❧❧❦

Poetry and the Poet

[A SONNET.]
(FOUND ON THE POET'S DESK.)

Weary, I open wide the antique pane
  I ope to the air
I ope to
I open to the air the antique pane

 And gaze $\begin{Bmatrix} \text{beyond?} \\ \text{across} \end{Bmatrix}$ the thrift-sown field of wheat,
          [commonplace?]
 A-shimmering green in breezes born of heat;
And lo!
And high

And my soul's eyes behold $\begin{Bmatrix} \text{a?} \\ \text{the} \end{Bmatrix}$ billowy main

Whose farther shore is Greece   strain
               again
               vain

[*Arcadia*—mythological allusion.—Mem.: *Lemprière*.]
 I see thee, Atalanta, vestal fleet,
 And look! with doves low-fluttering round her feet,

Comes Venus through the golden $\begin{Bmatrix} \text{fields of?} \\ \text{bowing} \end{Bmatrix}$ grain.

   (Heard by the Poet's neighbour.)

Venus be bothered—it's Virginia Dix!

   (Found on the Poet's door.)

> *Out on important business—back at 6.*

George Carlin (Contemporary)

~~∂~∂~~

FROM *Brain Droppings*

Things You Never See

- A puppet with a hard-on
- A butterfly with a swastika design
- The Latin word for *douche bag*
- Someone defecating in church
- A junkie with leisure time
- A serial killer with a light-up bow tie
- A mom-and-pop steel mill
- A shot glass full of carrot juice
- A bum with matching luggage
- Really interesting twins
- Condoms with pictures of the saints
- Two homosexuals who own a bait shop
- A pimp with a low profit margin
- A Rolls-Royce that's more than 50 percent primer paint

Baseball and Football

Baseball is different from any other sport; very different.

For instance, in most sports you score points or goals; in baseball you score runs.

In most sports the ball, or object, is put in play by the offensive team; in baseball the defensive team puts the ball in play, and only the defense is allowed to touch the ball. In fact, in baseball if an offensive player touches the ball intentionally, he's out; sometimes unintentionally, he's out.

Also: In football, basketball, soccer, volleyball, and all sports played with a ball, you score *with* the ball, and without the ball you can't score. In baseball the ball prevents you from scoring.

In most sports the team is run by a coach; in baseball the team is run by a manager; and only in baseball does the manager (or coach) wear the same clothing the players do. If you had ever seen John Madden in his Oakland Raiders football uniform, you would know the reason for this custom.

Now, I've mentioned football. Baseball and football are the two most popular spectator sports in this country. And, as such, it seems they ought to be able to tell us something about ourselves and our values. And maybe how those values have changed over the last 150 years. For those reasons, I enjoy comparing baseball and football:

Baseball is a nineteenth-century pastoral game.
Football is a twentieth-century technological struggle.

Baseball is played on a diamond, in a park. The baseball park!

Football is played on a gridiron, in a stadium, sometimes called Soldier Field or War Memorial Stadium.

Baseball begins in the spring, the season of new life.
Football begins in the fall, when everything is dying.

In football you wear a helmet.
In baseball you wear a cap.

Football is concerned with *downs*. "What down is it?"
Baseball is concerned with *ups*. "Who's up? Are you up? I'm not up! He's up!"

In football you receive a penalty.
In baseball you make an error.

In football the specialist comes in to kick.
In baseball the specialist comes in to relieve somebody.

Football has hitting, clipping, spearing, piling on, personal fouls, late hitting, and unnecessary roughness.
Baseball has the sacrifice.

* * *

Football is played in any kind of weather: Rain, snow, sleet, hail, fog . . . can't see the game, don't know if there is a game going on; mud on the field . . . can't read the uniforms, can't read the yard markers, the struggle will continue!

In baseball if it rains, we don't go out to play. "I can't go out! It's raining out!"

Baseball has the seventh-inning stretch.
Football has the two-minute warning.

Baseball has no time limit: "We don't know when it's gonna end!"
Football is rigidly timed, and it will end "even if we have to go to sudden death."

In baseball, during the game, in the stands, there's a kind of picnic feeling. Emotions may run high or low, but there's not that much unpleasantness.

In football, during the game in the stands, you can be sure that at least twenty-seven times you were perfectly capable of taking the life of a fellow human being.

And finally, the objectives of the two games are completely different:

In football the object is for the quarterback, otherwise known as the field general, to be on target with his aerial assault, riddling the defense by hitting his receivers with deadly accuracy in spite of the blitz, even if he has to use the shotgun. With short bullet passes and long bombs, he marches his troops into enemy territory, balancing this aerial assault with a sustained ground attack that punches holes in the forward wall of the enemy's defensive line.

In baseball the object is to go home! And to be safe! "I hope I'll be safe at home!"

Play Ball

Athletes like that physical shit. When they're pleased with each other they bump chests, butt heads, and bang forearms. Why don't they just punch each other in the fuckin' teeth? Wouldn't that be great? Teammates, I mean. After a touchdown pass, why doesn't the guy who caught the ball just go over and kick the quarterback right in the nuts? Same with a slam dunk in basketball. The guy who scores oughta grab a chair and beat the living shit out of the guy who fed him the ball. For about forty-five minutes. If this type of celebration were more common, the postgame show from the winners' locker room would be a lot livelier.

And I think there should be at least one sport where the object is to kill someone. A team sport. Deathball. Let's face it, athletes are mostly physical freaks with serious personality defects where competition is concerned, and they just love someone to "motivate" them. Well, what greater motivation can there be than trying to avoid being killed? It's a fuckin' natural! And for me, what could be more fun than watching one of these jackoffs motivate his ugly ass into an early grave every game?

Unnecessary Words

THERE IS A TENDENCY THESE DAYS TO COMPLICATE
SPEECH BY ADDING UNNECESSARY WORDS.
THE FOLLOWING PHRASES ALL CONTAIN
AT LEAST ONE WORD TOO MANY.

emergency situation
shower activity
surgical procedure
boarding process
flotation device
hospital environment
fear factor
free of charge

prison setting
peace process
intensity level
belief system
seating area
sting operation
evacuation process
rehabilitation process

risk factor
crisis situation
leadership role
learning process
rain event
confidence level
healing process
standoff situation

knowledge base   facial area   shooting incident
forest setting   daily basis   planning process
beverage items   blue in color

There Are No Times That Don't Have Moments Like These

Since 1983, more than thirty people have been killed in post office shootings. You know why? Because the price of stamps keeps changing. There's a lot of pressure. "How much are they now, Rob? Twenty-nine? Thirty-two? I can't keep track! Fuck it!" BANG BANG BANG BANG BANG BANG BANG BANG BANG!!!

On Opening Day, the President doesn't throw *out* the first ball. He throws it *in*. If he threw it out, it would land in the parking lot and someone would have to go get it.

Roz Chast (Contemporary)

FROM *The Four Elements*

FROM *Proof of Life on Earth*

James David Corrothers
(1869–1917)

❧❧❧

An Indignation Dinner

Dey was hard times jes fo' Christmas round our neighborhood one year;
So we held a secret meetin', whah de white folks couldn't
 hear,
To 'scuss de situation, an' to see what could be done
Towa'd a fust-class Christmas dinneh an' a little Christmas fun.

Rufus Green, who called de meetin', ris an' said: "In dis
 here town,
An' throughout de land, de white folks is a'tryin' to keep us
 down."
S' 'e: "Dey bought us, sold us, beat us; now dey 'buse us
 'ca'se we's free;
But when dey tetch my stomach, dey's done gone too fur
 foh me!

"Is I right?" "You sho is, Rufus!" roared a dozen hungry
 throats.
"Ef you'd keep a mule a-wo'kin', don't you tamper wid
 his oats.
Dat's sense," continued Rufus. "But dese white folks
 nowadays
Has done got so close and stingy you can't live on what
 dey pays.

* * *

"Here 'tis Christmas-time, an', folkses, I's indignant 'nough
  to choke.
Whah's our Christmas dinneh comin' when we's mos' completely broke?
I can't hahdly 'fo'd a toothpick an' a glass o' water. Mad?
Say, I'm desp'ret! Dey jes better treat me nice, dese white
  folks had!"

Well, dey 'bused de white folks scan'lous, till old Pappy
  Simmons ris,
Leanin' on his cane to s'pote him, on account his rheumatis',
An' s' 'e: "Chillun, whut's dat wintry wind a-sighin' th'ough
  de street
'Bout yo' wasted summeh wages? But, no matter, we
  mus' eat.

"Now, I seed a beau'ful tuhkey on a certain gemmun's fahm.
He's a-growin' fat an' sassy, an' a-struttin' to a chahm.
Chickens, sheeps, hogs, sweet pertaters—all de craps is fine
  dis year;
All we needs is a committee foh to tote de goodies here."

Well, we lit right in an' voted dat it was a gran' idee,
An' de dinneh we had Christmas was worth trabblin' miles
  to see;
An' we eat a full an' plenty, big an' little, great an' small,
Not beca'se we was dishonest, but indignant, sah. Dat's all.

Bill Cosby (Contemporary)

~~~ces~~~

FROM *Love & Marriage*

Till Talk Do You Part

In her endless effort to bring her husband out of the cave, the American wife will tell him, "The problem with you is you are not in touch with your feelings." She will tell him this right after he has tried to shotput his son to dramatize some parental point for which mere language lacked clarity. She will tell him this right after he has kicked in the television set as a fitting response to an overtime field goal against his home team. A man can spend an entire morning creatively running amuck; and when he is finished and the foam on his lips has dried, his wife will say, "The problem with you is you are not in touch with your feelings."

Although I'm not a psychologist (my doctorate is in education, my BA in the quarter-mile), it has always seemed to me that I am nicely in touch with my feelings, one of which is an urge to bounce pass the next woman who tells me I am not in touch with my feelings. Of course, what women often mean by this charge is that men don't know how to cry; but crying isn't always an indication of genuine feeling. If it were, then Jimmy Swaggart and Tammy Faye Bakker would be sensitivity's king and queen.

I sometimes think that women may be too involved in revelation, that perhaps a marriage is strained by just four words: not *The children aren't yours* but *How was your day?* It is often too much pressure on a man to ask him to keep giving the six o'clock news, especially when the only thing to report is the weather. What, for example, is a dentist to say when his wife inquires, *How was your day?*

I did six fillings, four root canals, and a small child spat in my eye.

Maybe the best answer a husband can give to *How was your day?* is *I spent it dreading that question.* Or maybe the husband should draw first and ask his *wife, How was your day?* Then, however, he is liable to hear the four grimmest words of all:

I had the children.

Camille never has to be a district attorney with me, for she has a way to learn what I'm thinking that even allows me to have a good meal.

"If I ever want to find out anything about you," she has said, "I'll invite five of your friends to dinner and just listen in."

By communicating indirectly, sometimes through a basketball team, Camille and I have been able to keep the mystery in our marriage, a quality that the marriage manuals consider important. Of course, these manuals say that communication is important too; and so, the answer seems to be that a couple should communicate mysteriously, each one making sure that the other rarely knows what he is talking about. Every time that Camille and I exchange *That's not what I'm* saying / *Then what's your* point?, we are moving further into foggy paradise.

In this happy pursuit of marital mystery, Camille and I sometimes *almost* have a conversation, but then she thinks better of the idea.

"I want to talk to you," she told me one evening in the kitchen.

"Fine," I said. "Let's do it right after I finish these chili dogs. I don't want to distract my mouth right now."

A few minutes later and a few pounds heavier, I walked into the living room, where she was standing by the fireplace, a stunning portrait of a great lady about to hold forth. I hoped I was equal to the subject. I hoped it was the Cleveland Browns.

"Here I am for the talking," I said. "What was it you wanted?"

"*You* know what I wanted," she replied. "Let's just leave it at that."

And she turned and went up to the bedroom, no doubt for a meeting with Godot.

Because Camille and I have wisely left each other in the dark so often, our marriage has been rich in surprise. It is an atmosphere in which my son can come to me and say, "Dad, I've decided I want to be more involved in politics."

"That's good," I reply.

"So I'm dropping out of college, changing my name to Raul, and joining the Contras."

"Then I guess you'll be wanting some advance allowance."

"Yes, please. Either pesos or traveler's checks."

"You know, this is . . . well, I guess you'd have to call it a surprise. *I* didn't know you wanted to become a Nicaraguan guerrilla. At least not this *semester*."

"Well, *Mom* has known it for months."

"She has?"

"Yes, she even says the Contras are the ideal group for me because I'm always against everything. Dad, if you and Mom did more talking, you'd be ready with a going-away present for me."

My son did not understand, however, that there is a method in the intermittent and semicoherent exchanges of information that Camille and I have: we are trying not to use up the conversation allotted to our marriage. Unaware that this conversational allotment governs every marriage, most young couples do not pace their tongues and suddenly find themselves in three-month lulls.

The next time you're in a restaurant, study some couple that seems to have been married for more than ten years. Watch them exchanging long desperate looks, each of them hoping that the numbing silence will be broken by a good grease fire or a holdup. And each of them is about to be driven to think the unthinkable:

We should have brought the children.

Camille and I bring the children. In fact, people have said that we are prisoners of the children because we bring them everywhere we go, from Las Vegas to the South of France. However, I can recall six times in our marriage when we left the children home. *Seven* times if you count the night that Camille walked out on me and I went after her without bothering to get a sitter.

Nevertheless, I have to admit that whenever Camille has suggested that we go off without the children for longer than an hour and a half, I say either, "But it's always more *fun* with the children along" or "Just be patient, dear. In just nine or ten or fifteen years, they'll all be married or in the armed forces and then we'll have the house back. That's our reason to keep *living*."

However, early one summer in our thirteenth year of marriage, my mother offered to stay with the children for a week so that Camille and I could go on a little vacation alone and recapture the magic of the honeymoon we had always planned to take. For a moment, I had considered having my mother take Camille for a week and letting *me* go off with the children, whose interests were closer to mine; but then I yielded to my yen for adventure and decided to see if Camille and I could make it alone, operating under the handicap of having to talk only to each other.

"Darling," I had said to her, "what would you say if I told you that we're going to take a vacation without the children?"

"I'd say you're a liar," she replied.

"And usually you'd be right, but my mother just offered to stay with them so we can get to know each other again—unless there's someone else you'd rather get to know."

"No, you'll do. But I thought you said it's always more fun with the kids along."

"So it won't be our greatest vacation, but at least it'll be all ours. Just the two of us, dancing away from Fat Albert."

As the moment of our departure approached, Camille and I conceived some rules for this romantic escapade:

- There could be no mention of the children.
- No photographs, tapes of cuteness, or report cards could be taken along.
- No one could become pregnant or in any other way involved with kids.

And so, one afternoon in July, we turned our two girls and our boy over to my mother and then drove out to a charming old inn on eastern Long Island. A few minutes after arriving, as I zipped up the back of Camille's dress before taking her to an elegant dinner, I said, "You look so young and lovely. No one could ever tell that you had two kid . . . um, kidneys. Sorry."

"That's okay," she said. "I miss them too, those precious kidneys. And that spleen."

"Courage," I said. "We can make it."

In the dining room, we found a corner table, where I sat down and began desperately trying to think of things to talk about. So far, I had two: the plight of the dollar and the plight of the whale. I would have to pace myself with them or my mouth would be retired before the soup.

After a silence of no more than five or ten minutes, I tenderly placed my hand on Camille's and said, "Have I ever told you, my darling, that they should let the dollar float?"

"How you *talk,* lover," she demurely replied.

"And speaking of floating, this is a tough time to be a whale, don't you think?"

She smiled helplessly, and then I said, "You look so young and lovely tonight."

"You've said that already, but I don't mind. If my loveliness is the bottom of your barrel, you can go with it for a day or two."

The pressure was getting to me now. How *could* parents keep themselves from talking about their children? I decided that there should be a clinic where addicts could taper off, first looking at photos of their own children, then gradually at someone else's, and finally at slides of vasectomies.

Once our appetizers came, we began to chew our way through a seemingly endless lull. I thought about my oldest daughter often telling me not to talk with a mouthful of food and I congratulated myself on avoiding a demerit from Camille by keeping the thought unexpressed.

"You know, the Owls could go all the way this year," I finally said.

"Some new migration?" she replied.

"The *Temple* Owls. All the way."

"That would be nice. All the way where?"

As a bird-watcher, Camille was no better than Denise. Was *any* woman wise enough to follow my Owls?

After the meal a romantic mood was upon us, so hand in hand we walked down to the beach under a sky full of stars. We went almost to the water's edge, and for four or five minutes nothing was said; but neither of us was trying now, for we both were transported by the awesome beauty of the universe. At last, however, from somewhere deep in my soul, a thought emerged and was given voice.

"Just think," I said. "At this very moment, under these very stars, a little Cosby is wetting the bed." And then I piteously cried, "Oh, honey, I *tried*! You don't *know* how I tried!"

"Don't hate yourself," she said. "I was just about to suggest that we gather some shells for them."

Frederick Swartout Cozzens
(1818–1869)

Our New Bedstead

I have bought me a new patent bedstead, to facilitate early rising, called a "wake-up." It is a good thing to rise early in the country. Even in the winter time it is conducive to health to get out of a warm bed by lamplight; to shiver into your drawers and slippers; to wash your face in a basin of ice-flakes; and to comb out your frigid hair with an uncompromising comb, before a frosty looking-glass. The only difficulty about it lies in the impotence of human will. You will deliberate about it and argue the point. You will indulge in specious pretences, and lie still with only the tip end of your nose outside the blankets; you will pretend to yourself that you *do* intend to jump out in a few minutes; you will tamper with the good intention, and yet indulge in the delicious luxury. To all this the "wake-up" is inflexibly and triumphantly antagonistic. It is a bedstead with a clock scientifically inserted in the head-board. When you go to bed you wind up the clock, and point the index-hand to that hour on the dial at which you wish to rise in the morning. Then you place yourself in the hands of the invention and shut your eyes.

You are now, as it were, under the guardianship of King Solomon and Doctor Benjamin Franklin. There is no need to recall those beautiful lines of the poet's—

> "Early to bed and early to rise,
> Will make a man healthy, wealthy, and wise."

Science has forestalled them. The "wake-up" is a combination of hard wood, hinges, springs, and clock-work, against sleeping late o' mornings. It is a bedstead with all the beautiful vitality of a flower—it opens with the dawn. If, for instance, you set the hand against six o'clock in the morning, at six the clock at the bed's head solemnly strikes a demitwelve on its sonorous bell. If you pay no attention to the monitor, or idly, dreamily endeavour to compass the coherent sequence of sounds, the invention, within the succeeding two minutes, drops its tail-board and lets down your feet upon the floor. While you are pleasantly defeating this attempt upon your privacy by drawing up your legs within the precincts of the blankets, the virtuous head-board and the rest of the bed suddenly rise up in protest; and the next moment, if you do not instantly abdicate, you are launched upon the floor by a blind elbow that connects with the crank of an eccentric, that is turned by a cord that is wound around a drum, that is moved by an endless screw, that revolves within the body of the machinery. So soon as you are turned out, of course, you waive the balance of the nap and proceed to dress.

"Mrs. Sparrowgrass," said I, contemplatively, after the grimy machinists had departed, "this machine is one of the most remarkable evidences of progress the ingenuity of man has yet developed. In this bedstead we see a host of cardinal virtues made practical by science. To rise early one must possess courage, prudence, self-denial, temperance, and fortitude. The cultivation of these virtues, necessarily attended with a great deal of trouble, may now be dispensed with, as this engine can entirely set aside, and render useless, a vast amount of moral discipline. I have no doubt in a short time we shall see the finest attributes of the human mind superseded by machinery. Nay, more; I have very little doubt that, as a preparatory step in this great progress, we shall have physical monitors of cast-iron and wheelwork to regulate the ordinary routine of duty in every family."

Mrs. Sparrowgrass said she did not precisely understand what I meant.

"For instance," said I, in continuation, "we dine every day, as a general thing, I mean. Now sometimes we eat too much, and how easy, how practicable it would be to regulate our appetites by a banquet-dial. The subject, having had the superficial area of his skull and the cubic capacity of his body worked out respectively by a licensed craniologist and by a licensed corporalogist, gets from each a certificate, which certificates are duly registered in the county clerk's office. From the county clerk he received a permit, marked, we will say, ten."

"Not ten pounds, I hope," said Mrs. S.

"No, my dear," I replied, "ten would be the average of his capacity. We will now suppose the chair, in which the subject is seated at dinner, rests upon a pendulous platform, over a delicate arrangement of levers, connected with an upright rod, that runs through the section of table in front of his plate, and this rod, we will suppose, is toothed into a ratchet-wheel, that moves the index of the banquet-dial. You will see at once that, as he hangs balanced in this scale, any absorption of food would be instantly indicated by the index. All then he is called upon to do is to watch the dial until the hand points to 'ten,' and then stop eating."

"But," said Mrs. Sparrowgrass, "suppose he shouldn't be half through?"

"Oh!" said I, "that would not make any difference. When the dial says he has had enough, he must quit."

"But," said Mrs. Sparrowgrass, "suppose he *would not* stop eating?"

"Then," said I, "the proper way to do would be to inform against him, and have him brought immediately before a justice of the peace, and if he did not at once swear that he had eaten within his limits, fine him, and seize all the victuals on his premises."

"Oh!" said Mrs. S., "you would have a law to regulate it, then?"

"Of course," said I, "a statute—a statutory provision, or provisionary act. Then, the principle once being established, you see how easily and beautifully we could be regulated by the simplest motive powers. All the obligations we now owe to society and to ourselves could be dispensed with, or rather transferred to, or vested in, some superior machine, to which we would be accountable by night and day. Nay, more than that, instead of sending representatives to legislate for us, how easy it would be to construct a legislature of bronze and wheel-work—an incorruptible legislature. I would suggest a hydraulic or pneumatic congress as being less liable to explode, and more easily graduated than one propelled by steam simply. All that would be required of us then would be to elect a state engineer annually, and he, with the assistance of a few underlings, could manage the automata as he pleased."

"I do not see," replied Mrs. Sparrowgrass, "how that would be an improvement upon the present method, from all I hear."

This unexpected remark of Mrs. S. surprised me into silence for a moment, but immediately recovering, I answered, that a hydraulic or pneumatic legislature would at least have this advantage—it would construct enactments for the State at, at least, one-fiftieth part of the present expense, and at the same time do the work better and quicker.

"Now, my dear," said I, as I wound up the ponderous machinery with a huge key, "as you are always an early riser, and as, of course, you will be up before seven o'clock, I will set the indicator at that hour, so that you will not be disturbed by the progress of science. It is getting to be very cold, my dear, but how beautiful the stars are to-night. Look at Orion and the Pleiades! Intensely lustrous in the frosty sky."

The sensations one experiences in lying down upon a complication of mechanical forces are somewhat peculiar if they are not entirely novel. I once had the pleasure, for one week, of sleeping over the boiler of a high-pressure Mississippi steamboat; and, as I knew in case of a blow up I should be the first to hear of it, I composed my mind as well as I could under the circumstances. But this reposing upon a bed of statics and dynamics, with the constant chirping and crawling of wheel-work at the bed's head, with a thought now and then of the inexorable iron elbow below, and an uncertainty as to whether the clock itself might not be too fast, or too slow, caused me to be rather reflective and watchful than composed and drowsy.

Nevertheless, I enjoyed the lucent stars in their blue depths, and the midnight moon, now tipping the Palisades with a fringe of silver fire, and was thinking how many centuries that lovely light had played upon those rugged ridges of trap and basalt, and so finally sinking from the reflective to the imaginative, and from the imaginative to the indistinct, at last reached that happy state of half consciousness, between half asleep and asleep, when the clock in the machine woke up, and suddenly struck eight. Of course I knew it was later, but I could not imagine why it should at all, as I presumed the only time of striking was in the morning by way of signal. As Mrs. S. was sound asleep, I concluded not to say anything to her about it; but I could not help thinking what an annoyance it would be if the clock should keep on striking the hours during the night. In a little while the bedclothes seemed to droop at the foot of the bed, to which I did not pay much attention, as I was just then engaged listening to the drum below, that seemed to be steadily engaged in winding up its rope and preparing for action. Then I felt the upper part of the patent bedstead rising up, and then I concluded to jump out, just as the iron elbow began to utter a cry like unto the cry of a steel Katydid, and did jump, but was accidentally preceded by the mattress, one bolster, two pillows, ditto blankets, a brace of threadbare linen sheets, one coverlid, the baby, one cradle (overturned), and Mrs. Sparrowgrass. To gather up these heterogeneous materials of comfort required some little time, and, in the meanwhile, the bedstead subsided. When we retired again, and were once more safely protected from the nipping cold, although pretty well cooled, I could not help speaking of the perfect operation of the bedstead in high terms of praise, although, by some accident, it had fulfilled its object a little earlier than had been desirable. As I am very fond of dilating upon a pleasant theme, the conversation was prolonged until Mrs. Sparrowgrass got sleepy, and the clock struck nine. Then we had to turn out again. We had to turn out every hour during the long watches of the night for that wonderful epitome of the age of progress.

When the morning came we were sleepy enough, and the next evening we concluded to replace the "wake-up" with a common, old-fashioned bedstead. To be sure I had made a small mistake the first night, in not setting the *"indicator"* as well as the *index* of the dial. But what of that? Who wants his rest, that precious boon, subjected to contingencies? When we go to sleep, and say our prayers, let us wake up according to our natures, and according to our virtues; some require more sleep, some less; we are not mere bits of mechanism after all; who knows what world we may chance to wake up in? For my part, I have determined not to be a humming-top, to be wound up and to run down, just like that very interesting toy one of the young Sparrow-grassii has just now left upon my table, minus a string.

Josephine Daskam (1876–1961)

FROM *The Woman Who Caught the Idea*

There was once a Woman whose Fiancé had a Decided Theory regarding the most Desirable Characteristics of the Sexes. This Theory, in a Word, was that a Woman should be Like a Clinging Vine, while a Man should Resemble a Sturdy Oak. For Many Years, therefore, the Woman had Practiced Clinging with Great Success. One day, However, her Fiancé grew Critical of her Method . . .

So they Broke off the Engagement. The Fiancé found a Progressive and Stimulating Woman who Agreed to Criticize him and March Abreast of him. The only Trouble with this was that Not Only did she March Abreast, but it Seemed Probable that she would Get Ahead. Also she had a Work of Her Own, which sometimes Interfered with His. . . .

* * *

So he Returned to his Old Love and said, "Let All Be as it was Before."

"I am Afraid that can Not be," she replied, Sadly. "Since I Lost You I have Given Up Clinging, and I have Caught Your Idea. I had to Sympathize with Someone, so I have Taken Up a Work of My Own. Judging from your Tone I think you Would Fail to Comprehend it. The Century is Progressing and Things can Never Be as they Were Before."

This teaches us that It's Well to Be On with the Old Love Before you are Off with the New.

FROM *Smith College Stories*

The Education of Elizabeth

I

FROM MISS ELIZABETH STOCKTON
TO MISS CAROLYN SAWYER

Lowell, Mass., Sept. 10, 189–.

My Dearest Carol: The thing we have both wished so much has happened! Papa has finally consented to let me go to college! It has taken a long time and a *great deal* of persuasion, and Mamma never cared *anything* about it, you know, herself. But I laid it before her in a way that I really am ashamed of! I never thought I'd do anything like it! But I *had* to, it seemed to me. I told her that she had often spoken of what a mistake Mrs. Hall made in letting Marjory come out so soon, and that I should *certainly* be unwilling to stay at Mrs. Meade's another year. I'm doing advanced work now, and I'm *terribly* bored. The girls all seem so very young, somehow! And I said that I couldn't come out till I was twenty-two, if I went to college. I teased so that she gave way, but we had a *terrible* siege with Papa. He is the *dearest* man in the world, but just a little *tiny* bit prejudiced, you know. He wants me to finish at Mrs. Meade's and then go abroad for a year or two. He wants me to do something with my music. But I told him of the *fine* Music School there was at Smith, and how much *harder* I should work there, *naturally*. He talked a good deal about the art advantages and travel and French—you know what I think about the *terrible narrowness* of a boarding-school education! It is *shameful,* that an intellectual girl of this century should be tied down to *French* and *Music*! And how can the scrappy little bit of gallery sight-seeing that I should do *possibly* equal four years of earnest, intelligent, *regular* college work? He said something about marriage—oh, dear! It is *horrible* that one should have to think of that! I told him, with a great deal of dignity and rather coldly, I'm afraid, that *my* life would be, I hoped, *something more* than the mere *evanescent glitter* of a *social butterfly*! I think it really impressed him. He said, "Oh, very well—very well!" So I'm coming, dearest, and you must write me all about what books I'd better get and just what I'd better know of the college customs. I'm *so* glad you're on the campus. You know Uncle Wendell knows the President very well indeed—he was in college with him—and, somehow or other, I've got a room in the Lawrence, though we did n't expect it so soon! I feel inspired already when I think of the chapel and the big Science Building and that *beautiful* library! I've laid out a course of work that Miss Beverly—that's the literature teacher—thinks very ambitious, but I am afraid she doesn't realize the intention of a *college,* which is a little different, I suppose, from a *boarding-school* (!) I have planned to take sixteen hours for the four years. I must say I think it's rather absurd to limit a girl to that who *really* is *perfectly* able to do more. Perhaps you could see the Register—if that's what it is—and tell him I could just as well take eighteen, and then I could do that other Literature. I must go to try on something—really, it's very hard to convince Mamma that Smith is n't a *summer resort*! Good-by, dearest, we shall have such *beautiful* times together—I'm sure you'll be as excited as I am. We shall *for once* see as much of each other as we want to—I wish I could study with you! I'm coming up on the 8.20 Wednesday morning.

> Devotedly yours,
>
> ELIZABETH.

FROM MISS CAROLYN SAWYER
TO MISS ELIZABETH STOCKTON

Lake Forest, Ill., Sept. 17, 189–.

Dear Bess: I'm very glad you're coming up—it's the only place in the world. I'm not going to be able to meet you—I'm coming back late this year—Mrs. Harte is going to give our crowd a house-party at Lakemere. Isn't that gay? I met Arnold Ritch this summer. He knows you, he said. I never heard you speak of him. He's perfectly *smooth*—his tennis is all right, too. For heaven's sake, don't try to take sixteen hours—on the campus, too! It will break you all up. You'll get on the Glee Club, probably—bring up your songs, by the way—and you'll want to be on the Team. Have you got that blue organdie? You'll want something about like that, pretty soon. If you can help it, don't get one of those Bagdad things for your couch. I'm deadly sick of mine. Get that portière thing you used to have on the big chair at home. It's more individual. We're getting up a little dance for the 26th. If you know any man you could have up, you can come—it will be a good chance to meet some of the upper-class girls. We may not be able to have it, though. Don't tell Kate Saunders about this, please. She'd ask Lockwood over from Amherst, and I've promised Jessie Holden to ask him for her. We shall probably have Sue for class president this year—I'm glad of it, too. There will be a decent set of ushers. I suppose you'll want me for your senior for the sophomore-senior thing. I'll keep that if you wish. I shall get up by the 24th. I'm in the Morris. Don't forget your songs.

Yours in haste,
C. P. S.

FROM MRS. HENRY STOCKTON
TO MRS. JOHN SAWYER

Lowell, Mass., Sept. 23, 189–.

Dear Ella: In spite of great uncertainty on my part and actual unwillingness on her father's, Lizzie has started for Smith. It seems a large undertaking, for four years, and I must say I would rather have left her at Mrs. Meade's. But her heart is set on it, and it is very hard to deny her. She argues so, too; really, the child has great ability, I think. She fairly convinced me. It has always seemed to me that a girl with good social surroundings, a good home library, and an intellectual home atmosphere does very well with four years at so good a school as Mrs. Meade's, and a little travel afterwards. Lizzie has quite a little musical talent, too, and I should have liked her to devote more attention to that. Very frankly, I cannot say that I have been able to see any improvement in Carrie since she went away. I suppose it will wear off, but when I saw her this summer she had a manner that I did not like so well as her very pleasant air three—no, two—years ago. It seemed a curious mixture of youth and decision, that had, however, no maturity in it. Katharine Saunders, too, seems to me so utterly irresponsible for a young woman of twenty-one, and yet so almost arrogant. I expected she would know a great deal, as she studied Greek before she went, but she told me that she always skipped the Latin and Greek quotations in books! She seems to be studying nothing but French and Literature and History; her father could perfectly well have taught her all that, and was anxious to, but she would hear nothing of it. She wanted the college life, she said. Ah, well, I suppose the world has moved on since we read Livy at Miss Hopkins'! I picked up a Virgil of Lizzie's yesterday and was astonished to find how it all came back. We felt very learned, then, but now it is nothing.

I hope Carrie will be good to my little girl and help her perhaps with her lessons—not that I fear Lizzie will need very much help! Miss Beverly assures me that she has never trained a finer mind. Her essay on Jane Austen was highly praised by Dr. Strong, the rector of St. Mary's. Of course, dear Ella, you won't resent my criticism of Carrie—I should never dream of it with any one but an old and valued friend, and I shall gladly receive the same from you. But Lizzie has always been all that I could wish her.

Yours with love,

SARAH B. STOCKTON.

From Mr. William B. Stockton
to Miss Elizabeth Stockton

Boston, Mass., Oct. 16, 189–.

My Dear Niece: Your mother advises me of your having just entered Smith Academy. I had imagined that your previous schooling would have been sufficient, but doubtless your parents know best. Your mother seems a little alarmed as to your success, but I have reassured her. I trust the Stockton blood. Whatever your surroundings may be, you can never, I am sure, set yourself a higher model than your mother. I have never known her to lack the right word or action under any circumstances, and if you can learn that in your schooling, your friends and relatives will be more than satisfied.

I enclose my cheque for fifty dollars ($50), in case you should have any special demand on your purse not met by your regular allowance. I remember many such in my own schooldays. Wishing you success in your new life, I remain,

Your affectionate uncle,
William B. Stockton.

From Miss Elizabeth Craigie
to Miss Elizabeth Stockton

New Haven, Conn., Oct. 21, 189–.

My Dear Elizabeth: Sarah tells me that you are going to college. I am sure I don't see why, but if you do, I suppose that is enough. Children are not what they used to be. It seems to me that four years at Mrs. Meade's should have been enough; neither your Aunt Hannah nor I ever went to college, though to be sure Hannah wanted to go to Mt. Holyoke Seminary once. I have never heard any one intimate that either of us was not sufficiently educated: I wonder that you could for one instant imagine such a thing! Not that I have any reason to suppose you ever did. However, that is neither here nor there. Your Aunt Hannah and I were intending to give you Mother's high shell-comb and her garnet set for Christmas. If you would prefer them now for any reason, you may have them. The comb is being polished and looks magnificent. An absurd thing to give a girl of your age, from my point of view. However, your Aunt Hannah thinks it best. I trust you will be very careful of your diet. It seemed to me that your complexion was not what it should have been when you came on this summer. I am convinced that it is nothing but the miscellaneous eating of cake and other sweets and over-education. There has been a young girl here from some college—I think it is Wellesley—and her complexion is disgraceful. Your Aunt Hannah and I never set up for beauties, but we had complexions of milk and roses, if I do say it. Hannah thinks that the garnets are unsuitable for you, but that is absurd. Mother was no older than you when she wore them, and looked very well, too, I have no doubt. I send you by express a box of Katy's doughnuts, the kind you like, very rich, and a chocolate cake. Also some salad and a loaf cake, Mrs. Harding's rule. I trust you will take sufficient exercise, and don't let your hands grow rough this winter. Nothing shows a lady so much as her hands. Would you like the garnets reset, or as Mother wore them? They are quite the style now, I understand. Hoping you will do well in your studies and keep well, I am,

Yours lovingly,
AUNT LIZZIE.

FROM MISS ELIZABETH STOCKTON
TO MR. ARNOLD RITCH, JR.

Lawrence House, Northampton, Mass., Nov. 1, 189–.

My Dear Arnold: It is only fair to you to tell you that it can never be. No, never! When I—if I did (which I can hardly believe)—allowed you to think anything else, I was a mere child. Life looks very different to me, now. It is quite useless to ask me—I must say that I am surprised that you have spoken to Papa. Nor do I feel called upon to give my reasons. I shall always be a very, very good friend to you, however, and very, very much interested in you.

In the first place, I am, or at least you are, far too young. The American woman of today is younger than her grandmother. I mean, of course, younger than her grandmother is now. That is, than she was then. Also I doubt if I could ever love you as you think you do. Love me, I mean. I am not a man's woman. I much prefer women. Really, Arnold, it is very strange how men bore me now that I have known certain women. Women are so much more interesting, so much more fascinating, so much more exciting! This will probably seem strange to you, but the modern woman I am sure is rapidly getting not to need men at all! I have never seen so many beautiful red-haired girls before. One sits in front of me in chapel, and the light makes an aureole of glory about her head. I wrote a theme about it that is going to be in the *Monthly* for November.

I hope that you won't feel that our dear old friendship of so many years is in any way changed. I shall never forget certain things—

I am enjoying my work very much, though it is easier than I had thought it would be, and the life is different in many ways. If I did not think that Miss Sawyer had probably invited you, I should be very glad to have you come up for the Christmas concert, but I suppose it is useless to ask you. I had no idea you were so fond of tennis!

Your friend always,
ELIZABETH WOLFE STOCKTON.

FROM MR. HENRY STOCKTON TO MISS ELIZABETH STOCKTON

Lowell, Mass., Nov. 1, 189–.

My Dear Elizabeth: Yours received and read with my usual attention and interest. I am glad that your college life continues to be pleasant, and that you have found so many friends. I was much interested, too, in the photograph of Miss Hunter. I find the blue prints are more common than I had supposed, for I had imagined that they were something quite new. It is certainly very accommodating in your teachers to allow themselves to be so generally photographed. Your mother seemed much pleased with Miss Hunter, and glad that you were in the house with her and liked her so much. I was surprised to see her so young in appearance. I had very foolishly imagined the typical old style "school-marm," I suppose. But it seems that she was graduated only a few years ago, herself.

Now, my dear Elizabeth, I am going to speak to you very seriously. I trust that you will take it in good part and re-member that nothing can be more to my interest than the real happiness and well-being of my daughter. The tone of your letters to both your mother and me has seemed for some weeks unsatisfactory. I mean that we have found in them a nervous, strained tone that troubles me exceedingly. I cannot see why you should close with such expressions as this (I copy verbatim): "Too tired to write more;" "All used up—lots of Latin to do—can only find time for a note;" "Tired to death because I'm not sleeping quite as well as usual, just now;" et cetera, et cetera.

I have been to see Mrs. Meade, and she assures me that your preparation was more than adequate: that your first year should prove very easy for you, *in Latin especially*. Now what does this mean? You left us well and strong, considering that you have always been a delicate girl. It was for that reason, as you know, that I particularly opposed your going to college.

But there is more. Mrs. Allen's daughter, Harriet, has been at home for some days to attend her sister's wedding. Your mother and I naturally seized the opportunity of inquiring after you, and after some questioning from us she admitted that you were not looking very well. She said that you seemed tired and were "going it a little too hard, perhaps." That seemed to me a remarkable expression to apply to a young girl! My endeavors to find out exactly what it meant resulted in nothing more explicit than that "Bess was trying to do too much."

Now, my dear girl, while we are naturally only too pleased that you should be striving to stand well in your classes, do not, I beg of you, imagine for one moment that any intellectual advancement you may win can compensate us or you for the loss of your health. You remember Cousin Will, who carried off six honors at Harvard and came home a nervous invalid. I fear that the Stockton temperament cannot stand the strain of too continued mental application.

I must stop now, to attend to some business matters, and I will add only this. Do not fail to remember my definite conditions, which have not altered since September. If you are not perfectly well at the Christmas holidays, you must remain with us. This may seem severe, but I am convinced, your mother also, that we shall be acting entirely for your good.

Yours aff.,
FATHER.

From Mr. Arnold Ritch, Sr., to Miss Marion Hunter

New York, N. Y., Nov. 4, 189–.

My Dear Miss Hunter: You may remember meeting, five years ago, in Paris, in the Louvre, an old American, who had the great pleasure of rendering you a trifling assistance in a somewhat embarrassing situation, and who had the further pleasure of crossing on the *Etruria* with you a month later. I was that man, and I remember that you said that if ever there should happen to be an occasion for it, you would be only too happy to return your imaginary debt.

If you really meant it, the occasion, strangely enough, has come. I know well enough from my lifelong friend, Richard Benton, whose family you have so often visited, that you are an extremely busy young woman, and I will state my case briefly. I never make half-confidences, and I rely implicitly on your discretion in the following clear statement. My only nephew and namesake, incidentally heir, has been for some time practically engaged to Miss Elizabeth Stockton, the daughter of an old friend. The engagement has been entirely satisfactory to all parties concerned, and was actually on the eve of announcement, when the young lady abruptly departed for Smith College.

My nephew is, though only twenty-four, unusually mature and thoroughly settled: he was deeply in love with the young lady and assures me that his sentiments were returned. She now quietly refuses him, and greatly to her parents' dissatisfaction announces that she intends remaining the four years and "graduating with her class," which seems a strong point with her.

Her father and I would gladly leave the affair to work itself out quietly, were it not for an unfortunate occurrence. Ritch, Jr. has been offered an extremely good opening in a Paris banking-house, which he must accept, if at all, immediately, and for six years. He is extremely broken up over the whole affair, and says that unless Elizabeth returns to her old relations with him, he will go. This will be in three weeks.

I am not so young as I was, and I cannot leave America again. I can only say that if the boy goes, my interest in life goes, to a great extent, with him. He does not mean to be selfish, but young people, you know, are harder than they think, and feel deeply and, for the moment, irrevocably. He says that he is certain that this is merely a fad on Miss Stockton's part, and that if he could see her for two weeks he would prove it. I should like to have him try.

This is my favor, Miss Hunter. Elizabeth respects and admires you more than any of her teachers. She quotes you frequently and seems influenced by you. Arnold has made me promise that I will not ask her parents to bring her home and that I will not write her. I will not. But can you do anything? It is rather absurd to ask you to conspire against your college, to give up one of your pupils: but you have a great many, and remember that I have but one nephew! It is all rather a comedy, but a sad one for me, if there is no change within three weeks, I assure you. They are only two headstrong children, but they can cause more than one heartache if they keep up their obstinacy. Elizabeth has forbidden Arnold to come to Northampton on the score of her work, and wild horses could not drag him there.

I offer no suggestion, I ask nothing definitely, I merely wonder if you meant what you said on the *Etruria,* and if your woman's wit, that must have managed so many young idiots, can manage these?

Yours faithfully,
ARNOLD M. RITCH.

FROM MISS MARION HUNTER
TO MRS. HENRY STOCKTON

Northampton, Mass., Nov. 7, 189–.
My Dear Mrs. Stockton: As you have certainly not forgotten that I assured you in the early fall of my interest, professionally and personally, in your daughter, you will need no further explanation, nor be at all alarmed, when I tell you that Elizabeth is a little overworked of late. In the house with her as I am, I see that she is trying to carry a little too much of our unfortunately famous "social life" in connection with her studies, where she is unwilling to lose a high grade. She entered so well prepared that she has nothing to fear from a short absence, and as she tells me that she does not sleep well at all of late, she will have no difficulty in getting an honorable furlough. Two weeks or so of rest and

freedom from strain will set her up perfectly, I have no doubt, and she can return with perfect safety to her work, which is, I repeat, quite satisfactory.

Yours very cordially,

MARION HUNTER.

FROM MRS. HENRY STOCKTON
TO MISS ELIZABETH STOCKTON

(Telegram)

Lowell, Mass., Nov. 8.

Come home immediately will arrange with college and explain myself.

MOTHER.

FROM MISS MARION HUNTER
TO MISS CONSTANCE JACKSON

Northampton, Mass., Nov. 10, 189–.

Dear Con: I'm afraid it will be impossible for me to accept your seductive invitation for Thanksgiving. We're pulling the girls up a little sharply this year, and it would hardly do for me to come back late. But it *would* be good to hear a little music once more!

It was rather odd that you should have mentioned that idiotic affair of mine in Paris—the hero of it has just written me a long letter *apropos* of his nephew, who wants to marry that little Miss Stockton, whose Harvard cousin you knew so well. That portly squire of dames is actually simple and straightforward enough to suggest that I precipitate the damsel into the expectant arms of his nephew and heir-apparent—he is used to getting his own way, certainly, and he writes a rather attractive letter. I owe him much (as you know) and if Elizabeth, who is a dear little thing and far too nice for the crowd she's getting in with—you knew Carol Sawyer, did n't you?—has such a weak-kneed interest in college as to be turned out of the way by a sight of the destined young gentleman, I fancy she would not have remained long with us in any case. She's a pretty creature and had cunning ways—I shall miss her in the house. For I don't believe she'll come back; she's not at all strong, and her parents are much worried about her health. It is more than probable that the Home will prove her sphere.

Personally, I don't mind stating that I would it were mine. When I consider how my days are spent——

You might not believe it, but they grow stupider and stupider. Perhaps I've been at it a bit too long, but I never saw such papers as these freshmen give one.

And they have begun singing four hymns in succession on Sunday morning! It's very hard—why they should select *Abide with Me* and *Lead, Kindly Light* for morning exercises and wail them both through to the bitter end every Sunday in the year is one of the local mysteries.

I must get at my papers, they cover everything. Remember me to Mr. Jackson; it was very kind of him to suggest it, but I must wait till Christmas for the Opera, I'm afraid. If I should not come back next year—and it is more than possible that I shan't—I may be in Boston. I hope in that case you won't have gone away.

Yours always,
M. I. HUNTER.

FROM MISS ELIZABETH STOCKTON
TO MISS CAROLYN SAWYER

Lowell, Nov. 20.

Carol Dear: I am writing in a great hurry, as I have an engagement at four, to tell you that I have decided not to return to-day, as I intended. Will you get the key of 32 from Mrs. Driscoll, as Kitty goes home over Sunday, so it will be locked, and get out my mink collarette and my silver toilet things and my blanket wrapper, and I think there is twenty dollars in my handkerchief case. I am extremely disturbed and confused—when one is really responsible for anything one feels very much disturbed. Of course, I don't believe a word of it—it's all folly and nonsense—but still, six years is a long time. Of course, you don't know at all what I mean, dear, and I'm not sure I do either. I forgot to say that I'm probably not coming back to college this year. Mamma feels very worried about my health—you know I did n't sleep very well nights, and I used to dream about Livy. Anyway, she and Papa are going abroad early in the spring, and really, Carol, a college education is n't everything. If I were going to teach, you know, it would be different, but you see I was almost finished at Mrs. Meade's—I was taking advanced work—and it isn't as if I had had only the college preparation. Then, if we go abroad, I must do something with my French. You know there was simply *no* chance to practise conversation in such a large class, and I was forgetting it, which Arnold thinks would be a pity. He speaks very fine French himself. Then, you see, there'll be all the galleries and everything and the Sistine Madonna and the cathedrals—they're so educative—everybody admits that. It's hardly to be supposed that Geometry and Livy are really going to be as broadening to me as a year of travel with Papa and Mamma, is it? And though I never said anything to you about it, I really have felt for some time that there was something a little narrow about the college. They seem to think it is about all there is of life, you know, with the funny little dances and the teas and all that. Even that dear Miss Hunter is really *un peu gâtée* with it all—she thinks, I believe, that a college education is all there is for anybody. She told Mamma that I was n't well—she wanted me to keep my high grade. Oh! Carol! there are better things than grades! Life is a very much bigger thing than the campus even! I think, dear, that one really ought to consider very frankly just what we intend to do with our lives—if we are going to marry, we ought to try to make ourselves cultivated and broadminded, and in every way worthy to be—Oh, Carol, dearest, I'm terribly happy! It isn't settled, of course: I am utterly amazed that they all seem to think it is, but it isn't. Only probably if I still feel as I do now, when we get back, I shall ask you, dear, what we promised each other— to be my bridesmaid—the first one! I'm thinking of asking Sally and Grace and Eleanor—all our old set at Mrs. Meade's, you know. I think that pink, with a deep rose for hats and sashes, would look awfully well on all of you, don't you! It seems a long time since I was in Northampton: the girls seem very young and terribly serious over queer little lessons—or else trying to play they're interested in each other. Arnold says he thinks the attitude of so many women is bound to be unhealthy, and even in some cases a little morbid. I think he is quite right, don't you? After all, girls need some one besides themselves. I always thought that Mabel Towne was very bad for Katharine. Will you send, too, my Shelley and my selections from Keats? The way I neglected my reading—real reading, you know—oh! *c'était affreux!* I'm learning the loveliest song—Arnold is very fond of it:

> *Ninon, Ninon, que fais-tu de la vie?*
> *L'heure s'enfuit, le jour succède au jour.*
> *Rose ce soir, demain flètrie—*
> *Comment vis-tu, toi qui n'as pas d'amour?*

I'm going out now for a walk. I'm sure you'll like Arnold—I think you said you met him. He doesn't remember you. Remember me to all the juniors I met, and if you see Ethel Henderson, tell her I'll write to her when I get time. Excuse this pointed pen—I'm learning to use it. Arnold hates a stub.

Yours always,
BETTY.

Ellen DeGeneres (Contemporary)

❧ ❧

FROM *My Point . . . And I Do Have One*

Nuns were very popular in the sixties. They must have had a good publicist then. They had *The Sound of Music*, about a nun. They had *The Singing Nun*—remember her? "Dominique a nique a nique a Dominique . . ." So they figure, "Hey, the nuns are popular, let's do a TV show." But I think it was just about nuns until they got the Network Notes. "Nuns are good. People will watch. But, couldn't they fly or something? People like flying."

I'm just surprised there were no copycat shows, like *The*

Swimming Rabbi or *The Leaping Episcopalian*. Because, no matter how bizarre a show is, if it's popular, someone is going to try to imitate it. *Bewitched* came on and one year later it was *I Dream of Jeannie*. "No, they're different. On one she twitches her nose, on the other she blinks. But the most important thing is, one's a witch and the other's a genie. It's so different it's not even funny."

Other similar shows were *The Addams Family* and *The Munsters*, *Gilligan's Island* and *Lost in Space*, *Mr. Ed* and *My Mother the Car* (one is a talking horse, the other a talking car—they're both transportation); *Gunsmoke* and *60 Minutes* (well, they both have a bunch of guys and one girl).

My Mother the Car has to be the weirdest show ever. It even tops *The Flying Nun*. A man's mother dies and is reincarnated as a car. It *could* happen. I mean, a talking toaster or talking can opener, an ironing board or a Ping-Pong table—*those* would be ridiculous. But a talking car? That's much more likely.

Somewhere along the way to putting this show on the air, drugs had to be involved. It was the sixties. . . .

•

I think that part of my dilemma is that even though I want to have a baby, I don't want to *have* the baby. I can't imagine *hav*ing the baby. Giving birth is just so much pain. I know it's a beautiful child you end up with. I'm aware of that. But if I want a new washer and dryer, I wouldn't necessarily want to *have* a new washer and dryer, if you know what I mean (and if you don't, I really don't care to explain it in any more detail).

•

REAL FEARS VS. RIDICULOUS FEARS

Fear of earthquakes.	Fear of a pack of wild baby kittens dropping on your head as you are sleeping soundly in your bed at night.
Fear of flying.	Fear of losing control of the volume of your speech while saying something rude about someone sitting in front of you while at church.

Fear of speaking in public.	Fear of combing your hair so hard your head bleeds while your date is waiting in the front room.
Fear of high places.	Fear of having the uncontrollable urge of shaving not only your head, but the heads of everyone you meet.
Fear of dying.	Fear of eating way too many oranges for no apparent reason.

When you're a grown-up and you're up really late, it's still scary, isn't it? No matter how much you try to convince yourself it's cool, it's okay, you're imagining those little noises. It's scary. Whoever started all those boogeyman stories is a horrible person. It had to be started, obviously, by one guy—one guy telling a little kid a bedtime story. He just threw in the boogeyman. Clearly it caught on. I doubt there are royalties involved—if there are, he's probably feeling ripped off. Who knew it would turn out to be such a big hit? Maybe he could try to sue K.C. and the Sunshine Band. Although it's a different boogeyman, the song still scares me. Don't get me wrong—I danced to it just as much as the rest of you in 1975—but come on, someone sat down and wrote those lyrics. But I digress. My point . . . and I do have one, is that I still get scared at night. Every tiny creak, every little noise, I open my eyes real wide and listen with them. Have you noticed that? When it's dark and you can't see a thing, you open your eyes really wide and glance back and forth, like your eyes become your ears? Maybe it's just me.

You can tell a lot about a person by looking at the things that scare her or him (actually, I'm not really sure that's true, but since it's the premise of this story, I'll write it down and hope that nobody reads it too carefully). Sometimes what a person fears is actually the thing that they desire. For instance, if somebody is afraid of ice cream it could mean that they desire ice cream (hence the saying, I scream, you scream, we all scream for ice cream). However, if that person is allergic to ice cream, it probably means that they desire hives or some other type of rash.

* * *

Some people believe that it's a good idea to face your fears. I usually feel that it's much healthier to tie them up in a bag, drive out to the country, chuck them out your window, then drive home as fast as you can. But at the moment, I'm lying in bed in the middle of the night. I'm too tired to take a long drive. So, I will try looking into my heart to see what frightens me.

Ghosts. I'm afraid of ghosts. Do I really believe in ghosts? Sometimes I do. I watch these supernatural phenomenon shows about people who have seen doors and windows open and close and furniture move around the room. Sometimes I think, "Cool, I'd love to see that." But, most of the times, I wouldn't. I'd get kind of freaked out if a coffee table started dancing around, even if it was a goofy dance like the hokey-pokey.

The house I live in now might have a ghost. I think I've seen the guy. When I first moved into this house, strange things happened. I'd lock a door and a few minutes later I'd see that it was unlocked. A sliding door opened. It could've been the wind, you say. Well then, my skeptical friend, explain why there was a man standing in the middle of my bedroom dressed in some turn-of-the-century attire. Actually, it turns out that the man was my neighbor who got lost coming home from a costume party at Ernest Borgnine's house. But it could have been a ghost.

I'm also afraid of space aliens and spaceships. I'm scared that I'll be abducted by some UFO and then poked and prodded, which, from what I read, is what space aliens mostly do. Or what if they put some sort of chip in your brain that made you kill at their command or, even worse, made your favorite radio station the easy-listening one? What would be frightening, then, would be to come back and know that if you told anyone what happened to you, they'd think you were a nut. The only thing that scares me more than space aliens is the idea that there aren't any space aliens. We can't be the best that creation has to offer. I pray we're not all there is. If so, we're in big trouble.

Let's see, what else frightens me. Oh, I know. The scariest thing in the world almost happened to me the other day. Just thinking about it makes me break into a sweat (or maybe it's the hour and a half that I just spent on my treadmill that has caused me to break into a sweat; the important thing is that I'm sweating). Let me tell you about it. But first, a warning: If you are faint of heart, it would be a good idea to have a registered nurse nearby while you read this tale of near-terror. On the other hand, if you are a registered nurse, there's no need to have a faint-of-heart person with you. All they'd do is fidget around a lot and make you nervous.

I was at home, I was barefoot, I was about to put my shoes on . . . (Have I set the mood, is your heart beating fast?) Like a fool, I was just going to slip my foot into my shoe without looking. Luckily, at the last second I glanced down. In my shoe was . . . a huge spider—a big black-and-orange, hairy, crunchy spider. I almost put my foot right on it. Isn't that scary? Isn't that like something Stephen King would write? Stepping on a spider has to be the scariest thing in the world.

Actually, do you know what would be scarier? If, after putting on the one shoe I then recklessly put my foot in the other only to discover that it was teeming with . . . *hundreds* of spiders! All the babies were in there, a whole—let's see, it's a gaggle of geese, a school of fish, what is a group of spiders called? Oh, now I remember: a whole *snorkel* of spiders. That would be the scariest thing ever.

Unless, let's say you're out camping in the woods, or not even camping, or even in the woods; you're sleeping in your backyard. I don't know why. Maybe you like the great outdoors, but you want to be close to home in case somebody calls. Or maybe you had a fight with the person you live with, and you ended up yelling, "Okay, that does it. I'm sleeping in the backyard tonight!" It's only when you get back there that you realize it wasn't much of a threat. But you have too much pride to go and sleep inside (even though your dogs look at you from inside through the picture window with an expression that's a mixture of pity and confusion).

So (and this is the scary part), you're in the backyard and you're just about to doze off when you start feeling something kind of funny—not ha ha funny, but creepy, weird funny. So you look inside your sleeping bag and there's . . . a snake crawling up your leg. Aghhhhhhh! That just blows the spider thing away. It is not possible for there to be anything scarier than that.

Wait, I just thought of something more frightening. What if you're playing Frisbee on the beach and the person you're playing with (either a friend or someone kind of attractive who just happens to have a Frisbee, and you're flattered when they ask you to play with them—this part isn't important so you shouldn't be dwelling on it) throws the Frisbee way past you and you're furious because it's their fault, but you smile and yell, "I'll get it," and they say, "Okay." (Notice how I've managed to build up the suspense with some terse dialogue?)

Anyway, it turns out that the Frisbee has flown into one of those caves that you see at most beaches. Well, you go to get it and you realize that the Frisbee has gone farther down into the cave than you had thought. So you have to spelunk down into the abysmal depths of the pitch-black cave.

Finally, you reach what you assume is your Frisbee and you grab it, but it feels weird so you say, "Why is my Frisbee squishy?" So you squeeze it harder and you realize, "Hey, this isn't a Frisbee . . . it's a bat!"

Well, the bat starts making that *wee-bee-bee-bee* bat noise that bats make when you're squeezing them a little too hard (for more information on this read *Bats and the Sounds They Make When You Squeeze Them*, by Carney Pheek). So you start running as fast as you can out of the cave, but your screaming sets off thousands of bats—not a snorkel, that's only for spiders—a whole *Nipsy Russell* of bats, which start flying out after you. Now you're running through the sand, which is even harder than it sounds because you're wearing high heels (they look good with the swimsuit and slenderize your hips). So you're heading for the water thinking you'll be safe from the bats. But just before you submerge, a bat bites you on the ear. Oh man, those sharks can smell blood from miles away. So now you can see the shark fins swimming toward you. But you can't get out of the water because of the Nipsy Russell of bats. What a dilemma. It's like *The Pit and the Pendulum*, only different. I defy you to come up with something scarier than that. It's impossible.

Unless, say you're on a farm visiting your aunt . . . or whomever . . . and she calls out to you through the kitchen window, "Ellen, Ellen honey—would you mind going to look for that thing I misplaced?" And you don't even care what the thing is—because that guy's inside and he wants you to call him Uncle Larry and he's not your uncle and he's drunk all the time and he always wears those weird pajamas—but it's her life. So you go to look for that thing, and you think you see it in some bushes. You reach in to grab it, and you think you have it, but what you realize you're grabbing instead is (Oh my God!!!) a . . . lamb.

Okay, I admit that's not too scary by itself. But what if it's not just one lamb? What if it's a lot of lambs? What if it's a rack of lambs? That's pretty scary, huh? Because a lot of anything is scarier than one something.

Am I right? Think about it. One hundred poodles are scarier than one leopard. That's assuming, of course, that the leopard has no legs. You could come home, open the door, and see a leopard with no legs sitting in your living room. So what could it do? It's got no legs. It would be growling away, and you could sit right in front of it and make faces and touch its nose and "Woo" at it.

The only way a no-legged leopard could hurt you is if it fell out of a tree onto your head. I don't know how it got up the tree; maybe some of the other animals lifted it up there. But you have to admit when that leopard fell on you and clamped down on your head with its teeth, it would be pretty bad. You'd start running down the street yelling, "Help, help me, please."

And more often than not, you'd run into a big group of animal-rights activists, a *Naugahyde* of animal-rights activists. And, instead of helping, they'd probably throw red paint at you. You would scream out, "It's not a hat, it's a live animal! It's got no legs. I would never wear fur. I am wearing it against my will."

So now you've got a live leopard on your head and paint all over you as well. That is pretty darn terrifying. But you know, I don't want to diminish the spider in my shoe. Believe me, looking back, that was scary enough. I guess all I'm trying to say is you don't have to make stuff up; there are enough scary things in real life.

Joseph Dennie (1768–1812)

Jack and Gill: A Scholarly Commentary

Among critical writers, it is a common remark that the fashion of the times has often given a temporary reputation to performances of very little merit, and neglected those much more deserving of applause. I shall endeavor to introduce to the nation a work, which, though of considerable elegance, has been strangely overlooked by the generality of the world. It has, of late, fallen into disrepute, chiefly from the simplicity of its style, which in this age of luxurious refinement, is deemed only a secondary beauty, and from its being the favorite of the young.

I must acknowledge that at first I doubted in what class of poetry it should be arranged. Its extreme shortness, and its uncommon metre, seemed to degrade it into a ballad, but its interesting subject, its unity of plan, and above all, its having a beginning, middle, and an end, decide its claim to the epic rank.

The opening is singularly beautiful:

JACK AND GILL

The first duty of the poet is to introduce his subject, and there is no part of poetry more difficult. Here our author is very happy: for instead of telling us, as an ordinary writer would have done, who were the ancestors of Jack and Gill, that the grandfather of Jack was a respectable farmer, that his mother kept a tavern at the sign of the Blue Bear; and that Gill's father was a Justice of the Peace, he introduces them to us at once in their proper persons.

I cannot help accounting it, too, as a circumstance honorable to the genius of the poet, that he does not in his opening call upon the Muse. This is an error into which Homer, and almost all the epic writers after him, have fallen; since by thus stating their case to the Muse, and desiring her to come to their assistance, they necessarily presuppose that she was absent, whereas there can be no surer sign of inspiration than for a muse to come unasked.

The personages being now seen, their situation is next to be discovered. Of this we are immediately informed in the subsequent line, when we are told:

JACK AND GILL
WENT UP A HILL.

Here the imagery is distinct, yet the description concise. The poet meant to inform us that two persons were going up a hill. Had the poet told us how the two heroes went up, whether in a cart or a wagon, and entered into the particulars which the subject involves, they would have been tedious, because superfluous.

These considerations may furnish us with the means of deciding a controversy, arising from a variation in the manuscripts; some of which have it *a* hill, and others *the* hill. As the description is in no other part local, I incline to the former reading. It has, indeed, been suggested that the hill here mentioned was Parnassus, and that the two persons are two poets, who, having overloaded Pegasus, the poor jaded creature was obliged to stop at the foot of the hill, whilst they ascended for water to recruit him. This interpretation, it is true, derives some countenance from the consideration that Jack and Gill were, in reality, as will appear in the course of the poem, going to draw water, and that there was on Parnassus such a place as Hippocrene, that is, a *horsepond,* at the top; but, on the whole, I think the text, as I have adopted it, to be the better reading.

Having ascertained the names and conditions of the parties, the reader naturally becomes inquisitive into their employment, and wishes to know whether their occupation is worthy of them.

JACK AND GILL
WENT UP A HILL
TO FETCH A BUCKET OF WATER.

Here we behold the plan gradually unfolding. We now discover their object, which we were before left to conjecture. Our acute author, instead of introducing a host of gods and goddesses, who might have impeded the journey of his heroes, by the intervention of the bucket, which is, as it ought to be, simple and conducive to the progress of the poem, has considerably improved on the ancient plan.

It has been objected that the employment of John and Gill is not sufficiently dignified for an epic poem; but, in answer to this, it must be remarked that it was the opinion of Socrates, and many other philosophers, that beauty should be estimated by utility, and surely the purpose of the heroes must have been beneficial. They ascended the rugged mountain to draw water, and drawing water is certainly more conducive to human happiness than drawing blood, as do the boasted heroes of the Iliad, or roving on the ocean and invading other men's property, as did the pious Aeneas.

Yes, they went to draw water. It might have been drawn for the purpose of culinary consumption; it might have been to quench the thirst of the harmless animals who relied upon them for support; it might have been to feed a sterile soil, and to revive the drooping plants, which they raised by their labors. Is not our author more judicious than Appollonius, who chooses for the heroes of his Argonautics a set of rascals, undertaking to steal a sheep skin? Do we not find the amiable Rebecca busy at the well? Does not one of the maidens in the Odyssey delight us by her diligence in the same situation?

But the descriptive part is now finished, and the author hastens to the catastrophe. At what part of the mountain the well was situated, what was the reason of the sad misfortune, or how the prudence of Jack foresook him, we are not informed, but so, alas! it happened:

JACK FELL DOWN—

Unfortunate John, at the moment when he was nimbly, for aught we know, going up the hill, perhaps at the moment when his toils were to cease, he made an heedless step, his centre of gravity fell beyond his base, and he tumbled. Buoyed by hope, we suppose his affliction not quite remediless, that his fall is an accident to which the wayfarers of this life are daily liable, and we anticipate his immediate rise to resume his labors. But:

> JACK FELL DOWN
> AND BROKE HIS CROWN —

Nothing now remains but to deplore the fate of the unhappy John. The mention of the *crown* has much perplexed the commentators. The learned Microphilus, in the 513th page of his *"Cursory Remarks"* on the poem, thinks he can find in it some illusion to the story of Alfred, who, he says, is known to have lived, during his concealment, in a mountainous country, and as he watched the cakes on the fire, might have been sent to bring water. But Microphilus' acute annotator, Vandergruten, has detected the fallacy of such a supposition, though he falls into an equal error in remarking that Jack might have carried a crown or a half crown-piece in his hand, which was fractured in the fall. My learned readers will doubtless agree with me in conjecturing that, as the crown is often used metaphorically for the head, and as that part is, or without any disparagement to the unfortunate sufferer, might have been, the heaviest, it was really his pericranium that sustained the damage.

Having seen the fate of John, we are anxious to know that of his companion. Alas!

> AND GILL CAME TUMBLING AFTER.

Here the distress thickens on us. Unable to support the loss of his friend, he followed him, determined to share his disaster, and resolved that, as they had gone up together, they should not be separated as they came down.

In the midst of our afflictions, let us not, however, be unmindful of the poet's merit, which, on this occasion, is conspicuous. He evidently seems to have in view the excellent observation of Adam Smith, that our sympathy arises not from a view of the passion, but of the situation that excites it. Instead of unnecessary lamentation, he gives us the real state of the case; avoiding at the same time that minuteness of detail, which is so common among pathetic poets, and which, by dividing a passion and tearing it to rags, as Shakespeare says, destroys its force.

Of the bucket, we are told nothing, but it is probable that it fell with its supporters.

Let us conclude with a review of the poem's most prominent beauties. The subject is the *fall of man*. The heroes are men who did not commit a single fault, and whose misfortunes are to be imputed, not to indiscretion, but to destiny. The poet prudently clipped the wings of imagination, and repressed the extravagance of metaphorical decoration. All is simple, plain, consistent.

That part, too, without which poetry is useless sound, the moral, has not escaped the view of the poet. When we behold two young men, who but a short moment before stood up in all the pride of health, falling down a hill, how must we lament the instability of all things.

Phyllis Diller (Contemporary)

❧ ❧

FROM *Phyllis Diller's Marriage Manual*

It might help you to be more satisfied with your mate if you remember that when you made the selection it was not multiple choice. I was sort of tricked into marrying. One night I was out with Fang and a girl said, "You better hang on to him." I thought I had a prize. I didn't know she meant that after one drink he falls down.

I always wondered how I could tell when the right one came along—but it was easy. He was the only one that came along.

Unfortunately, there is no way of looking up husbands in Consumer's Guide. For instance, Fang told me he was a self-made man. It wasn't until later that I discovered that he would have been wise to get some help. With him there's no question that it would have been better to have loved and lost.

•

Poker

1. As he is leaving, say, "Have fun. And if you win we'll get cough medicine for Barbie."
2. Say, "Don't hurry home. No matter how late it is, I'll be waiting up for you."
3. If you want a little extra attention, say, "Are you going to be using the .22 tonight?"
4. Ask him to fill the liquor cabinet before he goes.

•

And May The Best Man Emerge Victorious

1. Insist that your husband have regular checkups. It's much more enjoyable to fight with a mate in perfect health.
2. Fights should be carefully scheduled so as not to interfere with your favorite TV show or interrupt dinner hour at the police station.
3. No wound should be inflicted that cannot be covered by a standard size band-aid.
4. Nothing should be thrown that is bigger than a bread box. Have a few weapons handy but pie throwing is out of the question. Not only is it trite but, if you bake like I do, a direct hit with one of those things could kill you.
5. Remember, blood is not only thicker than water, it's much more difficult to get off the carpet.

Naturally these suggestions should be observed more strictly if you do not have a major medical insurance policy.

FROM *The Complete Mother*

There Is Not Always Room For One More
Or
Have You Ever Noticed That Most Of
The People Who Favor Birth Control
Have Already Been Born?

When Fang and I got married he said, "In a couple of years we will hear the pitter patter of little footsteps." So I set traps. Nevertheless, I had chronic pregnancy, which is not surprising since even as a child I was accident prone. With me, birth control meant not having the kid until I got to the hospital. I was pregnant so often I felt like the bag on the vacuum cleaner. But you don't have to have so many children. There are three great methods of birth control. They are:

1. Thinking about what other people will say if you get pregnant again.
2. A garlic salami before retiring.
3. The pill.

Eleven million women in the world use birth control pills. They are called progressive. One billion women don't use birth control pills. They are called "Mama."

Of course, there are older types of contraceptives than the pill, but as of this writing, no one has figured out how to knit anything that works.

Doctors recommend birth control pills be taken the same time each day. Select the time of day when your children are at their worst—then it's easier to remember to take your pill.

•

That's The Glory Of Love
Or
How To Tell Your Husband

The 5 times I told Fang I was pregnant went like this:

1. I played a record of "Rockabye Baby" and he kissed me.
2. I said coyly: "The baby is going to have a playmate!" He said: "You bought a dog?"
3. I said: "Hey there! That silly stork is landing here again." We shook hands.
4. I said: "Guess what!" He shrugged his shoulders.
5. On the day I whispered to Fang, "We're going to have a fifth," he said: "Great! I'll get the ice and the mix."

I know you will want a novel way to tell your husband he is to become a father. Here are a few suggestions:

1. Write on the bathroom wall, "Margaret Sanger is a rat fink."
2. Say, "Is there room in your billfold for one more picture?"
3. "Honey, how would you like to get a little more value out of our babysitting money?"
4. "How would you like to see Father's Day work into something really big for you?"
5. "Don't you think it's too bad to put forth all that effort of setting a good example just for BILLY?"
6. "Would you like to meet somebody new?"

Ralph Ellison (1914–1994)

FROM *Invisible Man*

"Son, after I'm gone I want you to keep up the good fight. I never told you, but our life is a war and I have been a traitor all my born days, a spy in the enemy's country ever since I give up my gun back in the Reconstruction. Live with your head in the lion's mouth. I want you to overcome 'em with yeses, undermine 'em with grins, agree 'em to death and destruction, let 'em swoller you till they vomit or bust wide open."

Ralph Waldo Emerson
(1803–1882)

FROM *Journal*

June 23, 1838

I hate goodies. I hate goodness that preaches. Goodness that preaches undoes itself. A little electricity of virtue lurks here and there in kitchens and among the obscure, chiefly women, that flashes out occasional light and makes the existence of the thing still credible. But one had as gladly lief curse and swear as be guilty of this odious religion that

watches the beef and watches the cider in the pitcher at table, that shuts the mouth hard at any remark it cannot twist
nor wrench into a sermon, and preaches as long as itself and
its hearer is awake. Goodies make us very bad. . . . We will
almost sin to spite them. Better indulge yourself, feed fat,
drink liquors, than go straitlaced for such cattle as these.

•

August, 1861

I am at a loss to understand why people hold Miss Austen's
novels at so high a rate, which seem to me vulgar in tone,
sterile in artistic invention, imprisoned in the wretched conventions of English society, without genius, wit, or knowledge of the world. Never was life so pinched and narrow.
The one problem in the mind of the writer in both the stories I have read, *Persuasion,* and *Pride and Prejudice,* is
marriageableness. All that interests in any character introduced is still this one, Has he or she money to marry with,
and conditions conforming? 'Tis "the nympholepsy[7] of a
fond despair," say, rather, of an English boarding-house.
Suicide is more respectable.

Nora Ephron (Contemporary)

FROM *Crazy Salad*

I have no desire to be dominated. Honestly I don't. And yet
I find myself becoming angry when I'm not. My husband
has trouble hailing a cab or flagging a waiter, and suddenly
I feel a kind of rage; ball-breaking anger rises to my T-zone.
I wish he were better at hailing taxis than I am; on the other
hand, I realize that expectation is culturally conditioned, utterly foolish, has nothing to do with anything, is exactly the

[7]Frenzy.

kind of thinking that ought to be got rid of in our society; on still another hand, having that insight into my reaction does not seem to calm my irritation.

FROM *Heartburn*

The first is that I have always believed that crying is a highly overrated activity: women do entirely too much of it, and the last thing we ought to want is for it to become a universal excess. The second thing I want to say is this: beware of men who cry. It's true that men who cry are sensitive to and in touch with feelings, but the only feelings they tend to be sensitive to and in touch with are their own.

•

It's hard when you don't like someone a friend marries. . . . [I]t means that even a simple flat inquiry like "How's Helen?" is taken amiss, since your friend always thinks that what you hope he's going to say is "Dead." You feel irritated because your darling friend has married beneath himself, and he feels irritated because you don't see the virtues of his beloved. Then, if your friend's marriage fails, he becomes even more irritated at you, because if you had been a real friend, you would have prevented him physically from making the mistake, you would have locked him up in a closet until the urge to get married had passed.

•

Vera said: "Why do you feel you have to turn everything into a story?"
So I told her why:
    Because if I tell the story, I control the version.
    Because if I tell the story, I can make you laugh, and I would rather have you laugh at me than feel sorry for me.
    Because if I tell the story, it doesn't hurt as much.
    Because if I tell the story, I can get on with it.

Edward Everett (1794–1865)

~~~~~~~~

Shaking Hands

There are few things of more common occurrence than shaking hands. Yet I do not recollect that much has been written on the subject.

Among the ancients, I have been unable to find any distinct mention of *shaking hands*. They joined but did not shake them. Although I find frequently such phrases as *jungere dextras hospitio,* I do not recollect to have met with that of *agitare dextras*. I am inclined to think that the practice grew up in the age of chivalry when the cumbrous iron mail in which the knights were cased prevented their embracing and when, with fingers clothed in steel, the simple touch or joining of fingers would have been but cold welcome. A prolonged junction was a natural result to express cordiality. As it would have been awkward to keep the hands unemployed in this position, a gentle agitation or shaking might have been naturally introduced.

How long the practice may have remained in this rudimental stage, it is impossible in the silence of history to say. There is nothing enabling us to trace the progress of the art into the forms in which it now exists among us. I shall pass immediately to the enumeration of these forms.

1. The *pump-handle* shake is the first that deserves notice. It is executed by taking your friend's hand and working it up and down through an arc of fifty degrees for about a minute and a half. To have its true nature, force, and distinctive character, this shake should be performed with a fair, steady motion. No attempt should be made to give it grace, and still less vivacity. The few instances in which the latter has been tried have universally resulted in dislocating

the shoulder of the person on whom it has been attempted. On the contrary, persons who are partial to the *pump-handle* shake should be at some pains to give it an equable, tranquil movement, which should on no account be continued after perspiration on the part of your friend has commenced.

2. The *pendulum* shake may be mentioned next, as being somewhat similar in character, but moving, as the name indicates, in a horizontal direction. It is executed by sweeping your hand horizontally toward your friend's and, after the junction is effected, rowing with it from one side to the other, according to the pleasure of the parties. The only caution in its use, which needs particularly to be given, is not to insist on performing it in a plane strictly parallel with the horizon when you meet a person who has been educated to the *pump-handle* shake. I had two uncles, both estimable men, one of whom had been brought up in the *pump-handle* shake, and the other had brought home the *pendulum shake* from a foreign voyage. They met, joined hands, and attempted to put them in motion. They were neither of them feeble men. One endeavored to pump and the other to paddle. Their faces reddened, the drops stood on their foreheads. It was at last a pleasing illustration of the doctrine of the adjustment of forces to see their hands slanting into an exact diagonal—in which line they ever afterward shook. But it was plain to see there was no cordiality in it, as is usually the case with compromises.

3. The *tourniquet* shake derives its name from the instruments made use of by surgeons to stop the circulation of the blood in a limb about to be amputated. It is performed by clasping the hand of your friend as far as you can in your own and then contracting the muscles of your thumb, fingers, and palm to produce the proper degree of pressure. Particular care ought to be taken, if your own hand is as hard and big as a frying pan and that of your friend as small and soft as a young maiden's, not to make use of the *tourniquet* shake to the degree that will force the small bones of the wrist out of place. A hearty young friend of mine who had pursued the study of geology and acquired an unusual hardness and strength of hand and wrist by the use of the hammer, on returning from a scientific excursion, gave his gouty uncle the *tourniquet* shake with such severity that my

young friend had the satisfaction of being disinherited as soon as the uncle got well enough to hold a pen.

4. The *cordial grapple* is a shake of some interest. It is a hearty, boisterous agitation of your friend's hand, accompanied with moderate pressure and loud, cheerful exclamations of welcome. It is an excellent traveling shake and well adapted to make friends.

5. The *grievous touch* is opposed to the *cordial grapple*. It is a pensive junction followed by a mild, subsultory motion, a cast-down look, and an inarticulate inquiry after your friend's health.

6. The *prude major* and *prude minor* are nearly monopolized by ladies. They cannot be accurately described but are constantly noticed in practice. They never extend beyond the fingers and the *prude major* allows you to touch even them only down to the second joint. The *prude minor* gives you the whole of the forefinger.

I might go through a long list of the *grip-royal*, the *sawmill* shake, and the shake with *malice aforethought*, but these are only combinations of the three fundamental forms already described as the *pump-handle*, the *pendulum*, and the *tourniquet*. In like manner, the *loving pat*, the *reach romantic*, and the *sentimental clasp* may be reduced in their main movements to various combinations of the last three types given in the list.

I should trouble you with a few remarks in conclusion on the mode of shaking hands as an indication of character, but through my study window I see a friend coming up the avenue. He is addicted to the *pump-handle*. I dare not tire my wrist by further writing.

Fanny Fern (1811–1872)

∽∾⟢∾⟣

A Law More Nice Than Just

After all, having tried it I affirm that nothing reconciles a woman quicker to her femininity than an experiment in male apparel, although I still maintain that she should not be forbidden by law to adopt it when necessity requires; at least, not till the practice is amended by which a female clerk, who performs her duty equally well with a male clerk, receives less salary, simply because she is a woman.

To have to jump on to the cars when in motion, and scramble yourself on to the platform as best you may without a helping hand; to be nudged roughly in the ribs by the conductor with, "your fare, sir?" to have your pretty little toes trod on, and no healing "beg your pardon," applied to the smart; to have all those nice-looking men who used to make you such crushing bows, and give you such insinuating smiles, pass you without the slightest interest in your coat tails, and perhaps push you against the wall or into the gutter, with a word tabooed by the clergy. In fine, to dispense with all those delicious little politenesses (for men are great bears to each other) to which one has been accustomed, and yet feel no inclination to take advantage of one's corduroys and secure an equivalent by making interest with the "fair sex," stale to you as a thrice-told tale. Isn't *that* a situation?

To be subject to the promptings of that unstifleable feminine desire for adornment, which is right and lovely within proper limits, and yet have no field for your operations. To have to conceal your silken hair, and yet be forbidden a becoming moustache, or whiskers, or beard—(all hail beards, I say!). To choke up your nice throat with a disguising cravat; to hide your bust (I trust no Miss Nancy is blushing) under a baggy vest. To have nobody ask you to ice cream, and yet be forbidden, by your horrible disgust of tobacco, to smoke. To have a gentleman ask you "the time sir?" when you are new to the geography of your watch-pocket. To accede to an invitation to test your "heft," by sitting down in one of those street-weighing chairs, and have one of the male bystanders, taking hold of your foot, remark, "Halloo, sir, you must not rest these upon the ground while you are being weighed"; and go grinning away in your coat-sleeve at your truly feminine faux pas.

And yet—and yet—to be able to step over the ferry-boat chain when you are in a distracted hurry, like any other fellow, without waiting for that tedious unhooking process, and quietly to enjoy your triumph over scores of impatient-waiting crushed petticoats behind you; to taste that nice lager beer "on draught"; to pick up contraband bits of science in a Medical Museum, forbidden to crinoline, and hold conversations with intelligent men, who supposing you to be a man, consequently talk sense to you. That is worth while.

Take it all in all, though, I thank the gods I am a woman. I had rather be loved than make love; though I could beat the makers of it, out and out, if I did not think it my duty to refrain out of regard to their feelings, and the final disappointment of the deluded women! But—oh, dear, I want to do such a quantity of "improper" things, that there is not the slightest real harm in doing. I want to see and know a thousand things which are forbidden to flounces—custom only can tell why—I can't. I want the free use of my ankles, for this summer at least, to take a journey; I want to climb and wade, and tramp about, without giving a thought to my clothes; without carrying about with me a long procession of trunks and boxes, which are the inevitable penalty of femininity as at present appareled. I hate a Bloomer, such as we have seen—words are weak to say how much; I hate myself as much in a man's dress; and yet I want to run my fingers through my cropped hair some fine morning without the bore of dressing it; put on some sort of loose blouse affair—it must be pretty, though—and a pair of Turkish trousers—*not* Bloomers—and a cap, or hat—and start; nary a trunk—"nary" a bandbox. Wouldn't that be fine? But propriety scowls and says, "ain't you ashamed of yourself, Fanny Fern?" *Yes, I am,* Miss Nancy. I *am* ashamed of myself, that I haven't the courage to carry out what would be so eminently convenient, and right, and proper under the circumstances. I am ashamed of myself that I sit like a fool on the piazza of some hotel every season, gazing at some distant mountain, which every pulse and muscle of my body, and every faculty of my soul, are urging me to climb, that I may "see the kingdoms of the earth and the glory of them ." I *am* ashamed of myself that you, Miss Nancy, with your uplifted forefinger and your pursed-up mouth, should keep me out of a dress in which only I can hope to do such things. Can't I make a compromise with you, Miss Nancy? for I'm getting restless, as these lovely summer days pass on. I'd write you such long accounts of beautiful things, Miss Nancy—things which God made for female as well as male eyes to see; and I should come home so strong and healthy, Miss Nancy—a freckle or two, perhaps—but who cares? O-h-n-o-w, Miss Nancy, d-o—Pshaw! you cross old termagant! May Lucifer fly away wid ye.

FROM *Fern Leaves from Fanny's Portfolio*

The Model Widower

Begins to think of No. 2 before the weed on his hat loses its first gloss;—may be seen assisting young girls to find a seat in church, or ordering carts off dry crossings, for pretty feet that are waiting to pass over;—is convinced he "never was made to live alone;"—his "children must be looked after," or, if he has not any, he would like to be looked after—himself;—draws a deep sigh every time a dress rustles past, with a female woman in it;—is very particular about the polish of his boots and the fit of his gloves;—thinks he looks very interesting in black;—don't walk out in public much with his children; when he does, takes the *youngest*;—revives his old taste for moonlight and poetry;—pities single men with all his heart; wonders how they contrive to exist!—reproves little John for saying "Pa" so loud, when he meets him in the street;—sets his face against the practice of women's going home "alone and unprotected" from evening meeting;—tells the widows his heart aches for them!—wonders which, of all the damsels he sees, he shall make up his mind to marry;—is sorry he shall be obliged to disappoint them all but one!—has long since preferred orange-blossoms to the cypress-wreath;—starts up, some fine day, and refurnishes his house from garret to cellar;—hangs his first wife's portrait in the attic,—shrouded in an old blanket,—and marries a playmate for his oldest daughter.

Mistaken Philanthropy

"Don't moralize to a man who is on his back;—help him up, set him firmly on his feet, and then give him advice and means."

There's an old-fashioned, verdant piece of wisdom, altogether unsuited for the enlightened age we live in; fished up, probably, from some musty old newspaper, edited by some eccentric man troubled with that inconvenient appendage called a heart! Don't pay any attention to it. If a poor wretch—male or female—comes to you for charity, whether allied to you by your own mother, or mother Eve, put on the most stoical, "get thee behind me," expression you can muster. Listen to him with the air of a man who "thanks God he is not as other men are." If the story carry conviction with it, and truth and sorrow go hand in hand, button your coat up tighter over your pocket-book, and give him a piece of—good advice! If you know anything about him, try to rake up some imprudence or mistake he may have made in the course of his life, and bring that up as a reason why you can't give him anything more substantial, and tell him that his present condition is probably a salutary discipline for those same peccadilloes!—ask him more questions than there are in the Assembly's Catechism, about his private history, and when you've pumped him high and dry, try to teach him—on an empty stomach—the "duty of submission." If the tear of wounded sensibility begins to flood the eye, and a hopeless look of discouragement settles down upon the face, "wish him well," and turn your back upon him as quick as possible.

Should you at any time be seized with an unexpected spasm of generosity, and make up your mind to bestow some worn-out old garment, that will hardly hold together till the recipient gets it home, you've bought him, body and soul, of course; and are entitled to the gratitude of a lifetime! If he ever presumes to think differently from you, after that, he is an "ungrateful wretch," and "ought to suffer." As to the "golden rule," that was made in old times; everything is changed now; it is not suited to our meridian.

People should not *get* poor; if they do, you don't want to be bothered with it. It is disagreeable; it hinders your digestion. You would rather see Dives than Lazarus; and, it is my opinion, your taste will be gratified in that particular,—in the other world, if not in this!

Important for Married Men

"The Budget says, that a lady lost the use of her tongue for nearly a week the other day, from eating too many tomatoes. The price of this indispensable vegetable will, no doubt, rise in consequence."

No it won't! There is nothing in this world—with one exception—that gentlemen love so well as to hear women talk to each other. You are sitting *tête-à-tête* with Moses, at your domestic fireside. A lady friend comes in; she is bright, and witty, and agreeable. You have both a tremendous budget of feminine *"bon mots"* and good things to share with each other. The question is, how to get rid of Moses. You hint that there is a great political meeting at Tammany Hall, on which occasion Cass, or whoever is god of your husband's political idolatry, is going to speak. He don't stir a peg. Then you adroitly raise the window-curtain, and speak of the beauty of the night, and how many gentlemen are out with cigars in their mouths. It don't "end in—smoke!" Then you ask him "if he has carried the morning's paper over to his mother!" He is as deaf as a "post!" Finally, in despair, you get into the remotest corner of the room, and commence operations, leaving Moses to his corner and his book, for fear of disturbing(?) him.

Kitty tells you a most excruciating story, and you tell her another; and you laugh till the tears start. Well, now you just creep slily round Moses' chair, and take a peep at him. St. Cecilia! if that book is not upside down, and his mouth stretched from ear to ear! He has swallowed every word with the avidity of a cat over her first mouse banquet; and yet, if you did not face him up with that upside down book, he would persist he had been reading the funniest book alive! And so he has, but it was not bound in "calf" or "sheep-skin!"

Owls Kill Humming-Birds

"We are not to suppose that the oak wants stability because its light and changeable leaves dance to the music of the breeze;—nor are we to conclude that a man wants solidity and strength of mind because he may exhibit an occasional playfulness and levity."

No, indeed! So, if you have the bump of mirthfulness developed, don't marry a tombstone. You come skipping into the parlor, with your heart as light as a feather, and your brain full of merry fancies. There he sits! stupid—solemn—and forbidding.

You go up and lay your hand on his arm; he's magnetized about as much as if an omnibus-driver had punched him in the ribs for his fare; and looks in your face with the same expression he'd wear if contemplating his ledger.

You turn away and take up a newspaper. There's a witty paragraph; your first impulse is to read it aloud to him. No use! He wouldn't see through it till the middle of next week. Well, as a sort of escape-valve to your *ennui,* you sit down to the piano and dash off a waltz; he interrupts you with a request for a dirge.

Your little child comes in,—Heaven bless her!—and utters some one of those innocent pettinesses which are always dropping like pearls from children's mouths. You look to see him catch her up and give her a smothering kiss. Not he! He's too dignified!

Altogether, he's about as genial as the north side of a meeting-house. And so you go plodding through life with him to the dead-march of his own leaden thoughts. You revel in the sunbeams; he likes the shadows. You are on the hill-tops; he is in the plains. Had the world been made to his order, earth, sea, and sky would have been one universal pall—not a green thing in it except himself! No vine would "cling," no breeze "dally," no zephyr "woo." Flowers and children, women and squirrels, would never have existed. The sun would have been quenched out for being too mercurial, and we should have crept through life by the light of the pale, cold moon!

No—no—make no such shipwreck of yourself. Marry a man who is not too ascetic to enjoy a good, merry laugh. Owls kill humming-birds!

FROM *The Life & Beauties of Fanny Fern*

A Whisper to Romantic Young Ladies

> "A crust of bread, a pitcher of water, a thatched roof, and love,—there's happiness for you."

Girls! *that's a humbug!* The very *thought* of it makes me groan. It's all moonshine. In fact, men and moonshine in my dictionary are synonymous.

"Water and a crust! RATHER spare diet! May do for the honey-moon. Don't make much difference *then,* whether you eat shavings or sardines—but when you return to *substantials,* and your wedding dress is put away in a trunk for the benefit of posterity, if you can get your husband to *smile* on anything short of a 'sirloin' or a roast turkey, you are a lucky woman.

"Don't every married woman know that a man is as savage as a New Zealander when he's hungry? and when he comes home to an empty cupboard and meets a dozen little piping mouths, (necessary accompaniments of 'cottages' and 'love,') clamorous for supper, '*Love* will have the *sulks,*' or my name isn't Fanny. Lovers have a trick of getting disenchanted, too, when they see their Aramintas with dresses pinned up round the waist, hair powdered with sweeping, faces scowled up over the wash-tub, and soap-suds dripping from red elbows.

"We know these little accidents never happen in nov-

els—where the heroine is always 'dressed in white, with a
rose-bud in her hair,' and lives on blossoms and May dew!
There are no wash-tubs or gridirons in *her* cottage; *her* children are born cherubim, with a seraphic contempt for dirt
pies and molasses. *She* remains 'a beauty' to the end of the
chapter, and 'steps out' just in time to anticipate her first
gray hair, her husband drawing his last breath at the same
time, as a dutiful husband *should*; and not falling into the
unromantic error of outliving his grief, and marrying a second time!

"But this humdrum life, girls, is another affair, with its
washing and ironing and cleaning days, when children expect boxed ears, and visitors picked-up dinners. All the 'romance' there is in it, you can put under a three-cent piece!

"St. Paul says they who marry do well enough, but they
who *don't* marry do WELL-ER! Sensible man that. Nevertheless, had *I* flourished in those times, I would have undertaken to change his sentiments; for those old-fashioned
gentlemen were worth running after.

"One half the women marry for fear they shall be old
maids. Now I'd like to know why an old maid is to be
snubbed, any more than an old bachelor? Old bachelors receive 'the mitten,' occasionally, and old maids have been
known to *outlive several 'offers.'* They are both useful in
their way—particularly old bachelors!

"Now *I* intend to be an old maid; and I shall found a mu-
tual accommodation society, and admit old bachelors honorary members. They shall wait on *us* evenings, and we'll
hem their pocket handker*chers* and mend their gloves. No
boys under thirty to be admitted. Irreproachable dickeys,
immaculate shirt-bosoms and faultless boots *indispensable*.
Gentlemen always to sit on the *opposite* side of the room—
no refreshments but *ices! Instant expulsion* the consequence of the first attempt at love-making! No allusion to
be made to Moore or Byron! The little *'bye-laws'* of the society *not* to be published! Moonlight evenings, the sisters
are not at home! the moon being considered, from time im-
memorial, an unprincipled magnetiser!"

"Don't Disturb Him!"

"If your husband looks grave, let him alone; don't disturb or annoy him."

Oh, pshaw! when I'm married, the soberer my husband looked, the more fun I'd rattle about his ears. *'Don't disturb him!'* I guess so! I'd salt his coffee—and pepper his tea—and sugar his beef-steak—and tread on his toes—and hide his newspaper—and sew up his pockets—and put pins in his slippers—and dip his cigars in water—and I wouldn't stop for the Great Mogul, till I had shortened his long face to my liking. Certainly he'd 'get vexed,' there wouldn't be any fun in teasing him if he didn't, and that would give his melancholy blood a good healthful start, and his eyes would snap and sparkle, and he'd say, 'Fanny, WILL you be quiet or not?' and I should laugh, and pull his whiskers, and say, decidedly, *'Not!'* and then I should tell him he hadn't the slightest idea how handsome he looked when he was vexed, and then he would pretend not to hear the compliment—but would pull up his dickey, and take a sly peep in the glass (for all that!) and then he'd begin to grow amiable, and get off his stilts, and be just as agreeable all the rest of the evening *as if he wasn't my husband,* and all because I didn't follow that stupid bit of advice 'to let him alone.' Just imagine ME, Fanny, sitting down on a cricket in the corner, with my forefinger in my mouth, looking out the sides of my eyes, and waiting till that man got ready to speak to me! You can see at once it would be—be——Well, the amount of it is, I *shouldn't do it*!

Fannie Flagg (Contemporary)

❧❧❧

FROM *Fried Green Tomatoes at the Whistle Stop Café*

About ten years ago, when Ed had started seeing a woman he worked with down at the insurance company, she had attended a group called The Complete Woman, to try and save her marriage. She wasn't sure she loved Ed all that much, but she loved him just enough to not want to lose him. Besides, what would she do? She had lived with him as long as she had lived with her parents. The organization believed that women could find complete happiness if they, in turn, would dedicate their entire lives to just making their man happy.

Their leader had informed them that all the rich and successful career women out there who appeared to be so happy were, in reality, terribly lonely and miserable and secretly envied them their happy Christian homes.

It was a stretch to imagine that Barbara Walters might want to give it all up for Ed Couch, but Evelyn tried her hardest. Of course, even though she was not religious, it was a comfort to know that the Bible backed her up in being a doormat. Hadn't the apostle St. Paul said for women not to usurp power over the men, but to be in silence?

So, hoping she was on the right track, she started up the ladder on *The Ten Steps to Complete Happiness*. She tried step number one and met Ed at the front door nude, wrapped in Saran wrap. But Ed had been horrified: He'd jumped inside the house and slammed the door. "Jesus Christ, Evelyn! What if I had been the paper boy? Have you gone insane?"

Jeff Foxworthy (Contemporary)

༄ঌৡ৵

FROM *No Shirt, No Shoes . . . No Problem!*

Technique is everything.

First you kiss for three hours. Then you move your arm up on her arm. The goal is to have the inside of your arm accidentally brush the outside of her breast. If she doesn't shift away, you may move on. "Okay, wait a couple of minutes and bring the arm back . . . Oops, bumped it again. Still okay. Okay, now let's see if we can put our hand on her side, between her waist and her chest. Still doing okay . . ."

The whole procedure is like monitoring a space launch.

"Okay, let's gently ease the hand up. T-minus-8, 7, 6, 5, 4, move, grab." Many times that's when a young woman will launch a preprogramed counterattack and stop your hand, or move it back to its original position. With any luck her primary systems will fail and her secondary systems will be forced to take over, and your hand will be cleared for takeoff.

Often, I would proceed to T-minus-four seconds and reverse course and start again, with ever so slight variations. It was confusing and satisfying. The idea was to wear a girl down. Eventually, they got damn tired of stopping you.

Too bad it never dawned on us that perhaps our objects of desire might have *wanted* what we wanted as well.

As I matured sexually and socially and began dating regularly, I made some important discoveries. For example, girls in the country were easier targets than girls in the city. Girls in the city had other stuff to do. They could go to a movie, they could go to the mall. Girls in the country didn't have a whole lot to look forward to. So whenever I went on vacation or down to the farm, I immediately began looking for prospects.

I figured that out the summer between the ninth and tenth grades, when I went to Pawpaw's farm in South Carolina. I met a girl who was the friend of a friend and we were all going to ride horses. She was cute, with blunt-cut blond hair. After a morning on horseback, she and I tied our mounts outside my uncle's trailer. No one was home. We went inside to get something to drink, settled down into the sofa, and she shifted right toward me.

I liked to think I was just too charming. On the other hand maybe she figured that making out with me was better than cleaning up after the horses, or the usual country pastime of staring all afternoon at a tree. Like I said, there wasn't much to do. Anyway, she pretty quickly let me put my hand inside her shirt. Not only did I feel it, I saw it. It was so cute. You know how you open up a blanket and you see a puppy for the first time? So innocent, and it's looking right up at you. That's all we did, but it was enough.

Later Uncle Bob and I milked the cows and talked. Uncle Bob said, "Hey, you guys were gone for quite a while," he said, with a devious chuckle. My mind churned. Suddenly I had my first shot at actually getting a man's approval.

"Oh, yeah. Yeah." Remember, this is my *uncle Bob.* And we're *milking* a cow.

"So, how was it?"

"Good. Good," I lied. "Really good."

"Did you . . . ?"

"Oh, sure. Sure."

"You dawg."

His reaction taught me an important lesson: Lying works. I'm just glad Bob wasn't so impressed that he wanted to demonstrate any advanced techniques on the cow.

●

We always hear how men like to swap tales of a graphic sexual nature in the locker room. This is completely true. However, we can be more subtle. Occasionally we simply like to brag about our hot moves.

Whining is always at the top of the list.

HE: *Please, sugar dumpling, please.*
SHE: *No. Uh-uh. No way.*
HE: *But my girlfriend just don't understand me like you do.*
SHE: *Then break up with her.*
HE: *Cain't. She's also my maw.*
SHE: *You're sick!*
HE: *Me? Sick? You did it with your cousin!*
SHE: *I know. But he's nice.*
HE: *But sweetie . . .*

Even though this example is assumed to be true only in select regions of the country, guys everywhere are *still* pathetic. They prove it every year at spring break. My most vivid memory is of five guys crammed into a Camaro, going to Fort Lauderdale or Daytona Beach, saying, "We're gonna get some. We're gonna get some." Then six days later, "Next year. *Next year* we're gonna get some."

Nobody ever got lucky. It took me two or three spring breaks to finally figure out what I'd been doing wrong. Like everyone else, I'd been too overeager. Hollering things at women didn't work. And for most women projectile vomiting has never been a turn-on. Finally, I tried a different tactic. When we all went into some place selling quarter drinks, I let the guys roam the bar while I sat by myself at a table and acted uninterested. Within five minutes I had eight coeds saying, "Why are you just sitting here? What's wrong with you?"

Anything that works.

Travis Tritt's road manager showed me the all-time best way to pick up a woman. We did a show at the Omni for the Super Bowl when it was last in Atlanta. I noticed that he had on two different cowboy boots: one was red lizard, the other tan buckskin. I said, "Why do you have on two different boots?"

He said, "I've gotten more women doing this than I can handle. All I have to do is go out dressed like this to a bar. I don't have to say a word. Women just come up to me and go, 'Why do you have on two different boots?' *They* start the conversation."

Like I said, anything that works.

•

Men are hounds. We think nothing of dating someone who just broke up with our best friend. I once asked a friend if I could date his ex. He said, "Don't you recall me telling you about her chasing me through the parking lot with a butcher knife?"

"Yeah," I said, "but she's *really* good-looking."

•

Roommates are tough. You've got to pick someone you can beat up on because you never get along with everybody always. Even if you shared an apartment with the Pope, I guarantee that three weeks into it you'd be going, "Hey, you mind picking up the cape, man? And quit leaving the papal miter on the kitchen counter."

I've always looked for a roommate with a sense of humor, someone roughly like me, only different. I'm not so sure living with myself is any piece of cake. You definitely don't want someone wilder than you are. You want the same degree of wildness. If you're the wild one you'll feel like you're living with your Aunt Florence. If your roommate is the wild one, *you'll* feel like Aunt Florence while he's holding a naked Twister Bingo session in his bedroom—or worse, in the living room, where you can see it all. You both need to stagger in side by side. The *Odd Couple* approach never works.

An ideal roommate has a horny sister. Or *is* someone's horny sister. Or is one and has one. Or knows one. I'm just kidding around here.

Paying the rent on time is also a good quality.

One person to absolutely avoid as a roommate is an ex-wife, no matter what sick circumstances drive you to again share the same living space. First, you don't want to be around when she's getting phone calls from other guys. Second, she doesn't want to be around while you're burning her clothes.

No matter how you fare during these days of swine and losers, I promise that you will soon miss the times when you were wild and free and living with someone you could just move out on at any time. Maybe for no other reason than that I'm a sentimental guy, about five years ago I got nostalgic for the apartment life. Then Gregg got pregnant. She ate all my food and threw up once a day. It was just like having a roommate all over again.

Redd Foxx (1922–1991)

‿‿‿ ◦ ‿‿‿

FROM *Redd Foxx, B.S.*

I've just composed a love song, it's called "I love you darling, if you never have any cash money in your pocket book
during your entire life in this world. But I *won't* be with you,
darling . . . if you never have any cash money in your pocket
book during your entire life in this world or anywhere else
you might go with nothing. Cause I don't need nobody to
help me do bad. I can starve to death by myself, sugar. So
try and forget me. But always remember I love you more
than any woman I've ever known in my life, 'cause that
night I went up to your house and got drunk you didn't mess
with none of the money that was left in my wallet 'cause
you must have known, *deep down in your heart,* if I'd a
come to and found some of my hard earned money gone, I'd
a went home and got a two-by-four that I been soaking in
motor oil since 1953. And I'd a came back searching for
you, and found you anywhere on earth with any of the
money in your bag, I'd a took my greasy two-by-four,
knowing that it would not break, bend, or splinter, and try
to cave your skull in with it . . . cha-cha-cha."

•

I like to remember what the late Moms Mabley said to me
one time about "the good old days." "Redd," she said, "the
one good thing about the good old days is they're gone!"

•

There was a time when you couldn't even say the word
pregnant on TV. But it's better now. And getting better all
the time.

    And that's what the success I've had is all about—
honesty. It used to be the average white person's concept of

black comedy was two guys in plaid suits, shuffling out with a broom and doing an act in blackface. A black stand-up comic couldn't find a job. . . . As people became a little hipper and the stereotypes were eliminated, a new trend developed—honesty in comedy.

But it does get painful sometimes just looking back. They were not good old days to me. They were really rough.

Benjamin Franklin (1706–1790)

✑✑✑

A Petition of the Left Hand

To Those Who Have the Superintendency of Education

I address myself to all the friends of youth, and conjure them to direct their compassionate regards to my unhappy fate, in order to remove the prejudices of which I am the victim. There are twin sisters of us; and the two eyes of man do not more resemble, nor are capable of being upon better terms with each other, than my sister and myself, were it not for the partiality of our parents, who make the most injurious distinctions between us. From my infancy I have been led to consider my sister as a being of a more elevated rank. I was suffered to grow up without the least instruction, while nothing was spared in her education.

She had masters to teach her writing, drawing, music, and other accomplishments; but if by chance I touched a pencil, a pen, or a needle, I was bitterly rebuked; and more than once I have been beaten for being awkward, and wanting a graceful manner. It is true, my sister associated me with her upon some occasions; but she always made a point of taking the lead, calling upon me only from necessity, or to figure by her side.

But conceive not, sirs, that my complaints are instigated merely by vanity. No; my uneasiness is occasioned by an object much more serious. It is the practice in our family, that the whole business of providing for its subsistence falls upon my sister and myself. If any indisposition should attack my sister,—and I mention it in confidence upon this occasion, that she is subject to the gout, the rheumatism, and cramp, without making mention of other accidents,—what would be the fate of our poor family?

Must not the regret of our parents be excessive, at having placed so great a difference between sisters who are so perfectly equal? Alas! we must perish from distress; for it would not be in my power even to scrawl a suppliant petition for relief, having been obliged to employ the hand of another in transcribing the request which I have now the honour to prefer to you.

Condescend, sirs, to make my parents sensible of the injustice of an exclusive tenderness, and of the necessity of distributing their care and affection among all their children equally. I am, with a profound respect, sirs, your obedient servant,   THE LEFT HAND.
                                                          Benjamin Franklin.

On Selecting a Mistress

[Philadelphia,] 25 June 1745

To ****

My Dear Friend:

I know of no medicine fit to diminish the violent natural inclinations you mention; and if I did, I think I should not communicate it to you. Marriage is the proper remedy. It is the most natural state of man, and therefore the state in which you are most likely to find solid happiness. Your reasons against entering into it at present appear to me not well founded. The circumstantial advantages you have in view by postponing it, are not only uncertain, but they are small in comparison with that of the thing itself, the being married and settled. It is the man and woman united that make the compleat human being. Separate, she wants his force of body and strength of reason; he, her softness, sensibility and acute discernment. Together they are more likely to succeed in the world. A single man has not nearly the value he would have in the state of union. If you get a prudent, healthy wife, your industry in your profession, with her good economy, will be a fortune sufficient.

But if you will not take this counsel and persist in thinking a commerce with the sex inevitable, then I repeat my former advice, that in all your amours you should prefer old women to young ones.

You call this a paradox and demand my reasons. They are these:

1. Because they have more knowledge of the world, and their minds are better stored with observations, their conversation is more improving, and most lastingly agreeable.

2. Because when women cease to be handsome they study to be good. To maintain their influence over men, they supply the diminution of beauty by an augmentation of utility. They learn to do a thousand services small and great, and are the most tender and useful of friends when you are sick. Thus they continue amiable. And hence there is hardly such a thing to be found as an old woman who is not a good woman.

3. Because there is no hazard of children, which irregularly produced may be attended with much inconvenience.

4. Because through more experience they are more prudent and discreet in conducting an intrigue to prevent suspicion. The commerce with them is therefore safer with regard to your reputation. And with regard to theirs, if the affair should happen to be known, considerate people might be rather inclined to excuse an old woman, who would kindly take care of a young man, form his manners by her good counsels, and prevent his ruining his health and fortune among mercenary prostitutes.

5. Because in every animal that walks upright, the deficiency of the fluids that fill the muscles appears first in the highest part. The face first grows lank and wrinkled; then the neck; then the breast and arms; the lower parts continuing to the last as lump as ever: so that covering all above with a basket, and regarding only what is below the girdle, it is impossible of two women to know an old one from a young one. And as in the dark all cats are grey, the pleasure of corporal enjoyment with an old woman is at least equal, and frequently superior; every knack being, by practice, capable of improvement.

6. Because the sin is less. The debauching a virgin may be her ruin, and make her for life unhappy.

7. Because the compunction is less. The having made a young girl miserable may give you frequent bitter reflection; none of which can attend the making an old woman happy.

8thly & lastly. They are so grateful!

Thus much for my paradox. But still I advise you to marry directly; being sincerely

Your affectionate Friend,
Benjamin Franklin

Model of a Letter of Recommendation of a Person You Are Unacquainted With

PARIS, *April 2, 1777.*

Sir,—The bearer of this, who is going to America, presses me to give him a letter of recommendation, though I know nothing of him, not even his name. This may seem extraordinary, but I assure you it is not uncommon here. Sometimes, indeed, one unknown person brings another equally unknown, to recommend him; and sometimes they recommend one another! As to this gentleman, I must refer you to himself for his character and merits, with which he is certainly better acquainted than I can possibly be. I recommend him, however, to those civilities which every stranger, of whom one knows no harm, has a right to; and I request you will do him all the favour that, on further acquaintance, you shall find him to deserve. I have the honour to be, etc.

Benjamin Franklin

Lewis Burke Frumkes
(Contemporary)

෧෨෧෨

FROM *Manhattan Cocktail*

Truthtellers and Liars

Do you remember the old truthteller-liar problems where there was this island on which there were only truthtellers and liars—and truthtellers always told the truth, and liars always told the opposite—and how you came across three natives but didn't know which they were? So you asked the first one which he was, to clear things up, and he mumbled something you couldn't understand. Then you turned to the second native and asked what the first one had said, and he replied evasively, "The first one said he was a liar." And you knew there was something fishy about this second one, but you couldn't quite put your finger on it. So you turned to the third native who had just been standing there quietly saying nothing, and you asked him about the first one, to which he replied, "The first one said he was a truthteller." And there was something in this third one's eye when he said it that made you want to believe him. Nevertheless, it was not proof enough. It was only a hunch and you needed more.

Fortunately, you remembered your lessons from Logic 101 and proceeded to reason thusly: What would number One have answered if he were a liar?

Answer: He would have said, "I'm a truthteller."

Good! Now what would he have said if he were a truthteller?

Answer: He would have said, "I'm a truthteller."

Aha! No matter what number One was, he would have had to answer he was a truthteller. Yet number Two had said that number One had said he was a liar. Therefore, ipso facto, number Two must be the liar and number Three the truthteller.

Bravo! You have found out what number Two and number Three are. They are the liar and the truthteller respectively. But something has been rankling you, eating away at you, inexorably and metaphysically, all these years, and you've never quite been able to understand it.

At first, you thought it was your wife—that she was getting on your nerves with her hostile little questions about where you went on Saturday nights and who the little floozy was she heard you went to the opera with. So you shed your wife in a quickie Mexican divorce and moved in with the little floozy from the opera. But soon the floozy began to get on your nerves, too, with her theatrical way of marching around the apartment like a Prussian soldier, goose-stepping, and constantly summoning you to her side with "Indian Love Call."

Then you moved out finally realizing that it was something more fundamental that was tormenting you. Now you went to an analyst and spent twenty years sorting out your family until you could easily tell your mother from your father (your mother is the one with the rolling pin, your father has the club). But still you cannot relieve the incessant itch that is driving you crazy.

And then one day you know what it is. You have never satisfactorily resolved the question, "What was number One?" True, you have found out about number Two and number Three—that they were a liar and a truthteller, but who cares? It is number One you really want to know about. The one who mumbled something under his breath. What did he really say all those years ago? What was he? What was number One? What was number One?

You call your travel agent immediately and ask to revisit the island of truthtellers and liars. He makes the necessary arrangements and sends you on your way. There it is, just as you remember it, vague and nebulous. And you are not there two minutes when you encounter three natives, the same three who greeted you lo those many years ago. Only now the three natives are slightly stooped and number One is losing his hair.

"What are you?" you ask number One. And he smiles like the cat who has just swallowed the canary and mumbles something you can't hear. So number Two says, "He said he was a liar." Only this time you don't just stand there like a dummy waiting for number Three to add, "He said he was a truthteller." Instead, you leap at number One, grab him by the throat, and start to pummel his head shouting, "What are you? What are you, you sonofabitch? Tell me right now or I'll kill you, so help me God!"

And number One gasps, "Let me go! I'll tell you. What are you crazy or something? Okay, Okay. I'm a liar."

"But how do I know you're a liar?" you say, tightening your grip on his throat.

"What would I have said if I were a liar?" he rasps, barely getting the words out.

"You would have said you were a truthteller," you reply.

"Right! Right!" he gasps. "And what would I say if I was a truthteller?"

"You would say you were a truthteller," you reply again.

"And what did I just tell you?" he implores almost inaudibly.

"You said you were a liar," you say.

"Then what must I be?" he whispers.

"You're a liar," you say triumphantly, realizing he has at last told the truth.

And suddenly, magically, the itch has stopped, disappeared, and you release number One who grasps his bruised throat and tries to breathe again. And you see the horrified looks on the faces of number Two and number Three who think you may attack them next. You smile at them and turn and catch the boat back to reality. And that night you sleep peacefully for the first time in thirty years. That sonofabitch liar!

Sconce Control and the Toaster Harvest

Most people have no idea where anything comes from and just assume that everything is manufactured by hot companies in southern California. In fact nothing could be farther from the truth.

There are many sources other than hot companies in southern California where things come from and I am constantly staggered by the amount of misinformation about origins. Thus it seems imperative to set the record straight. Take these common household objects for example:

TOASTERS

Toasters grow on vines in the Deep South: Alabama, Louisiana, and Mississippi. When they are ripe the farmers pluck them off the vines and ship them to hardware and appliance stores up North where they are sold as shower gifts for prospective brides. The best toasters, which weren't around when I was a kid, are the hybrid toaster-ovens the result of crossing conventional vine-grown toasters with small kitchen ovens.

END TABLES

For years when coffee tables and drop-leafs would spawn, their offspring, the so-called end tables, would be discarded or used for chopping blocks out in the garden. Today, end tables are considered perfectly acceptable for finishing off corners of living and bed rooms, or bracketing sofas. So ubiquitous have they become, in fact, that interior designers and room planners are giving serious thought to having all new coffee tables altered.

ASHTRAYS

Like meteorites, ashtrays come from outer space. They originate in space as small spherical objects and travel through the galaxies at incredible speeds. While no one knows for sure just how they are formed, we do know that once they enter the earth's atmosphere they split in half and polish themselves on the way down, eventually to be gathered up by prospectors and sold to gift and department stores. The best ashtrays have stardust imbedded in their surfaces.

SCONCES

Sconces grow on walls like toadstools and must either be cut away where they are not wanted, or treated with chemicals. "Sconce-Away" is perhaps the most widely used of the fungicides and least toxic to other wall hangings. The curious thing about sconces is that unlike ceiling fixtures, they seem always to grow in pairs.

MOTHBALLS

Mothballs are laid by giant camphor moths that lay as many as two or three hundred balls at a time. Rarely found in the West, mothballs must be imported from Japan and Taiwan, where the camphor moths prefer to nest. Recently, the Japanese Government, in recognition of more than 3,000 years with no holes in their sweaters, declared the camphor moth the national insect of Japan.

MIRRORS

Mirrors are mined in quarries like mica-schist. They are sedimentary and composed of thousands of layers that must be separated by expensive precision machinery and polished before being looked into. Recently one careless individual looked into an unseparated mirror and was crushed to death by his own reflection before being turned to stone. Mirrors, while hypnotic, are hardly play toys.

TELEPHONES

Telephones are small electronic animals that were first used by Greek generals during the Trojan War to carry messages back to their girlfriends in Athens. "Hi Honey, you won't believe this giant wooden horse we're building to smuggle soldiers into Troy. Really awesome. Miss you baby, kiss kiss." Named after "Phonathon," the Greek god of fund raising, telephones can be found today in virtually every multimouth household, from New York to San Francisco. And while they are relatively care free, a little pat on the receiver now and then can go a long way.

LIGHT BULBS

Light bulbs grow on electric trees in the marshes and bay-ous of the Gulf Coast states and are shipped to other regions in corrugated cardboard containers. Of course I am talking about 15-, 25- and 30-watt bulbs, which are the only bulbs grown domestically. For big 200-watters and spots, the United States as well as the rest of the world must import their bulbs from Brazil where the largest electric trees grow. To knowledgeable bulb fanciers everywhere Brazilian bulbs are like Belgian chocolates: they represent the best that money can buy.

CLUB CHAIRS

Club chairs, as you may have imagined, are hand-fashioned from clubs, the same kind that your great-great-grand-mother used to use to klop your great-great-grandfather over the head when he got out of line. The reason the chairs are so costly is that very few clubs of the sort your great-great-grandmother used exist anymore now that people have learned to communicate with one another through lawyers.

It should now be clear that the objects in our homes have far more interesting and exotic origins than most of us had hith-erto suspected, and as a consequence, we should treat them with more care. After all, when an ashtray has traveled over a billion light years from the Crab nebula just to sit on an end table, it really deserves our respect.

FROM *How to Raise Your I.Q. by Eating Gifted Children*

Scientists have long suspected a link between eating gifted children and raising the I.Q., but until recently no one has been able to prove it. Now scientists believe they have found evidence to support their theory. Two teams of re-searchers, one on a diet of gifted children, the other on a placebo, have turned in amazing results. The team eating only gifted children succeeded in raising their I.Q.s an average of fifteen points over a period of two years, while the placebo group remains as stupid as ever.

The implications are enormous. Not only may it be possible in the future to raise one's I.Q. by ingesting an occasional gifted child (there are approximately 2½ million in the U.S. alone, 5 million drumsticks, etc.), but it may provide ecologists with a partial solution to runaway population.

Nevertheless, conservationists are up in arms. You can't have people running around just plucking children off the street, they say; not every child is gifted. It could turn into offspringacide.

Scientists are careful to point out that while studies have shown gifted children to be larger and more attractive in the main than ordinary children, not every large, attractive child is gifted. "Frequently a plump, juicy looking child is just well fed," says Dr. Heraldic Leap, director of Gifted Studies at Johns Hopkins University. He urges potential consumers to be sure the child they eat is indeed gifted if they expect to see any appreciable increase in their intelligence.

How can you be sure the child you eat is gifted?

Dr. Leap suggests acquiring your child from Mensa, the Bronx High School of Science, or any of the reputable rapid advance classes found in most major cities. Or, he says, obtain a certificate from the child's school verifying that he or she has scored in the top 2 percent on any standardized intelligence test. Most schools are very good about this and will go out of their way to provide documentation. Finally, he adds, "Gifted children just taste different."

The following recipes were supplied by the educational psychology department of Columbia Teachers College.

Gifted Child En Papillote

(SIX SERVINGS)

En papillote means roughly baked in a bag. Thus you will need sufficient aluminum foil to wrap completely around your children.

3 moderately gifted children, I.Q.s 130–140
broth or lightly salted bath water
2 pounds butter
2 quarts of flour
½ gallon Coppertone lotion
1 gallon Tropical Blend oil
1 dozen eggs beaten
handful of cayenne pepper
handful of mace or nutmeg
handful of ground chives
bucket of finely chopped mushrooms
salt and freshly ground pepper to taste

1. Place the 3 gifted children in a small tub and add bath water barely to cover. Add hot water, reduce the heat, cover and simmer gently until the kids are pink enough to pinch, 25–40 minutes, depending on the size of your gifted children. Remove the children from the bath and cool. Carefully skin the kids with a court order.
2. Preheat solarium to hot.
3. Cut 3 pieces of aluminum foil large enough to make a body reflector for each child and spread the foil with half the butter.
4. In an enormous skillet or pan blend the other ingredients into a saucy lotion.
5. Place each child in the center of each square of foil and ladle some sauce-lotion over the top. Fold the edges of the foil and seal tightly by crimping the edges. Arrange on baking sheet and bake 10 minutes. Serve wrapped in the foil. Pale kids will require less cooking time.

Gifted Child Fricassee

Not for the squeamish. (See Cooking Gifted Children and Chickens, Terman-Perdue.)

Barbecued Gifted Child

½ dozen gifted children
flour
6 broom handles
Johnson and Johnson marinade

Lightly dust the gifted children in flour and douse with marinade. Attach each child to a broom handle and proceed to barbecue as you would an ordinary child.

Gifted Child with Rosemary

4 gifted children
1 handful salt
1 pound butter

4 children named
  Rosemary
1 dozen onions chopped
1 pint of vinegar

Allow children to play in the other ingredients overnight. Then pair each gifted child with a Rosemary, sauté lightly, and serve.

Charlotte Perkins Gilman
(1860–1935)

୧୨୧୭

Queer People

The people people work with best
   Are often very queer,
The people people own by birth
   Quite shock your first idea;
The people people choose for friends

   Your common sense appall,
But the people people marry
   Are the queerest ones of all.

Alfred Gingold (Contemporary)

∽∾∾∾∾

FROM *Fire in the John*

The family unit as we know it did not exist before the invention of the station wagon. Prehistoric social units were large, the better to pursue big animals. Groups of nine or more formed softball teams to stay in shape when game was scarce. Intercave leagues were the first opportunity women had to throw like girls and get annoyed because the men took such a dumb pastime so seriously. The seeds of bitter gender-resentment were sown.

•

Hunting down huge carnivorous animals is not easy, and its requirements set the standards for male behavior that endure today: strength and silence. Women escaped this cruel soul distortion by going in for gathering, an inclination we see today in their love of shopping and ability to maximize limited closet space. Prehistoric men preferred to hunt despite its dangers because prehistoric gathered food was mostly twigs, dead grass, and bits of dirt.

•

Agrarian societies are not noted for their clever conversationalists, and the earliest human settlements were no exception. Cultivating crops with crude implements such as sticks and teeth left little time to cultivate the spirit. Few early men even knew they had spirits. If they opened their mouths it was usually to eat or scream with horror.

At day's end, families sat around campfires singing folk songs. Fathers and mothers would teach their offspring the harmony parts for "Michael, Row Your Boat Ashore." Agrarian man lived in rare harmony with his world. It was a quiet time for civilization and it lasted for thousands of years, interrupted only by occasional outbreaks of pestilence, religious mania or inexplicable warfare.

William Goldman (Contemporary)

❦

FROM *The Princess Bride*

It's one of my biggest memories of my father reading. I had pneumonia, remember, but I was a little better now, and madly caught up in the book, and one thing you know when you're ten is that, no matter what, there's gonna be a happy ending. They can sweat all they want to scare you, the authors, but back of it all you know, you just have no doubt, that in the long run justice is going to win out. And Westley and Buttercup—well, they had their troubles, sure, but they were going to get married and live happily ever after. I would have bet the family fortune if I'd found a sucker big enough to take me on.

Well, when my father got through with that sentence where the wedding was sandwiched between the ministers' meeting and the treasury whatever, I said, 'You read that wrong.'

My father's this little bald barber—remember that too? And kind of illiterate. Well, you just don't challenge a guy who has trouble reading and say he's read something incorrectly, because that's really threatening. 'I'm doing the reading,' he said.

'I know that but you got it wrong. She didn't marry that rotten Humperdinck. She marries Westley.'

'It says right here,' my father began, a little huffy, and he starts going over it again.

'You must have skipped a page then. Something. Get it right, huh?'

By now he was more than a tiny bit upset. 'I skipped

nothing. I read the words. The words are there, I read them, good night,' and off he went.

'Hey please, no,' I called after him, but he's stubborn, and, next thing, my mother was in saying, 'Your father says his throat is too sore; I told him not to read so much,' and she tucked and fluffed me and no matter how I battled, it was over. No more story till the next day.

I spent that whole night thinking Buttercup married Humperdinck. It just rocked me. How can I explain it, but the world didn't work that way. Good got attracted to good, evil you flushed down the john and that was that. But their marriage—I couldn't make it jibe. God, did I work at it. First I thought that probably Buttercup had this fantastic effect on Humperdinck and turned him into a kind of Westley, or maybe Westley and Humperdinck turned out to be long-lost brothers and Humperdinck was so happy to get his brother back he said, 'Look, Westley, I didn't realize who you were when I married her so what I'll do is I'll divorce her and you marry her and that way we'll all be happy.' To this day I don't think I was ever more creative.

But it didn't take. Something was wrong and I couldn't lose it. Suddenly there was this discontent gnawing away until it had a place big enough to settle in and then it curled up and stayed there and it's still inside me lurking as I write this now.

The next night, when my father went back to reading and the marriage turned out to have been Buttercup's dream, I screamed 'I knew it, all along I knew it,' and my father said, 'So you're happy now, it's all right now, we can please continue?' and I said 'Go' and he did.

But I wasn't happy. Oh my ears were happy, I guess, my story sense was happy, my heart too, but in my, I suppose you have to call it 'soul', there was that damn discontent, shaking its dark head.

All this was never explained to me till I was in my teens and there was this great woman who lived in my home town, Edith Neisser, dead now, and she wrote terrific books about how we screw up our children—*Brothers and Sisters* was one of her books, *The Eldest Child* was another. Published by Harper. Edith doesn't need the plug, seeing, like I said, as she's no longer with us, but if there are any amongst you who are worried that maybe you're not being perfect parents, pick up one of Edith's books while there's still time. I knew her 'cause her kid Ed got his haircuts from my pop, and she was this writer and by my teens I knew, secretly, that was the life for me too, except I couldn't tell anybody. It was too embarrassing—barber's sons, if they hustled, maybe got to be IBM salesmen, but writers? No way. Don't ask me how, but eventually Edith discovered my shhhhhh ambition and from then on, sometimes, we would talk. And I remember once we were having iced tea on the Neisser porch and talking and just outside the porch was their badminton court and I was watching some kids play badminton and Ed had just shellacked me, and as I left the court for the porch, he said, 'Don't worry, it'll all work out, you'll get me next time' and I nodded, and then Ed said, 'And if you don't, you'll beat me at something else.'

I went to the porch and sipped iced tea and Edith was reading this book and she didn't put it down when she said, 'That's not necessarily true, you know.'

I said, 'How do you mean?'

And that's when she put her book down. And looked at me. And said it: 'Life isn't fair, Bill. We tell our children that it is, but it's a terrible thing to do. It's not only a lie, it's a cruel lie. Life is not fair, and it never has been, and it's never going to be.'

Would you believe that for me right then it was like one of those comic books where the light bulb goes on over Mandrake the Magician's head? 'It isn't!' I said, so loud I really startled her. 'You're right. It's not fair.' I was so happy if I'd known how to dance, I'd have started dancing. 'Isn't that great, isn't it just terrific?' I think along about here Edith must have thought I was well on my way toward being bonkers.

But it meant so much to me to have it said and out and free and flying—that was the discontent I endured the night my father stopped reading, I realized right then. That was the reconciliation I was trying to make and couldn't.

And that's what I think this book's about. All those Columbia experts can spiel all they want about the delicious satire; they're crazy. This book says 'life isn't fair' and I'm telling you, one and all, you better believe it. I got a fat spoiled son—he's not gonna nab Miss Rheingold. And he's always gonna be fat, even if he gets skinny he'll still be fat and he'll still be spoiled and life will never be enough to make him happy, and that's my fault maybe—make it all my fault, if you want—the point is, we're not created equal, for the rich they sing, life isn't fair. I got a cold wife; she's brilliant, she's stimulating, she's terrific; there's no love; that's okay too, just so long as we don't keep expecting everything to somehow even out for us before we die.

Look. (Grownups skip this paragraph.) I'm not about to tell you this book has a tragic ending, I already said in the very first line how it was my favorite in all the world. But there's a lot of bad stuff coming up, torture you've already been prepared for, but there's worse. There's death coming up, and you better understand this: some of the wrong people die. Be ready for it. This isn't Curious George Uses the Potty. Nobody warned me and it was my own fault (you'll see what I mean in a little) and that was my mistake, so I'm not letting it happen to you. The wrong people die, some of them, and the reason is this; life is not fair. Forget all the garbage your parents put out. Remember Morgenstern. You'll be a lot happier.

Okay. Enough. Back to the next. Nightmare time.

Margaret Halsey (Contemporary)

꧁❧

FROM *With Malice Toward Some*

Today, when one of my blanks said OCCUPATION, I wrote down *none,* though I suspected this would not do. A severe but courteous official confirmed this impression. So I crossed it out and wrote *parasite,* which, not to be too delicate about it, is what I am. This made the official relax a little and he himself put *housewife* in what space there was left. "Be a prince," I said. "Make it *typhoid carrier.*" But he only smiled and blotted out *parasite* so that it would not show.

•

I am a big girl now and too old to believe in Shakespeare.

•

We left the suitcases and went out to eat, as—if the smell in the corridors was any indication—it was Human Sacrifice Night at the hotel. Three-quarters of an hour of walking failed to disclose a restaurant which was still open. Just as I was saying tragically that we would have to go back to the room and eat toothpaste, Henry noticed a place of decidedly humble aspect which seemed in two minds about closing up. We hurried in, and an absent-minded waitress gave us a pot of tea, supplemented after fifteen minutes by a piece of steak which had evidently been put to bed for the night and resented being disturbed.

•

Humility is not my forte, and whenever I dwell for any length of time on my own shortcomings, they gradually begin to seem mild, harmless, rather engaging little things, not at all like the staring defects in other people's characters.

The poor man has all the machinery of an intellectual (the books, the attitudes and the vocabulary), but not juice enough to run it, which makes him bad-tempered.

•

American men look at women when (they think) the women are not aware of it; Englishmen do not look at them at all; but Frenchmen look at them with such thoroughness and intensity that you half expect them to approach and ask dubiously, "Is it washable?"

Lynn Harris (Contemporary)

∽⠀⠀∾

Worrywarts and All

When I found out that the American reporter who'd been abducted by the Serbs was my dear old friend David Rohde, I remained surprisingly calm.

Why?

Not because I wasn't worried about him, but because I didn't know how to worry about him. I already have worry soft-ware in my brain for everyday things, like minor illness and travel during inclement weather. You call, send cards, monitor the Weather Channel, look up telltale symptoms ("fatigue") in *Our Bodies, Our Selves*, whatnot.

But political imprisonment in Bosnia? I didn't know where to start.

Only one person would know what to do: my mother. My mother is the best worrier I know. Her worrying is epic, Olympic, encyclopedic. People in the hospital, on transatlantic flights, at midlife crossroads—all of them jostle for a spot on her elite Worry List. She knows everything: the chemical composition of the pesticide on your apple, the link between yogurt and breast cancer ("Eat only Stonyfield Farms," she once intoned cryptically), how far away you should sit from household appliances (notably, computers) that emit hazardous electromagnetic rays. When I moved to Brooklyn, she bought me two canisters—one for my bike— of pepper spray. She responds to any mention of the Brooklyn Blades, my women's ice hockey team, with an update on the condition of the Boston University player who recently wound up paralyzed from the neck down. She e-mails me about the latest in vitamin research (B6 is in; beta-carotene is out). (True story: I'd originally written "fish oil is in," but when mom happened to see a draft of this column while I was visiting home, she crossed it out and wrote in "B6.")

Problem was, when I heard that David had been taken prisoner, my parents were away in Argentina. Quite a project, the hostage crisis, for a novice worrier.

It crossed my mind to call my friend Kent's Aunt Barb, the only person who may have my mother beat, at least in terms of international worry protocol. When Kent went to China for a year, Aunt Barb devised a code that would elude the eyes of censoring captors. If Kent signed his letters with his first name, all was well. But if he used his middle name, she'd know he was in trouble. Kent then went to work for the CIA, so Barb really had her hands full.

Luckily, by the time I summoned the courage to call David's family, he'd just been released. (And a few months later, David won a Pulitzer for his efforts. I think his mom should have gotten one, too. By the way, he now covers Brooklyn—including the war-torn Park Slope Food Co-Op—for the *Times*—)

You have to realize that asking my mother for worrying assistance represents quite a breakthrough in our relationship, since I had long ago resolved never to be like her. As you can imagine, her worrying cramped my style during my formative years. She insisted on dropping me off right in front of school dances to make sure I "got there okay." If my destination eluded direct surveillance, I had to call when I got there. Curfews were set not so much in Eastern Standard Time, but rather in Guilt Mean Time ("You know I won't sleep until I hear you come in").

Then I went to college. My mother didn't always know where I was, what I was doing, and whether or not I washed my hands with anti-bacterial soap before and after I did it. And she didn't ask. I was becoming free to start living—and worrying—on my own.

So one night, I was lying there waiting for my then-boyfriend to come in from a rehearsal (don't worry, mom, it was only once, and he brought a sleeping bag). It was getting later and later, and I was getting madder and madder. I began to rehearse all the stinging, guilt-tipped barbs I'd hurl at him: "Where have you been . . . I was worried . . . You could have called . . . You know I won't sleep until I hear you come in . . ."

I sat up in bed. Oh, my God. It had happened.

I've fought it, but it's only gotten worse. I have developed an acute fear of raw chicken and now trail my housemate Jason around the kitchen with Comet and the "chicken" cutting board. I am trying to convince my housemate Chris to eat more vegetables, especially green leafy anti-carcinogens. In our apartment, I have instituted The Noon Rule: whoever "doesn't come home" must call by noon the next day so the others know [not] to worry. I tsk-tsk at bicyclists and in-line skaters without helmets. If I forget to say "Drive carefully," it occurs to me that if there is an accident, it will be my fault. After I did a reporting assignment in a pediatric emergency room, every stove-top saucepan, moving vehicle, and untied shoelace became, in my eyes, an instrument of death.

I reached my worry zenith the day I went on an ice-skating outing with a group of under-served kids. We had to herd them through the busy subway and along the Central Park South sidewalk, across the street, and into Wollman Rink in Central Park—and then let them loose to navigate on untied skates with blades that couldn't cut butter. Can you imagine? My heart nearly stopped every time one of our young charges stepped off the curb.

And as I raced around the rink from kid to kid, picking one up and tightening another's laces, I felt the cells on the back of my head starting to divide into two sharp eyes.

It was time to tell my mother what had happened. I told her about my day and apologized for making fun of her all those years, assuming she'd welcome her heir with open arms to the world of worriers.

I was wrong.

Triumphant, mocking, satisfied, she responded, "Ha, ha."

So I guess we're equal. Almost. My mother has now gone on to worry that I'm worring too much. "I wish sometimes you could relax," she tells me, with no trace of irony. Yes, she's still the master, but I'm learning. And when she's worrying about me, I'm still her testy daughter. This kidnapped-reporter thing does give me a little mileage in that regard, I must say. Now, if I ever get another perilous reporting assignment in, God forbid, the NYPD vs. FDNY hockey game, or the food co-op, I can say, "Relax, Mom, it's not like I'm sneaking into Srebrenica! . . . Oh, and by the way, how far away from my computer am I supposed to be sitting?"

Bret Harte (1836–1902)

❧⊱∾⊰❧

The Haunted Man

A Christmas Story by Ch–r–s D–ck–n–s

PART I
THE FIRST PHANTOM

Don't tell me that it wasn't a knocker. I had seen it often enough, and I ought to know. So ought the three o'clock beer, in dirty high-lows, swinging himself over the railing, or executing a demoniacal jig upon the doorstep; so ought the butcher, although butchers as a general thing are scornful of such trifles; so ought the postman, to whom knockers of the most extravagant description were merely human weaknesses, that were to be pitied and used. And so ought, for the matter of that, etc., etc., etc.

But then it was *such* a knocker. A wild, extravagant, and utterly incomprehensible knocker. A knocker so mysterious and suspicious that Policeman X 37, first coming upon it, felt inclined to take it instantly in custody, but compromised with his professional instincts by sharply and sternly noting it with an eye that admitted of no nonsense, but confidently expected to detect its secret yet. An ugly knocker; a knocker with a hard, human face, that was a type of the harder human face within. A human face that held between its teeth a brazen rod. So hereafter, in the mysterious future should be held, etc., etc.

But if the knocker had a fierce human aspect in the glare of day, you should have seen it at night, when it peered out of the gathering shadows and suggested an ambushed figure; when the light of the street lamps fell upon it, and wrought a play of sinister expression in its hard outlines; when it seemed to wink meaningly at a shrouded figure who, as the night fell darkly, crept up the steps and passed into the mysterious house; when the swinging door disclosed a black passage into which the figure seemed to lose itself and become a part of the mysterious gloom; when the night grew boisterous and the fierce wind made furious charges at the knocker, as if to wrench it off and carry it away in triumph. Such a night as this.

It was a wild and pitiless wind. A wind that had commenced life as a gentle country zephyr, but wandering through manufacturing towns had become demoralised, and reaching the city had plunged into extravagant dissipation and wild excesses. A roistering wind that indulged in Bacchanalian shouts on the street corners, that knocked off the hats from the heads of helpless passengers, and then fulfilled its duties by speeding away, like all young prodigals,—to sea.

He sat alone in a gloomy library listening to the wind that roared in the chimney. Around him novels and story-books were strewn thickly; in his lap he held one with its pages freshly cut, and turned the leaves wearily until his eyes rested upon a portrait in its frontispiece. And as the wind howled the more fiercely, and the darkness without fell blacker, a strange and fateful likeness to that portrait appeared above his chair and leaned upon his shoulder. The Haunted Man gazed at the portrait and sighed. The figure gazed at the portrait and sighed too.

"Here again?" said the Haunted Man.

"Here again," it repeated in a low voice.

"Another novel?"

"Another novel."

"The old story?"

"The old story."

"I see a child," said the Haunted Man, gazing from the pages of the book into the fire,—"a most unnatural child, a model infant. It is prematurely old and philosophic. It dies in poverty to slow music. It dies surrounded by luxury to slow music. It dies with an accompaniment of golden water and rattling carts to slow music. Previous to its decease it makes a will; it repeats the Lord's Prayer, it kissed the 'boofer lady.' That child"——

"Is mine," said the phantom.

"I see a good woman, undersized. I see several charming women, but they are all undersized. They are more or less imbecile and idiotic, but always fascinating and undersized. They wear coquettish caps and aprons. I observe that feminine virtue is invariably below the medium height, and that it is always babyish and infantine. These women"——

"Are mine."

"I see a haughty, proud, and wicked lady. She is tall and queenly. I remark that all proud and wicked women are tall and queenly. That woman"——

"Is mine," said the phantom, wringing his hands.

"I see several things continually impending. I observe that whenever an accident, a murder, or death is about to happen, there is something in the furniture, in the locality, in the atmosphere, that foreshadows and suggests it years in advance. I cannot say that in real life I have noticed it,—the perception of this surprising fact belongs"——

"To me!" said the phantom. The Haunted Man continued, in a despairing tone—

"I see the influence of this in the magazines and daily papers; I see weak imitators rise up and enfeeble the world with senseless formula. I am getting tired of it. It won't do, Charles! it won't do!" and the Haunted Man buried his head in his hands and groaned. The figure looked down upon him sternly: the portrait in the frontispiece frowned as he gazed.

"Wretched man," said the phantom, "and how have these things affected you?"

"Once I laughed and cried, but then I was younger. Now, I would forget them if I could."

"Have then your wish. And take this with you, man whom I renounce. From this day henceforth you shall live with those whom I displace. Without forgetting me, 'twill be your lot to walk through life as if we had not met. But first, you shall survey these scenes that henceforth must be yours. At one to-night, prepare to meet the phantom I have raised. Farewell!"

The sound of its voice seemed to fade away with the dying wind, and the Haunted Man was alone. But the firelight flickered gaily, and the light danced on the walls, making grotesque figures of the furniture.

"Ha, ha!" said the Haunted Man, rubbing his hands gleefully; "now for a whiskey punch and a cigar."

Cynthia Heimel (Contemporary)

❦

FROM *Get Your Tongue Out of My Mouth, I'm Kissing You Good-bye*

The Baby Machine

Girls! Want to have a baby? No man in sight? Here's why it's hard:

Your body doesn't want to. I recently read somewhere that our bodies are still geared for the Stone Age, that we have to jog and lift weights because our bodies still think that any minute now we're going to be running from a lion or hefting a dead seal on our shoulders, and we go to seed if we don't approximate these antics.

Our hormones, too, were formed back in the Stone Age, affecting our every thought. There were no Stone Age feminists. Women just didn't have the time for marches and petitions and legislation, they were too busy trying to discover fire. Therefore, when your modern self-actualized girl suddenly goes all goopy at the sight of minuscule Reeboks, her brain may well decide that it's time for motherhood. No matter that she's single and thirty-six; she has, after all, only one life. But when her brain informs her body of this decision, her body is shocked.

"Excuse me," her body snarls, "but where's the fellah? No way I'm going through nine months of intense vulnerability without a dude with a club to protect me."

At which point your modern girl feels a cold, heavy dread in the pit of her stomach, a dread which, freely translated, means that all the teensy Reeboks in all the world will never be enough to lead her to the turkey baster. . . .

What's a Guy to Do?

I'm still trying to figure out why men are in such trouble.

Oh, come on, you know you are. You're bewildered, insecure, and terribly nervous. You're confused not only about how to act with women, but how to relate to the entire world. You've been buffeted by constant social and sexual conflicts and have lost control of all inner equilibrium.

I see you on talk shows attempting to explain yourself to audiences of sneering women. I see you pouring into twelve-step meetings, where you try to cry in front of people. But worst of all, I'm starting to see you at bookstores furtively buying self-help books.

The buying of a self-help book is the most desperate of all human acts. It means you've lost your mind completely: You've entrusted your mental health to a self-aggrandizing twit with a psychology degree and a yen for a yacht. It means you're having a major identity crisis.

Women did this a while ago, when our sex was having an identity crisis that lasted for oh, a decade. We didn't know who we were supposed to be, so we mainlined annoying tomes like *Women Who Love Too Much*. But then along came Anita Hill. She was the ignition that switched on everywoman's brain. Before Anita, we were all whining, "What's wrong with me? Where can I find a book to fix me?" After Anita, we all decided, "Wait a minute! It isn't me after all! Women are *still* being fucked over in our society!"

We're feeling much better now, thank you.

But men are feeling worse. You've been through a lot of identity-battering in the last twenty years:

First, you had to unlearn everything you were ever taught about women when feminism came along. You thought that you were supposed to grow up, get married, and immediately become the captain of the ship, the breadwinner. All that responsibility was scary, but a man had to do what a man had to do.

Then you were told that that was all wrong and how dare you? It was time to give up half your power to women or else.

Some of you became recalcitrant pigs, but many of you tried. You tried to be sensitive, you tried to learn the new language of women, you tried to gently abdicate your heavy mantle of responsibility, you tried to treat women as equal.

Then you were told that that was all wrong and how come you were all such wimps? What woman wanted a man she could walk all over?

So then you all bought motorcycle jackets and grew little ponytails and sported a three-day growth of beard and tried to be neotough. The message was "No broad better push me around, and if she does, well, I'll . . . I'll be sensitive and caring."

That didn't work, because women were going through their aforementioned crisis around then and nothing you did pleased us. Nothing.

Then along came Robert Bly and the masculinist movement and suddenly many of you found yourself spending nights in the woods, sweating and beating drums. Or at least reading about it.

But that felt just too goofy, and you had bigger problems. The economy plunged disastrously and many people lost jobs. Maybe not you. But maybe you soon. Plus women were charging you with sexual harassment and date rape. Maybe not you. But maybe you soon.

At this point in history, does it feel like you can't do anything right?

It's time to realize that there's nothing wrong with you. Well, there's plenty wrong with *some* of you. Men who abuse women, men who take the anger in their souls out on women, men who think of women as sex objects to be used and discarded should not even be allowed to be called men. But most of you are well-meaning but hopelessly befuddled.

So you're buying self-help books, you're blaming yourselves for your own unhappiness, you think you have some fatal flaw that reading some book will put right.

But it's not you. Society is fucking you over. Society has taken away all possible role models.

The last role model you had was "breadwinner, captain of the family." You could go ahead and become that, or you could become some kind of James Dean/Jack Nicholson guy and rebel against everything and run away. Either choice gave you a built-in structure in your attitudes toward women: You were either totally responsible or totally irresponsible. Either choice was sanctioned by society.

Now these choices have been systematically destroyed and replaced with nothing. There's nothing you're supposed to be, there's nothing to rebel against being.

You're working in a void, without identity, and the only messages you receive are negative: Don't be a pig, don't be a wimp.

Many of you have taken refuge in careers, defining yourselves solely by your jobs. This doesn't work anymore either. You're having heart attacks, you're getting fired.

Okay, I'm not a man. But I have been through a period of my life where it was either reinvent yourself or kill yourself. And I say it's time for a masculine revolution.

This means you've got to stop listening to anybody. Stop listening to a society which tells you you're powerful when in fact a couple of rich guys control everything. Stop listening to beer commercials which instruct you to be a moron. Stop listening to women who don't know what the hell they want but want you to give it to them anyway. Follow your best instincts. Figure out what's important to you.

Maybe you could reinvent the concept of fatherhood. Everybody seems to be decrying the lack of fathers, nobody seems to know what fathers are supposed to do. Maybe you can drop that heavy cloak of "manliness" that keeps you acting silent and strong when you want to be gossipy and playful.

Oh, don't listen to me, either. Just make it up as you go along. Just stop moping before we all go insane.

Ernest Hemingway (1899–1961)

❧❧❧

FROM *A Farewell to Arms*

I know I did not love Catherine Barkley nor had any idea of loving her. This was a game, like bridge, in which you said things instead of playing cards. Like bridge you had to pretend you were playing for money or playing for some stakes. Nobody had mentioned what the stakes were. It was all right with me.

O. Henry (1862–1910)

❧❧❧

The Ransom of Red Chief

It looked like a good thing: but wait till I tell you. We were down South, in Alabama—Bill Driscoll and myself—when this kidnapping idea struck us. It was, as Bill afterward expressed it, "during a moment of temporary mental apparition"; but we didn't find that out till later.

There was a town down there, as flat as a flannel-cake, and called Summit, of course. It contained inhabitants of as undeleterious and self-satisfied a class of peasantry as ever clustered around a Maypole.

Bill and me had a joint capital of about six hundred dollars, and we needed just two thousand dollars more to pull off a fraudulent town-lot scheme in Western Illinois with. We talked it over on the front steps of the hotel. Philoprogenitiveness, says we, is strong in semi-rural communities; therefore, and for other reasons, a kidnapping project ought to do better there than in the radius of newspapers that send reporters out in plain clothes to stir up talk about such things. We knew that Summit couldn't get after us with anything stronger than constables and, maybe, some lackadaisical bloodhounds and a diatribe or two in the *Weekly Farmers' Budget.* So, it looked good.

We selected for our victim the only child of a prominent citizen named Ebenezer Dorset. The father was respectable and tight, a mortgage fancier and a stern, upright collection-plate passer and forecloser. The kid was a boy of ten, with bas-relief freckles, and hair the color of the cover of the magazine you buy at the news-stand when you want to catch a train. Bill and me figured that Ebenezer would melt down for a ransom of two thousand dollars to a cent. But wait till I tell you.

About two miles from Summit was a little mountain, covered with a dense cedar brake. On the rear elevation of this mountain was a cave. There we stored provisions.

One evening after sundown, we drove in a buggy past old Dorset's house. The kid was in the street, throwing rocks at a kitten on the opposite fence.

"Hey, little boy!" says Bill, "would you like to have a bag of candy and a nice ride?"

The boy catches Bill neatly in the eye with a piece of brick.

"That will cost the old man an extra five hundred dollars," says Bill, climbing over the wheel.

That boy put up a fight like a welter-weight cinnamon bear; but, at last, we got him down in the bottom of the buggy and drove away. We took him up to the cave, and I hitched the horse in the cedar brake. After dark I drove the buggy to the little village, three miles away, where we had hired it, and walked back to the mountain.

Bill was pasting court-plaster over the scratches and bruises on his features. There was a fire burning behind the big rock at the entrance of the cave, and the boy was watching a pot of boiling coffee, with two buzzard tail-feathers stuck in his red hair. He points a stick at me when I come up, and says:

"Ha! cursed paleface, do you dare to enter the camp of Red Chief, the terror of the plains?"

"He's all right now," says Bill, rolling up his trousers and examining some bruises on his shins. "We're playing Indian. We're making Buffalo Bill's show look like magic-lantern views of Palestine in the town hall. I'm Old Hank, the Trapper, Red Chief's captive, and I'm to be scalped at daybreak. By Geronimo! that kid can kick hard."

Yes, sir, that boy seemed to be having the time of his life. The fun of camping out in a cave had made him forget that he was a captive himself. He immediately christened me Snake-eye, the Spy, and announced that, when his braves returned from the warpath, I was to be broiled at the stake at the rising of the sun.

Then we had supper; and he filled his mouth full of bacon and bread and gravy, and began to talk. He made a during-dinner speech something like this:

"I like this fine. I never camped out before; but I had a pet 'possum once, and I was nine last birthday. I hate to go to school. Rats ate up sixteen of Jimmy Talbot's aunt's speckled hen's eggs. Are there any real Indians in these woods? I want some more gravy. Does the trees moving make the wind blow? We had five puppies. What makes your nose so red, Hank? My father has lots of money. Are the stars hot? I whipped Ed Walker twice, Saturday. I don't like girls. You dassent catch toads unless with a string. Do oxen make any noise? Why are oranges round? Have you got beds to sleep on in this cave? Amos Murray has got six toes. A parrot can talk, but a monkey or a fish can't. How many does it take to make twelve?"

Every few minutes he would remember that he was a pesky redskin, and pick up his stick rifle and tiptoe to the mouth of the cave to rubber for the scouts of the hated paleface. Now and then he would let out a war-whoop that made Old Hank the Trapper shiver. That boy had Bill terrorized from the start.

"Red Chief," says I to the kid, "would you like to go home?"

"Aw, what for?" says he. "I don't have any fun at home. I hate to go to school. I like to camp out. You won't take me back home again, Snake-eye, will you?"

"Not right away," says I. "We'll stay here in the cave awhile."

"All right!" says he. "That'll be fine. I never had such fun in all my life."

We went to bed about eleven o'clock. We spread down some wide blankets and quilts and put Red Chief between us. We weren't afraid he'd run away. He kept us awake for three hours, jumping up and reaching for his rifle and screeching: "Hist! pard," in mine and Bill's ears, as the fancied crackle of a twig or the rustle of a leaf revealed to his young imagination the stealthy approach of the outlaw band. At last, I fell into a troubled sleep, and dreamed that I had been kidnapped and chained to a tree by a ferocious pirate with red hair.

Just at daybreak, I was awakened by a series of awful screams from Bill. They weren't yells, or howls, or shouts, or whoops, or yawps, such as you'd expect from a manly set of vocal organs—they were simply indecent, terrifying, humiliating screams, such as women emit when they see ghosts or caterpillars. It's an awful thing to hear a strong, desperate, fat man scream incontinently in a cave at daybreak.

I jumped up to see what the matter was. Red Chief was sitting on Bill's chest, with one hand twined in Bill's hair. In the other he had the sharp case-knife we used for slicing bacon; and he was industriously and realistically trying to take Bill's scalp, according to the sentence that had been pronounced upon him the evening before.

I got the knife away from the kid and made him lie down again. But, from that moment, Bill's spirit was broken. He laid down on his side of the bed, but he never closed an eye again in sleep as long as that boy was with us. I dozed off for a while, but along toward sun-up I remembered that Red Chief had said I was to be burned at the stake at the rising of the sun. I wasn't nervous or afraid; but I sat up and lit my pipe and leaned against a rock.

"What you getting up so soon for, Sam?" asked Bill.

"Me?" says I. "Oh, I got a kind of pain in my shoulder. I thought sitting up would rest it."

"You're a liar!" says Bill. "You're afraid. You was to be burned at sunrise, and you was afraid he'd do it. And he would, too, if he could find a match. Ain't it awful, Sam?

Do you think anybody will pay out money to get a little imp like that back home?"

"Sure," said I. "A rowdy kid like that is just the kind that parents dote on. Now, you and the Chief get up and cook breakfast, while I go up on the top of this mountain and reconnoitre."

I went up on the peak of the little mountain and ran my eye over the contiguous vicinity. Over towards Summit I expected to see the sturdy yeomanry of the village armed with scythes and pitchforks beating the countryside for the dastardly kidnappers. But what I saw was a peaceful landscape dotted with one man ploughing with a dun mule. Nobody was dragging the creek; no couriers dashed hither and yon, bringing tidings of no news to the distracted parents. There was a sylvan attitude of somnolent sleepiness pervading that section of the external outward surface of Alabama that lay exposed to my view. "Perhaps," says I to myself, "it has not yet been discovered that the wolves have borne away the tender lambkin from the fold. Heaven help the wolves!" says I, and I went down the mountain to breakfast.

When I got to the cave I found Bill backed up against the side of it, breathing hard, and the boy threatening to smash him with a rock half as big as a cocoanut.

"He put a red-hot boiled potato down my back," explained Bill, "and then mashed it with his foot; and I boxed his ears. Have you got a gun about you, Sam?"

I took the rock away from the boy and kind of patched up the argument. "I'll fix you," says the kid to Bill. "No man ever yet struck the Red Chief but he got paid for it. You better beware!"

After breakfast the kid takes a piece of leather with strings wrapped around it out of his pocket and goes outside the cave unwinding it.

"What's he up to now?" says Bill, anxiously. "You don't think he'll run away, do you, Sam?"

"No fear of it," says I. "He don't seem to be much of a home body. But we've got to fix up some plan about the ransom. There don't seem to be much excitement around Summit on account of his disappearance; but maybe they haven't realized yet that he's gone. His folks may think he's spending the night with Aunt Jane or one of the neighbors. Anyhow, he'll be missed to-day. To-night we must get a message to his father demanding the two thousand dollars for his return."

Just then we heard a kind of war-whoop, such as David might have emitted when he knocked out the champion Goliath. It was a sling that Red Chief had pulled out of his pocket, and he was whirling it around his head.

I dodged, and heard a heavy thud and a kind of a sigh from Bill, like a horse gives out when you take his saddle off. A niggerhead rock the size of an egg had caught Bill just behind his left ear. He loosened himself all over and fell in the fire across the frying pan of hot water for washing the dishes. I dragged him out and poured cold water on his head for half an hour.

By and by, Bill sits up and feels behind his ear and says: "Sam, do you know who my favorite Biblical character is?"

"Take it easy," says I. "You'll come to your senses presently."

"King Herod," says he. "You won't go away and leave me here alone, will you, Sam?"

I went out and caught that boy and shook him until his freckles rattled.

"If you don't behave," says I, "I'll take you straight home. Now, are you going to be good, or not?"

"I was only funning," says he, sullenly. "I didn't mean to hurt Old Hank. But what did he hit me for? I'll behave, Snake-eye, if you won't send me home, and if you'll let me play the Black Scout to-day."

"I don't know the game," says I. "That's for you and Mr. Bill to decide. He's your playmate for the day. I'm going away for a while, on business. Now, you come in and make friends with him and say you are sorry for hurting him, or home you go, at once."

I made him and Bill shake hands, and then I took Bill aside and told him I was going to Poplar Grove, a little village three miles from the cave, and find out what I could about how the kidnapping had been regarded in Summit. Also, I thought it best to send a peremptory letter to old man Dorset that day, demanding the ransom and dictating how it should be paid.

"You know, Sam," says Bill, "I've stood by you without batting an eye in earthquakes, fire and blood—in poker games, dynamite outrages, police raids, train robberies, and cyclones. I never lost my nerve yet till we kidnapped that two-legged skyrocket of a kid. He's got me going. You won't leave me long with him, will you, Sam?"

"I'll be back some time this afternoon," says I. "You must keep the boy amused and quiet till I return. And now we'll write the letter to old Dorset."

Bill and I got paper and pencil and worked on the letter while Red Chief, with a blanket wrapped around him, strutted up and down, guarding the mouth of the cave. Bill begged me tearfully to make the ransom fifteen hundred dollars instead of two thousand. "I ain't attempting," says he, "to decry the celebrated moral aspect of parental affection, but we're dealing with humans, and it ain't human for anybody to give up two thousand dollars for that forty-pound chunk of freckled wildcat. I'm willing to take a chance at fifteen hundred dollars. You can charge the difference up to me."

So, to relieve Bill, I acceded, and we collaborated a letter that ran this way:

EBENEZER DORSET, ESQ.:

We have your boy concealed in a place far from Summit. It is useless for you or the most skillful detectives to attempt to find him. Absolutely, the only terms on which you can have him restored to you are these: We demand fifteen hundred dollars in large bills for his return; the money to be left at midnight to-night at the same spot and in the same box as your reply—as hereinafter described. If you agree to these terms, send your answer in writing by a solitary messenger to-night at half-past eight o'clock. After crossing Owl Creek on the road to Poplar Grove, there are three large trees about a hundred yards apart, close to the fence of the wheat field on the right-hand side. At the bottom of the fence-post, opposite the third tree, will be found a small pasteboard box.

The messenger will place the answer in this box and return immediately to Summit.

If you attempt any treachery or fail to comply with our demand as stated, you will never see your boy again.

If you pay the money as demanded, he will be returned to you safe and well within three hours. These terms are final, and if you do not accede to them no further communication will be attempted.

TWO DESPERATE MEN.

I addressed this letter to Dorset, and put it in my pocket. As I was about to start, the kid comes up to me and says:

"Aw, Snake-eye, you said I could play the Black Scout while you was gone."

"Play it, of course," says I. "Mr. Bill will play with you. What kind of a game is it?"

"I'm the Black Scout," says Red Chief, "and I have to ride to the stockade to warn the settlers that the Indians are coming. I'm tired of playing Indian myself. I want to be the Black Scout."

"All right," says I. "It sounds harmless to me. I guess Mr. Bill will help you foil the pesky savages."

"What am I to do?" asks Bill, looking at the kid suspiciously.

"You are the hoss," says Black Scout. "Get down on your hands and knees. How can I ride to the stockade without a hoss?"

"You'd better keep him interested," said I, "till we get the scheme going. Loosen up."

Bill gets down on his all fours, and a look comes in his eye like a rabbit's when you catch it in a trap.

"How far is it to the stockade, kid?" he asks, in a husky manner of voice.

"Ninety miles," says the Black Scout. "And you have to hump yourself to get there on time. Whoa, now!"

The Black Scout jumps on Bill's back and digs his heels in his side.

"For Heaven's sake," says Bill, "hurry back, Sam, as soon as you can. I wish we hadn't made the ransom more than a thousand. Say, you quit kicking me or I'll get up and warm you good."

I walked over to Poplar Grove and sat around the post-office and store, talking with the chaw-bacons that came in to trade. One whisker-ando says that he hears Summit is all upset on account of Elder Ebenezer Dorset's boy having been lost or stolen. That was all I wanted to know. I bought some smoking tobacco, referred casually to the price of black-eyed peas, posted my letter surreptitiously, and came away. The postmaster said the mail-carrier would come by in an hour to take the mail to Summit.

When I got back to the cave Bill and the boy were not to be found. I explored the vicinity of the cave, and risked a yodel or two, but there was no response.

So I lighted my pipe and sat down on a mossy bank to await developments.

In about half an hour I heard the bushes rustle, and Bill wabbled out into the little glade in front of the cave. Behind him was the kid, stepping softly like a scout, with a broad grin on his face. Bill stopped, took off his hat, and wiped his face with a red handkerchief. The kid stopped about eight feet behind him.

"Sam," says Bill, "I suppose you'll think I'm a renegade, but I couldn't help it. I'm a grown person with masculine proclivities and habits of self-defense, but there is a time when all systems of egotism and predominance fail. The boy is gone. I sent him home. All is off. There was martyrs in old times," goes on Bill, "that suffered death rather than give up the particular graft they enjoyed. None of 'em ever was subjugated to such supernatural tortures as I have been. I tried to be faithful to our articles of depredation; but there came a limit."

"What's the trouble, Bill?" I asks him.

"I was rode," says Bill, "the ninety miles to the stockade, not barring an inch. Then, when the settlers was rescued, I was given oats. Sand ain't a palatable substitute. And then, for an hour I had to try to explain to him why there was nothin' in holes, how a road can run both ways, and what makes the grass green. I tell you, Sam, a human can only stand so much. I takes him by the neck of his clothes and drags him down the mountain. On the way he kicks my legs black and blue from the knees down; and I've got to have two or three bites on my thumb and hand cauterized.

"But he's gone"—continues Bill—"gone home. I showed him the road to Summit and kicked him about eight feet nearer there at one kick. I'm sorry we lose the ransom; but it was either that or Bill Driscoll to the madhouse."

Bill is puffing and blowing, but there is a look of ineffable peace and growing content on his rose-pink features.

"Bill," says I, "there isn't any heart disease in your family, is there?"

"No," says Bill, "nothing chronic except malaria and accidents. Why?"

"Then you might turn around," says I, "and have a look behind you."

Bill turns and sees the boy, and loses his complexion and sits down plump on the ground and begins to pluck aimlessly at grass and little sticks. For an hour I was afraid of his mind. And then I told him that my scheme was to put the whole job through immediately and that we would get the ransom and be off with it by midnight if old Dorset fell in with our proposition. So Bill braced up enough to give the kid a weak sort of a smile and a promise to play the Russian in a Japanese war with him as soon as he felt a little better.

I had a scheme for collecting that ransom without danger of being caught by counterplots that ought to commend itself to professional kidnappers. The tree under which the answer was to be left—and the money later on—was close to the road fence with big, bare fields on all sides. If a gang of constables should be watching for any one to come for the note, they could see him a long way off crossing the fields or in the road. But no, sirree! At half-past eight I was up in that tree as well hidden as a tree toad, waiting for the messenger to arrive.

Exactly on time, a half-grown boy rides up the road on a bicycle, locates the pasteboard box at the foot of the fence-post, slips a folded piece of paper into it, and pedals away again back toward Summit.

I waited an hour and then concluded the thing was square. I slid down the tree, got the note, slipped along the fence till I struck the woods, and was back at the cave in another half an hour. I opened the note, got near the lantern, and read it to Bill. It was written with a pen in a crabbed hand, and the sum and substance of it was this:

Two Desperate Men.

Gentlemen: I received your letter to-day by post, in regard to the ransom you ask for the return of my son. I think you are a little high in your demands, and I hereby make you a counter-proposition, which I am inclined to believe you will accept. You bring Johnny home and pay me two hundred and fifty dollars in cash, and I agree to take him off your hands. You had better come at night, for the neighbors believe he is lost, and I couldn't be responsible for what they would do to anybody they saw bringing him back. Very respectfully,

EBENEZER DORSET.

"Great pirates of Penzance," says I; "of all the impudent—"

But I glanced at Bill, and hesitated. He had the most appealing look in his eyes I ever saw on the face of a dumb or a talking brute.

"Sam," says he, "what's two hundred and fifty dollars, after all? We've got the money. One more night of this kid will send me to a bed in Bedlam. Besides being a thorough gentleman, I think Mr. Dorset is a spendthrift for making us such a liberal offer. You ain't going to let the chance go, are you?"

"Tell you the truth, Bill," says I, "this little he ewe lamb has somewhat got on my nerves too. We'll take him home, pay the ransom, and make our getaway."

We took him home that night. We got him to go by telling him that his father had bought a silver-mounted rifle and a pair of moccasins for him, and we were to hunt bears the next day.

It was just twelve o'clock when we knocked at Ebenezer's front door. Just at the moment when I should have been abstracting the fifteen hundred dollars from the box under the tree, according to the original proposition, Bill was counting out two hundred and fifty dollars into Dorset's hand.

When the kid found out we were going to leave him at home he started up a howl like a calliope and fastened himself as tight as a leech to Bill's leg. His father peeled him away gradually, like a porous plaster.

"How long can you hold him?" asks Bill.

"I'm not as strong as I used to be," says old Dorset, "but I think I can promise you ten minutes."

"Enough," says Bill. "In ten minutes I shall cross the Central, Southern, and Middle Western States, and be legging it trippingly for the Canadian border."

And, as dark as it was, and as fat as Bill was, and as good a runner as I am, he was a good mile and a half out of Summit before I could catch up with him.

Nicole Hollander (Contemporary)

FROM *The Whole Enchilada*

FROM *Female Problems*

Eeek! It's Kathie Lee

WHAT
WAS
THAT
NOISE?

I fear exercise, flying, great heights, walking around alone at night, musical comedy, small dark places, roaches and mice, cash machines that run out of money, sudden noises, new neighbors, cocktail parties, foreign languages, stolen credit cards, credit bureaus, the IRS, bombs at airports, airline food, bingo, stuffing from inside the turkey, dentists, highway construction, vicious dogs, gangs of eight-year-old boys, nursing homes, dense forests, getting locked out of my apartment without shoes, deserts, empty highways, pierced nipples, abandoned motels, running out of gas, miniskirts, spiked heels, mold, Republicans, killer bees, spit on the sidewalk, Fundamentalists, graffiti, snowstorms, cold weather, humidity, gum disease, telephone calls after 9:00 P.M., large bodies of water, people who talk a lot, mysterious tinfoil packages in the back of the refrigerator, the FBI, shy people, washing machines that overflow, frozen pipes, walking across an open field during a thunderstorm, ant invasions, piles of ironing, sudden attacks of lust, electrical outlets, tomatoes without flavor, mobile homes during a hurricane, runaway horses, maps, cruise control, hockey pucks, masseuses who crack your neck, getting trapped in a sauna, car jackers, men in suits, crying babies, cruel landlords, crooked mechanics, Freddy Krueger, insurance companies, needles, tongue depressors, plastic bags, and Florida. . . . But please, O powerful one, O ruler of the body, please don't make me fear hot dogs with everything, on a poppyseed bun; ice cream laced with chocolate and nuts; thick steaks; garlic bread with butter; two eggs over easy with bacon, hash browns, and a side of sausage; or meat loaf with gravy.

Notes from the traveler who Whines

I like to travel in my bathrobe.

Well, a really bad trip is where you die, am I right? Anything less: dysentery, loss of your passport, bugged hotel rooms, insects the size of ponies, mud slides, frostbite, and outright rudeness are the stuff of good stories when you get back home. The recollection of near disaster is the only thing that will remove the glassy look from a friend's eyes as you recount your trip to Afghanistan or Iowa. Well, I'm not doing it. It's not worth it.

James Morris was with Edmund Hillary when he reached the summit of Mount Everest. That same intrepid man later had a sex change operation and became Jan Morris. Fearful journeys, both, but Ms. Morris is addicted to exploring and has never had a bad experience.

I have had bad experiences in Elmhurst, Illinois. Like soufflé, I do not travel well. I whine. My IQ goes down. I forget to look both ways. I can get lost taking a new way home from the office. London defeated me. I panic over trifles. I became comatose in a hotel in Santa Monica because there was an odd stain on the ceiling and the spreads felt clammy. I had to be half-carried to the plane. (A plane, oh my God, I'm on a plane. Well, it was either that or live in Santa Monica forever.)

So I am unable to visit the rain forest, take a solo trip around the globe in a tiny boat, or see the pyramids in old Algiers. I will never exchange courteous speech and gifts with chieftains in Samoa or get a haircut in Kashmir. If I were by profession a governess, you would not find me in a forbidding mansion on a moor in a windswept corner of England, even though I was down on my luck and the master of the house was terribly good-looking and stern.

I am an armchair traveler of a very limited kind. I like to read books about awful trips. I loved *Forgotten Fatherland*. The author searches for the lost colony of Elisabeth Nietzsche in Paraguay and suffers mightily from aggressive biting insects and a diet composed solely of protein. The

English seem to excel at this kind of writing. Bless them. I keep a copy of *Bad Trips* (edited by Keith Fraser) at my bedside. I leaf through it when I feel the urge to travel. It calms me and confirms to me the rightness of my abject wimpiness. Even for armchair traveling I impose strict limits. I don't watch films in which young people are imprisoned in Turkey for minor drug offenses or where women disguise themselves in chadors and escape with their daughters from alien cultures. Makes me nervous.

Most trips involve plane travel. I hate that. A friend of mine was offered a free trip to Uzbekistan. She couldn't pass it up. Well, who could? Many of us have longed to go to a theater festival in Uzbekistan all our adult lives. She said she thought of me when, on the second or fifth leg of the journey, her plane, experiencing mechanical difficulties, landed at an unmarked airfield. After quite a while, in which no one in authority communicated anything and the passengers were not allowed off the aircraft, a long ladder was placed against the wing. A man climbed up the ladder and hit something sharply with a hammer and they took off again.

Marietta Holley (1836–1926)

FROM *The Widder Doodle's Courtship*

I Wish I Was a Widder
by Betsey Bobbet

Oh, "Gimlet," back again I float
    With broken wings, a weary bard;
I cannot write as once I wrote,
    I have to work so very hard.
So hard my lot, so tossed about,
My muse is fairly tuckered out.

My muse aforesaid, once hath flown,
　　But now her back is broke, and breast;
And yet she fain would crumble down
　　On "Gimlet" pages she would rest;
And sing plain words as there she's sot
Haply they'll rhyme, and haply not.

I spake plain words in former days,
　　No guile I showed, clear was my plan;
My gole it matrimony was.
　　My earthly aim it was a man.
I gained my man, I won my gole,
Alas, I feel not as I fole.

Yes, ringing through my maiden thought
　　This clear voice rose, "Oh come up higher"
To speak plain truth with cander fraught,
　　To married be, was my desire.
Now sweeter still this lot doth seem
To be a widder is my theme.

For toil hath claimed me for her own,
　　In wedlock I have found no ease;
I've cleaned and washed for neighbors round;
　　And took my pay in beans and pease;
In boiling sap no rest I took
Or husking corn in barn and stook.

Or picking wool from house to house,
　　White-washing, painting, papering,
In stretching carpets, boiling souse,
　　E'en picking hops it hath a sting
For spiders there assembled be,
Mosqueetoes, bugs, and etcetree.

I have to work, oh! very hard;
　　Old Toil, I know your breadth, and length.
I'm tired to death; and in one word
　　I have to work beyond my strength,
And mortal men are very tough
To get along with—nasty, rough.

Yes, tribulation's doomed to her
   Who weds a man, without no doubt
In peace a man is singuler
   His ways, they are past finding out,
And oh! the wrath of mortal males
To paint their ire, earth's language fails.

And thirteen children in our home
   Their buttons rend, their clothes they burst.
Much bread and such do they consume;
   Of children they do seem the worst;
And Simon and I do disagree,
He's prone to sin continualee.

On Marriage

"Good land!" says I, "is marryin' the only theme that any-body can lay holt of?" says I, "it seems to me it would be the best way to lay holt of duty now, and then, if a bo come, lay holt of him. If they ketch a bo with such a hook as they are a-fishin' with now, what kind of a bo will it be? Nobody but a fool would lay holt of a hook baited with dime novels and pups. Learn your girls to be industrious, and to respect themselves. They can't now, Delila Ann, I know they can't. No woman can feel honorable and reverential toward them-selves, when they are foldin' their useless hands over their empty souls, waitin' for some man, no matter who, to marry 'em and support 'em. When in the agony of suspense and fear, they have narrowed down to this one theme, all their hopes and prayers, Good Lord; *anybody!*"

"But when a woman lays holt of life in a noble, earnest way, when she is dutiful, and cheerful, and industrious, God-fearin', and self-respectin', though the world sinks, there is a rock under her feet that won't let her down far enough to hurt her any. If love comes to her to brighten her pathway, so much the better. She will be ready to receive them roy-ally, and keep him when she gets him. Some folks don't know how to use love worth a cent. But no matter whether she be single or double, I am not afraid of her future."

FROM *Josiah Allen's Wife*

Josiah said he wanted to look at a mowin' machine, and as I hadn't been to the Woman's Pavilion only to take a cursory view of it, I thought now was my time, and so I went through it with a proud and happy heart. Yes, I can truly say without lyin' that my emotions as I went through that buildin' was larger in size and heftier in weight than any emotions I had enjoyed sense I had been to the Sentinal. Feelin' such feelins for my sect as I felt, holdin' their honor and prosperity, and success nearer to my heart, than to any earthly object, (exceptin' Josiah) I suppose if anybody could have looked inside of my mind as I wandered through them rooms, they would have seen a sight they never would have forgot the longest day they ever lived; I s'pose it would have skairt 'em most to death if they wasn't used to seein' emotions performin'. Oh! such proud and lofty feelins as I did enjoy a seein' the work of my sect from all over the length and breadth of the world. The wonderful, useful inventions of the sect, showin' the power and solid heft of her brains; the beautiful works of art showin' her creative artist soul, and provin' plain the healthy and vigorous state of her imagination. The wonderful wood carvin', and dainty fancy needle work, and embroideries of all kinds you can imagine, showin' the stiddy, patient, persistent powers of her hands and fingers; and what was fur more interestin' to me of all, was the silent exhibit at the south entrance, showin' what sort of a heart she has within her, a record of eight hundred and twenty-two large noble sized charities, organized and carried on by the sect which a certain person once Smith, is proud to say she belongs to.

Oh! I can truly say that I felt perfectly beautiful, a goin' through them noble halls, a seein' everything and more too, (as it were) from doll's shoes, and pictures of poseys, and squirrels, and five little pigs, up to the Vision of St. Christopher, and a big statute of Eve standin' with her arm over her face, hidin' the shame in it. There was Injun basket work, perfectly beautiful, and settin' by the side of it weavin' her baskets sot as dignified and good appearin' a woman, (though dark complexioned) as any nation of the world sent to the Sentinal. I bought a little basket of her right there on the spot, for I liked her looks, and she handed me out her card:

Margaret Kesiah, Obkine Injun of Canada.

And there was napkins, the linen of which was wove by my friend, the Widder Albert; and as I looked at 'em, I thought gently to myself: how many wimmen who haint got a Right, and don't want one, could spin linen equal to this? And then amongst every other way to honor and glorify my sect that could be thought of, there was a female woman all carved out of butter. I had thought in my proud spirited hautiness of soul that I could make as handsome butter balls, and flower 'em off as nobby as any other woman of the age. But as I looked at that beautiful roll of butter all flattened out into such a lovely face, I said to myself in firm axents, though mild: "Samantha, you have boasted your last boast over butter balls."

There was some bright happy pictures, and some that wasn't. One was of a sick child and its mother out in the desert alone with the empty water jug standin' by 'em. The mother holdin' the feeble little hands, and weepin' over him. Her heart was a desert, and she was in a desert, which made it hard for her, and hard for me too, and I was jest puttin' my hand into my pocket after my white cotton handkerchief, when somebody kinder hunched me in the side, and lookin' round, there was that very female lecturer I see at New York village. Says she: "Come out where it is more quiet, Josiah Allen's wife; I want to have a little talk with you."

She looked perfectly full of talk, but says I: "I haint only jest commenced lookin' round at the splendid doins in this buildin' " says I, "I don't want to stir out of this house for 13 or 14 hours."

Says she, "You can come again, but I *must* have a talk with you."

Says I, "Feelin' as I do, wont you excuse me mom?"

But she wouldn't excuse me, and seein' she was fairly sufferin' to talk, I led the way to a rendezvoo where I promised Josiah to be, not knowin' how long she would talk when she got at it, for—though I am very close mouthed myself—I know well the failins of my sect in that respect. The very moment we sot down on the pleasant and secluded bench I took her to, she begun:

"What do you think of men meetin' here to celebrate

National Independance and the right of self-government, when they hold half of their own race in political bondage?"

Says I, firmly, "I think it is a mean trick in 'em."

Says she, bitterly: "Can't you say sunthin' more than that?"

"Yes," says I, "I can, and will; it is mean as pusly, and meaner."

Says she, "What do you think of their meetin' here and glorifyin' the sentiment up to the heavens in words, 'true government consists in the consent of the governed,' and tramplin' it practically down to the dust under their feet? What do you think of this great ado over grantin' the makin' of our laws to the Irishman jest out of prison, whom they dislike and despise—and denyin' these rights to intelligent, native-born citizens, whom they love and respect? What do you think of their taxin' the christian and earnest souled woman, worth half a million, and leave it to men, not worth the shoes they wear to the pole, the ignorant, and the vicious, to vote how that money shall be used; she, by the work of her hands or brains, earnin' property to be used in this way, in makin' and enforcin' laws she despises and believes to be ruinous, and unjust in the sight of God and man. What do you think of this?" says she.

Says I, with a calm but firm dignity: "I think pusly is no meaner."

"Oh!" says she, turnin' her nose in the direction of the Main Buildin' and shakin' her brown lisle thread fist at it, "how I despise men! Oh, how sick I be of 'em!" And she went on for a long length of time, a callin' 'em every name I ever heerd men called by, and lots I never heerd on, from brutal whelps, and roarin' tyrants, down to lyin' sneakin' snipes; and for every new and awful name she'd give 'em, I'd think to myself: why, my Josiah is a man, and Father Smith was a man, and lots of other relatives, and 4 fathers on my father's side. And so says I:

"Sister, what is the use of your runnin' men so?" says I, mildly, "it is only a tirin' yourself; you never will catch 'em, and put the halter of truth onto 'em, while you are a runnin' 'em so fearfully; it makes 'em skittish and baulky." Says I, "Men are handy in a number of ways, and for all you seem to despise 'em so, you would be glad to holler to some man if your horse should run away, or your house git a fire, or the ship go to sinkin', or anything."

Says she, "Men are the most despiseable creeters that ever trod shoe leather."

"Well," says I, calmly, "take wimmen as a race, mom, and they don't cherish such a deadly aversion to the other sect as you seem to make out they do; quite the reverse and opposite. Why, I have seen wimmen act so, a follerin' of 'em up, pursuin' of 'em, clingin' to 'em, smilin' almost vacantly at 'em; I have seen 'em act and behave till it was more sickenin' than thoroughwort to my moral stomach. Says I, "I cherish no such blind and almost foolish affection for 'em as a sect, (one, I almost worship) but I have a firm, reasonable, meetin'-house esteem for 'em, as a race. A calm, firm regard, unmoved and stiddy as a settin' hen; I see their faults, plainly, very—as my Josiah will testify and make oath to; and I also see their goodnesses, their strength, their nobilities, and their generosities—which last named are as much more generous than ourn, as their strength is stronger."

Says I, "Pause a moment, mom, in your almost wild career of runnin' men down, to think what they have done; look round the world with your mind's eye, and see their work on land and sea. See the nations they have founded; see the cities stand where there used to be a wilderness; see the deserts they have made to blossom like a rosy; see the victories they have got over time and space,—talkin' from one end of the world to the other in a minute, and travellin' almost as quick, through mountains and under the water, and every thing. See how old ocian herself—who used to roar defiance at 'em—was made by 'em to bile herself up into steam to git the victory over herself. And in spite of the thunder that tried to scare 'em out, see how they have drawd the lightnin' out of the heavens to be their servant. Look there," says I, pintin' my forefinger eloquently towards the main Halls: Machinery, Agricultural—and so 4th—"see the works of that sect you are runnin' so fearfully; see their time-conquerin', labor-savin' inventions, see—"

"I won't see," says she, firmly, and bitterly. "I won't go near any of their old machines; I'll stand by my sect, I'll stick to the Woman's Pavilion. I haint been nigh Machinery

Hall, nor the Main Buildin', nor the Art Gallery, nor I won't neither."

"I have," says I, in triumphant, joyful tones, "I have been lost in 'em repeatedly, and expect to be again. I have been destracted and melted down in 'em, and have been made almost perfectly happy, for the time bein', to see the wonderful fruits of men's intellects; the labor of strong heads and hearts; to see the works of men's genius, and en-terprise, and darin'; the useful, the beautiful and grand, the heroic and sublime. Why I have been so lifted up that I didn't know but I should go right up through the ruff, (over 200 pounds in all). I have been elevated and inspired as I don't expect to be elevated and lifted up again for the next 100 years. And lookin' round on what I see, and thinkin' what I thought, it made me so proud and happy, that it was a sweet thought to me that my Josiah was a man."

"Oh shaw!" says she, "you had better be a lookin' at the Woman's Pavilion, than lookin' on what them snipes have done."

Says I, "Do you take me for a natteral fool mom? Do you s'pose I am such a fool or such a luny, that every time I have looked at the Woman's Pavilion, and gloried over the works of her hands and brains, I haint felt jest so—only more so?" Says I, "That buildin' stands there to-day as a solid and hefty proof that wimmen are sunthin' more than the deli-cate, and helpless zephyrs and scraphines, that they have been falsely pointed out to be." Says I, "It is a great scien-tific fact, that if men go to canterin' blindly down that old pathway of wimmen's weakness and unfitness for labor and endurance and inability to meet financial troubles and dis-couragements again, they must come bunt up ag'inst that buildin' and recognize it as a solid fact, and pause before it respectfully, ponderin' what it means, or else fall. They can't step over it, their legs haint long enough."

And says I, "It is earnest thought and work that has filled it, and that is what wimmen want to do—to do more, and say less. No stream can rise higher than its fountain; a uni-verse full of laws to elevate wimmen can't help her, unless she helps herself. Sufferagin' will do a good deal, but it haint a goin' to fill up a empty soul, or a vacant frivolous mind. There are thoughts that have got to turn right square round and travel another road; there is tattin' and bobinet lace to be soared over; there is shoulder blades that has got to be put to the wheel. Every flag on the buildin' seems to float out like good deeds and noble eloquent thoughts, while the gabriel ends stand firm under 'em, like the firm, solid motives and principles that great and good deeds have got to wave out from, in order to amount to anything."

"But," says she, "the mean snipes won't let us vote."

Says I calmly, "That's so; they haint willin' all on 'em, to give us the right of sufferagin' jest at present, and as I have said, and say now, it is mean as pusly in 'em. But it don't look so poor in them as it does in the wimmen that oppose it, a fightin' ag'inst their own best interests. It seems to me that any conscientious, intelligent woman, who took any thought for herself and her sect, would want a Right to—"

Here she hollered right out interruptin' me; says she: "Less vote! less take a hammer and go at the men, and make them let us vote this minute."

Says I, "I'd love to convince men of the truth, but it haint no use to take a hammer and try to knock unwelcome truths into anybody's head, male or female. The idee may be good, and the hammer may be a moral, well meanin' hammer; but you see the dander rise up in the head that is bein' hit, and makes a impenetrable wall, through which the idee can't go; that is a great philosophical fact, that can't be sailed round, or climbed over. And it is another deep scientific principle, that you can't git two persons to think any more of each other or think any nearer alike by knockin' their heads together. Nobody can git any water by breakin' up a chunk of ice with a axe; not a drop; you have got to thaw it out gradual; jest like men's and wimmen's prejudices in the cause of Wimmen's Rights. Public sentiment is the warm fire that is a goin' to melt this cold hard ice of injustice that we are contendin' ag'inst; laws haint good for much if public opinion don't stand behind 'em pushin' 'em onward to victory."

"I wont wait a minute," says she, "I will vote."

But I argued with her; says I: "Sister, you are well meanin', no doubt, but you ort to remember that the battle haint always to the swift." Says I, "It wont harm none of us to foller Nater's ways a little more close; and Nater is a female that—if she is ruther slow motioned—generally has her way in the end to an uncommon degree. You don't catch her gittin' mad, wild, impatient, tearin' open a kernel of corn, or grain of wheat, or anything, and growin' a stalk out of it sudden and at once. No! jest like all patient toilers for the Right, she plants the seed, and then lets it take time to swell out, and git full to bustin' with its own convictions and desires to grow, till it gits so sick of the dark ground where it is hid, and longs so for the light and the free air above it, that it can't be kep' back a minute longer, but soars right up of its own free will and accord, towards the high heavens and the blessed sunlight. But if seeds haint good for nothin', they wont come up; all the sunshine and rain on earth can't make 'em grow, nor cultivators, nor horse rakes, nor nothin'.

"And so with principles. Lots of folks spend most of their days a plantin' seeds that wont come up. What is worthless wont amount to nothin'—in accordance with that great mathematical fact, that scientific folks like me apply to lots of things, and find that it comes right every time—that ort from ort leaves nothin', and nothin' to carry. But if the idee is true and has got life in it, no matter how dark the mould that covers it, it is morally bound to sprout—positively bound to, and can't be hindered. Don't you know, when a big forest has been cut down, berry bushes will spring right up, seem to have stood all ready to spring up for the refreshin' of men and wimmen just as quick as the shadders of the tall trees had got offen 'em; curious, but so it is. Who knows how many centuries them seeds have laid there a waitin' their time to grow, gittin' sick of the shadders mebby, but jest a waitin' with considerable patience after all.

"And thinkin' of these things mom, ort to make us considerable patient too, willin' to work, and willin' to wait; knowin' that gittin' mad and actin' haint a goin' to help us a mite; knowin' that the seeds of good and right, planted with tears and prayers, are bound to spring up triumphant; knowin' that the laughin' and cold sneers of the multitude haint a goin' to frost bite 'em; knowin' that the tears of weakness, and weariness, and loneliness, fallin' from human eyes over the hoe handle in plantin' time, only moistens the sod, and kinder loosens it up first-rate. And that even the ashes of persecution, and all the blood that falls in righteous cause, only nourishes the snowy flowers and golden grain of the future. Mebby it is our mission to clear away trees and stumps—sort o' wood choppers, or sawyers—I don't care a mite what I am called. We may never see the seed spring up; we may not be here when it breaks through the dark mould triumphant; but somebody will see it; happy skies will bend over it; happy hearts will hail it; and if Freedom, Truth, and Justice is remembered, what matters it if Josiah Allen's wife is forgotten."

Says she, "I *will* hammer 'em."

I declare for't I had forgot where I was, and who I was, and who she was, and who Josiah was—I was carried away such a distance by my emotions. But her remark soared up like a brass pin or a tack nail, and pierced my wrapped mood. I see I hadn't convinced her, her eyes looked wild and glarin'.

"Well," says I, "if you do you will probable have the worst of it, besides injurin' the hammer."

Jest at that very minute I see Josiah a comin', and I watched that beloved and approachin' form for mebby half or two thirds of a minute, and when I looked round again she was gone, and I was glad on't; I never liked her looks. And in a few minutes Miss Bean come too, and says she: "Don't you want to go and see some relicks?"

Says I, "I haint particular either way. Bein' a respectable married woman with a livin' pardner of my own, I shant make no move either way, I shant run towards 'em or from 'em. Havin' lived a vegetable widow for so many years, I s'pose *you* feel different about relicks."

Says she, "I mean relicks from Jerusalem and other old places, made out of wood from Mount Olive, and the cross, and the Holy Sepulchre, and so 4th." And then she kinder whispered to me: "They do say that they have used up more than ten cords of stovewood right here in the village of Filadelphy, a makin' relicks for Turks to sell—Turks right from Ireland." Says she, "You are so awful patriotic you ort to see George Washington's clothes, and old Independence Hall, and Liberty bell."

Says I in agitated axents: "Cousin Bean has George Washington got any clothes here to the Sentinal?"

"Yes," says she, "they are in the United States Government Buildin'."

I gripped holt of her hand, and says I, "Lead me there instantly!" and she led the way to the buildin'.

But though I see everything on my way and more too seeminly, I didn't seem to sense anything as it should be sensed, till I stood before them relicks; and then, oh! what feelins I did feel as I see that coat and vest that George had buttoned up so many times over true patriotism, truthfulness, and honor. When I see the bed he had slept on, the little round table he had eat on, the wooden bottomed chair he had sot down on, the belluses he had blowed the fire with in cold storms and discouragements; and then to see the bed quilts worked by his own mother, and to think what powerful emotions, what burnin' plans, what eager hopes, and what dark despairs they had covered up in 76. And then to see—a layin' on the bed—the cane that Benjamin give to George, and to see George's glasses and candle stick, and trunks and etcetery. Why, they all rousted up my mind so, that I told Josiah I must see Independance Hall before I slept, or I wouldn't answer for the consequences.

Oliver Wendell Holmes

(1809–1894)

❧ ❧ ❧

FROM *The Autocrat of the Breakfast Table*

—All generous minds have a horror of what are commonly called "facts." They are the brute beasts of the intellectual domain. Who does not know fellows that always have an ill-conditioned fact or two which they lead after them into decent company like so many bull-dogs, ready to let them slip at every ingenious suggestion, or convenient generalization, or pleasant fancy? I allow no "facts" at this table. What! Because bread is good and wholesome and necessary and nourishing, shall you thrust a crumb into my windpipe while I am talking? Do not these muscles of mine represent a hundred loaves of bread? and is not my thought the abstract of ten thousand of these crumbs of truth with which you would choke off my speech?

[The above remark must be conditioned and qualified for the vulgar mind. The reader will of course understand the precise amount of seasoning which must be added to it before he adopts it as one of the axioms of his life. The speaker disclaims all responsibility for its abuse in incompetent hands.]

This business of conversation is a very serious matter. There are men that it weakens one to talk with an hour more than a day's fasting would do. Mark this that I am going to say, for it is as good as a working professional man's advice, and costs you nothing: It is better to lose a pint of blood from your veins than to have a nerve tapped. Nobody measures your nervous force as it runs away, nor bandages your brain and marrow after the operation.

There are men of *esprit* who are excessively exhausting to some people. They are the talkers who have what may be called *jerky* minds. Their thoughts do not run in the natural order of sequence. They say bright things on all possible subjects, but their zigzags rack you to death. After a jolting half-hour with one of these jerky companions, talking with a dull friend affords great relief. It is like taking the cat in your lap after holding a squirrel.

What a comfort a dull but kindly person is, to be sure, at times! A ground-glass shade over a gas-lamp does not bring more solace to our dazzled eyes than such a one to our minds.

"Do not dull people bore you?" said one of the lady-boarders,—the same that sent me her autograph-book last week with a request for a few original stanzas, not remembering that "The Pactolian" pays me five dollars a line for every thing I write in its columns.

"Madam," said I, (she and the century were in their teens together,) "all men are bores, except when we want them. There never was but one man whom I would trust with my latch-key."

"Who might that favored person be?"

"Zimmermann."

—The men of genius that I fancy most have erectile heads like the cobra-di-capello. You remember what they tell of William Pinkney, the great pleader; how in his eloquent paroxysms the veins of his neck would swell and his face flush and his eyes glitter, until he seemed on the verge of apoplexy. The hydraulic arrangements for supplying the brain with blood are only second in importance to its own organization. The bulbous-headed fellows that steam well when they are at work are the men that draw big audiences and give us marrowy books and pictures. It is a good sign to have one's feet grow cold when he is writing. A great writer and speaker once told me that he often wrote with his feet in hot water; but for this, *all* his blood would have run into his head, as the mercury sometimes withdraws into the ball of a thermometer.

—You don't suppose that my remarks made at this table are like so many postage-stamps, do you,—each to be only once uttered? If you do, you are mistaken. He must be a poor creature that does not often repeat himself. Imagine the author of the excellent piece of advice, "Know thyself," never alluding to that sentiment again during the course of a protracted existence! Why, the truths a man carries about with him are his tools; and do you think a carpenter is bound to use the same plane but once to smooth a knotty board with, or to hang up his hammer after it has driven its first nail? I shall never repeat a conversation, but an idea often. I shall use the same types when I like, but not commonly the same stereotypes. A thought is often original, though you have uttered it a hundred times. It has come to you over a new route, by a new and express train of associations.

Sometimes, but rarely, one may be caught making the same speech twice over, and yet be held blameless. Thus, a certain lecturer, after performing in an inland city, where dwells a *Littératrice* of note, was invited to meet her and others over the social teacup. She pleasantly referred to his many wanderings in his new occupation. "Yes," he replied, "I am like the Huma, the bird that never lights, being always in the cars, as he is always on the wing."—Years elapsed. The lecturer visited the same place once more for the same purpose. Another social cup after the lecture, and a second meeting with the distinguished lady. "You are constantly going from place to place," she said.—"Yes," he answered, "I am like the Huma,"—and finished the sentence as before. What horrors, when it flashed over him that he had made this fine speech, word for word, twice over! Yet it was not true, as the lady might perhaps have fairly inferred, that he had embellished his conversation with the Huma daily during that whole interval of years. On the contrary, he had never once thought of the odious fowl until the recurrence of precisely the same circumstances brought up precisely the same idea. He ought to have been proud of the accuracy of his mental adjustments. Given certain factors, and a sound brain should always evolve the same fixed product with the certainty of Babbage's calculating machine.

—What a satire, by the way, is that machine on the mere mathematician! A Frankenstein-monster, a thing without brains and without heart, too stupid to make a blunder; that turns out results like a cornsheller, and never grows any wiser or better, though it grind a thousand bushels of them!

I have an immense respect for a man of talents *plus* "the mathematics." But the calculating power alone should seem to be the least human of qualities, and to have the smallest amount of reason in it; since a machine can be made to do the work of three or four calculators, and better than any one of them. Sometimes I have been troubled that I had not a deeper intuitive apprehension of the relations of numbers. But the triumph of the ciphering hand-organ has consoled me. I always fancy I can hear the wheels clicking in a calculator's brain. The power of dealing with numbers is a kind of "detached lever" arrangement, which may be put into a mighty poor watch. I suppose it is about as common as the power of moving the ears voluntarily, which is a moderately rare endowment.

—Little localized powers, and little narrow streaks of specialized knowledge, are things men are very apt to be conceited about. Nature is very wise; but for this encouraging principle how many small talents and little accomplishments would be neglected! Talk about conceit as much as you like, it is to human character what salt is to the ocean; it keeps it sweet, and renders it endurable. Say rather it is like the natural unguent of the sea-fowl's plumage, which enables him to shed the rain that falls on him and the wave in which he dips. When one has had *all* his conceit taken out of him, when he has lost *all* his illusions, his feathers will soon soak through, and he will fly no more.

•

—I wonder if you know the *terrible smile*? [The young fellow whom they call John winked very hard, and made a jocular remark, the sense of which seemed to depend on some double meaning of the word *smile*. The company was curious to know what I meant.]

There are persons—I said—who no sooner come within sight of you than they begin to smile, with an uncertain movement of the mouth, which conveys the idea that they are thinking about themselves, and thinking, too, that you are thinking they are thinking about themselves,—and so look at you with a wretched mixture of self-consciousness, awkwardness, and attempts to carry off both, which are betrayed by the cowardly behaviour of the eye and the tell-tale weakness of the lips that characterize these unfortunate beings.

—Why do you call them unfortunate, Sir?—asked the divinity-student.

Because it is evident that the consciousness of some imbecility or other is at the bottom of this extraordinary expression. I don't think, however, that these persons are commonly fools. I have known a number, and all of them were intelligent. I think nothing conveys the idea of *underbreeding* more than this self-betraying smile. Yet I think this peculiar habit as well as that of *meaningless blushing*, may be fallen into by very good people who meet often, or sit opposite each other at table. A true gentleman's face is infinitely removed from all such paltriness,—calm-eyed, firm-mouthed. I think Titian understood the look of a gentleman as well as anybody that ever lived. The portrait of a young man holding a glove in his hand, in the Gallery of the Louvre, if any of you have seen that collection, will remind you of what I mean.

—Do I think these people know the peculiar look they have?—I cannot say; I hope not; I am afraid they would never forgive me, if they did. The worst of it is, the trick is catching; when one meets one of these fellows, he feels a tendency to the same manifestation. The Professor tells me there is a muscular slip, a dependence of the *platysma myoides*, which is called the *risorius Santorini*.

—Say that once more,—exclaimed the young fellow mentioned above.

The Professor says there is a little fleshy slip called Santorini's laughing muscle. I would have it cut out of my face, if I were born with one of those constitutional grins upon it. Perhaps I am uncharitable in my judgment of those sour-looking people I told you of the other day, and of these smiling folks. It may be that they are born with these looks, as other people are with more generally recognized deformities. Both are bad enough, but I had rather meet three of the scowlers than one of the smilers.

—There is another unfortunate way of looking, which is peculiar to that amiable sex we do not like to find fault with. There are some very pretty, but, unhappily, very ill-bred women, who don't understand the law of the road with regard to handsome faces. Nature and custom would, no doubt, agree in conceding to all males the right of at least two distinct looks at every comely female countenance, without any infraction of the rules of courtesy or the sentiment of respect. The first look is necessary to define the person of the individual one meets so as to avoid it in passing. Any unusual attraction detected in a first glance is a sufficient apology for a second,—not a prolonged and impertinent stare, but an appreciating homage of the eyes, such as a stranger may inoffensively yield to a passing image. It is astonishing how morbidly sensitive some vulgar beauties are to the slightest demonstration of this kind. When a *lady* walks the streets, she leaves her virtuous-indignation countenance at home; she knows well enough that the street is a picture-gallery, where pretty faces framed in pretty bonnets are meant to be seen, and everybody has a right to see them.

—When we observe how the same features and style of person and character descend from generation to generation, we can believe that some inherited weakness may account for these peculiarities. Little snapping-turtles snap—so the great naturalist tells us—before they are out of the egg-shell. I am satisfied, that, much higher up in the scale of life, character is distinctly shown at the age of—2 or—3 months.

—My friend, the Professor, has been full of eggs lately. [This remark excited a burst of hilarity, which I did not allow to interrupt the course of my observations.] He has been reading the great book where he found the fact about the little snapping-turtles mentioned above. Some of the things he has told me have suggested several odd analogies enough.

There are half a dozen men, or so, who carry in their brains the *ovarian eggs* of the next generation's or century's civilization. These eggs are not ready to be laid in the form of books as yet; some of them are hardly ready to be put into the form of talk. But as rudimentary ideas or inchoate tendencies, there they are; and these are what must form the future. A man's general notions are not good for much, unless he has a crop of these intellectual ovarian eggs in his own brain, or knows them as they exist in the minds of others. One must be in the *habit* of talking with such persons to get at these rudimentary germs of thought; for their development is necessarily imperfect, and they are moulded on new patterns, which must be long and closely studied. But these are the men to talk with. No fresh truth ever gets into a book.

—A good many fresh lies get in, anyhow,—said one of the company.

I proceeded in spite of the interruption.—All uttered thought, my friend, the Professor, says, is of the nature of an excretion. Its materials have been taken in, and have acted upon the system, and been reacted on by it; it has circulated and done its office in one mind before it is given out for the benefit of others. It may be milk or venom to other minds; but, in either case, it is something which the producer has had the use of and can part with. A man instinctively tries to get rid of his thought in conversation or in print so soon as it is matured; but it is hard to get at it as it lies imbedded, a mere potentiality, the germ of a germ, in his intellect.

—Where are the brains that are fullest of these ovarian eggs of thought?—I decline mentioning individuals. The producers of thought, who are few, the "jobbers" of thought, who are many, and the retailers of thought, who are numberless, are so mixed up in the popular apprehension, that it would be hopeless to try to separate them before opinion has had time to settle. Follow the course of opinion on the great subjects of human interest for a few generations or centuries, get its parallax, map out a small arc of its movement, see where it tends, and then see who is in advance of it or even with it; the world calls him hard names, probably;

but if you would find the *ova* of the future, you must look into the folds of his cerebral convolutions.

[The divinity-student looked a little puzzled at this suggestion, as if he did not see exactly where he was to come out, if he computed his arc too nicely. I think it possible it might cut off a few corners of his present belief, as it has cut off martyr-burning and witch-hanging;—but time will show,—time will show, as the old gentleman opposite says.]

William Dean Howells
(1837–1920)

Kitty Answers

It was dimmest twilight when Kitty entered Mrs. Ellison's room, and sank down on the first chair in silence.

"The Colonel met a friend at the St. Louis, and forgot about the expedition, Kitty," said Fanny, "and he only came in half-an-hour ago. But it's just as well; I know you've had a splendid time. Where's Mr. Arbuton?"

Kitty burst into tears.

"Why, has anything happened to him?" cried Mrs. Ellison, springing towards her.

"To him? No! What should happen to *him*?" Kitty demanded, with an indignant accent.

"Well, then, has anything happened to *you*?"

"I don't know if you can call it *happening*. But I suppose you'll be satisfied now, Fanny. He's offered himself to me."

Kitty uttered the last words with a sort of violence, as if, since the fact must be stated, she wished it to appear in the sharpest relief.

"Oh, dear!" said Mrs. Ellison, not so well satisfied as the successful match-maker ought to be. So long as it was a marriage in the abstract, she had never ceased to desire it; but as the actual union of Kitty and this Mr. Arbuton, of whom, really, they knew so little, and of whom, if she searched her heart, she had as little liking as knowledge, it was another affair. Mrs. Ellison trembled at her triumph, and began to think that failure would have been easier to bear. Were they in the least suited to each other? Would she like to see poor Kitty chained for life to that impassive egotist, whose very merits were repellent, and whose modesty even seemed to convict and snub you? Mrs. Ellison was not able to put the matter to herself with moderation, either way; doubtless she did Mr. Arbuton injustice now.

"Did you accept him?" she whispered feebly.

"Accept him?" repeated Kitty. "No!"

"Oh, dear!" again sighed Mrs. Ellison, feeling that this was scarcely better, and not daring to ask further.

"I'm dreadfully perplexed, Fanny," said Kitty, after waiting for the questions which did not come, "and I wish you'd help me think."

"I will, darling. But I don't know that I'll be of much use. I begin to think I'm not very good at thinking."

Kitty, who longed chiefly to get the situation more distinctly before herself, gave no heed to this confession, but went on to rehearse the whole affair. The twilight lent her its veil; and in the kindly obscurity she gathered courage to face all the facts, and even to find what was droll in them.

"It was very solemn, of course, and I was frightened; but I tried to keep my wits about me, and *not* to say yes, simply because that was the easiest thing. I told him that I didn't know,—and I don't; and that I must have time to think,—and I must. He was very ungenerous, and said he had hoped I had already had time to think; and he couldn't seem to understand, or else I couldn't very well explain, how it had been with me all along."

"He might certainly say you had encouraged him," Mrs. Ellison remarked, thoughtfully.

"Encouraged him, Fanny? How can you accuse me of such indelicacy?"

"Encouraging isn't indelicacy. The gentlemen *have* to be encouraged, or of course they'd never have any courage. They're so timid, naturally."

"I don't think Mr. Arbuton is very timid. He seemed

to think that he had only to ask as a matter of form, and I had no business to say anything. What has he ever done for me? And hasn't he often been intensely disagreeable? He oughtn't to have spoken just after overhearing what he did. It was horrid to do so. He was very obtuse, too, not to see that girls can't always be so certain of themselves as men, or, if they are, don't know they are as soon as they're asked."

"Yes," interrupted Mrs. Ellison, "that's the way with girls. I do believe that most of them—when they're young like you, Kitty—never think of marriage as the end of their flirtations. They'd just like the attentions and the romance to go on for ever, and never turn into anything more serious; and they're not to blame for that, though they *do* get blamed for it."

"Certainly," assented Kitty eagerly, "that's it; that's just what I was saying; that's the very reason why girls must have time to make up their minds. *You* had, I suppose."

"Yes, two minutes. Poor Dick was going back to his regiment, and stood with his watch in his hand. I said no, and called after him to correct myself. But, Kitty, if the romance had happened to stop without his saying anything, you wouldn't have liked that either, would you?"

"No," faltered Kitty; "I suppose not."

"Well, then, don't you see? That's a great point in his favour. How much time did you want, or did he give you?"

"I said I should answer before we left Quebec," answered Kitty, with a heavy sigh.

"Don't you know what to say now?"

"I can't tell. That's what I want you to help me think out."

Mrs. Ellison was silent for a moment before she said, "Well, then, I suppose we shall have to go back to the very beginning."

"Yes," assented Kitty, faintly.

"You did have a sort of fancy for him the first time you saw him, didn't you?" asked Mrs. Ellison coaxingly, while forcing herself to be systematic and coherent, by a mental strain of which no idea can be given.

"Yes," said Kitty, yet more faintly, adding, "but I can't tell just what sort of a fancy it was. I suppose I admired him for being handsome and stylish, and for having such exquisite manners."

"Go on," said Mrs. Ellison; "and after you got acquainted with him?"

"Why, you know we've talked that over once already, Fanny."

"Yes, but we oughtn't to skip anything now," replied Mrs. Ellison, in a tone of judicial accuracy, which made Kitty smile.

But she quickly became serious again, and said, "Afterwards I couldn't tell whether to like him or not, or whether he wanted me to. I think he acted very strangely for a person in—love. I used to feel so troubled and oppressed when I was with him. He seemed always to be making himself agreeable under protest."

"Perhaps that was just your imagination, Kitty."

"Perhaps it was; but it troubled me just the same."

"Well, and then?"

"Well, and then after that day of the Montgomery expedition he seemed to change altogether, and to try always to be pleasant, and to do everything he could to make me like him. I don't know how to account for it. Ever since then he's been extremely careful of me, and behaved—of course without knowing it—as if I belonged to him already. Or maybe I've imagined that too. It's very hard to tell what has really happened the last two weeks."

Kitty was silent, and Mrs. Ellison did not speak at once. Presently she asked, "Was his acting as if you belonged to him disagreeable?"

"I can't tell. I think it was rather presuming. I don't know why he did it."

"Do you respect him?" demanded Mrs. Ellison.

"Why, Fanny, I've always told you that I did respect some things in him."

Mrs. Ellison had the facts before her, and it rested upon her to sum them up, and do something with them. She rose to a sitting posture, and confronted her task.

"Well, Kitty, I'll tell you. I don't really know what to think. But I can say this: if you liked him at first, and then didn't like him, and afterwards he made himself more agreeable, and you didn't mind his behaving as if you belonged to him, and you respected him, but after all didn't think him fascinating——"

"He *is* fascinating—in a kind of way. He was, from the

beginning. In a story his cold, snubbing, putting-down ways would have been perfectly fascinating."

"Then why didn't you take him?"

"Because," answered Kitty, between laughing and crying, "it isn't a story, and I don't know whether I like him."

"But do you think you might get to like him?"

"I don't know. His asking brings all the doubts I ever had of him, and that I've been forgetting the past two weeks. I can't tell whether I like him or not. If I did, shouldn't I trust him more?"

"Well, whether you are in love or not, I'll tell you what you *are,* Kitty," cried Mrs. Ellison, provoked with her indecision, and yet relieved that the worst, whatever it was, was postponed thereby for a day or two.

"What?"

"You're——"

But at this important juncture the colonel came lounging in, and Kitty glided out of the room.

"Richard," said Mrs. Ellison, seriously, and in a tone implying that it was the colonel's fault, as usual, "you know what has happened, I suppose?"

"No, my dear, I don't; but no matter: I will presently, I daresay."

"Oh, I wish for once you wouldn't be so flippant. Mr. Arbuton has offered himself to Kitty."

Colonel Ellison gave a quick, sharp whistle of amazement, but trusted himself to nothing more articulate.

"Yes," said his wife, responding to the whistle, "and it makes me perfectly wretched."

"Why, I thought you liked him."

"I didn't *like* him; but I thought it would be an excellent thing for Kitty."

"And won't it?"

"She doesn't know."

"Doesn't know?"

"No."

The colonel was silent, while Mrs. Ellison stated the case in full, and its pending uncertainty. Then he exclaimed vehemently as if his amazement had been growing upon him. "This is the most astonishing thing in the world! Who would ever have dreamt of that young iceberg being in love?"

"Haven't I *told* you all along he was?"

"Oh yes, certainly! but that might be taken either way, you know. You would discover the tender passion in the eye of a potato."

"Colonel Ellison," said Fanny, with sternness, "why do you suppose he's been hanging about us for the last four weeks? Why should he have stayed in Quebec? Do you think he pitied *me,* or found *you* so very agreeable?"

"Well, I thought he found us just tolerable, and was interested in the place."

Mrs. Ellison made no direct reply to this pitiable speech, but looked a scorn which, happily for the colonel, the darkness hid. Presently she said that bats did not express the blindness of men, for any bat could have seen what was going on.

"Why," remarked the colonel, "I did have a momentary suspicion that day of the Montgomery business; they both looked very confused when I saw them at the end of that street, and neither of them had anything to say; but that was accounted for by what you told me afterwards about his adventure. At the time I didn't pay much attention to the matter. The idea of his being in love seemed too ridiculous."

"Was it ridiculous for you to be in love with me?"

"No; and yet I can't praise my condition for its wisdom, Fanny."

"Yes! that's *like* men. As soon as one of them is safely married, he thinks all the love-making in the world has been done for ever, and he can't conceive of two young people taking a fancy to each other."

"That's something so, Fanny. But granting—for the sake of argument merely—that Boston has been asking Kitty to marry him, and she doesn't know whether she wants him, what are we to do about it? *I* don't like him well enough to plead his cause; do you? When does Kitty think she'll be able to make up her mind?"

"She's to let him know before we leave."

The colonel laughed. "And so he's to hang about here on uncertainties for two whole days! That *is* rather rough on him. Fanny, what made you so eager for this business?"

"Eager? I *wasn't* eager."

"Well, then,—reluctantly acquiescent?"

"Why, she's so literary and that."

"And what?"

"How insulting! Intellectual, and so on; and I thought she would be just fit to live in a place where everybody is literary and intellectual. That is, I thought that, if I thought anything."

"Well," said the colonel, "you may have been right on the whole, but I don't think Kitty is showing any particular force of mind, just now, that would fit her to live in Boston. My opinion is, that it's ridiculous for her to keep him in suspense. She might as well answer him first as last. She's putting herself under a kind of obligation by her delay. I'll talk to her——"

"If you do, you'll kill her. You don't know how she's wrought up about it."

"Oh, well, I'll be careful of her sensibilities. It's my duty to speak with her. I'm here in the place of a parent. Besides, don't I know Kitty? I've almost brought her up."

"Maybe you're right. You're all so queer that perhaps you're right. Only do be careful, Richard. You must approach the matter very delicately, indirectly, you know. Girls are different, remember, from young men, and you mustn't be blunt. Do manoeuvre a little, for once in your life."

"All right, Fanny; you needn't be afraid of my doing anything awkward or sudden. I'll go to her room pretty soon, after she is quieted down, and have a good, calm, old, fatherly conversation with her."

The colonel was spared this errand; for Kitty had left some of her things on Fanny's table, and now came back for them with a lamp in her hand. Her averted face showed the marks of weeping; the corners of her firm-set lips were downward bent, as if some resolutions which she had taken were very painful. This the anxious Fanny saw; and she made a gesture to the colonel which any woman would have understood to enjoin silence, or, at least, the utmost caution and tenderness of speech. The colonel summoned his *finesse* and said, cheerily, "Well, Kitty, what's Boston been saying to you?"

Mrs. Ellison fell back upon her sofa as if shot, and placed her hands over her face.

Kitty seemed not to hear her cousin. Having gathered up her things, she bent an unmoved face and an unseeing gaze full upon him, and glided from the room without a word.

"Well, upon my soul," cried the colonel, "this is a pleasant, nightmarist, sleep-walking, Lady-Macbethish, little transaction. Confound it, Fanny! this comes of your wanting me to manoeuvre. If you'd let me come straight *at* the subject, like a *man*——"

"*Please,* Richard, don't say anything more now," pleaded Mrs. Ellison in a broken voice. "You can't help it, I know; and I must do the best I can, under the circumstances. Do go away for a little while, darling! Oh dear!"

Langston Hughes (1902–1967)

≈≈≈

FROM *Laughing to Keep from Crying*

We all ordered fish and settled down comfortably to shocking our white friends with tales about how many Negroes there were passing for white all over America. We were determined to *épater le bourgeois* real good via this white couple we had cornered, when the woman leaned over the table in the midst of our dissertations and said, "Listen, gentlemen, you needn't spread the word, but me and my husband aren't white either. We've just been *passing* for white for the last fifteen years."

"What?"

"We're colored, too, just like you," said the husband. "But it's better passing for white because we make more money."

Well, that took the wind out of us. It took the wind out of Caleb, too. He thought all the time he was showing some fine white folks Harlem—and they were as colored as he was!

Caleb almost never cursed. But this time he said, "I'll be damned!"

Then everybody laughed. And laughed! We almost had hysterics. All at once we dropped our professionally self-conscious "Negro" manners, became natural, ate fish, and talked and kidded freely like colored folks do when there are no white folks around. We really had fun then, joking about that red-haired guy who mistook a fair colored woman for white. After the fish we went to two or three more night spots and drank until five o'clock in the morning.

Finally we put the light-colored people in a taxi heading downtown. They turned to shout a last good-by. The cab was just about to move off, when the woman called to the driver to stop.

She leaned out the window and said with a grin, "Listen, boys! I hate to confuse you again. But, to tell the truth, my husband and I aren't really colored at all. We're white. We just thought we'd kid you by passing for colored a little while—just as you said Negroes sometimes pass for white."

She laughed as they sped off toward Central Park, waving, "Good-by!"

Zora Neale Hurston (1891–1960)

಄ೲ

FROM *Their Eyes Were Watching God*

The more people in there the more ridicule he poured over her body to point attention away from his own. So one day Steve Mixon wanted some chewing tobacco and Janie cut it wrong. She hated that tobacco knife anyway. It worked very stiff. She fumbled with the thing and cut way away from the mark. Mixon didn't mind. He held it up for a joke to tease Janie a little.

"Looka heah, Brother Mayor, whut yo' wife done took and done." It was cut comical, so everybody laughed at it. "Uh woman and uh knife—no kind of uh knife, don't b'long tuhgether." There was some more good-natured laughter at the expense of women.

Jody didn't laugh. He hurried across from the post office side and took the plug of tobacco away from Mixon and cut it again. Cut it exactly on the mark and glared at Janie.

"I god amighty! A woman can stay round uh store till she get old as Methusalem and still can't cut a little thing like a plug of tobacco! Don't stand dere rollin' yo' pop eyes at me wid yo' rump hangin' nearly to yo' knees!"

A big laugh started off in the store but people got to thinking and stopped. It was funny if you looked at it right quick, but it got pitiful if you thought about it awhile. It was like somebody snatched off part of a woman's clothes while she wasn't looking and the streets were crowded. Then too, Janie took the middle of the floor to talk right into Jody's face, and that was something that hadn't been done before.

"Stop mixin' up mah doings wid mah looks, Jody. When you git through tellin' me how tuh cut uh plug uh tobacco, then you kin tell me whether mah behind is on straight or not."

"Wha—whut's dat you say, Janie? You must be out yo' head."

"Naw, Ah ain't outa mah head neither."

"You must be. Talkin' any such language as dat."

"You de one started talkin' under people's clothes. Not me."

"Whut's de matter wid you, nohow? You ain't no young girl to be gettin' all insulted 'bout yo' looks. You ain't no young courtin' gal. You'se uh ole woman, nearly forty."

"Yeah, Ah'm nearly forty and you'se already fifty. How come you can't talk about dat sometimes instead of always pointin' at me?"

"T'ain't no use in gettin' all mad, Janie, 'cause Ah mention you ain't no young gal no mo'. Nobody in heah ain't lookin' for no wife outa yuh. Old as you is."

"Naw, Ah ain't no young gal no mo' but den Ah ain't no old woman neither. Ah reckon Ah looks mah age too. But Ah'm uh woman every inch of me, and Ah know it. Dat's uh whole lot more'n *you* kin say. You big-bellies round here and put out a lot of brag, but 'tain't nothin' to it but yo' big voice. Humph! Talkin' 'bout *me* lookin' old! When you pull down yo' britches, you look lak de change uh life."

"Great God from Zion!" Sam Watson gasped. "Y'all really playin' de dozens tuhnight."

Molly Ivins (Contemporary)

FROM *Molly Ivins Can't Say That, Can She*

State of the States

Speaking of Baton Rouge, when David Duke, the newest member of the Louisiana Legislature, was the chief chees and sheet-washer for the Knights of the Ku Klux Klan, he took the Dale Carnegie course in how to win friends and influence people. Honest. At the time, the case of the Klansman who took the Carnegie course (where they teach you to say heartily, 'Gosh, isn't this a good party?' and 'My, aren't we having a lot of fun?') seemed to be just another reason not to write fiction.

Lubbock: Seat of Rebellion

One thing I like about Lubbock is that people there know what sin is. There's more confusion on that issue than many people realize, with all this bushwa about being nonjudgmental. The advantage of being able to identify sin is that you can go out and do it, and enjoy it.

Honky Tonking

Many cultures have popular song forms that reflect the people's concerns. In Latin cultures the *corridos*, written by immortal poets such as Garcia Lorca, give voice to the yearnings of the voiceless. In our culture, 'Take This Job and Shove It' serves much the same function. If you want to take the pulse of the people in this country, listen to country-western music.

Yet a surprising number of men are alarmed by the thought of a witty woman. . . . Margaret Atwood, the Canadian novelist, once asked a group of women at a university why they felt threatened by men. The women said they were afraid of being beaten, raped, or killed by men. She then asked a group of men why they felt threatened by women. They said they were afraid women would laugh at them.

Henry James (1843–1916)

FROM *The Portrait of a Lady*

'You know, if you don't like Lockleigh—if you think it's damp or anything of that sort—you need never go within fifty miles of it. It's not damp, by the way; I've had the house thoroughly examined; it's perfectly safe and right. But if you shouldn't fancy it you needn't dream of living in it. There's no difficulty whatever about that; there are plenty of houses. I thought I'd just mention it, some people don't like a moat, you know. Good-bye.'

'I adore a moat,' said Isabel. 'Good-bye.'

•

Madame Merle tossed away the music with a smile. 'What's your idea of success?"

'You evidently think it must be a very tame one. It's to see some dream of one's youth come true. . . . I began to dream very young,' Isabel smiled

'Ah, if you mean the aspirations of your childhood—that of having a pink sash and a doll that could close her eyes.'

'No, I don't mean that.'

'Or a young man with a fine moustache going down on his knees to you.'

'No, nor that either,' Isabel declared with still more emphasis.

Madame Merle appeared to note this eagerness. 'I suspect that's what you do mean. We've all had the young man with the moustache. He's the inevitable young man; he doesn't count.'

Erica Jong (Contemporary)

~~~

FROM *Fear of Flying*

We drove to the hotel and said goodbye. How hypocritical to go upstairs with a man you don't want to fuck, leave the one you do sitting there alone, and then, in a state of great excitement, fuck the one you don't want to fuck while pretending he's the one you do. That's called fidelity. That's called monogamy. That's called civilization and its discontents.

•

I was a little appalled at my own promiscuity, that I could go from one man to another and feel so glowing and intoxicated. I knew I would have to pay for it later with the guilt and misery which I alone know how to give myself in such good measure. But right now I was happy. I felt properly appreciated for the first time. Do two men perhaps add up to one whole person?

•

Bennett's careful, compulsive, and boring steadfastness was my own panic about change, my fear of being alone, my need for security. Adrian's antic manners and ass-grabbing was the part of me that wanted exuberance above all. I had never been able to make peace between the two halves of myself. All I had managed to do was suppress one half (for a while) at the expense of the other. I had never been happy with the bourgeois virtues of marriage, stability, and work above pleasure. I was too curious and adventurous not to chafe under those restrictions. But I also suffered from night terrors and attacks of panic at being alone. So I always wound up living with somebody or being married.

Besides I really believed in pursuing a longstanding and deep relationship with one person. I could easily see the sterility of hopping from bed to bed and having shallow affairs with lots of shallow people. I had had the unutterably dismal experience of waking up in bed with a man I couldn't bear to talk to—and that was certainly no liberation either. But still, there just didn't seem to be any way to get the best of both exuberance and stability into your life. The fact that greater minds than mine had pondered these issues and come up with no very clear answers didn't comfort me much either. It only made me feel that my concerns were banal and commonplace. If I were really an exceptional person, I thought, I wouldn't spend hours worrying my head about marriage and adultery. I would just go out and snatch life with both hands and feel no remorse or guilt for anything. My guilt only showed how thoroughly bourgeois and contemptible I was. All my worrying this sad old bone only showed my ordinariness.

•

The ultimate sexist put-down: the prick which lies down on the job. The ultimate weapon in the war between the sexes: the limp prick. The banner of the enemy's encampment: the prick at half-mast. The symbol of the apocalypse: the atomic warhead prick which self-destructs. *That* was the basic inequity which could never be righted: not that the male had a wonderful added attraction called a penis, but that the female had a wonderful all-weather cunt. Neither storm nor sleet nor dark of night could faze it. It was always there, always ready. Quite terrifying, when you think about it. No wonder men hated women. No wonder they invented the myth of female inadequacy.

•

Why should a bad marriage have been so much more compelling than no marriage? Why had I clung to my misery so? Why did I believe it was all I had?

As I read the notebook, I began to be drawn into it as into a novel. I almost began to forget that I had written it. And then a curious revelation started to dawn. I stopped blaming myself; it was that simple. Perhaps my finally running away was not due to malice on my part, nor to any disloyalty I need apologize for. Perhaps it was a kind of loyalty to myself. A drastic but necessary way of changing my life.

You did not have to apologize for wanting to own your own soul. Your soul belonged to you—for better or for worse. When all was said and done, it was all you had.

Marriage was tricky because in some ways it was always a *folie à deux.* At times you scarcely knew where your own lunacies left off and those of your spouse began. You tended to blame yourself too much, or not enough, or for the wrong things. And you tended to confuse dependency with love.

I went on reading and with each page I grew more philosophical. I knew I did not want to return to the marriage described in that notebook. If Bennett and I got back together again, it would have to be under very different circumstances. And if we did not, I knew I would survive.

No electric light bulb went on in my head with that recognition. Nor did I leap into the air and shout *Eureka*! I sat very quietly looking at the pages I had written. I knew I did not want to be trapped in my own book.

It was also heartening to see how much I had changed in the past four years. I was able to send my work out now. I was not afraid to drive. I was able to spend long hours alone writing. I taught, gave lectures, traveled. Terrified of flying as I was, I didn't allow that fear to control me. Perhaps someday I'd lose it altogether. If some things could change, so could other things. What right had I to predict the future and predict it so nihilistically? As I got older I would probably change in hundreds of ways I couldn't foresee. All I had to do was wait it out.

It was easy enough to kill yourself in a fit of despair. It was easy enough to play the martyr. It was harder to do nothing. To endure your life. To wait.

I slept. I think I actually fell asleep with my face pressed to my spiral notebook. I remember waking up in the blue hours of early morning and feeling a spiral welt on the side of my cheek. Then I pushed away the notebook and went back to sleep.

And my dreams were extravagant. Full of elevators, platforms in space, enormously steep and slippery staircases, ziggurat temples I had to climb, mountains, towers, ruins . . . I had some vague sense that I was *assigning* myself dreams as a sort of cure. I remember once or twice waking and then falling back to sleep thinking: "Now I will have the dream which makes my decision for me." But what was the decision I sought? Every choice seemed so unsatisfactory in one way or another. Every choice excluded some other choice. It was as if I were asking my dreams to tell me who I was and what I ought do do. I would wake with my heart pounding and then sink back to sleep again. Maybe I was hoping I'd wake up somebody else.

Fragments of those dreams are still with me. In one of them, I had to walk a narrow plank between two skyscrapers in order to save someone's life. Whose? Mine? Bennett's? Chloe's? The dream did not say. But it was clear that if I failed, my own life would be over. In another, I reached inside myself to take out my diaphragm, and there, floating over my cervix, was a large contact lens. Womb with a view. The cervix was really an eye. And a nearsighted eye at that.

Then I remember the dream in which I was back in college preparing to receive my degree from Millicent McIntosh. I walked up a long flight of steps which looked more like the steps of a Mexican temple than the steps of Low Library. I teetered on very high heels and worried about tripping over my gown.

As I approached the lectern and Mrs. McIntosh held out a scroll to me, I realized that I was not merely graduating but was to receive some special honor.

"I must tell you that the faculty does not approve of this," Mrs. McIntosh said. And I knew then that the fellowship conferred on me the right to have three husbands simultaneously. They sat in the audience wearing black caps and gowns: Bennett, Adrian, and some other man whose face was not clear. They were all waiting to applaud when I got my diploma.

"Only your high academic achievement makes it impossible for us to withhold this honor," Mrs. McIntosh said, "but the faculty hopes you will decline of your own volition."

"But why?" I protested. "Why *can't* I have all three?"

After that I began a long rationalizing speech about marriage and my sexual needs and how I was a poet not a secretary. I stood at the lectern and ranted at the audience. Mrs.

McIntosh looked soberly disapproving. Then I was picking my way down the steep steps, half crouching and terrified of falling. I looked into the sea of faces and suddenly realized that I had forgotten to take my scroll. In a panic I knew that I had forfeited everything: graduation, my fellowship grant, my harem of three husbands.

The final dream I remember is strangest of all. I was walking up the library steps again to reclaim my diploma. This time it was not Mrs. McIntosh at the lectern, but Colette. Only she was a black woman with frizzy reddish hair glinting around her head like a halo.

"There is only one way to graduate," she said, "and it has nothing to do with the number of husbands."

"What do I have to do?" I asked desperately, feeling I'd do anything.

She handed me a book with my name on the cover. "That was only a very shaky beginning," she said, "but at least you *made* a beginning."

I took this to mean I still had years to go.

"Wait," she said, undoing her blouse. Suddenly I understood that making love to her in public was the real graduation, and at the moment it seemed like the most natural thing in the world. Very aroused, I moved toward her. Then the dream faded.

Judith Katz (Contemporary)

❦❧

FROM *Running Fiercely Toward a High Thin Sound*

Sarah reached up and pinched my cheek. "So you're the maid of honor. Let me set you ladies up in dressing room three."

It took me a minute to remember they were talking about me, that I was the honor maiden. Nonetheless, when Sarah led us to a far corner of the bridal boutique, I followed. Sarah jingled a huge ring of keys and unlocked a white door. "You go in and make yourselves comfortable. Mimi will be in to fit you in a minute."

"It's lovely, isn't it?" my mother gestured broadly at the small private room. Mirrors covered three walls, a white shag rug was on the floor. The furniture was early Barbie doll—two plump white hassocks and a satin couch.

"I hope you have a decent bra on," my mother said as I unbuttoned my shirt. I suddenly couldn't remember if I had on any bra at all, but before I could pull my shirt back on the door swung open and there stood Mimi, who must have been Sarah's depressed twin. She had a tape measure around her neck, a long pink dress slug over one arm, and a pair of white linen pumps clutched between her thick fingers. Sighing deeply, Mimi hung the dress on a chrome hook and set the shoes down at my feet. Then she kneeled in front of me and with the help of a shoe horn slipped my foot into one of the pumps.

"Like a glove," Mimi said as she got me into the other shoe.

"I don't think I can walk." I stood and wobbled from one end of the dressing room to another.

"A little practice, you'll be fine," my mother said.

"Besides, you'll kick them off as soon as the dancing starts."

I was surprised to hear my sister Electa's voice. She hadn't said a word since we got into the department store.

"She won't kick them off," my mother argued.

"I probably will," I answered, disturbed at the whine in my voice, "but still, I have to walk down the aisle—"

"Don't worry, Janie, we've got a nice strong best man for you to lean on when it comes to that." Electa winked conspiratorially.

Best man? I never even considered I'd have to wobble on some strange guy's arm on top of every other thing. "But I still have to stand up at the altar teetering—"

"For God's sake," burst my mother, "the heel is only a half inch—less than that. You can practice standing. It won't kill you—"

"I could break my neck," I said softly.

"Yes, think of the headlines," Electa said, "FEMINIST SISTER DIES IN TRAGIC HIGH HEEL ACCIDENT: 'I DIDN'T THINK IT COULD HAPPEN HERE' SAYS SHOCKED BRIDE."

"Alright, Electa, cut the comedy," my mother said. "Mimi, the shoes fit. Let's try the dress."

"*Oi,* the dress."

"It's not gonna kill you to wear a dress and heels and look like a *mentsh* for five hours."

"It totally contradicts my political world view."

"Stop talking nonsense. Mimi! The dress."

The dress was worse than I'd imagined. The sleeves were sheer, the bodice and hem frilly. I cringed at the thought of wearing it in public. "Electa, this is a real girly outfit."

"I know, Jane. I'm sorry, but it's the best of what they're offering this year."

"What's wrong with it?" my mother wanted to know. "A dress is for girls to wear. What were you expecting? Lace overalls?"

"It's just so—"

"Feminine?" my mother sneered. "Look, we haven't got all day. Try it on."

I slipped out of the rest of my clothes. To my relief, I had remembered to wear a bra and if it wasn't clean, my mother didn't notice. I climbed into the dress, which pinched at the waist as my mother zipped it.

"It's too small, Ma."

She pulled up at the zipper, and my sister Electa empathetically held her breath. Mimi the seamstress evilly fingered the pins in the cushion on her wrist.

"It really doesn't fit," I said weakly.

"It fits. With a different bra—you know, it wouldn't hurt to lose a few pounds before the wedding anyway . . . *oi* . . . there." My mother triumphantly slipped the zipper all the way shut. I saw myself in the three dressing room mirrors. I recognized the face, but I couldn't place the body anywhere. "Ma, if I turn purple because I can't breathe it's gonna spoil the effect."

"You only have to wear it once. It's fine."

"I'm gonna faint."

"Alright, we can let it out, can't we, Mimi? Jane, take it off."

Mimi unzipped, and I dutifully stepped out of the dress.

My mother snatched the dress out of Mimi's hands and carefully examined the seams. "There's plenty here to play with."

"Ma," Electa looked our mother in the eye, "let Jane try the next size."

"It will fit like a tent."

"Please, can we try the next size?" Electa asked the seamstress directly, by-passing my mother, taking matters into her own bride-to-be hands.

Mimi returned in a few minutes bearing another gown exactly like the first but bigger. I numbly climbed into it. It zipped like a charm but hung oddly in strange places.

"What did I tell you," my mother said triumphantly, "a tent."

Electa again went over my mother's head. "Mimi, what's easier? To take in or let out?"

"In my professional opinion, it would be easier to find a style that fit the young lady to begin with."

A tear formed in the corner of my eye. Electa sat back in her chair with her head in her hands. "This is impossible. I can't find one dress that looks good on five different women!"

"Try the smaller size again."

"Ma, I can't fit in the smaller size."

"Can't means *won't."*

I stood looking at myself in the larger dress. I pressed my eyes in to hold back a fit of crying. Electa touched my shoulder. "Really, Jane, it's not so bad."

"The smaller one is better," my mother said flatly. "Jane, try the smaller one just one last time."

I stood paralyzed in the middle of the dressing room.

"Really," said my mother, "I just want to prove a point. Please step into this."

She held the dress open like an envelope. I looked at Electa who looked at Mimi who silently washed her hands of the entire matter. Then Mimi unzipped the bigger gown and held it while I carefully stepped out.

The other women held their breath as I wedged myself

into the first dress. My mother once again tugged at the zipper.

"It's gonna rip."

My mother squeezed the flesh of my back in under the zipper and yanked. "I could use a little cooperation. Pull your tummy in."

"It's in as far as it will go."

"Mommy," Electa pulled herself up to her full height, which in the space of the dressing room was rather impressive. "I'm not going to watch you torture Jane one more minute. Jane, you put on the large dress. Mimi, you pin it."

My mother threw up her hands and sat in a corner where she sulked until the pinning was complete. Normally I would have been nervous that she was going to lapse into her depression again, but right now I had troubles of my own.

"It's not my fault I can't fit into a size-eleven dress."

"No comment," my mother muttered.

She was still alive, and I was an adolescent again. The fluorescent light made my skin green, my teeth yellow, my face puffy and full of tear streaks. I wobbled in my white linen pumps while Mimi took pin after pin from her pin cushion wrist watch, poked, adjusted, and sighed.

At last, the seamstress got up off her knees. She dusted her hands and opened them to my reflection in the mirror. "You look like a million," she said.

Even through the straight pins, I could see that the dress looked better, although it was nothing I would ever choose for myself.

I picked my way out of the dress. My mother said, "Don't scratch yourself. If you get blood on that dress it's ruined."

I put my own clothes on but still could not recognize myself in the bridal boutique mirrors.

"You look exhausted," said my mother. "C'mon. I'm gonna buy you girls some lunch."

Bel Kaufman (Contemporary)

FROM *Up the Down Staircase*

I know homework is essential to our well being, and I did it but I got into a fight with some kid on the way to school and he threw it in the gutter.

My dog chewed it up.

I didn't know we were supposed to do it.

I fell asleep on the subway because I stayed up all night doing my homework, so when it stopped at my station I ran through the door not to be late & left it on the seat on the subway.

The cat chewed it up and there was no time to do it over.

Why I Didn't Do It. When you tell us to bring a book report I do not like it because I have to go to the library and get a book to read it. It will take me about two month or more to read it and I have to owe money to them and it adds up. . . .
As I was taking down the assignment my ballpoint stopped.

I had to study French so didn't have time to study English.

I did it but left it home by mistake.

If a teacher wants to know something why doesn't she look it up herself instead of making we students do it? We benefit ourselves more by listening to her, after all, she's the teacher!

* * *

The baby spilled milk on it.

My brother took "my" homework instead of "his."

I have to work after school and they kept me til midnight.

The page was missing from my book.

Even though I brought in a legal note for absence he sent me back. That's why I'm unprepared.

I had to take care of my three siblings because my mother is in the hospital.

I lost my book & just found it.

There's no room in my house now my uncle moved in and I have to sleep in the hall and couldn't use the kitchen table.

Some one stole it.

What homework?

My dog pead on it.

Garrison Keillor (Contemporary)

Marooned

I remember exactly when the marriage took a weird turn. I was on the examining table with my shorts draped around my ankles and my tail pointing high in the air and Dr. Miller surveying my colon through a cold steel periscope and making *hmmmm* sounds, his ballpoint pen scratching on a notepad, and at this delicate moment, he said, softly, "Do I strike you as a selfish person?"

"No . . . why?" I asked. The periscope felt like it was about six feet up me and I'm only five-foot-eight.

"I took a personal-inventory test in that book about getting ahead that everybody's reading—you know, the book that I heard you're related to the author of," he said. According to the test, he said, he was rather selfish.

I groaned, feeling the excavation of the Holland Tunnel within me, but of course I knew which book he meant. My dumbbell brother-in-law Dave's book, that's which one.

He told me Dave's book had meant a lot to him. "I never buy books other than science fiction," he confided, "but my partner Jamie gave it to me for my birthday and I opened it up and I couldn't put the rascal down. Heck of a book." Meanwhile, *the periscope was way up there in my hinder, probing parts of me I had been unaware of until now.* "He says that what holds us back is fear, and that fear is selfish, and that getting ahead is a problem of *getting outside yourself,*" and he gave the periscope a little nudge for emphasis. "You have to really *focus* on a goal outside yourself in order to succeed. My goal is to open a restaurant. Jamie's a wonderful cook. Chinese and Mexican, what do you think?"

I felt sore afterward. I went home and told Julie that a person as dim as my proctologist was exactly who Dave's book was aimed at, one ream job deserves another, and so forth. I was steamed.

She said, "You've always resented Dave, Danny, and you know why? I'll tell you why. Because your life is in Park and the key isn't even in the ignition. You're totally into negativity, Danny. You stopped growing twenty-six years ago. And how would I know? Because I'm your wife, that's how I know."

Twenty-six years ago I graduated from the University of Minnesota journalism school with honors, the editor of the Minnesota *Daily,* and got a job as a professional copywriter at a Minneapolis ad agency. Dave Grebe was a clerk in his dad's stationery store, peddling birthday cards. He and I played basketball on a Lutheran church team; that's how I met his sister Julie; she picked him up after the game because he'd lost his driver's license for drunk driving. He was twenty, big and porky and none too bright, just like now. "I'd sure like to get the heck out of stationery, I hate the smell of it, mucilage especially, and the damn perfume, it's like someone vomited after eating fruit," Dave remarked to me more than once.

So I was not too surprised when, one fine day, Dave walked away from his job and shaved his head clean and moved to a commune in south Minneapolis, living with sixteen other disciples of the Serene Master Diego Tua, putting on the sandals of humility and the pale-green robe of constant renewal. "I have left your world, Danny," he told me on the phone.

Julie, who had become my wife, thought that Dave "just needed to get away for a while." I pointed out to her that the Tuans were fanatics who roamed the airport jingling bells and droning and whanging on drums, collecting money to support their master and his many wives and concubines. The Tuans believed that they held the secrets of the universe and everyone else was vermin.

Julie thought they were Buddhists of some sort.

"They could be Buddhists or nudists or used-car salesmen who like to dress up in gowns, but whatever they are, they're working your brother like a puppet on a string."

She thought that Dave was only doing what he felt was best for him. Subject closed. So I did double duty for a few years—was a copywriter *and* kept the Grebe stationery store going—and Dave went around droning and whanging and dinging and making a holy nuisance of himself.

"We are God's roadblocks," said the Happy Master, Diego himself, "warning the people that the bridge is washed out." His real name was Tim U. Apthed; he chose the name Diego, *Die—ego,* and crunched his initials into a surname, and founded a church for jerks. My agency, Curry, Cosset, Dorn, flew me to Atlanta or Boston or Chicago occasionally, and I'd come running through the terminal to catch a plane and hear the drums and bells and there were the Tuans in the middle of the concourse, holding up their signs, "Your Life Is a Lie," and chanting, "Only two ways, one false, one true. Only one life, which way are you? Back! back! turn away from your lies! And God will give you a beautiful surprise!" and I'd be trying to squeeze through the crowd of shaven men including my blissful brother-in-law and get on board the plane. It was like Run, Sheep, Run.

"Well, when he talks about people being so materialistic, I think he has a good point," said Julie.

Then, fifteen years ago, Mr. Grebe died of a cerebral hemorrhage—clapped his hand to his forehead one morning and said, "Oh mercy. Call Ann and tell her I'll be late," and fell over dead onto the ballpoint-pen rack. The rest of us were living in the felt-tip era but Mr. Grebe never gave up on ballpoints, which worked better on carbon paper, he explained patiently, ignoring the fact that photocopying had replaced carbons. The family was devastated at the loss of this vacuous and bewildered man. They mourned for weeks, during which I was the bulwark, arranging the funeral, paying the bills, ordering stock, and Dave sat in a corner weeping. They never found out who Ann was.

Dave left the Tuans and let his hair grow out and went to work at the Wm. Grebe Stationery Shop. Every few days he'd call up and say, "I don't know how I can ever make it up to everyone for the terrible things I've done."

You get sick of remorse when it becomes a broken record. Dave kept saying, "You've been so great, Danny, and I've been a jerk. I don't know why God lets me live." After a few months of it, I told him that I didn't know either but that he could take his guilt and put it where the sun don't shine. He reported this to Julie. She vindictively canceled our vacation trip to the Bahamas. "I can never forgive you for saying that to my brother," she said, and she was right, she couldn't.

Meanwhile, Dave, who once had renounced material things, took over Wm. Grebe, stocked it with felt tips and expanded into malls and branched out into discount book-selling, got rich in about three years, and became one smooth guy: bought a Hasselblad camera, Finnish furniture, a Steinway, a Martin guitar, four Harleys, a Peterbilt truck, an original Monet (*Girl with Light Hair*), and next thing I knew he was going around giving pep talks to Kiwanis clubs, and then, he wrote his book about getting ahead, *Never Buy a Bottle of Rat Poison That Comes with Gift Coupons*. It sold more copies than there are rats in Rio (millions). He turned Tuanism inside out and restated it in capitalist terms, and made low cash flow seem like a denial of God's love.

On the same day that an interview with Dave appeared on the front page of *The Wall Street Journal,* I got canned at the agency. Twenty-five years I had labored at Curry, Cosset, Dorn, and on a Monday morning, as I sharpened my No. 2 pencil, a twenty-nine-year-old guy in a red bow tie leaned over the wall of my work cubicle and said, "The folks at Chippy called and cut back on the campaign, Danny, I'm going to have to let you go for a while."

"Are you sure?" That's all I could think to say. A quarter-century with the company—"Are you sure?" He was sure.

I crawled home, bleeding, and Julie was glued to the TV, watching Dave talk about the irrelevance of suffering. It was a videotape, not a live appearance, but even so, she did not turn it off when she heard my tragic news. She said, "That's too bad," and then, "I'm so proud of him. This is one of his new videotapes. He's going to put out twelve of them. He just seems to touch a chord in people, don't you think? People can't help but respond to him. It's a natural gift." She recommended that I study *Rat Poison* to give me the confidence to find a new job and wait for his next book, *How to Find Your Rear End Without Using Both Hands.*

"Your brother," I said, "is one of the world's biggest b.s.ers."

This was when Julie decided that we needed to face up to my problems. "You are a dark cloud in my life, Danny. A small dark cloud," she said.

I don't know what she meant by that. I'm a happy guy who loves life, it's just that I have a moony face. A guy can't help it that his face won't light up. Inside, I'm like a kid with a new bike. Though being flushed down the toilet while your brother-in-law is getting rich certainly puts a crimp in a guy's hose. Dave was hot. I was dead. For twenty-five years, I had been a happy guy who created dancing ketchup commercials, who made high-fiber bran flakes *witty,* who wrote those coffee commercials in which the husband and wife share a golden moment over a cup of java. I brought lucidity to capitalism, and Dave brought gibberish, and he walked off with the prize.

The next day, Julie told me that Dave thought we should go away and be alone and he'd given her fifteen thousand dollars so we could charter a fifty-foot schooner for a two-week cruise off Antigua, where we could try to put the marriage back together.

"Fifteen thousand dollars would come in handy in other ways than blowing it on a cruise," I pointed out. "We could invest it. I'm unemployed, you know."

"Aren't you willing to invest in our marriage?" she said.

"We could *buy* a boat for that kind of money and sail every weekend." She said that fifteen thousand wasn't enough to pay her to get into a boat with me at the tiller.

"Remember the time we drifted powerless down the Mississippi because you put oil in the gas tank? Remember how you tried to rig up an overcoat on an oar to make a sail? Remember how we drifted toward that oncoming coal barge and stood and waved our arms and cried out in our pitiful voices?"

Ten years had not dimmed her memory of that afternoon. So off we flew to Antigua.

We flew first-class, in those wide upholstered seats, where everything is sparkly and fresh and lemony and candles flicker on the serving cart. A painful reminder of how cheery life can be for the very rich, people like Dave. The flight attendants wore gold-paisley sarongs slit up the side and pink-passion lipstick, they were Barnard graduates (*cum laude*) in humanities, and they set a vase of fresh roses on my table, along with the seviche and salmon loaf and crab puffs with Mornay sauce, and they leaned over me, their perfect college-educated breasts hanging prettily in place, and they whispered, "You've got a nice butt. You ever read Kant?" I knew that they only flirted with me because I was holding a first-class ticket; I wanted to say, "I'm forty-seven, I'm broke, ashamed, in pain, on the verge of divorce, and sponging off a despised relative. I've hit bottom, babes. Buzz off."

We stayed one night at Jumby Bay, dropping a bundle, and headed off by cab to the Lucky Lovers Marina, and there, at the end of the dock, lay the *Susy Q*. I put my arm around Julie, who was shivering despite the bright sunshine and eighty-five degrees.

"Is that a schooner or a ketch?" I said.

"It's a yawl," she replied. It was hard not to notice the frayed rigging and rusted hardware, the oil slick around the stern, the sail in a big heap on deck, and what appeared to be sneaker treadmarks along the side of the hull. But we had put down a deposit of fifteen hundred dollars already, so we banished doubt from our minds.

"Hello! Anybody below?" I hollered. There was a muffled *yo,* and a beautiful young man poked up his head from the cockpit and smiled. His golden curls framed his Grecian-god-like face, his deep tan set off by a green T-shirt that said "Montana . . . The Big Sky." He was Rusty, our captain, he said. "I was just making your bed downstairs. Come on down. Your room's up front!"

This struck me as odd, that he said *downstairs* instead of *below decks,* and I mentioned this to Julie as we stowed our bags in the cabin. "How can you get upset about poor word choice when our marriage is on the rocks?" she asked.

The *Susy Q* cleared port and sailed west toward Sansevar Trist, and she and I sat below discussing our marriage, which I have always believed is not a good idea for Julie and me. My experience tells me that we should shoot eight-ball, sit in a hot tub, go to the zoo, rake the lawn, spread warm oil on each other's bodies, do anything but talk about our marriage, but she is a fan of those articles like "How Lousy Is Your Marriage: A 10-Minute Quiz That Could Help You Improve It" and of course the first question is, "Are you and your husband able to sit down and discuss your differences calmly and reasonably?" *No! Of course not! Are you kidding? Who discusses these things without screaming? Name one person!* So she launched off on a reasonable discussion of differences, and two minutes later we're screeching and hissing and slamming doors so hard the pictures fall off the walls. We simply are unable to discuss our marriage—does that make us terrible people? Our marriage is like the Electoral College: it works okay if you don't think about it.

"Do you love me?" Julie asked, as the boat rocked in the swell, Rusty thumping around on deck overhead.

"How do you mean that?"

"I mean, is it worth it to try to stick together? Marriages have their rough passages. It's only worth it if there's love. If there isn't why waste time trying to patch this up."

"Do you love me?"

"I asked first."

"How come I'm the one who has to say if I love you or not? Why is it always up to me?"

There was a loud thump above, like somebody kicking the side, and then Rusty let out a cry, "Oh shoot!" I poked my head up out of the hatch. "It's the steering thing," he said. The tiller had broken off and was now bobbing in our wake. I told him to lash an oar in its place and come around and retrieve the tiller, and I ducked back down into the cabin. Julie was sitting on the bunk, her back to the bulkhead, her trim brown legs drawn up.

"I better go up and help Rusty," I said.

"You can't run away, Danny," she said. "It's a simple question. Do you love me or not? What's so hard about that?"

I flopped down on the chair. "Why can't we *converse* about this in a calm friendly way instead of getting into a shooting match over every little thing—"

"A little thing," she said. "Our love. A little thing. Oh right. Sure. Great way to start off a vacation. Our love, a little thing."

There was a loud *cra-a-a-ack* above, like a sequoia falling, and a muffled splash. I stuck my head up. The sail was gone, and the mast. "I was gonna turn right and the whole thing broke and fell off," he said, shaking his head. "Boy, that was something!" He shrugged and grinned, like he'd just burned the toast. "Oh well, we still got a motor." I told him to come about and retrieve the sail and mast and then head for port.

I told Julie that we had serious problems above and maybe we should postpone our talk. She said we had been postponing it for twenty years.

I was about to tell her how full of balloon juice she was, and then I heard the motor turn over, a dry raspy sound, like gravel going down a chute, and I realized the *Susy Q* was going nowhere. Still, it wasn't as aggravating as Miss Priss there, sitting and telling me about my marriage.

"Dave recommended a great book to me and it opened my eyes. *The Silent Chrysalis.* I read it twice. Danny, in some way my love for you is a symptom of my denial of myself, an attempt to make myself invisible."

The starter cranked over once and wheezed and coughed a deep dry cough.

Julie's eyes locked with mine. "We need to change that love from something angry to a *mature* love," she said. "I can't use you as an instrument of my self-hatred."

What is that supposed to mean? I asked.

"Dave thinks you're trapped in a lingering infantile narcissism, like a lot of guys. I don't know. I can't speak to that. Only you can."

How does a stationery-store clerk suddenly become the expert on American men? I wondered, but then Rusty's face appeared in the hatch, a mite taut around the eyes. "We may have to ditch the boat in a minute, you guys. We're coming real close to the reef, I think. The water looks sort of bubbly out there."

Julie grabbed my arm when I got up to go topside. "You're not going to just walk away from this one, Danny. You're going to face up to what's wrong, which is your selfishness. Your selfishness is a *fact,* Danny. Let's stop denying it. Let's deal with it."

Rusty's voice was hoarse. "Come on, folks."

I poked my head up. The Great Navigator had an odd horrified expression on his face, and his chin was aquiver. He wore an orange life jacket. "Want me to take the helm?" I asked.

"No helm left to take, and there's big jagged rocks up ahead, folks, so if you see a cushion, better grab on to it. This is not a test."

There was a distant roar of waves that was not as distant as before.

I ducked down and told Julie we were about to abandon ship. "If you can't deal with the truth, Danny, then I can't be married to you," said Julie, softly. "I don't want a marriage based on a lie."

I was just about to tell her that she wouldn't have that problem much longer, when there was a jagged ripping tearing crunching sound from just below our feet, and the boat lurched to a dead stop. Water began boiling up from below. I grabbed Julie and hoisted her through the hatch, grabbed a carry-on bag and a couple cushions, and took Julie by the hand, and we jumped into the water. Rusty was already on shore, waving to us. It was shallow, all right; the water frothed around our feet on the jagged coral, but it wasn't too hard wading in to shore, a beautiful white sandy beach that curved around and around a very pretty island—uninhabited, we soon discovered. "Well," said Rusty, "looks like you guys may get a little more than two weeks. Nice place, too." And he glanced down at Julie. Her T-shirt was wet from the surf, and her breasts shone through. He looked at her a long time, I thought.

We made a hut from palm fronds and the jibsail. Julie had brought her purse and suntan oil and four books about marriage and communication, and I had dragged in our suitcase and a bottle of Campari, and Rusty had salvaged the oregano, sweet basil, rosemary, chives, coriander, cayenne pepper, paprika, orange zest, nutmeg, cinnamon, pine nuts, bay leaf, marjoram, tarragon, caraway, and saffron.

"The boat sinks and you rescue the spice rack?" I cried. "You're the captain and your boat goes down and you come ashore with the spice rack?"

Rusty looked at Julie. "Just because we're marooned on an island doesn't mean the food has to be bland and tasteless," he said.

She nodded. "It's no dumber than bringing a bottle of Campari. You don't like Campari," she said. "You only like beer."

And an hour later, Julie had made beds out of pine boughs and Rusty had carved a salad bowl from a stump and tossed a salad in it—"Just some ferns and breadfruit and hearts of palm," he said. He had also baked a kelp casserole over an open fire. Julie thought it was the best salad in salad history. Actually, it was okay. "And this casserole!" she cried. "I have never tasted kelp that tasted like this kelp tastes. What's the secret?"

"Paprika," he said.

Julie couldn't get over it. She said, "Danny couldn't even boil an egg. I kept offering to teach him, but he never wanted to learn."

It was hard not to notice that she was talking about me in the past tense.

"No, Danny couldn't have made a salad like this in a million years. Are you kidding? Not him," she chortled. "No, no, no, no, no."

We sat under the palm tree as the sun went down, and

Julie and Rusty talked about the American novel, how they didn't care for Updike, who had never written strong women characters and was hung up on male menopause and had no ear for dialogue.

"No ear for dialogue?" I cried.

"No ear for dialogue," she said.

"John Updike? No ear for dialogue? Are you kidding me? Updike? That's what you said, right? Updike? His dialogue? No ear?"

"He has none," she said.

"None. Updike."

"Right."

"I can't believe this," I said. "You're sitting here under this palm tree and saying the John Updike—*the* John Updike, who wrote the Rabbit books—that he has no ear for *dialogue*? Tell me something. If John Updike has no ear for dialogue, then who do you think *does* have an ear for dialogue?"

Rusty looked at Julie. "Maya Angelou. Alice Walker. Doris Lessing," he said.

"Doris Lessing," I said.

"Yes," she said. "Doris Lessing."

"An ear for dialogue," I said. I stood up. "You know, I must be going deaf, but I could swear you just said Doris Lessing. Or did you say Arthur Schlesinger?" I kicked a little dirt toward Rusty.

"I said, Doris Lessing," he said.

It was the first of many discussions where I was in the minority. One morning, over a dried-seaweed breakfast, Julie said she thought there is such a thing as a "masculine personality" and that it is basically controlling and violent. Rusty agreed. "But some of us are working to change that," he said. Julie felt that men are inherently competitive, i.e. linear, hierarchical, and women are circular, i.e. radiant. "I never thought of it that way before," said Rusty. Julie and Rusty started meditating together every morning, sitting on the beach facing the east. "Hey, mind if I sit in?" I said, cheerfully.

Julie squinted up at me. "I think you'd block the unity of the experience," she said.

Rusty nodded.

"Well, far be it from me to block anyone's unity," I said, and walked away.

That night, Julie and Rusty were cooking a bark soup and she looked up at me and said, "Rusty is such an inspiration. I'm glad this happened."

I grabbed her arm. "This numbskull who ran the boat onto the rock is an inspiration?"

Rusty confronted me later that night, after Julie went to sleep. "I've decided to take Julie away from you," he said. "You two do nothing but fight, and she's obviously attracted to me, so if she and I paired up, at least there'd be two happy people on this island. It makes more sense that way. Two out of three isn't bad. So why don't you go and sleep in the jungle someplace. This tent is for Julie and me."

I said, "Okay, you're right," and I turned and bent down and picked up my Campari bottle and then whirled and swung it straight up into his nuts and he staggered back and I threw a handful of dirt in his eyes. He bent down, blinded, and I kicked him as hard as I could in the gut, and he went *whooomph,* like a needle sliding across a record, and down he went, and I picked him up and threw him into the ocean and suddenly the water was whipped to a froth by thousands of tiny carnivorous fish and the frenzy went on for half a minute and subsided and whatever was left of Rusty sank bubbling to the bottom.

It wasn't the Zen way but it got the job done.

Julie was distraught in the morning. She dashed around the island screaming his name. "What have you done to him, Danny?" she shrieked.

"He fell in the water and the fish ate him," I said.

"You killed him!"

"Nothing ever dies. He is at one with the fish."

Two weeks later, when the big cruise ship saw us and anchored a half-mile to leeward and sent in a launch to take us off, Julie had calmed down and was almost ready to talk to me again. I could tell. I yelled up to her where she sat on the ledge of the rocky promontory, "You know something? I think the secret of marriage is that you can't change the person you love. You have to love that person the way he or she is. Well, here I am!"

"You got that out of a book," she called back. It was the first time she'd spoken to me in two weeks.

A man in officer whites with big tufts of hair on his chest was on the launch. He said, "You the couple who went down with the *Susy Q*? Where's the captain?"

"He drowned," I said. Julie said nothing. She still has said nothing about Rusty to me at all, and nothing about our marriage, but we have had sex more often than any time since we were twenty-four. It has been nice. I definitely think there is a vital connection between anger and an exciting sex life.

When we got back to the States, I saw a newspaper in the Newark airport with a picture of Dave on the front page glowering at the photographer and trying to stiff-arm him. He had been arrested for fondling a couple of fifteen-year-old girls in his swimming pool at his birthday party and was charged with six counts of sexual assault. I chuckled, but it was a low chuckle, and Julie didn't hear it. We were back two days and a publisher offered me $50,000 for a book about our "desert-island" experience. "Nah," I said, "nothing happened. Worst part was having to go around in a wet bathing suit." Since returning, I have done little except be a help and a support to Dave and Julie and the whole Grebe family. I have been a monster of pity and understanding and quiet strength. I have been there for them every moment in their terrible suffering. Dave sat weeping in our kitchen and told us, "I've been under so much stress, and it was like it was somebody else unfastening those girls' straps, and I was only watching." I said, "Don't feel you have to talk about it." He told me that he didn't know what he would ever do without the strength I gave him in this awful crisis. "It's my pleasure," I said, sincerely.

Florynce Kennedy (Contemporary)

One-liners

When a male heckler called out "Are you a lesbian?" she immediately replied, "Are you my alternative?"

•

There's a lady in the dentist's chair who is pretty nervous about what's going on. The dentist works on her for about three minutes and all of a sudden he realizes that she has managed to obtain a very tight grip on his testicles, and she's squeezing just short of agony. So he stops and says, "What is this?" and she says, "We are not going to hurt each other, are we, doctor?"

•

I'm just a loud-mouthed middle-aged colored lady . . . and a lot of people think I'm crazy. Maybe you do too, but I never stop to wonder why I'm not like other people. The mystery to me is why more people aren't like me.

•

When women began wearing pants there was a tremendous backlash. I can remember—I was still practicing law at that time—going to court in pants and the judge's remarking that I wasn't properly dressed, that the next time I came to court I should be dressed like a lawyer. He's sitting there in a long black dress gathered at the yoke, and I said, "Judge, if you won't talk about what I'm wearing, I won't talk about what you're wearing."

Jean Kerr (Contemporary)

❧❧❧

FROM *How I Got to Be Perfect*

Can This Romance Be Saved?
LOLITA AND HUMBERT CONSULT
A MARRIAGE COUNSELOR

It was a mistake to read Vladimir Nabokov's *Lolita* and the "Can This Marriage Be Saved?" column in the *Ladies' Home Journal* on the same evening. The total effect was a little confusing.

The counselor interviews Humbert, and reports his *side of the story:*

Humbert was a tall, graying man. The natural pallor of his skin was perhaps accentuated by the drabness of his present garb. With his quiet, old-world charm he made me welcome in the cells and spoke quite readily of his broken romance.

"Doctor, picture—if you will—my darling, my nymphet, my Lolita, her scrawny, brown, twelve-year-old legs splashed all over with daubs of Mercurochrome, which spread like roses under the little white wings of Band-Aids.

"To watch her sit at the kitchen table and play jacks was to know what Aristotle meant by pity and terror and to feel with Oedipus, arriving blind and gutted at Colonus. The jacks in her grubby paws flew into the air like little prisms of silver, like stars. And when sometimes it happened, as often it did, that the small rubber ball dropped from her hands into the butter dish (my darling was not very well co-ordinated), the stream of four-letter words that poured from her adorable mouth would have dazzled a fishmonger.

"Ah, Lolita—the snap, snap, splat of her bubble gum (she chewed twelve hours a day, my lamb did) will echo down the corridors of all my dreams. Even in hell (*is* there a hell, shall we talk theology, Doctor?) I will be bedeviled (forgive the pun; it was intended) by visions of the precious one who curled up so sweetly in my lap after I gave her five dollars.

"My conscience, that wary censor, that watchdog of memory, permits me to recall only the happy hours, when Lolita lay at my feet poring over movie magazines and munching candied apples (alas, she often brought these— the apples—to bed). Her bright eyes sparkled as she gorged herself on pictures of pulchritudinous Rock or Tab or Guy (surely I invent these names) here photographed in a limed-oak study, there caught spread-armed and godlike on a surfboard.

"It has been suggested that after her mother's most timely demise I forced my attentions on this angel-nymphet. (Idle roomers beget idle rumors.) But I swear to you that I did no more than kidnap her from that summer camp, right under the toothy smiles of the lady counselors (fat, middle-aged sows, all of them, twenty-two or older). It was little Lolita, accomplished beyond her years, who seduced poor old Humbert. It was the fly, if you will, who gobbled up the spider. You must remember that I was worn down from poring over scholarly journals (did you know, dear Doctor, that Dante's Beatrice was a nymphet of thirteen?) and weakened by the atrociously poor food provided by the series of mental institutions to which I was periodically committed. On the other hand, my little lamb chop was in fighting trim, lean and lithe from playing hopscotch. Oh, Lolita, oh those nights, *mon Dieu!* (that's French, Doctor; I'm a very educated fellow).

"Imagine my horror when my darling, who—what is the vulgar phrase?—who had it made, who had handsome, hairy Humbert in the palm of her tiny hand, left, scrammed, vamoosed, ran off. And ran off, would you believe it, with the first fat, balding slob who promised her a glimpse of Hamburger Heaven. And I, all alone, bewailed my outcast state and troubled the deaf deities with my burping, noisy grief. Ah, laugh if you will, but hath not a pervert eyes, hands, senses, passions, and affections? Do you wonder that I killed him?

"And here I am, behind bars which contain me and enclose me like my own parentheses. Yesterday and yesterday and yesterday I was always her victim, Doctor. An unlikely story, you say, and yet you may have observed how it sells."

The counselor interviews Lolita, and reports her *side of the story:*

I would not say that my first interview with twelve-year-old Lolita was entirely successful. In the first place, she was busy manipulating her Yo-Yo and seemed reluctant to talk. After I had gained her confidence, she opened up a little.

"Look, Doc, it was a nightmare from the beginning. The night he swiped me from that camp and took me to the motel, do you know what he did to me? First of all, you've gotta get the picture that there's nothing in this room but the double bed and one bureau. So what happens? Humbert takes the three big drawers for his stuff and leaves me with those two little tiny drawers on top. I couldn't even get all my hair ribbons in. Was I burned up!

"I'll say this. He could be sweet enough when he wanted to. But as soon as we got out of bed in the morning, my troubles began. Boy did he overwork the togetherness bit. All this jazz about 'sharing' nearly drove me out of my little pink mind. If I went out on the front sidewalk to skip rope, *he* had to skip rope. We had to cut down the clothesline to get a rope big enough for him. Boy, you should have seen him, huffing and puffing and getting his big clodhoppers all tangled up in the rope. If I had an onion sandwich, you bet your life Big Daddy had to have an onion sandwich. He'd pile on the onions and then, as soon as he got it all down, he'd turn absolutely green and have to drink *gallons* of Bromo-Seltzer. All this time he'd be groaning and saying, 'You see, mah puhteet, I'd do anything for you—anything.' I'd come right out and tell him, 'Look, Pops, if you wanna do me a real favor, go to the movies and leave me alone for two hours.' Then he'd start to cry and say I was just trying to get rid of him. That guy cried so much he should have had windshield wipers for those glasses.

"But the worst of all was the way he hogged things. On Sunday morning, who used to toddle out in his pajamas and

grab all the funnies first? Mr. Geritol. Of course by the time
I got hold of them, they were an absolute mess. He used to
pretend that he just wanted to know what I was reading. But
he didn't fool me. A forty-year-old yakking it up over Moon
Mullins—I ask you. If you want the inside story, Doc, I'm
looking for a more mature man."

The counselor gives his advice:

At first glance it seemed as though these two people were
poles apart. To begin with, there was the vast difference in
their ages. Obviously it was difficult for an experienced girl
like Lolita to put up with Humbert's childishness.

However, as our interviews continued, I was quick to notice that they had a number of important things in common.
For instance, Humbert, as a child, suffered from an "absent"
mother. That is to say, his mother died when he was eighteen months old, and so, quite naturally, he hated her. As a
counselor, I was able to show Humbert that his rebellious
attitude stemmed in large part from the fact that, as a child,
he lacked that symbol of sensual pleasure, the cookie jar.
Resentful at being abandoned by his mother, he was trying
to penalize all other women who, in his fantasies, became
"cookies." Humbert was quick to acknowledge the truth of
my diagnosis. "Doctor," he said, "that's a new one on me."

Lolita, on the other hand, had a "present" mother who
danced attendance on her night and day. Naturally she hated
her. The mother, with that obtuseness so often found among
females of the lower middle classes, made a fetish of propriety. Consequently, she was unsympathetic to twelve-
year-old Lolita's valiant efforts to form a sexual alliance
with an older man. And, what was worse, she constantly interfered with Lolita's natural development by saying things
like "Don't leave the soap in the bathtub" or "Get your fingers out of the plate." Is it any wonder that Lolita has spent
her whole life trying to get her fingers in the plate?

The solution for this pair did not come all at once. But as
our sessions drew to a close I felt that the future looked
brighter for both of them. Lolita has agreed to stop bringing
candied apples to bed. (The onion sandwiches are no longer
a problem; since Lolita's gall bladder operation she is no
longer able to tolerate raw onions.)

On his side, Humbert has agreed to stay in prison. With

time off for good behavior, he can look forward to a parole in forty-five years. At this time he will be eighty-five and should be sufficiently mature to shoulder his responsibilities. Lolita will wait. (I have decided to take her into my home as a ward.) In the meantime, she is optimistic. As she herself expressed it, "With my luck, he'll get out of the clink."

Good luck to you both, Lolita and Humbert.

Out of Town with a Show

OR WHAT TO DO UNTIL THE PSYCHIATRIST COMES

I used to love to go out of town with a show—you miss so much at home. Oh, the exhilaration of being in Philadelphia just as the air is turning nippy, and knowing that somebody else back in Larchmont will have to find the storm windows. Indeed when I was younger and still in love with room service, I felt, like any other red-blooded American housewife, that a whole day spent rewriting the first act was a small price to pay for the privilege of having somebody else make my breakfast and bring it up to me on a tray. I don't know just when the truth caught up with me. But I have noticed recently that the mere thought of going to Boston with a musical causes me to tremble and drop small objects.

Many people have asked me—well, my father has asked me several times—why playwrights have to take a show out of town to try it out. Can't they tell anything from rehearsals?

The truth is that the playwright learns a great deal from rehearsals. He learns that the play is brave, haunting, luminous, tender, and hilarious, and that a cardboard container of coffee sent in from the delicatessen costs thirty cents. Everybody tells him how great the play is—the producer's secretary, the press agent's wife, the leading lady's mother. In fact, after spending only twenty minutes peering at a rehearsal from the back of an empty theater, they are so choked up with the magic of it all that they can barely vocalize. They squeeze the author's trembling hand and mutter hoarsely, "This is it, Sam—it can't miss." Not wishing to dispel the universal euphoria, Sam dismisses as unlikely his own secret theory that the play was badly cast, is being badly directed, and may have been badly written. Soon he is making discreet inquiries as to when the balloting closes for the Pulitzer Prize, and finally he comes home to tell his wife, "Honey, I don't see how it can miss."

And that's why he goes to Philadelphia: so he can see how it can miss.

Out of town the first thing he is up against is Murphy's Law. In Abe Burrows' definition, Murphy's Law states simply: if something *can* go wrong, it will. Now you wouldn't think it to look at me, but I just happen to be the world's expert on the things that can go wrong out of town. That's why I've taken up finger painting. The doctor says it will help me to forget. But while I can still remember, I would like to point out a few of the simpler rules for survival, for those of you who may be thinking of writing a play. And it's no use pretending that you have no intention of writing a play. There are distraught playwrights locked away in the Touraine Hotel this minute who, as recently as last year, were decently and profitably employed by Young and Rubicam or the Chock Full o' Nuts Company.

Learn to Cope with Room Service

We will start with the idea that the play will have to be entirely rewritten (there is no other possibility). This means that you will have to spend twenty-two hours out of every day closeted in a small hotel room with a rented typewriter and a very bad reproduction of a Utrillo.

Entombed as he is, the playwright usually makes the foolish mistake of supposing that he can count on room service to sustain the slender thread of life. This is patently ridiculous, as anyone who has ever waited three hours for two pots of black coffee will know. The thing to do is to bring along a couple of Care packages, or even a tin of biscuits. This will eliminate that air of panic which brings out the beast in room service, and will allow you to order with the proper air of detachment. With any luck, you may stun the girl on the other end of the wire into instant action. A good method is to begin by asking her what day it is. Greet the news that it is Thursday with real appreciation. Then say, in an offhand, casual way, "Thursday, eh? Well, look, sometime over the weekend send me up a chicken sandwich, but there's no rush, I won't be checking out until the end of the month." Sometimes you'll get it in ten minutes.

The worst possible thing you can do, however, is to throw yourself on her mercy and suggest that you are dying of starvation. I know one playwright who swears he could have fixed that play if he hadn't spent all his time calling to inquire what had happened to his breakfast. And a pitiful sight he was, too—a large man of fifty-four shrieking into the telephone, "Yeah, yeah, yeah—I'm the scrambled eggs in 412!" Many writers of comedies exhaust their best energies composing humorous insults to hurl at room service (one I know went so far as to send a large funeral wreath to the kitchen "in memory of all those who have passed away in the last twenty-four hours"). I've never been up to anything so daring or original. I'm not the rugged type, and in the total absence of food, sleep, and clean laundry I tend to sink into childish incoherence. I take the phone in faltering hand and say, with what I assume in my enfeebled state to be dignity, "Hello, Room Service, is this Room Service— well, you're the *worst Room Service I ever met!*"

I know one hotel in Philadelphia (name supplied on request) in which there is only one possible way to get room service. If you take off your clothes, climb into the shower, and begin to lather, the boy will start banging on the door with your tray. You will go through a great many bath towels in this way, which will lead to further quarreling with the maid, but at least you'll get something to eat.

Stay Out of the Lobby

Most authors waste a great deal of valuable energy slinking about the lobby during intermissions in a foolish effort to overhear the comments of the paying customers. They do this, mind you, even on those occasions when the audience has coughed and muttered throughout the entire first act with an animosity that has caused the actors to fear for their safety and the producer to leave town. Even in these circumstances the playwright somehow imagines that he will overhear a tall, distinguished man (clearly a United States senator) say to his companion, "Egad, Helen, it's plays like this that make theatergoing worth while."

Alas, this never happens. The people who attend the theater in tryout towns do not seem to recognize their obligation to discuss what they have just seen. Indeed, there is
something downright perverse in the way they persist in believing that they are free to chat about their own affairs.
Should you rub shoulders with a vivacious group out on the
sidewalk, all you'll hear is a lady saying, "That's Jim for
you, he *will* drink manhattans when he knows how I hate to
drive the station wagon."

When I was in Philadelphia some years ago with a
comedy called *King of Hearts*, I brushed so close to so
many strangers that it's a wonder I wasn't arrested for so-
liciting. However, in two weeks of eavesdropping I heard
only one remark that was in any way relevant to the show.
This happened when a lady got up after the first act with dismay written all over her perplexed face. She turned to her
husband and said plaintively, "George, this *can't* be *Dial M
for Murder*!"

Even this wasn't as devastating as the experience a friend
of mine had in Wilmington. It was opening night of his new
melodrama, and after the second act he flew to his lookout
in the lobby, where he was rewarded by hearing two couples
actually discussing the play. "Well, Bill," asked the first
man, "how do you like it?" My friend held his breath. Bill's
answer was not long in coming. "You'd better ask Grace,"
he said, "she stayed awake."

Another reason authors should stay out of the lobby is
that they look so terrible. Our playwright friend Sam, who
is normally so natty that he has actually posed for a vodka
advertisement, will turn up in the Shubert lobby in Philadelphia looking as unshaven, unkempt, and unstrung as the
end man in a police lineup. In this condition he will strike
terror into the hearts of the visiting investors, who will conclude that he is not likely to live long enough to finish the
rewrite. He will also come under the inspection of some acquaintance who will take the trouble to write to his poor old
mother and announce, "Sam is hitting the bottle again, or
else he's got hepatitis."

One season I spent three weeks in Boston with a musical,
and of course went rapidly to seed. Now, a certain random,
helter-skelter look is absolutely native to me. But on this occasion I sank into a really spectacular state of disrepair. I

looked like a wire-service photo that would go nicely under the caption "She Survived Death March." Dear friends would take me aside and say, "I know all about the second act, but you do have a comb, don't you?" In any case it was clear that in my derelict condition I couldn't be seen moping about the lobby, so I used to stand behind a pillar that was additionally sheltered by a large palm. It was in this retreat that I was accosted one night by a young man I had never seen before but who was evidently a classmate of my brother's. "Well, hel-lo!" he said, all sunny smiles of recognition, "aren't you Frankie's sister, Jean Kerr?" I was quite naturally outraged. "Nonsense," I said, summoning all the dignity I could muster, "she's a much younger person."

Insist That All Midnight Conferences Be Held in Somebody Else's Hotel Room

Each night after the performance it is customary for all members of the production staff to meet with the author to discuss the somber past, the doubtful future, and the plain fact that the new comedy scene which just went into the show is falling rather flatter than the old one. This session, coming as it does at the end of a perfect day, may loosen your last grip on sanity. It is nevertheless obligatory. The producer insists upon it because he is still trying to persuade you to cut that God-awful scene at the end of the first act and because he is reluctant to go down to the bar and join his friends who have come from New York to see the show. (The friends will say, "I'm gonna level with you, Lou—close it," which is why, in the theater, auld acquaintances are oft forgot and never brought to mind.) And most playwrights accept the inevitable nightly post-mortem because they have learned that it is one tenth of one per cent less taxing to talk about the rewrite than to do the rewrite.

However, all of this talking should definitely be done in the producer's suite. Should the merry little band assemble in your room, not only will you have to sign the tab for all those chicken sandwiches and all that scotch, but, what is more to the point, you will have cut off your escape hatch.

Sooner or later as soft voices die and tempers rise, the director (or maybe the producer) will see fit to add to the many true remarks spoken in jest. "Look, Sam," he will say, still smiling, "we all know the first act is lousy—what you don't seem to realize is that the *second* act stinks." At this moment you should be free to arise and go without a backward glance. It might take twenty minutes if you have to throw them all out of your room.

These nuggets of advice I am dispensing so freely are all, as you can see, concerned with protecting the sanity of the playwright. Playwrights are an unstable crew at best, and they tend to become unglued in the face of the most trivial mishaps. I remember one who was carted right back to Menninger's because, at the climactic moment of his play, the bit player who had to call for the police cried out loudly and clearly, "Help! There's been a murder—call the poloose!"

But if the author, standing at the back of the house gnashing his teeth, is painfully aware that the leading man has just answered the telephone before it rang, the audience tends to remain blissfully unconscious of technical mishaps, unless, of course, the leading lady actually tumbles off the stage into the first row of the orchestra. In this connection I recall an experience I had while tending an ailing musical in Philadelphia. For complicated reasons of the plot there was a big snowstorm effect at the finale of the show. One night the ropes that controlled the snow bags (enormous canvas bags filled with tiny pellets of white paper) somehow became intertwined with the ropes that pulled up the main curtain, so that from the beginning of the second act it snowed—gently, evenly, peacefully, down through the crystal chandeliers of the ballroom, all over the sunny farm scene, without pause during the nightclub scene, it snowed on the just and unjust alike. Indeed, the prodigal flurries continued right up to the moment, at the very end of the show, when the leading lady had to say, "It's snowing, Max." She said the line looking up to the empty heavens, because by that time, naturally, we were fresh out of snow—and I sat there with my face buried in my hands, praying for guidance. When I dashed outside, still feeling murderous, I stumbled into a friend who was seeing the show for the first time. "Oh, Lord," I said, "you would have to catch this performance. Of course things go wrong every night, but this—this is the worst, the absolute worst!" He surprised me by being entirely philosophical about the whole matter. "You worry too much," he said, patting my shoulder. "Sure I noticed she was flat on that first song, but I don't think anybody else did."

By the way, many of the problems that cause faintness and loss of appetite out of town begin with simple mistakes in casting. Some performers that should never, in any circumstances, be cast are:

1. Known alcoholics. You will have trouble enough with the unknown ones.

2. Small children. It's not just that, unless, happily, they are orphans, you will have to cope with their mothers. Much worse is the fact that children, being quicker, brighter, and in a better state of preservation than their elders, can and do memorize the entire script in three days. Thereafter they conceive it to be their civic duty to prompt the star any time and every time he seems to be groping for a word. This unwise practice not only exposes the child to unsuitable language but, in general, lowers the morale and defeats the efforts of the director to create a tight ship with a happy crew.

3. Dogs. Dogs, of course, don't have mothers, which makes them a little easier to deal with, though not much. I was once connected with a production that required the services of a large English sheepdog. We began rehearsals with a beast that was supposed to be so highly trained that I imagined he would be able to do the rewrite. As it turned out, he was not trained even in the conventional sense. The circumstances over which he had no control eventually elicited howls of outrage from the manager of the theater in which we were rehearsing and resulted in our being urged—in the most intemperate language imaginable—to "go hire another hall." Furthermore, this same unfortunate animal had a tendency to bite the actors during performance, which not only lost him audience sympathy but lost us several actors.

He was replaced out of town by an enchanting dog who, unlike her predecessor, was well adjusted and secure, and limited her nibbling to the bits of liver we deposited at various key points on the set. However, she commanded a salary that was well in excess of that paid to most of the company, a circumstance which did not endear her to the other performers, several of whom claimed that, in any case, she had a habit of scratching her ears on their best lines. (I don't think she did this deliberately, but then you never know; and so far as these actors were concerned, they were already unhinged from having to compete with two very cute child actors who crept into any hearts conceivably left vacant by that dog.)

In addition to talking about the pitfalls that must be side-stepped, I might say a word about the really bad moments that may be inevitable. Many playwrights have recorded their despair at being required to attend the premature closing in New York. And this is a very grim occasion for the playwright. Since objectivity doesn't begin to set in for about six months, he still doesn't grasp what happened. The play may be a poor thing, alas, but it's his own, and around the dear ruin each wish of his heart is entwined verdantly still.

To me, however, there is a worse moment. This occurs during one of the final performances out of town, after all of the changes have been made. You stand at the back of the house and observe the results of all the work, all the sleepless nights, the conferences, the rehearsals, the arguments. And the show is better, oh, definitely better, and the audience seems to be enjoying it. You should be happy—and then, suddenly, you experience a brief but exquisitely painful moment of clarity in which you realize that what you are seeing is not really the show you had in mind at all.

This always reminds me of a story about a friend of mine. One Easter she had to prepare dinner for fifteen people, counting children and relatives. For reasons of economy she decided to make a ham loaf instead of the traditional baked ham. Obviously it was going to be four times the trouble, since the recipe for the ham loaf was extremely elaborate: there were a dozen different ingredients and the whole thing had to be made in advance and allowed to "set" overnight in pineapple juice. But she went gamely ahead, convinced that she was going to produce something tastier than baked ham, if not indeed a gourmet's dish. As she took the square pink loaf out of the oven, a sinister thought crossed her mind. She cut off a little slice and tasted it, her worst suspicions confirmed. In tears she flew out of the kitchen to find her husband. "Oh, Frank," she said, "do you know what I've *got*? I've got Spam!"

All I can say is God love you, honey, if you're in Philadelphia and you've got Spam.

The Conversation Gap

Of course, I have no statistics, and nobody ever tells me anything. But I suspect one reason marriages break up is that some wives, after spending a full hour in rich, deeply shared silence with the beloved, are apt to remark, "In heaven's name, *say* something, will you?"

The problem stems quite naturally from the fact that women speak because they wish to speak, whereas a man speaks only when driven to speech by something outside himself—like, for instance, he can't find any clean socks, or he has just read in a headline that Con Edison is asking for a new rate increase. A wife who really feels cheerful and chatty early in the morning (a circumstance that can be explained only by a faulty metabolism) can always inveigle her husband into conversation by using a little imagination and by learning to snap up cues. She might say, "Speaking of clean socks reminds me, did you read Anatole Broyard's review of *Humboldt's Gift*?" Now he's on the spot. He has to say something, even if it is only to comment on the total absence of any connection between his socks and *Humboldt's Gift*.

I have a rather engaging little trick for stirring my own husband into statement. I just quote a few lines from the balcony scene of *Romeo and Juliet*.

"He speaks," I say in mock lyrical tones, "but he says nothing. What of that? His eye discourses. I will answer *it*." Thus prodded, he is apt to say things he will have to retract later, but there are risks to everything.

Actually, if you had wanted a husband who would be a stimulating conversationalist, you should have married a mechanic or even a gardener—certainly not an author or a professional man or, last of all, a lecturer. When we got married, my husband was a lecturer and professor of drama and I used to imagine the stimulating, intellectual conversation we were going to have at breakfast. Like this:

ME: That play last night was interesting, didn't you think?
HIM: Very. Of course, the author is still heavily in debt to

Chekhov—the despairing protagonist, the shackling environment, the complete stasis in the third act, and, of course, the total absence of climax.

ME: Yes, he has an almost kinetic sense of atmosphere, but he never licked the story line.

HIM: Licked it? He should have joined it.

(Appreciative chuckles all around)

This, however, is a transcript of the actual conversation:

HIM: (Despairingly) I'll bet this is diet bread.

ME: What's the matter with diet bread?

HIM: (After a pause) Everything. Why don't we eat things other people eat?

ME: Such as—

HIM: (Passionately) Those flat sticky things with jam inside them. Or muffins. Why don't we ever have muffins?

ME: (Evenly) Very well, dear, we'll have muffins.

HIM: (Suspiciously) Oh, I know you. You'll get diet muffins.

We really should have our own radio show.

It's interesting to observe the phenomenon that will cause a husband who hasn't opened his yap in weeks suddenly to find the gift of speech. Just order a new coat that differs in any way at all from the last five coats you have owned and watch Big Chief Still Waters blossom into Alistair Cooke, a veritable fount of articulation. "Yes, I know it's the new style, but we haven't got a space ship yet. Oh, I see, all the fullness in the back is *supposed* to make you look as if you're standing in a head wind! Well, never mind. It'll be economical, anyway—in the summer you can take it to the beach and use it as a cabana." Etc.

There is a cure for this. Just take him with you when you go to Bonwit Teller's. Once you deposit him on that chaste Empire sofa in Misses' Suits, his whole attitude will change—not to mention his pulse, temperature, and rate of breathing. Precisely what causes men to go into shock in Bonwit's I can't imagine. My husband keeps looking from right to left in a state of ashen panic, as though he feared at any moment one of those elegant salesladies was going to snatch him and set his hair. But at any rate he brings a more judicious attitude to the subject of high style. "Yeah, yeah," he mutters at my first appearance from the depths of the dressing room, "it looks great, let's get out of here."

Some men do most of their talking at the movies ("Good Lord, I knew I was in for *Moby Dick,* but you didn't say there was going to be forty minutes of cartoons!"). My father is a man like that. The most he has spoken in thirty years was on a certain unfortunate occasion when my mother (who can't remember the titles of movies) took him for the second time in three weeks to see Bob Hope in *Son of Paleface.*

But let's get down to cases:

How to Talk to a Man When He's Snoring

When I speak of snoring I do not refer to the simple, rhythmic snorp-bleet, snorp-bleet to which every loyal, understanding wife should adjust. I am here talking of snoring which has the range and crescendo of a musical composition—where you can actually detect a verse, two choruses, and a release. I used to give my husband a gentle shove and whisper, "Honey, turn over—you're snoring." The result was that he turned over and in two minutes was snoring louder than before, while I lay awake for hours planning a separation and wondering what we were going to do about the children and all those monogrammed towels.

Then I learned the trick, which is to get the snorer interested. Don't make statements. Ask questions. Shake him and say, "Darling, what are you trying to say?" Eventually, after a few incoherent "huh, huhs" and "what, whats," he'll ask, "What do you mean, what am I trying to say?" After a few more equally pointless questions and answers he will be so cross that it will be at least fourteen minutes before he'll be able to snore again, giving you ample time to get to sleep first.

How to Talk to a Man in a Fashionable Restaurant

I once read an interview with the Duchess of Windsor in which she said that she and the Duke hated to eat in public restaurants because they had to converse so animatedly and affect such feverish interest in each other—lest rumors start that they were estranged—that she never could enjoy a bite of her dinner. It ought to be (but somehow it isn't) helpful to tell yourself that you're not the Duchess of Windsor and that nobody is even the tiniest bit interested in whether you and your husband have spoken since 1963. The point is that in a restaurant (like Sardi's, for instance) where you are surrounded by the tinkling laughter of beautiful models engaged in vivacious conversation with movie actors, you do feel somehow that you can't just sit there, specters at the feast, looking like two people who have just learned that their 1976 income tax return is being investigated. Of course there are lots of things on your mind that you could say ("Well, you saw that Chris got D in Health Habits again," or, "The exterminator says our new bugs are silverfish") but this doesn't seem to be the time or the place.

A couple I knew have solved the problem beautifully. She just tells him the story of "The Three Bears," a narrative which is admirable for the purpose because of its many rising inflections. And he helps her out by occasionally interjecting a remark like "By George, you mean she ate every last bite of the baby bear's porridge?" Do try it some time. Anybody overhearing you will conclude that you are discussing a new television spectacular—either that, or you're both a little bit dotty. If you should be concerned about this aspect of the matter, or if you should happen to intercept a stunned glance from the waiter, you can always drop in a covering remark like "Woody Allen—*there's* your Baby Bear!"

How to Talk to a Man When He's Taking a Shower

Here you have a captive audience and an ideal opportunity to tell a husband a number of things that you don't want him to hear. (Later on you can say, "Of course, I told you, you just don't listen!") There is no limit to the amount of unwelcome information you can get off your chest at one clip in these circumstances: "The man from Macy's was here and I took thirty dollars out of your wallet," and "Betty called, she and George are going to drop in," and "This is our weekend to take care of the school rabbit."

How to Talk to a Man on the Telephone, Long Distance

When a man calls you from Tulsa, he invariably makes the mistake of calling either from a public bar or from his mother's living room. Neither setting is exactly conducive to a free exchange of ideas. There, within earshot of his fellow revelers or his mother, he can hardly say the one thing you want to hear, which is that he misses you terribly, it's been a nightmare, a nightmare! and he's never going to make a trip alone again. For that matter, you can't tell him you miss him either, because the children are there with you and they become downright alarmed at any hint that their parents have preserved this degrading adolescent attachment so far into senility. So, if you're not careful, it's going to be a total loss of five dollars and eighty-five cents.

Don't, whatever you do, launch into that foolish litany of last-minute health bulletins: "Yes, I'm fine, yes, Chris is fine, yes, Gilbert is fine, etc." Let it be understood in advance that if one of the children should be rushed to the hospital for an emergency appendectomy, you'll mention it.

Use the time to clear up some matter that has really been troubling you. Explain that you finally saw *The Bridge on the River Kwai* on television and that it was marvelous, marvelous, but you didn't understand the ending. Get him to explain it. Did Alec Guinness mean to set off that dynamite or didn't he? What about William Holden? Who really killed him? This is important. When William Holden gets shot, a woman wants to know the facts. Later, when you hang up, you may discover that you've forgotten to ask what time his plane arrives at La Guardia, but the call won't have been a total loss.

How to Talk to a Man Before a Party

There are two occasions when a wife absolutely expects that a loyal husband will cleave to her side: when she's having a baby and when she's having a party. (It's interesting to note that the announcements on both occasions always seem to imply that these are joint projects, but, when it comes right down to it, who has that baby and who has that party? You do.) No one expects a husband to go out in the kitchen and stuff eggs, but he might try being a moral support during that horrible, hollow half hour before the first guest arrives. There you are, wandering aimlessly about from ashtray to ashtray, suddenly feeling as strange and as lost as if you had just checked into a motel in downtown Pittsburgh. And one of the reasons you can't rely on your husband for a comforting remark is that this is precisely the moment he chooses to lay a few asphalt tiles on the floor of the rumpus room.

If you should stand on your rights and say "Don't you

disappear anywhere at all, just stay right here!" he will eventually lighten the tension by muttering "Great Scott, you forgot limes!" What he should say, of course, is something soothing like "Darling, you look charming in that dress. It reminds me of the night we met, do you remember? You were dancing with Hugh, and I came in with Connie and Leo . . . ."

The last time we had a party I suggested this constructive line of conversation to my husband. He claimed that he'd once said something very similar, and what I said was "In heaven's name, stop chattering about the night we met and go get some ice."

How to Talk to a Man After You've Told Him That if He Doesn't Stop Fiddling with That Old Toaster He Is Going to Blow a Fuse, and He Does.

There is no way. Just light a candle and count ten or your blessings, whichever is greater.

James Kincaid (Contemporary)

FROM *Eroticism Is a Two-Way Street, and I'm Working Both Sides*

Maturity, you and I agree, is, at bottom, an erotic realism, the graceful and becoming acknowledgement that Sophia Loren will not, after all these years, come to the door and tear our clothes from us, right off us, all of them. No she won't. Had she been likely to do so, she would have done it by now. She isn't coming. Stop thinking about whether she should have come or whether she would have come had she had any sense or all the time you wasted preparing for her or whether you are not justified in writing her a very angry letter. We (You and I) are mature and have put away childish things. We laugh at the idea of Sophia Loren coming to our door, though she is still so heart-stoppingly beautiful and would have such a good time with us were she somehow only to drop by when she is here and she wouldn't after all have to stay so long (she is often in Los Angeles, you know, and so am I).

•

My point is that, however virile flesh-and-blood teachers (you, me) may be, the part they are required to play allows them only bumbling impotence. Our culture provides but one erotic script for the pedagogue, and it's a farce.

•

One qualification: the teachers of the very young are often knockouts, men and women alike. Gorgeous kindergarten teachers are the rule; but they become progressively less thinkable as sexual partners as the students get older and more capable of thinking that sexual partners are what they'd like to have. By junior high it's a mockery, by high school preposterous. Graduate education is an exposure to full-scale god-awful revulsion; it's a wonder the highly-educated propagate. Those who go on to be deans and presidents enter another species altogether, a reptilian order where cross-fertilization with the human is not to be thought on.

Alan King (Contemporary)

FROM *Help! I'm a Prisoner in a Chinese Bakery*

After You Say "I Do" . . . You Don't

Has it ever occurred to you that the greatest loves of history and literature had one thing in common? The boy and the girl never got married. . . .

Not only don't they get married, they virtually never see each other. The lovers are always kept apart by family, society, wars, crusades, the black plague, or they're married to someone else. If you want to read about love and marriage, you've gotta go out and buy two separate books.

Romeo and Juliet, they got married. They spent one night together and the next day he committed suicide. Then she committed suicide. I'm trying to figure out what went on in that bedroom. . . .

I don't ever remember being single. My wife and I were kids together. . . . We grew up in the same slum together. . . .

I remember how much her father was against our marriage. He wanted her to marry a doctor, and, now that I look back on it, he was right. She should have married a doctor. It's the only way I could ever have gotten even with the medical profession. Furthermore, her father didn't want her to get married below her station. Jeanette's station was Fourteenth Street, and I had to get off at Eighth Street. That was six blocks below her station. . . .

He had one more standard question. They've always gotta ask it. It's part of the ritual.

"Will you support my daughter in the manner to which she's accustomed?"

"Sure," I replied. "We're moving in with you."

. . . We danced with both arms around one another. Jeanette put her head on my shoulder and closed her eyes. Each time we twirled, I moved her a little closer to the door.

. . . past Aunt Bessie who was stuffing her purse with cold hors d'oeuvres.

. . . past Uncle Max who was stuffing his pockets with the stainless-steel silverware.

. . . past Aunt Sonia who was stuffing a floral centerpiece up the back of Uncle Herman's tuxedo.

. . . past a waiter who was fighting with my father-in-law. "AND I'M TELLING YA, THE TIPS ARE NOT INCLUDED WITH THE MEAL."

Robert Klane (Contemporary)

❧❧❧

FROM *Where's Poppa?*

"Now, Coach Williams," the defense attorney began, "how did you come to be employed by the Memphis Maulers?"

Coach Williams answered immediately. "Well, to tell you the truth," he started, "I knew that the Memphis Maulers were the worst football team in the world. I knew that they needed a winner. So I contacted the management and told them that I could produce a world championship team for them in one year."

"That's quite a promise to make, isn't it, Coach Williams?" the defense attorney asked.

"Normally it would be," Coach Williams said, "but I already had a team ready to go. A team I had been working with for years. I just asked the management to come and take a look at them."

"And did they?" the defense attorney asked.

"They sure did," Coach Williams said. "They was desperate for a winner, all right." He laughed. "Anyway, they come and looked the boys over, and when they saw the material I had for them, they signed me on the spot."

"And what was this team they saw?"

Coach Williams smiled proudly. "A special one," he said. "These boys were hand-picked. I was convinced for a long time that I could build the greatest football team in the world if I got the players young enough and teached them nothing else but to play football."

"I see," the defense attorney said. "And how old were these football players when you selected them?"

Coach Williams smiled again. "Oh they weren't football players when I picked them. They was just boys. Big boys."

"But how old were they?" the defense attorney asked again.

"I guess about nine or ten," Coach Williams answered. "I got them from all over the country. I just kept looking until I found the biggest and fastest boys in the country."

"And their parents gave you permission to take them?"

"No," Coach Williams said, "I just took them."

Hocheiser sat up straight. He started riffling his notes.

"You took them?" the defense attorney asked.

"Yeah," Coach Williams answered. "I took them."

"Without asking their parents?"

"I didn't see no need to," Coach Williams said. "I knew they'd all be thanking me once I made them rich as football players. None of these kids were too bright anyhow."

"Don't you think you were assuming a lot?" the defense attorney asked.

"I had to get them young," Coach Williams said. "I wanted them to learn the game of football the right way."

Hocheiser was turning pale. He knew nothing of what was now being revealed by the defense.

The defense attorney went on. "And your way was the right way."

"Correct," Coach Williams said. "I put them in a special training camp. These boys lived, ate and slept nothing but football. Hell, by the time they were fifteen they was ready for the pros."

"But don't you think," the defense attorney asked, "that these boys were missing a lot of things in life?"

"That's crazy talk," Coach Williams snapped. "I gave these boys the best of everything. Why, I fed them nothing but the finest raw meat. I fed the boys right."

The defense attorney looked at Coach Williams. "Coach Williams," he said, "didn't you notice that the boys were a little different from most people after having lived nothing but football for so long?"

"No," Coach Williams said, "I can't say that I did. They was damm good football players, that's all, and when they was ready, I contacted the Memphis Maulers."

The defense attorney went on. "Well then, answer this for me. After being with you for ten years, could they or could they not speak English as we know it?"

Coach Williams started to get excited. "They didn't have

to speak no damm English. They just had to play football. Besides," he added in a note of triumph, "the quarterback could speak."

"Speak?" the defense attorney asked. "English?"

"Well," Coach Williams said, "he could say numbers." Coach Williams looked over at Hocheiser. "What's this all about, anyway?"

Hocheiser looked up from his pile of notes. "I was just about to ask you the same thing," he said.

"Well, it's not important," Coach Williams shouted. "What's important is that the boys could play football. Goddamn, they could play football. The contract said they had to play football, not give speeches."

The judge rapped for order. "Please continue," he said to the defense attorney.

"Thank you, your honor." The defense attorney smiled. "Now then, Coach Williams, let's get on to the first game your team played as professionals."

"All right."

"Wouldn't you say that it was a rather violent game?"

Coach Williams smashed his hand down on the arm of his chair. "Football is a violent sport," he said. "I trained my boys to play it that way."

"Don't you think you might have overtrained them?"

"No, not at all."

"Do you recall, Coach Williams, any sort of unusual disturbance when your team first took the field?"

"I don't think so," Coach Williams said.

"You don't remember," the defense attorney said, "that some of your players ran up into the stands and started hitting and kicking a lot of spectators?"

"They was just up for the game," Coach Williams said. "Just up for the game, that's all."

"That's all?" the defense attorney asked.

"Listen," Coach Williams said, "people who go to football games like to see violence. They saw it."

The defense attorney shook his head. Hocheiser shook his head. "Let's get back to the game," the defense attorney said. "What happened on the first play from scrimmage?"

Coach Williams looked around the courtroom. "I don't remember," he said.

"Well," the defense attorney said, "let me see if I can

refresh your memory. Do you have a fullback on your team named Tommy 'No Hands' Crespiak?"

"Yes, I do." Coach Williams smiled. "The best damn fullback that ever was."

The defense attorney continued. "And why do they call him 'No Hands'?"

"Because he carried the football in his mouth."

"In his mouth?" the defense attorney asked unbelievingly.

"Yep," Coach Williams said. "That's the way I teached him. That left two hands free to knock the tacklers out of his way. Damn effective, too." Coach Williams demonstrated with an imaginary ball. "All the quarterback had to do was stick the ball in Tommy's mouth, and off he went, both arms swinging away."

"I see," the defense attorney said. "And did this lead to any unusual happenings?"

"Nothing serious," Coach Williams said.

"But didn't the quarterback fumble on the first play of the game?"

"Yes."

"And wasn't Tommy 'No Hands' Crespiak supposed to get the ball on that play?"

"Yes."

"And when he didn't get the ball, didn't he bite off the quarterback's head?"

A groan escaped from Hocheiser's mouth.

"Maybe he did," Coach Williams said, "but he ran it in for a touchdown."

"But it was the quarterback's head," the defense attorney protested.

"He never should have fumbled that ball," Coach Williams explained. "Tommy was expecting something in his mouth. He couldn't help it if it was the quarterback's head instead of the ball. He had a job to do and he did it."

Hocheiser felt faint. He started to gather up his papers and put them away. "Your honor," he said.

"Be quiet," the judge told him.

"And what happened when the rest of the players on your team saw all that blood?" the defense attorney asked.

"Now you can't blame them for that," Coach Williams told him. "I suppose I should have fed them before the game. They were hungry, that's all."

"So they jumped on him and ate him."

"Picked him clean," Coach Williams admitted.

"Your honor," Hocheiser began, "I would like to withdraw myself . . ."

"Sit down and be quiet," the judge told him.

"But he never told me any of this," Hocheiser protested.

"Shut up," the judge said.

The defense attorney went on. "Now, Coach Williams, won't you admit that the half-time show you planned for the game was a little unusual?"

Coach Williams slammed his hand down on the arm of the chair again. "They like violence," he shouted. "They come to see violence, not no namby-pamby game."

"Would you mind telling the court, Coach Williams, what that half-time program was?"

"Yessir," Coach Williams said, "it was a hanging."

"You hanged someone during the half-time?"

"That's right," Coach Williams said. "I thought it would make good publicity. Besides, those fans want violence, they don't want to see no sissy band prancing around."

"But what about the person you hanged?" the defense attorney asked. "Didn't he object?"

"Hell no," Coach Williams answered. "We did it fair and square. We drew a number and the person with the lucky number got hung."

"Your honor," Hocheiser screamed, "I didn't know. I swear I didn't know."

"One hundred dollars for contempt of court," the judge said.

The defense attorney spoke up. "Your honor, in light of this testimony I move that the case against my client, the Memphis Maulers, be dismissed."

"So moved."

"Your honor," Hocheiser yelled, "please listen to me."

"Throw him out."

Tony Kornheiser (Contemporary)

〰〰〰

FROM *Pumping Irony*

Chic Coffee: Say It Ain't So, Joe

In the '50s, the craze was ice cream. Every weekend the family went out for ice-cream sundaes and banana splits, and then your dad dropped dead at forty-eight, his arteries all plumped up like kielbasa, and so we reconsidered our diets and opted for something less frivolous and more nourishing, and in the '60s, the craze was . . . pizza. Pizza was also horrible for your health, inasmuch as it consisted essentially of bread (for useless bulk) and cheese (for circulatory blockage), tomato paste (for color), yeast (for infections), and those red-and-yellow-flake peppers (for boils and blisters on the roof of the mouth). Eventually, diet gurus began to enter our lives, and in the '70s, the craze was salad bars, which featured "three-bean salad" (garbanzo, fatouli, and ganoozi beans) and other fine ethnic delicacies you would not feed a hamster. No one really liked salad bars, other than the manufacturer of Plexiglas sneeze guards. In the '80s, the fad was enterprises dedicated to the production and sales of fresh chocolate chip cookies, as though chocolate chip cookies were some product of great quality and sophistication in which absolute freshness was required for the true connoisseur, as opposed to some brown glob that tastes perfectly good when it comes in a bag from Keebler.

Now it's coffee.

People actually go *out* for coffee. Like it's a movie. Like it's entertainment.

All across America, every store that goes out of business is replaced by a Starbucks or a Quartermaine's or some other fancy coffee chain featuring this week's special: Peruvian Monkeyfoot Decaf. (Which comes, by the way, with a thick foamy head that would make Budweiser jealous, and takes up two thirds of the cup, so when you pierce the canopy of foam, you realize you've paid four dollars for two sips. Which is why they call it Star-BUCKS.)

Fran Lebowitz (Contemporary)

◈◈◈◈

FROM *Social Studies*

Things

To put it rather bluntly, I am not the type who wants to go back to the land—I am the type who wants to go back to the hotel. This state of affairs is at least partially due to the fact that nature and I have so little in common. We don't go to the same restaurants, laugh at the same jokes or, most significant, see the same people. . . .

First of all, nature is by large to be found out of doors, a location where, it cannot be argued, there are never enough comfortable chairs. Secondly, for fully half of the time it is day out there, a situation created by just the sort of harsh overhead lighting that is so unflattering to the heavy smoker. Lastly, and most pertinent to this discourse, is the fact that natural things are by their very definition wild, unkempt and more often than not crawling with bugs. Quite obviously, then, natural things are just the kind of things that one does not strive to acquire. *Objets d'art* are one thing; *objets d'nature* are not.

Sinclair Lewis (1885–1951)

୬ଇଡ୍‌ ଡ୍‌ନ

FROM *Babbitt*

Often of a morning Babbitt came bouncing and jesting in to breakfast. But things were mysteriously awry to-day. As he pontifically tread the upper hall he looked into Verona's bedroom and protested, "What's the use of giving the family a high-class house when they don't appreciate it and tend to business and get down to brass tacks?"

He marched upon them: Verona, a dumpy brown-haired girl of twenty-two, just out of Bryn Mawr, given to solicitudes about duty and sex and God and the unconquerable bagginess of the gray sports-suit she was now wearing. Ted—Theodore Roosevelt Babbitt—a decorative boy of seventeen. Tinka—Katherine—still a baby at ten, with radiant red hair and a thin skin which hinted of too much candy and too many ice cream sodas. Babbitt did not show his vague irritation as he tramped in. He really disliked being a family tyrant, and his nagging was as meaningless as it was frequent. He shouted at Tinka, "Well, kittiedoolie!" It was the only pet name in his vocabulary, except the "dear" and "hon." with which he recognized his wife, and he flung it at Tinka every morning.

He gulped a cup of coffee in the hope of pacifying his stomach and his soul. His stomach ceased to feel as though it did not belong to him, but Verona began to be conscientious and annoying, and abruptly there returned to Babbitt the doubts regarding life and families and business which had clawed at him when his dream-life and the slim fairy girl had fled.

Verona had for six months been filing-clerk at the Gruensberg Leather Company offices, with a prospect of becoming secretary to Mr. Gruensberg and thus, as Babbitt defined it, "getting some good out of your expensive college education till you're ready to marry and settle down."

But now said Verona: "Father! I was talking to a classmate of mine that's working for the Associated Charities—oh, Dad, there's the sweetest little babies that come to the milk-station there!—and I feel as though I ought to be doing something worth while like that."

"What do you mean 'worth while'? If you get to be Gruensberg's secretary—and maybe you would, if you kept up your shorthand and didn't go sneaking off to concerts and talkfests every evening—I guess you'll find thirty-five or forty bones a week worth while!"

"I know, but—oh, I want to—contribute— I wish I were working in a settlement-house. I wonder if I could get one of the department-stores to let me put in a welfare-department with a nice rest-room and chintzes and wicker chairs and so on and so forth. Or I could—"

"Now you look here! The first thing you got to understand is that all this uplift and flipflop and settlement-work and recreation is nothing in God's world but the entering wedge for socialism. The sooner a man learns he isn't going to be coddled, and he needn't expect a lot of free grub and, uh, all these free classes and flipflop and doodads for his kids unless he earns 'em, why, the sooner he'll get on the job and produce—produce—produce! That's what the country needs, and not all this fancy stuff that just enfeebles the will-power of the working man and gives his kids a lot of notions above their class. And you—if you'd tend to business instead of fooling and fussing— All the time! When I was a young man I made up my mind what I wanted to do, and stuck to it. . . .

. . . realize I don't appreciate how profoundly you think and what a splendid brain and vocabulary you have. Just—splendid."

But Verona was irritating. "Dad," she worried, "how do you know that public ownership of utilities and so on and so forth will always be a failure?"

Mrs. Babbitt reproved, "Rone, I should think you could see and realize that when your father's all worn out with orating, it's no time to expect him to explain these complicated subjects. I'm sure when he's rested he'll be glad to explain it to you. Now let's all be quiet and give Papa a chance to get ready for his next speech. Just think! Right now they're gathering in Maccabee Temple, and *waiting* for us!"

David Ross Locke (1833–1888)

❦❦❦

Woman's Place

I adore woman, but I want her to keep her place. In considering this woman question, I take the conservative standpoint. From the beginning, woman has occupied a dependent position. The Turks, logical fellows, denied her a soul, and made her an object of barter and sale. The American Indians made of her a beast of burden. In America, since we have extended the area of civilization by butchering the Indians, we have copied both. In our higher walks of life, she is a toy to be played with, and is bought and sold; in the lower strata she bears the burdens and does the drudgery of servants. But I am sure that her present condition is her proper condition, for it has always been so.

Man, it will be observed, was created first, showing conclusively that he was intended to take precedence of woman. A schoolmistress of mine once denied the correctness of this conclusion. "If there is anything in being first," she said, "man must acknowledge the supremacy of the goose, for according to Genesis, the fowl was first created."

Such an argument, of course, I reject with scorn.

My research indicates that Eve was the ideal woman. She knew her place. She did not even keep a kitchen girl. At least, I find no record of anything of the kind. Probably at that time the emigration from Ireland was setting in other directions. Eve was no strong-minded female, and never got out of her legitimate sphere. I have searched the Book of

Genesis faithfully, and I defy anyone to find it recorded therein that Eve ever made a public speech, or expressed any desire to practice law or medicine, or sit in the legislature. What a crushing, withering, scathing, blasting rebuke to the Dickinsons, Stantons, Blackwells, and Anthonys of this degenerate day!

I find in the Bible many arguments against the equality of woman with man in point of intellectual power. The serpent tempted Eve, not Adam. Why did he select Eve? Ah, why, indeed! He is a most consummate judge of character, and that he has never failed to select for his work the most fitting instruments. When America was to be betrayed the first time, Satan selected Benedict Arnold, and when the second betrayal of the Republic was determined upon, he knew where Jefferson Davis lived. When there is a fearful piece of jobbery to get through Congress or the New York legislature, he never fails to select precisely the right persons for the villainy. Possibly he is not entitled to credit for discrimination in these last-mentioned bodies, for he could not very well go wrong, blindfolded and with both hands tied—but this is a digression.

Satan selected Eve because the woman was weaker than the man, and therefore best for his purpose. This reckless female, my old schoolmistress, insisted that Satan approached Eve first because he knew that woman was not afraid of the Devil. But I reject this explanation as irrelevant.

At this point, however, we must stop. Should we go on, we would find that Eve, the weak woman, tempted Adam, the strong man, with distinguished success, which would leave us in this predicament: Satan, stronger than Eve, tempted her to indulge in fruit. Eve's weakness was demonstrated by her falling a victim to temptation. Eve tempted Adam; Adam yielded to Eve; therefore—but I shall dismiss Adam and Eve with the remark that if Satan had been considerate of the feelings of the conservatives, his best friends, by the way, in all ages, he would have tempted Adam first and caused Adam to tempt Eve.

As a conservative, I must say that the inferiority of the sex is easy of demonstration. It has been said that the mother forms the character of the man so long, that the proposition has become axiomatic. If this be true, we can crush those who prate of the equality of woman, by holding up to the gaze of the world the inferior men she has formed. Look at the Congress of the United States! By their works ye shall know them.

Pocahontas has been held up as a sample of female strength of mind. I don't deny that she displayed some decision of character, but it was fearfully unwomanly. When her father raised his club over the head of the astonished Smith, instead of rushing in so recklessly, she should have said, "Please, pa, don't." Her recklessness was immense. Suppose Pocahontas had been unable to stay the blow, where would our Miss have been then?—she never would have married Rolfe. What would the first families of Virginia have done for somebody to descend from?

The disturbing female, my former schoolmistress, of whom I have spoken once or twice, maintains that women's qualifications entitle them to vote. I answer that such is not the case. For example, my friend is learned. She has read the Constitution of the United States. She excels in political lore the great majority of our representatives in Congress. Nevertheless, I protest against her voting for several reasons:

1. She cannot sing bass. Her voice is pitched higher than the male voice, which indicates feminine weakness of mind.
2. Her form is graceful rather than strong.
3. She delights in millinery goods.
4. She can't grow whiskers.

In all of these points nature has made a distinction between the sexes which cannot be overlooked.

Unless women keep to their sphere, dependent on men for all things, they would be as miserable as Jay Gould is, with an ungobbled railroad. Let every woman marry and marry as soon as possible. Then she is provided for. Then the ivy has her oak. Then, if her husband is a good man, a kind man, an honest man, a sober man, an industrious man, and if he has a good business and drives it, and meets with no misfortunes, and never yields to temptations, why, then, the maid promoted to be his wife will be tolerably certain to, at least, have all that she can eat, and all that she can wear, as long as he continues so.

If there be more women than there are men, I don't know what they can do unless they make shirts at twelve and a half cents each, and live gorgeously on the proceeds of their toil. If one man concludes that he won't marry at all, it's bad for another woman, unless some man's wife dies and he marries again. That might equalize it, but for two reasons: It compels the woman to wait for a husband until she possibly concludes it isn't worth while. Furthermore, husbands die as fast as wives, which brings a new element into the field—widows. And, pray, what chance has an inexperienced man against a widow determined upon a second husband?

However, this strange woman, of whom I have spoken, remarked that she wanted women to have an opportunity to stand alone in case she could not marry or her husband proved incompetent to support her. She demanded for woman, in short, employment at anything she was capable of doing, and pay precisely the same that men receive for the same labor, provided she does it as well.

This is a clear flying in the face of Providence! It is utterly impossible that any woman can do any work as well as men. Nature decreed it otherwise. Ask the clerks at Washington, whose muscular frames, whose hardened sinews, are employed at from twelve hundred to three thousand dollars per annum, at the arduous and exhausting labor of writing in books and counting money, and cutting out extracts from newspapers, and endorsing papers and filing them, what they think of that?

I asked her sternly, "Are you willing to go to war? Did you shoulder a musket in the late unpleasantness?"

She merely asked me if I carried a musket in the late war? Certainly I did not. I had too much presence of mind to volunteer. Nor did the majority of those holding official position. Like Job's charger, they snuffed the battle afar off—some hundreds of miles—and slew the haughty Southron on the stump, or by hired substitute. But there is this difference: We *could* have gone, while women could not. And it is better that it is so. In the event of another bloody war, one so desperate as to require all the patriotism of the country to show itself, I do not want my wife to go to the tented field, even though she have the requisite physical strength. No, indeed! I want her to stay at home—with me.

In the matter of wages, I do not see how it is to be helped.

The woman who teaches a school receives, if she has thoroughly mastered the requirements of the position, say, six hundred dollars a year, while a man occupying the same position, filling it with equal ability, receives twice that amount, and possibly three times. But what is this to me? As a man of business, my duty to myself is to get my children educated at the least possible expense. As there are very few things women are permitted to do, and as, for every vacant place, there are a hundred women eager for it, their pay—as a matter of course—is brought down to a fine point.

There are immutable laws governing all these things—the laws of supply and demand. Christ, whose mission was with the poor, made other laws, but Christ is not allowed to have anything to do with business. Selfishness is older than Christ, and we conservatives stick close to the oldest.

As I said some minutes ago, if the men born into the world would marry at twenty-one, each a maiden of eighteen, and take care of her properly, and never get drunk or sick, or anything of that inconvenient sort, and both would be taken at precisely the same time with consumption, yellow fever, cholera, or any of those ailments, and employ the same physician, that they might go out of the world at the same moment, it would be well. The men would then take care of the women. Women are themselves to blame for a great part of the distress they experience. There is work for them, if they would only do it. The kitchens of the country are not half supplied with intelligent labor, and therein is a refuge for all women in distress. I assert that nothing but foolish pride, which is sinful, keeps the daughters and widows of insolvency out of kitchens, where they may have happy underground homes and three dollars per week, by merely doing six hours per day more labor than hod-carriers average.

Failing the kitchen, women may canvass for books, though that occupation, like a few others, equally profitable, brings them into continual contact with the lords of creation, and thus has a drawback in the fact that some men leer into the face of every woman who strives to do business for herself, as though she were a moral leper.

Failing all these, as I have touched upon before, she may, at least, take to the needle. At this last occupation, she is certain to meet no competition, save from her own sex. In all my experience, and it has been extensive, I never yet saw a man making pantaloons at twelve and one half cents a pair.

But women will not all submit. Refusing to acknowledge the position in life nature fixed for them, they rebel, and unpleasantness takes place. An incident which fell under my observation recently, beautifully illustrates this.

A young lady, named Jane Evans, I believe, had sustained the loss of both her parents. Jane purchased some needles, and renting a room in the uppermost part of a building in a secluded section of New York, commenced a playful effort to live by making shirts, at eighteen cents each. She was situated, I need not say, pleasantly for one of her class. Her room was not large, it is true, but as she had no cooking stove or bedstead, what did she want of a large room? She had a window, which did not open, but as there was no glass in it, she had no occasion to open it. This building commanded a beautiful view of the back parts of other buildings similar in appearance, and the sash kept out a portion of the smell. In this delightful retreat, she sat and sat and sewed and sewed. Sometimes, in her zeal, she would sew till late in the night, and she was always at her work very early in the morning. She paid rent promptly, for the genial old gentleman of whom she leased her room had a sportive habit of kicking girls into the street who did not pay promptly. She managed every now and then, did this economical girl, to purchase a loaf of bread, which she ate.

One Saturday night, she took her bundle of work to the delightful man who employed her. Jane had labored sixteen hours per day on them, and she had determined, as Sunday was close at hand, to have for her breakfast, in addition to her bread, a small piece of mutton. Mutton! Luxurious living destroyed Ancient Rome!

Her employer found fault with the making of these shirts. "They are not properly sewed," he said, and he could not, in consequence, pay her. Jane then, injudiciously cried about it, and her employer who was, and is, possessed of a tender heart, and cannot bear to see a woman cry, kicked her out of his store into the snow.

What did this wicked girl do? Did she go back and ask pardon of her good, tender-hearted employer? Not she! On the contrary, she clenched her hands, and, passing by a baker's shop, stole a loaf of bread, and, brazen thing that she was, she ate it in front of the shop! She said she was hungry, though it was subsequently proven that she had eaten within forty-eight hours.

Justice was swift upon the heels of the desperate wretch—it always is, by the way, close behind the heels of the friendless. She was arrested by a policeman and conveyed to the Tombs, was herded into a cell in which there were other women who had progressed farther than she had. She was arraigned for petty larceny and sent to jail for sixty days.

Now, see how surely evildoers come to bad ends. The wretched Jane—this fearfully depraved Jane—unable, after such a manifestation of depravity, to hold up her head, fell into bad ways. Remorse for the stealing of that loaf of bread so preyed upon her, that she wandered about the streets of New York for five days, asking for work, and finally threw herself off a wharf. Had she continued working cheerily, sewing shirts, accepting the situation like a Christian, taking life as she found it, would she have thrown herself off a dock? Never!

So you see demonstrated the mischief that comes from women attempting to move out from their sphere. Women who do not want to steal bread, and be arrested, and go off wharves, must take pay as it is offered, whether they get anything to eat or not. Had this wretched girl gone back contentedly to her room, and starved to death cheerfully, she would not have stolen bread, and would have saved the City of New York the expense and trouble of fishing her out of the East River.

Alas! Such women always make trouble.

Anita Loos (1893–1981)

‿‿⁓∘⁓‿‿

FROM *Kiss Hollywood Goodby*

I recall an occasion on the set where the camera was to cease grinding abruptly at a moment when Jean [Harlow] started to remove her jacket. But for some reason the boy in charge of the clap-board failed to give the signal to cut, so Jean "innocently" continued to take off her jacket, under which she was nude to the waist. Nudity was rarely seen in those days, and Jean's had the startling quality of an alabaster statue. Visitors on the set scarcely believed their eyes. The lighting crew almost fell out of the flies in shock. Wide-eyed in her "apology," Jean addressed the director. "I'm sorry, but nobody gave the order to cut."

Every MGM movie was taken out to one of the Los Angeles suburbs for a preview. . . .

The initial preview of *Red-Headed Woman* took place in Glendale on that momentous date in June of 1932. Irving and I hid out in that suburban audience with our ears nervously tuned for its reaction. And during the first ten minutes we were deeply disturbed, for the audience was as confused as Jack Conway had been. It didn't know whether to laugh at our sex pirate or not, and, as every producer of comedy knows, a half-laugh is worse than none at all. Only after the movie was well along did the audience catch on and begin to enjoy the jokes.

There was no need to wait for postcards on that movie. Irving called me to his office the first thing next morning. "Look," said he, "I'd like you to contrive a prologue which will tip the audience off that the movie's a comedy." I proceeded to concoct a scene which showed Jean describing to her girl friend the all-abiding depth of her love for her married boss; as proof of which Jean revealed a photo of her loved one on a flashy dime-store garter.

Our second preview was in Pasadena and the movie started off with the garter scene. That did it! Laughs began at once and never ceased to mount to the end of the film.

When *Red-Headed Woman* was released, it instantly catapulted Jean Harlow into stardom. The picture enjoyed all sorts of fringe successes. It won the award of *Vanity Fair* magazine as the best film of the year; and the London office of MGM reported that the royal family kept a copy at Buckingham Palace for entertaining guests after dinner. Among its many distinctions, *Red-Headed Woman* made film history because it brought on more stringent censorship and caused massive difficulties to the industry for years to come. It outraged ladies' clubs throughout the land, but not because of any episode which might be termed salacious. It was because our heroine, the bad girl of whom all good husbands dream, ended her career as many such scalawags do, rich, happy, and respected, without ever having paid for her sins.

FROM *Gentlemen Prefer Blondes*

Dorothy said that she did not say anything more about me being a debutant at Little Rock, because after all Dorothy knows that I really did not make any debut in Little Rock, because just when it was time to make my debut, my gentleman friend Mr. Jennings became shot, and after the trial was over and all of the Jury had let me off, I was really much too fatigued to make any debut.

So then Dorothy said, why don't we throw a party now and you can become a debutant now and put them all in their place, because it seems that Dorothy is dying for a party. So that is really the first sensible suggestion that Dorothy has made yet, because I think that every girl who is engaged to a gentleman who has a fine old family like Henry, had really ought to be a debutant. So I told her to come right over and we would plan my debut but we would keep it very, very quiet and give it tomorrow night, because if Henry heard I was making my debut he would come up from Pennsylvania and he would practically spoil the party, because all Henry has to do to spoil a party is to arrive at it.

So Dorothy came over and we planned my debut. So first we decided to have some engraved invitations engraved, but it always takes quite a little time to have invitations engraved, and it would really be foolish because all of the gentlemen we were going to invite to my debut were all members of the Racquet Club, so I could just write out a notice that I was having a debut and give it to Willie Gwynn and have Willie Gwynn post it on the Racquet Club board.

So Willie Gwynn posted it on the club board and then he called me up and he told me that he had never seen so much enthusiasm since the Dempsey-Firpo fight, and he said that the whole Racquet Club would be there in a body. So then we had to plan about what girls we would ask to my debut. Because I have not seemed to meet so many society women yet because of course a girl does not meet society women until her debut is all over, and then all the society women all come and call on a debutant. But I know practically all of the society men, because practically all of the society men belong to the Racquet Club, so after I have the Racquet Club at my debut, all I have to do to take my real place in society is to meet their mothers and sisters, because I know practically all of their sweethearts now.

But I always seem to think that it is delightful to have quite a lot of girls at a party, if a girl has quite a lot of gentlemen at a party, and it is quite delightful to have all the girls from the Follies, but I really could not invite them because, after all, they are not in my set. So then I thought it all over and I thought that even if it was not etiquette to invite them to a party, it really would be etiquette to hire them to come to a party and be entertainers, and after they were entertainers they could mix in to the party and it really would not be a social error.

So then the telephone rang and Dorothy answered it and it seems that it was Joe Sanguinetti, who is almost the official bootlegger for the whole Racquet Club, and Joe said he had heard about my debut and if he could come to my debut and bring his club which is the Silver Spray Social Club of Brooklyn, he would supply all of the liquor and he would guarantee to practically run the rum fleet up to the front door.

So Dorothy told him he could come, and she hung up the telephone before she told me his proposition, and I became quite angry with Dorothy because, after all, the Silver Spray

Social Club is not even mentioned in the Social Register and it has no place at a girl's debut. But Dorothy said by the time the party got into swing, anyone would have to be a genius if he could tell whether he belonged to the Racquet Club, the Silver Spray Social Club, or the Knights of Pythias. But I really was almost sorry that I asked Dorothy to help plan my debut, except that Dorothy is very good to have at a party if the police come in, because Dorothy always knows how to manage the police, and I never knew a policeman yet who did not finish up by being madly in love with Dorothy. So then Dorothy called up all of the reporters on all of the newspapers and invited them all to my debut, so they could see it with their own eyes.

So Dorothy says that she is going to see to it that my debut lands on the front page of all of the newspapers, if we have to commit a murder to do it.

June 19th:

Well, it has been three days since my debut party started but I finally got tired and left the party last night and went to bed because I always seem to lose all of my interest in a party after a few days, but Dorothy never loses her interest in a party and when I woke up this morning Dorothy was just saying goodbye to some of the guests. I mean Dorothy seems to have quite a lot of vitality, because the last guests of the party were guests we picked up when the party went to take a swim at Long Beach the day before yesterday, and they were practically fresh, but Dorothy had gone clear through the party from beginning to end without even stopping to go to a Turkish bath as most of the gentlemen had to do. So my debut has really been very novel, because quite a lot of the guests who finished up at my debut were not the same guests that started out at it, and it is really quite novel for a girl to have so many different kinds of gentlemen at her debut.

•

Willie Gwynn's sister was having a dance at the Gwynn estate on Long Island, and Willie Gwynn said that all of the eligible gentlemen in New York were conspicuous by their absents at his sister's party, because they were all at my party. So it seems as if I am really going to be quite a famous hostess if I can just bring my mind to the point of being Mrs. Henry Spoffard, Jr.

FROM *But Gentlemen Marry Brunettes*

Well, just going into the old Breene family mansion on Fifth Avenue, ought to make a girl feel as if she was getting somewheres. Because you have to be shown through three separate doors, and the first two of them are *iron*. But when Charlie showed Dorothy through them, all Dorothy could think of was that the Breene family were giving themselves three separate chances to throw her out, and she began to lose some of her self-possession.

Well, after they got past the third door, the butler started to lead them through quite a long, hollow hallway that had nothing to relieve it but some life size crockery baby elephants that only made Dorothy feel more unimpressive. But they finally reached the old family libery, and under an electric lamp, sat the father of Charlie Breene. But Dorothy says that, after all that suspence, Charlie's Father was not such a climax. I mean, he is the kind of a gentleman who has never done anything in his life, either one way or another. And the Breene family were always holding him up to Charlie as an example of what he could keep from doing if he would only concentrate his mind on it.

Well, Dorothy looked Mr. Breene over, and she began to feel quite a little better. And Mr. Breene told Dorothy that he was pleased to meet her, because somebody had taken him to a Follies once five years ago, and he really could not remember when he had ever had such an enjoyable evening. So Dorothy spoke up and said, "If you feel that way about it, why don't you take a long chance, and try going again?" So Mr. Breene said that that was really quite a bright idea, and he wondered why he had never thought of it.

And while he was wondering, Mrs. Breene came in. Well, Mrs. Breene was really more than sweet to Dorothy, for she made conversation just as if Dorothy were an equal. And first she asked Dorothy her opinion of quite a few rare old first editions of anteek classic books they had in their libery. And when Mrs. Breene asks for an opinion, she is always polite enough to stop, and wait for a reply. But Dorothy did not have any, and the atmosphere became quite strained. I mean, Dorothy does not know enough about etiquette to know that any time a girl feels like she has nothing to say, the best thing to do is to ask for a glass of water. And asking for a glass of water, where it was quite inconvenient to find one, would have made Dorothy feel quite important.

Well, after Mrs. Breene saw that Dorothy had become as uncomftable as she could be in a libery, she invited her into the Art gallery, to show her a new picture she just bought by the famous Spanish artist called Zuluago. And Mrs. Breene told Dorothy to look it over carefully, and then tell her what she thought of its' "chiarusquero." Well, Dorothy had practically no thoughts on the subjeck, but she suddenly got quite a bright idea, and asked Charlie what *he* thought of it. So Charlie spoke up and said, "By Jove, I don't know what it is." Well, of course, it made Mrs. Breene look quite small that any son of hers was so uncultured. So she really had to bite her lip. But she became sweeter than ever to Dorothy and told her that she had arranged quite a little surprise for her. And the suprise was that she had invited Jefferson Breene, the famous uncle of Charlie, who is not only the head of the whole Breene family, but one of the most impressive Americans of the Age, to come and look her over at dinner.

Well, while they were waiting for Jefferson Breene to arrive and look Dorothy over, the famous debutant, Muriel Devanant came in and did it. Well, Muriel seemed to be delighted with Dorothy from the start, for she greeted her in quite a hearty tone, and shook Dorothy's hand in quite a strong grasp that Dorothy says reminded her of a homesick Elk meeting one of his kind in some foreign climb. But the way that Dorothy acted was the depths of being uncultured. For she backed away from Muriel, in defence, and began to look toward an exit. So finally even Charlie noted her disturbants, and he got Dorothy off on one side, and wanted to know if anything was the matter. And Dorothy said "Nothing that an earthquake couldn't clear up." But Charlie did not understand what she was getting at. And he began to look at Dorothy askance.

Well, finally it seemed to be dinner time, and Mrs. Breene said they would not wait for Mr. Jefferson Breene, because when a gentleman holds the affairs of the Nation in his pocket, he is likely to be late at any moment. So Mrs. Breene led them through 5 or 6 large size salons with quite slippery floors and small Armenian rugs, and Dorothy says that the only diffrence between her and Eliza crossing the ice, was that Mrs. Breene had forgotten to order blood hounds.

Well, Dorothy said they finally arrived at the old oaken dining room, where the table was all laid out in her honor, to look like a funeral. And just as they were sitting down, the great Jefferson Breene himself came in. But when he made his entrants, Dorothy realized that she had already met him, at the apartment of a girl in the Follies called Gloria. Only at the apartment of Gloria he went under the nom de plume of Mr. Jones. Well, when Jefferson Breene was intraduced to Dorothy he was really quite surprised. But he did not seem to want to mention their previous acquaintence before the family. So he said "grace" instead.

Well, during dinner, Jefferson Breene gave Dorothy quite a confidential talk about the evils of modern life, and he finally brought up the subjeck of having met Dorothy at Gloria's apartment. So he explained to Dorothy that his interest in Gloria was to help a girl from doing wrong. Because he said that he had a theory that if gentlemen would give girls expensive apartments, and automobiles and jewelry as a reward to *keep* from doing wrong, instead of visa versa, the world would really be a better place. So he told Dorothy that that was what he was doing to Gloria. But Dorothy held her tongue, because she says the only reply she could think up to that old bird, couldn't be spoken out loud in a refined home.

Well, then Mrs. Breene started in to ask Dorothy questions about the habits of girls in the Follies. Because it seems that Mrs. Breene was so broad minded, that she did not care how much she learned about Life. But Dorothy says that Mrs. Breene had the idea that Follies girls were about the same as red ants, and Dorothy did not know enough about red ants to answer her questions. Well, Dorothy tried to give Charlie a sign to think up a quick excuse to get out as soon as dinner was over. But Charlie did not understand, because it seems that he thought they were giving Dorothy a pleasant evening.

Well, dinner was no sooner over than the string quartet arrived. And then Society people began to pour in for the musical evening. And Mrs. Breene was so sweet to Dorothy that she picked out the most titled aristocrats to introduce her to, even if Dorothy did not know what to call them. But instead of taking the opertunity of making friends, Dorothy only let everybody see her misery. And the kind of an expression that Dorothy wears on her face when she is on the verge of standing more than she can bear, almost gives a person the impression that she is cross eyed. So the Society people began to leave Dorothy severly alone. And Mrs. Breene kept Charlie busy putting small gilt chairs all over the salon so that he could not join Dorothy and keep her company. And every time he looked at Dorothy across the salon, she was sitting all alone, looking quite unpopular, with a very unbecoming expression on her countenance. And I am really afraid that Charlie was beginning to wonder.

Well, finally Mrs. Breene came over to Dorothy and told her that she ought to smile, and enjoy herself and join in the conversation. But Dorothy does not know how to make an effort, and smile in Society, like the rest of us have to do. And finally the string quartet started in to play something that was called on the program a Bach Fudge, and Dorothy started to feel even worse.

But by this time, Mrs. Breene's own troubles began. Because nothing that Mrs. Breene could do would make those music lovers keep quiet. And just as soon as she got one set to hold their tongues in the hall, another set would start talking about themselves in the salon. And Mrs. Breene would have to crowd her way through all the gilt chairs, to tell them to "Hush!"

But, by that time, the music lovers in the hall would be at it again. And Mrs. Breene would try to hush them at a distants. But it was really like water rolling off of a duck's back. So then she would have to make her way back through all the gilt chairs in order to hush them again in the hallway. And she had to work like a Trojan, without really getting anywheres. And the looks of the string quartet kept getting blacker and blacker.

And finally things even got worse. Because somebody discovered that the butler was laying out champagne in the libery. And a regular Exodus started to occur in that direction, until there were only 4 people left in the salon, and they were the string quartet. So Mrs. Breene became almost frantick. And she rushed toward the libery, but by the time she got there, it was jammed to the door with music lovers. Well, she finally worked her way through the crowd, and

told them that the champagne would *not* be opened until the
music was over, so they might just as well make up their
minds to listen to the string quartet. So she pushed them all
out and locked the door, and they finally decided to go back
to the salon and be quiet. But Mrs. Breene did not know that
one of the guests was locked up in the libery with the butler
and all of that champagne. And, of course, the guest that
was locked up, was Dorothy.

Well, it seems that the butler and Dorothy started right in
to become friendly. For he was in quite a Bolshivistic state
of mind himself, because, by rights it should have been his
night out. And it seems that he was a German butler who
loved music, so he had bought himself a ticket to Lowan-
grin at the opera. But, of course, he had to give it up. And
he could not even hear the string quartet, because they had
to shut the libery door on account of the way the guests behaved. So he seemed to think that, in this world, it was only
the wealthy who were allowed to love music. So he and
Dorothy took a drink to forget their troubles.

Well, the champagne was of the very best, so they had
some more, and the first thing Dorothy knew, she began
to cheer up and feel better. And Dorothy says, that by the
time the string quartet got through their program, she had
reached a state where she could have been happy in a
swamp. So she emerged from the libery and made her way
back through the party, smiling to the right and left, and
greeting people heartily that she had not even had an intra-
duction to.

Well, when she reached the salon, it seems that Dorothy
decided to do a dance of some new step she had learned in
the Follies. I mean, nobody had even asked her, but strange
to say, instead of everybody being annoyed, they were all
delighted. And they started to applaud. So then Dorothy decided to sing the comick version of a song that some of the
girls had composed in the privacy of their own dressing
room, that was not even meant to be sung in the Follies,
much less a salon. But instead of being shocked, those music lovers were even more delighted, and they started to
crowd back into the salon in such large numbers that the
string quartet, that was trying its best to get out of the salon,
nearly had its shello smashed.

Well, Dorothy became the Life of the party. And Charlie

Breene stood by in pride and watched her with the love light in his eyes. And Mrs. Breene finally had to step in and take Dorothy by the arm, and make her stop. Because she told her guests that they must not allow the dear child to overtax herself.

Well, then Dorothy started to say "good-night" to her Hostess, and quite a few guests still crowded around to listen, because by this time Dorothy had gained quite a little reputation as a "Bon Mot." So Mrs. Breene was really more than sweet to Dorothy, and she took her by the hand, and seemed to want to hold quite a little conversation. But Dorothy could not understand what she was saying because Mrs. Breene could not seem to help from breaking out into French. Well, Dorothy had learned quite a few Mexican words when she was in the Southern part of California, so Dorothy says she came right back at her in Mexican. But Dorothy really ought not to have talked Mexican to such a refined Social leader as Mrs. Breene, because hardly any society leaders know Mexican, and Dorothy was so ignorant that she did not know that it is the depths of low breeding to hold a conversation in Mexican, when the one you are holding it with does not understand the Mexican landguage.

Well, Dorothy says she finally told Mrs. Breene, in Mexican, to "help herself to the chili," and then she took Charlie by the hand and bowed herself out. And the last she saw of Mrs. Breene, she was standing in the midst of guests who admired Dorothy, gritting her teeth, and telling Charlie that he must bring his little friend again some time.

Well, when they got out, Charlie was in the seventh Heaven, because it was the first time that his Mother had ever aproved of any Follies girl enough to ask her to come again. And everybody else was so full of enthusiasm about Dorothy, that Charlie was very, very proud. So he asked her to become his bride.

Well, Dorothy, as usual, was skeptical. Because she had gotten an idea that Mrs. Breene's enthusiasm was forced, and might break down before the alter. So she asked Charlie for time to think the proposition over. But Dorothy says that she really was intreeged by the idea of being able to return Mrs. Breene's hospitality by inviting *her* to their wedding breakfast. So, I mean, sometimes even a girl like Dorothy gets an impults that is sweet.

"Moms" Mabley (1894–1975)

~∞∞∞∞~

Stand-up Routines

One day she was sitting on the porch and I said, "Granny, how old does a woman get before she don't want no more boyfriends?" (She was around 106 then.) She said, "I don't know, Honey. You have to ask somebody older than me." She said, "A woman is a woman as long as she lives; there's a certain time in a man's life when he has to go to a place called over the hill."

•

Now his sporting days are over, and his tail light is out,
And what used to be his sex appeal now is just his water spout.
So that's the story, alas and alack,
When he's squeezed out the toothpaste, he just can't squeeze it back.

So if we want to make whoopie, don't wait until—
We get—over the hill, over the hill.

•

My daddy liked him so I had to marry that old man. My daddy should have married him; he the one liked him *(laughter)*. The nearest thing to death you ever seen in your life. His shadow weighed more than he did. He got out of breath threading a needle. And UGLY! He was so ugly he hurt my feelings. . . . He was so ugly he had to tip up on a glass to get a drink of water. . . . I thought he never would die. . . . I shouldn't talk like that about him though. He's dead. They say you shouldn't say nothing about the dead unless you can say something good. He's dead, GOOD!

My slogan is if it don't fit don't force it. In other words, if you can't make it, don't fake it. Let somebody else take it. . . . I'd rather pay a young man's way from here to California than to tell an old man the distance. . . . Don't get me wrong, it ain't no disgrace to come from the South. But it's a disgrace to go back down there.

Merrill Markoe (Contemporary)

FROM *What the Dogs Have Taught Me*

Stupid Women, Stupid Choices

Put on alert by my foolproof "dumb-movie sensory system"— a highly developed sixth sense that reminds me to stay away from movies with titles containing numbers or accompanied by the words *produced by Simpson and Bruckheimer*— I had been purposely avoiding *Pretty Woman*. But *Pretty Woman* was the thing that wouldn't die. I kept seeing ads that called it "the feel-good hit of the season." And then it was rereleased so everyone would have a chance to see it *again*. And then came a barrage of new ads proclaiming that at long last the movie was available on videocassette.

Finally, I started to hear that ten-year-old girls were watching it over and over, and this was when I began to get concerned, because my own ten-year-old girl fantasy fixations were the early starting point for a whole lot of trouble later on. So I gave in and saw the darn thing, and my short review is this: It really sucks and it pissed me off.

To recap briefly, the amazingly appealing Julia Roberts plays the most improbable hooker in the history of unlikely TV and movie hookers. She might as well have been portraying the Bean Goddess from Neptune, so unhookerlike is her character. (In fact, what we have here is the first true Disney hooker! The story could almost have been serialized on the old *Mickey Mouse Club* with Annette in the starring role!)

Anyway, here's the hooker dressed like Rocker Barbie, leading a life just a tad less brutal, alienating or problematic than that of any cosmetics counter saleswoman when she encounters repressed, handsome, egomaniac john Richard Gere. This man has just been dumped by his girlfriend because, she says, she is "sick of being at his beck and call." So he decides to hire this (wink, wink) *hooker* to be his temporary social companion. And as it turns out, not only does she not have any kind of a "beck and call" problem, something about this situation causes her to blossom, flower and *thrive!* Even though he never offers her anything in the way of emotional interaction, that doesn't affect her *incredible joie de vivre!* Because she's just so darned full of this drug-free, childlike wonderment at life! Wow! A hotel lobby! Yikes! Room service! A hat! A dress! A *really big* bathtub! Oh, my God! Pinch me! I'm dreaming!

Because this is a movie, she pretty soon falls in love with this guy. And now, when he offers to *pay* her to stay, she is hurt and packs up to leave. "It's just not good enough anymore," she says to him. "I want *the whole fairy tale*!!" (And I'm thinking to myself, *Excuse me, but where was I when they rewrote the fairy tale to start, "Once upon a time, in a land far, far away, there was this hooker . . ."?*)

Anyway, these are the easy, lighthearted reasons to hate the movie. That it is evil and loathsome to glorify hooking and sociopathic men is kind of obvious. But the ending was the final straw. Moved to the kind of white-knight behavior that I have never seen exhibited, even in the name of love, by a human male of any race, creed or religion anywhere except in a movie, the Richard Gere character shows up at the last minute to *rescue* Julia Roberts and bring us to the super-disgusting last line. As he lifts her into his arms, she says, "And now I'll rescue you right back."

That was when the uncontrollable barfing started for me. Because I knew that the guys who made this movie were all patting themselves on the back, thinking that the line added some kind of Nineties contemporary woman's egalitarian spin to the proceedings. I really got revved up, thinking about the insanity of that mainstay of Hollywood romantic plot devices: *rescuing*.

(You: "Gee, Merrill is certainly very grumpy today. I wonder if she's getting enough potassium and magnesium.")

It's certainly a time-honored tradition to have women be the *rescued* party. (Cinderella and Sleeping Beauty spring to mind.) But the fantasies that had the tightest hold on me involved the woman as the *rescuer*. In my preteen years I went repeatedly to see *West Side Story* because I had the hots for all the (wink, wink) teenage gang members. They were the first versions of a fantasy prototype that I have always found a real winner—I speak of the wounded, brooding, tough-guy loner with the mysterious tragic past, running, ever running, from unjust circumstances, his sad eyes the only clue to the horrible lack of love that has driven him to unfortunate acts of rage, rebellion, and self-destruction. Now he is hurt, and dangerous to everyone except that one woman whose love might make a difference. It is she he can come to in the middle of the night as he hides from the "authorities" who have wronged him. Together they will walk through the turbulent weather, joint observers of life's cruelties, until he kisses her with such ferocity that she has no choice but to devote her very being to trying to save him.

Various versions of this scenario accompanied me through my girlhood in the form of James Dean, Clint Eastwood or even the young Bob Dylan; then, more recently, Sean Penn, Gary Oldman or Johnny Depp. (Girlhood nothing; I was mesmerized *last weekend* by the several male cast members who have been doing this dance on *Twin Peaks.*) And that got me to thinking, *Who are these guys playing? Who are these wounded, brooding guys in real life?* Finally, I realized that wounded, brooding loners in real life are the emotionally crippled, paranoid, narcissistic guys with drug and alcohol and commitment problems who drove the woman of the Eighties into a frenzy, writing, reading and buying that endless series of bestselling books with the long, annoying titles. I refer, of course, to the *Men Who Hate Women and the Women Who Love Them,* etc., genre.

Just about all these books are devoted to the premise that rescuing is not only futile, it is *impossible* (because someone can rescue himself, but no one can rescue another person). These books contain chapter after chapter of advice on how to rebuild your decimated life and your shattered self-esteem—just two of the cute little by-products of your full-out rescuing attempt. In fact, in the past decade we have become a nation of Twelve-Step Programs (AA, ACOA, CODA, etc.), each set up to instruct participants in how to regain their sanity and stop rescuing.

(You again: "Gee, Merrill really *is* grumpy today. I'll bet she isn't getting enough vitamin B complex. Someone should check.")

If the characters in *Pretty Woman* had lived real people's lives, here is how the story would have continued after the movie. Longing to feel more legitimate, the Julia Roberts character would succeed in getting the Richard Gere character to marry her. And, feeling more legitimized, she would begin to build a sense of identity, power and self-worth, all of which would become threatening to the Richard Gere character even though she would be imagining that it made her more appealing. After all, the only reason she never moved in this direction before was her unfortunate social circumstances. Of course, she also loses interest in being at his beck and call, which is maybe when she notices that he has begun to withdraw emotionally. But who can blame him? He feels hurt and betrayed. This is not the woman he married. And so he secretly starts searching for another naive, joie-de-vivre-driven, beck-and-call girl to serve his needs. In other words, if I am not mistaken, *Pretty Woman* turns into the story of Donald and Ivana Trump and Marla Maples!

Well! Now that I have proven how pernicious this whole rescuing business can be (in fact, it's even at the core of that most pathetic of female situations—waiting for the unhappily trapped married man), then what, oh what, you are probably wondering, are we to put in its place? How do we rebuild our romantic fantasies? Well, I think there is a solution. And, as they say on the sitcoms, "It's kinda crazy but it just might work."

Here it is: Entertain the notion that the rescuing isn't what we crave. After all, there's a lot of *work*. Couldn't it be the theatrical behavior? All of those appealing facial expressions and great moves are being totally wasted on the wrong bunch of guys. And so I call for a national retraining program in which pleasant, good-natured accountants and management trainees can learn to pout and brood and wear leather jackets. One class could be devoted to the dramatic uses of staring into nature—the pounding surf, the driving rain, the howling wind. Learn which seasonal precipitate is right for you.

In other words, if we could just get the good, well-intentioned but dowdy guys to take all this over, it would be a whole lot easier and more doable than trying to get women like me to stop falling in love with the screwed-up, weaselly guys who use that behavior to such good effect.

Well, it's just an idea. I'm off now to see about some kind of meditation plan and maybe consult with a dietician.

An Insider's Guide
to the American Woman

The first item in my collection of the greatest irritants of the early Nineties is the June 1990 issue of *Esquire* featuring "The Secret Life of the American Wife." On the cover is a partially clothed woman, anatomically labeled with such questions as "HER LIPS: Can you trust what they say?" and "HER BRA: What *really* keeps it up?"

I'm not surprised to learn that men are still mystified by women. Certainly women are still utterly baffled by men. But what I found so infuriating this time around was the type of thing the (presumably college-educated) editors and writers were pretending to find so gosh-darned unfathomable. And their approach! So *retro,* so Fifties, so "Honey, now dry those tears and how about we take you downtown and buy you something sparkly?"

The lead article ("Your Wife: An Owner's Manual") offered pseudoscientific dissections of such feminine mysteries as "HER HANDBAG: Its capacity and contents" and "HER PLUMBING: General Diagnostics." If this is how far men have come in their knowledge of women—to wide-eyed wonderment at the contents of her purse and dumbfounded speechlessness at the thought of "female plumbing"—well, I personally think now is as good a time as any to throw in the towel.

My suggestion to men is, *Stop trying* to comprehend that which is clearly too complicated for you. Let me kindly state that it no longer really matters whether or not you understand. I just don't think you should worry your pretty little heads about it for another moment. Instead, simply *memorize* the following information and blindly incorporate it into your thinking, much as one might deal with an elusive scientific concept, such as $E = mc^2$.

MERRILL'S FUN FACTS TO KNOW AND TELL ABOUT WOMEN

I. WOMEN AND THE ENGLISH LANGUAGE. To a woman, the words "I had a great time. I'll call you" translate roughly to mean, "He said he had a great time. He'll call me." So, if you *say* those words, expect to *make* a call to the woman to whom you have said them. If this does not fit into your plans, *do not say those words.* (I know this is confusing. Just memorize it and do it. There's nothing more to discuss.)

Women have other quirky language-oriented notions. For instance, to a woman the words "I love you" represent a heartfelt expression of the intensely fond feelings you have for her. At least, this kind of thing will be what the woman has in mind when *she* utters the words, and so she will not be pleased if your response is "Thank you" or "I know."

There is an interesting truth behind some of this that may be hard to grasp: Women *like* to talk about personal things. In fact, they actually *listen* when a man does just that. Why? Well, because women believe that a conversation can go beyond a simple exchange of sports scores! Yes! They do! In fact, women who meet for the first time on a checkout line will often have more intimate conversations with each other than they have had with men to whom they have been married for two or three decades. They do this voluntarily! Why? Because they find it *enjoyable*!

Now that you understand this, realize that the answer to "Hi, honey. What did you do today?" is *not* "I don't know. Nothing."

II. WOMEN AND FOOD. Most women are on a diet, thinking about going on a diet or wondering if they should think about going on a diet. In a free-market economy, a majority of women will order a salad on a majority of dining-out occasions. If a man wishes a woman to change her eating habits and make them more like his own, he need only repackage the food he would like to see eaten as a salad. For example, most women would feel okay about sitting down to a hot-fudge-sundae salad or a pizza salad.

It is not necessary to inquire whether a woman would like something for dessert. The answer is, *yes,* she *would* like something for dessert, but she would like *you* to order it so she can pick at it with her fork. She does not want you to call attention to this by saying, "If you wanted a dessert, why didn't you order one?" You must understand, she *has* the dessert she wants. The dessert she wants is contained *within* yours!

Bear in mind also that she wants you to keep pace with her and prefers you to eat at least half of your dessert because she does *not* want the responsibility of having eaten most of it.

III. THEIR ENTERTAINMENT NEEDS. Unlike men, most women are not endlessly in search of opportunities to watch things crash and blow up. Women tend to prefer movies teeming with human intrigue and personal foible to movies where someone breaks through a plate glass window with a car, or breaks a plate glass window with his fist, or breaks someone's head with his fist in a car, or breaks someone's fist with a plate glass window. We're just wacky that way.

IV. WOMEN'S ABLUTIONS (and why they take so long). The amount of time a woman takes to prepare for a date with a man is in direct proportion to the amount of time she has spent observing that man staring saucer-eyed at other women who have put in at least the aforementioned amount of preparation time on their date. If a man would like to see one decrease, so too must the other.

V. THEIR PLUMBING. How much should you know? Women are the ones who do not have a penis and did not even have to undergo painful penis-removal surgery to accomplish this. As a result, they will require more frequent stops on a long car trip.

Once a month women find themselves strangely depressed and taking a long hard look at where they've made a wrong turn in life. They will ruminate over such dilemmas as "Perhaps the reason I'm depressed is that I really need to find a better job, but I guess I'm afraid to change because I have such low self-esteem, which comes from my childhood when my mother always used to tell me blah blah blah

blah blah." Then they realize they have just gotten their period, which snuck up on them in the form of a mood change. So if you get involved with a woman, don't be surprised when you find it sneaking up on you as well.

There are very simple ways to give a woman an orgasm. These involve specific manipulations of "the plumbing." If you suspect that you don't know what you're doing but think you are bluffing effectively and/or you notice that it is taking more than a half hour, please be advised that you're fooling *no one*. It's just that most women are too polite and too concerned about the frailties of the male ego to say anything. So ask the owner of "the plumbing" to provide you with some helpful tips!!! And save everyone involved a couple of long, painful hours!!! And by the way . . . if you *do* suspect that you don't know what you're doing, for God's sake, don't do it *harder*.

VI. WOMEN AND LOVE. I have heard men say that they don't mind the idea of breast implants in a woman because, after all, big breasts are big breasts. (Actually what I have heard men say is slightly coarser.) On the other hand, I have never met a woman who would rather be with a man in a toupee than a bald man.

This ability to accept and embrace the less-than-ideal, this generosity of spirit, has a downside—the tendency to be attracted to psychos. We know better, we're not proud of this, and we have spent decades learning that we would *really* rather be with nice men. But any man who has a problem attracting women because they think he is too nice would do well to augment his usual behavior with anguished exhalations of barely controlled rage.

In case you haven't noticed, women take sex just a tad more personally than do guys. For a woman, the only working definition of a one-night stand is a night spent with a guy who turned out to be a total weenie. The degree of any date's success can be easily determined by the degree of obsession it causes in the woman. If you would like to test this, introduce yourself to some of her good friends. If they aren't already sick of hearing your name, *the date didn't go that well.*

Once women are in love, they can be easily manipulated because they're so overwhelmed with feelings of insecurity. Many will happily take responsibility for everything that goes wrong, as in: "If he isn't happy it's my fault" and "If I'm not happy it's my fault."

Now that you know this, be a good guy and don't take unfair advantage. *Own up to stuff you know is your fault.* You might as well, anyway, because there is still another female phenomenon that ensures you'll be living on borrowed time if you don't.

VII. WOMEN AND THERAPY. Women are naturally attracted to therapy. Yes, it's true! If they don't get expensive one-on-one counseling, they will read self-help books and magazine articles or listen to radio and TV shows that discuss these issues or talk to and get advice from their friends who have done some or all of the above. Women do this because therapy actually involves so many of the things they enjoy: personal idiosyncrasy, a chance to talk dramatically about themselves and a good starting point for future conversations with friends or anyone they might meet in the checkout line.

VIII. THEIR PURSES, THEIR BRAS. A woman learns at a young age that she will be expected to carry the equivalent of a suitcase everywhere she goes for the rest of her life. And so she plans accordingly, secure in the knowledge that she will permanently have at her disposal anything, under a certain size, she might need in an emergency. This means that no matter what unexpected event or disaster she encounters, a woman will always have enough makeup to look really cute.

As far as the bra goes . . . give me a break, okay? *Give me a fucking break.*

The Marx Brothers
FROM *A Night at the Opera*

GROUCHO: I just remembered—I came back here looking for somebody. You don't know who it is, do you?
CHICO: Funny—it just slipped my mind.

GROUCHO *(Snapping his fingers):* I remember now—the greatest tenor in the world, that's what I'm after!

CHICO: That's funny. I am his manager.

GROUCHO: Whose manager?

CHICO: The greatest tenor in the world.

GROUCHO: The fellow that sings at the opera here?

CHICO: Sure!

GROUCHO: What's his name?

CHICO: What do you care? Some Italian name—I can't pronounce it. What you want with him?

GROUCHO: Well, I'd like to offer him a job. Would he be interested?

CHICO: I don't know, but *I'm* interested. That's the main thing. What sort of job?

GROUCHO: With the New York Opera. America is waiting to hear him sing.

CHICO: Well, he can sing loud, but he can't sing that loud.

GROUCHO: Well, I think we can get America to meet him halfway. The main thing is, can he sail tomorrow night?

CHICO: If you pay him enough money, he can sail *last* night. How much you pay him?

GROUCHO *(Aside):* Let's see—a thousand dollars a night. I'm entitled to a little profit. *(To* CHICO) How about ten dollars a night?

(CHICO *laughs scornfully.*)

CHICO: Ten dollars! . . . *(A quick change of mood)* All right. I'll take it.

GROUCHO: That's fine. Of course, I want a ten percent commission for putting the deal over.

CHICO: And I get ten percent as his manager.

GROUCHO: Well, that leaves eight dollars. Say he sings once a week—that's eight dollars a week clear profit for him.

CHICO *(Considering a week):* He sends five dollars home to his mother.

GROUCHO: Well, that still leaves him three dollars.

CHICO: Three dollars. Can he live in New York on that?

GROUCHO: Like a prince—of course, he won't be able to eat, but he can live like a prince. Oh, I forgot to tell you. He'll have to pay income tax on that three dollars.

CHICO: Income tax?

GROUCHO: Yes, there's a federal tax and the state tax and there may be a city tax. And, naturally, a sales tax.

CHICO: How much does that all come to?

GROUCHO: Well, I figure if he doesn't sing too often, he can break even.

CHICO: All right. We'll take it.

•

GROUCHO *(Holding contract farther and farther away):* I can read, but I can't see it. If my arms were a little longer, I could read it . . . Ah, here we are. Now pay attention to this first clause. *(Reads)* "The party of the first part shall be known in this contract as the party of the first part." How do you like that? Pretty neat, eh?

CHICO: No, that'sa no good.

GROUCHO *(Indignantly):* What's the matter with it?

CHICO *(Conciliatorily):* I don't know—let's hear it again.

GROUCHO: "The party of the first part shall be known in this contract as the party of the first part."

CHICO: It sounds a little better this time.

GROUCHO: Well, it grows on you. Want to hear it once more?

CHICO: Only the first part.

GROUCHO: The *party* of the first part?

CHICO: No. The *first part* of the party of the first part.

GROUCHO: Well, it says, "The first part of the party of the first part shall be known in this contract—" Look! Why should we quarrel about a thing like that? *(He tears off the offending clause)* We'll take it right out.

CHICO *(Tearing the same clause out of his contract):* Sure, it's too long anyhow. Now what have we got left?

GROUCHO: Well, I've got about a foot and a half . . . Now, then: "The party of the second part shall be known in this contract as the party of the second part."

CHICO: Well, I don't know. I don't like the second party, either.

GROUCHO: You should have come to the first party. We didn't get home till around four in the morning. *(Slight pause)* I was blind for three days.

CHICO: Look, couldn't the first part of the second party be the second part of the first party? Then we got something.

Jackie Mason (Contemporary)

FROM *The World According to Me*

There was a time I didn't know who I was. Thank God, now I know. I don't know if you heard about it. I went to a psychiatrist. I'm not ashamed to admit it. It's because I didn't know who I was. He took one look at me and said right away. "This is not you."

I said, "If this is not me, then who is it?"

He said, "I don't know either."

I said, "Then what do I need you for?"

He said, "To find out who you are."

I said to myself, "If I don't know who I am, how do I know who to look for? And even if I find me, how do I know it's me? Besides, if I want to look for me, why do I need him? I can look myself. Or I could take my friends. We'd know where I was. Besides, what if I find the real me and I find out he's even worse than me? Why do I need him? I don't make enough for myself . . . I need a partner? Ten years ago I'd be glad to look for anybody. Now I'm doing good. Why should I look for him? He needs help? Why doesn't he look for me?"

He said, "The search for the real you will have to continue. That'll be a hundred dollars, please."

I said to myself, "If this is not the real me, why should I give *him* a hundred dollars? *I'll* look for the real me. Let *him* give him a hundred dollars. . . . But what if I find the real me and he doesn't think it's worth a hundred dollars? Then I've stuck my money with the real him."

Then I said, "For all I know the real me might be going to another psychiatrist altogether. Might even be a psychiatrist himself. Wouldn't it be funny if you're the real me and you owe *me* a hundred dollars?"

I said, "I'll tell you what. I'll charge you fifty dollars and we'll call it even."

H. L. Mencken (1880–1956)

∽∾∾∾

FROM *Prejudices: First Series*

The Blushful Mystery

I
SEX HYGIENE

The literature of sex hygiene, once so scanty and so timorous, now piles mountain high. There are at least a dozen formidable series of books of instruction for inquirers of all ages, beginning with "What Every Child of Ten Should Know" and ending with "What a Woman of Forty-five Should Know," and they all sell amazingly. Scores of diligent authors, some medical, some clerical and some merely shrewdly chautauqual, grow rich at the industry of composing them. One of these amateur Havelock Ellises had the honor, during the last century, of instructing me in the elements of the sacred sciences. He was then the pastor of a fourth-rate church in a decaying neighborhood and I was sent to his Sunday-school in response to some obscure notion that the agony of it would improve me. Presently he disappeared, and for a long while I heard nothing about him. Then he came into sudden prominence as the author of such a series of handbooks and as the chief stockholder, it would seem, in the publishing house printing them. By the time he died, a few years ago, he had been so well rewarded by a just God that he was able to leave funds to establish a missionary college in some remote and heathen land.

This holy man, I believe, was honest, and took his platitudinous compositions quite seriously. Regarding other contributors to the literature it may be said without malice that their altruism is obviously corrupted by a good deal of hocus-pocus. Some of them lecture in the chautauquas, peddling their books before and after charming the yokels. Others, being members of the faculty, seem to carry on medical practice on the side. Yet others are kept in profitable jobs by the salacious old men who finance vice crusades. It is hard to draw the line between the mere thrifty enthusiast and the downright fraud. So, too, with the actual vice crusaders. The books of the latter, like the sex hygiene books, are often sold, not as wisdom, but as pornography. True enough, they are always displayed in the show-window of the small-town Methodist Book Concern—but you will also find them in the back-rooms of dubious second-hand book-stores, side by side with the familiar scarlet-backed editions of Rabelais, Margaret of Navarre and Balzac's "Droll Tales." Some time ago, in a book advertisement headed "Snappy Fiction," I found announcements of "My Battles With Vice," by Virginia Brooks—and "Life of My Heart," by Victoria Cross. The former was described by the publisher as a record of "personal experiences in the fight against the gray wolves and love pirates of modern society." The book was offered to all comers by mail. One may easily imagine the effects of such an offer.

But even the most serious and honest of the sex hygiene volumes are probably futile, for they are all founded upon a pedagogical error. That is to say, they are all founded upon an attempt to explain a romantic mystery in terms of an exact science. Nothing could be more absurd: as well attempt to interpret Beethoven in terms of mathematical physics—as many a fatuous contrapuntist, indeed, has tried to do. The mystery of sex presents itself to the young, not as a scientific problem to be solved, but as a romantic emotion to be accounted for. The only result of the current endeavor to explain its phenomena by seeking parallels in botany is to make botany obscene. . . .

2
ART AND SEX

One of the favorite notions of the Puritan mullahs who specialize in this moral pornography is that the sex instinct, if suitably repressed, may be "sublimated" into the higher sorts of idealism, and especially into aesthetic idealism. That notion is to be found in all their books; upon it they ground the theory that the enforcement of chastity by a huge force of spies, stool pigeons and police would convert the republic into a nation of incomparable uplifters, forward-lookers and artists. All this, of course, is simply pious fudge. If the notion were actually sound, then all the great artists of the world would come from the ranks of the hermetically repressed, *i.e.*, from the ranks of Puritan old maids, male and female. But the truth is, as every one knows, that the great artists of the world are never Puritans, and seldom even ordinarily respectable. No virtuous man—that is, virtuous in the Y. M. C. A. sense—has ever painted a picture worth looking at, or written a symphony worth hearing, or a book worth reading, and it is highly improbable that the thing has ever been done by a virtuous woman. The actual effect of repression, lamentable though it may be, is to destroy idealism altogether. The Puritan, for all his pretensions, is the worst of materialists. Passed through his sordid and unimaginative mind, even the stupendous romance of sex is reduced to a disgusting transaction in physiology. As artist he is thus hopeless; as well expect an auctioneer to qualify for the Sistine Chapel choir. All he ever achieves, taking pen or brush in hand, is a feeble burlesque of his betters, all of whom, by his hog's theology, are doomed to hell.

3
A LOSS TO ROMANCE

Perhaps the worst thing that this sex hygiene nonsense has accomplished is the thing mourned by Agnes Repplier in "The Repeal of Reticence." In America, at least, innocence has been killed, and romance has been sadly wounded by the same discharge of smutty artillery. The flapper is no longer naïve and charming; she goes to the altar of God with a learned and even cynical glitter in her eye. The veriest school-girl of to-day, fed upon Forel, Sylvanus Stall, Reginald Wright Kauffman and the Freud books, knows as much as the midwife of 1885, and spends a good deal more time discharging and disseminating her information. All this, of course, is highly embarrassing to the more romantic and ingenuous sort of men, of whom I have the honor to be one. We are constantly in the position of General Mitchener in Shaw's one-acter, "Press Cuttings," when he begs Mrs. Farrell, the talkative charwoman, to reserve her confidences for her medical adviser. One often wonders, indeed, what women now talk of to doctors. . . .

Please do not misunderstand me here. I do not object to this New Freedom on moral grounds, but on aesthetic grounds. In the relations between the sexes all beauty is founded upon romance, all romance is founded upon mystery, and all mystery is founded upon ignorance, or, failing that, upon the deliberate denial of the known truth. To be in love is merely to be in a state of perceptual anaesthesia—to mistake an ordinary young man for a Greek god or an ordinary young woman for a goddess. But how can this condition of mind survive the deadly matter-of-factness which sex hygiene and the new science of eugenics impose? How can a woman continue to believe in the honor, courage and loving tenderness of a man after she has learned, perhaps by affidavit, that his haemoglobin count is 117%, that he is free from sugar and albumen, that his blood pressure is 112/79 and that his Wassermann reaction is negative? . . . Moreover, all this new-fangled "frankness" tends to dam up, at least for civilized adults, one of the principal well-springs of art, to wit, impropriety. What is neither hidden nor forbidden is seldom very charming. If women, continuing their present tendency to its logical goal, end by going stark naked, there will be no more poets and painters, but only dermatologists and photographers. . . .

4

SEX ON THE STAGE

The effort to convert the theater into a forum of solemn sex discussion is another abhorrent by-product of the sex hygiene rumble-bumble. Fortunately, it seems to be failing.

A few years ago, crowds flocked to see Brieux's "Les Avariés," but to-day it is forgotten, and its successors are all obscure. The movement originated in Germany with the production of Frank Wedekind's "Frühlings Erwachen." The Germans gaped and twisted in their seats for a season or two, and then abandoned sex as a horror and went back to sex as a comedy. This last is what it actually should be, at least in the theater. The theater is no place for painful speculation; it is a place for diverting representation. Its best and truest sex plays are not such overstrained shockers as "Le Mariage d'Olympe" and "Damaged Goods," but such penetrating and excellent comedies as "Much Ado About Nothing" and "The Taming of the Shrew." In "Much Ado" we have an accurate and unforgettable picture of the way in which the normal male of the human species is brought to the altar—that is, by the way of appealing to his hollow vanity, the way of capitalizing his native and ineradicable asininity. And in "The Taming of the Shrew" we have a picture of the way in which the average woman, having so snared him, is purged of her resultant vainglory and bombast, and thus reduced to decent discipline and decorum, that the marriage may go on in solid tranquillity.

The whole drama of sex, in real life, as well as on the stage, revolves around those two enterprises. One-half of it consists of pitting the native intelligence of women against the native sentimentality of men, and the other half consists of bringing women into a reasonable order, that their superiority may not be too horribly obvious. To the first division belong the dramas of courtship, and a good many of those of marital conflict. In each case the essential drama is not a tragedy but a comedy—nay, a farce. In each case the conflict is not between imperishable verities but between mere vanities and pretensions. This is the essence of the comic: the unmasking of fraud, its destruction by worse fraud. Marriage, as we know it in Christendom, though its utility is obvious and its necessity is at least arguable, is just such a series of frauds. It begins with the fraud that the impulse to it is lofty, unearthly and disinterested. It proceeds to the fraud that both parties are equally eager for it and equally benefited by it—which actually happens only when two Mondays come together. And it rests thereafter upon the fraud that what is once agreeable (or tolerable) remains agreeable ever thereafter—that I shall be exactly the same man in 1938 that I am to-day, and that my wife will be the same woman, and intrigued by the merits of the same man. This last assumption is so outrageous that, on purely evidential and logical grounds, not even the most sentimental person would support it. It thus becomes necessary to reënforce it by attaching to it the concept of honor. That is to say, it is held up, not on the ground that it is actually true, but on the ground that a recognition of its truth is part of the bargain made at the altar, and that repudiation of this bargain would be dishonorable. Here we have honor, which is based upon a sense of the deepest and most inviolable truth, brought in to support something admittedly not true. Here, in other words, we have a situation in comedy, almost exactly parallel to that in which a colored bishop whoops "Onward, Christian Soldiers!" like a calliope in order to drown out the crowing of the rooster concealed beneath his chasuble.

In all plays of the sort that are regarded as "strong" and "significant" in Greenwich Village, in the finishing schools and by the newspaper critics, connubial infidelity is the chief theme. Smith, having a wife, Mrs. Smith, betrays her love and trust by running off with Miss Rabinowitz, his stenographer. Or Mrs. Brown, detecting her husband, Mr. Brown, in lamentable proceedings with a neighbor, the grass widow Kraus, forgives him and continues to be true to him in consideration of her children, Fred, Pansy and Little Fern. Both situations produce a great deal of eye-rolling and snuffling among the softies aforesaid. Yet neither contains the slightest touch of tragedy, and neither at bottom is even honest. Both, on the contrary, are based upon an assumption that is unsound and ridiculous—the assumption, to wit, that the position of the injured wife is grounded upon the highest idealism—that the injury she suffers is directed at her lofty and impeccable spirit—that it leaves her standing in an heroic attitude. All this, soberly examined, is found to be untrue. The fact is that her moving impulse is simply a desire to cut a good figure before her world—in brief, that plain vanity is what animates her.

This public expectation that she will endure and renounce is itself hollow and sentimental, and so much so that it can seldom stand much strain. If, for example, her heroism goes beyond a certain modest point—if she carries it to the extent of complete abnegation and self-sacrifice—her reward is not that she is thought heroic, but that she is thought weak and foolish. And if, by any chance, the external pressure upon her is removed and she is left to go on with her alleged idealism alone—if, say, her recreant husband dies and some new suitor enters to dispute the theory of her deathless fidelity—then it is regarded as down-right insane for her to continue playing her artificial part.

In frank comedy we see the situation more accurately dealt with and hence more honestly and more instructively. Instead of depicting one party as revolting against the assumption of eternal fidelity melodramatically and the other as facing the revolt heroically and tragically, we have both criticizing it by a good-humored flouting of it—not necessarily by act, but by attitude. This attitude is normal and sensible. It rests upon genuine human traits and tendencies. It is sound, natural and honest. It gives the comedy of the stage a high validity that the bombastic fustian of the stage can never show, all the sophomores to the contrary notwithstanding.

When I speak of infidelity, of course, I do not mean only the gross infidelity of "strong" sex plays and the divorce courts, but that lighter infidelity which relieves and makes bearable the burdens of theoretical fidelity—in brief, the natural reaction of human nature against an artificial and preposterous assumption. The assumption is that a sexual choice, once made, is irrevocable—more, that all desire to revoke it, even transiently, disappears. The fact is that no human choice can ever be of that irrevocable character, and that the very existence of such an assumption is a constant provocation to challenge it and rebel against it.

What we have in marriage actually—or in any other such contract—is a constant war between the impulse to give that rebellion objective reality and a social pressure which puts a premium on submission. The rebel, if he strikes out, at once collides with a solid wall, the bricks of which are made up of the social assumption of his docility, and the mortar of which is the frozen sentimentality of his own lost yesterday—his fatuous assumption that what was once agreeable to him would be always agreeable to him. Here we have the very essence of comedy—a situation almost exactly parallel to that of the pompous old gentleman who kicks a plug hat lying on the sidewalk, and stumps his toe against the cobblestone within.

Under the whole of the conventional assumption reposes an assumption even more foolish, to wit, that sexual choice is regulated by some transcendental process, that a mysterious accuracy gets into it, that it is limited by impenetrable powers, that there is for every man one certain woman. This sentimentality not only underlies the theory of marriage, but is also the chief apology for divorce. Nothing could be more ridiculous. The truth is that marriages in Christendom are determined, not by elective affinities, but by the most trivial accidents, and that the issue of those accidents is relatively unimportant. That is to say, a normal man could be happy with any one of at least two dozen women of his acquaintance, and a man specially fitted to accept the false assumptions of marriage could be happy with almost any presentable woman of his race, class and age. He is married to Marie instead of to Gladys because Marie definitely decided to marry him, whereas Gladys vacillated between him and some other. And Marie decided to marry him instead of some other, not because the impulse was irresistibly stronger, but simply because the thing seemed more feasible. In such choices, at least among women, there is often not even any self-delusion. They see the facts clearly, and even if, later on, they are swathed in sentimental trappings, the revelation is not entirely obliterated.

Here we have comedy double distilled—a combat of pretensions, on the one side, perhaps, risen to self-hallucination, but on the other side more or less uneasily conscious and deliberate. This is the true soul of high farce. This is something not to snuffle over but to roar at.

Alice Duer Miller (1874–1942)

❧

FROM *Are Women People?*

Our Own Twelve Anti-suffragist Reasons

1. Because no woman will leave her domestic duties to vote.
2. Because no woman who may vote will attend to her domestic duties.
3. Because it will make dissension between husband and wife.
4. Because every woman will vote as her husband tells her to.
5. Because bad women will corrupt politics.
6. Because bad politics will corrupt women.
7. Because women have no power of organization.
8. Because women will form a solid party and out-vote men.
9. Because men and women are so different that they must stick to different duties.
10. Because men and women are so much alike that men, with one vote each, can represent their own views and ours too.
11. Because women cannot use force.
12. Because the militants did use force.

Why We Oppose Pockets for Women

1. Because pockets are not a natural right.
2. Because the great majority of women do not want pockets. If they did they would have them.

3. Because whenever women have had pockets they have not used them.
4. Because women are required to carry enough things as it is, without the additional burden of pockets.
5. Because it would make dissension between husband and wife as to whose pockets were to be filled.
6. Because it would destroy man's chivalry toward woman, if he did not have to carry all her things in his pockets.
7. Because men are men, and women are women. We must not fly in the face of nature.
8. Because pockets have been used by men to carry tobacco, pipes, whiskey flasks, chewing gum and compromising letters. We see no reason to suppose that women would use them more wisely.

Why We Oppose Women Travelling in Railway Trains

1. Because travelling in trains is not a natural right.
2. Because our great-grandmothers never asked to travel in trains.
3. Because woman's place is the home, not the train.
4. Because it is unnecessary; there is no point reached by a train that cannot be reached on foot.
5. Because it will double the work of conductors, engineers and brakemen who are already overburdened.
6. Because men smoke and play cards in trains. Is there any reason to believe that women will behave better?

Why We Oppose Votes for Men

1. Because man's place is the armory.
2. Because no really manly man wants to settle any question otherwise than by fighting about it.
3. Because if men should adopt peaceable methods women will no longer look up to them.
4. Because men will lose their charm if they step out of their natural sphere and interest themselves in other matters than feats of arms, uniforms and drums.

5. Because men are too emotional to vote. Their conduct at baseball games and political conventions shows this, while their innate tendency to appeal to force renders them peculiarly unfit for the task of government.

The Universal Answer

Oh, there you go again,
Invading man's domain!
It's Nature's laws, you know, you are defying.
Don't fancy that you can
Be really like a man,
So what's the use of all this fuss and trying?
It seems to me so clear,
That women's highest sphere
Is being loving wives and patient mothers.
Oh, can't you be content
To be as you were meant?
For { souls
{ books belong to husbands and to
{ votes   [brothers.

What Every Woman Must Not Say

"I don't pretend I'm clever," he remarked,
    "or very wise,"
And at this she murmured, "Really," with
    the right polite surprise.
"But women," he continued, "I must own
    I understand;
Women are a contradiction—honorable
    and underhand—
Constant as the star Polaris, yet as change-
    able as Fate,
Always flying what they long for, always
    seeking what they hate."
"Don't you think," began the lady, but he
    cut her short: "I see
That you take it personally—women always
    do," said he.

"You will pardon me for saying every
    woman is the same,
Always greedy for approval, always sensi-
    tive to blame;
Sweet and passionate are women; weak in
    mind, though strong in soul;
Even you admit, I fancy, that they have no
    self-control?"
"No, I don't admit they haven't," said the
    patient lady then,
"Or they could not sit and listen to the non-
    sense talked by men."

Margaret Mitchell (1900–1949)

FROM *Gone With the Wind*

A startling thought this, that a woman could handle business matters as well as or better than a man, a revolutionary
thought to Scarlett who had been reared in the tradition that
men were omniscient and women none too bright. Of
course, she had discovered that this was not altogether true
but the pleasant fiction still stuck in her mind. Never before
had she put this remarkable idea into words. She sat quite
still, with the heavy book across her lap, her mouth a little
open with surprise, thinking that during the lean months at
Tara she had done a man's work and done it well. She had
been brought up to believe that a woman alone could accomplish nothing, yet she had managed a plantation without men to help her until Will came. Why, why, her mind
stuttered, I believe women could manage everything in the
world without men's help.

Pat Mora (Contemporary)

Prayer to the Saints
Oración a los Santos

At sixteen I began to pray to you, old friends,
    for a handsome man who would never stray.
        Devoutly, I'd say,
Saint Peter the Apostle,
    please grant me this miracle,
Saint Raphael, the Archangel,
    remove every obstacle,
San José, dear father,
    may he frown at liquor
Saint Clare,
    for Mother, could he be a millionaire,
Saint John Nepomuk,
    my few faults may he overlook,
Santa María Magdalena,
    que a veces me sirva mi cena,
Saint Christopher,
    may he my figure prefer,
Our Lady of Remedies,
    could he avoid my father's frugalities,
Saint Francis,
    please don't make him a pessimist,
Saint Anne,
    could he be a very handsome man,
Saint Anthony,
    may he know the art of flattery,
Santa Bárbara, protector against lightning,
    make him good at dancing,

Saint Genevieve,
    may he never plot to deceive,
Saint Blaise,
    let him shower me with praise,
Saint Jerome,
    have him build me my dream-home,
San Pascual,
    como él que no haya igual,
Saint Patrick,
    could he be a lovesick Catholic,
Saint Gertrude the Great,
    forgive me, but make him passionate,
Saint Lucy,
    suggest he kiss me secretly,
Saint Martin,
    may my smile turn him to gelatin,
Santa Teresita,
    que me traiga florecitas,
Saint Agnes,
    make him love me with wild excess,
Saint James,
    por favor, nudge him this love to proclaim,
Saint Rose,
    have him soon propose,
Saint Elizabeth,
    may we celebrate our fiftieth,
Saint Jude,
    let me soon be wooed,
Saint Stephen,
    please remind all the santos
        to find me a husband soon. Ah, men.
    Amen.

Ogden Nash (1902–1971)

FROM *Good Intentions*

Not George Washington's, Not Abraham Lincoln's, But Mine

Well, here I am thirty-eight,
Well, I certainly thought I'd have longer to wait.
You just stop in for a couple of beers,
And gosh, there go thirty-seven years.
Well, it has certainly been fun,
But I certainly thought I'd have got a lot more done.
Why if I had been really waked up and alive,
I could have been a Congressman since I was
    twenty-one or President since I was thirty-five.
I guess I know the reason my accomplishments are
    so measly:
I don't comprehend very easily.
It finally dawned on me that in life's race I was off
    to a delayed start
When at the age of thirty-three I had to be told that
    I could swim faster if I'd keep my fingers
    together instead of spreading them apart,
And I was convinced that precociousness was not
    the chief of my faults
When it was only last winter that I discovered that
    the name of that waltz that skaters waltz to is
    "The Skaters' Waltz."
After thirty-seven years I find myself the kind of
    man that anybody can sell anything to,
And nobody will ever tell anything to.
Whenever people get up a party of which I am to be

a member to see some picture which I don't want
to see because I am uninterested in the situation
that Scarlett and Mr. Chips are estranged over,
Why my head is what it is arranged over.
Contrariwise, I myself not only can't sell anybody
anything,
I can't even ever tell anybody anything.
I have never yet had a good gossip bomb all poised
and ready to burst
That somebody hasn't already told everybody first.
Yes, my career to date has certainly been a fiasco;
It would not have made a thrilling dramatic
production for the late Oliver Morosco or the late
David Belasco.
But in spite of the fact that my career has been a
fiasco to date,
Why I am very proud and happy to be thirty-eight.

Bill Nye (1850–1896)

❦

FROM *Remarks by Bill Nye*

Habits of a Literary Man

The editor of an Eastern health magazine, having asked for
information relative to the habits, hours of work, and style
and frequency of feed adopted by literary men, and several
parties having responded who were no more essentially
saturated with literature than I am, I now take my pen in
hand to reveal the true inwardness of my literary life, so that
boys, who may yearn to follow in my footsteps and wear a
laurel wreath the year round in place of a hat, may know
what the personal habits of a literary party are.

I rise from bed the first thing in the morning, leaving my couch not because I am dissatisfied with it, but because I cannot carry it with me during the day.

I then seat myself on the edge of the bed and devote a few moments to thought. Literary men who have never set aside a few moments on rising for thought will do well to try it.

I then insert myself into a pair of middle-aged pantaloons. It is needless to say that girls who may have a literary tendency will find little to interest them here.

Other clothing is added to the above from time to time. I then bathe myself. Still this is not absolutely essential to a literary life. Others who do not do so have been equally successful.

Some literary people bathe before dressing.

I then go down stairs and out to the barn, where I feed the horse. Some literary men feel above taking care of a horse, because there is really nothing in common between the care of a horse and literature, but simplicity is my watchword. T. Jefferson would have to rise early in the day to eclipse me in simplicity. I wish I had as many dollars as I have got simplicity.

I then go in to breakfast. This meal consists almost wholly of food. I am passionately fond of food, and I may truly say, with my hand on my heart, that I owe much of my great success in life to this inward craving, this constant yearning for something better.

During this meal I frequently converse with my family. I do not feel above my family; at least, if I do, I try to conceal it as much as possible. Buckwheat pancakes in a heated state, with maple syrup on the upper side, are extremely conducive to literature. Nothing jerks the mental faculties around with greater rapidity than buckwheat pancakes.

After breakfast the time is put in to good advantage looking forward to the time when dinner will be ready. From 8 to 10 A.M., however, I frequently retire to my private library hot-bed in the hay mow, and write 1,200 words in my forthcoming book, the price of which will be $2.50 in cloth and $4 with Russia back.

I then play Copenhagen with some little girls 21 years of age, who live near by, and of whom I am passionately fond.

After that I dig some worms, with a view to angling. I then angle. After this I return home, waiting until dusk, however, as I do not like to attract attention. Nothing is more distasteful to a truly good man of wonderful literary acquirements, and yet with singular modesty, than the coarse and rude scrutiny of the vulgar herd.

In winter I do not angle. I read the "Pirate Prince" or the "Missourian's Mash," or some other work, not so much for the plot as the style, that I may get my mind into correct channels of thought. I then play "old sledge" in a rambling sort of manner. I sometimes spend an evening at home, in order to excite remark and draw attention to my wonderful eccentricity.

I do not use alcohol in any form, if I know it, though sometimes I am basely deceived by those who know of my peculiar prejudice, and who do it, too, because they enjoy watching my odd and amusing antics at the time.

Alcohol should be avoided entirely by literary workers, especially young women. There can be no more pitiable sight to the tender hearted, than a young woman of marked ability writing an obituary poem while under the influence of liquor.

I knew a young man who was a good writer. His penmanship was very good, indeed. He once wrote an article for the press while under the influence of liquor. He sent it to the editor, who returned it at once with a cold and cruel letter, every line of which was a stab. The letter came at a time when he was full of remorse.

He tossed up a cent to see whether he should blow out his brains or go into the ready-made clothing business. The coin decided that he should die by his own hand, but his head ached so that he didn't feel like shooting into it. So he went into the ready-made clothing business, and now he pays taxes on $75,000, so he is probably worth $150,000. This, of course, salves over his wounded heart, but he often says to me that he might have been in the literary business to-day if he had let liquor alone.

The Wail of a Wife

"Ethel" has written a letter to me and asked for a printed reply. Leaving off the opening sentences, which I would not care to have fall into the hands of my wife, her note is about as follows:

"——————Vt., Feb. 28, 1885.

"MY DEAR SIR: *******************************
***** [Tender part of letter omitted for obvious reasons.]
Would it be asking too much for me to request a brief reply
to one or two questions which many other married women
as well as myself would like to have answered?

I have been married now for five years. To-day is the anniversary of my marriage. When I was single I was a teacher
and supported myself in comfort. I had more pocket-money
and dressed fully as well if not better than I do now. Why
should girls who are abundantly able to earn their own
livelihood struggle to become the slave of a husband and
children, and tie themselves to a man when they might be
free and happy?

I think too much is said by the men in a light and flippant
manner about the anxiety of young ladies to secure a home
and a husband, and still they do deserve a part of it, as I feel
that I do now for assuming a great burden when I was comparatively independent and comfortable.

Now, will you suggest any advice that you think would
benefit the yet unmarried and self-supporting girls who are
liable to make the same mistake that I did, and thus warn
them in a manner that would be so much more universal in
its range, and reach so many more people than I could if I
should raise my voice? Do this and you will be gratefully
remembered by

ETHEL."

It would indeed be a tough, tough man who could ignore
thy gentle plea, Ethel; tougher far than the pale, intellectual
hired man who now addresses you in this private and un-
derhanded manner, unknown to your husband. Please destroy this letter, Ethel, as soon as you see it in print, so that
it will not fall into the hands of Mr. Ethel, for if it should, I
am gone. If your husband were to run across this letter in the
public press I could never look him in the eye again.

You say that you had more pocket-money before you
were married than you have since, Ethel, and you regret
your rash step. I am sorry to hear it. You also say that you
wore better clothes when you were single than you do now.

You are also pained over that. It seems that marriage with you has not paid any cash dividends. So that if you married Mr. Ethel as a financial venture, it was a mistake. You do not state how it has affected your husband. Perhaps he had more pocket-money and better clothes before he married than he has since. Sometimes two people do well in business by themselves, but when they go into partnership they bust higher than a kite, if you will allow me the free, English translation of a Roman expression which you might not fully understand if I should give it to you in the original Roman.

Lots of self-supporting young ladies have married and had to go very light on pin-money after that, and still they did not squeal, as you, dear Ethel. They did not marry for revenue only. They married for protection. (This is a little political bon mot which I thought of myself. Some of my best jokes this spring are jokes that I thought of myself.)

No, Ethel, if you married expecting to be a dormant partner during the day and then to go through Mr. Ethel's pantaloons pocket at night and declare a dividend, of course life is full of bitter, bitter regret and disappointment. Perhaps it is also for Mr. Ethel. Anyhow, I can't help feeling a pang of sympathy for him. You do not say that he is unkind or that he so far forgets himself as to wake you up in the morning with a harsh tone of voice and a yearling club. You do not say that he asks you for pocket-money, or, if so, whether you give it to him or not.

Of course I want to do what is right in the solemn warning business, so I will give notice to all simple young women who are now self-supporting and happy, that there is no statute requiring them to assume the burdens of wifehood and motherhood unless they prefer to do so. If they now have abundance of pin-money and new clothes, they may remain single if they wish without violating the laws of the land. This rule is also good when applied to young and self-supporting young men who wear good clothes and have funds in their pockets. No young man who is free, happy and independent, need invest his money in a family or carry a colicky child twenty-seven miles and two laps in one night unless he prefers it. But those who go into it with the right spirit, Ethel, do not regret it.

I would just as soon tell you, Ethel, if you will promise that it shall go no farther, that I do not wear as good clothes as I did before I was married. I don't have to. My good clothes have accomplished what I got them for. I played them for all they were worth, and since I got married the idea of wearing clothes as a vocation has not occurred to me.

Please give my kind regards to Mr. Ethel, and tell him that although I do not know him personally, I cannot help feeling sorry for him.

FROM *Bill Nye and Boomerang*

Suggestions for a School of Journalism

A number of friends having personally asked me to express an opinion upon the matter of an established school of journalism, as spoken of by ex-Mayor Henry C. Robinson, of Hartford, Connecticut, and many more through the West who are strangers to me personally, having written me to give my views upon the subject, I have consented in so far that I will undertake a simple synopsis of what the course should embrace.

I most heartily indorse the movement, if it may be called such at this early stage. Knowing a little of the intricacies of this branch of the profession, I am going to state fully my belief as to its importance, and the necessity for a thorough training upon it. We meet almost everywhere newspaper men who are totally unfitted for the high office of public educators through the all-powerful press. The woods is full of them. We know that not one out of a thousand of those who are to-day classed as journalists is fit for that position.

I know that to be the case, because people tell me so.

I cannot call to mind to-day, in all my wide journalistic acquaintance, a solitary man who has not been pronounced an ass by one or more of my fellow-men. This is indeed a terrible state of affairs.

In many instances these harsh criticisms are made by those who do not know, without submitting themselves to a tremendous mental strain, the difference between a "lower case" q and the old Calvinistic doctrine of unanimous damnation, but that makes no difference; the true journalist should strive to please the masses. He should make his whole life a study of human nature and an earnest effort to serve the great reading world collectively and individually.

This requires a man, of course, with similar characteristics and the same general information possessed by the Almighty, but who would be willing to work at a much more moderate salary.

The reader will instantly see how difficult it is to obtain this class of men. Outside of the mental giant who writes these lines and two or three others, perhaps——

But never mind. I leave a grateful world to say that, while I map out a plan for the ambitious young journalist who might be entering upon the broad arena of newspaperdom, and preparing himself at a regularly established school for that purpose.

Let the first two years be devoted to meditation and prayer. This will prepare the young editor for the surprise and consequent profanity which in a few years he may experience when he finds in his boss editorial that God is spelled with a little g, and the peroration of the article has been taken out and carefully locked up between a death notice and the announcement of the birth of a cross-eyed infant.

The ensuing five years should be spent in becoming familiar with the surprising and mirth-provoking orthography of the English language.

Then would follow three years devoted to practice with dumb bells, sand bags and slung shots, in order to become an athlete. I have found in my own journalistic history more cause for regret over my neglect of this branch than any other. I am a pretty good runner, but aside from that I regret to say that as an athlete I am not a dazzling success.

The above course of intermediate training would fit the student to enter upon the regular curriculum.

Then set aside ten years for learning the typographical art perfectly, so that when visitors wish to look at the composing room, and ask the editor to explain the use of the "hell box," he will not have to blush and tell a gauzy lie about its being a composing stick. Let the young journalist study the mysteries of type setting, distributing, press work, galleys, italic, shooting sticks, type lice and other mechanical implements of the printer's department.

Five years should be spent in learning to properly read and correct proof, as well as how to mark it on the margin like a Chinese map of the Gunnison country.

At least fifteen years should then be devoted to the study of American politics and the whole civil service. This time could be extended five years with great profit to the careful student who wishes, of course, to know thoroughly the names and records of all public men, together with the relative political strength of each party.

He should then take a medical course and learn how to bind up contusions, apply arnica, court plaster or bandages, plug up bullet holes and prospect through the human system for buck shot. The reason of this course which should embrace five years of close study, is apparent to the thinking mind.

Ten years should then be devoted to the study of law. No thorough metropolitan editor wants to enter upon his profession without knowing the difference between a writ of *mandamus* and other styles of profanity. He should thoroughly understand the entire system of American jurisprudence, and be as familiar with the more recent decisions of the courts as New York people are with the semi-annual letter of Governor Seymour declining the Presidency.

The student will by this time begin to see what is required of him and will enter with greater zeal upon his adopted profession.

He will now enter upon a theological course of ten years. He can then write a telling editorial on the great question of What We Shall Do To Be Saved without mixing up Calvin and Tom Paine with Judas Iscariot and Ben Butler.

The closing ten years of the regular course might be profitably used in learning a practical knowledge of cutting cord wood, baking beans, making shirts, lecturing, turning double handsprings, preaching the gospel, learning how to make a good adhesive paste that will not sour in hot weather, learning the art of scissors grinding, punctuation, capitalization, prosody, plain sewing, music, dancing, sculpting, etiquette, how to win the affections of the opposite sex, the ten commandments, every man his own teacher on the violin, croquet, rules of the prize ring, parlor magic, civil engineering, decorative art, calsomining, bicycling, base ball, hydraulics, botany, poker, calisthenics, high-low jack, international law, faro, rhetoric, fifteen-ball pool, drawing and painting, mule skinning, vocal music, horsemanship, plastering, bull whacking, etc., etc., etc.

At the age of 95 the student will have lost that wild, reckless and impulsive style so common among younger and less experienced journalists. He will emerge from the school with a light heart and a knowledge-box loaded up to the muzzle with the most useful information.

The hey day and the springtime of life will, of course, be past, but the graduate will have nothing to worry him any more, except the horrible question which is ever rising up before the journalist, as to whether he shall put his money into government four per cents or purchase real estate in some growing town.

FROM *Baled Hay*

The Man Who Interrupts

I do not, as a rule, thirst for the blood of my fellow-man. I am willing that the law should in all ordinary cases take its course, but when we begin to discuss the man who breaks into a conversation and ruins it with his own irrelevant ideas, regardless of the feelings of humanity, I am not a law and order man. The spirit of the "Red Vigilanter" is roused in my breast and I hunger for the blood of that man.

Interrupters are of two classes: First, the common plug who thinks aloud, and whose conversation wanders with his so-called mind. He breaks into the saddest and sweetest of sentiment, and the choicest and most tearful of pathos, with the remorseless ignorance that marks a stump-tail cow in a dahlia bed. He is the bull in my china shop, the wormwood in my wine, and the kerosene in my maple syrup. I am shy in conversation, and my unfettered flights of poesy and sentiment are rare, but this man is always near to mar it all with a remark, or a marginal note, or a story of a bit of politics, ready to bust my beautiful dream and make me wish that his name might be carved on a marble slab in some quiet cemetery, far away.

Dear reader, did you ever meet this man—or his wife? Did you ever strike some beautiful thought and begin to reel it off to your friends only to be shut off in the middle of a sentence by this choice and banner idiot of conversation? If so, come and sit by me, and you may pour your woes into my ear, and I in turn will pour a few gallons into your listening ear.

I do not care to talk more than my share of the time, but I would be glad to arrive at a conclusion just to see how it would seem. I would be so pleased and so joyous to follow up an anecdote till I had reached the "nub," as it were, to chase argument home to conviction, and to clinch assertion with authority and evidence.

The second class of interrupters is even worse. It consists of the man—and, I am pained to state, his wife also—who see the general drift of your remarks and finish out your story, your gem of thought or your argument. It is very seldom that they do this as you would do it yourself, but they are kind and thoughtful and their services are always at hand. No matter how busy they may be, they will leave their own work and fly to your aid. With the light of sympathy in their eyes, they rush into the conversation, and, partaking of your own zeal, they take the words from your mouth, and cheerfully suck the juice out of your joke, handing back the rind and hoping for reward. That is where they get left, so far as I am concerned. I am almost always ready to repay rudeness with rudeness, and cold preserved gall with such acrid sarcasm as I may be able to secure at the moment. No one will ever know how I yearn for the blood of the interrupter. At night I camp on his trail, and all the day I thirst for his warm life's current. In my dreams I am cutting his scalp loose with a case-knife, while my fingers are twined in his clustering hair. I walk over him and promenade across his abdomen as I slumber. I hear his ribs crack, and I see his tongue hang over his shoulder as he smiles death's mirthful smile.

I do not interrupt a man no more than I would tell him he lied. I give him a chance to win applause or decomposed eggs from the audience, according to what he has to say, and according to the profundity of his profound. All I want is a similar chance and room according to my strength. Common decency ought to govern conversation without its being necessary to hire an umpire armed with a four-foot club, to announce who is at the bat and who is on deck.

It is only once in a week or two that the angel troubles the waters and stirs up the depths of my conversational powers, and then the chances are that some leprous old nasty toad who has been hanging on the brink of decent society for two weeks, slides in with a low kerplunk, and my fair blossom of thought that has been trying for weeks to bloom, withers and goes to seed, while the man with the chilled steel and copper-riveted brow, and a wad of self-esteem on his intellectual balcony as big as an inkstand, walks slowly away to think of some other dazzling gem, and thus be ready to bust my beautiful phantom, and tear out my high-priced bulbs of fancy the next time I open my mouth.

The Youmorist

"You are an youmorist, are you not?" queried a long-billed pelican addressing a thoughtful, mental athlete, on the Milwaukee & St. Paul road the other day.

"Yes, sir," said the sorrowful man, brushing away a tear. "I am an youmorist. I am not very much so, but still I can see that I am drifting that way. And yet I was once joyous and happy as you are. Only a few years ago, before I was exposed in this malady, I was as blithe as a speckled yearling, and recked not of aught—nor anything else, either. Now my whole life is blasted. I do not dare to eat pie or preserves, and no one tells funny stories when I am near. They regard me as a professional, and when I get in sight the 'scrub nine' close up and wait for me to entertain the crowd and waddle around the ring."

"What do you mean by that?" murmured the purple-nosed interrogation point.

"Mean? Why, I mean that whether I'm drawing a salary or not, I'm expected to be the 'life of the party.' I don't want to be the life of the party. I want to let some one else be the life of the party. I want to get up the reputation of being as cross as a bear with a sore head. I want people to watch their children for fear I'll swallow them. I want to take my low-cut-evening-dress smile and put it in the bureau drawer, and tell the world I've got a cancer in my stomach, and the heaves and hypochondria, and a malignant case of leprosy."

"Do you mean to say that you do not feel facetious all the time, and that you get weary of being a youmorist?"

"Yes, hungry interlocutor. Yes, low-browed student, yes. I am not always tickled. Did you ever have a large, angry, and abnormally protuberent boil somewhere on your person where it seemed to be in the way? Did you ever have such a boil as a traveling companion, and then get introduced to people as an youmorist? You have not? Well, then, you do not know all there is of suffering in this sorrow-streaked world. When wealthy people die why don't they endow a cast-iron castle with a draw-bridge to it and call it the youmorists' retreat? Why don't they do some good with their money instead of fooling it away on those who are comparatively happy?"

"But how did you come to git to be an youmorist?"

"Well, I don't know. I blame my parents some. They might have prevented it if they'd taken it in time, but they didn't. They let it run on till it got established, and now it's no use to go to the Hot Springs or to the mountains, or have an operation performed. You let a man get the name of being an youmorist and he doesn't dare to register at the hotels, and he has to travel anonymously, and mark his clothes with his wife's name, or the public will lynch him if he doesn't say something youmorous.

"Where is your boy to-night?" continued the gloomy humorist. "Do you know where he is? Is he at home under your watchful eye, or is he away somewhere nailing the handles on his first little joke? Parent, beware. Teach your boy to beware. Watch him night and day, or all at once, when he is beyond your jurisdiction, he will grow pale. He will have a far-away look in his eye, and the bright, rosy lad will have become the flat-chested, joyless youmorist.

"It's hard to speak unkindly of our parents, but mingled with my own remorse I shall always murmur to myself, and ask over and over, why did not my parents rescue me while they could? Why did they allow my chubby little feet to waddle down to the dangerous ground on which the sad-eyed youmorist must forever stand?

"Partner, do not forget what I have said to-day. Whether your child be a son or daughter, it matters not. Discourage the first sign of approaching humor. It is easier to bust the backbone of the first little, tender jokelet that sticks its head through the virgin soil, than it is to allow the slimy folds of your son's youmorous lecture to be wrapped about you, and to bring your gray hairs with sorrow to the grave."

My Cabinet

I have made a small collection of wild, western things during the past seven years, and have put them together, hoping some day, when I get feeble, to travel with the aggregation and erect a large monument of kopecks for my executors, administrators and assigns forever.

Beginning with the skull of old Hi-lo-Jack-and-the-game, a Sioux brave, the collection takes in my wonderful bird, known as the Walk-up-the-creek, and another *rara avis,* with carnivorous bill and web feet, which has astonished everyone except the taxidermist and myself. An old grizzly bear hunter—who has plowed corn all his life and don't know a coyote from a Maverick steer—looked at it last fall and pronounced it a "king-fisher," said he had killed one like it a year ago. Then I knew that he was a pilgrim and a stranger, and that he had bought his buckskin coat and bead-trimmed moccasins at Niagara Falls, for the bird is constructed of an eagle's head, a canvas back duck's bust and feet, with the balance sage hen and baled hay.

Last fall I desired to add to my rare collection a large hornet's nest. I had an embalmed tarantula and her porcelain-lined nest, and I desired to add to these the gray and airy home of the hornet. I procured one of the large size after cold weather and hung it in my cabinet by a string. I forgot about it until this spring. When warm weather came, something reminded me of it. I think it was a hornet. He jogged my memory in some way and called my attention to it. Memory is not located where I thought it was. It seemed as though whenever he touched me he awakened a memory— a warm memory with a red place all around it.

Then some more hornets came and began to rake up old personalities. I remember that one of them lit on my upper lip. He thought it was a rosebud. When he went away it looked like a gladiola bulb. I wrapped a wet sheet around it . . . .

How to Put Up a Stove-Pipe

Putting up stove-pipe is easy enough, if you only go at it right. In the morning, breakfast on some light, nutritious diet, and drink two cups of hot coffee; after which put on a suit of old clothes—or new ones, if you can get them on time—put on an old pair of buckskin gloves, and, when everything is ripe for the fatal blow, go and get a good hardware man who understands his business. If this rule be strictly adhered to, the gorgeous eighteen-karat-stem-winding profanity of the present day may be very largely diminished, and the world made better.

Fun of Being a Publisher

Being a publisher is not all sunshine, joy and johnny-jump-ups, although the gentle and tractable reader may at times think so.

A letter was received two years ago by the publishers of this book, on the outside of which was the request to the "P. Master of Chicago to give to the most reliable man in Chicago and oblige."

The P. Master thereupon gave the letter to Messrs. Belford, Clarke & Co., who have sent it to me as a literary curiosity. I want it to go down to posterity, so I put it in this great work. I simply change the names, and where words are too obscure, doctor them up a little:

BUTLER, Bates county, Mo., Jan. the 2, 1881.
I have a novle fresh and pure from the pen, wich I would like to be examined by you. I wish to bring it before the public the ensuing summer. I have wrote a good deal for the press, and always with great success. I wrote once an article on the growth of pie plant wich was copied fur and wide. You may have heard of me through my poem on "The Cold, Damp Sea or the Murmuring Wave and its Sad Kerplunk."

I dashed it off one summer day for the Scabtown *Herald*.

In it, I enter the fair field of fancy and with exquisite word-painting, I lead the reader on and on till he forgets that breakfast is ready, and follows the thrilling career of Algonquin and his own fair-haired Sciataca through page after page of delirious joy and poetic rithum.

In this novle, I have wove a woof of possibilities, criss-crossed with pictures of my own wild, unfettered fancy, which makes it a work at once truthful and yet sufficiently unnatural to make it egorly sot for by the great reading world.

The plot of the novle is this:

Algonquin is a poor artist, who paints lovely sunsets and things, nights, and cuts cordwood during the day, struggling to win a competence so that he can sue for the hand of Sciataca, the wealthy daughter of a plumber.

She does not love him much, and treats him coldly; but he perseveres till one of his exquisite pictures is egorly snapt up by a wealthy man at $2. The man afterwards turns out to be Sciataca's pa.

He says unkind things of Algonquin, and intimates that he is a better artist in four-foot wood than he is as a sunset man. He says that Algonquin is more of a Michael Angelo in basswood than anywhere else, and puts a wet blanket on Sciataca's love for Algonquin.

Then Sciataca grows colder than ever to Algonquin, and engages herself to a wealthy journalist.

Just as the wedding is about to take place, Algonquin finds that he is by birth an Ohio man. Sciataca repents and marries her first love. He secures the appointment of governor of Wyoming, and they remove to Cheyenne.

Then there are many little bursts of pictureskness and other things that I would like to see in print.

I send also a picture of myself which I would like to have in the book. Tell the artist to tone down the freckles so that the features may be seen by the observer, and put on a diamond pin, so that it will have the appearance of wealth, which the author of a book generally wears.

It is not wrote very good, but that won't make any difference when it is in print.

When the reading public begins to devour it, and the scads come rolling in, you can deduct enough for to pay your expenses of printing and pressing, and send me the balance by post-office money order. Please get it on the market as soon as possible, as I need a Swiss muzzlin and some other togs suitable to my position in liturary circles.

Yours truly, LUELLA BLINKER.

The Secret of Health

Health journals are now asserting, that to maintain a sound constitution you should lie only on the right side. The health journals may mean well enough; but what are you going to do if you are editing a Democratic paper?

Household Recipes

To remove oils, varnishes, resins, tar, oyster soup, currant jelly, and other selections from the bill of fare, use benzine, soap and chloroform cautiously with whitewash brush and garden hose. Then hang on wood pile to remove the pungent effluvia of the benzine.

To clean ceilings that have been smoked by kerosene lamps, or the fragrance from fried salt pork, remove the ceiling, wash thoroughly with borax, turpentine and rain water, then hang on the clothes line to dry. Afterward pulverize and spread over the pie plant bed for spring wear.

To remove starch and roughness from flatirons, hold the iron on a large grindstone for twenty minutes or so, then wipe off carefully with a rag. To make this effective, the grindstone should be in motion while the iron is applied. Should the iron still stick to the goods when in use, spit on it.

To soften water for household purposes, put in an ounce of quicklime in a certain quantity of water. If it is not sufficient, use less water or more quicklime. Should the immediate lime continue to remain deliberate, lay the water down on a stone and pound it with a base ball club.

To give relief to a burn, apply the white of an egg. The yolk of the egg may be eaten or placed on the shirt bosom, according to the taste of the person. If the burn should occur on a lady, she may omit the last instruction.

To wash black silk stockings, prepare a tub of lather, composed of tepid rain water and white soap, with a little ammonia. Then stand in the tub till dinner is ready. Roll in a cloth to dry. Do not wring, but press the water out. This will necessitate the removal of the stockings.

If your hands are badly chapped, wet them in warm water, rub them all over with Indian meal, then put on a coat of glycerine and keep them in your pockets for ten days. If you have no pockets convenient, insert them in the pocket of a friend.

An excellent liniment for toothache or neuralgia, is made of sassafras, oil of organum and a half ounce of tincture of capsicum, with half a pint of alcohol. Soak nine yards of red flannel in this mixture, wrap it around the head and then insert the head in a haystack till death comes to your relief.

To remove scars or scratches from the limbs of a piano, bathe the limb in a solution of tepid water and tincture of sweet oil. Then apply a strip of court plaster, and put the piano out on the lawn for the children to play horse with.

Woolen goods may be nicely washed if you put half an ox gall into two gallons of tepid water. It might be well to put the goods in the water also. If the mixture is not strong enough, put in another ox gall. Should this fail to do the work, put in the entire ox, reserving the tail for soup. The ox gall is comparatively useless for soup, and should not be preserved as an article of diet.

What is Literature?

A squash-nosed scientist from away up the creek, asks, "What is literature?" Cast your eye over these logic-imbued columns, you sun-dried savant from the remote precincts. Drink at the never-failing BOOMERANG springs of forgotten lore, you dropsical wart of a false and erroneous civilization. Read our "Address to the Duke of Stinking Water," or the "Ode to the Busted Snoot of a Shattered Venus De-Milo," if you want to fill up your thirsty soul with high-priced literature. Don't go around hungering for literary pie while your eyes are closed and your capacious ears are filled with bales of hay.

Table Manners of Children

Young children who have to wait till older people have eaten all there is in the house, should not open the dining-room door during the meal and ask the host if he is going to eat all day. It makes the company feel ill at ease, and lays up wrath in the parents' heart.

Children should not appear displeased with the regular

courses at dinner, and then fill up on pie. Eat the less expensive food first, and then organize a picnic in the preserves afterward.

Do not close out the last of your soup by taking the plate in your mouth and pouring the liquid down your childish neck. You might spill it on your bosom, and it enlarges and distorts the mouth unnecessarily.

When asked what part of the fowl you prefer, do not say you will take the part that goes over the fence last. This remark is very humorous, but the rising generation ought to originate some new table jokes that will be worthy of the age in which we live.

Children should early learn the use of the fork, and how to handle it. This knowledge can be acquired by allowing them to pry up the carpet tacks with this instrument, and other little exercises, such as the parent mind may suggest.

The child should be taught at once not to wave his bread around over the table, while in conversation, or to fill his mouth full of potatoes, and then converse in a rich tone of voice with some one out in the yard. He might get his dinner down his trachea and cause his parents great anxiety.

In picking up a plate or saucer filled with soup or with moist food, the child should be taught not to parboil his thumb in the contents of the dish, and to avoid swallowing soup bones or other indigestible debris.

Toothpicks are generally the last course, and children should not be permitted to pick their teeth and kick the table through the other exercises. While grace is being said at table, children should know that it is a breach of good breeding to smouge fruit cake just because their parents' heads are bowed down, and their attention for the moment turned in another direction. Children ought not to be permitted to find fault with the dinner, or fool with the cat while they are eating. Boys should, before going to the table, empty all the frogs and grasshoppers out of their pockets, or those insects might crawl out during the festivities, and jump into the gravy.

If a fly wades into your jelly up to his gambrels, do not mash him with your spoon before all the guests, as death is at all times depressing to those who are at dinner, and retards digestion. Take the fly out carefully, with what naturally adheres to his person, and wipe him on the table cloth.

It will demonstrate your perfect command of yourself, and afford much amusement for the company. Do not stand up in your chair and try to spear a roll with your fork. It is not good manners to do so, and you might slip and bust your crust, by so doing. Say "thank you," and "much obliged," and "beg pardon," wherever you can work in these remarks, as it throws people off their guard, and gives you an opportunity to get in your work on the pastry and other bric-a-brac near you at the time.

Dorothy Parker (1893–1967)

FROM *Complete Stories*

The Garter

There it goes! That would be. That would happen to me. I haven't got enough trouble. Here I am, a poor, lone orphan, stuck for the evening at this foul party where I don't know a soul. And now my garter has to go and break. That's the kind of thing they think up to do to me. Let's see, what shall we have happen to her now? Well, suppose we make her garter break; of course, it's an old gag, but it's always pretty sure-fire. A lot they've got to do, raking up grammar-school jokes to play on a poor, heartsick orphan, alone in the midst of a crowd. That's the bitterest kind of loneliness there is, too. Anybody'll tell you that. Anybody that wouldn't tell you that is a rotten egg.

This couldn't have happened to me in the perfumed sanctity of my boudoir. Or even in the comparative privacy of the taxi. Oh, no. That would have been too good. It must wait until I'm cornered, like a frightened rat, in a room full of strangers. And the dressing-room forty yards away—it might as well be Sheridan. I would get that kind of break.

Break, break, break, on thy cold gray stones, O sea, and I
would that my tongue could utter the thoughts that arise in
me. Boy, do I would that it could! I'd have this room emptied in thirty seconds, flat.

Thank God I was sitting down when the crash came.
There's a commentary on existence for you. There's a
glimpse of the depths to which a human being can sink. All
I have to be thankful for in this world is that I was sitting
down when my garter busted. Count your blessings over,
name them one by one, and it will surprise you what the
Lord hath done. Yeah. I see.

What is a person supposed to do in a case like this? What
would Napoleon have done? I've got to keep a cool head on
my shoulders. I've got to be practical. I've got to make
plans. The thing to do is to avert a panic at all costs. Tell the
orchestra for God's sake to keep on playing. Dance, you
jazz-mad puppets of fate, and pay no attention to me. I'm all
right. Wounded? Nay, sire, I'm healthy. Oh, I'm great.

The only course I see open is to sit here and hold on to it,
so my stocking won't come slithering down around my ankle. Just sit here and sit here and sit here. There's a rosy future. Summer will come, and bright, bitter Autumn, and
jolly old King Winter. And here I'll be, hanging on to this
damned thing. Love and fame will pass me by, and I shall
never know the sacred, awful joy of holding a tiny, warm
body in my grateful arms. I may not set down imperishable
words for posterity to marvel over; there will be for me nor
travel nor riches nor wise, new friends, nor glittering adventure, nor the sweet fruition of my gracious womanhood.
Ah, hell.

Won't it be nice for my lucky hosts, when everybody else
goes home, and I'm still sitting here? I wonder if I'll ever
get to know them well enough to hang my blushing head
and whisper my little secret to them. I suppose we'll have to
get pretty much used to one another. I'll probably live a
long time; there won't be much wear on my system, sitting
here, year in, year out, holding my stocking up. Maybe they
could find a use for me, after a while. They could hang hats
on me, or use my lap for an ash-tray. I wonder if their lease
is up, the first of October. No, no, no, now I won't hear a
word of it; you all go right ahead and move, and leave me
here for the new tenants. Maybe the landlord will do me

over for them. I expect my clothes will turn yellow, like Miss
Havisham's, in *Great Expectations,* by Charles Dickens, an
English novelist, 1812–1870. Miss Havisham had a broken
heart, and I've got a broken garter. The Frustration Girls.
The Frustration Girls on an Island, The Frustration Girls at
the World's Fair, The Frustration Girls and Their Ice-Boat,
The Frustration Girls at the House of All Nations. That's
enough of that. I don't want to play that any more.

To think of a promising young life blocked, halted, shattered by a garter! In happier times, I might have been able to
use the word "garter" in a sentence. Nearer, my garter thee,
nearer to thee. It doesn't matter; my life's over, anyway. I
wonder how they'll be able to tell when I'm dead. It will be
a very thin line of distinction between me sitting here holding my stocking, and just a regulation dead body. A dead,
damp, moist, unpleasant body. That's from *Nicholas Nick-
leby*. What am I having, anyway—An Evening with Dickens? Well, it's the best I'll get, from now on.

If I had my life to live over again, I'd wear corsets;
corsets with lots of firm, true, tough, loyal-hearted garters
attached to them all the way around. You'd be safe with
them; they wouldn't let you down. I wouldn't trust a round
garter again as far as I could see it. I or anybody else. Never
trust a round garter or a Wall Street man. That's what life
has taught me. That's what I've got out of all this living. If
I could have just one more chance, I'd wear corsets. Or
else I'd go without stockings, and play I was the eternal
Summer girl. Once they wouldn't let me in the Casino at
Monte Carlo because I didn't have any stockings on. So I
went and found my stockings, and then came back and lost
my shirt. Dottie's Travel Diary: or Highways and Byways
in Picturesque Monaco, by One of Them. I wish I were in
Monte Carlo right this minute. I wish I were in Carcas-
sonne. Hell, it would look like a million dollars to me to be
on St. Helena.

I certainly must be cutting a wide swath through this
party. I'm making my personality felt. Creeping into every
heart, that's what I'm doing. Oh, have you met Dorothy
Parker? What's she like? Oh, she's terrible. God, she's poi-
sonous. Sits in a corner and sulks all evening—never opens
her yap. Dumbest woman you ever saw in your life. You
know, they say she doesn't write a word of her stuff. They

say she pays this poor little guy, that lives in some tenement on the lower East Side, ten dollars a week to write it and she just signs her name to it. He has to do it, the poor devil, to help support a crippled mother and five brothers and sisters; he makes buttonholes in the daytime. Oh, she's terrible.

Little do they know, the blind fools, that I'm all full of tenderness and affection, and just aching to give and give and give. All they can see is this unfortunate exterior. There's a man looking at it now. All right, baby, go on and look your head off. Funny, isn't it? Look pretty silly, don't I, sitting here holding my knee? Yes, and I'm the only one that's going to hold it, too. What do you think of that, sweetheart?

Heaven send that no one comes over here and tries to make friends with me. That's the first time I ever wished that, in all my life. What shall I do if anyone comes over? Suppose they try to shake hands with me. Suppose somebody asks me to dance. I'll just have to rock my head and say, "No spik Ingles," that's all. Can this be me, praying that nobody will come near me? And when I was getting dressed, I thought, "Maybe this will be the night that romance will come into my life." Oh, if I only had the use of both my hands, I'd just cover my face and cry my heart out.

That man, that man who was looking! He's coming over! Oh, now what? I can't say, "Sir, I have not the dubious pleasure of your acquaintance." I'm rotten at that sort of thing. I can't answer him in perfect French. Lord knows I can't get up and walk haughtily away. I wonder how he'd take it if I told him all. He looks a little too Brooks Brothers to be really understanding. The better they look, the more they think you are trying to get new with them, if you talk of Real Things, Things That Matter. Maybe he'd think I was just eccentric. Maybe he's got a humane streak, somewhere underneath. Maybe he's got a sister or a mother or something. Maybe he'll turn out to be one of Nature's noblemen.

How do you do? Listen, what would you do if you were I, and . . . ?

The Little Hours

Now what's this? What's the object of all this darkness all over me? They haven't gone and buried me alive while my back was turned, have they? Ah, now would you think they'd do a thing like that! Oh, no, I know what it is. I'm awake. That's it. I've waked up in the middle of the night. Well, isn't that nice. Isn't that simply ideal. Twenty minutes past four, sharp, and here's Baby wide-eyed as a marigold. Look at this, will you? At the time when all decent people are just going to bed, I must wake up. There's no way things can ever come out even, under this system. This is as rank as injustice is ever likely to get. This is what brings about hatred and bloodshed, that's what *this* does.

Yes, and you want to know what got me into this mess? Going to bed at ten o'clock, that's what. That spells ruin. T-e-n-space-o-apostrophe-c-l-o-c-k: ruin. Early to bed, and you'll wish you were dead. Bed before eleven, nuts before seven. Bed before morning, sailors give warning. Ten o'clock, after a quiet evening of reading. Reading—there's an institution for you. Why, I'd turn on the light and read, right this minute, if reading weren't what contributed toward driving me here. I'll show it. God, the bitter misery that reading works in this world! Everybody knows that— everybody who *is* everybody. All the best minds have been off reading for years. Look at the swing La Rochefoucauld took at it. He said that if nobody had ever learned to read, very few people would be in love. There was a man for you, and that's what *he* thought of it. Good for you, La Rochefoucauld; nice going, boy. I wish I'd never learned to read. I wish I'd never learned to take off my clothes. Then I wouldn't have been caught in this jam at half-past four in the morning. If nobody had ever learned to undress, very few people would be in love. No, his is better. Oh, well, it's a man's world.

La Rochefoucauld, indeed, lying quiet as a mouse, and me tossing and turning here! This is no time to be getting all steamed up about La Rochefoucauld. It's only a question of minutes before I'm going to be pretty darned good and sick of La Rochefoucauld, once and for all. La Rochefoucauld this and La Rochefoucauld that. Yes, well, let me tell you that if nobody had ever learned to quote, very few people would be in love with La Rochefoucauld. I bet you I don't know ten souls who read him without a middleman. People pick up those scholarly little essays that start off "Was it not that lovable old cynic, La Rochefoucauld, who said . . ."

and then they go around claiming to know the master backwards. Pack of illiterates, that's all they are. All right, let them keep their La Rochefoucauld, and see if I care. I'll stick to La Fontaine. Only I'd be better company if I could quit thinking that La Fontaine married Alfred Lunt.

I don't know what I'm doing mucking about with a lot of French authors at this hour, anyway. First thing you know, I'll be reciting *Fleurs du Mal* to myself, and then I'll be little more good to anybody. And I'll stay off Verlaine too; he was always chasing Rimbauds. A person would be better off with La Rochefoucauld, even. Oh, damn La Rochefoucauld. The big Frog. I'll thank him to keep out of my head. What's he doing there, anyhow? What's La Rochefoucauld to me, or he to Hecuba? Why, I don't even know the man's first name, that's how close I ever was to *him*. What am I supposed to be, a hostess to La Rochefoucauld? That's what *he* thinks. Sez he. Well, he's only wasting his time, hanging around here. I can't help him. The only other thing I can remember his saying is that there is always something a little pleasing to us in the misfortunes of even our dearest friends. That cleans me all up with Monsieur La Rochefoucauld. *Maintenant c'est fini, ça.*

Dearest friends. A sweet lot of dearest friends *I've* got. All of them lying in swinish stupors, while I'm practically up and about. All of them stretched sodden through these, the fairest hours of the day, when man should be at his most productive. Produce, produce, produce, for I tell you the night is coming. Carlyle said that. Yes, and a fine one *he* was, to go shooting off his face on production. *Oh,* Thomas Carli-yill, what I know about *you*-oo! No, that will be enough of that. I'm not going to start fretting about Carlyle, at this stage of the game. What did he ever do that was so great, besides founding a college for Indians? (That one ought to make him spin.) Let him keep his face out of this, if he knows what's good for him. I've got enough trouble with that lovable old cynic, La Rochefoucauld—him and the misfortunes of his dearest friends!

The first thing I've got to do is get out and ship me up a complete new set of dearest friends; that's the first thing. Everything else can wait. And will somebody please kindly be so good as to inform me how I am ever going to meet up with any new people when my entire scheme of living is out of joint—when I'm the only living being awake while the rest of the world lies sleeping? I've got to get this thing adjusted. I must try to get back to sleep right now. I've got to conform to the rotten little standards of this sluggard civilization. People needn't feel that they have to change their ruinous habits and come my way. Oh, no, no; no, indeed. Not at all. I'll go theirs. If that isn't the woman of it for you! Always having to do what somebody else wants, like it or not. Never able to murmur a suggestion of her own.

And what suggestion has anyone to murmur as to how I am going to drift lightly back to slumber? Here I am, awake as high noon what with all this milling and pitching around with La Rochefoucauld. I really can't be expected to drop everything and start counting sheep, at my age. I hate sheep. Untender it may be in me, but all my life I've hated sheep. It amounts to a phobia, the way I hate them. I can tell the minute there's one in the room. They needn't think that I am going to lie here in the dark and count their unpleasant little faces for them; I wouldn't do it if I didn't fall asleep again until the middle of next August. Suppose they never get counted—what's the worst that can happen? If the number of imaginary sheep in this world remains a matter of guesswork, who is richer or poorer for it? No, sir; *I'm* not their scorekeeper. Let them count themselves, if they're so crazy mad after mathematics. Let them do their own dirty work. Coming around here, at this time of day, and asking me to count them! And not even *real* sheep, at that. Why, it's the most preposterous thing I ever heard in my life.

But there must be *something* I could count. Let's see. No, I already know by heart how many fingers I have. I could count my bills, I suppose. I could count the things I didn't do yesterday that I should have done. I could count the things I should do today that I'm not going to do. I'm never going to accomplish anything; that's perfectly clear to me. I'm never going to be famous. My name will never be writ large on the roster of Those Who Do Things. I don't do anything. Not one single thing. I used to bite my nails, but I don't even do that any more. I don't amount to the powder to blow me to hell. I've turned out to be nothing but a bit of flotsam. Flotsam and leave 'em—that's me from now on. Oh, it's all terrible.

Well. This way lies galloping melancholia. Maybe it's

because this is the zero hour. This is the time the swooning soul hangs pendant and vertiginous between the new day and the old, nor dares confront the one or summon back the other. This is the time when all things, known and hidden, are iron to weight the spirit; when all ways, traveled or virgin, fall away from the stumbling feet, when all before the straining eyes is black. Blackness now, everywhere is blackness. This is the time of abomination, the dreadful hour of the victorious dark. For it is always darkest— Was it not that lovable old cynic, La Rochefoucauld, who said that it is always darkest before the deluge?

There. Now you see, don't you? Here we are again, practically back where we started. La Rochefoucauld, we are here. Ah, come on, son—how about your going your way and letting me go mine? I've got my work cut out for me right here; I've got all this sleeping to do. Think how I am going to look by daylight if this keeps up. I'll be a seamy sight for all those rested, clear-eyed, fresh-faced dearest friends of mine—the rats! My *dear*, whatever have you been doing; I thought you were so good lately. Oh, I was helling around with La Rochefoucauld till all hours; we couldn't stop laughing about your misfortunes. No, this is getting too thick, really. It isn't right to have this happen to a person, just because she went to bed at ten o'clock once in her life. Honest, I won't ever do it again. I'll go straight, after this. I'll never go to bed again, if I can only sleep now. If I can tear my mind away from a certain French cynic, *circa* 1650, and slip into lovely oblivion. 1650. I bet I look as if I'd been awake since then.

How do people go to sleep? I'm afraid I've lost the knack. I might try busting myself smartly over the temple with the night-light. I might repeat to myself, slowly and soothingly, a list of quotations beautiful from minds profound; if I can remember any of the damn things. That might do it. And it ought effectually to bar that visiting foreigner that's been hanging around ever since twenty minutes past four. Yes, that's what I'll do. Only wait till I turn the pillow; it feels as if La Rochefoucauld had crawled inside the slip.

Now let's see—where shall we start? Why—er—let's see. Oh, yes, I know one. This above all, to thine own self be true and it must follow, as the night the day, thou canst not then be false to any man. Now they're off. And once they get started, they ought to come like hot cakes. Let's see. Ah, what avail the sceptered race and what the form divine, when every virtue, every grace, Rose Aylmer, all were thine. Let's see. They also serve who only stand and wait. If Winter comes, can Spring be far behind? Lilies that fester smell far worse than weeds. Silent upon a peak in Darien. Mrs. Porter and her daughter wash their feet in sodawater. And Agatha's Arth is a hug-the-hearth, but my true love is false. Why did you die when lambs were cropping, you should have died when apples were dropping. Shall be together, breathe, and ride, so one day more am I deified, who knows but the world will end tonight. And he shall hear the stroke of eight and not the stroke of nine. They are not long, the weeping and the laughter; love and desire and hate I think will have no portion in us after we pass the gate. But none, I think, do there embrace. I think that I shall never see a poem lovely as a tree. I think I will not hang myself today. Ay tank Ay go home now.

Let's see. Solitude is the safeguard of mediocrity and the stern companion of genius. Consistency is the hobgoblin of little minds. Something is emotion remembered in tranquility. A cynic is one who knows the price of everything and the value of nothing. That lovable old cynic is one who—oops, there's King Charles's head again. I've got to watch myself. Let's see. Circumstantial evidence is a trout in the milk. Any stigma will do to beat a dogma. If you would learn what God thinks about money, you have only to look at those to whom He has given it. If nobody had ever learned to read, very few people—

All right. That fixes it. I throw in the towel right now. I know when I'm licked. There'll be no more of this nonsense; I'm going to turn on the light and read my head off. Till the next ten o'clock, if I feel like it. And what does La Rochefoucauld want to make of that? Oh, he *will,* eh? Yes, he will! He and who else? La Rochefoucauld and *what* very few people?

Sam Pickering, Jr. (Contemporary)

ᘓᓂᓂᘒᘒᘒ

FROM *Living to Prowl*

Book Tour

Reading occasionally influences life. In the *Hartford Courant* I read an article describing a book tour made by Kaye Gibbons. To publicize her novel *Sights Unseen*, Gibbons visited thirty cities. *Walkabout Year*, my latest collection of essays, appeared in early October. "Damn," I said to Vicki, putting the paper down on the kitchen table, "I bet my Australia book would sell better if I went on a tour." "Then go on one," Vicki said, bending over and slipping a tray of cinnamon buns into the oven. I followed Vicki's advice. I walked out of the kitchen into the hall. From a hook in the closet, I removed the Akubra hat that I bought in Cairns three years ago. Then I strolled through the woods to the Cup of Sun, the first stop on my tour. I drank two cups of coffee, ate a bran muffin, and talked to Mary, Ellen, George, and Roger. Later that morning Eliza played soccer at Spring Hill. I wore the hat to the game. "Just in from the outback?" Chuck said when he saw me. "No," I said, "I'm on a book tour, and this is my second appearance." "Oh," Chuck said, pausing before asking, "do you think the girls will win today?" "Yes," I said. I watched the game. The girls won 4–0. When I returned home, I hung the Akubra back on the hook in the closet. The tour was over, or at least the actual tour ended. My imaginary tour, however, was in full swing, stretching not just through thirty cities but through all my days, not only shaping sights unseen but so quickening them that they cast bright shadows across the hours.

Children force parents to see clearly. In a family the sun

often rises and sets at high noon, preventing parents from dreaming and transforming shadows into the stuff of life. Recently the president of the United States spoke at the University of Connecticut. "Daddy," Eliza said at dinner one night, "the parents of lots of my friends received invitations to meet the president. You write books. Why weren't you invited?" Before I answered, Edward spoke. "Many people write books," he said; "Dad's not important." Edward told the truth, something that brings book tours to abrupt ends. Because my applications are always rejected, I no longer apply for literary fellowships. Now, instead of becoming gloomy as I fill out forms and realize that no matter my words the applications will fail, I only dream of success. I imagine the pages fellowships will enable me to write. When I get up from my desk after not completing an application, I feel invigorated. I am ready to wander hill and field and spinning loops through the air turn falling leaves into necklaces, strings of jewels: yellow sugar maple and black locust, crimson red maple, orange hickory, and bronze beech. Keeping imagination vital is not easy. This fall I turned down two speaking engagements because the fees offered were modest. In contrast I agreed to speak on four occasions for free. "The honorariums were so low they made me feel ordinary," I explained to Vicki. "When a person doesn't receive a fee, he is free to create an imaginary self. Money does not define him and reduce him to the everyday." "But," Edward said when I finished the explanation, "if you made the speeches, you would earn enough to buy Mommy the new refrigerator she wants."

Writers whose tours take them to faraway places meet lots of literary folk. On my tour I met only one other writer, and that was Eliza. On Eliza's desk I found an account of Hungry Bert, a young vole who spent his summer playing games instead of stocking a larder for the winter. During the first week of winter Bert stripped the shelves of his storeroom. Forced to leave his burrow to search for food, Bert suffered from the cold. " 'Just look at my hands; they are frozen,' Bert exclaimed; 'even the marrow of my bones is blue from cold!' 'That's what you get from playing kick-the-acorn instead of collecting insects for the winter!' cried a goose, flying south." Luck enabled Bert to survive "the winter of '93," as Eliza phrased it. Early in the fall a squirrel abandoned a flea-infested nest. In a corner of the nest Bert discovered a cache of acorns.

In late September fleas infested our yard. In jumping from the grass to George and Penny, they hopped into dinner table conversation. From there they bounced into Eliza's writings. While cleaning Eliza's room, I found a poem under the bed. The poem was entitled "Poppies." "The poppies grow gaily out upon the green, / Their colors are sapphires and a rosy sheen. / They bob and dance so gracefully in the blowing breeze, / While listening to the music and singing with the fleas. / If I were but a poppy in a field of grass, / I know a flute I'd play, not a horn of brass."

After book tours writers often get mail. Despite the appearance of *Walkabout Year*, I received few letters this fall. Only after my tour ended did the mail bring letters that touched on writing matters. One day I received two letters. Announcing the publication of a magazine devoted to elementary school matters, the first letter began, "Dear Literature Professional." An old friend and a literary amateur who had written a box of books wrote the second letter. Some time ago he suffered a stroke, and I wrote him, wishing him good health and describing the happy hours I spent watching the children play soccer. "Your soccer-parent days remind me of my son and me years ago," my friend said. "Now all my grandchildren are college graduates and ready to improve an imperfect world. Alas."

Unlike most writers on tour, schedule did not buckle me tightly to place and time. "Your tour," Vicki said, "sounds more like a detour." "Yes," I said, "that's the best kind of tour." One morning I drifted through Carthage, Tennessee. I didn't sign copies of my book, but I learned that Alice Blair, the fairest bud ever to bloom in the gritty soil around Mayflower, had married William Whicker from Nashville. Whicker was from a wealthy family. He grew up in a big house on Craighead and graduated from Wallace School after which he spent two lean years at Vanderbilt. Rich men often make poor husbands, and Whicker did not appreciate Alice, thinking her roots ran shallower than those of people blossoming in West Nashville. One night after she labored over dinner, Alice asked, "Darling, do I cook as well as your mother?" "My dear girl," Whicker responded, turning his fork sideways and digging at a kernel of corn lodged next to the first premolar on the left side of his face, "I come from an old and distinguished family. My mother was not a cook." Old and distinguished the Whickers may have been; brainy they were not. Before the wedding Whicker's brother Baxley visited the Blairs in Mayflower. Alice's father Nunnley was a deacon in the local church. On Sunday night Baxley accompanied Nunnley to a meeting of the church vestry. A parishioner had left the church a substantial bequest, and the vestry debated whether to spend the money on a chandelier or on a piano. Out of courtesy the vestry solicited Baxley's opinion. "If I was you," Baxley said, excavating a seam of golden wax running through his inner ear, "I'd buy a piano. You are mighty deep in the country, and you aren't going to find anybody out here who can play a chandelier."

Carthage itself enjoyed Indian summer, that quiet time between the last of the summer camp meetings and the first of the winter revivals. Taking advantage of the theological calm, Slubey Garts started a collection of sermons. "Folks tell that you are writing a book," Googoo Hooberry said to Slubey one afternoon. "Yes," Slubey answered, "although I'm just a poor weak worm creeping after Christ, I'm trying to do a little something at it." "Well," Googoo said, "keep going. You have just as much right to make a book as them that knows how." Slubey had not progressed far when I visited Carthage. He had decided on a title, written part of an invocation, and filled a spiral notebook with jottings. The title was *Like to a Saltlick,* the phrase being taken from "Come back to Christ like a saltlick," an invitation Slubey often issued during services at the Tabernacle of Love, spreading his arms wide, gazing upward, and staggering slightly, looking like, Turlow Gutheridge said, "he was carrying a giant turnip to the Smith County Fair."

Slubey liked music. He often said, "you can lead a congregation to the collection plate but without some whooping and hollering they'll just stand there." In the invocation Slubey combined his affection for music with what he thought was the dangerous spread of Catholicism in Tennessee, particularly in Nashville. "After Nashville, Carthage; after Carthage, the world," Proverbs Goforth declared one Sunday. In the invocation Slubey stated that *papist* and *Romanist* disagreed not only with his soul but also with his ear. In order to make his prose more euphonic and more pleasing to God and man, he was changing, he wrote, the *-ist* ending of *papist* and *Romanist* to *-ite,* thus producing *papite* and *Romanite.* "Christ did not build his cathedral on a cabbage stump, but on words," Slubey said, explaining that in changing *-ist* to *-ite* he was following "the divine pencil." "Edomites, Moabites, and Ammonites," he said, wandered the Holy Land, "not Edomists, Moabists, and Ammonists." "Elijah was a Tishbite, not a Tishbist; Ephron was a Hittite, not a Hittist, and Bildad was a Shuite, not a Shuist." I told Slubey that I didn't think linguists would adopt his changes. But I could be wrong. After I told Josh about Slubey's proposal, he embraced the notion wholeheartedly and immediately began calling Communists, Communites, and feminists, feminites.

Despite the invocation Slubey's notes implied that the book would contain only one critique of papite practices. Under the heading "Relics and Bamboozle" appeared a list, "pickled tongues, candied noses, and ears in aspic" followed by "the hook that caught the great fish which swallowed Jonah, the bag from one of Pharaoh's lean kine, and three hairs from the tail of the ass that Jesus rode into Jerusalem." The rest of the sermons appeared to be standard moral fare. Under "Anger," Slubey wrote, "Describe the red-mouthed man." Beneath "Spewing Hate" *Humility* appeared, followed by "bowing to a dwarf will not prevent a man from standing up again." On another page, one that I assumed referred to Gluttony, he wrote, "John the Baptist fed on locusts, but today people are not satisfied with chocolate-covered raspberries or strawberries; they want chocolate-covered watermelons." "Lazy folks," he wrote on the next page, "water the horse with the milk bucket. In spring they don't drain fields, and instead of corn they raise frogs." Under "Ravages of Cupid," he warned, "bedroom slippers are made out of banana skins. Only wingtips can ferry the soul over the bottomless ocean of corruption." Watery metaphors lay beached throughout Slubey's notes. "Many lewdsters," he wrote, "awash on the flood of sin consider sending a note to God in a bottle, begging for help and forgiveness. Alas, wine fills all the bottles in their basements, and instead of praying to God they worship drink and sink under the waves." On the same page appeared an anecdote. Although Slubey ran a pencil through the names, I was able to decipher "Horace Armitage" and

"Enos Mayfield's Inn." Horace, it seems, appeared at the inn late one Saturday night. Drunk and short of money, he slapped a Gideon Bible on the bar "as security for drink." When Enos refused to accept the bible, Horace was incensed. "Why you refuse God's own word!" he shouted, staggering toward the door. "You must be an infidel."

My tour did not flow smoothly. Fatherhood forced me to return to Storrs for soccer games. On the Sunday of Columbus Day weekend, I got up at six o'clock in order to drive Edward to Lebanon for a tournament that began at eight. I returned home at 6:45 that evening, Eliza's last game having started in Willimantic at 5:10 in the afternoon. Sarah Dorr was Eliza's best friend. Sarah played on the same team as Eliza, and often I drove the girls to games. Afterward they enjoyed insulting each other, Eliza calling Sarah "doorknob" and Sarah responding with "nosepicker." When soccer did not kick books out of mind, Josh burst into my office. "Great god!" he exclaimed last Tuesday. "The woods are full of men in drag and carrying guns. Don't think about going on one of your inspirational little rambles now." "In drag?" I asked. "Yes," he said, "flaming queens in gray and green outfits." "Camouflage," I said; "the men are hunters dressed in camouflage." "No!" Josh shouted. "Soldiers wear camouflage, and no war is being fought in Mansfield. The men are queens." Early in October myth was on Josh's mind. "Remember Pygmalion," he said, "the sculptor who carved a statue of a beautiful woman and then fell so in love with his creation that he kissed it, whereupon the gods blessed him and turned her into flesh and blood?" "Sure," I said. "Supposedly, Pygmalion and his bride lived happily ever after." "Well," Josh continued, "that wouldn't happen in today's feminite environment. Now the statue would accuse Pygmalion of sexual harassment and sue him for kissing without permission."

Josh is fond of silly stories, and yesterday he insisted upon my listening to an account of a mother snake and her nineteen snakelings. The snakelings spent days practicing hissing, perfecting their technique in a pit dug for them by their mother. One day when the mother had to slither out to crawl a couple of errands, she sent her children to the den of Mrs. Pot, a neighbor. Mrs. Pot was out of her den, but when she returned and found the snakelings hissing in her pit, she sent them home. When they crawled through the front hole, the babies' mother asked why they came home so soon. "Mrs. Pot sent us," the snakelings cried. "Why that ungrateful coluber," the mother exclaimed. "Who assisted her the last time she suffered from ecdysis and couldn't see? Who nursed her when she bruised her fangs against the heel of man? Who does Mrs. Pot think she is? Her family is new to this range. Who showed her all the vole runs? Why I remember when the Pots didn't have a pit to hiss in."

I had heard Josh's story before. Instead of boring, however, repetition reassures, implying that life is comfortably circular, not linear. Yesterday's event will be tomorrow's happening, and no regimen of zeal or moral earnestness can alter the cycle. Rather than thrusting forward into the unknown, carrying banners proclaiming "progress" and "development," the person who believes life circular can relax, and riding the wheel of days, marvel at the dust pitched up by spinning time. On my tour I traveled a familiar October landscape. Fields appeared shaved, the corn stalks chopped into silage. From Horsebarn Hill the land rumpled outward in embers, trees flaming red and orange through ashy mists. In depressions between rows of stalks, lamb's quarters glowed, the stems claret and the flowers purple. Low bush huckleberry spilled down a slope in a red haze. Beneath leaves yellow crystals glittered like small sparks. In woods hayscented and New York ferns crumpled. Color leached out of fronds, transforming them into ghostly remnants of the green that rolled like water through spring. Down the hill behind the sheep barn cinnamon ferns turned ochre, looking as if they had been burned by a damp fire, cindered and rusted at the same time. Bundles of satiny sweet everlasting glowed in the dull light. Bushy and purple-stemmed asters drifted across vision looking as fragile as cirrus clouds. Canada geese honked overhead, the sound almost too familiar to hear. In contrast calls of crows jerked into awareness like wrenches tugging frozen bolts. A collar of alders pressed against the woods. Resembling gauze bandages, woolly aphids wrapped around twigs. The larvae of striped alder sawfly clung in circles to the margins of leaves and on cold mornings glistened like glazed doughnuts.

Leaves bunched across the forest floor in shag rugs. The foliage thinned. The woods turned yellow, and shadows became wispy. As sunlight sifted through black birch and sugar maple, it lost body and absorbing color floated lightly over the understory like a throw of weary lace. Thickets of spicebush turned hollows yellow. Along the border of the woods, green dried out of beaked hazelnut. For a moment the leaves turned yellow. Then splotches spread across them like measles, at first appearing red and proud but then shrinking into brown crust.

Because I had no appointments, I drifted across days. Instead of signing books, I looked for, if not the signatures, at least traces of others. On a dead star-nosed mole flies laid eggs in clutches, resembling bundles of shiny white spindles. Sagging on a spicebush were three heart-shaped balloons, all with "Happy Anniversary" printed on them. A hedge of pink hibiscus blossomed across the front of one balloon. On the second balloon horticultural artists forced peonies out of season and into the company of chicory and goldenrod. A wicker basket opened like a ventricle on the last balloon. Roses burst over the rim of the basket in scarlet spurts while in the middle of the basket a dove huddled on a nest, an anniversary being a time when home is where the heart is and when feeling pulses stronger than thought.

I followed whim through days. One damp morning I watched leaves drizzle into the Fenton River. Some surfed the air, riding up over a finger of breeze then quickly dipping and coasting into the water. Others swung through circles resembling drops tossed out by a sprinkler. Some leaves from red maples turned like corkscrews. Others with long stems fell like arrows. The river was low, and leaves drifted slowly downstream, bunching against rocks and ledges, and in worn bends rumpling together, resembling quilts pushed against headboards. Hemlocks grew along the river bank, and needles hooked leaves, seeming to reel them in and wear them as ornaments. I walked up from the river to the raspberry field. A woodcock broke cover and flying low circled behind me. A flock of yellow-rumped warblers hurried through the scrub. Sulfur shelf fungus bloomed on a log. The leaves of staghorn sumac resembled artists' palettes running with color, green near the stems, deep orange in the middle, and red at the tips. Northern red oak grew at the edge of the field. Color swept out from then drew back into the big leaves, shimmering, making me think Neats Foot oil had been rubbed into them. White pines towered behind the oaks. Tops of the trees were green, but nearer the ground branches had broken off, and the trunks resembled heavy culverts, at their bases needles oozing out in an overflow of orange.

To see how season signed October I toured at different times. Early in the morning fibrous mists floated over lowlands. A tuft of reed canary grass resembled a scythe, the panicle bending the stem into a blade. Inside the curve hung a spider web, droplets of water silver on the silk, creating the illusion of motion, making the grass swish through the air. A bumblebee quivered chilled and dying on top of a field thistle. Seeds spilled out of milkweed in damp mats, resembling sheets of water that had frozen, melted, and frozen again, this last time into cloudy sheaves. At midday I forced my hands into open milkweed pods. The pods felt warm and oily. Sometimes I shook stalks, and a frolic of clouds blew out of the pods. Below the white hairs seeds hung swollen, arches of yellow at the bases of the hairs curving over them like minute rainbows. On Queen Anne's lace umbrels folded inward so seeds could dry. Lady bugs nested in the umbrels, the prickly seeds blankets around them. I did not tell Josh or Slubey about touring early October. Queen Anne's lace, Josh would have warned, was just the bit of nifty to spice up the gowns of men trolling the woods with guns and dressed fit to kill, hoping for a slice of the old venison. Slubey would have preached to me, accusing me of turning nature into god. I can hear Slubey now. "Instead of listening to the rustle of leaves, harken to the rustle of angels' wings."

Book tours, as Slubey might have put it, "pry open the portals of the head." At the end of a tour writers return home, having seen and heard the stuff of new stories. One evening during the middle of my tour, I drove Eliza to soccer practice. As I drove along the dirt road past the town dump, Eliza asked a question. "Daddy," she said, "what is Communism?" "Communism was," I said, "a theory of government. Like all theories it promised people better lives." I explained that the gap between theory and practice was vast, primarily, I said, because humans were flawed creatures. Self always got in the way when people tried to implement theory. "Instead of being our brothers' keepers," I said, "we have become our brothers' exploiters." "Communism," I continued, promised "a fairer distribution of income. If the United States were a Communist country," I said, "I would not have the money to send you to Camp Wohelo in Maine each summer. But then some of the poor children in Hartford might have better lives." "That doesn't sound bad to me, Daddy," Eliza said. "I don't know why Americans hate Communism so much."

The practice field was four miles from our house, so I stayed at the field and talked to parents. Most parents were threads from the same financial and social fabric: doctors, teachers, lawyers, and artists. A few parents did not have means, however. On the weekend Eliza's team was scheduled to play in a tournament. The entrance fee for the tournament was fifteen dollars a child. "Is Sally looking forward to the tournament?" I said to a mother. "She'd like to play," the mother answered slowly, "but we can't come up with the fifteen dollars. Bill broke his arm six weeks ago. He hasn't worked since, and we don't have insurance." Sally played in the tournament. Afterward she baked me an apple pie. The pie was sweet. Still, as I ate it, my mind scrolled back to the conversation with Eliza. "Fifteen dollars," I thought, "from each according to his abilities. To each according to his need. Communites could teach us a lesson."

The narrative weather changed rapidly during my tour. While some stories were cloudy, others were sunny. The morning after the tournament I went to the Cup of Sun, and Ellen told me a story about Robbie, the five-year-old son of a friend. This fall Robbie started kindergarten. When he got on the bus the first day, he asked the bus driver his name. "Just call me Mr. Bus Driver," the man said. "Isn't it wonderful, Daddy," Robbie said to his father later, "that Mr. and Mrs. Driver named their little boy Bus, and when he grew up, he became a bus driver?" "Yes, son," the father said, "that's wonderful." As children age, stories told about them remain wondrous, albeit the tone changes. Edward's soccer team played most games on a field below the middle school. Parents parked cars at the school. We sat on a railing at the edge of the parking lot, watched the games, and talked about our children, then life itself. Twelve and thirteen, the boys on the team had grown prickly. "Ryan," a mother recounted, "never wears shoes out of the locker room. Last Wednesday when the temperature was below freezing, he walked barefoot across the parking lot. When he got to the car, he said, 'Boy, I'm cold.' 'Maybe, if you wore your shoes, you would be warmer,' I suggested. 'Why are you always trying to ruin my life!' he shouted, getting into the backseat and slamming the door."

Halloween is a week away, and at the Cup of Sun this morning, friends and I dallied through muffins and coffee, talking about costumes. One year when I was a graduate student, I bought several pairs of inflatable buttocks. I strapped them to my chest and backside and went to a party as an ass. Another time I purchased a plague of rubber flies. I glued a swarm to my face. Afterward I attached threads to the wings of another swarm and hung them from the brim of a battered Cavanaugh hat. Then I went to a party as Fly Face, a character from the Dick Tracy comic strip. "Costumes are fun," Mary said; "years ago a friend convinced his sweetheart to dress like a girl scout for a Halloween party. She put the outfit on in my friend's apartment, and they never got to the party." "Sort of like your book tour," George said; "you never got out of Mansfield." "Still, I bet you had almost as much fun as that scout master," Ellen said. "More," I said. "I had much more fun."

Sylvia Plath (1932–1963)

෨෨ඁ෨

FROM *The Bell Jar*

Suddenly, after I finished a poem, he said, "Esther, have you ever seen a man?"

The way he said it I knew he didn't mean a regular man or a man in general, I knew he meant a man naked.

"No," I said. "Only statues."

"Well, don't you think you would like to see me?"

I didn't know what to say. My mother and my grandmother had started hinting around to me a lot lately about what a fine, clean boy Buddy Willard was, coming from such a fine, clean family, and how everybody at church thought he was a model person, so kind to his parents and to older people, as well as so athletic and so handsome and so intelligent.

All I heard about, really, was how fine and clean Buddy was and how he was the kind of a person a girl should stay fine and clean for. So I didn't really see the harm in anything Buddy would think up to do.

"Well, all right, I guess so," I said.

I stared at Buddy while he unzipped his chino pants and took them off and laid them on a chair and then took off his underpants that were made of something like nylon fishnet.

"They're cool," he explained, "and my mother says they wash easily."

Then he just stood there in front of me and I kept staring at him. The only thing I could think of was turkey neck and turkey gizzards and I felt very depressed.

Buddy seemed hurt I didn't say anything. "I think you ought to get used to me like this," he said. "Now let me see you."

But undressing in front of Buddy suddenly appealed to me about as much as having my Posture Picture taken at college, where you have to stand naked in front of a camera, knowing all the time that a picture of you stark naked, both full view and side view, is going into the college gym files to be marked A B C or D depending on how straight you are.

"Oh, some other time," I said.

Edgar Allan Poe (1809–1849)

~~~~~~

How to Write a Blackwood Article

In the name of the Prophet—figs!
Cry of Turkish fig-pedler

I presume everybody has heard of me. My name is the Signora Psyche Zenobia. This I know to be a fact. Nobody but my enemies ever calls me Suky Snobbs. I have been assured that Suky is but a vulgar corruption of Psyche, which is good Greek, and means "the soul" (that's me, I'm *all* soul), and sometimes "a butterfly," which latter meaning undoubtedly alludes to my appearance in my new crimson satin dress, with the sky-blue Arabian *mantelet,* and the trimmings of green *agraffas,* and the seven flounces of orange-colored *auriculas.* As for Snobbs—any person who should look at me would be instantly aware that my name wasn't Snobbs. Miss Tabitha Turnip propagated that report through sheer envy. Tabitha Turnip indeed! Oh, the little wretch! But what can we expect from a turnip? Wonder if she remembers the old adage about "blood out of a turnip, etc." (Mem.: put her in mind of it the first opportunity.) (Mem. again—pull her nose.) Where was I! Ah! I have been assured that Snobbs is a mere corruption of Zenobia, and that Zenobia was a queen (so am I. Dr. Moneypenny always calls me the Queen of Hearts), and that Zenobia, as well as Psyche, is good Greek, and that my father was "a Greek," and that consequently I have a right to our patronymic, which is Zenobia, and not by any means Snobbs. Nobody but Tabitha Turnip calls me Suky Snobbs. I am the Signora Psyche Zenobia.

As I said before, everybody has heard of me. I am that very Signora Psyche Zenobia so justly celebrated as corresponding secretary to the "Philadelphia, Regular, Exchange, Tea, Total, Young, Belles, Lettres, Universal, Experimental, Bibliographical, Association, To, Civilize, Humanity." Dr. Moneypenny made the title for us, and says he chose it because it sounded big, like an empty rumpuncheon. (A vulgar man that sometimes, but he's deep.) We all sign the initials of the society after our names, in the fashion of the R.S.A., Royal Society of Arts—the S.D.U.K., Society for the Diffusion of Useful Knowledge, etc., etc. Dr. Moneypenny says that S stands for *stale,* and that D.U.K. spells duck (but it don't), and that S.D.U.K. stands for Stale Duck, and not for Lord Brougham's Society; but then Dr. Moneypenny is such a queer man that I am never sure when he is telling me the truth. At any rate we always add to our names the initials P.R.E.T.T.Y.B.L.U.E.B.A.T.C.H.—that is to say, Philadelphia, Regular, Exchange, Tea, Total, Young, Belles, Lettres, Universal, Experimental, Bibliographical, Association, To, Civilize, Humanity—one letter for each word, which is a decided improvement upon Lord Brougham. Dr. Moneypenny will have it that our initials give our true character, but for my life, I can't see what he means.

Notwithstanding the good offices of the Doctor, and the strenuous exertions of the Association to get itself into notice, it met with no very great success until I joined it. The truth is, members indulged in too flippant a tone of discussion. The papers read every Saturday evening were characterized less by depth than buffoonery. They were all whipped syllabub. There was no investigation of first causes, first principles. There was no investigation of anything at all. There was no attention paid to that great point, the "fitness of things." In short, there was no fine writing like this. It was low—very! No profundity, no reading, no metaphysics, nothing which the learned call spirituality and which the unlearned choose to stigmatize as cant. (Dr. M. says I ought to spell "cant" with a capital K—but I know better.)

When I joined the Society it was my endeavor to introduce a better style of thinking and writing, and all the world knows how well I have succeeded. We get up as good papers now in the P.R.E.T.T.Y.B.L.U.E.B.A.T.C.H. as any to be found even in "Blackwood." I say "Blackwood," because I have been assured that the finest writing, upon every subject, is to be discovered in the pages of that justly celebrated magazine. We now take it for our model upon all themes, and are getting into rapid notice accordingly. And, after all, it's not so very difficult a matter to compose an article of the genuine "Blackwood" stamp, if one only goes properly about it. Of course I don't speak of the political articles. Everybody knows how *they* are managed, since Dr. Moneypenny explained it. Mr. Blackwood has a pair of tailor's-shears, and three apprentices who stand by him for orders. One hands him the "Times" another the "Examiner," and a third a Gulley's "New Compendium of Slang-Whang." Mr. B— merely cuts out and intersperses. It is soon done: nothing but "Examiner," "Slang-Whang," and "Times;" then "Times," "Slang-Whang," and "Examiner;" and then "Time," "Examiner," and "Slang-Whang."

But the chief merit of the magazine lies in its miscellaneous articles; and the best of these come under the head of what Dr. Moneypenny calls the *bizarreries* (whatever that may mean) and what everybody else calls the *intensities*. This is a species of writing which I have long known how to appreciate, although it is only since my late visit to Mr. Blackwood (deputed by the Society) that I have been made aware of the exact method of composition. This method is very simple, but not so much so as the politics. Upon my calling at Mr. B—'s, and making known to him the wishes of the Society, he received me with great civility, took me into his study and gave me a clear explanation of the whole process.

"My dear madam," said he, evidently struck with my majestic appearance, for I had on the crimson satin, with the green *agraffas*, and orange-colored *auriculas*, "my *dear* madam," said he, "sit down. The matter stands thus. In the first place, your writer of intensities must have very black ink, and a very big pen, with a very blunt nib. And, mark me, Miss Psyche Zenobia!" he continued, after a pause, with the most impressive energy and solemnity of manner, "mark me!—*that pen—must—never be mended!* Herein, madam, lies the secret, the soul, of intensity. I assume upon myself to say, that no individual, of however great genius, ever wrote with a good pen—understand me—a good article. You may take it for granted that when manuscript can be read it is never worth reading. This is a leading principle in our faith, to which if you cannot readily assent, our conference is at an end."

He paused. But, of course, as I had no wish to put an end to the conference, I assented to a proposition so very obvious, and one, too, of whose truth I had all along been sufficiently aware. He seemed pleased, and went on with his instructions.

"It may appear invidious in me, Miss Psyche Zenobia, to refer you to any article, or set of articles, in the way of model or study; yet perhaps I may as well call your attention to a few cases. Let me see. There was 'The Dead Alive,' a capital thing! the record of a gentleman's sensations when entombed before the breath was out of his body; full of taste, terror, sentiment, metaphysics, and erudition. You would have sworn that the writer had been born and brought up in a coffin. Then we had the 'Confessions of an Opium-eater'—fine, very fine!—glorious imagination—deep philosophy—acute speculation—plenty of fire and fury, and a good spicing of the decidedly unintelligible. That was a nice bit of flummery, and went down the throats of the people delightfully. They would have it that Coleridge wrote the paper—but not so. It was composed by my pet baboon, Juniper, over a rummer of Hollands and water, 'hot, without sugar.' " (This I could scarcely have believed had it been anybody but Mr. Blackwood, who assured me of it.) "Then there was 'The Involuntary Experimentalist,' all about a gentleman who got baked in an oven, and came out alive and well, although certainly done to a turn. And then there was 'The Diary of a Late Physician,' where the merit lay in a good rant, and indifferent Greek—both of them taking things with the public. And then there was 'The Man in the Bell,' a paper, by the bye, Miss Zenobia, which I cannot sufficiently recommend to your attention. It is the history of a young person who goes to sleep under the clapper of a church bell, and is awakened by its tolling for a funeral. The sound drives him mad, and, accordingly, pulling out his tablets, he gives a record of his sensations. Sensations are the great things, after all. Should you ever be drowned or hung, be sure and make a note of your sensations; they will be worth to you ten guineas a sheet. If you wish to write forcibly, Miss Zenobia, pay minute attention to the sensations."

"That I certainly will, Mr. Blackwood," said I.

"Good!" he replied. "I see you are a pupil after my own heart. But I must put you *au fait* to the details necessary in composing what may be denominated a genuine 'Blackwood' article of the sensation stamp, the kind which you will understand me to say I consider the best of all purposes.

"The first thing requisite is to get yourself into such a scrape as no one ever got into before. The oven, for instance,—that was a good hit. But if you have no oven or big bell at hand, and if you cannot conveniently tumble out of a balloon, or be swallowed up in an earthquake, or get stuck fast in a chimney, you will have to be contented with simply imagining some similar misadventure. I should prefer, however, that you have the actual fact to bear you out. Nothing so well assists the fancy as an experimental knowledge of the matter in hand. 'Truth is strange,' you know, 'stranger than fiction'—besides being more to the purpose."

Here I assured him I had an excellent pair of garters, and would go and hang myself forthwith.

"Good!" he replied, "do so; although hanging is somewhat hackneyed. Perhaps you might do better. Take a dose of Brandreth's pills, and then give us your sensations. However, my instructions will apply equally well to any variety of misadventure, and on your way home you may easily get knocked in the head, or run over by an omnibus, or bitten by a mad dog, or drowned in a gutter. But to proceed.

"Having determined upon your subject, you must next consider the tone, or manner, of your narration. There is the tone didactic, the tone enthusiastic, the tone natural— all commonplace enough. But then there is the tone laconic, or curt, which has lately come much into use. It consists in short sentences. Somehow thus: Can't be too brief. Can't be too snappish. Always a full stop. And never a paragraph.

"Then there is the tone elevated, diffusive, and interjectional. Some of our best novelists patronize this tone. The words must be all in a whirl, like a humming-top, and make a noise very similar, which answers remarkably well instead of meaning. This is the best of all possible styles where the writer is in too great a hurry to think.

"The tone metaphysical is also a good one. If you know any big words this is your chance for them. Talk of the Ionic and Eleatic schools—of Archytas, Gorgias, and Alcmæon. Say something about objectivity and subjectivity. Be sure and abuse a man named Locke. Turn up your nose at things in general, and when you let slip anything a little *too* absurd, you need not be at the trouble of scratching it out, but just add a foot-note, and say that you are indebted for the above profound observation to the *Kritik der reinen Vernunft*, or to the *Metaphysische Anfangsgrunde der Naturwissenschaft*. This will look erudite and—and—and frank.

"There are various other tones of equal celebrity, but I shall mention only two more, the tone transcendental and the tone heterogeneous. In the former the merit consists in seeing into the nature of affairs a very great deal farther than anybody else. This second sight is very efficient when properly managed. A little reading of the 'Dial' will carry you a great way. Eschew, in this case, big words; get them as small as possible, and write them upside down. Look over Channing's poems and quote what he says about a 'fat little man with a delusive show of Can.' Put in something about the Supernatural Oneness. Don't say a syllable about the Infernal Twoness. Above all, study innuendo. Hint everything—assert nothing. If you feel inclined to say 'bread and butter,' do not by any means say it outright. You may say anything and everything *approaching* to 'bread and butter.' You may hint at buckwheat cake, or you may even go so far as to insinuate oatmeal porridge, but if bread and butter be your real meaning, be cautious, my *dear* Miss Psyche, not on any account to say 'bread and butter'!"

I assured him that I should never say it again as long as I lived. He kissed me, and continued:

"As for the tone heterogeneous, it is merely a judicious mixture, in equal proportions, of all the other tones in the world, and is consequently made up of everything deep, great, odd, piquant, pertinent, and pretty.

"Let us suppose now you have determined upon your incidents and tone. The most important portion—in fact, the soul of the whole business, is yet to be attended to; I allude to *the filling up*. It is not to be supposed that a lady, or gentleman either, has been leading the life of a bookworm. And yet above all things it is necessary that your article have an air of erudition, or at least afford evidence of extensive general reading. Now I'll put you in the way of accomplishing this point. See here!" (pulling down some three or four ordinary-looking volumes, and opening them at random). "By casting your eye down almost any page of any book in the world, you will be able to perceive at once a host of little scraps of either learning or *bel-esprit-ism,* which are the very thing for the spicing of a 'Blackwood' article. You might as well note down a few while I read them to you. I shall make two divisions: first, *Piquant Facts for the Manufacture of Similes; and second, Piquant Expressions to be introduced as occasion may require.* Write now!"— and I wrote as he dictated.

"PIQUANT FACTS FOR SIMILES. 'There were originally but three Muses—Melete, Mneme, Aœde—meditation, memory, and singing.' You may make a great deal of that little fact if properly worked. You see it is not generally known, and looks *recherché.* You must be careful and give the thing with a downright improviso air.

"Again. 'The river Alpheus passed beneath the sea, and emerged without injury to the purity of its waters.' Rather stale that, to be sure, but, if properly dressed and dished up, will look quite as fresh as ever.

"Here is something better. 'The Persian Iris appears to some persons to possess a sweet and very powerful perfume, while to others it is perfectly scentless.' Fine that, and very delicate! Turn it about a little, and it will do wonders. We'll have something else in the botanical line. There's nothing goes down so well, especially with the help of a little Latin. Write!

" '*The Epidendrum Flos Aeris,* of Java, bears a very beautiful flower, and will live when pulled up by the roots. The natives suspend it by a cord from the ceiling, and enjoy its fragrance for years.' That's capital! That will do for the Similes. Now for the Piquant Expressions.

"PIQUANT EXPRESSIONS. *'The venerable Chinese novel Ju-Kiao-Li.'* Good! By introducing these few words with dexterity you will evince your intimate acquaintance with the language and literature of the Chinese. With the aid of this you may possibly get along without either Arabic, or Sanskrit, or Chickasaw. There is no passing muster, however, without Spanish, Italian, German, Latin, and Greek. I must look you out a little specimen of each. Any scrap will answer, because you must depend upon your own ingenuity to make it fit into your article. Now write!

" '*Aussi tendre que Zaïre'*—as tender as Zaïre—French.

Alludes to the frequent repetition of the phrase, *la tendre Zaïre*, in the French tragedy of that name. Properly introduced, will show not only your knowledge of the language, but your general reading and wit. You can say, for instance, that the chicken you were eating (write an article about being choked to death by a chicken-bone) was not altogether *aussi tendre que Zaïre*. Write!

> *'Ven muerts tan ascondida,*
> *Que no te sienta venir,*
> *Porque el plazer del morir*
> *No me torne à dar la vida.'*

That's Spanish, from Miguel de Cervantes. 'Come quickly, O death! but be sure and don't let me see you coming, lest the pleasure I shall feel at your appearance should unfortunately bring me back again to life.' This you may slip in quite *à propos* when you are struggling in the last agonies with the chicken-bone. Write!

> *'Il pover' huomo che non sen' era accorto,*
> *Andava combattendo, ed era morto.'*

That's Italian, you perceive—from Ariosto. It means that a great hero, in the heat of combat, not perceiving that he had been fairly killed, continued to fight valiantly, dead as he was. The application of this to your own case is obvious; for I trust, Miss Psyche, that you will not neglect to kick for at least an hour and a half after you have been choked to death by that chicken-bone. Please to write!

> *'Und sterb' ich doch, so sterb' ich denn*
> *Durch sie—durch sie!'*

That's German—from Schiller. 'And if I die, at least I die— for thee—for thee!' Here it is clear that you are apostrophizing the *cause* of your disaster, the chicken. Indeed, what gentleman (or lady either) of sense, *wouldn't* die, I should like to know, for a well-fattened capon of the right Molucca breed, stuffed with capers and mushrooms, and served up in a salad-bowl, with orange-jellies *en mosaïques*.

Write! (You can get them that way at Tortoni's.)—Write, if you please!

"Here is a nice little Latin phrase, and rare one (one can't be too *recherché* or brief in one's Latin, it's getting so common)—*ignoratio elenchi.* He has committed an *ignoratio elenchi,* that is to say, he has understood the words of your proposition, but not the idea. The man was a *fool,* you see. Some poor fellow whom you addressed while choking with that chicken-bone, and who therefore didn't precisely understand what you were talking about. Throw the *ignoratio elenchi* in his teeth, and at once you have him annihilated. If he dare to reply, you can tell him from Lucan (here it is) that speeches are mere *anemonæ verborum,* anemone words. The anemone, with great brilliance, has no smell. Or, if he begin to bluster, you may be down upon him with *insomnia Jovis,* reveries of Jupiter—a phrase which Silius Italicus (see here!) applies to thoughts pompous and inflated. This will be sure and cut him to the heart. He can do nothing but roll over and die. Will you be kind enough to write?

"In Greek we must have something pretty—from Demosthenes, for example. Ἀνήρ δ φεύγων καὶ πάλιν μαχήσε′′′ται. (Aner o pheugon kai palin makesetai.) There is a tolerably good translation of it in 'Hudibras'—

> *'For he that flies may fight again,*
> *Which he can never do that's slain.'*

In a 'Blackwood' article nothing makes so fine a show as your Greek. The very letters have an air of profundity about them. Only observe, madam, the astute look of that Epsilon! That Phi ought certainly to be a bishop! Was ever there a smarter fellow than that Omicron? Just twig that Tau! In short, there is nothing like Greek for a genuine sensation-paper. In the present case your application is the most obvious thing in the world. Rap out the sentence, with a huge oath, and by way of ultimatum at the good-for-nothing dunder-headed villain who couldn't understand your plain English in relation to the chicken-bone. He'll take the hint and be off, you may depend upon it."

These were all the instructions Mr. B— could afford me

upon the topic of question, but I felt they would be entirely sufficient. I was, at length, able to write a genuine "Blackwood" article, and determined to do it forthwith. In taking leave of me, Mr. B— made a proposition for the purchase of the paper when written; but, as he could offer me only fifty guineas a sheet, I thought it better to let our society have it than sacrifice it for so paltry a sum. Notwithstanding this niggardly spirit, however, the gentleman showed his consideration for me in all other respects, and indeed treated me with the greatest civility. His parting words made a deep impression upon my heart, and I hope I shall always remember them with gratitude.

"My dear Miss Zenobia," he said, while the tears stood in his eyes, "is there *any*thing else I can do to promote the success of your laudable undertaking? Let me reflect! It is just possible that you may not be able, so soon as convenient, to—to—get yourself drowned, or—choked with a chickenbone, or—or hung,—or bitten by a—but stay! Now I think me of it, there are a couple of very excellent bull-dogs in the yard—fine fellows, I assure you—savage, and all that— indeed just the thing for your money—they'll have you eaten up, *auriculas* and all, in less than five minutes (here's my watch!)—and then only think of the sensations! Here! I say—Tom!—Peter!—Dick, you villain!—let out those"— but as I was really in a great hurry, and had not another moment to spare, I was reluctantly forced to expedite my departure, and accordingly took leave *at once*—somewhat more abruptly, I admit, than strict courtesy would have otherwise allowed. . . .

Roger Price (Contemporary)

~~~~~~~~~

FROM *The Great Roob Revolution*

. . . We are all, as a whole, as a nation, dumb. We simply don't know very much. We are educated only in the way that a chimpanzee who sits at a table and drinks from a saucer is educated compared to a baboon. Our schools have trained us in the techniques of modern living, they have turned out excellent technologists, engineers, professional people, but they have not educated us.

Except for the fragmentary and specialized knowledge associated with our work, we have only the most superficial information about the world. We do not read well* and we do not read books. Except for a few childish folk tales, we know nothing whatever about history, and being ignorant of the past, we have no realistic idea of the future. We are surrounded by, and entirely dependent on, a technology which we cannot understand. We are intellectually *passive,* watching and listening but never understanding or remembering. Our memories are so weak that the introduction of a simple zip code causes a near panic and evokes angry howls of "I don't like it." We remember only that we are Americans, so we must therefore be educated. But can you identify, even vaguely, Charlemagne? Can you extract a simple square root? Do you know what a square root *is*? What is the capital of Illinois? Who were, in order, the last six Presidents of the United States? How much is eight times eight?†

---

*As we identify quality with quantity, we also equate speed with proficiency. Hence the ridiculous "speed-reading" courses.
†Sixty-four!

Ishmael Reed (Contemporary)

∽∾∾∽

Sermonette

a poet was busted by a topless judge
his friends went to morristwn nj & put
black powder on his honah's doorstep
black powder into his honah's car
black powder on his honah's briefs
tiny dolls into his honah's mind

by nightfall his honah could a go go no mo
his dog went crazy & ran into a crocodile
his widow fell from a wall &
hanged herself
his daughter was run over by a black man
coming home for the wakes the two boys
skidded into mourning
all the next of kin's teeth fell out

gimmie dat ol time
                         religion
it's good enough
            for me!

Agnes Repplier (1855-1950)

❦

FROM *Essays in Miniature*

Battle of the Babies

A warfare has been raging in our midst, the echoes of which have hardly yet died sullenly away upon either side of the Atlantic. It has been a bloodless and un-Homeric strife, not without humorous side-issues, as when Pistol and Bardolph and Fluellen come to cheer our anxious spirits at the siege of Harfleur. Its first guns were heard in New York, where a modest periodical, devoted to the training of parents, opened fire upon those time-honored nursery legends which are presumably dear to the hearts of all rightly constituted babies. The leader of this gallant foray protested vehemently against all fairy tales of a mournful or sanguinary cast, and her denunciation necessarily included many stories which have for generations been familiar to every little child. She rejected *Red Riding Hood*, because her own infancy was haunted and embittered by the evil behavior of the wolf; she would have none of *Bluebeard*, because he was a wholesale fiend and murderer; she would not even allow the pretty *Babes in the Wood*, because they tell a tale of coldhearted cruelty and of helpless suffering; while all fierce narratives of giants and ogres and magicians were to be banished ruthlessly from our shelves. Verily, reading will be but gentle sport in the virtuous days to come.

Now it chanced that this serious protest against nursery lore fell into the hands of Mr. Andrew Lang, the most lighthearted and conservative of critics, and partial withal to tales of bloodshed and adventure. How could it be otherwise with one reared on the bleak border land, and familiar from infancy with the wild border legends that Sir Walter knew and loved; with stories of Thomas the Rhymer, and the plundering Hardens, and the black witches of Loch Awe! It was natural that with the echoes of the old savage strife ringing in his ears, and with the memories of the dour Scottish bogies and warlocks lingering in his heart, Mr. Lang could but indifferently sympathize with those anxious parents who think the stories of Bluebeard and Jack the Giant Killer too shocking for infant ears to hear. Our grandmothers, he declared, were not ferocious old ladies, yet they told us these tales, and many more which we were none the worse for hearing. "Not to know them is to be sadly ignorant, and to miss that which all people have relished in all ages." Moreover, it is apparent to him, and indeed to most of us, that we cannot take even our earliest steps in the world of literature, or in the shaded paths of knowledge, without encountering suffering and sin in some shape; while, as we advance a little further, these grisly forms fly ever on before. "Cain," remarks Mr. Lang, "killed Abel. The flood drowned quite a number of persons: David was not a stainless knight, and Henry VIII was nearly as bad as Bluebeard. Several deserving gentlemen were killed at Marathon. Front de Bœuf came to an end shocking to sensibility, and to Mr. Ruskin." The *Arabian Nights*, *Pilgrim's Progress*, *Paul and Virginia*—all the dear old nursery favorites must, under the new dispensation, be banished from our midst; and the rising generation of prigs must be nourished exclusively on *Little Lord Fauntleroy*, and other carefully selected specimens of milk-and-water diet.

The prospect hardly seems inviting; but as the English guns rattled merrily away in behalf of English tradition, they were promptly met by an answering roar from this side of the water. A Boston paper rushed gallantly to the defense of the New York periodical, and gave Mr. Lang—to use a pet expression of his own—"his kail through the reek." American children, it appears, are too sensitively organized to endure the unredeemed ferocity of the old fairy stories. The British child may sleep soundly in its little cot after hearing about the Babes in the Wood; the American infant is prematurely saddened by such unmerited misfortune. "If a consensus of American mothers could be taken," says the Boston writer, "our English critic might be infinitely disgusted to know in how many nurseries these cruel tales must be changed, or not told at all to the children of less savage generations. No mother nowadays tells them in their unmitigated brutality."

Is this true, I wonder, and are our supersensitive babies reared perforce on the optimistic version of Red Riding Hood, where the wolf is cut open by the woodman, and the little girl and her grandmother jump out, safe and sound? Their New England champion speaks of the "intolerable misery"—a very strong phrase—which he suffered in infancy from having his nurse tell him of the Babes in the Wood; while the Scriptural stories were apparently every whit as unbearable and heartbreaking. "I remember," he says, "two children, strong, brave man and woman now, who in righteous rage plucked the Slaughter of the Innocents out from the family Bible." This was a radical measure, to say the least, and if many little boys and girls started in to expurgate the Scriptures in such liberal fashion, the holy book would soon present a sadly mutilated appearance. Moreover, it seems to me that such an anecdote, narrated with admirable assurance, reveals very painfully the lack of a fine and delicate spirituality in the religious training of children; of that grace and distinction which are akin to saintship, and are united so charmingly in those to whom truth has been inseparably associated with beauty. There is a painting by Ghirlandaio hanging over the altar in the chapel of the Foundling Asylum in Florence. It represents the Adoration of the Magi, and kneeling by the side of the Wise Men is a little group of the Holy Innocents, their tiny garments stained with blood, their hands clasped in prayer; while the Divine Child turns from his mother's embraces, and from the kings' rich gifts to greet the little companions who have yielded up their spotless lives for him. Now, surely those lean, brown Florentine orphans, who have always before their eyes this beautiful and tender picture, absorb through it alone a religious sentiment unfelt by American children who are familiar only with the ugly and inane prints of American Sunday-schools, in which I have known the line, "My soul doth magnify the Lord," to be illustrated by a man with a magnifying-glass in his hand. Possibly our Sunday-school scholars, being more accurately instructed as to dates, could inform the little Florentines that the Innocents were not slaughtered until after the Magi had returned to the East. But no child who had looked day after day upon Ghirlandaio's lovely picture—more appealing in its pathos than Holman Hunt's brilliant and jocund Triumph of the Innocents—could desire to pluck "in righteous rage" that chapter from the Bible. He would have at least some dim and imperfect conception of the spiritual meaning, the spiritual joy, which underlie the pain and horror of the story.

This reflection will help us in some measure to come to a decision, when we return to the vexed problem of nursery tales and legends. I believe it is as well to cultivate a child's emotions as to cultivate his manners or his morals, and the first step in such a direction is necessarily taken through the stories told him in infancy. If a consensus of mothers would reject the good old fairy tales "in their unmitigated brutality," a consensus of men of letters would render a different verdict; and such men, who have been children in their time, and who look back with wistful delight upon the familiar figures who were their earliest friends, are entitled to an opinion in the case. How admirable was the "righteous rage" of Charles Lamb, when he wanted to buy some of these same brutal fairy stories for the little Coleridges, and could find nothing but the correct and commonplace literature which his whole soul abhorred! "Mrs. Barbauld's and Mrs. Trimmer's nonsense lay in piles about," he wrote indignantly to papa Coleridge, "and have banished all the old classics of the nursery. Knowledge, insignificant and vapid as Mrs. Barbauld's books convey, must, it seems, come to a child in the shape of knowledge; and his empty noddle must be turned with conceit of his own powers when he has learnt that a horse is an animal, and that Billy is better than a horse, and such like; instead of that beautiful interest in wild tales which made the child a man, while all the time he suspected himself to be no bigger than a child."

Just such a wild tale, fantastic rather than beautiful, haunted Châteaubriand all his life—the story of Count Combourg's wooden leg, which, three hundred years after its owner's death, was seen at night walking solemnly down the steep turret stairs, attended by a huge black cat. Not at all the kind of story we would select to tell a child nowadays. By no means! Even the little Châteaubriand heard it from peasant lips. Yet in after years, when he had fought the battle of life, and fought it with success; when he had grown gray, and illustrious, and disillusioned, and melancholy, what should come back to his mind, with its old pleasant flavor of terror and mystery, but the vision of Count Combourg's wooden leg taking its midnight constitutional, with the black cat stepping softly on before? So he notes it gravely down in his Memoirs, just as Scott notes in his diary the pranks of Whippity Stourie, the Scotch bogie that steals at night into open nursery windows; and just as Heine, in gay, sunlit Paris, recalls with joy the dark, sweet, sombre tales of the witch and fairy haunted forests of Germany.

These are impressions worth recording, and they are only a few out of many which may be gathered from similar sources. That which is vital in literature or tradition, which has survived the obscurity and wreckage of the past, whether as legend, or ballad, or mere nursery rhyme, has survived in right of some intrinsic merit of its own, and will not be snuffed out of existence by any of our precautionary or hygienic measures. We could not banish Bluebeard if we would. He is as immortal as Hamlet, and when hundreds of years shall have passed over this uncomfortably enlightened world, the children of the future—who, thank Heaven, can never, with all our efforts, be born grown up—will still tremble at the bloodstained key, and rejoice when the big brave brothers come galloping up the road. We could not even rid ourselves of Mother Goose, though she, too, has her mortal enemies, who protest periodically against her cruelty and grossness. We could not drive Punch and Judy from our midst, though Mr. Punch's derelictions have been the subject of much serious and adverse criticism. It is not by such barbarous rhymes or by such brutal spectacles that we teach a child the lessons of integrity and gentleness, explain our nursery moralists, and probably they are correct. Moreover, Bluebeard does not teach a lesson of conjugal felicity, and Cinderella is full of the world's vanities, and Puss in Boots is one long record of triumphant effrontery and deception. An honest and self-respecting lad would have explained to the king that he was not the Marquis of Carabas at all; that he had no desire to profit by his cat's ingenious falsehoods, and no weak ambition to connect himself with the aristocracy. Such a hero would be a credit to our modern schoolrooms, and lift a load of care from the shoulders of our modern critics. Only the children would have none of him, but would turn wistfully back to those brave old tales which are their inheritance from a splendid past, and of which no hand shall rob them.

FROM *Counter-Currents*

I pick up a very serious and very well-written book on the Brontë sisters, and am told that if I would "touch the very heart of the mystery that was Charlotte Brontë" (I had never been aware that there was anything mysterious about this famous lady), I will find it—save the mark!—in her passionate love for children.

"We are face to face here, not with a want, but with an abyss, depth beyond depth of tenderness, arid longing, and frustration; with a passion that found no clear voice in her works because it was one with the elemental nature in her, undefined, unuttered, unutterable!"

It was certainly unuttered. It was not even hinted at in Miss Brontë's novels, nor in her voluminous correspondence. Her attitude toward children—so far as it found expression—was the arid but pardonable attitude of one who had been their reluctant caretaker and teacher. If, as we are now told, "there were moments when it was pain for Charlotte to see the children born of and possessed by other women," there were certainly hours—so much she makes clear to us—in which the business of looking after them wearied her beyond her powers of endurance. It is true that Miss Brontë said a few, a very few friendly words about these little people. She did not, like Swift, propose that babies should be cooked and eaten. But this temperate regard, this restricted benevolence, gives us no excuse for wallowing in sentiment at her expense.

Will Rogers (1879–1935)

~~~~~~~

FROM *The Writings of Will Rogers*

Let Us Pray They Don't Find Out What's the Matter with the Movies

I can't write about the movies for I don't know anything about them, and I don't think anybody else knows anything about them.

It's the only business in the world that nobody knows anything about. Being in them don't give any more of an inkling about them than being out of them.

They, just a few months ago in New York, had a convention to discuss ways and means of regulating them and fixing a few of the things that they thought was worrying the industry. Well, it didn't get anywhere for nobody knew what was worrying the industry.

Everybody knew what was worrying him personally, but there was no two things that was worrying the same person.

The exhibitor said he wanted better pictures for less money; the producer said he wanted better stories and better directors and better actors for less money.

The actor said: "You are not giving me a fair share of what I draw at the box office." Will Hays said: "They got to be cleaner."

The exhibitor says: "If you get them too clean nobody is interested in them."

The novelist says: "What's the use of selling them a story, they don't make the story they buy."

The Scenario Staff says: "It reads good but it won't photograph." The exchange salesmen say: "The exhibitors are a dumb lot, they don't know what their audiences do want."

The exhibitors say: "We may be dumb, but we know how to count up. Give us pictures where there is something to count up."

The so-called intellectual keeps saying: "Why don't they give us something worthwhile in the movies that we can think about."

The regular movie fan says: "Give us something to see, never mind think about. If we wanted to think we wouldn't come in here."

The old married folks say: "Give us something besides all this love sick junk, and the fadeout behind a willow tree."

The young folks that pay the rent on these temples of uplift say: "Give us some love and romance; what do we care about these pictures with a lot of folks trying to show what they do in life. We will get old soon enough without having to see it now."

Wall Street says: "We want more interest on our money."

The producers say: "Look at the fun you are having by being in this business. Didn't we give you a pass through the studio, what do you want for your money?"

The actors that aren't working say: "They don't want actors any more, they only want types."

The actors that are working say: "Thank God they are beginning to realize it's us actors they want and not just somebody that looks like the part."

Everybody is trying to offer suggestions how to regulate the business and bring it down on a sane basis. They are not going to bring it back on a sane basis. It will keep right on going just like it is now. It was never meant to be sane. It grows and gets bigger in spite of every known handicap.

You can't get a picture so poor but there will be an audience growing up somewhere that will like it, and you can't get one so good but what they will be forty per cent of the people that see it that won't like it. If it wasn't that way everybody in the world would go to see one picture. So they better quit monkeying with the business and let it alone. It's odd now, but it's odd in all of us movie people's favor.

The exhibitor that says he isn't making as much money as he used to, means that he is not making as much as he did last year or the year before but he doesn't mean that he is not making as much as he was before he got into this business.

The producer who says things are getting tough in the

picture business, you suggest to him to go back into his original line of business and he will punch you in the jaw.

And the same with the actor, or anyone connected with the business, and the same also with the audience. He starts beefing about poor pictures, when he was never able to go before and get as much amusement for twenty, thirty, forty or fifty cents. He can't go into any other amusement business and better himself. If he could he would do it. He is doing better than he ever was in his life before.

He used to have to go to the gallery and sit in peanut hulls up to his chin, and come down a long stairs into a dark alley after the show, for more money than he can sit in a wonderful upholstered seat that he didn't even know existed till the movie man built his theater.

It's breaking pretty soft for audiences the same as for movie actors and producers and exhibitors.

Then the highbrow that says pictures are the bunk, let him try and find something that will beat them for twenty-five cents. There is no other branch of amusement in the world that has been brought right to his own little town, or if in a city, to his nearest street corner.

They are not bringing opera to your door step, or spoken drama to your neighborhood. You have to go to the city to get them. So don't start yapping about pictures. There is no law in the world that makes you go to them. No sir, you go to them because there is nothing that has yet been invented that can compare with them for the money.

These fan magazines are always yowling about, "What's the matter with the movies?" Try and get any of these editors to go back into their old newspaper work at their old salaries.

No sir, the movie business is a "cuckoo" business made by "cuckoo" people for "cuckoo" audiences, and as about eighty per cent of the world is "cuckoo" anyway they fill a spot that nothing will ever replace unless somebody invents something more "cuckoo."

Everybody is trying to find out what's the matter with them. If they ever do find out they will ruin their own business.

The movies have only one thing that may ever dent them in any way, and that is when the people in them, or the people going to them, ever start taking them seriously. That was one wonderful thing about dear Marcus Loew. He made more money out of them than anybody, and he had the greatest sense of humor of any producer of them. But he always said, "I don't know what they are all about, and the more I learn about them, the less I know."

So go ahead, work hard, and do the best you can, but don't try to hold a clinic over the body.

Call them "arts and sciences" but do so with your tongue in your cheek. Everything that makes money and gives pleasure is not art. If it was, bootlegging would be the highest form of artistic endeavor.

So let's everybody connected with them, and everybody that loves to go see them, as we go to our beds at night, pray to our Supreme Being, that he don't allow it to be found out what is the matter with the movies, for if he ever does, we will all be out of a job.

The Older We Men Get,
the More Cuckoo We Are

All I know is just what I read in the papers. Say did a fashion Magazine ever fall into your hands? I don't mean a woman's fashion one, Lord we have all spent half our life looking at "Laungerie" adds. But what I mean did a men's fashion Magazine ever drop across your trail? Well my Wife dug one up somewhere, and she has got a pretty good sense of humor, and I heard her giggling at this thing, and asked what it was, and I am telling you that it was a great big prosperous Magazine. There must be flocks of 'em that take that stuff serious.

Now if you have ever landed a good job, couldent seem to grab off your second million, couldent get so tropical with the Ladies, why it was because maby you dident have on the following, as that is given in the Magazine as the "Real ultra Calf's brains": "Black jacket single breasted, fairly shapely, it buttons with two medium wide notch lapels. The waist coat is double breasted, narrow in its lap, with a likable roll in its collar, and a much waisted look. Below the jacket and waistcoat, are mull grey trousers without pleats or turn ups. These have a double stripe. One line of white the other of biscuit color. The stripes are far enough apart to not jarr.

The boots are black, the lowers are varnished with de-Gniche varnish, mixed with a little claret to make the enameled more brilliant, and pliable, the button tops are of dull finish French calfskin."

Now you farmers that's been hollering for relief, maby that's what's the matter with you, you havent had this "de-Gniche varnish mixed with a little claret." That may be just the Mary McHaughen bill you are looking for. It says: "Below the waistcoat and jacket appear the trousers." Now you Democrats that havent got anywhere in years maby you havent been wearing your trousers below your waistcoat. In fact some of you maby havent had trousers either above or below. They say the boots are black, and then it says they button. Did you ever see a button boot? It looks like the buttons would catch on the brush when you are riding through the mosquite. There is one place in there where it says it has a "waisted look." Say I have been in style all my life and dident know it if that waisted look means what it says.

Did you ever have trousers with a biscuit colored stripe? Say there is not two women that make biscuits the same color, so any stripe is biscuit colored. And then it says, "The stripes of Biscuit and white are not close enough to jarr." Now just how close will one stripe jarr another one? Some will jarr evidently quicker than others, so you got to be careful, you may have on a pair of pants, and you feel something funny and it's your pants jarring. They are just liable to jarr right off you can't tell. There is nothing worse than a jarring pair of pants.

It tells about how the men of Palm Beach that are "Well dressed" change five times a day. "Green is the color that has made it's appearance in men's jackets, Lovatts blue green, grey greens, lapels are of a stubby character, as made by English tailors, small patterned neckwear in foulard continues." So watch your jackets. Lack of a pea green jacket has held many a good man back. Now don't by any chance throw away your old foulard ties, they are going to get some mileage out of them. You take a good small pattern tie on a smooth neck, and it ought to do from two to five hundred cocktails without showing wear. Of course on a rough neck, it will gradually wear itself frayed at the edges.

Have you given any thought much to your bathrobe? There is a thing that you must decide on. They have "bright colored terry robes, and elaborate designs, and solid color contrasted trimmings." Those are mostly worn by men that buy on margins. I have become so discouraged over the selection of my bathrobe that I sometimes think I will just get out of the tub and get right into my clothes, like I have been doing, and not monkey with one of the things.

There is a new cocoanut straw hat that is being worn by just a few of the very smartly dressed men of Palm Beach and Nassau: It's got a high "puggarree" band and a "careless" curl to the brim. Maby it will help you get your Ford order through quicker if you only had a touch of "Puggarree" to your old lid.

Now boneheads like you and I can't imagine sane people taking all this junk serious, but they do. Why if a tie has one more dot in it than the one worn by Tony Biddle, their day is spoiled. Talk about women being vain, and always primping, why say men will make a sucker out of any woman when it comes to thinking he is about the grapes, a Corset manufacturer told me that if it was not for men's corsets they would have to go out of business. Can you imagine a big hulk going in getting a corset fitted? No Sir, we can't laugh at the women any more. Men are getting their nails manicured, and even pointed and colored. They are henna'ing their hair. They are watching their diet. They are reducing everything but their head. And the funny part the older and the funnier looking they are the more Cuckoo they are. They will be rougeing their lips, and powdering their noses next.

Here is an ad in the Magazine that you will get a kick out of. "From the Montmarte, Hollywood's most fashionable Cafe, rendevoux of the smart set of Hollywood. Where the stars dine and dance comes the exclusive styles that go into Hollywood Clothes, Styles that are swagger, flattering, chosen by men to whom appearance is everything painstakingly tailored in selected fabrics, $20.00 and $25.00. A few extra Ultra at $30.00."

Maby that's what has kept you out of the movies you dident have one of those "Extra Ultra suits" at $30.00. Then there is some "Snappy" top coats at $8.00. Cost you more to check 'em than it would to buy 'em, but I am telling you men are watching their styles. That's why they all look so funny.

The Lady Mosquito Is Busy, Thanks

Well all I know is just what I read in the papers. We are always reading statistics and figures. Half of America do nothing but prepare Propaganda for the other half to read. Insurance Companies have Guys figure out the very day you will die. (In fact they won't insure till they have it investigated and find out.) Then you like a Sucker go bet them you will live longer than that. The Government can tell you how much wheat is going to be raised next year.

Everything is figured out down to a Gnat's tooth according to some kind of statistics. Course nobody knows if the figures are right or not, you have no way of checking up on 'em. But just the other day a fellow in Atlantic City, New Jersey come through with some statistics that really ought to set us all thinking. It wasent one of those "The average working Girl makes $33 a week spends $10 for board $12 for silk stockings and the rest for lip sticks."

This was professor Thomas J. Headlee, Dr. Professor and Chief "Entomologist." (That word will stop you ignorant ones. But we got a fifty-fifty break I don't know what it means either.)

Well he delivered this address at a Convention of the New Jersey Exterminators Association duly assembled in the very heart of the Mosquito belt. So I gather from that that an Entomologist is a man that has devoted his life to a study that must include this Jersey product. He has either given his life's work for or against the Mosquito. Now it's not only what this fellow said that is of such vital interest to all of us. It's the surprise that New Jersey had such an organization called, "The New Jersey Mosquito Exterminators Inc." Anyone who has ever visited that State could not possibly understand how there could be an organization devoted to the annihalitation of those Komical little rascals. And if they have got such a Society what have they been doing? Where have they been exterminating and when?

But you see that's what they been doing is holding dinners. All you do in America nowadays is get a name for some kind of Organization, then you start holding dinners. An Organization without a dinner is just impossible. Now the only Mosquitos exterminated was at the dinner. Well during the scratching and shipping and singing of the mosquitos at this Dinner, Mr. Headlee read off the following authoritative statistics.

"The normal productivity of one lone Female house Mosquito in one year is 159,875,000,000 offspring."

Now you statistic hounds get that. (There is four sets of those three figures.) So according to my remembrance of Ray's "elementary" Arithmatic, that runs us up into the Billions. So that first 159 you see there ain't nothing but BILLIONS. Now just wait and let that soak in awhile, 159 billions of offsprings.

You Mothers that think you have done something for your race when you have brought into the World two to 8 or 10 young Hyenas, you certainly can't boast after reading what the Female Mosquito has done to leave her imprint on the ankles of humanity. Now I don't know what was done at the dinner about it. Perhaps they all signed a pledge to all go out and during the coming year to exterminate as early in the season as possible one Female Mosquito, thereby lessening the yearly yield by 158 billion.

Now wait a minute. You ain't heard nothing yet. "Only half of these, or 79,937,500,000 should be counted as Pests, for they are the active, buzzing, biting, and egg laying females. The others are mere Males which do not bite and are harmless. These figures which are based on the known rate of Mosquito reproduction and which disregard infantile mortality, indicate the urgent need for control measures that begin early in the season."

Now Women, what have you got to say for yourselves? Get that, the Males are harmless, they don't bite, Buzz or lay eggs. That's great. It makes me proud I am a Male. That fellow Kipling had it right when he wrote, (or maby it was Shakespeare, or Lady Astor, or somebody over there) "The Female of the Specie is more deadly than the Male." Women denied it then and there was a great mess raised about it. But this Jersey entomologist has finally got the dope on 'em.

Now we are getting down to the "Nubbin" or main part and like all Speakers he dident explain that. It is this. He told you to "go out and exterminate a Female as early in life as possible." But he dident tell you how to distinguish the female from the Male. You are liable to go out with the best intentions in the World and kill one, and what might it turn out to be but an innocent Male. A poor Male Mosquito, that had never done a soul a wrong all its life. It had never sung to you, it had never bit you, it had never laid eggs on you. In fact it had gone through life acting in a Gentlemanly way, and here it is killed. Why? Because you havent been taught to distinguish the sex. He has given up his life this poor Mosquito has just as a Martyr to the ignorance of the human race.

What we need is Literature of two kinds. One to teach us readily to realize the sex, and the other is Pamphlets for the Female Mosquitos on Birth Control. Show them that they are not only doing their part but they are going over their Quota. Teach them that the days of the big families in Mosquitos are past, that what we want is "Fewer and better Mosquitos." Try and get 'em to move out of Jersey and to Fifth and Park Avenue New York and let 'em see there that being prolific in offsprings is only for the "Lower Classes."

Don't try to kill off the Females. Educate 'em up to modern ways. They are not so crazy about laying eggs, it's just because they think it's their duty to do it. Course the whole thing is kinder mysterious to me. I don't see how the Female can be the one that Lays all the eggs, raises all the young, does all the biting, and still has time to sing. Now some of these must kinder overlap. Now they can't bite and sing at the same time. We know that from experience. They generally don't start singing about it till the biting is over, then they crow about it. If the biting hasent been good they won't sing. I have noticed that.

Now when do they find time to raise all these children? There must be times when they can't be singing or biting. Now the way this Entomologist has left us now about the only way we have left open to do is watch a Mosquito till he bites you and then destroy him. (I mean her.) In other words, if he bites you he is a Her, and if he sings, he is a Her. Watch him and see if he lays an egg, then it's a Her.

But if he just sits around all day and don't do anything, why about the only conclusion we can come to is that it is a HE. Don't kill him, he does no harm, he just sits and revels in the accomplishments of his Wife. So when you find a Male the best thing to do is just to sit there and wait till his Wife comes between bites. "How does the Male live?" That's what they going to take up at the next dinner.

Helen Rowland (1875–1950)

❧❧❧❧

FROM *Reflections of a Bachelor Girl*

Kissing a girl, without first telling her that you love her, is as small and mean as letting a salesman take you for a free ride in an automobile when you have no intention of buying it.

•

Flinging yourself at a man's head is like flinging a bone at a cat; it doesn't fascinate him, it frightens him.

•

Men say they admire a woman with high ideals and principles; but it's the kind with high heels and dimples that a wife hesitates to introduce to her husband.

•

Never worry for fear you have broken a man's heart; at the worst it is only sprained and a week's rest will put it in perfect working condition again.

•

Nothing can exceed the grace and tenderness with which men make love—in novels—, except the off-hand commonplaceness with which they do it in real life.

•

About the only sign of personal individuality that the average woman is allowed to retain after she marries is her toothbrush.

•

A man seldom discovers that he hasn't married his affinity until his wife begins to get crow's feet around the eyes.

•

Odd how a man always gets remorse confused with reform; a cold bath, a dose of bromo-selzer, and his wife's forgiveness will make him feel so moral that he will begin to patronize you.

•

Husbands are like the pictures in the anti-fat advertisements—
so different before and after taking.

•

There are moments when the meanest of women may feel a
sisterly sympathy for her husband's first wife.

•

A woman may have a great deal of difficulty getting married the first time, but after that it's easy, because where one
man leads the others will follow like a flock of sheep.

•

When you see what some girls marry, you realize how they
must hate to work for a living.

•

There is no such thing as a confirmed bachelor in the countries where harems are fashionable.

•

It isn't tying himself to one woman that a man dreads when
he thinks of marrying; it's separating himself from all the
others.

•

It's the men who are least particular about their own morals
who are the most particular about a woman's; if Satan
should come up here seeking a wife, he would probably demand an angel with gilt wings instead of a nice congenial
little devil.

•

What do they know—about one another that makes every
man who kisses a girl warn her so darkly and impressively
not to trust any of the others?

•

Poverty is only a relative affair, after all; it is X minus the
things you want.

•

The woman who is wedded to an art and also to a man pays
the full penalty for that kind of bigamy.

•

Some men are born for marriage, some achieve marriage;
but all of them live in the deadly fear that marriage is going
to be thrust upon them.

•

A summer resort is a place where a man will resort to anything from croquet to cocktails for amusement and where a girl will resort to anything from a half-grown boy to an aged paralytic for an escort.

•

When a man becomes a confirmed old bachelor it is not because he has never met the one woman he could live with, but because he has never met the one woman he couldn't live without.

•

Don't fancy a man is serious merely because he treats you to French dinners and talks sentiment; wait until he begins to take you to cheap tables d'hôte and talks economy.

•

It is one of the mockeries of matrimony that the moment two people begin to be awfully courteous to one another round the house it is a sign they are awfully mad.

FROM *Book of Flirts*

Marvellous, oh, my Daughter, is the way of a man with women; for every man hath a *method* and each his favorite *stunt*. And the stunt that he hath found to work successfully with one damsel shall be practised upon each in turn, even unto the finest details thereof.

Behold, one man shall come unto thee saying:

"How foolish are the sentimentalists! But, as for *me*, my motives are altruistic and disinterested; and a woman's *friendship* is what I most desire." Yet, I charge thee, seek among his women "friends" and thou shalt not find an *homely* damsel in all their number.

For this is the *platonic* stunt. . . .

Yet observe how still another seeketh to be more subtle.

Mark how he sitteth afar off and talketh of love in the *abstract*; how he calleth three times a week, yet remaineth always *impersonal*; how he praiseth the shape of thine hand and admireth thy rings, yet toucheth not so much as the *tips* of thy fingers.

"Lo," he thinketh in his heart, "I shall keep her guessing. Yea, I shall wrack her soul with thoughts of how I may be brought to subjection. And when she can no longer contain her curiosity, then will she seek to *lure* me, and I shall gather her in mine arms."

And this is the *elusive* stunt.

. . . Each of these is but as a chainstitch unto a rose pattern, beside him that playeth the *frankly devoted.*

For all women are unto him as one woman—and that one *putty.*

FROM *It Must Be Thrilling to Be a Man*

It must be thrilling to be a man!

It must be wonderful always to get the best food, the best service and all the waiter's attention. . . .

It must be wonderful to feel that your morals are not your own responsibility, and that it is up to some woman to "guide you to heaven." . . .

It must be thrilling to know that you will always be "as young as you feel," and that you will be fascinating just as long as you have a few strands of hair left to plaster across your forehead.

It must be comforting to face forty without the slightest fear that you will be out of the "vamping" class—and to believe at fifty that a girl of nineteen loves you for yourself alone!

It must be consoling to know that, no matter how poor or plain, or passé you may be, you can always find some woman willing to dine with you, flirt with you—and even to marry you! . . .

It must be delightful to be able to carry all your belongings in your pockets, instead of having to struggle with a hand-bag, a vanity case, a change-purse, and half a dozen other pieces of "junk." . . .

It must be wonderful to know that, when you die, if you have managed to keep out of jail and the newspaper, everybody will speak of you as a "good man."

It must be wonderful to have someone believe everything you tell her!

It must be *wonderful* to be a man!

Rita Rudner (Contemporary)

✒∽❀∽✒

FROM *Naked Beneath My Clothes*

Inhuman Nature

I'm a pretty nice person. I'm not a bad person. I'm no Mother Teresa. I'm somewhere between Mother Teresa and Hitler. I try to be the best person I can be, but I'm constantly letting myself down. Human nature is largely something that has to be overcome. Lots of the little things in life that give me pleasure are usually connected with someone else's misfortune. Not big misfortunes, not even misfortunes, more inconveniences; little victories in my life that keep me going. Before you start to hate me, let me give you a few examples and see if they sound familiar.

1. You're standing on line for a very popular movie. You're worried about whether or not you will get in. You wait ten minutes. You turn around. You are no longer at the end of the line. There are now at least thirty people behind you who have less chance of getting in than you do, and if they do, you will almost certainly get a better seat. What is your reaction? Do you say to the people behind you, "Hey, you can all get in front of me, I can see this movie tomorrow night." No, you gloat—admit it, you gloat . . . or am I the only one?

2. I'm staying in a hotel, and while walking down the corridor I always peek in other people's hotel rooms to see if they are nicer than mine. If their room is nicer, I rationalize to myself, "It's just a room, I'm going to be sleeping in it most of the time." However, if my room is nicer, I think, "Ha ha, I got a better room, ha, ha, ha, ha, ha, ha, ha, ha." I revert to a three-year-old and say "ha" far too many times.

3. We all know that life isn't fair; but restaurant service should be. When I sit down at a restaurant and the people who sit down fifteen minutes after me get served first, I'm furious, unless I'm the later person who has gotten served. I don't wait and say, "I'm not eating until the people who got here before me are taken care of." I eat. I eat, and it's especially delicious.

4. There are few things that have given me more joy than Geraldo Rivera being hit in the nose by a chair. It still gives me the giggles when I think about the bandage. I don't like Geraldo Rivera, but I would never wish him harm. I just think it's the chair that makes the image special. A fist would have been too common and a blender too disturbing, but a chair and a nose coming together when the nose belonged to Geraldo Rivera, that was a delight.

5. This is something that must not go farther than this book. Sometimes, when I'm in an elevator and I see someone running toward it, I . . . I . . . I pretend I can't find the Open Door button. There, I said it. It has nothing to do with the character of the person who wants to come in. I don't even particularly want to be alone. I just don't want to press the button.

6. When I'm driving down the street and see someone else fixing a flat tire, I sit a little taller. I know someday that will be me out there, but it hasn't happened yet, so I'm still able to chuckle.

7. In traffic there is only one rule that is a constant. The lane of traffic that you are in is the lane of traffic that isn't moving. If I were in the lane of traffic that was moving, I'm sure I would be happy about it, but this personally has never happened to me.

8. I'm in the movie theater, a woman with an enormous head sits down directly in front of the person sitting next to me. I am amused, but only for a few seconds before she changes her mind and sits directly in front of me.

9. One of my very best friends who has never been able to gain weight (poor thing) recently gained ten pounds and had to go on a diet. Glee. I call her and laugh and hang up. (She does deserve it; all those years of complaining to me about the horrors of having to drink a chocolate shake every day.)

10. My husband found a gray hair on his head. He was upset. I had it framed.

There are more things about myself that I'm ashamed of,

but I'm going to stop here, just in case it's not really human
nature . . . and I'm the only one.

Carl Sandburg (1878–1967)

❦

Is Wisdom a Lot of Language?

Apes, may I speak to you a moment?
Chimpanzees, come hither for words.
Orangoutangs, let's get into a huddle.
Baboons, lemme whisper in your ears.
Gorillas, do yuh hear me hollerin' to yuh?
And monkeys! monkeys! get this chatter—

For a long time men have plucked letters
Out of the air and shaped syllables.
And out of the syllables came words
And from the words came phrases, clauses.
Sentences were born—and languages.
(The Tower of Babel didn't work out—
it came down quicker than it went up.)
Misunderstandings followed the languages,
Arguments, epithets, maledictions, curses,
Gossip, backbiting, the buzz of the bazoo,
Chit chat, blah blah, talk just to be talking,
Monologues of members telling other members
How good they are now and were yesterday,
Conversations missing the point,
Dialogues seldom as beautiful as soliloquies,
Seldom as fine as a man alone, a woman by herself
Telling a clock, "I'm a plain damn fool."

Read the dictionary from A to Izzard today.
Get a vocabulary. Brush up on your diction.
See whether wisdom is just a lot of language.

One Parting

Why did he write to her,
"I can't live with you"?
And why did she write to him,
"I can't live without you"?
For he went west, she went east,
And they both lived.

Henry W. Shaw (1818–1885)

◦◦◦

Amerikans

Amerikans love caustick things; they would prefer turpentine tew colone-water, if they had tew drink either.

So with their relish of humor; they must hav it on the half-shell with cayenne.

An Englishman wants hiz fun smothered deep in mint sauce, and he iz willin tew wait till next day before he tastes it.

If you tickle or convince an Amerikan yu hav got tew do it quick.

An Amerikan luvs tew laff, but he don't luv tew make a bizzness ov it; he works, eats, and haw-haws on a canter.

I guess the English hav more wit, and the Amerikans more humor.

We havn't had time, yet, tew bile down our humor and git the wit out ov it.

The English are better punsters, but i konsider punning a sort ov literary prostitushun in which future happynesz iz swopped oph for the plezzure ov the moment.

Thare iz one thing i hav noticed: evryboddy that writes expeckts tew be wize or witty—so duz evrybody expect tew be saved when they die; but thare iz good reason tew beleave that the goats hereafter will be in the majority, just az the sheep are here.

Don't forget *one* thing, yu hav got tew be wize before yu kan be witty; and don't forget *two* things, a single paragraff haz made sum men immortal, while a volume haz bin wuss than a pile-driver tew others—but what would Amerikans dew if it want for their sensashuns?

Sumthing new, sumthing startling iz necessary for us az a people, and it don't make mutch matter what it iz—a huge defalkashun—a red elephant—or Jersee clams with pearls in them will answer if nothing better offers.

Englishmen all laff at us for our sensashuns, and sum ov them fret about it, and spred their feathers in distress for us, az a fond and foolish old hen, who haz hatched out a setting ov ducks' eggs, will stand on the banks ov a mill pond, wringing her hands in agony to see her brood pitch in and take a sail. *She* kant understand it, but the *Ducks* know awl about it.

N.B.—Yu kan bet 50 dollars the Ducks know all about it.

N.B.—Yu kan bet 50 dollars more that it makes no difference who hatches out an Amerikan, the fust thing he will do, iz to pitch into sumthin.

N.B.—No more bets at present.

Jean Shepherd (Contemporary)

⤳⤳✦⤳⤳

FROM *Wanda Hickey's Night of Golden Memories and Other Disasters*

Now we were deep in the heart of the thrill-ride section of the fair. The Ferris wheel reached high up into the dark sky, its spokes outlined in colored light bulbs, jerking upward and stopping and jerking and jerking upward again. It loomed over us like a huge illuminated snowflake.

"I wanna go on the Ferris wheel!" Randy whined for the 317th time. This time, he was not to be denied.

My father bought a ticket from the man in the little booth. Off my brother went through the turnstile and into a wobbly car the color of a grape. A minute later, he was laughing down at us and sticking his tongue out as he swept up ecstatically into the night. Every few seconds, the wheel would stop and unload a car. We stood around and waved every time he went past.

Finally, the grape car stopped at the bottom. We could see the attendant in blue coveralls swing the gate open. He seemed to be arguing with the occupant. The attendant finally hollered out to the guy in the box office:

"HEY, JAKE! THIS KID WON'T GET OUT!"

"Oh, fer Chrissake, what now?" the old man muttered.

"NOW, YOU GET OUT. YOU HAD ENOUGH," said the attendant.

"WHAAAAAAAA!"

The attendant reached in and wrenched him out, fighting and kicking every inch of the way. My father took over the battle, dragging him out into the midway.

"I WANNA GO ON AGAIN!!" he screamed, but to no avail.

The big wheel started up without him as we moved on to the next attraction, Randy struggling at every step.

We tried to hurry past a merry-go-round swarming with little kids and mothers, but it was no use. Randy threatened to throw himself under it if he didn't get to ride on it. I stood with my father as he whirled round and round beside my mother, sitting on a black swan with a yellow beak. He tried to do a headstand as *The Man on the Flying Trapeze* played over and over and over and over. After the sixth ride, we managed to pull him off. He emerged slightly pale but still game. We ate a red candy cane apiece, thus setting the stage for total disaster.

My father never went on rides unless they were real gut busters. He had ventured unflinchingly onto roller coasters so violent as to turn away strong men, quaking in fear. He spotted one of his old favorites, an evil contraption known as the Whirligig Rocket Whip. We had been warned of its presence long before we arrived on the scene. Screams of horror and the flashing light of the emergency ambulance led us to the killer ride of them all.

At every fair or amusement park, there is one ride that is

the yokel equivalent of the main bull ring in Madrid. This is where callow-faced youths and gorilla-armed icemen prove their virility to their admiring women. The Rocket Whip was a classic of its kind. It consisted of two bullet-shaped cars, one yellow, one red, attached to the ends of rotating arms. It revolved simultaneously clockwise and up and down. At the same time, the individual cars rotated in their own orbits. The old man, spotting the Rocket Whip, strained forward like a fire horse smelling smoke.

"Are you sure you should go on that?" My mother held back.

"Aw, come on. It'll do the kids good. Blow the stink off 'em." She didn't answer, just gazed up in fear at the mechanical devil that was now about to take on passengers. The yellow car rested near the ground, its wire-mesh door invitingly open.

He bought three tickets from the operator, who sat near the turnstile in a rocking chair, the control lever at his side.

"Let's go, kids."

We piled into the car. It was simplicity itself; two hard metal seats and a bar that clamped down over the laps of the occupants, so that their bodies didn't become actually dismembered. We sat stationary for a long moment. High above us, the occupants of the red car gazed down at us—upside down—waiting for Thor's hammer to descend.

The man yanked the lever and it began. Slowly at first, we began to spin. The landscape outside our wire-mesh cage blurred as we gained speed. We leaped skyward, up, up; paused briefly at the top of the arc at what looked like thousands of feet above ground level, then plunged straight down. Just as we neared the earth, we were whipped upward again. By this time, the car, caught by enormous forces, had begun spinning centrifugally on its own. We were trapped in a giant cream separator.

There were brief flashes of dark sky, flashing lights, gaping throngs, my old man's rolling eyes, his straw hat sailing around the interior of the car.

"Oh, no, fer Chrissake!" he yelled. A shower of loose change—quarters, nickels, dimes, pennies—sprayed out of his pockets, filled the car for an instant and was gone, spun out into the night.

"Oh, Jesus Christ! No!" he yelled again, as his brown-and-white marbled Wearever fountain pen with his name on it, given to him by the bowling team, flew out of his pocket and disappeared into the night.

Higher and higher we flew, swooping low to scream upward again. My kid brother, chalk white, whimpered piteously. I hung onto the iron bar, certain that my last hour had arrived. My head thumped the back of the car steadily as it spun.

"Ain't this fun, kids? Wow, what a ride!" shouted the old man, sweating profusely. He made a grab for his hat as it sailed past.

"Wave to Ma, kids! There she is!"

It was then that the operator turned the power on full. Everything that had gone before was only a warm-up. Our necks snapped back as the Rocket Whip accelerated. I was not touching the seat at any point. Jack-knifed over the bar, I saw that one of my shoes had been wrenched off my foot. At that moment, with no warning, my kid brother let it all go. His entire day's accumulation of goodies, now marinated and pungent, gushed out in a geyser. The car spun crazily. The air was filled with atomized spray of everything he had ingested for the past 24 hours. Down we swooped.

"My new pongee shirt!"

Soaked from head to foot, the old man struggled frantically in his seat to get out of the line of fire. It was no use. I felt it coming, too. I closed my eyes and the vacuum forces of outer space just dragged it all out of me like a suction pump. From a million miles away, I heard my old man shouting something, but it didn't matter. All I knew was that if I didn't hold onto that bar, it would be all over.

We gradually spun to a stop and finally the wire-mesh door opened. My feet touched the blessed earth. On rubbery legs, clinging weakly together, the three of us tottered past the turnstile as other victims were clamped into the torture chamber we had just left.

"Great ride, eh, folks? I left you on a little longer, 'cause I could see the kids was really enjoyin' it," said the operator, pocketing the last of my father's change as we passed through the turnstile.

"Thanks. It sure was great," said the old man with a weak

smile, a bent cigarette hanging from his lips. He always judged a ride by how sick it made him. The nausea quotient of the Rocket Whip was about as high as they come.

We sat on a bench for a while to let the breeze dry off the old man's shirt, and so that our eyes could get back into focus. From all around us we could hear the whoops and hollers of people going up and down and sideways on the other rides.

There was one across from the Rocket Whip that my kid brother, who had great recuperative powers, *had* to go on. We didn't have the strength to stop him. It was a big barrel made out of some kind of shiny metal and it spun around like a cocktail shaker on its side. The people were screaming and yelling; their skirts were flying up, their shoes falling off. Randy loved it. We hung around and waited until they threw him out.

Allan Sherman (1924–1973)

∽⌇∾

FROM *The Rape of the A.P.E.* *

. . . American language, an exquisitely forked tongue which enabled the speaker to remain always polite and smiling, though his message be lethal. *Basic APE* was a brilliant code, a shorthand route to competitive success. We all became fluent in it; some of us managed to be eloquent.

Basic APE	*English Translation*
She's a nice girl.	She's got buck teeth.
She's a nice girl with a great personality.	She's also cross-eyed.

* A.P.E.: American Puritan Ethie

Betty Smith (1896–1972)

◈

FROM *A Tree Grows in Brooklyn*

Sissy wasn't working that day. Knowing that the children would be left alone locked in the rooms, she decided to keep them company.

She knocked at the door calling out that she was Aunt Sissy. Francie opened the door on the chain to make sure before she let her in. The children swarmed over Sissy smothering her with hugs. They loved her. To them, she was a beautiful lady who always smelled sweet, wore beautiful clothes and brought them amazing presents.

Today she brought a sweet-smelling cedar cigar box, several sheets of tissue paper, some red and some white, and a jar of paste. They sat around the kitchen table and went to work decorating the box. Sissy outlined circles on the paper with a quarter and Francie cut them out. Sissy showed her how to make them into little paper cups by molding the circles around the end of a pencil. When they had a lot of cups made, Sissy drew a heart on the box cover. The bottom of each red cup was given a dab of paste and the cup was pasted on the penciled heart. The heart was filled in with red cups. The rest of the lid was filled in with white. When the top was finished it looked like a bed of closely-packed white carnations with a heart of red ones. The sides were filled in with white cups and the inside lined with red tissue. You never could tell it had been a cigar box, it was that beautiful. The box took up most of the afternoon.

Sissy had a chop suey date at five and she got ready to leave. Francie clung to her and begged her not to go. Sissy hated to leave, yet she didn't want to miss her date. She searched in her purse for something to amuse them in her absence. They stood at her knee helping her look. Francie spied a cigarette box and pulled it out. On the cover was a picture of a man lying on a couch, knees crossed, one foot dangling in the air and smoking a cigarette which made a big smoke ring over his head. In the ring was a picture of a girl with her hair in her eyes and her bust popping out of her dress. The name on the box was *American Dreams*. It was out of the stock at Sissy's factory.

The children clamored for the box. Sissy reluctantly let them have it after explaining that the box contained cigarettes and was only to hold and to look at and not under any circumstances to be opened. They must not touch the seals, she said.

After she left, the children amused themselves for a time by staring at the picture. They shook the box. A dull swishing mysterious sound resulted.

"They is snakes in there and not zingarettes," decided Neeley.

"No," corrected Francie. "Worms are in there. Live ones."

They argued, Francie saying the box was too small for snakes and Neeley insisting that they rolled-up snakes like herring in a glass jar. Curiosity grew to such a pitch that Sissy's instructions were forgotten. The seals were so lightly pasted, it was a simple matter to pull them off. Francie opened the box. There was a sheet of soft dulled tin foil over the contents. Francie lifted the foil carefully. Neeley prepared to crawl under the table if the snakes became active. But there were neither snakes, worms nor cigarettes in the box and its contents were very uninteresting. After trying to devise some simple games, Francie and Neeley lost interest, clumsily tied the contents of the box to a string, trailed the string out of the window and finally secured the string by shutting the window on it. They then took turns jumping on the denuded box and became so absorbed in breaking it into bits that they forgot all about the string hanging out of the window.

Consequently, there was a great surprise waiting for Johnny when he sauntered home to get a fresh dicky and collar for his evening's job. He took one look and his face burned with shame. He told Katie when she came home.

Katie questioned Francie closely and found out everything. Sissy was condemned. That night after the children had been put to bed and Johnny was away working, Katie sat in her dark kitchen with blushes coming and going. Johnny went about his work with a dull feeling that the world had come to an end.

Evy came over later in the evening and she and Katie discussed Sissy.

"That's the end, Katie," said Evy, "the very end. What Sissy does is her own business until her own business makes a thing like this happen. I've got a growing girl, so have you, we mustn't let Sissy come into our homes again. She's bad and there's no getting around it."

"She's good in many ways," temporized Katie.

"You say that after what she did to you today?"

"Well . . . I guess you're right. Only don't tell Mother. She doesn't know how Sissy lives and Sissy is her eye-apple."

When Johnny came home, Katie told him that Sissy was never to come to their house again. Johnny sighed and said he guessed that was the only thing to do. Johnny and Katie talked away the night, and in the morning they had their plans all made for moving when the end of the month came . . .

In the summer of that same year, Johnny got the notion that his children were growing up ignorant of the great ocean that washed the shores of Brooklyn. Johnny felt that they ought to go out to sea in a ship. So he decided to take them for a rowboat ride at Canarsie and do a little deep sea fishing on the side. He had never gone fishing and he'd never been in a rowboat. But that's the idea he got.

Weirdly tied up with this idea, and by a reasoning process known only to Johnny, was the idea of taking Little Tilly along on the trip. Little Tilly was the four-year-old child of neighbors whom he had never met. In fact, he had never seen Little Tilly but he got this idea that he had to make something up to her on account of her brother Gussie. It all tied up with the notion of going to Canarsie.

Gussie, a boy of six, was a murky legend in the neighborhood. A tough little hellion, with an over-developed under-lip, he had been born like other babies and nursed at his mother's great breasts. But there, all resemblance to any child, living or dead, ceased. His mother tried to wean him when he was nine months old but Gussie wouldn't stand for it. Denied the breast, he refused a bottle, food or water. He lay in his crib and whimpered. His mother, fearful that he would starve, resumed nursing him. He sucked contentedly, refusing all other food, and lived off his mother's milk until he was nearly two years old. The milk stopped then because his mother was with child again. Gussie sulked and bided his time for nine long months. He refused cow's milk in any form or container and took to drinking black coffee.

Little Tilly was born and the mother flowed with milk again. Gussie went into hysterics the first time he saw the baby nursing. He lay on the floor, screaming and banging his head. He wouldn't eat for four days and he refused to go to the toilet. He got haggard and his mother got frightened. She thought it wouldn't do any harm to give him the breast just once. That was her big mistake. He was like a dope fiend getting the stuff after a long period of deprivation. He wouldn't let go.

He took all of his mother's milk from that time on and Little Tilly, a sickly baby, had to go on the bottle.

Gussie was three years old at this time and big for his age. Like other boys, he wore knee pants and heavy shoes with brass toe tips. As soon as he saw his mother unbutton her dress, he ran to her. He stood up while nursing, an elbow on his mother's knee, his feet crossed jauntily and his eyes roving around the room. Standing to nurse was not such a remarkable feat as his mother's breasts were mountainous and practically rested in her lap when released. Gussie was indeed a fearful sight nursing that way and he looked not unlike a man with his foot on a bar rail, smoking a fat pale cigar.

The neighbors found out about Gussie and discussed his pathological state in hushed whispers. Gussie's father got so that he wouldn't sleep with his wife; he said that she bred monsters. The poor woman figured and figured on a way to wean Gussie. He *was* too big to nurse, she decided. He was going for four. She was afraid his second teeth wouldn't come in straight.

One day she took a can of stove blackening and the brush and closed herself in the bedroom where she copiously blackened her left breast with the stove polish. With a lipstick she drew a wide ugly mouth with frightening teeth in the vicinity of the nipple. She buttoned her dress and went into the kitchen and sat in her nursing rocker near the window. When Gussie saw her, he threw the dice, with which he had been playing, under the washtubs and trotted over for feeding. He crossed his feet, planted his elbow on her knee and waited.

"Gussie want tiddy?" asked his mother wheedlingly.

"Yup!"

"All right. Gussie's gonna get nice tiddy."

Suddenly she ripped open her dress and thrust the horribly made-up breast into his face. Gussie was paralyzed with fright for a moment, then he ran away screaming and hid under the bed where he stayed for twenty-four hours. He came out at last, trembling. He went back to drinking black coffee and shuddered every time his eyes went to his mother's bosom. Gussie was weaned.

The mother reported her success all over the neighborhood. It started a new fashion in weaning called, "Giving the baby the Gussie."

Johnny heard the story and contemptuously dismissed Gussie from his mind. He was concerned about Little Tilly. He thought she had been cheated out of something very important and might grow up thwarted. He got a notion that a boat ride off the Canarsie shore might wipe out some of the wrong her unnatural brother had done her. He sent Francie around to ask could Little Tilly go with them. The harassed mother consented happily.

The next Sunday, Johnny and the three children set out for Canarsie. Francie was eleven years old, Neeley ten and Little Tilly well past three. Johnny wore his tuxedo and derby and a fresh collar and dicky. Francie and Neeley wore their everyday clothes. Little Tilly's mother, in honor of the day, had dressed her up in a cheap but fancy lace dress trimmed with dark pink ribbon.

On the trolley ride out, they sat in the front seat and Johnny made friends with the motorman and they talked politics. They got off at the last stop which was Canarsie and found their way to a little wharf on which was a tiny shack; a couple of water-logged rowboats bobbed up and down on the frayed ropes which held them to the wharf. A sign over the shack read:

"Fishing tackle and boats for rent."

Underneath was a bigger sign which said:

FRESH FISH TO TAKE HOME FOR SALE HERE.

Johnny negotiated with the man and, as was his way, made a friend of him. The man invited him into the shack for an eye opener saying that he himself only used the stuff for a night cap.

While Johnny was inside getting his eyes opened, Neeley and Francie pondered how a night cap could also be an eye opener. Little Tilly stood there in her lace dress and said nothing.

Johnny came out with a fishing pole and a rusty tin can filled with worms in mud. The friendly man untied the rope from the least sorry of the rowboats, put the rope in Johnny's hand, wished him luck and went back to his shack.

Johnny put the fishing stuff into the bottom of the boat and helped the children in. Then he crouched on the wharf, the bit of rope in his hand and gave instructions about boats.

"There is always a wrong and a right way to get on a boat," said Johnny, who had never been on any boat except an excursion boat once. "The right way is to give the boat a shove and then jump in it before it drifts out to sea. Like this."

He straightened up, pushed the boat from him, leaped . . . and fell into the water. The petrified children stared at him. A second before, papa had been standing on the dock above them. Now he was below them in the water. The water came to his neck and his small waxed mustache and derby hat were in the clear. His derby was still straight on his forehead. Johnny, as surprised as the children, stared at them a moment before he said:

"Don't any of you damned kids dare to laugh!"

He climbed into the boat almost upsetting it. They didn't dare laugh aloud but Francie laughed so hard inside that her ribs hurt. Neeley was afraid to look at his sister. He knew that if their eyes met, he'd burst out laughing. Little Tilly said nothing. Johnny's collar and dicky were a sodden paperish mess. He stripped them off and threw them overboard. He rowed out to sea waveringly, but with silent dignity. When he came to what he thought was a likely spot, he announced that he was going to "drop anchor." The children were disappointed when they discovered that the romantic phrase simply meant that you threw a lump of iron attached to a rope overboard.

Horrified, they watched papa squeamishly impale a muddy worm on the hook. The fishing started. It consisted in baiting the hook, casting it dramatically, waiting awhile, pulling it up minus worm and fish and starting the whole thing over again.

The sun grew bright and hot. Johnny's tuxedo dried to a stiff wrinkled greenish outfit. The children started to get a whopping case of sunburn. After what seemed hours, papa announced to their intense relief and happiness that it was time to eat. He wound up the tackle, put it away, pulled up the anchor and made for the wharf. The boat seemed to go in a circle which made the wharf get further away. Finally they made shore a few hundred yards further down. Johnny tied up the boat, told the children to wait in it and went ashore. He said he was going to treat them to a nice lunch.

He came back after a while walking sideways, carrying hot dogs, huckleberry pie and strawberry pop. They sat in the rocking boat tied to the rotting wharf, looked down into the slimy green water that smelled of decaying fish, and ate. Johnny had had a few drinks ashore which made him sorry that he had hollered at the kids. He told them they could laugh at his falling into the water if they wanted to. But somehow, they couldn't bring up a laugh. The time was past for that. Papa was very cheerful, Francie thought.

"This is the life," he said. "Away from the maddening crowd. Ah, there's nothing like going down to the sea in a ship. We're getting away from it all," he ended up cryptically.

After their amazing lunch, Johnny rowed them out to sea again. Perspiration poured down from under his derby and the wax in the points of his mustache melted causing the neat adornment to change into disorganized hair on his upper lip. He felt fine. He sang lustily as he rowed:

Sailing, sailing, over the bounding main.

He rowed and rowed and kept going around in a circle and never did get out to sea. Eventually his hands got so blistered that he didn't feel like rowing any more. Dramatically he announced that he was going to pull for the shore. He pulled and pulled and finally made it by rowing in smaller and smaller circles and making the circles come near the wharf. He never noticed that the three children were pea green in the spots where they were not beet red from the sunburn. If he had only known it, the hot dogs, huckleberry pie, strawberry pop and worms squirming on the hook weren't doing them much good.

At the wharf, he leaped to the dock and the children followed his example. All made it excepting Tilly who fell into the water. Johnny threw himself flat on the dock, reached in and fished her out. Little Tilly stood there, her lace dress wet and ruined, but she said nothing. Although it was a broiling hot day, Johnny peeled off his tuxedo jacket, knelt down and wrapped it around the child. The arms dragged in the sand. Then Johnny took her up in his arms and strode up and down the dock patting her back soothingly and singing her a lullaby. Little Tilly didn't understand a thing of all that happened that day. She didn't understand why she had been put into a boat, why she had fallen into the water or why the man was making such a fuss over her. She said nothing.

When Johnny felt that she was comforted, he set her down and went into the shack where he had either an eye opener or a night cap. He bought three flounders from the man for a quarter. He came out with the wet fish wrapped in a newspaper. He told his children that he had promised to bring home some fresh-caught fish to mama.

"The principal thing," said papa, "is that I am bringing home fish that were caught at Canarsie. It makes no difference who caught them. The point is that we went fishing and we're bringing home fish."

His children knew that he wanted mama to think he caught the fish. Papa didn't ask them to lie. He just asked them not to be too fussy about the truth. The children understood.

They boarded one of those trolley cars that had two long benches facing each other. They made a queer row. First there was Johnny in green wrinkled salt stiff pants, an undershirt full of big holes, a derby hat and a disorderly mustache. Next came Little Tilly swallowed up in his coat with salt water dripping from under it and forming a brackish pool on the floor. Francie and Neeley came next. Their faces were brick red and they sat very rigid trying not to be sick.

People got on the car, sat across from them and stared curiously. Johnny sat upright, the fish in his lap, trying not to think of the holes in his exposed undershirt. He looked over the heads of the passengers pretending to study an Ex-Lax advertisement.

More people got on, the car got crowded but no one would sit next to them. Finally one of the fish worked its way out of the sodden newspaper and fell on the floor where it lay slimily in the dust. It was too much for Little Tilly. She looked into the fish's glazed eye, said nothing but vomited silently and thoroughly all over Johnny's tuxedo jacket. Francie and Neeley, as if waiting for that cue, also threw up. Johnny sat there with two exposed fish in his lap, one at his feet and kept staring at the ad. He didn't know what else to do.

When the grisly trip was ended, Johnny took Tilly home feeling that his was the responsibility of explaining. The mother never gave him a chance to explain. She screamed when she saw her dripping be-fouled child. She snatched the coat off, threw it into Johnny's face and called him a Jack-the-Ripper. Johnny tried and tried to explain but she wouldn't listen. Little Tilly said nothing. Finally Johnny got a word in edgewise.

"Lady, I think your little girl has lost her speech."

Whereupon the mother went into hysterics. "You did it, you did it," she screamed at Johnny.

"Can't you make her say something?"

The mother grabbed the child and shook her and shook her. "Speak!" She screamed. "Say something." Finally Little Tilly opened her mouth, smiled happily and said.

"T'anks."

Katie gave Johnny a tongue lashing and said that he wasn't fit to have children. The children in question were alternating between the chills and hot flashes of a bad case of sunburn. Katie nearly cried when she saw the ruin of Johnny's only suit. It would cost a dollar to get it cleaned, steamed and pressed and she knew it would never be the same again. As for the fish, they were found to be in an advanced state of decay and had to be thrown into the garbage can.

The children went to bed. Between chills and fever and bouts of nausea, they buried their heads under the covers and laughed silently and bed-shakingly at the remembrance of papa standing in the water.

Johnny sat at the kitchen window until far into the night trying to figure out why everything had been so wrong. He had sung many a song about ships and going down to the sea in them with a heave ho and a heave to. He wondered why it hadn't turned out the way it said in songs. The children should have returned exhilarated and with a deep and abiding love for the sea and he should have returned with a fine mess of fish. Why, oh why hadn't it turned out the way it did in a song? Why did there have to be his blistered hands and his spoiled suit and sunburn and rotting fish and nausea? Why didn't Little Tilly's mother understand the intention and overlook the result? He couldn't figure it out—he couldn't figure it out.

The songs of the sea had betrayed him.

Charles H. Smith (Bill Arp)
(1826–1903)

Tell and Kiss

They used to have a kissing game up there in the mountains that they still keep up over in East Tennessee. This is the way they practiced it:

A lot of big-limbed, powerful young men and apple-cheeked, buxom girls gather and select one of their number as master of ceremonies. He takes his station in the center of the room, while the rest pair off and parade around him. Suddenly one young woman will throw up her hands and say:

"I'm a-pining."

The master of ceremonies takes it up and the following dialogue takes place:

"Miss Arabella Jane Apthorp says she's a-pining. What is Miss Arabella Jane Apthorp a-pining for?"

"I'm a-pining for a sweet kiss."

"Miss Arabella Jane Apthorp says she's a-pining for a sweet kiss. Who is Miss Arabella Jane Apthorp a-pining for a sweet kiss from?"

She blushes and giggles but forces herself to say, "I'm a-pining for a sweet kiss from Mr. William Arp."

Mr. William Arp now walks up manfully and relieves the fair Arabella's pining by a smack that sounds like a three-year-old steer drawing his hoof out of the mud.

Then a young man will be taken with a sudden pining which, after the usual exchange of questions and answers, reveals the name of the maiden who causes the gnawing and pining. She coyly retreats outdoors, only to be chased, overtaken, captured, and forcibly compelled to relieve her captor's distress.

At one of these entertainments I attended, there was a remarkably beautiful young woman who had been married about a month. Her husband was present, a huge, beetle-browed, black-eyed young mountaineer, with a fist like a ham. The boys fought shy of the bride for fear of the anger of her hulking spouse.

The game went on for some time, when symptoms of anger developed in the giant. Striding into the middle of the room, he said:

"My wife is as purty an nice an sweet as any gal here. You-uns has knowed her all her life. This game has been a-goin on half an hour, an nobody has pined for her once. If somebody don't pine for her purty *soon*, boys, thar will be trouble!"

She was the belle of the ball after that. Everybody pined for her.

Gloria Steinem (Contemporary)

⤜⤏⤜⤏

FROM *If Men Could Menstruate*

So what would happen if suddenly, magically, men could menstruate and women could not?

Clearly, menstruation would become an enviable, boast-worthy, masculine event:

Men would brag about how long and how much.

Young boys would talk about it as the envied beginning of manhood. Gifts, religious ceremonies, family dinners, and stag parties would mark the day.

To prevent monthly work loss among the powerful, Congress would fund a National Institute of Dysmenorrhea. Doctors would research little about heart attacks, from which men were hormonally protected, but everything about cramps.

Sanitary supplies would be federally funded and free. Of course, some men would still pay for the prestige of such commercial brands as Paul Newman Tampons, Muhammad Ali's Rope-a-Dope Pads, John Wayne Maxi Pads, and Joe Namath Jock Shields—"For Those Light Bachelor Days."

Statistical surveys would show that men did better in sports and won more Olympic medals during their periods.

Generals, right-wing politicians, and religious fundamentalists would cite menstruation ("*men*-struation") as proof that only men could serve God and country in combat ("You have to give blood to take blood"), occupy high political office ("Can women be properly fierce without a monthly cycle governed by the planet Mars?"), be priests, ministers, God Himself ("He gave this blood for our sins"), or rabbis ("Without a monthly purge of impurities, women are unclean").

Male liberals or radicals, however, would insist that women are equal, just different; and that any woman could join their ranks if only she were willing to recognize the primacy of menstrual rights ("Everything else is a single issue") or self-inflict a major wound every month ("You *must* give blood for the revolution").

Street guys would invent slang ("He's a three-pad man") and "give fives" on the corner with some exchange like "Man, you lookin' *good*!"

"Yeah, man, I'm on the rag!"

TV shows would treat the subject openly. (*Happy Days:* Richie and Potsie try to convince Fonzie that he is still "The Fonz," though he has missed two periods in a row. *Hill Street Blues:* The whole precinct hits the same cycle.) So would newspapers. (SUMMER SHARK SCARE THREATENS MENSTRUATING MEN. JUDGE CITES MONTHLIES IN PARDONING RAPIST.)

Men would convince women that sex was *more* pleasurable at "that time of the month." Lesbians would be said to fear blood and therefore life itself, though all they needed was a good menstruating man.

Medical schools would limit women's entry ("they might faint at the sight of blood").

Of course, intellectuals would offer the most moral and logical arguments. Without that biological gift for measuring the cycles of the moon and planets, how could a woman master any discipline that demanded a sense of time, space, mathematics—or the ability to measure anything at all? In philosophy and religion, how could women compensate for being disconnected from the rhythm of the universe? Or for their lack of symbolic death and resurrection every month?

Menopause would be celebrated as a positive event, the symbol that men had accumulated enough years of cyclical wisdom to need no more.

Liberal males in every field would try to be kind. The fact that "these people" have no gift for measuring life, the liberals would explain, should be punishment enough.

Pam Stone (Contemporary)

❦

On Female Problems

I'm not much of a Southern belle. Southern women tend to be real demure. They don't like to talk about anything graphic. I had a girlfriend who told me she was in the hospital for female problems. I said, "Get real! What does that mean?" She says, "You know, *female* problems." I said, "What? You can't parallel park? You can't get credit?"

Harriet Beecher Stowe
(1811–1896)

❦

FROM *Love Versus Law*

When a young lady states that she is not going to believe a thing, good judges of human nature generally give up the case; but Miss Silence, to whom the language of opposition and argument was entirely new, could scarcely give her ears credit for veracity in the case; she therefore repeated over exactly what she said before, only in a much louder tone of voice, and with much more vehement forms of asseveration—a mode of reasoning which, if not strictly logical, has at least the sanction of very respectable authorities among the enlightened and learned.

Frank Sullivan (1892–1976)

❧❧❧

The Cliché Expert Testifies on Love

Q—Mr. Arbuthnot, as an expert in the use of the cliché, are you prepared to testify here today regarding its application in topics of sex, love, matrimony, and so on?

A—I am.

Q—Very good. Now, Mr. Arbuthnot, what is love?

A—Love is blind.

Q—Good. What does love do?

A—Love makes the world go round.

Q—Whom does a young man fall in love with?

A—With the Only Girl in the World.

Q—Whom does a young woman fall in love with?

A—With the Only Boy in the World.

Q—When do they fall in love?

A—At first sight.

Q—How?

A—Madly.

Q—They are then said to be?

A—Victims of Cupid's darts.

Q—And he?

A—Whispers sweet nothings in her ear.

Q—Who loves a lover?

A—All the world loves a lover.

Q—Describe the Only Girl in the World.

A—Her eyes are like stars. Her teeth are like pearls. Her lips are ruby. Her cheek is damask, and her form divine.

Q—Haven't you forgotten something?

A—Eyes, teeth, lips, cheek, form—no, sir, I don't think so.

Q—Her hair?

A—Oh, certainly. How stupid of me. She has hair like spun gold.

Q—Very good, Mr. Arbuthnot. Now will you describe the Only Man?

A—He is a blond Viking, a he-man, and a square shooter who plays the game. There is something fine about him that rings true, and he has kept himself pure and clean so that when he meets the girl of his choice, the future mother of his children, he can look her in the eye.

Q—How?

A—Without flinching.

Q—Are all the Only Men blond Vikings?

A—Oh, no. Some of them are dark, handsome chaps who have sown their wild oats. This sort of Only Man has a way with a maid, and there is a devil in his eye. But he is not a cad; he would not play fast and loose with an Only Girl's affections. He has a heart of gold. He is a diamond in the rough. He tells the Only Girl frankly about his Past. She understands—and forgives.

Q—And marries him?

A—And marries him.

Q—Why?

A—To reform him.

Q—Does she reform him?

A—Seldom.

Q—Seldom what?

A—Seldom, if ever.

Q—Now, Mr. Arbuthnot, when the Only Man falls in love, madly, with the Only Girl, what does he do?

A—He walks on air.

Q—Yes, I know, but what does he do? I mean, what is it he pops?

A—Oh, excuse me. The question, of course.

Q—Then what do they plight?

A—Their troth.

Q—What happens after that?

A—They get married.

Q—What is marriage?

A—Marriage is a lottery.

Q—Where are marriages made?

A—Marriages are made in Heaven.

Q—What does the bride do at the wedding?

A—She blushes.

Q—What does the groom do?

A—Forgets the ring.

A—After the marriage, what?

A—The honeymoon.

Q—Then what?

A—She has a little secret.

Q—What is it?

A—She is knitting a tiny garment.

Q—What happens after that?

A—Oh, they settle down and raise a family and live happily ever afterward, unless—

Q—Unless what?

A—Unless he is a fool for a pretty face.

Q—And if he is?

A—Then they come to the parting of the ways.

Q—Mr. Arbuthnot, thank you very much.

A—But I'm not through yet, Mr. Untermyer.

Q—No?

A—Oh, no. There is another side to sex.

Q—There is? What side?

A—The seamy side. There are, you know, men who are wolves in sheep's clothing and there are, alas, lovely women who stoop to folly.

Q—My goodness! Describe these men you speak of, please.

A—They are snakes in the grass who do not place woman upon a pedestal. They are cads who kiss and tell, who trifle with a girl's affections and betray her innocent trust. They are cynics who think that a woman is only a woman, but a good cigar is a smoke. Their mottoes are "Love 'em and leave 'em" and "Catch 'em young, treat 'em rough, tell 'em nothing." These cads speak of "the light that lies in woman's eyes, and lies—and lies—and lies." In olden days they wore black, curling mustachios, which they twirled, and they invited innocent Gibson girls to midnight suppers, with champagne, at their bachelor apartments, and said, "Little girl, why do you fear me?" Nowadays they have black, patent-leather hair, and roadsters, and they drive up to the curb and say, "Girlie, can I give you a lift?" They are fiends in human form, who would rob a woman of her most priceless possession.

Q—What is that?

A—Her honor.

Q—How do they rob her?

A—By making improper advances.

Q—What does a woman do when a snake in the grass tries to rob her of her honor?

A—She defends her honor.

Q—How?

A—By repulsing his advances and scorning his embraces.

Q—How does she do that?

A—By saying, "Sir, I believe you forget yourself," or "Please take your arm away," or "I'll kindly thank you to remember I'm a lady," or "Let's not spoil it all."

Q—Suppose she doesn't say any of those things?

A—In that case, she takes the first false step.

Q—Where does the first false step take her?

A—Down the primrose path.

Q—What's the primrose path?

A—It's the easiest way.

Q—Where does it lead?

A—To a life of shame.

Q—What is a life of shame?

A—A life of shame is a fate worse than death.

Q—Now, after lovely woman has stooped to folly, what does she do to the gay Lothario who has robbed her of her most priceless possession?

A—She devotes the best years of her life to him.

Q—Then what does he do?

A—He casts her off.

Q—How?

A—Like an old shoe.

Q—Then what does she do?

A—She goes to their love nest, then everything goes black before her, her mind becomes a blank, she pulls a revolver, and gives the fiend in human form something to remember her by.

Q—That is called?

A—Avenging her honor.

Q—What is it no jury will do in such a case?

A—No jury will convict.

Q—Mr. Arbuthnot, your explanation of the correct application of the cliché in these matters has been most instructive, and I know that all of us cliché-users here will know exactly how to respond hereafter when, during a conversation, sex—when sex—when—ah—

A—I think what you want to say is "When sex rears its ugly head," isn't it?

Q—Thank you, Mr. Arbuthnot. Thank you very much.

A—Thank *you*, Mr. Untermyer.

The Cliché Expert Testifies on Literary Criticism

Q—Mr. Arbuthnot, you are an expert in the use of the cliché as applied to literary criticism?

A—I am tóld that I am, sir.

Q—We shall soon find out. What is this object, marked Exhibit A, which I hold?

A—That is a book.

Q—Good. What kind of book is it?

A—It is a minor American classic. Truly a prose epic.

Q—And what kind of document is it?

A—It is a valuable human document.

Q—Very good, Mr. Arbuthnot. Please continue.

A—It is a book in which the results of painstaking—or scholarly—research are embodied and it should interest all thoughtful readers. This reviewer could not put it down.

Q—Why not?

A—Because of its penetrating insight into the ever-present problem of international relationships. It is a sincere and moving study of an American family against the background of a small college town, and it is also a vivid and full-blooded portrayal of the life of that true child of nature, the Southern Negro.

Q—How is it written?

A—It is written with sympathy, pathos, and kindly humor. It throws a clear light on a little-understood subject and is well worth reading.

Q—How is it illustrated?

A—Profusely. It is original in conception, devoid of sentimentality, highly informative, consistently witty, and rich in color. Place it on your required-reading list.

Q—Why?

A—Because it strikes a new note in fiction. Mystery and suspense crowd its pages. The author has done an encyclopedic job of blending fact and fiction, and the result is an authentic drama of social revolution, a definite contribution to proletarian literature, and an important addition to frontier literature.

Q—Told with a wealth of what?

A—Told with a wealth of detail.

Q—And how portrayed?

A—Realistically portrayed, in staccato prose. For sheer brilliance of style there has been nothing like it since "Moby Dick." Rarely does a narrative move at such a fast pace.

Q—What is it a shrewd comment on?

A—The American scene. It marks a red-letter day in American literature. It is capital entertainment.

Q—What pervades it?

A—A faint tinge of irony.

Q—And how is it translated?

A—Ably. It is a penetrating study in abnormal psychology, and unlike most scientific works, it is written in language understandable to the layman. It belongs in the front rank of modern picaresque literature. Ideology.

Q—I beg your pardon?

A—I said ideology. Also catharsis, and nuances of feeling.

Q—What about them?

A—Well, they have to come in somewhere.

Q—I see. Now, to return to the minor American classic, Mr. Arbuthnot. Would you call it a subtle and arresting piece of work?

A—Certainly I would. Why do you suppose I'm an expert in the use of the cliché? I'd also call it an honest attempt to depict, a remarkable first novel, a veritable masterpiece, a genuine contribution to literature, a really fine study in contemporary manners, a thrilling saga of life in frontier days, and the most impressive study of degeneration since Zola. It bids fair to go down as one of the great biographies of all time, including "Moby Dick." In short, it has unusual merit.

Q—How does it augur?

A—It augurs well for the future of the author.

Q—And how does it end?

A—It ends upon a distinct note of despair. It is a work of art.

Q—I'm glad you liked it, Mr. Arbuthnot.

A—Who said I liked it?

Q—Well, didn't you like it?

A—Certainly not.

Q—Why not?

A—Because it is, one fears, mawkishly sentimental and, one regrets, faintly pretentious. It is destructive rather than constructive. Curiously enough, it does not carry conviction. Strangely enough, it lacks depth. Oddly enough, the denouement is weak. It is to be regretted that the title is rather misleading and it need hardly be pointed out that the book as a whole lacks cohesion and sparkle. I am very much afraid, one regrets, that it falls definitely into the hammock school of fiction. And of course, like all first novels, it is autobiographical. Frankly, it doesn't quite come off.

Q—I'm glad you told me. I won't buy it.

A—Ah, but in spite of its faults it contains much of real value, and in the opinion of the present reviewer it would be the long-awaited great American novel except for one serious defect.

Q—What is that?

A—It lacks an index.

Q—Mr. Arbuthnot, it is easy to see that you have earned your spurs in the field of literary criticism. So much for the book. Now, observe this object I hold here in my hand, marked Exhibit B. What is it?

A—That? *That* is an *author.*

Q—Whose are those italics, Mr. Arbuthnot?

A—The italics are mine.

Q—What kind of author is this?

A—A promising young author who will bear watching.

Q—What does he write?

A—Powerful first novels. Or important first novels.

Q—What kind of story-teller is he?

A—He's a born story-teller.

Q—What kind of satirist is he?

A—A satirist of the first order.

Q—Tell us more about this interesting creature.

A—Well, he cannot be lightly dismissed. He is undoubtedly

to be reckoned with, one feels, as a definite force in American literature.

Q—Why?

A—Because his work plainly shows the influence of Joyce, Hemingway, Proust, Gertrude Stein, and Virginia Woolf. Here is an authentic talent from which we may expect great things, for he is a writer of no mean ability and he knows whereof he writes.

Q—So what do you do?

A—So I hail him. And I acclaim him. He has a keen ear for the spoken word. He also has a flair. He sets out to tell. He deals with themes, or handles them. He captures moods. His execution is brilliant, his insight is poetic, his restraint is admirable, and he has a sense of values. He writes hard-bitten, full-bodied, fine-grained novels of the soil, with a telling use of the American language. There is something almost uncanny in his ability to look into men's souls. Not since "Moby Dick" has an American author displayed such a knowledge of human nature. And he paints a vivid word picture and works on a vast canvas.

Q—How?

A—With consummate artistry. He writes with commendable frankness.

Q—Using what kind of style?

A—Using a limpid prose style. He has a real freshness of approach that stamps him as an artist in the true sense of the word. He culls his material, and his niche in the hall of literary fame seems secure.

Q—I'm glad you like him, Mr. Arbuthnot.

A—But I don't.

Q—No? Why not?

A—Because his talent is plainly superficial and ephemeral. He has an unfortunate habit of allowing his personality to obtrude. His book is badly documented, and not the least of his many irritating mannerisms is his addiction to inexcusable typographical errors. His book is full of clichés, and he does not make his characters live and feel and breathe. And he writes with one eye on Hollywood.

Q—You mean to tell me that a cad like that has the audacity to call himself an author?

A—Well, now, don't be too hard on him. Although he decidedly does not justify his early promise, it is as yet too early to evaluate his work. Want to know about the plot?

Q—Yes, indeed. What about the plot?

A—The plot is like Mae West.

Q—I give up. Why?

A—Because it is well rounded and fully developed. But unlike Mae West, it is marred by structural weaknesses.

Q—What kind of structural weaknesses?

A—Inherent structural weaknesses. It is motivated, of course. And its threads are cunningly woven into a harmonious texture by the deft hand of a skilled literary craftsman.

Q—Just one thing more, Mr. Arbuthnot. How many kinds of readers are there?

A—Four: casual, average, gentle, and constant.

Q—Mr. Arbuthnot, I think that about finishes. I can't thank you enough for having come here today to help us out.

A—It has been a pleasure—a vivid, fascinating, significant, vigorous, timely, urbane, breath-taking, mature, adequate, nostalgic, unforgettable, gripping, articulate, engrossing, poignant, and adult pleasure to be of service to you, sir.

Robert Sullivan (Contemporary)

❧ ❧ ❧

Mulligans and Ms. Lewinsky:
An Object Lesson for History

The moment that I first heard about Monica S. Lewinsky I said to myself, well, sure, absolutely, no question about it. I can still, even today, vividly recall an early discussion on this topic between my wife and myself. Luci was just finishing her take on the subject—". . . and another thing, buster, I don't care *what* the Bible says, that kind of behavior outside *this* home means *big* trouble"—when I followed with, "Of course, dear. Goes without saying, dear.

"And you know what, sweetie? Saying that this kind of thing doesn't *count* is precisely the type of wacky distinction our friend Clinton *would* make. It's just like with the mulligans."

My wife, not wanting an explanation, didn't ask for one. But I've thought about this further as time has gone by, and have become ever more firmly convinced: If the President's handlers—not to mention, we—had paid a little closer attention to their man's behavior on the golf course, they would've been more on their toes, and perhaps could've headed off not only impeachment but the Lewinsky mess entire. They could have spared the country a lot of pain back then. With a little watchfulness, we might avoid similar pain in the future.

I had, before Ms. Lewinsky came onstage, been watching President Clinton's game—his golf game—for six years, and while I'd seen his swing improve admirably—particularly the follow-through, which had become high and strong—I had noticed that the fellow had been resolutely unable to conquer his seemingly pathological mulliganitis. What did it say about a man that he just couldn't help but shave strokes, *even when the whole world was watching*? Did it, perhaps, say something dangerous?

Tim Russert, too, wondered about that even before the *scandale*. Russert chatted with the President on the fiftieth anniversary edition of *Meet the Press* in early 1998. First, the host showed results of his program's poll of American attitudes toward Clinton—for instance, that many more of his countrymen pictured the President playing golf (40 percent) than saw him in jogging shorts or even eating at McDonald's; Clinton-as-golfer was second in image only to Clinton-as-saxophone-player (43 percent). This wasn't all that surprising: The President was and always had been an enthusiastic, unapologetic golfer, nothing like the top-secret swinger that his idol, John F. Kennedy, once had been. (JFK, wanting to project a vigorous, energetic persona to the electorate in order to counter the country-club image of Eisenhower, Nixon and Republicans generally, kept his superb game—perhaps the best-ever of a U.S. President—largely in the closet.)

Anyway . . . On *Meet the Press* Russert steered the interview along the curvy roads of domestic policy and foreign affairs. And then, as time wound down, he started tossing softballs. He asked questions about eating, about Martha's Vineyard, about daughter Chelsea and, finally, about golf.

"I've gotten better since being President," said Mr. Clinton, unaware that this was a pretty disquieting thought. "It's mostly because I've gotten to play with better golfers." I was hoping that Russert would follow-up with a question about the President's good friend Greg Norman: What *did* happen at the Shark's house in Hobe Sound, Fla., when Clinton "slipped" on the stairs and broke his foot? (Kenneth Starr subsequently sniffed around for videotapes of the President's Florida visit, and the rumor-mill suggested an extra-Oval-Office assignation with Monica.) But instead, Russert went on to the subject of handicaps. "Twelve, thirteen—something like that," answered the President. With any mulligans? Russert pressed.

Mr. Clinton's eyes went steely. He took one of those pauses of his. He set his chin.

"One, now."

I believed that like I believe in July snow, in winged pigs, in my own ability to stay dry on the 12th hole of Augusta.

For those who are innocent of golf: "Mulligan" is a term that refers to a shot that needn't be counted. It is usually granted by one golfer to another, usually at the first tee, usually after a drive has hooked left, usually into thick forest. The thinking goes, golfers are not yet properly warmed up, so they should be allowed one bad swipe—like a warm-up frame at the bowling alley. The golfer, taking advantage of his mulligan, tees the ball up a second time and proceeds to hit his "first" shot of the day. Clinton was, therefore, putting himself foursquare in the tradition of honorable golf by answering "one, now." That's what an honorable golfer takes, in re. mulligans: one.

But there was, of course, a problem—a credibility problem. In trying to figure out the sitting Presidential handicap for their 1996 book *Presidential Lies: The Illustrated His-*

tory of White House Golf, Shepherd Campbell and Peter Landau wrote: "The answer is clouded by the matter of mulligans, which he uses freely. . . . Clinton admits to one mulligan per round. But others put the number higher. It is said, for instance, that with friends in Little Rock the standard arrangement was for one extra tee shot and two extra fairway shots per nine holes." As we now know, such an arrangement is Little Rock all over.

Do I think the President continued to shave six per 18 throughout his residency at 1600 Pennsylvania? I'm afraid I do, yes.

Once the Lewinsky affair became news, I tried to piece together what I knew about the golf, in order to develop this correlative theory about mulligans and Ms. Lewinsky. I got tapes of the Russert interview, and looked hard at the President's eyes. From the 'Net I pulled the good reporting of CBS News' Mark Knoller, who was to Clinton's golf game what Boswell was to Johnson. If anyone has figured this out, I felt, Knoller will have. The Knoller files turned up a lot of information that was undeniably fascinating, if only marginally useful. Knoller said, for instance, that during Mr. Clinton's 17-day vacation in Jackson Hole, Wyo., in 1995, the President spent 55 hours and 36 minutes playing 206 holes of golf, scoring an average of 85.1, while in 1997 on Martha's Vineyard he spent 48 hours, 31 minutes, playing 180 holes in an average of 82.73 strokes per round. By crunching Knoller's statistics, I learned some fairly certain things about the Presidential game. To wit: that Mr. Clinton's foursome proceeds at a pace of five hours per round, a notion that would have horrified the Presidential predecessor, George Bush, who used to play a shoot-and-scoot game at Kennebunkport that the press termed "polo golf." (GWB and three buddies once completed 18 in an hour, 42 minutes.)

But there were some things about Bill Clinton's game that we simply cannot know, Knoller admitted. The first time the President reported breaking 80 was on a course in San Diego, Knoller told *Sports Illustrated,* "when no one was there to see it." The correspondent pointed out that "the press doesn't have access to most of the holes he plays, so a lot of times I have to take him at his word." Knoller's statistical model was, therefore, intrinsically flawed—Knoller admitted as much. He said rather sadly that when President Clinton claimed a Martha's Vineyard 79 early in his second term, "that was immediately cast into doubt because we saw him take three tee shots on the 1st hole."

When I read those words my first reaction was "eureka!" and my second was sadness. Clearly, the President had not conquered his mulliganitis while in office. Poor, pathetic soul.

Was this, I asked myself, really such a big deal? I sought to take my analysis a step further, I sought to develop some context. I returned to *Presidential Lies* and learned that Lyndon Johnson played a golf game that was wholly constructed around the concept of the mulligan. If LBJ didn't like a shot—any shot—he just dropped a ball and hit another shot. If he didn't like that one, he dropped again.

However, Johnson didn't really care about golf, and never made public his goals. Bill Clinton's longing to break 80 was famous in his first term; it was an object of desire second only to health-care reform (and, we now know, one young intern).

Then too, if you asked LBJ how his game was, vis-a-vis mulligans, he would *not* have replied, "One, now, sonny-boy." He would have given a square answer: "Many as I want, I'm the goddam President!"

I was haunted by the image on my monitor: There sat President Clinton, all but wagging his finger at Tim Russert, all but saying, "I have never, ever had as much as two gimme shots in one round of that game, that game of golf."

I realized then with great clarity that there was, indeed, something serious to be said about Mr. Clinton's mulliganitis—something about duplicity, chronic self-delusion, a genetic incapacity for truth-telling. Also, as directly related to the Lewinsky situation: Something about calling a thing other than what it truly is, in fact calling it in a way that makes it vanish entirely, that makes it *not count*. Poof!—it was never there. Oral sex is not sex and so it goes away, it is erased, it is . . . a mulligan.

But, you see, a golf shot is not a mulligan, it's a golf shot. A golf shot exists to be counted, to be toted on a scorecard. Count it, count 'em all. Similarly, an act which might cause the spouse to shy some crockery at your head—count that too.

That's the narrow moral, which is perhaps finally evident to Mr. Clinton. Perhaps not; I wouldn't bet either way, and it matters little, now, in any event.

As for a more general message that might be of some use to us as a society, as a Union, it is this: Let's pay attention. Bill Clinton's golf game fairly shouted for us to be *en garde,* yet we remained heedless. It was our own fault, as much as his, what happened back then. It should never happen again.

Judy Tenuta (Contemporary)

FROM *The Power of Judyism*

Once I was riding my bike and my mom was waving to me from the window. She said, "Judy, soon your body will change."

I said, "I know—puberty."

She said, "No, that Good Humor truck."

One day . . . my mom chained me to the high chair while my baby sister Blambo was still in it. Nice. I'm flattening my kid sister while Mom is obsessively perm-rodding me. . . . I was transformed into a mini Bride of Frankenstein. Imagine this frizzy-topped freak the night before my very first day of school. . . . That morning I sat in the front yard crying my baby eyes out and Eddie Crader delivered the *Oakleaves* newspaper into my hair. At lunchtime the kids in my class hung me from my feet and whacked my hornet's head with a bat while shouting, "Where's our presents, piñatahead?"

All the great love stories are based on some poor pining plankton who can't pounce on the petite princess of his dreams. Look at *Wuthering Heights*. Do you think for one minute that if Cathy surrendered to Heathcliff he would be half as crazy about her? No way. He was in love with his fantasy of that floozie. Even after Cathy marries some society squid that she doesn't love, Heathcliff pursues her and says, "Cathy, nothing can come between our love; not even you." What a great line. Women the world over dream about such passionate prose from some pumped-up parasite.

Cathy says, "Heathcliff, I'm married. Why did you come after me?"

He says, "Because you willed it."

Could you hemorrhage, heifers?

Heathcliff repeats, "I'm here because you willed it, Cathy." How could she not melt? I'm yelling, "Cathy, you fool, lay down already, loosen your lovesick loins." But Cathy is no fool, she knows that as a true romantic, giving in to love would be the death of lust. So she spurns Heathcliff again and he is even more mental about possessing her.

Why can't we petite flowers in the real world find a passionate love puppy like Heathcliff? Because they do not exist. Neither do Romeos or Othellos. These guys can afford to be passionate about their Juliets and Desdemonas because they don't have to earn a living like every other mortal toad.

Henry David Thoreau (1817–1862)

❧ ❧ ❧

FROM *Journal*

JOURNAL / JUNE 17, 1853

Here have been three ultrareformers, lecturers on Slavery, Temperance, the Church, etc., in and about our house and Mrs. Brooks's the last three or four days—A. D. Foss, once a Baptist minister in Hopkinton, N.H.; Loring Moody, a sort of traveling pattern-working chaplain; and H. C. Wright, who shocks all the old women with his infidel writings. Though Foss was a stranger to the others, you would have thought them old and familiar cronies. (They happened here together by accident.) They addressed each other constantly by their Christian names, and rubbed you continually with the greasy cheeks of their kindness. They would not keep their distance, but cuddle up and lie spoon fashion with you, no matter how hot the weather nor how narrow the bed—chiefly———. I was awfully pestered with his benignity; feared I should get greased all over with it past restoration; tried to keep some starch in my clothes. Wright wrote a book called *A Kiss for a Blow*,* and he behaved as if there were no alternative between these, or as if I had given him a blow. I would have preferred the blow, but he was bent on giving me the kiss, when there was neither quarrel nor agreement between us. I wanted that he should straighten his back, smooth out those ogling wrinkles of benignity about his eyes, and, with a healthy reserve, pronounce something in a downright manner. It was difficult to keep clear in his slimy benignity, with which he sought to cover you before he swallowed you and took you fairly into his bowels.

It would have been far worse than the fate of Jonah. I do not wish to get any nearer to a man's bowels than usual. They lick you as a cow her calf. They would fain wrap you about with their bowels. ——— addressed me as "Henry" within one minute from the time I first laid eyes on him, and when I spoke, he said with drawling, sultry sympathy, "Henry, I know all you would say; I understand you perfectly; you need not explain anything to me"; and to another, "I am going to dive into Henry's inmost depths." I said, "I trust you will not strike your head against the bottom." He could tell in a dark room, with his eyes blinded and in perfect stillness, if there was one there whom he loved. One of the most attractive things about the flowers is their beautiful reserve. The truly beautiful and noble puts its lover, as it were, at an infinite distance, while it attracts him more strongly than ever. I do not like the men who come so near with their bowels. It is the most disagreeable kind of snare to be caught in. Men's bowels are far more slimy than their brains. They must be ascetics indeed who approach you by this side.

*Henry C. Wright, *A Kiss for a Blow; or, A Collection of Stories for Children; Showing Them How to Prevent Quarreling.* Boston: Dow & Jackson, 1842.

What a relief to have heard the ring of one healthy reserved tone! With such a forgiving disposition, as if he were all the while forgiving you for existing. Considering our condition or habit of soul—maybe corpulent and asthmatic—maybe dying of atrophy, with all our bones sticking out—is it kindness to embrace a man? They lay their sweaty hand on your shoulder, or your knee, to magnetize you.

James Thurber and E. B. White
(1896–1961)(1899–1985)

FROM *Is Sex Necessary? Or,*
Why You Feel the Way You Do

The Sexual Revolution

It was the heyday of monogamy, and in order to contemplate marriage, it was necessary for a man to decide on One Particular Woman. This he found next to impossible, for the reason that he had unconsciously set up so many mental barriers and hazards.

Let me mention a few.

The fear that his fiancée might get fat inside of a few years. To any mentally alert man, this thought was a strong deterrent. Quite often the man met the girl's parents. He would quickly size up her mother and make a mental calculation as to how long it would be before the daughter was in the same boat. Somehow, it took the bloom off the romance. . . .

The use of a word, phrase, or punctuation mark by his fiancée that annoyed him. . . .

I am thinking at the moment of the case of a young man who, in his junior year in college, had found the girl he believed ideal for him to marry, and then one day learned,

quite by accident, that she was in the habit of using the word
"Howdy" as a form of salutation. He did not like "Howdy,"
although he did not know why. Days and nights he spent
trying to reconcile himself to the idea of it, weighing the
young lady's extreme beauty and affability against her one
flaw. In the end he decided he could not stomach it, and
broke the troth. . . .

The suspicion that if he waited twenty-four hours, or possibly less, he would likely find a lady even more ideally
suited to his taste than his fiancée. Every man entertained
such a suspicion. Entertained it royally. He was greatly
strengthened in his belief by the fact that he kept catching a
fleeting glimpse of this imaginary person—in restaurants,
in stores, in trains. To deny the possibility of her existence
would be, he felt, to do a grave injustice to her, to himself,
and to his fiancée. Man's unflinching desire to give himself
and everybody else a square deal was the cause of much of
his disturbance.

John Trumbull (1750–1831)

⸙

FROM *The Progress of Dulness,*
1772–1773

A College Education

Two years thus spent in gathering knowledge,
The lad sets forth t'unlade at college,
While down his sire and priest attend him,
To introduce and recommend him;
Or if detain'd, a letter's sent
Of much apocryphal content,
To set him forth, how dull soever,
As very learn'd and very clever;

A genius of first emission,
With burning love for erudition;
So studious he'll outwatch the moon
And think the planets set too soon.
He had but little time to fit in;
Examination too must frighten.
Depend upon't he must do well,
He knows much more than he can tell;
Admit him, and in little space
He'll beat his rivals in the race;
His father's incomes are but small,
He comes now, if he comes at all.

   So said, so done, at college now
He enters well, no matter how;
New scenes awhile his fancy please,
But all must yield to love of ease.
In the same round condemn'd each day,
To study, read, recite and pray;
To make his hours of business double—
He can't endure th' increasing trouble;
And finds at length, as times grow pressing,
All plagues are easier than his lesson.
With sleepy eyes and count'nance heavy,
With much excuse of *non paravi*,
Much absence, *tardes* and *egresses*,
The college-evil on him seizes.
Then ev'ry book, which ought to please,
Stirs up the seeds of dire disease;
Greek spoils his eyes, the print's so fine,
Grown dim with study, or with wine;
Of Tully's Latin much afraid,
Each page, he calls the doctor's aid;
While geometry, with lines so crooked,
Sprains all his wits to overlook it.
His sickness puts on every name
Its cause and uses still the same;
'Tis tooth-ache, cholic, gout or stone,
With phases various as the moon;
But though through all the body spread,
Still makes its cap'tal seat, the head.
In all diseases, 'tis expected,
The weakest parts be most infected.

Mark Twain (1835–1910)

❧

Speech on the Babies

[At the banquet, in Chicago, given by the army of the Tennessee to their first commander, General U. S. Grant, November 1879. The fifteenth regular toast was "The Babies—as they comfort us in our sorrows, let us not forget them in our festivities."]

I like that. We have not all had the good fortune to be ladies. We have not all been generals, or poets, or statesmen; but when the toast works down to the babies, we stand on common ground. It is a shame that for a thousand years the world's banquets have utterly ignored the baby, as if he didn't amount to anything. If you will stop and think a minute—if you will go back fifty or one hundred years to your early married life, and recontemplate your first baby—you will remember that he amounted to a good deal, and even something over. You soldiers all know that when that little fellow arrived at family headquarters you had to hand in your resignation. He took entire command. You became his lackey, his mere body-servant, and you had to stand around too. He was not a commander who made allowances for time, distance, weather, or anything else. You had to execute his orders whether it was possible or not. And there was only one form of marching in his manual of tactics, and that was the double-quick. He treated you with every sort of insolence and disrespect, and the bravest of you didn't dare say a word. You could face the death-storm at Donelson and Vicksburg, and give back blow for blow; but when he clawed your whiskers, and pulled your hair, and twisted your nose, you had to take it. When the thunders of war were sounding in your ears, you set your faces toward the batteries and advanced with steady tread; but when he turned on the terrors of his war-whoop, you advanced in the other direction, and mighty glad of the chance too. When he called for soothing-syrup, did you venture to throw out any side remarks about certain services being unbecoming an officer and a gentleman? No. You got up and *got* it. When he ordered his pap-bottle, and it was not warm, did you talk back? Not you. You went to work and *warmed* it. You even descended so far in your menial office as to take a suck at that warm, insipid stuff yourself, to see if it was right—three parts water to one of milk, and a touch of sugar to modify the colic, and a drop of peppermint to kill those immortal hiccoughs. I can taste the stuff yet. And how many things you learned as you went along! Sentimental young folks still take stock in that beautiful old saying, that when the baby smiles in his sleep, it is because the angels are whispering to him. Very pretty, but too thin—simply wind on the stomach, my friends. If the baby proposed to take a walk at his usual hour, two o'clock in the morning, didn't you rise up promptly and remark, with a mental addition which would not improve a Sunday-school book *much*, that that was the very thing you were about to propose yourself?

Oh! you were under good discipline, and as you went fluttering up and down the room in your undress uniform, you not only prattled undignified baby-talk, but even turned up your martial voices and tried to *sing*!—"Rock-a-by baby in the tree-top," for instance. What a spectacle for an army of the Tennessee! And what an affliction for the neighbours, too; for it is not everybody within a mile around that likes military music at three in the morning. And when you had been keeping this sort of thing up two or three hours, and your little velvet-head intimated that nothing suited him like exercise and noise, what did you do? ("Go on!") You simply *went* on until you dropped in the last ditch. The idea that a *baby* doesn't *amount* to anything! Why, *one* baby is just a house and a front yard full by itself. *One* baby can furnish more business than you and your whole Interior Department can attend to. He is enterprising, irrepressible, brimful of lawless activities. Do what you please, you can't make him stay on the reservation. Sufficient unto the day is one baby. As long as you are in your right mind don't you ever pray for twins. Twins amount to a permanent riot, and there ain't any real difference between triplets and an insurrection.

Yes, it was high time for a toast-master to recognise the importance of the babies. Think what is in store for the present crop! Fifty years from now we shall all be dead, I trust, and then this flag, if it still survive (and let us hope it may), will be floating over a Republic numbering 200,000,000 souls, according to the settled laws of our increase. Our present schooner of State will have grown into a political leviathan—a *Great Eastern*. The cradled babies of to-day will be on deck. Let them be well trained, for we are going to leave a big contract on their hands.

Among the three or four million cradles now rocking in the land are some which this nation would preserve for ages as sacred things, if we could know which ones they are. In one of these cradles the unconscious Farragut of the future is at this moment teething—think of it!—and putting in a world of dead earnest, unarticulated, but perfectly justifiable profanity over it, too. In another the future renowned astronomer is blinking at the shining Milky Way with but a languid interest—poor little chap!—and wondering what has become of that other one they call the wet-nurse. In another the future great historian is lying—and doubtless will continue to lie until his earthly mission is ended. In another the future president is busying himself with no profounder problem of state than what the mischief has become of his hair so early; and in a mighty array of other cradles there are now some 60,000 future office-seekers, getting ready to furnish him occasion to grapple with that same old problem a second time. And in still one more cradle, somewhere under the flag, the future illustrious commander-in-chief of the American armies is so little burdened with his approaching grandeurs and responsibilities as to be giving his whole strategic mind at this moment to trying to find out some way to get his big toe into his mouth—an achievement which, meaning no disrespect, the illustrious guest of this evening turned *his* entire attention to some fifty-six years ago; and if the child is but a prophecy of the man, there are mighty few who will doubt that he *succeeded*.

Fenimore Cooper's Literary Offenses

The Pathfinder and *The Deerslayer* stand at the head of Cooper's novels as artistic creations. There are others of his works which contain parts as perfect as are to be found in these, and scenes even more thrilling. Not one can be compared with either of them as a finished whole.

The defects in both of these tales are comparatively slight. They were pure works of art. *Prof. Lounsbury.*

The five tales reveal an extraordinary fullness of invention.

. . . One of the very greatest characters in fiction, Natty Bumppo. . . .

The craft of the woodsman, the tricks of the trapper, all the delicate art of the forest, were familiar to Cooper from his youth up. *Prof. Brander Matthews.*

Cooper is the greatest artist in the domain of romantic fiction yet produced by America. *Wilkie Collins.*

It seems to me that it was far from right for the Professor of English Literature in Yale, the Professor of English Literature in Columbia, and Wilkie Collins to deliver opinions on Cooper's literature without having read some of it. It would have been much more decorous to keep silent and let persons talk who have read Cooper.

Cooper's art has some defects. In one place in *Deerslayer*, and in the restricted space of two-thirds of a page, Cooper has scored 114 offenses against literary art out of a possible 115. It breaks the record.

There are nineteen rules governing literary art in the domain of romantic fiction—some say twenty-two. In *Deerslayer* Cooper violated eighteen of them. These eighteen require:

1. That a tale shall accomplish something and arrive somewhere. But the *Deerslayer* tale accomplishes nothing and arrives in the air.

2. They require that the episodes of a tale shall be necessary parts of the tale, and shall help to develop it. But as the

Deerslayer tale is not a tale, and accomplishes nothing and arrives nowhere, the episodes have no rightful place in the work, since there was nothing for them to develop.

3. They require that the personages in a tale shall be alive, except in the case of corpses, and that always the reader shall be able to tell the corpses from the others. But this detail has often been overlooked in the *Deerslayer* tale.

4. They require that the personages in a tale, both dead and alive, shall exhibit a sufficient excuse for being there. But this detail also has been overlooked in the *Deerslayer* tale.

5. They require that when the personages of a tale deal in conversation, the talk shall sound like human talk, and be talk such as human beings would be likely to talk in the given circumstances, and have a discoverable meaning, also a discoverable purpose, and a show of relevancy, and remain in the neighborhood of the subject in hand, and be interesting to the reader, and help out the tale, and stop when the people cannot think of anything more to say. But this requirement has been ignored from the beginning of the *Deerslayer* tale to the end of it.

6. They require that when the author describes the character of a personage in his tale, the conduct and conversation of that personage shall justify said description. But this law gets little or no attention in the *Deerslayer* tale, as Natty Bumppo's case will amply prove.

7. They require that when a personage talks like an illustrated, gilt-edged, tree-calf, hand-tooled, seven-dollar Friendship's Offering in the beginning of a paragraph, he shall not talk like a negro minstrel in the end of it. But this rule is flung down and danced upon in the *Deerslayer* tale.

8. They require that crass stupidities shall not be played upon the reader as "the craft of the woodsman, the delicate art of the forest," by either the author or the people in the tale. But this rule is persistently violated in the *Deerslayer* tale.

9. They require that the personages of a tale shall confine themselves to possibilities and let miracles alone; or, if they venture a miracle, the author must so plausibly set it forth as to make it look possible and reasonable. But these rules are not respected in the *Deerslayer* tale.

10. They require that the author shall make the reader feel a deep interest in the personages of his tale and in their fate;

and that he shall make the reader love the good people in the tale and hate the bad ones. But the reader of the *Deerslayer* tale dislikes the good people in it, is indifferent to the others, and wishes they would all get drowned together.

11. They require that the characters in a tale shall be so clearly defined that the reader can tell beforehand what each will do in a given emergency. But in the *Deerslayer* tale this rule is vacated.

In addition to these large rules there are some little ones. These require that the author shall

12. *Say* what he is proposing to say, not merely come near it.

13. Use the right word, not its second cousin.

14. Eschew surplusage.

15. Not omit necessary details.

16. Avoid slovenliness of form.

17. Use good grammar.

18. Employ a simple and straightforward style.

Even these seven are coldly and persistently violated in the *Deerslayer* tale.

Cooper's gift in the way of invention was not a rich endowment; but such as it was he liked to work it, he was pleased with the effects, and indeed he did some quite sweet things with it. In his little box of stage-properties he kept six or eight cunning devices, tricks, artifices for his savages and woodsmen to deceive and circumvent each other with, and he was never so happy as when he was working these innocent things and seeing them go. A favorite one was to make a moccasined person tread in the tracks of the moccasined enemy, and thus hide his own trail. Cooper wore out barrels and barrels of moccasins in working that trick. Another stage-property that he pulled out of his box pretty frequently was his broken twig. He prized his broken twig above all the rest of his effects, and worked it the hardest. It is a restful chapter in any book of his when somebody doesn't step on a dry twig and alarm all the reds and whites for two hundred yards around. Every time a Cooper person is in peril, and absolute silence is worth four dollars a minute, he is sure to step on a dry twig. There may be a hundred handier things to step on, but that wouldn't satisfy Cooper. Cooper requires him to turn out and find a dry twig;

and if he can't do it, go and borrow one. In fact, the Leather-stocking Series ought to have been called the Broken Twig Series.

I am sorry there is not room to put in a few dozen instances of the delicate art of the forest, as practised by Natty Bumppo and some of the other Cooperian experts. Perhaps we may venture two or three samples. Cooper was a sailor—a naval officer; yet he gravely tells us how a vessel, driving toward a lee shore in a gale, is steered for a particular spot by her skipper because he knows of an *undertow* there which will hold her back against the gale and save her. For just pure woodcraft, or sailorcraft, or whatever it is, isn't that neat? For several years Cooper was daily in the society of artillery, and he ought to have noticed that when a cannon-ball strikes the ground it either buries itself or skips a hundred feet or so; skips again a hundred feet or so—and so on, till finally it gets tired and rolls. Now in one place he loses some "females"—as he always calls women—in the edge of a wood near a plain at night in a fog, on purpose to give Bumppo a chance to show off the delicate art of the forest before the reader. These mislaid people are hunting for a fort. They hear a cannon-blast, and a cannon-ball presently comes rolling into the wood and stops at their feet. To the females this suggests nothing. The case is very different with the admirable Bumppo. I wish I may never know peace again if he doesn't strike out promptly and *follow the track* of that cannon-ball across the plain through the dense fog and find the fort. Isn't it a daisy? If Cooper had any real knowledge of Nature's ways of doing things, he had a most delicate art in concealing the fact. For instance: one of his acute Indian experts, Chingachgook (pronounced Chicago, I think), has lost the trail of a person he is tracking through the forest. Apparently that trail is hopelessly lost. Neither you nor I could ever have guessed out the way to find it. It was very different with Chicago. Chicago was not stumped for long. He turned a running stream out of its course, and there, in the slush in its old bed, were that person's moccasin tracks. The current did not wash them away, as it would have done in all other cases—no, even the eternal laws of Nature have to vacate when Cooper wants to put up a delicate job of woodcraft on the reader.

We must be a little wary when Brander Matthews tells us

that Cooper's books "reveal an extraordinary fullness of invention." As a rule, I am quite willing to accept Brander Matthews's literary judgments and applaud his lucid and graceful phrasing of them; but that particular statement needs to be taken with a few tons of salt. Bless your heart, Cooper hadn't any more invention than a horse; and I don't mean a high-class horse, either; I mean a clothes-horse. It would be very difficult to find a really clever "situation" in Cooper's books, and still more difficult to find one of any kind which he has failed to render absurd by his handling of it. Look at the episodes of "the caves"; and at the celebrated scuffle between Magua and those others on the table-land a few days later; and at Hurry Harry's queer water-transit from the castle to the ark; and at Deerslayer's half-hour with his first corpse; and at the quarrel between Hurry Harry and Deerslayer later; and at—but choose for yourself; you can't go amiss.

If Cooper had been an observer his inventive faculty would have worked better; not more interestingly, but more rationally, more plausibly. Cooper's proudest creations in the way of "situations" suffer noticeably from the absence of the observer's protecting gift. Cooper's eye was splendidly inaccurate. Cooper seldom saw anything correctly. He saw nearly all things as through a glass eye, darkly. Of course a man who cannot see the commonest little everyday matters accurately is working at a disadvantage when he is constructing a "situation." In the *Deerslayer* tale Cooper has a stream which is fifty feet wide where it flows out of a lake; it presently narrows to twenty as it meanders along for no given reason, and yet when a stream acts like that it ought to be required to explain itself. Fourteen pages later the width of the brook's outlet from the lake has suddenly shrunk thirty feet, and become "the narrowest part of the stream." This shrinkage is not accounted for. The stream has bends in it, a sure indication that it has alluvial banks and cuts them; yet these bends are only thirty and fifty feet long. If Cooper had been a nice and punctilious observer he would have noticed that the bends were oftener nine hundred feet long than short of it.

Cooper made the exit of that stream fifty feet wide, in the first place, for no particular reason; in the second place, he narrowed it to less than twenty to accommodate some Indians. He bends a "sapling" to the form of an arch over this narrow passage, and conceals six Indians in its foliage. They are "laying" for a settler's scow or ark which is coming up the stream on its way to the lake; it is being hauled against the stiff current by a rope whose stationary end is anchored in the lake; its rate of progress cannot be more than a mile an hour. Cooper describes the ark, but pretty obscurely. In the matter of dimensions "it was little more than a modern canal-boat." Let us guess, then, that it was about one hundred and forty feet long. It was of "greater breadth than common." Let us guess, then, that it was about sixteen feet wide. This leviathan had been prowling down bends which were but a third as long as itself, and scraping between banks where it had only two feet of space to spare on each side. We cannot too much admire this miracle. A low-roofed log dwelling occupies "two-thirds of the ark's length"—a dwelling ninety feet long and sixteen feet wide, let us say—a kind of vestibule train. The dwelling has two rooms—each forty-five feet long and sixteen feet wide, let us guess. One of them is the bedroom of the Hutter girls, Judith and Hetty; the other is the parlor in the daytime, at night it is papa's bedchamber. The ark is arriving at the stream's exit now, whose width has been reduced to less than twenty feet to accommodate the Indians—say to eighteen. There is a foot to spare on each side of the boat. Did the Indians notice that there was going to be a tight squeeze there? Did they notice that they could make money by climbing down out of that arched sapling and just stepping aboard when the ark scraped by? No, other Indians would have noticed these things, but Cooper's Indians never notice anything. Cooper thinks they are marvelous creatures for noticing, but he was almost always in error about his Indians. There was seldom a sane one among them.

The ark is one hundred and forty-feet long; the dwelling is ninety feet long. The idea of the Indians is to drop softly and secretly from the arched sapling to the dwelling as the ark creeps along under it at the rate of a mile an hour, and butcher the family. It will take the ark a minute and a half to pass under. It will take the ninety-foot dwelling a minute to pass under. Now, then, what did the six Indians do? It would take you thirty years to guess, and even then you would have to give it up, I believe. Therefore, I will tell you what the Indians did. Their chief, a person of quite extraordinary intellect for a Cooper Indian, warily watched the canal-boat as it squeezed along under him, and when he had got his calculations fined down to exactly the right shade, as he judged, he let go and dropped. And *missed the house*! That is actually what he did. He missed the house, and landed in the stern of the scow. It was not much of a fall, yet it knocked him silly. He lay there unconscious. If the house had been ninety-seven feet long he would have made the trip. The fault was Cooper's not his. The error lay in the construction of the house. Cooper was no architect.

There still remained in the roost five Indians. The boat has passed under and is now out of their reach. Let me explain what the five did—you would not be able to reason it out for yourself. No. 1 jumped for the boat, but fell in the water astern of it. Then No. 2 jumped for the boat, but fell in the water still farther astern of it. Then No. 3 jumped for the boat, and fell a good way astern of it. Then No. 4 jumped for the boat, and fell in the water *away* astern. Then even No. 5 made a jump for the boat—for he was a Cooper Indian. In the matter of intellect, the difference between a Cooper Indian and the Indian that stands in front of a cigar-shop is not spacious. The scow episode is really a sublime burst of invention; but it does not thrill, because the inaccuracy of the details throws a sort of air of factitiousness and general improbability over it. This comes of Cooper's inadequacy as an observer.

The reader will find some examples of Cooper's high talent for inaccurate observation in the account of the shooting-match in *The Pathfinder*.

A common wrought nail was driven lightly into the target, its head having been first touched with paint.

The color of the paint is not stated—an important omission, but Cooper deals freely in important omissions. No, after all, it was not an important omission; for this nail-head is a *hundred yards from* the marksmen, and could not be seen by them at that distance, no matter what its color might be. How far can the best eyes see a common house-fly? A hundred yards? It is quite impossible. Very well; eyes that cannot see a house-fly that is a hundred yards away cannot see an ordinary nail-head at that distance, for the size of the two objects is the same. It takes a keen eye to see a fly or a nail-head at fifty yards—one hundred and fifty feet. Can the reader do it?

The nail was lightly driven, its head painted, and game called. Then the Cooper miracles began. The bullet of the first marksman chipped an edge of the nail-head; the next man's bullet drove the nail a little way into the target—and removed all the paint. Haven't the miracles gone far enough now? Not to suit Cooper; for the purpose of this whole scheme is to show off his prodigy, Deerslayer-Hawkeye-Long-Rifle-Leatherstocking-Pathfinder-Bumppo before the ladies.

"Be all ready to clench it, boys!" cried the Pathfinder, stepping into his friend's tracks the instant they were vacant. "Never mind a new nail; I can see that, though the paint is gone, and what I can see I can hit at a hundred yards, though it were only a mosquito's eye. Be ready to clench!"

The rifle cracked, the bullet sped its way, and the head of the nail was buried in the wood, covered by the piece of flattened lead.

There, you see, is a man who could hunt flies with a rifle, and command a ducal salary in a Wild West show today if we had him back with us.

The recorded feat is certainly surprising just as it stands; but it is not surprising enough for Cooper. Cooper adds a touch. He has made Pathfinder do this miracle with another man's rifle; and not only that, but Pathfinder did not have even the advantage of loading it himself. He had everything against him, and yet he made that impossible shot; and not only made it, but did it with absolute confidence, saying, "Be ready to clench." Now a person like that would have undertaken that same feat with a brickbat, and with Cooper to help he would have achieved it, too.

Pathfinder showed off handsomely that day before the ladies. His very first feat was a thing which no Wild West show can touch. He was standing with the group of marksmen, observing—a hundred yards from the target, mind; one Jasper raised his rifle and drove the center of the bull's-eye. Then the Quartermaster fired. The target exhibited no result this time. There was a laugh. "It's a dead miss," said Major Lundie. Pathfinder waited an impressive moment or two; then said, in that calm, indifferent, know-it-all way of his, "No, Major, he has covered Jasper's bullet, as will be seen if any one will take the trouble to examine the target."

Wasn't it remarkable! How *could* he see that little pellet fly through the air and enter that distant bullet-hole? Yet that is what he did; for nothing is impossible to a Cooper person. Did any of those people have any deep-seated doubts about this thing? No; for that would imply sanity, and these were all Cooper people.

The respect for Pathfinder's skill and for his *quickness and accuracy of sight* [the italics are mine] was so profound and general, that the instant he made this declaration the spectators began to distrust their own opinions, and a dozen rushed to the target in order to ascertain the fact. There, sure enough, it was found that the Quartermaster's bullet had gone through the hole made by Jasper's, and that, too, so accurately as to require a minute examination to be certain of the circumstance, which, however, was soon clearly established by discovering one bullet over the other in the stump against which the target was placed.

They made a "minute" examination; but never mind, how could they know that there were two bullets in that hole without digging the latest one out? for neither probe nor eyesight could prove the presence of any more than one bullet. Did they dig? No; as we shall see. It is the Pathfinder's turn now; he steps out before the ladies, takes aim, and fires.

"If one dared to hint at such a thing," cried Major Duncan, "I should say that the Pathfinder has also missed the target!"

As nobody had missed it yet, the "also" was not necessary; but never mind about that, for the Pathfinder is going to speak.

"No, no, Major," said he, confidently, "that *would* be a risky declaration. I didn't load the piece, and can't say what was in it; but if it was lead, you will find the bullet driving down those of the Quartermaster and Jasper, else is not my name Pathfinder."

A shout from the target announced the truth of this assertion.

Is the miracle sufficient as it stands? Not for Cooper. The Pathfinder speaks again, as he "now slowly advances toward the stage occupied by the females":

"That's not all, boys, that's not all; if you find the target touched at all, I'll own a miss. The Quartermaster cut the wood, but you'll find no wood cut by that last messenger."

The miracle is at last complete. He knew—doubtless *saw*—at the distance of a hundred yards—that his bullet had passed into the hole *without fraying the edges*. There were now three bullets in that one hole—three bullets embedded processionally in the body of the stump back of the target. Everybody knew this—somehow or other—and yet nobody had dug any of them out to make sure. Cooper is not a close observer, but he is interesting. He is certainly always that, no matter what happens. And he is more interesting when he is not noticing what he is about than when he is. This is a considerable merit.

The conversations in the Cooper books have a curious sound in our modern ears. To believe that such talk really ever came out of people's mouths would be to believe that there was a time when time was of no value to a person who thought he had something to say; when it was the custom to spread a two-minute remark out to ten; when a man's mouth was a rolling-mill, and busied itself all day long in turning four-foot pigs of thought into thirty-foot bars of conversational railroad iron by attenuation; when subjects were seldom faithfully stuck to, but the talk wandered all around and arrived nowhere; when conversations consisted mainly of irrelevancies, with here and there a relevancy, a relevancy with an embarrassed look, as not being able to explain how it got there.

Cooper was certainly not a master in the construction of dialogue. Inaccurate observation defeated him here as it defeated him in so many other enterprises of his. He even failed to notice that the man who talks corrupt English six days in the week must and will talk it on the seventh, and

can't help himself. In the *Deerslayer* story he lets Deerslayer talk the showiest kind of book-talk sometimes, and at
other times the basest of base dialects. For instance, when
some one asks him if he has a sweetheart, and if so, where
she abides, this is his majestic answer:

"She's in the forest—hanging from the boughs of the
trees, in a soft rain—in the dew on the open grass—the
clouds that float about in the blue heavens—the birds that
sing in the woods—the sweet springs where I slake my
thirst—and in all the other glorious gifts that come from
God's Providence!"

And he preceded that, a little before, with this:

"It consarns me as all things that touches a fri'nd consarns a fri'nd."

And this is another of his remarks:

"If I was Injin born, now, I might tell of this, or carry in
the scalp and boast of the expl'ite afore the whole tribe; or if
my inimy had only been a bear"—[and so on].

We cannot imagine such a thing as a veteran Scotch
Commander-in-Chief comporting himself in the field like a
windy melodramatic actor, but Cooper could. On one occasion Alice and Cora were being chased by the French
through a fog in the neighborhood of their father's fort:

"Point de quartier aux coquins!" cried an eager pursuer,
who seemed to direct the operations of the enemy.
"Stand firm and be ready, my gallant 60ths!" suddenly
exclaimed a voice above them; "wait to see the enemy; fire
low, and sweep the glacis."
"Father! father!" exclaimed a piercing cry from out the
mist; "it is I! Alice! thy own Elsie! spare, O! save your
daughters!"
"Hold!" shouted the former speaker, in the awful tones of
parental agony, the sound reaching even to the woods, and
rolling back in solemn echo. " 'Tis she! God has restored

me my children! Throw open the sally-port; to the field, 60ths, to the field! pull not a trigger, lest ye kill my lambs! Drive off these dogs of France with your steel!"

Cooper's word-sense was singularly dull. When a person has a poor ear for music he will flat and sharp right along without knowing it. He keeps near the tune, but it is *not* the tune. When a person has a poor ear for words, the result is a literary flatting and sharping; you perceive what he is intending to say, but you also perceive that he doesn't *say* it. This is Cooper. He was not a word-musician. His ear was satisfied with the *approximate* word. I will furnish some circumstantial evidence in support of this charge. My instances are gathered from half a dozen pages of the tale called *Deerslayer*. He uses "verbal" for "oral"; "precision" for "facility"; "phenomena" for "marvels"; "necessary" for "predetermined"; "unsophisticated" for "primitive"; "preparation" for "expectancy"; "rebuked" for "subdued"; "dependent on" for "resulting from"; "fact" for "condition"; "fact" for "conjecture"; "precaution" for "caution"; "explain" for "determine"; "mortified" for "disappointed"; "meretricious" for "factitious"; "materially" for "considerably"; "decreasing" for "deepening"; "increasing" for "disappearing"; "embedded" for "inclosed"; "treacherous" for "hostile"; "stood" for "stooped"; "softened" for "replaced"; "rejoined" for "remarked"; "situation" for "condition"; "different" for "differing"; "insensible" for "unsentient"; "brevity" for "celerity"; "distrusted" for "suspicious"; "mental imbecility" for "imbecility"; "eyes" for "sight"; "counteracting" for "opposing"; "funeral obsequies" for "obsequies."

There have been daring people in the world who claimed that Cooper could write English, but they are all dead now—all dead but Lounsbury. I don't remember that Lounsbury makes the claim in so many words, still he makes it, for he says that *Deerslayer* is a "pure work of art." Pure, in that connection, means faultless—faultless in all details—and language is a detail. If Mr. Lounsbury had only compared Cooper's English with the English which he writes himself—but it is plain that he didn't; and so it is likely that he imagines until this day that Cooper's is as clean and compact as his own. Now I feel sure, deep down in my heart, that Cooper wrote about the poorest English that exists in our language, and that the English of *Deer-slayer* is the very worst that even Cooper ever wrote.

I may be mistaken, but it does seem to me that *Deerslayer* is not a work of art in any sense; it does seem to me that it is destitute of every detail that goes to the making of a work of art; in truth, it seems to me that *Deerslayer* is just simply a literary *delirium tremens*.

A work of art? It has no invention; it has no order, system, sequence, or result; it has no life-likeness, no thrill, no stir, no seeming of reality; its characters are confusedly drawn, and by their acts and words they prove that they are not the sort of people the author claims they are; its humor is pathetic; its pathos is funny; its conversations are—oh! indescribable; its love-scenes odious; its English a crime against the language.

Counting these out, what is left is Art. I think we must all admit that.

A Cooper Indian who has been washed is a poor thing, and commonplace; it is the Cooper Indian in his paint that thrills. Cooper's extra words are Cooper's paint—his paint, his feathers, his tomahawk, his warwhoop.

In the two-thirds of a page elsewhere referred to, wherein Cooper scored 114 literary transgressions out of a possible 115, he appears before us with all his things on. As follows, the italics are mine—they indicate violations of Rule 14:

In a minute he was once fastened to the tree, *a helpless object of any insult or wrong that might be offered. So eagerly did every one now act, that nothing was said.* The fire was immediately lighted *in the pile, and the end of all was anxiously expected.*

It was not the intention of the Hurons *absolutely* to destroy *the life of* their victim by *means of* fire. They designed merely to put his *physical* fortitude to the severest proofs it could endure, short of that extremity. In the end, they fully intended to carry his scalp into their village, but it was their wish first to break down his resolution, and to reduce him to *the level of* a complaining sufferer. With this view, the pile of brush *and branches* had been placed at a *proper* distance, *or one* at which it was thought the heat would soon become intolerable, though *it might* not *be* immediately dangerous. *As often happened, however, on these occasions,* this distance had been miscalculated, and the flames *began to wave their forked tongues in a proximity to the face of the victim that* would have proved fatal in another instant had not Hetty rushed through the crowd, armed with a stick, and scattered the blazing pile *in a dozen directions*. More than one hand was raised to strike the *presumptuous* intruder to the earth; but the chiefs prevented the blows by reminding their *irritated* followers of the state of her mind. Hetty, herself, was insensible to the risk she ran; but, *as soon as she had performed this bold act, she* stood looking about her in frowning resentment, as if to rebuke the *crowd of attentive savages for their cruelty.*

'God bless you, dear*est sister,* for that brave and ready act,' murmured Judith, *herself unnerved so much as to be incapable of exertion;* 'Heaven itself has sent you on its holy errand.'

Number of words, 320; necessary ones, 220; words wasted by the generous spendthrift, 100.

In our day those 100 unnecessary words would have to come out. We will take them out presently and make the episode approximate the modern requirement in the matter of compression.

If we may consider each unnecessary word in Cooper's report of that barbecue a separate and individual violation of Rule 14, then that rule is violated 100 times in that report. Other rules are violated in it. Rule 12, two instances;[1] Rule 13, three instances;[2] Rule 15, one instance;[3] Rule 16, two instances;[4] Rule 17, one or two little instances;[5] the Report in its entirety is an offense against Rule 18[6]—also against Rule 16. Total score, about 114 violations of the laws of literary art out of a possible 115.

Let us now bring forward the Report again, with the most

---

[1] Rule 12: "*Say* what he is proposing to say, not merely come near it."

[2] Rule 13: "Use the right word, not its second cousin."

[3] Rule 15: "Not omit necessary details."

[4] Rule 16: "Avoid slovenliness of forms."

[5] Rule 17: "Use good grammar."

[6] Rule 18: "Employ a simple and straightforward style."

of the unnecessary words knocked out. By departing from
Cooper's style and manner, all the facts could be put into
150 words, and the effects heightened at the same time—
this is manifest, of course—but that would not be desirable.
We must stick to Cooper's language as closely as we can:

In a minute he was once more fastened to the tree. The
fire was immediately lighted. It was not the intention of the
Hurons to destroy Deerslayer's life by fire; they designed
merely to put his fortitude to the severest proofs it could endure short of that extremity. In the end, they fully intended
to take his life, but it was their wish first to break down his
resolution and reduce him to a complaining sufferer. With
this view the pile of brush had been placed at a distance at
which it was thought the heat would soon become intolerable, without being immediately dangerous. But this distance had been miscalculated; the fire was so close to the
victim that he would have been fatally burned in another instant if Hetty had not rushed through the crowd and scattered the brands with a stick. More than one Indian raised
his hand to strike her down but the chiefs saved her by reminding them of the state of her mind. Hetty herself was insensible to the risk she ran; she stood looking about her in
frowning resentment, as if to rebuke the savages for their
cruelty.

'God bless you, dear!' cried Judith, 'for that brave and
ready act. Heaven itself has sent you on its holy errand, and
you shall have a chromo.'

Number of words, 220—and the facts are all in.

II

Young Gentlemen: In studying Cooper you will find it
profitable to study him in detail—word by word, sentence
by sentence. For every sentence of his is interesting. Interesting because of its make-up; its peculiar make-up, its
original make-up. Let us examine a sentence or two, and
see. Here is a passage from Chapter XI of *The Last of the
Mohicans*, one of the most famous and most admired of
Cooper's books:

*   *   *

Notwithstanding the swiftness of their flight, one of the Indians had found an opportunity to strike a straggling fawn with an arrow, and had borne the more preferable fragments of the victim, patiently on his shoulders, to the stopping-place. Without any aid from the science of cookery, he was immediately employed in common with his fellows, in gorging himself with this digestible sustenance. Magua alone sat apart, without participating in the revolting meal, and apparently buried in the deepest thought.

This little paragraph is full of matter for reflection and inquiry. The remark about the swiftness of the flight was unnecessary, as it was merely put in to forestall the possible objection of some over-particular reader that the Indian couldn't have found the needed "opportunity" while fleeing swiftly. The reader would not have made that objection. He would care nothing about having that small matter explained and justified. But that is Cooper's way; frequently he will explain and justify little things that do not need it and then make up for this by as frequently failing to explain important ones that do need it. For instance he allowed that astute and cautious person, Deerslayer-Hawkeye, to throw his rifle heedlessly down and leave it lying on the ground where some hostile Indians would presently be sure to find it—a rifle prized by that person above all things else in the earth—and the reader gets no word of explanation of that strange act. There was a reason, but it wouldn't bear exposure. Cooper meant to get a fine dramatic effect out of the finding of the rifle by the Indians, and he accomplished this at the happy time; but all the same, Hawkeye could have hidden the rifle in a quarter of a minute where the Indians could not have found it. Cooper couldn't think of any way to explain why Hawkeye didn't do that, so he just shirked the difficulty and did not explain at all. In another place Cooper allowed Heyward to shoot at an Indian with a pistol that wasn't loaded—and grants us not a word of explanation to how the man did it.

No, the remark about the swiftness of their flight was not necessary; neither was the one which said that the Indian found an opportunity; neither was the one which said he *struck* the fawn; neither was the one which explained that it was a "straggling" fawn; neither was the one which said the striking was done with an arrow; neither was the one which said the Indian bore the "fragments"; nor the remark that they were preferable fragments; nor the remark that they were *more* preferable fragments; nor the explanation that they were fragments of the "victim"; nor the over-particular explanation that specifies the Indian's "shoulders" as the part of him that supported the fragments; nor the statement that the Indian bore the fragments patiently. None of those details has any value. We don't care what the Indian struck the fawn with; we don't care whether it was a straggling fawn or an unstraggling one; we don't care which fragments the Indian saved; we don't care why he saved the "more" preferable ones when the merely preferable ones would have amounted to just the same thing and couldn't have been told from the more preferable ones by anybody, dead or alive; we don't care whether the Indian carried them on his shoulders or in his handkerchief; and finally, we don't care whether he carried them patiently or struck for higher pay and shorter hours. We are indifferent to that Indian and all his affairs.

There was only one fact in that long sentence that was worth stating, and it could have been squeezed into these few words—and with advantage to the narrative, too:

"During the flight one of the Indians had killed a fawn, and he brought it into camp." You will notice that "During the flight one of the Indians had killed a fawn and he brought it into camp," is more straightforward and business-like, and less mincing and smirky, than it is to say "Not-withstanding the swiftness of their flight, one of the Indians had found an opportunity to strike a straggling fawn with an arrow, and had borne the more preferable fragments of the victim, patiently on his shoulders, to the stopping-place." You will notice that the form "During the flight one of the Indians had killed a fawn and he brought it into camp" holds up its chin and moves to the front with the steady stride of a grenadier, whereas the form "Notwithstanding the swiftness of their flight, one of the Indians had found an opportunity to strike a straggling fawn with an arrow, and had borne the more preferable fragments of the victim, patiently on his shoulders, to the stopping-place," simpers along with an airy, complacent, monkey-with-a-parasol gait which is not suited to the transportation of raw meat.

I beg to remind you that an author's way of setting forth a matter is called his Style, and that an author's style is a main part of his equipment for business. The style of some authors has variety in it, but Cooper's style is remarkable for the absence of this feature. Cooper's style is always grand and stately and noble. Style may be likened to an army, the author to its general, the book to the campaign. Some authors proportion an attacking force to the strength or weakness, the importance or unimportance, of the object to be attacked; but Cooper doesn't. It doesn't make any difference to Cooper whether the object of attack is a hundred thousand men or a cow; he hurls his entire force against it. He comes thundering down with all his battalions at his back, cavalry in the van, artillery on the flanks, infantry massed in the middle, forty bands braying, a thousand banners streaming in the wind; and whether the object be an army or a cow you will see him come marching sublimely in, at the end of the engagement, bearing the more preferable fragments of the victim patiently on his shoulders, to the stopping-place. Cooper's style is grand, awful, beautiful; but it is sacred to Cooper, it is his very own, and no student of the Veterinary College of Arizona will be allowed to filch it from him.

In one of his chapters Cooper throws an ungentle slur at one Gamut because he is not exact enough in his choice of words. But Cooper has that failing himself, as was remarked in our first Lecture. If the Indian had "struck" the fawn with a brick, or with a club, or with his fist, no one could find fault with the word used. And one cannot find much fault when he strikes it with an arrow; still it sounds affected, and it might have been a little better to lean to simplicity and say he shot it with an arrow.

"Fragments" is well enough, perhaps, when one is speaking of the parts of a dismembered deer, yet it hasn't just exactly the right sound—and sound is something; in fact sound is a good deal. It makes the difference between good music and poor music, and it can sometimes make the difference between good literature and indifferent literature. "Fragments" sounds all right when we are talking about the wreckage of a breakable thing that has been smashed; it also sounds all right when applied to cat's-meat; but when we use it to describe large hunks and chunks like the fore- and hind-quarters of a fawn, it grates upon the fastidious ear.

"Without any aid from the science of cookery, he was immediately employed, in common with his fellows, in gorging himself with this digestible sustenance."

This was a mere statistic; just a mere cold, colorless statistic; yet you see Cooper has made a chromo out of it. To use another figure, he has clothed a humble statistic in flowing, voluminous and costly raiment, whereas both good taste and economy suggest that he ought to have saved these splendors for a king, and dressed the humble statistic in a simple breech-clout. Cooper spent twenty-four words here on a thing not really worth more than eight. We will reduce the statistic to its proper proportions and state it in this way:

"He and the others ate the meat raw."

"Digestible sustenance" is a handsome phrase, but it was out of place there, because we do not know these Indians or care for them; and so it cannot interest us to know whether the meat was going to agree with them or not. Details which do not assist a story are better left out.

"Magua alone sat apart, without participating in the revolting meal," is a statement which we understand, but that is our merit, not Cooper's. Cooper is not clear. He does not say who it is that is revolted by the meal. It is really Cooper himself, but there is nothing in the statement to indicate that it isn't Magua. Magua is an Indian and likes raw meat.

The word "alone" could have been left out and space saved. It has no value where it is.

I must come back with some frequency, in the course of these Lectures, to the matter of Cooper's inaccuracy as an Observer. In this way I shall hope to persuade you that it is well to look at a thing carefully before you try to describe it; but I shall rest you between times with other matters and thus try to avoid over-fatiguing you with that detail of our theme. In *The Last of the Mohicans* Cooper gets up a stirring "situation" on an island flanked by great cataracts—a lofty island with steep sides—a sort of tongue which projects downstream from the midst of the divided waterfall. There are caverns in this mass of rock, and a party of Cooper people hide themselves in one of these to get away from some hostile Indians. There is a small exit at each end of this cavern. These exits are closed with blankets and the light excluded. The exploring hostiles back themselves up against the blankets and rave and rage in a blood-curdling way, but they are Cooper Indians and of course fail to discover the blankets; so they presently go away baffled and disappointed. Alice, in her gratitude for this deliverance, flings herself on her knee to return thanks. The darkness in there must have been pretty solid; yet if we may believe Cooper, it was a darkness which could not have been told from daylight; for here are some nice details which were visible in it:

"Both Heyward and the more tempered Cora witnessed the act of involuntary emotion with powerful sympathy, the former secretly believing that piety had never worn a form so lovely as it had now assumed in the youthful person of Alice. Her eyes were radiant with the glow of grateful feelings; the flush of her beauty was again seated on her cheeks, and her whole soul seemed ready and anxious to pour out its thanksgivings, through the medium of her eloquent features. But when her lips moved, the words they should have uttered appeared frozen by some new and sudden chill. Her bloom gave place to the paleness of death; her soft and melting eyes grew hard, and seemed contracting with horror; while those hands which she had raised, clasped in each other, towards heaven, dropped in horizontal lines before her, the fingers pointed forward in convulsed motion."

It is a case of strikingly inexact observation. Heyward and the more tempered Cora could not have seen the half of it in the dark that way.

I must call your attention to certain details of this work of art which invite particular examination. "Involuntary" is surplusage, and violates Rule 14.[1] All emotion is involuntary when genuine, and then the qualifying term is not needed; a qualifying term is needed only when the emotion is pumped-up and ungenuine. "Secretly" is surplusage, too; because Heyward was not believing out loud, but all to himself; and a person cannot believe a thing all to himself without doing it privately. I do not approve of the word "seated," to describe the process of locating a flush. No one can seat a

[1] Rule 14 "Eschew surplusage."

flush. A flush is not a deposit on an exterior surface, it is a something which squashes out from within.

I cannot approve of the word "new." If Alice had had an old chill, formerly, it would be all right to distinguish this one from that one by calling this one the new chill; but she had not had any old chill, this one was the only chill she had had, up till now, and so the tacit reference to an old anterior chill is unwarranted and misleading. And I do not altogether like the phrase "while those hands which she had raised." It seems to imply that she had some other hands—some other ones which she had put on a shelf a minute so as to give her a better chance to raise those ones; but it is not true; she had only the one pair. The phrase is in the last degree misleading. But I like to see her extend these ones in front of her and work the fingers. I think that that is a very good effect. And it would have almost doubled the effect if the more tempered Cora had done it some, too.

John Updike (Contemporary)

Under the Microscope

It was not his kind of pond; the water tasted slightly acid. He was a Cyclops, the commonest of copepods, and this crowd seemed exotically cladoceran—stylish water-fleas with transparent carapaces, all shimmer and bubbles and twitch. His hostess, a magnificent Daphnia fully an eighth of an inch tall, her heart and cephalic ganglion visibly pulsing, welcomed him with a lavish gesture of her ciliate, branching antennae; for a moment he feared she would eat him. Instead she offered him a platter of living desmids. They were bright green in color and shaped like crescents, hourglasses, omens. "Who do you know here?" Her voice was a distinct constant above the din. "Everybody knows

you, of course. They've read your books." His books, taken all together, with generous margins, would easily have fitted on the period that ends this sentence.

The Cyclops modestly grimaced, answered "No one," and turned to a young specimen of water-mite, probably *Hydrachna geographica,* still bearing ruddy traces of the larval stage. "Have you been here long?" he asked, meaning less the party than the pond.

"Long enough." Her answer came as swiftly as a reflex. "I go back to the surface now and then; we breathe air, you know."

"Oh I know, I envy you." He noticed she had only six legs. She was newly hatched, then. Between her eyes, arranged in two pairs, he counted a fifth, in the middle, and wondered if in her he might find his own central single optic amplified and confirmed. His antennules yearned to touch her red spots; he wanted to ask her, *What do you see?* Young as she was, partially formed, she appeared, alerted by his abrupt confession of envy, ready to respond to any question, however presuming.

But at that moment a monstrous fairy shrimp, an inch in length and extravagantly tinted blue, green, and bronze, swam by on its back, and the water shuddered. Furious, the Cyclops asked the water-mite, "Who invites *them*? They're not even in our scale."

She shrugged permissively, showing that indeed she had been here long enough. "They're entomostracans," she said, "just like Daphnia. They amuse her."

"They're going to eat her up," the Cyclops predicted.

Though she laughed, her fifth eye gazed steadily into his wide lone one. "But isn't that what we all want? Subconsciously, of course."

"Of course."

An elegant, melancholy
flatworm was passing *hors
d'œuvres*. The Cyclops
took some diatoms, cracked
their delicate shells of
silica, and ate them. They

tasted golden brown. Growing hungrier,
he pushed through to the serving table and
had a Volvox in algae dip. A shrill little rotifer, his head cilia whirling, his three-
toothed mastax chattering, leaped up
before him, saying, with the mixture of
put-on and pleading characteristic of this
pond, "I wead all

your wunnaful books, and I have a
wittle bag of pomes I wote myself,
and I would wove it, *wove* it if you
would wead them and wecommend
them to a big bad pubwisher!" At a
loss for a civil answer, the Cyclops
considered the rotifer silently, then
ate him. He tasted slightly acid.

The party was thickening. A host
of protozoans drifted
in on a raft of sphagnum moss: a trumpet-
shaped Stentor, apparently famous and inter-
locked with a lanky, bleached Spirostomum; a
claque of paramœcia, swishing back and forth
tickling the crustacea on the backs of their
knees; an old Voticella, a plantlike animalcule
as dreary, the Cyclops thought, as the batch of
puffs rooted to the flap of last year's *succès
d'estime*. The kitchen was crammed with ostra-
cods and flagellates engaged in mutually consuming conversation, and over in a corner, beneath an African mask, a
great brown hydra, the real thing, attached by its sticky foot
to the hissing steam radiator, rhythmically swung its tentacles here and there until one of them touched, in the circle of
admirers, something appetiz-
ing; then the poison sacs ex-
ploded, the other tentacles
contracted, and the prey was stuffed into the hydra's

swollen coelenteron, which gluttony had stretched to a transparency that veiled the preceding meals like polyethylene film protecting a rack of dry-cleaned suits. Hairy with bacteria, a Simocephalus was munching a rapt nematode. The fairy shrimps, having multiplied, their crimson tails glowing with hæmoglobin, came cruising in from the empty bedrooms. The party was thinning.

Suddenly fearful, fearing he had lost her forever, the Cyclops searched for the water-mite, and found her miserably crouching in a corner, quite drunk, her seventh and eighth legs almost sprouted. "What do you see?" he now dared ask.

"Too much," she answered swiftly. "Everything. Oh, it's horrible, horrible."

Out of mercy as much as appetite, he ate her. She felt prickly inside him. Hurriedly—the rooms were almost depleted, it was late—he sought his hostess. She was by the doorway, her antennae frazzled from waving goodbye, but still magnificent, Daphnia, her carapace a liquid shimmer of psychedelic pastel. "Don't go," she commanded, expanding, "I have a *minus*cule favor to ask. Now that my children, all thirteen billion of them, thank God, are off at school, I've taken a part-time editing job, and my first real break is this manuscript I'd be *so* grateful to have you read and comment on, whatever comes into your head, I admit it's a little long, maybe you can skim the part where Napoleon invades Russia, but it's the first *ef*fort by a perfectly delightful midge larva I know you'd enjoy meeting—"

"I'd adore to, but I can't," he said, explaining, "my eye. I can't afford to strain it, I have only this one . . ." He trailed off, he felt, feebly. He was beginning to feel permeable, acidic.

"You poor dear," Daphnia solemnly pronounced, and ate him.

And the next instant, a fairy shrimp, oaring by inverted, casually gathered her into the trough between his eleven pairs of undulating gill-feet and passed her toward his brazen mouth. Her scream, tinier than even the dot on this "i," was unobserved.

During the Jurassic

Waiting for the first guests, the iguanodon gazed along the path and beyond, toward the monotonous cycad forests and the low volcanic hills. The landscape was everywhere interpenetrated by the sea, a kind of metallic blue rottenness that daily breathed in and out. Behind him, his wife was assembling the *hors d'oeuvres,* As he watched her, something unintended, something grossly solemn, in his expression made her laugh, displaying the leaf-shaped teeth lining her cheeks. Like him, she was an ornithischian, but much smaller—a compsognathus. He wondered, watching her race bipedally back and forth among the scraps of food (dragonflies wrapped in ferns, cephalopods on toast), how he had ever found her beautiful. His eyes hungered for size; he experienced a rage for sheer blind size.

The stegosauri, of course, were the first to appear. Among their many stupid friends these were the most stupid, and the most punctual. Their front legs bent outward and their little filmy-eyed faces virtually skimmed the ground; the upward sweep of their  backs was gigantic, and the double rows of giant bone plates along the spine clicked together in the sway of their cumbersome gait. With hardly a greeting, they dragged their tails, quadruply spiked, across the threshold and maneuvered themselves toward the bar, which was tended by a minute and shapeless mammal hired for the evening.

Next came the allosaurus, a carnivorous bachelor whose dangerous aura and needled grin excited the female herbivores; then Rhamphorhynchus, a pterosaur whose much admired "flight" was in reality a clumsy brittle glide ending in an embarrassed bump and trot. The iguanodon despised these pterosaurs' pretensions, thought grotesque the precarious elongation of the single finger from which their levitating membranes were stretched, and privately believed that the less handsomely underwritten archaeopteryx, though sneered at as unstable and feathered, had more of a future. The hypsilophodon, with her graceful hands and branch-gripping feet, arrived escorted by the timeless crocodile—an incongruous pair, but both were recently divorced. Still the iguanodon gazed down the path.

Behind him, the conversation gnashed on a thousand things—houses, mortgages, lawns, fertilizers, erosion, boats, winds, annuities, capital gains, recipes, education, the day's tennis, last night's party. Each party was consumed by discussion of the previous one. Their lives were subject to constant cross-check. When did you leave? When did *you* leave? We'd been out every night this week. We had an amphibious babysitter who had to be back in the water by one. Gregor had to meet a client in town, and now they've reduced the Saturday schedule, it means the 7:43 or nothing. Trains? I thought they were totally extinct. Not at all. They're coming back, it's just a matter of time until the government . . . In the long range of evolution, they are still the most efficient . . . Taking into account the heat-loss/weight ratio and assuming there's no more glaciation . . . Did you know—I think this is fascinating—did you know that in the financing of those great ornate stations of the eighties and nineties, those real monsters, there was no provision for amortization? They weren't amortized at all, they were financed on the basis of eternity! The railroad was conceived of as the end of Progress! *I* think—though not an expert—that the key word in this over-all industrio-socio-what-have-you-oh nexus or syndrome or bag or whatever is *overextended.* Any competitorless object *bloats.* Personally, I miss the trolley cars. Now don't tell me I'm the only creature in the room old enough to remember the trolley cars!

The iguanodon's high pulpy heart jerked and seemed to split; the brontosaurus was coming up the path.

Her husband, the diplodocus, was with her. They moved together, rhythmic twins, buoyed by the hollow assurance of the huge. She paused to tear with her lips a clump of leaf from an overhanging paleocycas. From her deliberate grace the iguanodon received the impression that she knew he was watching her. Indeed, she had long guessed his love, as had her husband. The two saurischians entered his party with the languid confidence of the specially cherished. In the teeth of the iguanodon's ironic stance, her bulk, her gorgeous size, enraptured him, swelled to fill the massive ache he carried when she was not there. She rolled outward across his senses—the dawn-pale underparts, the reticulate skin, the vast bluish muscles whose management required a second brain at the base of her spine.

Her husband, though even longer, was more slenderly built, and perhaps weighed less than twenty-five tons. His very manner was attenuated and tabescent. He had recently abandoned an orthodox business career to enter the Episcopalian seminary. The regression—as the iguanodon felt it—seemed to make his wife more prominent, less supported, more accessible.

How splendid she was! For all the lavish solidity of her hips and legs, the modelling of her little flat diapsid skull was delicate. Her facial essence appeared to narrow, along the diagrammatic points of her auricles and eyes and nostrils, toward a single point, located in the air, of impermutable  refinement and calm. This irreducible point was, he realized, in some sense her mind: the focus of the minimal interest she brought to play upon the inchoate and edible green world flowing all about her, buoying her, bathing her. The iguanodon felt himself as an upright speckled stain in this world. He felt himself, under her distant dim smile, impossibly ugly: his mouth a sardonic chasm, his throat a pulsing curtain of scaly folds, his body a blotched bulb. His feet were heavy and horny and three-toed and his thumbs—strange adaptation!—were erect rigidities of pointed bone. Wounded by her presence, he savagely turned on her husband.

"Comment va le bon Dieu?"

"Ah?" The diplodocus was maddeningly good-humored. Minutes elapsed as stimuli and reactions travelled back and forth across his length.

The iguanodon insisted. "How are things in the supernatural?"

"The supernatural? I don't think that category exists in the new theology."

"N'est-ce pas?" What *does* exist in the new theology?"

"Love. Immanence as opposed to transcendence. Works as opposed to faith."

"Work? I had thought you had quit work."

"That's an unkind way of putting it. I prefer to think that I've changed employers."

The iguanodon felt in the other's politeness a detestable aristocracy, the unappealable oppression of superior size. He said gnashingly, "The Void pays wages?"

"Ah?"

"You mean there's a living in nonsense? I said nonsense. Dead, fetid nonsense."

"Call it that if it makes it easier for you. Myself, I'm not a fast learner. Intellectual humility came rather natural to me. In the seminary, for the first time in my life, I feel on the verge of finding myself."

"Yourself? That little thing? *Cette petite chose?* That's all you're looking for? Have you tried pain? Myself, I have found pain to be a great illuminator. *Permettez-moi.*" The iguanodon essayed to bite the veined base of the serpentine throat lazily upheld before him; but his teeth were too specialized and could not tear flesh. He abraded his lips and tasted his own salt blood. Disoriented, crazed, he thrust one thumb deep into a yielding gray flank that hove through the smoke and chatter of the party like a dull wave. But the nerves of his victim lagged in reporting the pain, and by the time the distant head of the diplodocus was notified, the wound would have healed.

The drinks were flowing freely. The mammal crept up to him and murmured that the dry vermouth was running out. The iguanodon told him to use the sweet. Behind the sofa the stegosauri were Indian-wrestling; each time one went over, his spinal plates raked the recently papered wall. The hypsilophodon, tipsy, perched on a banister; the allosaurus darted forward suddenly and ceremoniously nibbled her tail. On the far side of the room, by the great slack-stringed harp, the compsognathus and the brontosaurus were talking. He was drawn to them: amazed that his wife would presume to delay the much larger creature; to insert herself, with her scrabbling nervous motions and chattering leaf-shaped teeth, into the crevices of that queenly presence. As he drew closer to them, music began. His wife confided to him, "The salad is running out." He murmured to the bronto-saurus, *"Chère madame, voulez-vous danser avec moi?"*

Her dancing was awkward, but even in this awkward-ness, this ponderous stiffness, he felt the charm of her abun-dance. "I've been talking to your husband about religion," he told her, as they settled into the steps they could do.

"I've given up," she said. "It's such a deprivation for me and the children."

"He says he's looking for himself."

"It's so selfish," she blurted. "The children are teased at school."

"Come live with me."

"Can you support me?"

"No, but I would gladly sink under you."

"You're sweet."

"Je t'aime."

"Don't. Not here."

"Somewhere, then?"

"No. Nowhere. Never." With what delightful precision did her miniature mouth encompass these infinitesimal concepts!

"But I," he said, "but I lo—"

"Stop it. You embarrass me. Deliberately."

"You know what I wish? I wish all these beasts would disappear. What do we see in each other? Why do we keep getting together?"

She shrugged. "If they disappear, we will too."

"I'm not so sure. There's something about us that would survive. It's not in you and not in me but between us, where we almost meet. Some vibration, some enduring cosmic factor. Don't you feel it?"

"Let's stop. It's too painful."

"Stop dancing?"

"Stop being."

"That is a beautiful idea. *Une belle idée.* I will if you will."

"In time," she said, and her fine little face precisely fitted this laconic promise; and as the summer night yielded warmth to the multiplying stars, he felt his blood sympa-thetically cool, and grow thunderously, fruitfully slow.

Judith Viorst (Contemporary)

ᘛᙣᘚᘖ

Self-Improvement Program

I've finished six pillows in Needlepoint,
And I'm reading Jane Austen and Kant,
And I'm up to the pork with black beans in
    Advanced Chinese Cooking.
I don't have to struggle to find myself
For I already know what I want.
I want to be healthy and wise and extremely good-
    looking.

I'm learning new glazes in Pottery Class,
And I'm playing new chords in Guitar,
And in Yoga I'm starting to master the lotus position.
I don't have to ponder priorities
For I already know what they are:
To be good-looking, healthy, and wise,
And adored in addition.

I'm improving my serve with a tennis pro,
And I'm practicing verb forms in Greek,
And in Primal Scream Therapy all my frustrations
    are vented.
I don't have to ask what I'm searching for
Since I already know that I seek
To be good-looking, healthy, and wise,
And adored.
And contented.

I've bloomed in Organic Gardening,
And in Dance I have tightened my thighs,

And in Consciousness Raising there's no one
    around who can top me.
And I'm working all day and I'm working all night
To be good-looking, healthy, and wise.
And adored.
And contented.
And brave.
And well-read.
And a marvelous hostess,
Fantastic in bed,
And bilingual,
Athletic,
Artistic . . .
Won't someone please stop me?

Jane Wagner (Contemporary)

FROM *The Search for Signs of Intelligent Life in the Universe*

J B About a month ago, I was shown some
U E   products designed to
D A improve the sex lives of suburban
I S   housewives. I got so
T L   excited,
H E I just had to come on public access and tell
    Y   you about it. To
    look at *me,* you'd *never suspect* I was a
     semi-nonorgasmic
    woman. This means it was *possible* for me to
     have an orgasm—
    but highly unlikely.

    To me, the term "sexual freedom" meant freedom
    from having to

have sex. And then along came Good Vibrations.
    And was I
surprised! Now I am a regular
Cat on a Hot Tin Roof. . . .

think of it as a kind of
Hamburger Helper for the boudoir.

Can you afford one, you say?
Can you afford *not* to have one, I say. . . .

Ladies, it simply takes the guesswork out of
    making love.

"But doesn't it kill romance?" you say.
And I say,
"What doesn't?"

A sobering thought, Eileen:
What if, right at this very moment,
I *am* living up to my full potential?

I've about reached the conclusion if I'm ever going
    to make
something of my life, chances are it won't be
    through work.
It will have to be through personal growth stuff.

Go for the burn!

I've been trying to get into positive thinking in a
    really big way.
Frankly, I think it's my only hope.

My seminar leader said to me, "Chrissy, you
    should learn
to be happy
one day at a time." But what I learned from that is
    that you can
also be *miserable*
one day at a time.

*   *   *

This seminar I'm in, Eileen, has opened me up like
   some kind of
bronchial *spray.* I got clear:
my expectations about life are simply way too high.
   So are yours,
I bet, Eileen, because we
are all being *force-fed* a lot of false hopes about
   romance,
success, sex, life—you name it.

My seminar leader said to me, "Chrissy, you are a
   classic
'false hope' case" . . . because not only do I not
   have a very firm
grasp on reality, see,
but I have sort of a loose grip on my fantasies, too.

We had this exercise, Eileen.
We played this mind game called
"We know everything we need to know
if only we knew it."
We were told to be silent and our minds would tell
us whatever we needed to know.

I flashed on the time I lost my contact lens. There
   I was
looking for my contact lens
which I couldn't find
because I had lost my contact lens.
I thought: Wow, the story of my *life.*

You can't expect insights, even the big ones,
to suddenly make you understand
everything. But I figure: Hey, it's a step if they
   leave you
confused
in a deeper way.

The seminar ends tonight. To get us to face
   our fears,
we're supposed to walk over this bed of really red-
   hot coals—

barefoot. Quite a test! You name
it; I've feared it.
Except walking over hot coals . . . I never had
    that fear
till just now.

I'm working on overcoming my fears, Eileen,
but it's not easy.
At the Phobia Institute once,
this guy in group told about a friend who was
    terrified
of driving on the freeway,
but finally she conquered her fear and got so she
    thought
nothing of driving on the freeway.
And guess what?
She died
in a freeway accident.
That story has always stuck with me.

But *my* fears are more subtle. Like I fear being out
    of work,
and yet when I'm working, I have this constant fear
of being fired. The worst fear I have
is that this feeling I once had may come back.

At the lockers

Once . . . I've been wanting to tell someone this,
    Eileen . . .
once I came *this* close
to committing suicide.
That's how down and low I felt.
I would have, too. There was just one thing
    stopped me.
Fear. I was just plain too afraid.
So, if I ever did commit suicide, I'd have to be so
    desperate
I wouldn't even let fear of suicide
stand in my way.

*   *   *

And yet if I could overcome a fear like that
I could overcome
all my fears, I bet.

And then, of course—
and here's the irony—probably
if I weren't afraid, I'd really want to live.
Only, by then, if I'd really conquered my fear of
    suicide,
it might be too late.
I might already, you know,
have done it.

Life can be so ironic. Sometimes, to make any move
at all seems totally pointless. I bet the worst part about
dying is the part where your whole life passes before
you.

I hope I don't ever feel that low again. At the moment,
I feel pretty up about the work I'm doing on myself. I
used to be so sensitive; sometimes I would think of
the Kennedy family and I would just burst out in tears.
I'm not so sensitive anymore; I don't burst out in tears
as much as I used to and I hardly ever think of the
Kennedys anymore. So these seminars have been
good for me, Eileen, which is more than I can say for
any job I've ever had.

Course, *I* don't want to be a seminar-*hopper*;
    like this
ex-friend I used to know. She had no time for
    *any*thing but
self-improvement. She felt she had outgrown
    everyone,
especially *me*. Behind my back, she told this person
    that *I* was
Upwardly
Immobile. Asshole. And then, to add insult to
    injury,
she said it to my face. That did it—
I get enough insults on job interviews.

* * *

Well, I guess I'll see you tomorrow. How they
  lied about
this health club! Talk about false hopes. "The *place*
  to get
thin and meet good-looking men." The good-
  looking men here
are mostly looking at themselves.

I have never gotten so much as a date for
  cappuccino.

Yet I keep coming. I'm keeping really fit, I tell myself.
But the truth is,
I pig out one week and starve the next.

I have gained and lost
the same ten pounds
so many times over and over again
my cellulite must have déjà vu.

And all that business about exercise releasing
  endorphins.
I have not felt so much as *one* endorphin being
  released. Once
more, false hopes.

But hey, if it weren't for false hopes, the
  economy would
just collapse, I bet. Oh. I better hurry. My job
  interview! This
time I could get lucky. Requires no skills;
I'll just be hooking people up to
bio-feedback machines. At least I won't be lying
  to them.
Well, slinkydinks, I'm outta here.

AT THE DOCTOR'S

L You're sure, Doctor?
Y Pre*men*strual syndrome?
N I mean, I'm getting divorced.
    My mother's getting divorced.

I'm raising twin boys.
I have a lot of job pressure—
I've got to find one.
The ERA didn't pass,
not long ago I lost a very dear friend, and . . . and
my husband is involved . . .
not just involved, but in love, I'm afraid . . .
   with this
woman . . .
who's quite a bit younger than I am.

And you *think* it's my *period*
and *not* my life?

Mae West (1893–1980)

One-liners

Is that a pistol in your pocket or are you just happy to
see me?

•

. . . Why don't you come up and see me sometime? Come
up on Wednesday, that's amateur night. . . .
   Trust me, hundreds already have.

•

When women go wrong, men go right after them.

•

A hard man is good to find.

•

He who hesitates is last.

•

Give a man a free hand and he'll run it all over you.

•

Why should I be good when I'm packing them in by being bad?

•

FROM *Pleasure Man*

Dolores is learning the meaning of the word repentance. It is how you feel when you get caught.

•

Nellie knows people are divided into the goods and the bads. The thing is not to be caught with the goods.

•

Poor Mary Ann! She gave the guy an inch and now he thinks he's a ruler.

•

FROM *The Constant Sinner*

When Babe Gordon had told the Bearcat she had been to church, it never occurred to her that she was lying. That is, it had no moral significance for her. To Babe, a lie was simply something one told to gain an advantage, to get what one wanted by the shortest route. . . . Bearcat was now convinced that she was a good girl, had character; and now, no matter what Charlie said against her, if she were careful Bearcat would always believe in her.

Babe was the living example of all that is immoral, when viewed through conventional eyes. But she herself was unmoral. For her, morals did not exist. She would not have known what a moral was if it could be made to dance naked in front of her.

•

A distinguished looking tall man, with snow-white hair and well-groomed body, got into the cab with a dame who was highly rouged and expensively attired from shoes to the beautiful summer fur-piece about her shoulders. He caught snatches of their conversation.

"But I don't want to stop at the Plaza for tea," the man was saying, irritably. "You just want to show off that new fur I bought you."

"Please, honey," the girl begged.

"No, no. I'd be bored stiff. Let's go up to the apartment."

"But I don't want to go up there yet. It's too early."

"What has the time got to do with it? We can't get anything to drink at the Plaza." . . .

"All right, then," the girl said. "If you don't take me to
the Plaza, I won't be nice to you the way you like, any
more."

"Oh, I say now, Zelda," the man argued. "That's not
sporting, after I've given you so much."

"Well, I don't care," said the girl. "I just won't be nice
that way any more, that's all."

"Oh, good lord!" the man exclaimed, anxiously. "Well,
all right." He rapped on the taxi window with his stick. "I
say, my man."

"Yeah?" the Bearcat answered as he choked down the
speed of the car.

"Drive us to the Plaza—the Plaza!"

"Oh, you darling!" cried the girl.

FROM *A Bio-Bibliography*

I like movies about strong women. I was the first liberated
woman, y' know. No guy was gonna get the best of me,
that's what I wrote all my scripts about.

•

You must be good and tired.
West: No, just tired.

•

I'm not a little girl from a little town making good in a
big town. I'm a big girl from a big town making good in
a little town.

•

Hatcheck girl: Goodness, what lovely diamonds.
West: Goodness had nothing to do with it, dearie.

•

It takes two to get one in trouble.

•

I've been things and seen places.

•

When I'm good, I'm very good, but when I'm bad, I'm
better.

•

I used to be Snow White but I drifted.

•

It's not the men in my life, but the life in my men that counts.

•

Too much of a good thing can be wonderful.

•

Keep cool and collect.

•

Between two evils I always pick the one I never tried before.

•

I always say keep a diary and one day it will keep you.

•

I generally avoid temptation. Unless I can't resist it.

•

If young girls knew more about love and didn't take it so seriously, it would be better for them.

•

I have never minded foreign films, but who needs dirty foreign films? We can do better dirty films ourselves.

•

Some mousy women have more oomph in their hip pocket than a lot of beautiful women have in their whole bodies.

•

Politics? I keep up with what's going on. Although I'm not much for politics myself. But I always know a good party man when I see one. . . .

Edith Wharton (1862–1937)

FROM *The Age of Innocence*

An unalterable and unquestioned law of the musical world required that the German text of French operas sung by

Swedish artists should be translated into Italian for the clearer understanding of English-speaking audiences.

The immense accretion of flesh which had descended on her in middle life like a flood of lava on a doomed city had changed her from a plump active little woman with a neatly-turned foot and ankle into something as vast and august as a natural phenomenon.

To let her talk about familiar and simple things was the easiest way of carrying on his own independent train of thought. . . . Archer had reverted to all his old inherited ideas about marriage. It was less trouble to conform with the tradition and treat May exactly as all his friends treated their wives than to try to put into practice the theories with which his untrammelled bachelorhood had dallied. There was not use in trying to emancipate a wife who had not the dimmest notion that she was not free.

FROM *The House of Mirth*

"Ah, there's the difference—a girl must [marry], a man may if he chooses." She surveyed him critically. "Your coat's a little shabby—but who cares? It doesn't keep people from asking you to dine. If I were shabby no one would have me; a woman is asked out as much for her clothes as for herself. The clothes are the background, the frame, if you like: they don't make success, but they are a part of it. Who wants a dingy woman? We are expected to be pretty and well-dressed till we drop—and if we can't keep it up alone, we have to go into partnership."

•

It amused her to think that any one as rich as Mr. Percy Gryce should be shy; but she was gifted with treasures of indulgence for such idiosyncrasies, and besides, his timidity might serve her purpose better than too much assurance. She had the art of giving self-confidence to the embarrassed, but she was not equally sure of being able to embarrass the self-confident.

She waited till the train had emerged from the tunnel and was racing between the ragged edges of the northern suburbs. Then, as it lowered its speed near Yonkers, she rose from her seat and drifted slowly down the carriage. As she passed Mr. Gryce, the train gave a lurch, and he was aware of a slender hand gripping the back of his chair. He rose with a start, his ingenuous face looking as though it had been dipped in crimson: even the reddish tint in his beard seemed to deepen.

The train swayed again, almost flinging Miss Bart into his arms. She steadied herself with a laugh and drew back; but he was enveloped in the scent of her dress, and his shoulder had felt her fugitive touch.

"Oh, Mr. Gryce, is it you? I'm so sorry—I was trying to find the porter and get some tea."

She held out her hand as the train resumed its level rush, and they stood exchanging a few words in the aisle. Yes— he was going to Bellomont. He had heard she was to be of the party—he blushed again as he admitted it. And was he to be there for a whole week? How delightful!

But at this point one or two belated passengers from the last station forced their way into the carriage, and Lily had to retreat to her seat.

"The chair next to mine is empty—do take it," she said over her shoulder; and Mr. Gryce, with considerable embarrassment, succeeded in effecting an exchange which enabled him to transport himself and his bags to her side.

"Ah—and here is the porter, and perhaps we can have some tea."

She signalled to that official, and in a moment, with the ease that seemed to attend the fulfilment of all her wishes, a little table had been set up between the seats, and she had helped Mr. Gryce to bestow his encumbering properties beneath it.

When the tea came he watched her in silent fascination while her hands flitted above the tray, looking miraculously fine and slender in contrast to the coarse china and lumpy bread. It seemed wonderful to him that any one should perform with such careless ease the difficult task of making tea in public in a lurching train. He would never have dared to order it for himself, lest he should attract the notice of his fellow-passengers; but, secure in the shelter of her conspicuousness, he sipped the inky draught with a delicious sense of exhilaration.

Lily, with the flavour of Selden's caravan tea on her lips, had no great fancy to drown it in the railway brew which seemed such nectar to her companion; but, rightly judging that one of the charms of tea is the fact of drinking it together, she proceeded to give the last touch to Mr. Gryce's enjoyment by smiling at him across her lifted cup.

"Is it quite right—I haven't made it too strong?" she asked solicitously; and he replied with conviction that he had never tasted better tea.

"I daresay it is true," she reflected; and her imagination was fired by the thought that Mr. Gryce, who might have sounded the depths of the most complex self-indulgence, was perhaps actually taking his first journey alone with a pretty woman.

It struck her as providential that she should be the instrument of his initiation. Some girls would not have known how to manage him. They would have over-emphasized the novelty of the adventure, trying to make him feel in it the zest of an escapade. But Lily's methods were more delicate. She remembered that her cousin Jack Stepney had once defined Mr. Gryce as the young man who had promised his mother never to go out in the rain without his overshoes; and acting on this hint, she resolved to impart a gently domestic air to the scene, in the hope that her companion, instead of feeling that he was doing something reckless or unusual, would merely be led to dwell on the advantage of always having a companion to make one's tea in the train.

But in spite of her efforts, conversation flagged after the tray had been removed, and she was driven to take a fresh measurement of Mr. Gryce's limitations. It was not, after all, opportunity but imagination that he lacked: he had a mental palate which would never learn to distinguish between railway tea and nectar. There was, however, one topic she could rely on: one spring that she had only to touch to set his simple machinery in motion. She had refrained from touching it because it was a last resource, and she had relied on other arts to stimulate other sensations; but as a settled look of dullness began to creep over his candid features, she saw that extreme measures were necessary.

"And how," she said, leaning forward, "are you getting on with your Americana?"

His eye became a degree less opaque: it was as though an

incipient film had been removed from it, and she felt the pride of a skillful operator.

"I've got a few new things," he said, suffused with pleasure, but lowering his voice as though he feared his fellow-passengers might be in league to despoil him.

She returned a sympathetic enquiry, and gradually he was drawn on to talk of his latest purchases. It was the one subject which enabled him to forget himself, or allowed him, rather, to remember himself without constraint, because he was at home in it, and could assert a superiority that there were few to dispute. Hardly any of his acquaintances cared for Americana, or knew anything about them; and the consciousness of this ignorance threw Mr. Gryce's knowledge into agreeable relief. The only difficulty was to introduce the topic and to keep it to the front; most people showed no desire to have their ignorance dispelled, and Mr. Gryce was like a merchant whose warehouses are crammed with an unmarketable commodity.

But Miss Bart, it appeared, really did want to know about Americana; and moreover, she was already sufficiently informed to make the task of farther instruction as easy as it was agreeable. She questioned him intelligently, she heard him submissively; and, prepared for the look of lassitude which usually crept over his listeners' faces, he grew eloquent under her receptive gaze. The "points" she had the presence of mind to glean from Selden, in anticipation of this very contingency, were serving her to such good purpose that she began to think her visit to him had been the luckiest incident of the day. She had once more shown her talent for profiting by the unexpected, and dangerous theories as to the advisability of yielding to impulse were germinating under the surface of smiling attention which she continued to present to her companion.

Mr. Gryce's sensations, if less definite, were equally agreeable. He felt his confused titillation with which the lower organisms welcome the gratification of their needs, and all his senses floundered in a vague well-being, through which Miss Bart's personality was dimly but pleasantly perceptible.

Mr. Gryce's interest in Americana had not originated with himself: it was impossible to think of him as evolving any taste of his own. An uncle had left him a collection already noted among bibliophiles; the existence of the collection was the only fact that had ever shed glory on the name of Gryce, and the nephew took as much pride in his inheritance as though it had been his own work. Indeed, he gradually came to regard it as such, and to feel a sense of personal complacency when he chanced on any reference to the Gryce Americana. Anxious as he was to avoid personal notice, he took, in the printed mention of his name, a pleasure so exquisite and excessive that it seemed a compensation for his shrinking from publicity.

To enjoy the sensation as often as possible, he subscribed to all the reviews dealing with book-collecting in general, and American history in particular, and as allusions to his library abounded in the pages of these journals, which formed his only reading, he came to regard himself as figuring prominently in the public eye, and to enjoy the thought of the interest which would be excited if the persons he met in the street, or sat among in travelling, were suddenly to be told that he was the possessor of the Gryce Americana.

Most timidities have such secret compensations, and Miss Bart was discerning enough to know that the inner vanity is generally in proportion to the outer self-deprecation. With a more confident person she would not have dared to dwell so long on one topic, or to show such exaggerated interest in it; but she had rightly guessed that Mr. Gryce's egoism was a thirsty soil, requiring constant nurture from without. Miss Bart had the gift of following an undercurrent of thought while she appeared to be sailing on the surface of conversation; and in this case her mental excursion took the form of a rapid survey of Mr. Percy Gryce's future as combined with her own. The Gryces were from Albany, and but lately introduced to the metropolis, where the mother and son had come, after old Jefferson Gryce's death, to take possession of his house in Madison Avenue—an appalling house, all brown stone without and black walnut within, with the Gryce library in a fire-proof annex that looked like a mausoleum. Lily, however, knew all about them: young Mr. Gryce's arrival had fluttered the maternal breasts of New York, and when a girl has no mother to palpitate for her she must needs be on the alert for herself. Lily, therefore, had not only contrived to put herself in the young man's way, but had made the acquaintance of Mrs. Gryce, a monumental woman with the voice of a pulpit orator and a mind preoccupied with the iniquities of her servants, who came sometimes to sit with Mrs. Peniston and learn from that lady how she managed to prevent the kitchen-maid's smuggling groceries out of the house. Mrs. Gryce had a kind of impersonal benevolence: cases of individual need she regarded with suspicion, but she subscribed to Institutions where their annual reports showed an impressive surplus. Her domestic duties were manifold, for they extended from furtive inspections of the servants' bedrooms to unannounced descents to the cellar; but she had never allowed herself many pleasures. Once, however, she had had a special edition of the Sarum Rule printed in rubric and presented to every clergyman in the diocese; and the gilt album in which their letters of thanks were pasted formed the chief ornament of her drawing-room table.

Percy had been brought up in the principles which so excellent a woman was sure to inculcate. Every form of prudence and suspicion had been grafted on a nature originally reluctant and cautious, with the result that it would have seemed hardly needful for Mrs. Gryce to extract his promise about the overshoes, so little likely was he to hazard himself abroad in the rain. After attaining his majority, and coming into the fortune which the late Mr. Gryce had made out of a patent device for excluding fresh air from hotels, the young man continued to live with his mother in Albany; but on Jefferson Gryce's death, when another large property passed into her son's hands, Mrs. Gryce thought that what she called his "interests" demanded his presence in New York. She accordingly installed herself in the Madison Avenue house, and Percy, whose sense of duty was not inferior to his mother's, spent all his week days in the handsome Broad Street office where a batch of pale men on small salaries had grown grey in the management of the Gryce estate, and where he was initiated with becoming reverence into every detail of the art of accumulation.

As far as Lily could learn, this had hitherto been Mr. Gryce's only occupation, and she might have been pardoned for thinking it not too hard a task to interest a young man who had been kept on such low diet. At any rate, she felt herself so completely in command of the situation that she yielded to a sense of security in which all fear of Mr. Rosedale, and of the difficulties on which that fear was contingent, vanished beyond the edge of thought.

The stopping of the train at Garrisons would not have distracted her from these thoughts, had she not caught a sudden look of distress in her companion's eye. His seat faced toward the door, and she guessed that he had been perturbed by the approach of an acquaintance; a fact confirmed by the turning of heads and general sense of commotion which her own entrance into a railway-carriage was apt to produce.

She knew the symptoms at once, and was not surprised to be hailed by the high notes of a pretty woman, who entered the train accompanied by a maid, a bull-terrier, and a footman staggering under a load of bags and dressing-cases.

"Oh, Lily—are you going to Bellomont? Then you can't let me have your seat, I suppose? But I *must* have a seat in this carriage—porter, you must find me a place at once. Can't some one be put somewhere else? I want to be with my friends. Oh, how do you do, Mr. Gryce? Do please make him understand that I must have a seat next to you and Lily."

Mrs. George Dorset, regardless of the mild efforts of a traveller with a carpet-bag, who was doing his best to make room for her by getting out of the train, stood in the middle of the aisle, diffusing about her that general sense of exasperation which a pretty woman on her travels not infrequently creates.

She was smaller and thinner than Lily Bart, with a restless pliability of pose, as if she could have been crumpled up and run through a ring, like the sinuous draperies she affected. Her small pale face seemed the mere setting of a pair of dark exaggerated eyes, of which the visionary gaze contrasted curiously with her self-assertive tone and gestures; so that, as one of her friends observed, she was like a disembodied spirit who took up a great deal of room.

Having finally discovered that the seat adjoining Miss Bart's was at her disposal, she possessed herself of it with a farther displacement of her surroundings, explaining meanwhile that she had come across from Mount Kisco in her motor-car that morning, and had been kicking her heels for an hour at Garrisons, without even the alleviation of a cigarette, her brute of a husband having neglected to replenish her case before they parted that morning.

"And at this hour of the day I don't suppose you've a single one left, have you, Lily?" she plaintively concluded.

Miss Bart caught the startled glance of Mr. Percy Gryce, whose own lips were never defiled by tobacco.

"What an absurd question, Bertha!" she exclaimed, blushing at the thought of the store she had laid in at Lawrence Selden's.

"Why, don't you smoke? Since when have you given it up? What—you never— And you don't either, Mr. Gryce? Ah, of course—how stupid of me—I understand."

And Mrs. Dorset leaned back against her travelling cushions with a smile which made Lily wish there had been no vacant seat beside her own.

•

Bridge at Bellomont usually lasted till the small hours; and when Lily went to bed that night she had played too long for her own good.

Feeling no desire for the self-communion which awaited her in her room, she lingered on the broad stairway, looking down into the hall below, where the last card-players were grouped about the tray of tall glasses and silver-collared decanters which the butler had just placed on a low table near the fire.

The hall was arcaded, with a gallery supported on columns of pale yellow marble. Tall clumps of flowering plants were grouped against a background of dark foliage in the angles of the walls. On the crimson carpet a deer-hound and two or three spaniels dozed luxuriously before the fire, and the light from the great central lantern overhead shed a brightness on the women's hair and struck sparks from their jewels as they moved.

There were moments when such scenes delighted Lily, when they gratified her sense of beauty and her craving for the external finish of life; there were others when they gave a sharper edge to the meagerness of her own opportunities. This was one of the moments when the sense of contrast was uppermost, and she turned away impatiently as Mrs. George Dorset, glittering in serpentine spangles, drew Percy Gryce in her wake to a confidential nook beneath the gallery.

It was not that Miss Bart was afraid of losing her newly acquired hold over Mr. Gryce. Mrs. Dorset might startle or dazzle him, but she had neither the skill nor the patience to effect his capture. She was too self-engrossed to penetrate the recesses of his shyness, and besides, why should she care to give herself the trouble? At most it might amuse her to make sport of his simplicity for an evening—after that he would be merely a burden to her, and knowing this, she was far too experienced to encourage him. But the mere thought of that other woman who could take a man up and toss him aside as she willed, without having to regard him as a possible factor in her plans, filled Lily Bart with envy. She had been bored all the afternoon by Percy Gryce—the mere thought seemed to waken an echo of his droning voice—but she could not ignore him on the morrow, she must follow up her success, must submit to more boredom, must be ready with fresh compliances and adaptabilities, and all on the bare chance that he might ultimately decide to do her the honor of boring her for life.

FROM *The Custom of the Country*

Mrs. Fairford made no tactless allusions to her being a new-comer in New York—there was nothing as bitter to the girl as that—but her questions as to what pictures had interested Undine at the various exhibitions of the moment, and which of the new books she had read, were almost as open to suspicion, since they had to be answered in the negative. Undine did not even know that there were any pictures to be seen, much less that "people" went to see them; and she had read no new book but "When The Kissing Had to Stop," of which Mrs. Fairford seemed not to have heard. On the theater they were equally at odds, for while Undine had seen "Oolaloo" fourteen times, and was "wild" about Ned Norris in "The Soda-Water Fountain," she had not heard of the famous Berlin comedians who were performing Shakespeare at the German Theatre, and knew only by name the clever American actress who was trying to give "repertory" plays with a good stock company. The conversation was revived for a moment by her recalling that she had seen Sarah Bernhardt in a play she called "Leg-long," and another which she pronounced "Fade"; but even this did not carry them far, as she had forgotten what both plays were about and had found the actress a good deal older than she expected.

•

His mother and sister of course wanted him to marry. They had the usual theory that he was "made" for conjugal bliss: women always thought that of a fellow who didn't get drunk and have low tastes. Ralph smiled at the idea as he sat crouched among his secret treasures. Marry—but whom, in the name of light and freedom? The daughters of his own race sold themselves to the Invaders; the daughters of the Invaders bought their husbands as they bought an opera-box. It ought all to have been transacted on the Stock Exchange. His mother, he knew, had no such ambitions for him: she would have liked him to fancy a "nice girl" like Harriet Ray. Harriet Ray was neither vulgar nor ambitious. She regarded Washington Square as the birthplace of Society, knew by heart all the cousinships of early New York, hated motor-cars, could not make herself understood on the telephone, and was determined, if she married, never to receive a divorced woman. As Mrs. Marvell often said, such girls as Harriet were growing rare. Ralph was not sure about this. He was inclined to think that, certain modifications allowed for, there would always be plenty of Harriet Rays for unworldly mothers to commend to their sons; and he had no desire to diminish their number by removing one from the ranks of the marriageable.

•

She had read in the "Boudoir Chat" of one of the Sunday papers that the smartest women were using the new pigeon-blood notepaper with white ink; and rather against her mother's advice she had ordered a large supply, with her monogram in silver. It was a disappointment, therefore, to find that Mrs. Fairford wrote on the old-fashioned white sheet, without even a monogram—simply her address and telephone number. It gave Undine rather a poor opinion of Mrs. Fairford's social standing, and for a moment she thought with considerable satisfaction of answering the note on her pigeon-blood paper. Then she remembered Mrs. Heeny's emphatic commendation of Mrs. Fairford, and her pen wavered. What if white paper were really newer than pigeon-blood? It might be more stylish, anyhow. Well, she didn't care if Mrs. Fairford didn't like red paper—*she* did!

Frances Miriam Whitcher
(1812–1852)

❦

Hezekiah Bedott

He was a wonderful hand to mortalize, husband was, specially after he begun to enjoy poor health. He made an observation once, when he was in one of his poor turns, that I shall never forget the longest day I live.

He says to me one winter evenin as we was a-settin by the fire—I was a-knittin. I was always a great knitter—and he was smokin, though the doctor used to tell him he'd be better off to leave tobacco alone. When he was well, he used to take his pipe and smoke a spell after he'd got the chores done up, and when he warn't well, he used to smoke the biggest part of the time.

Well, he took his pipe out of his mouth and turned toward me, and I knowed somethin was comin, for he had a particular way of lookin round when he was a-goin to say anything uncommon. Well, he says to me, "Silly,"—my name was Prisilly, naturally, but he generally called me "Silly" because 'twas handier, you know—well, he says to me, "Silly," and he looked pretty solemn, I tell you! He had a solemn countenance, and after he got to be deacon 'twas more so, but since he'd lost his health he looked solemner than ever, and certainly you wouldn't wonder at it if you knew how much he underwent. He was troubled with a pain in his chest and mazin weakness in the spine of his back, besides the pleurisy in his side, and bein broke of his rest of nights because he was put to it for breath when he laid down. Why, it's an unaccountable fact that when that man died he hadn't seen a well day in fifteen year, though when he was married and for five or six year after, I shouldn't desire to see a ruggeder man than he was. But the time I'm a-speakin of, he'd been out of health nigh upon ten year, and, oh dear sakes! How he had altered since the first time I ever see him! That was to a quiltin to Squire Smith's a spell before Sally was married. I'd no idea *then* that Sal Smith was a-goin to be married to Sam Pendergrass. She'd been keepin company with Mose Hewlitt for better'n a year, and everybody said *that* was a settled thing and lo and behold! All of a sudden she up and took Sam Pendergrass. Well, that was the first time I ever see my husband, and if anybody'd a-told me then that I should ever marry him, I should a-said—

But lawful sakes! I was a-goin to tell you what he said to me that evenin, and when a body begins to tell a thing I believe in finishin on it some time or other. Some folks have a way of talkin round and round and round for evermore. Now there's Miss Jenkins, she that was Poll Bingham before she was married—but what husband said to me was this. He says to me, "Silly."

Says I, "What?" I didn't say, "What, Hezekiah?" for I didn't like his name. The first time I ever heard it I near killed myself a-laughin. "Hezekiah Bedott!" says I. "Well, I would give up if I had such a name!" But then, you know, I had no more idea of marryin the feller than you have this minute of marryin the governor. I suppose you think it's curious we should name our oldest son Hezekiah. Well, we done it to please Father and Mother Bedott. It's his name, and he and Mother Bedott both used to think that names had ought to go down from generation to generation. But we always called him Kiah, you know. That boy *is* a blessin! I ain't the only one that thinks so, I guess. Now, don't you ever tell anybody that I said so, but between you and me, I rather guess that if Kesiah Winkle thinks she's a-goin to catch Kiah Bedott, she is a *little* out of her reckonin!

Well, husband he says to me, "Silly." And says I, "What?" though I'd no idea what he was a-goin to say, didn't know but what it was somethin about his sufferins, though he warn't apt to complain, but used to say that he wouldn't wish his worst enemy to suffer one minute as he did all the time, but that can't be called grumblin—think it can? Why, I've seen him when you'd a-thought no mortal could a-helped grumblin, but *he* didn't. He and me went once in the dead of winter in a one-hoss sleigh out to see a sister of his. You know the snow is deep in this section of the country. Well, the hoss got stuck in one of them snow banks, and there we set, unable to stir, and to cap it all, husband was took with a dreadful crick in his back. Now that is what I call a predicament! Most men would a-swore, but husband didn't. We might a-been settin there to this day, far as *I* know, if there hadn't a-happened to come along a mess of men in a double team, and they pulled us out.

But husband says to me—I could see by the light of the fire, for there didn't happen to be any candle burnin, if I don't disremember, though my memory is sometimes rather forgetful, but I know we weren't apt to burn candles exceptin' when we had company—I could see by the light of the fire that his mind was uncommon solemnized. Says he to me, "Silly."

I says to him, "What?"

He says to me, says he, "We're all poor creatures."

N. P. Willis (1806–1867)

❧ ❧

Miss Albina McLush

I have a passion for fat women. If there is anything I hate in life it is what dainty people call a spirituelle. Motion—rapid motion—a smart, quick, squirrel-like step, a pert, voluble tone—in short, a lively girl—is my exquisite horror! I would as lief have a diable petit dancing his infernal horn-pipe on my cerebellum as to be in the room with one. I have tried before now to school myself into liking these parched peas of humanity. I have followed them with my eyes, and attended to their rattle till I was as crazy as a fly in a drum. I have danced with them, and romped with them in the country, and periled the salvation of my "white tights" by sitting near them at supper. I swear off from this moment. I do. I won't—no—hang me if ever I show another small, lively, spry woman a civility.

Albina McLush is divine. She is like the description of the Persian beauty by Hafiz: "Her heart is full of passion and her eyes are full of sleep." She is the sister of Lurly McLush, my old college chum, who, as early as his sophomore year, was chosen president of the *Dolce far niente* Society—no member of which was ever known to be surprised at anything (the college law of rising before breakfast excepted). Lurly introduced me to his sister one day, as he was lying upon a heap of turnips, leaning on his elbow with his head in his hand, in a green lane in the suburbs. He had driven over a stump, and been tossed out of his gig, and I came up just as he was wondering how in the d—l's name he got there! Albina sat quietly in the gig, and when I was presented, requested me, with a delicious drawl, to say nothing about the adventure—it would be so troublesome to relate it to everybody! I loved her from that moment. Miss McLush was tall, and her shape, of its kind, was perfect. It was not a fleshy one exactly, but she was large and full. Her skin was clear, fine-grained and transparent; her temples and forehead perfectly rounded and polished, and her lips and chin swelling into a ripe and tempting pout like the cleft of a bursted apricot. And then her eyes—large, liquid and sleepy—they languished beneath their long black fringes as if they had no business with daylight—like two magnificent dreams, surprised in their jet embryos by some bird-nesting cherub. Oh! it was lovely to look into them!

She sat, usually, upon a fauteuil, with her large, full arm embedded in the cushion, sometimes for hours without stirring. I have seen the wind lift the masses of dark hair from her shoulders when it seemed like the coming to life of a marble Hebe—she had been motionless so long. She was a model for a goddess of sleep as she sat with her eyes half-closed, lifting up their superb lids slowly as you spoke to her, and dropping them again with the deliberate motion of a cloud, when she had murmured out her syllable of assent. Her figure, in a sitting posture, presented a gentle declivity from the curve of her neck to the instep of the small round foot lying on its side upon the ottoman. I remember a fellow's bringing her a plate of fruit one evening. He was one of your lively men—a horrid monster, all right angles and activity. Having never been accustomed to hold her own plate, she had not well extricated her whole fingers from her handkerchief before he set it down in her lap. As it began to slide slowly toward her feet, her hand relapsed into the muslin folds, and she fixed her eye upon it with a kind of indolent surprise, drooping her lids gradually till, as the fruit scattered over the ottoman, they closed entirely, and a liquid jet line was alone visible through the heavy lashes. There was an imperial indifference in it worthy of Juno

Miss McLush rarely walks. When she does, it is with the deliberate majesty of a Dido. Her small, plump feet melt to the ground like snowflakes; and her figure sways to the indolent motion of her limbs with a glorious grace and yieldingness quite indescribable. She was idling slowly up the Mall one evening just at twilight, with a servant at a short distance behind her, who, to while away the time between his steps, was employing himself in throwing stones at the cows feeding upon the Common. A gentleman, with a natural admiration for splendid person, addressed her. He might have done a more eccentric thing. Without troubling herself to look at him, she turned to her servant and requested him, with a yawn of desperate ennui, to knock that fellow down! John obeyed his orders; and, as his mistress resumed her lounge, picked up a new handful of pebbles, and tossing one at the nearest cow, loitered lazily after.

Such supreme indolence was irresistible. I gave in—I—who never before could summon energy to sigh—I—to whom a declaration was but a synonym for perspiration—I—who had only thought of love as a nervous complaint, and of women but to pray for a good deliverance—I—yes—I—knocked under. Albina McLush! Thou were too exquisitely lazy. Human sensibilities cannot hold out forever.

I found her one morning sipping her coffee at twelve, with her eyes wide open. She was just from the bath, and her complexion had a soft, dewy transparency, like the cheek of Venus rising from the sea. It was the hour, Lurly had told me, when she would be at the trouble of thinking. She put away with her dimpled forefinger, as I entered, a cluster of rich curls that had fallen over her face, and nodded to me like a waterlily swaying to the wind when its cup is full of rain.

"Lady Albina," said I, in my softest tone, "how are you?"

"Bettina," she said, addressing her maid in a voice as clouded and rich as the south wind on an Aeolian, "how am I today?"

The conversation fell into short sentences. The dialogue became a monologue. I entered upon my declaration. With the assistance of Bettina, who supplied her mistress with cologne, I kept her attention alive through the incipient circumstances. Symptoms were soon told. I came to the avowal. Her hand lay reposing on the arm of the sofa half-buried in a muslin foulard. I took it up and pressed the cool soft fingers to my lips—unforbidden. I rose and looked into her eyes for confirmation. Delicious creature—she was asleep!

Herman Wouk (Contemporary)

~~~~

FROM *City Boy*

. . . they arrived at Golden's Restaurant on Southern Boulevard without exchanging another word.

Herbie's heart glowed within him at the sight of the steaks, fruits, layer cakes, and thickly creamed pastries in the glittering show window of Golden's, while Mr. Bookbinder, seeing Powers, Louis Glass, and Krieger seated at a table near the window, suddenly wondered whether bringing Herbie had not been a foolish deed. An impulse to honor the boy, a vague sense that he was in the habit of neglecting him, and an equally cloudy notion that the time had come to give his son the baptism of fire of a real business discussion had combined to cause his act. Now he sensed an urge to send him home. But Jacob Bookbinder was not in the habit of altering his resolutions. In fact, it was his way to quell his own hesitancy with grim pleasure. "Do it and see," was his favorite word to himself. He had invited Herbie to dinner at Golden's, and dinner at Golden's Herbie would have.

"Come, my boy, I see we're late," he said, and led his son inside.

Introducing Herbie was as awkward as his father expected, but he met the astonished glances of the others squarely and explained that he was rewarding his boy with a treat because he had skipped. Louis Glass, a fat, rubicund man with a black mustache, shook Herbie's hand and congratulated him. He had seen many youngsters ripen into clients yielding fees. Powers, already out of sorts at being dragged up to the Bronx after dark, permitted himself to look annoyed as he rapped the ash out of his pipe and thrust it into a pocket.

Krieger delivered his views as follows: "Same father, same son. Haybie big future. Maybe not go too fast better. Little fat boy in college better maybe not. Slow and steady turtle beat rabbit. Haybie different naturally. Smart is very fine—"

The table had places only for four. As Mr. Krieger rattled on, the waiter moved a narrow serving table alongside, projecting into the aisle. Here Herbie sat, looking like an extremely unnecessary appendage to the group. Menus were placed in the hands of the diners, and the men ordered their meals carelessly and quickly.

No so Herbie.

"What should I have, Pa?" he said nervously, bewildered by the menu.

"You're old enough to order for yourself. Have whatever you want."

Herbie ran his eye up and down the page and got a confused impression of a meal composed of sponge cake, pastry, smoked salmon, goulash, vegetables in sour cream, roast chicken, chopped herring, prunes, and ice cream.

"I—I'm not very hungry," he faltered.

"Then skip down to the main course. That's all we're having," said the father, and indicated a section of the bill of fare with his finger.

This was a help. But having to choose among lamb chops, broiled chicken, roast duck, steak, and so forth was still torture—not less for the youngster than for the waiter, a squat, bitter-faced bald man in greasy black trousers and spotted gray cotton jacket. This functionary shifted from foot to foot while Herbie puzzled; he yawned, he rapped his pencil against the order pad, he went "ha-hem" several times, and he stared malevolently at the boy, obviously wishing him far away and in bad health.

"Come, Herbie, the man can't stand there forever," said the father.

Powers said, "The kid evidently doesn't know what he wants. Order for him."

"I'll have the boiled haddock," Herbie burst out all at once, picking the item under his eye at that instant.

Everybody, even the waiter, looked amazed.

"Don't be silly, boy," said Jacob Bookbinder. "Boiled haddock, with all those delicious meat dishes to pick from? Come, take a steak."

But Herbie felt that his self-respect, his whole grip on manhood, depended on his sticking to the haddock now, although he loathed it. "Can't a guy order what he wants?" he complained. "I ordered boiled haddock, and that's what I'd like."

"Give him boiled haddock," said his father with a shrug. The waiter pried the bill of fare out of Herbie's spasmodically clutching fingers and walked off. Herbie gloomily watched the stooped back disappear through the swinging kitchen doors, and cursed his own folly.

The consequences were worse than he imagined. Golden's was mainly a meat restaurant. The fish was a desultory item placed on the menu for the rare customer who insisted on fish. Soon the waiter reappeared with four sizzling steaks that smelled heavenly, and a plate containing a pair of round blobs, white and green. The white was the haddock, buried under a thick flour sauce; the green was an unexpected horror, creamed spinach, which came with the fish. As the waiter put Herbie's plate down he winked, and all the men laughed. Herbie felt a blush rise to his face.

"That fish looks disgusting," said his father. "Waiter, take that mess away and bring the boy some lamb chops."

"Pa, please, this is just what I want," cried Herbie angrily. He placed his hand protectingly against the plate, and the gluey white mass trembled a little. The boy's throat crawled at the prospect of eating it. But he was going to eat it or die.

"After all, Bookbinder, he's grown up," said Powers with a grin. "Didn't he just skip to the eighth grade?"

Herbie's father glanced at the young man from Manhattan with narrowed eyes.

"All right, my boy," he said to Herbie. "But as long as you ordered it, eat it."

And Herbie, who understood his father's appeal not to disgrace him, ate it, with all the men watching him. Not a morsel of spinach or haddock remained. Heroes in other books do more noble and colorful deeds, but Herbie Bookbinder stands or falls as a hero for swallowing down every trace of those two ghastly mounds, green and white, and smacking his lips over them.

"Well, Bookbinder," said Powers when the steaks were eaten, leaning back and packing his pipe from an alligator-skin pouch, "do we talk business or do you send the boy home first?"

"The boy's doing no harm," retorted Bookbinder, "unless you other gentlemen object to him."

There was a difficult pause.

"Why, I think," said Louis Glass heartily, "that it'll do Herbie good to hear a business talk. Hear a business talk. Nothing like starting early in life, early in life, eh, Herbie?" He slapped the boy lightly on the back, and lit a cigar.

The waiter brought dessert. It was a house custom at Golden's to serve French pastry on a little flat stand, which was placed on the table when coffee was served, and left there. The stand accommodated eight pieces. The waiter simply counted the number missing at the close of the meal, and charged for them on the bill. None of the men accepted a piece when the waiter offered it to them, so he set the little stand down before Herbie and departed. The boy felt his shattered appetite pull itself together as he surveyed the eight creamy pastries, all of different shapes and colors.

Louis Glass polished the pince-nez that hung on a black ribbon around his neck. "Well, gentlemen, I see no reason why we can't settle our business between the time we start our coffee and finish it. Start our coffee and finish it," he said.

"That'll suit me beautifully," remarked Powers. "I'm late for a theater party now."

Bookbinder and Krieger said nothing.

Herbie tentatively selected a chocolate-covered cylinder filled with whipped cream, and sank his teeth into it. He seemed to hear chimes of Paradise. By comparison with this, the frap itself sank out of sight.

"There's only one thing to be discussed," went on Louis Glass. "I've described to you, Bookbinder, the advantages that will accrue to both you and Krieger from a merger of Bronx River with Interborough. I've made it as clear as I can that Interborough, which is now the largest ice company in New York, will guarantee to give both of you top executive positions. As I happen to be their attorney, I am speaking with some authority, with some authority. I have also given you my opinion that the so-called blue paper is a totally irregular document, no more than a scratch-pad memorandum, in effect, which does not transfer in due and proper form any stocks to you, and have advised you that if you choose to stand on it your stand will be overthrown in court. Overthrown in court."

During this speech, Herbie finished the whipped-cream roll in three rapturous bites. He now chose a charming oval piece entirely covered with green and chocolate cream, and bit into it.

"Your decision, then, as I see it," proceeded the lawyer, waving away clouds of blue smoke from Powers' fast-puffing pipe, "must be the sensible one of accepting this great increase in your good fortunes—I refer to the merger—or the highly dubious one of a court fight as to whether you or Mr. Powers has control of the Place, which I have stated you will lose. Stated you will lose."

Herbie heard these words dimly through the fog of ecstasy conjured up by French pastry, and wondered why Mr. Glass had the habit of acting as his own echo. But he forgot the perplexity as the last bite of mint and chocolate vanished, leaving him with the urgent question, which cake to eat next. The boy was not aware that these things would have to be paid for. They had been set before him like a bowl of fruit at home, and so he regarded them. After the haddock horror, it seemed to him that the only way to retrieve the glory of a restaurant meal was to consume as many pastries as he could hold. So he selected a chocolate éclair, and went to work on it.

When the lawyer finished talking, Bookbinder and

Krieger looked at each other. Herbie's father started to speak, but Krieger hastily and loudly broke in, "I say this way. Blue paper maybe yes, maybe no, who say for sure? I say peaceable. Executive position ten thousand a year very fine, maybe three thousand not so fine. But peaceable black and white on paper how much guaranteed? All gentlemen, word good as gold, but black and white on paper not yet. Thirty years in the ice business always black and white more peaceable. Mr. Glass very fine explain, everybody good friends all stick together. I say this way—"

(The éclair gone, Herbie commenced a rapid demolition of a round brown pastry that looked rather like a potato but was filled with exquisite orange-flavored cream.)

"If I understand you correctly, Mr. Krieger," interrupted Louis Glass, "I believe you need say no more. Interborough is prepared to guarantee in writing, as a condition of the merger, both of your salaries at"—he glanced at Powers, who continued puffing at his pipe and gave a tiny nod—"five thousand a year, merely as a beginning. Merely as a beginning."

"You understand him wrong, and what he said meant nothing," exclaimed Jacob Bookbinder, his expression so drawn and belligerent that he hardly resembled the man who had been smiling at his son a little while before. Herbie had seen this expression, which he thought of as his father's "business face," more than once, and it terrified him. He paid more attention to the talk now, as he absently began to eat a flaky yellow Napoleon. . . .

Herbie could not follow the duel and lost interest. For some reason the Napoleon did not taste as good to him as the first four pastries had. He finished it quickly and began on a cherry tart. And now he became aware of a new disturbing fact: the waiter was standing near by, staring at him with a mixture of horror and fascination. With each bite he took of the tart the waiter's eyes seemed to open wider. Herbie could not imagine what the man was looking at. He glanced uneasily at his suit to see if a blotch of food had fallen on it, and looked behind him, but evidently there was no marvel in sight but himself, a perfectly ordinary boy. The waiter's eyes made him self-conscious. He gobbled down the tart, not enjoying it very much, and reached for something he had been saving, a morsel consisting of four walls of solid chocolate brimful of coffee-colored cream. As he bit into it he saw with some discomfort that the waiter's jaw dropped open and he actually grew pale. He concluded the man must be sick—probably from the food in this miserable restaurant. Herbie was feeling none too well himself. The beautiful chocolate cake somehow tasted not much better than the boiled haddock had, and was just as gluey.

The conversation had jumped ahead several notches during Herbie's preoccupation with the waiter. He tried to pick up the thread, nibbling at the pastry more and more slowly. Powers was saying, "—certainly don't see why I had to come uptown at night to hear this same foolish story. I thought you men had come to your senses."

"I cannot help calling it most ill-advised, most ill-advised," the lawyer said, crushing out his half-smoked cigar. "I assure you the blue paper as it stands is worthless. In my opinion, Mr. Powers would be justified in proceeding to sell Bronx River Ice, but we must recognize that as the attorney for Interborough I cannot advise them to purchase a property, title to which is in any way doubtful. Any way doubtful. . . ."

"Yes, I'm a crazy businessman," Bookbinder shot back. "I want to remain a businessman, instead of becoming Burlingame's assistant."

"Pa."

The word came faintly from Herbie's direction. His father turned and looked at him.

"Pa, I don't feel good."

Herbie slumped in his chair, looking straight ahead with dull eyes. In one listless hand hanging at his side was a fragment of chocolate cake. The color of the boy's face was not unlike that of the creamed spinach he had eaten.

"Lord in heaven! He's sick. Why did you have to eat that rotten fish, boy?" said the father in great distress.

"Mister, don't you blame our food!" shouted the waiter. He advanced to the table and raised his right hand high. "I hope I drop dead if that boy didn't eat seven pieces of French pastry. Seven pieces, mister! I saw him with my own eyes. From that even an elephant would get sick. I personally don't feel good from watching him."

Herbie stood up unsteadily.

"I guess I'll go home, Pa," he said. His stomach seemed

to him to be rippling like a lake in a breeze; he could see mistily before his eyes the colored images of all the pastries he had eaten, swimming slowly around; and the word "frap" kept repeating itself in his brain—frap, frap, frap—and was somehow the most loathsome sound that man had ever uttered.

"Come, my boy, I'll take you." Bookbinder jumped up and grasped the boy's arm. "Gentlemen, our business was finished anyway, so excuse me for leaving like this. Mr. Powers, believe me you'll live to thank me for keeping our business in our own hands. Krieger, pay my check. Good night."

He rushed the boy outside and stood with him at the curb, signaling for a taxi. But none came at once, and Herbert, teetering on the curb, endured all the agonies of a rough sea voyage and then suddenly enjoyed the sovereign relief that comes of leaning over the rail. His father sympathetically gave him aid, and then walked the pale shaky boy home. Fresh air was better for him, now, than a taxi. The walk gradually revived Herbie, and through the darkness of his discomfort the drift of the business talk began to come back to him.

"Pa," he said timidly, "can Mr. Powers really sell the Place and throw you an' Mr. Krieger out?"

"Don't you worry about that," said Bookbinder. But his face was tense and sad. "Forget everything you heard, Herbie. For you it's castor oil and bed."

And thus, with castor oil, bed, and a chilly awareness that he had failed to distinguish himself, ended Herbie Bookbinder's first evening as a man among men.

Author Biographies

Scott Adams (Contemporary)

Born and raised in Windham, New York, Adams received a B.A. in Economics from Hartwick College in 1979 and an MBA from the University of California at Berkeley in 1986. His experiences in the workplace, particularly at Crocker Bank and at Pacific Bell in the San Francisco Bay Area, inspired his famous comic strip Dilbert. Adams has described his cartoon hero as a composite of many of his past co-workers. He has published more than a dozen collections of Dilbert strips, and Dilbert appears in 1700 newspapers in 51 countries.

George Ade (1866–1944)

George Ade was born in Indiana and read Mark Twain's books as a child. His first publication, a school composition titled "A Basket of Potatoes," appeared in the *Gazette* in 1881. He attended Purdue University on a scholarship and graduated in 1887. He moved to Chicago in 1890 and wrote for the Chicago *Morning News*, which changed its name to the *News-Record*, and eventually to the *Record*. He wrote columns in collaboration with John McCutcheon until 1897. A collection of Ade's "Artie" sketches appeared in 1896 under the title *Artie, a Story of Streets and Town*; *Artie* led to his "discovery" by William Dean Howells. Ade started writing his "Fables" in 1897; the collections *Fables in Slang* (1899) and *More Fables* (1900) followed. The Fables were soon syndicated and more than a dozen collections were eventually published. Ade also found some success as a playwright; he wrote *The Sultan of Sulu* (1902),

Peggy from Paris (1903), *The College Widow* (1904), and *The Old Town* (1910), among other plays.

Louisa May Alcott (1832–1888)

Louisa May Alcott was the daughter of Bronson Alcott, well-known Transcendentalist, abolitionist, and educational reformer; her childhood provided not only the material for much of her best-known work, but the experience of poverty that shaped her determination to be self-supporting. Her early positions as a governess, companion, domestic servant and Civil War nurse are treated in *Work: A Story of Experience* (1861); later, she was able to support herself and her family through her writing. Alcott is most famous for her children's novels, especially the classic *Little Women* (1868), *Little Men* (1871), and *Jo's Boys* (1886), but she also wrote sensation stories and gothic thrillers, either anonymously or under a pseudonym, as well as more "serious" works for adults. Her second novel, *Moods*, deals with adultery and divorce; *Transcendental Wild Oats* (1873) is based on Alcott's experience at Fruitlands, a short-lived Utopian community established by her father. She never married, but remained close to her family and devoted much energy to such causes as women's suffrage. Some of her other works are *Hospital Sketches* (1863), *An Old-Fashioned Girl* (1870), *Eight Cousins* (1875), and *Rose in Bloom* (1876).

Woody Allen (Contemporary)

Allen was born Allen Stewart Konigsberg in New York City. An extremely prolific screenwriter and film director, Allen began his career in show business as a comedy writer for television. His first produced screenplay, *What's New Pussycat?*, was made into a movie in which he starred in 1965. *Take the Money and Run* (1969) marked his debut as director of his own material. His major films include *Play It Again, Sam* (1972); *Annie Hall* (1977), which received four Academy Awards, including Best Picture; *Manhattan* (1979); *Zelig* (1983); *Hannah and Her Sisters* (1986); and *Husbands and Wives* (1992).

Regina Barreca (Contemporary)

A short biography of the editor appears elsewhere in this volume.

Dave Barry (Contemporary)

A celebrated syndicated columnist and successful humorist, Dave Barry was born in New York State. He won the Pulitzer Prize for Commentary in 1988. His titles include *Dave Barry's Guide to Marriage and/or Sex* (1987), *Dave Barry Talks Back* (1991), *Dave Barry Does Japan* (1992), *Dave Barry Is Not Making This Up* (1994), *Dave Barry in Cyberspace* (1996), *Dave Barry Is from Mars and Venus* (1997), and *Dave Barry Turns 50* (1998).

Lynda Barry (Contemporary)

Born in Wisconsin, Barry grew up in Seattle and became the first member of her Filipino-American family to go to college. She was a fine arts major at Evergreen State College in Olympia, Washington, in 1977 when she started drawing cartoons following a breakup with her boyfriend. Barry began her collaboration with *Esquire* in the early 1980s and her work was soon syndicated in weekly newspapers like the *Village Voice* and *L.A. Weekly* throughout the country. She adapted her novel *The Good Times Are Killing Me* (1988) for the stage in 1991. Barry's titles include *Girls & Boys* (1981), *The Fun House* (1987), *Heap Big Dysfunctional World* (1990), *My Perfect Life* (1992), and *It's So Magic* (1994).

Robert Benchley (1889–1945)

One of the most famous members of the Algonquin Round Table group, Benchley was born in Worcester, Massachusetts, and received a degree from Harvard in 1912. In addition to collaborating with numerous magazines in New York in the 1920s, Benchley worked in Hollywood as a radio and film actor, writer, and producer. He won an Academy Award in 1936 for his short film *How to Sleep*. His titles include *20,000 Leagues Under the Sea or, David*

Copperfield, Benchley—or Else, Pluck and Luck, Love Conquers All, and *My Ten Years in a Quandary and How They Grew.*

Elizabeth Berg (Contemporary)

Elizabeth Berg, who lives in Massachusetts, is the best-selling author of *Joy School, Durable Goods, Talk Before Sleep, Range of Motion*, and *The Pull of the Moon.* She won the 1997 New England Book Sellers' Award for fiction, and her novels have met with wide critical acclaim. Berg's work tends to focus on relationships and other aspects of ordinary, everyday life. "I'd rather read—and write—about people in kitchens than in Paris," she has said. "I think all the depth we need can be found in simple life."

Jennifer Berman (Contemporary)

Jennifer Berman is a nationally syndicated cartoonist whose work appears in both major dailies and alternative weeklies, as well as magazines such as *Ms., Harper's, Mademoiselle* and *Glamour.* Her cartoons often appear for the first time in her line of postcards. Berman's books include *Why Dogs Are Better Than Men, Adult Children of Normal Parents*, and *Why Dogs Are Better Than Republicans* (1996). She lives in Chicago.

Ambrose Bierce (1842–1913 or 14?)

The man who would later be known as the "Wickedest Man in San Francisco" was born in Ohio, grew up in Indiana, and worked as a printer's assistant on the anti-slavery newspaper *Northern Indianian* between the ages of fifteen and seventeen. He studied at the Kentucky Military Institute in 1859 and enlisted for the Civil War, during which he was involved in most of the deadliest battles. Bierce was severely wounded and discharged in 1865. The following year, he joined a mapping expedition covering the territories between Nebraska and California. He began working as a professional writer in San Francisco in 1867; he quickly became well known for his weekly column, "The Town Crier," in the *Newsletter.* At the height of his popularity, he was famous for his humorous writings from San Francisco to London, where he lived between 1872 and 1875, and where his first three books appeared under the pseudonym Dod Grile. He was editor of the weekly magazine *Wasp* between 1881 and 1886. His books include *Tales of Soldiers and Civilians* (1891), *Fantastic Fables* (1899), *Write It Right* (1909), and *The Cynic's Word Book* (1906), later reprinted as *The Devil's Dictionary* (1911). Bierce died in mysterious circumstances in Mexico, where he was last seen on December 26, 1913.

Amy Bloom (Contemporary)

Amy Bloom's highly acclaimed first book, *Come To Me: Stories* (1993), was a National Book Award Finalist and was also a finalist for the *Los Angeles Times* Fiction Award. Her novel *Love Invents Us*—described by the *Los Angeles Times* as "lyrical and funny"—was also welcomed with considerable praise. Bloom's stories have appeared in such publications as *The New Yorker*, *Story*, *Antaeus*, and *River City*; they have been anthologized in *Best American Stories* of 1991 and 1992 and in the 1994 *O. Henry Prize Story Collection*. Bloom is also a contributing editor for *New Woman* and the *Boston Review of Books*. She lives in Connecticut.

Elayne Boosler (Contemporary)

Elayne Boosler, a popular comedian, has performed her stand-up routine in countless venues. Her first television special, *Party of One*, aired in 1986, and was followed by *Broadway Baby*, *Top Tomata*, and *Live Nude Girls*. She has also made numerous appearances on such shows as *Politically Incorrect*, *The Today Show*, and *Crossfire*. The *New York Times* once commented of her, "How refreshing, a woman who doesn't have to tear her own skin off for our amusement."

Hugh Henry Brackenridge (1748–1816)

Born in Scotland, Brackenridge moved to the United States as a child and was raised in York County, Pennsylvania. He studied law at Princeton and was all his life committed to the idea of an educated population. The man who would later be known as the "worst of the Whiskey Rebels" lived for twenty years in the then frontier town of Pittsburgh from 1781 to 1801. During that time he wrote satires, essays and poems and published his most famous work, a satire of the New Republic entitled *Modern Chivalry* (1792). He was committed to, and deeply involved with, the democratic experiment but his years on the frontier as a justice of the Supreme Court of Pennsylvania severely tested his democratic ideals. In addition to his professional involvement with the law, Brackenridge founded the *United States Magazine* and contributed to the *Pittsburgh Gazette*. He also published *The Rising Glory of America*, a mixture of his political and literary interests.

Mel Brooks (Contemporary)

Brooks was born Melvin Kaminsky in Brooklyn, New York. He served during World War II and organized shows for his fellow servicemen. He began working as a stand-up comedian in the Catskills when he returned to the United States after the war. In the 1950s Brooks worked as a television writer with Neil Simon, Woody Allen, and Carl Reiner. He teamed up with Reiner in 1960 for the popular routines called "The 2000 Year Old Man"; Brooks and Reiner made a hit record and appeared on numerous televisions shows to perform these routines. Brooks went on to win three Grammy Awards for this landmark role. In the late 1960s, Brooks turned his attention to movies. He won an Academy Award for his screenplay *The Producers*. Brooks's films as director include *Blazing Saddles* (1973), *Young Frankenstein* (1974), *Silent Movie* (1976), and *Space Balls* (1987). His production company, Brooksfilms, is responsible for more serious movie fare such as *84 Charing Cross Road*, starring his wife, Anne Bancroft.

Claude Brown (Contemporary)

Claude Brown was born in New York City; his parents had migrated North from South Carolina in search of work. He grew up in Harlem and became a member of a street gang by the age of ten. He was sent to the Wiltwyck school for delinquent boys but at thirteen he was back on the streets and shot during an attempted bank robbery. Brown graduated from high school in 1957, played jazz in Greenwich Village, and received a degree from Howard University in 1965. That same year he published his highly regarded autobiography, *Manchild in the Promised Land.* The book met with instant success and turned Brown into a prominent voice in American letters. His second book, *Children of Ham* (1976), was less successful but Brown remains active in social causes.

Charles Farrar Browne · "Artemus Ward" (1834–1867)

Browne was born in Waterford, Maine, and at the age of thirteen he became an apprentice at the *Weekly Democrat* in Lancaster, New Hampshire. He later wrote for the Boston weekly *Carpet-Bag*, then moved to Ohio and worked in the printing trade until he became an editor at the Cleveland *Plain Dealer* in 1857. He invented the persona of Artemus Ward in the pages of the *Dealer.* Browne left Cleveland three years later and began working as a regular contributor for *Vanity Fair.* He traveled extensively until his death, of tuberculosis, in 1867. He was an important figure in American humor during the Civil War era, and his lectures, which probably influenced Mark Twain, met with popular success from San Francisco to London. Browne's books include *Artemus Ward; His Book* (1862), *Artemus Ward; His Travels* (1865), and *Artemus Ward Among the Fenians* (1866). His *Collected Works* appeared in 1870.

Christopher Buckley (Contemporary)

A novelist, essayist, and humorist, Buckley contributes regularly to the *New York Times*, the *Washington Post*, and *The New Yorker.* His titles include the satire *The White House Mess*, the novel *Thank You for Smoking* (1994), and *Steaming to Bamboola.* He lives in Washington, D.C., and works as the editor of *Forbes FYI Magazine.*

H. C. Bunner (1855–1896)

Well known in the late nineteenth century as a short-story writer, parodist, and essayist, Bunner was born in Oswego, New York, where he grew up until he moved with his family to New York City in 1865. He attended prep school and was planning to enroll at Columbia University, but financial problems forced him to leave school in 1871 and work for a wine importer. He started contributing short essays to periodicals and in 1877 he became the editor of *Puck: The Comic Weekly*, a position he kept until his death. Bunner settled with his family in New Jersey in 1887 and died of tuberculosis in 1896. His titles include *A Woman of Honor* (1883), *Story of a New York House* (1887), *"Made in France": French Tales Retold With a United States Twist* (1893), *The Suburban Sage* (1896), and *Love in Old Clothes and Other Stories* (1897).

George Carlin (Contemporary)

George Carlin's career in comedy began in radio, at age nineteen, while he was in the Air Force. He went on to make appearances on numerous television shows, including a number of HBO specials in the 1970s and 80s. Carlin is perhaps best known for his "Seven Words You Can't Say on Television" monologue; his often controversial humor is known for its intelligence and irreverence as well as its profanity. Carlin's 1972 album *FM & AM* received a Grammy Award; later recordings include *Class Clown* (1986) and *Parental Advisory—Explicit Lyrics* (1990). He won Cable-Ace awards for the shows *Doin' It Again* and *Jammin' in New York*—which also won a Grammy Award for best spoken-word comedy album. Carlin is also the author of *Brain Droppings* (1997).

Roz Chast (Contemporary)

Chast was born in Brooklyn and decided to become a cartoonist after discovering Charles Addams at the age of eight. She received a B.F.A. from the Rhode Island School of Design in 1977 and published cartoons in *The Village Voice* and *National Lampoon* before finding a permanent home for her work at *The New Yorker* in 1979. Her cartoons have been collected in more than seven volumes, including *Proof of Life on Earth* (1991). She has also illustrated children's books, including *Now Everybody Hates Me*.

James David Corrothers (1869–1917)

James Corrothers was born in Michigan; his parents were of mixed African and European American descent. He attended Northwestern University and became a school teacher. His friend Paul Dunbar encouraged him to write poetry and his dialect verse was published in the *Century Magazine*. He wrote humorous "negro" reports for the *Chicago Journal* and other newspapers; these pieces were later collected in the volume *The Black Cat Club* (1902). He became a Methodist minister until he was unjustly expelled from his church; he later became a Baptist, then a Presbyterian. He published an autobiography, *In Spite of the Handicap*, in 1916. He was famous in his time as a spokesman for the black community.

Bill Cosby (Contemporary)

Bill Cosby's long and successful career began on the nightclub circuit before Cosby landed a part on the television series *I Spy*, for which he eventually won three Emmy Awards for best actor. His later T.V. shows include *The Bill Cosby Show*, *Cos*, and the enormously popular series *The Cosby Show*. He has won five Grammy Awards for best comedy album; his albums include *Bill Cosby Is a Very Funny Fellow . . . Right?*, *I Started Out as a Child*, and *Wonderfulness*. He has also appeared in a number of feature films. His books include *Fatherhood* (1993), *Love and Marriage* (1989), and *Kids Say the Darndest Things* (1998).

Frederick Swartout Cozzens (1818–1869)

Born in New York City, Frederick Cozzens combined two unlikely professions, that of author and wine merchant. He considered literature only an avocation, yet he published essays, sketches, and poems throughout his life. In 1847 he published *Yankee Doodle*, a humorous imitation of Spenser.

For eight years he contributed anonymously to the *Knicker-bocker Magazine*. He published his miscellaneous writings in the volume *Prismatics* in 1853 under the pseudonym of his ancestor Richard Haywarde. He was most famous in his century for his *Sparrowgrass Papers*, a humorous take on the city man's experiences in rural Yonkers. He also created the monthly *Wine Press* magazine.

Josephine Dodge Daskam [Bacon] (1876–1961)

Josephine Bacon used her maiden name, Daskam, for most of her publications. A prolific author of short stories, novels, articles, and poems, she graduated from Smith College in 1898 and published her *Smith College Stories* in 1900. She raised three children while contributing to magazines like *Harper's Bazaar*, *Ladies' Home Journal*, and the *Saturday Evening Post*. One of Bacon's most popular books was *The Memoirs of a Baby* (1904), her satire on baby care and child-rearing. In her serious fiction, Bacon dealt with the New Woman and her struggle to gain a more equal status in society. She wrote the words to the "Hymn for the Nations" for the United Nations and compiled the *Girl Scout National Handbook* (1920). Her works include *Fables for the Fair* (1901), *Domestic Adventures* (1907), and *Kathy* (1934).

Ellen DeGeneres (Contemporary)

Ellen DeGeneres was born in Louisiana and moved to Texas with her mother after her parents' divorce. She attended the University of New Orleans but left before the end of her first semester. She supported her struggling career as a stand-up comic by working as a hostess, waitress, oyster shucker, clerical worker, and house painter. Her first big break happened in 1986 when she appeared on the *Tonight Show* hosted by Johnny Carson. DeGeneres's television sitcom *These Friends of Mine* first aired in 1994; it was soon revamped and renamed *Ellen*. The show and its star made social history when the Emmy-nominated "coming out" episode aired in April 1997. DeGeneres became the first openly gay actress to play a gay lead character on American television. In addition to her stand-up and television work, DeGeneres has also appeared in several movies. Her best-selling *My Point . . . And I Do Have One*, was published in 1995.

Joseph Dennie (1768–1812)

Known in the nineteenth century as "the American Addison," Joseph Dennie grew up in Boston during the exciting years preceding the Revolution. His parents were involved in his education and gave him free rein in their extensive library. He attended Harvard and began writing poetry and essays in 1788. He passed the bar examination in 1794 and opened a law office in Charlestown, New Hampshire. Despite his official career as a lawyer, Dennie found time to write essays for various papers like the *Eagle* and the *Boston Centinel*; the *Federal Orrery* published his satire in 1795. He also became involved with publishing as writer and editor for the *Farmer's Museum* magazine, published out of Walpole, New Hampshire. He wrote the regular *Lay Preacher* essays in the *Farmer's Museum*; these essays, inspired by Sterne's *Sermons of Yorick*, were later printed in two volumes in 1796 and 1816 and established his literary reputation. He moved to Philadelphia, then the nation's capital, and wrote regularly for the *Gazette of the United States*. His most lasting contribution to American letters may be his *Port Folio*, a weekly magazine patterned after the English *Tatler* for which he served as writer and editor from the first issue in 1801 until 1808. The magazine had a nation-wide circulation; Dennie used it to spread his love of literature and to exert his influence on his country's budding culture. He died of cholera in Philadelphia; his tombstone reads: "He devoted his life to the literature of his Country."

Phyllis Diller (Contemporary)

She was born Phyllis Driver and after raising five children she became a stand-up comic at the age of thirty-seven with the encouragement of her husband. Her first success as a comedian happened at San Francisco's Purple Onion club in 1955. She went on to star in three television series and in *Hello, Dolly!* on Broadway. She created a persona on stage very different from her real-life personality. In addition to her stage performances, Diller wrote several best-selling books, including *The Complete Mother*, *Phyllis Diller's Marriage Manual*, and *The Joys of Aging and How to Avoid Them*.

Ralph Ellison (1914–1994)

Ralph Ellison was born in Oklahoma; his father died when he was only three but his mother, significantly, led protests and campaigned for black civil rights while working as a domestic servant. Ellison studied music at the Tuskegee Institute for a year and then went to New York in order to earn more money for college; there he met some of the people involved in the Harlem Renaissance, as well as Richard Wright, who encouraged him to write. Ellison worked for the Work Projects Administration as a researcher with the New York Federal Writers' Project from 1938 to 1942. In 1944 he received a Rosenfeld Fellowship to work on a novel, and for seven years Ellison worked on *Invisible Man*, which was published in 1952. The novel became a best-seller and won the National Book Award; it also established Ralph Ellison's position as an important American voice and enabled him to spend the ensuing years teaching and lecturing. He later published two collections of essays, *Shadow and Act* (1964) and *Going to the Territory* (1986).

Ralph Waldo Emerson (1803–1882)

A poet, preacher, and essayist, Emerson had a tremendous influence on the works of nineteenth-century writers like Thoreau, Whitman, and Frederick Douglass, among many others. Born and raised in Massachusetts, Emerson was educated at home and at the Boston Latin school, and he attended Harvard on a scholarship. He trained as a minister at Harvard Divinity School, but resigned from the ministry after six years. Throughout his career as a writer, he supported and encouraged fellow authors like Bronson Alcott and Margaret Fuller, while publishing his own essays like the classic "Nature" and "The American Scholar." Emerson died of tuberculosis in Concord, Massachusetts.

Nora Ephron (Contemporary)

A journalist, novelist, screenwriter, and film director, Nora Ephron was born in New York City and grew up in Los Angeles, where her parents worked as a screenwriting team. She turned the story of her public divorce from the Watergate journalist Carl Bernstein into the novel *Heartburn* (1983), later made into a movie with Meryl Streep and Jack Nicholson. Since the late 1980s, Ephron has worked primarily as a screenwriter and film director. In addition to the script for *When Harry Met Sally*, her films as director include *This Is Your Life*, with Julie Kavner; *Sleepless in Seattle*, with Tom Hanks and Meg Ryan; *Michael*, with John Travolta; and *You've Got Mail*, reuniting the popular duo Hanks and Ryan. These films have established Ephron as one of the most powerful women directors in Hollywood. She lives in New York City with her husband, the screenwriter Nicholas Pileggi.

Edward Everett (1794–1865)

Edward Everett was born in Dorchester, Massachusetts, and was admitted to Harvard at the tender age of thirteen, in 1807. He graduated first in his class in 1811 and entered the Divinity School. He was ordained and began practicing as a minister in Boston only to resign after one year. Everett decided to travel to Europe; he met Lord Byron and Walter Scott in England on his way to Germany, where he also met Goethe. He attended the University of Gottingen; there he studied the Bible, then antiquities. He started teaching at Harvard upon returning to the United States and became editor of the *North American Review* from 1820 to 1824. He promoted the arts, literature, and the theater in the magazine's pages, and Emerson praised his articles. He entered politics in 1824 and eventually served four terms as Governor of Massachusetts and ten years in Congress. He was also minister to England from 1841 to 1845, and President of Harvard.

Fanny Fern (1811–1872)

Fanny Fern was born Sara Payson Willis in Portland, Maine, and grew up in Boston. She attended Hartford Female Seminary and married for the first time in 1837. Her husband died without any money in 1846, leaving her with two children. She married a widower with two children of his own, Samuel Farrington, in 1849, but the marriage was a mistake and she left him in 1851 to earn her living through writing. Her first articles appeared in the Boston *Olive Branch* and *True Flag* in 1851. By the following year, Fern was working as a columnist for the *New York Musical World and Times*. She published her first collection of essays, *Fern Leaves from Fanny's Portfolio*, in 1853. Her autobiographical novel *Ruth Hall* appeared in 1854. She became a columnist for the New York *Ledger* and married James Parton in 1856. She wrote her columns, often on taboo or controversial subjects like prostitution and divorce, until her death. Her publications include a second novel, *Rose Clark* (1856), three children's books, and numerous essay collections.

Fannie Flagg (Contemporary)

Fannie Flagg began writing and producing for television when she was nineteen; later she began acting, as well, in television, the theater, and films. Eventually deciding that she had allowed herself to get sidetracked from what she really wanted to be doing, Flagg quit acting in 1980 and has devoted herself to writing ever since. Much of her writing is set in the south, where she grew up, although she now lives in California. Her novels *Daisy Fay and the Miracle Man* and *Fried Green Tomatoes at the Whistle Stop Cafe* were both best-sellers, and Flagg was nominated for an Academy Award for her script for the film adaptation of *Fried Green Tomatoes.* Her most recent novel is *Welcome to the World, Baby Girl* (1998). "I suffer from what most humorists do," Flagg has remarked, "a deep need to be taken seriously."

Jeff Foxworthy (Contemporary)

Foxworthy was born in Atlanta, Georgia, and attended the Georgia Institute of Technology for three years. He worked as a computer repairman before setting out to make it as a comedian. Foxworthy first appeared in an Atlanta comedy club in 1982; his first national exposure was a spot on an HBO special starring Rodney Dangerfield in 1989. By 1991, he was a regular on the Comedy Central program *Comics Only.* His first solo special, *Jeff Foxworthy: You Might Be a Redneck,* also aired in 1991. His publications include *You Might Be a Redneck If. . . , Red Ain't Dead, Hick Is Chic: A Guide to Etiquette for the (Grossly) Unsophisticated,* and *Games Rednecks Play.* He starred in the sitcom *The Jeff Foxworthy Show* from 1995 to 1997. The passage here first appeared in his 1996 autobiography titled *No Shirt, No Shoes, No Problem.*

Redd Foxx (1922–1991)

Redd Foxx, a St. Louis-born African American comedian, began his career on the night-club circuit, taking odd jobs to support himself. By 1968 he had made a name for himself in Las Vegas. In 1970 Foxx appeared in a film called *Cotton Comes to Harlem,* which led to his being cast in the hugely successful television show *Sanford and Son.* The show ran until 1977, and Foxx followed it up with *The Redd Foxx Comedy Hour* (1977–78) and the *Red Foxx Show,* among others. In 1977 he co-edited *The Redd Foxx Encyclopedia of Black Humor.*

Benjamin Franklin (1706–1790)

The legendary author of the *Autobiography* was born in Boston and began publishing essays at age sixteen in his brother's newspaper, *The New England Courant,* under a pseudonym. Philosopher, inventor, philanthropist, pamphleteer, and politician, Franklin penned *Poor Richard's Almanac* (1733–1738), *Proposals Relating to the Education of Youth in Pennsylvania* (1749), and *A Narrative of the Late Massacres* (1764). He spent twenty years in London and wrote satires of England's low opinion of America.

Franklin also served as minister to France during the American Revolution and returned to America in 1785. His most famous speech was written for the Constitutional Convention in Philadelphia in 1787. He died before completing his celebrated *Autobiography*, written and revised between 1771 and 1789.

Lewis Burke Frumkes (Contemporary)

Frumkes teaches at Marymount Manhattan College where he is also director of the Writing Center. He contributes to numerous magazines and newspapers and hosts a weekly radio program featuring interviews with celebrities. His books include *How to Raise Your I.Q. by Eating Gifted Children* (1979) and *Manhattan Cocktail* (1989).

Charlotte Perkins Gilman (1860–1935)

Charlotte Perkins Gilman was one of the most important intellectuals in the women's movement from the 1890s to the 1920s; she wrote and lectured on women's rights and other social reform issues. During her life she was best known for sociological studies like *Women and Economics* (1898), an ambitious analysis of the social status of women that promoted a radical restructuring of the public and private spheres. Now she is most famous for "The Yellow Wallpaper," a disturbing short story based on her experience of Dr. Weir Mitchell's "rest cure" following a bout of severe depression. Gilman was divorced from her husband and married her cousin, George Houghton Gilman, in 1900. Her works include *The Home* (1904), *Human Work* (1904), *Man-Made World* (1911), a magazine called *The Forerunner* (1910–16) for which she wrote all the copy (including the feminist Utopian novel *Herland* in 1915), and hundreds of short stories.

Alfred Gingold (Contemporary)

Alfred Gingold, a popular humorist, is the author of a number of works, notably *Fire in the John* (1991), a parody of the men's movement, and *The House Trap*. With Helen Rogan, he wrote *Brooklyn's Best: Sightseeing, Shopping, Eat-*

ing, and Happy Wandering in the Borough of Kings (1998)
and *Cool Parent's Guide to All of New York: Excursions and
Activities in and Around Our City That Your Children Will
Love and You Won't Think Are Too Bad* (1998). He is also
the co-editor of *Snooze: The Best of Our Magazine* (1986).

William Goldman (Contemporary)

Goldman was born in Highland Park, Illinois, and is most
famous for his Academy Award–winning screenplays, *Butch
Cassidy and the Sundance Kid* (1969) and *All the President's
Men* (1976). His screenplay for the detective thriller *Harper*
(1966), starring Paul Newman, gave him his first success in
Hollywood, but he had been a published novelist since 1957.
His novels include *Magic* and *The Princess Bride* (1973),
which he adapted for the screen. Goldman's publications
also include humorous behind-the-scene books about the
entertainment industry, *Adventures in the Screen Trade* and
The Season: A Candid Look at Broadway. His most recent
screenplays include *Misery* (1991), adapted from Stephen
King's novel, and *Maverick* (1994), a western starring Mel
Gibson. Goldman continues to work in Hollywood as an un-
credited script doctor.

Margaret Halsey (Contemporary)

Margaret Halsey grew up outside of Yonkers, New York,
and entered Skidmore College in 1926 as a secretarial science major. Although she established a reputation as a humorous columnist on campus, she abandoned this pursuit
after college, taking jobs as a stenographer, a dictaphone
operator for a real estate company, and a secretary. A job in
the editorial department at Simon and Schuster turned out
to be the break she needed: the letters she wrote back to the
publisher during a trip to England with her husband led to
the commissioning of the book from which our selection
is excerpted, and thus began her writing career. Margaret
Halsey's work as a novelist, social critic and humorist fo-
cuses on a wide range of social and political issues. She is
the author of *With Malice Toward Some* (1938), *Some of My
Best Friends Are Soldiers* (1944), *Color Blind* (1946), *This
Demi-Paradise: A Westchester Diary* (1960), *The Pseudo-*

Ethic (1963), and *No Laughing Matter: The Autobiography of a WASP.*

Lynn Harris (Contemporary)

Lynn Harris is co-creator of the cybersuperhero *Breakup Girl* and author of the forthcoming *Breakup Girl to the Rescue!* (Little, Brown, 2000) as well as *He Loved Me, He Loves Me Not: A Guide to Fudge, Fury, Free Time, and Life Beyond the Breakup* (Avon, 1996). A standup comic, Harris also delivers advice to the lovelorn in print, radio, and television. She is a regular contributor to the New York *Daily News* as well as to numerous national magazines.

Bret Harte (1836–1902)

Bret Harte dominated the literary world of the West and his publications are innumerable. As the founding editor of the *Overland Monthly*, he helped promote the careers of a generation of western writers. Harte was born in Albany, New York, and moved to New York City with his mother at age nine after his father's death. He quit school at thirteen to work as a clerk and moved to the San Francisco Bay Area in 1854. Harte wrote for the *Golden Era*, a literary weekly, and began writing a series of condensed novels in the burlesque style, taking as his satirical targets the works of Dickens, Wilkie Collins, and James Fenimore Cooper. He later moved to England, where he enjoyed a greater popularity than he did in his native United States, and where he died of throat cancer in 1902. His works include *The Luck of Roaring Camp and Other Sketches* (1870), *The Story of a Mine* (1877), *On the Frontier* (1884), and *Suzy: A Story of the Plains* (1893). *The Writings of Bret Harte*, in twenty volumes, appeared between 1896 and 1914.

Cynthia Heimel (Contemporary)

An American humorist and feminist, Heimel has published essays on gender relations and columns in numerous magazines. She is a regular contributor to *Playboy*. Her titles include *Sex Tips for Girls* (1983), *But Enough About You* (1986), *If You Can't Live Without Me, Why Aren't You Dead*

Yet? (1991), *Get Your Tongue Out of My Mouth, I'm Kissing You Good-bye* (1993), and *When Your Phone Doesn't Ring, It'll Be Me* (1995).

Ernest Hemingway (1899–1961)

Ernest Hemingway was born in Oak Park, Illinois. He worked as a reporter for the *Kansas City Star* before serving as an ambulance driver on the Italian front during World War I. In the 1920s, he became European correspondent for the *Toronto Star* in Paris, where he was part of a circle of famous expatriate artists including F. Scott Fitzgerald and Gertrude Stein. Hemingway wrote about this expatriate colony in the memoir *A Moveable Feast* (1964). His fiction met with immediate success and he was hailed as a prominent voice of his "lost generation." His numerous titles include *In Our Time* (1925), *The Sun Also Rises* (1926), *A Farewell to Arms* (1929), *For Whom the Bell Tolls* (1940), and *The Old Man and the Sea* (1952). Hemingway won the Pulitzer Prize for fiction in 1952 and the Nobel Prize for Literature in 1954. Plagued throughout his life with bouts of depression, he killed himself on his ranch in Ketchum, Idaho, in 1961.

O. Henry (1862–1910)

O. Henry, a well-known short story writer, was born William Sydney Porter; he invented the pseudonym under which he became famous after being released from prison, where he had been serving a sentence for embezzlement. Before establishing himself as a writer, Porter worked as a pharmacist, a draftsman, a bank teller, and finally a feature writer for the *Houston Post*, where he wrote anecdotal sketches. He moved to New York in 1902, after his release, and for several years published a story a week in the New York *World*. O. Henry's first collection of stories, *Cabbages and Kings*, appeared in 1904 and was followed by such works as *The Four Million* (1906), *The Trimmed Lamp* (1907), *Heart of the West* (1907), and *Whirligigs* (1910), which contains the classic story "The Ransom of Red Chief." In all, O. Henry published ten collections and over six hundred short stories during his life, as well as several posthumous works; his stories range from tales of ordinary New Yorkers to tall tales and stories of Western adventure.

Nicole Hollander (Contemporary)

A cartoonist famous for her love of cats and her feminist humor, Hollander grew up in Chicago and studied painting at the University of Illinois at Urbana-Champaign. Her first cartoon strip, *The Feminist Funnies*, appeared in 1976. Her first collection of cartoons, *I'm in Training to Be Tall and Blonde*, was published in 1979. Hollander's cartoon alter-ego Sylvia first appeared in 1980. *Sylvia* is syndicated in over sixty newspapers and has inspired a line of greeting cards, a play, and more than a dozen books. Hollander's titles include *The Whole Enchilada* (1976) and *Female Problems: An Unhelpful Guide* (1995).

Marietta Holley "Josiah Allen's Wife" (1836–1926)

A famous literary humorist often compared to Mark Twain in her time but largely forgotten until feminist scholars recently rediscovered her work, Marietta Holley was born on the family farm in Jefferson County, New York. At twenty-one she published her first story, "Piety," in the *Jefferson County Journal*. She first used the pseudonym "Josiah Allen's Wife" in her story "Fourth of July in Jonesville" published in *Peterson's Magazine* in 1869. Holley sent writing samples to the important publisher Elisha Bliss, who became her mentor and editor and encouraged her to write *My Opinions and Betsey Bobbet's* (1873). She created the persona of Samantha, the "rustic philosopher farm wife of wit and gumption," as a covert vehicle for her particular brand of feminist humor. Holley wrote a dozen Samantha books between 1887 and 1913, tackling in them feminist issues such as the economic dependence of women and their lack of political power, as well as social problems of her day like temperance, children's rights, and poverty. At the height of her fame, she commanded fees as high as $14,000 per book, and "Betsey Bobbet" clubs were created around the country to read and act out parts of her books. She died of cancer at home, in the fifteen-room Victorian house she built on her family's land.

Oliver Wendell Holmes (1809–1894)

Oliver Wendell Holmes taught anatomy and physiology at Harvard Medical School—and served as the first dean of Harvard Medical School, from 1847 to 1853—but he is best known as a poet and essayist. Holmes is the author of such classics of American humor as "Old Ironsides" (1830), "The Chambered Nautilus" (1858), and *The Autocrat of the Breakfast Table* (1858). He also helped to found, along with James Russell Lowell, the influential magazine the *Atlantic Monthly* in 1857.

William Dean Howells (1837–1920)

Howells was arguably the most influential figure in American literature in the late nineteenth century. He grew up in frontier Ohio and received little formal schooling. He worked as an apprentice in his family print shop and became an autodidact. In 1860 he was commissioned to write a campaign biography of Abraham Lincoln; that same year, his first book of poetry was published. The Lincoln biography led to his appointment as consul in Venice during the Civil War. He published a volume of sketches titled *Venetian Life* in 1866. Howells moved to Boston and worked as assistant editor for the *Atlantic Monthly* in 1866; five years later he became editor-in-chief of the magazine. His power and influence in that post helped the careers of many writers, among which were his friends Henry James and Mark Twain, and also Sarah Orne Jewett, Charles Chestnutt, and Paul Dunbar. Howells's literary criticism was collected in the volume *Criticism and Fiction* in 1871. His novels, which include *The Rise of Silas Lapham* (1885) and *A Hazard of New Fortunes* (1890), address the social and economic problems of a changing America.

Langston Hughes (1902–1967)

Langston Hughes was born in Joplin, Missouri, and grew up in Kansas. He read the poetry of Paul Dunbar and Carl

Sandburg as a child and he began writing poetry himself under the influence of their work. Hughes attended Columbia
University for a year, then left to work on a ship and traveled extensively in Europe and Africa before returning to
New York and establishing himself in Harlem, where he
quickly became an important figure of the Harlem Renaissance. His first poem was published in the *Crisis* in 1921;
his first collection of poetry, *The Weary Blues*, appeared
two years later. His titles include the coming-of-age novel
Not Without Laughter (1930), *The Ways of White Folks*
(1934), and the poetry collections *Shakespeare in Harlem*
(1942), and *Montage of a Dream Deferred* (1951).

Zora Neale Hurston (1891–1960)

Zora Neale Hurston, born in the African American town of
Eatonville, Florida, went on to become one of the most important figures of the Harlem Renaissance. Her writing is
dedicated to the preservation and celebration of African
American culture, as was the very persona she created. Best
known for the novel *Their Eyes Were Watching God* (1937),
Hurston is also the author of *Dust Tracks on the Road*
(1942), an autobiography; *Mules and Men* (1935), a collection of folklore; *Tell My Horse—Voodoo Gods, an Inquiry*
(1938), an anthropological work; and *Jonah's Gourd Vine*
(1934), *Moses, Man of the Mountain* (1939), and *Seraph on
the Suwanee* (1948), all works of fiction. Hurston spent her
last years alone and in poverty, but her literary reputation
was revived largely through the work of Alice Walker in the
1970s.

Molly Ivins (Contemporary)

A journalist, humorist, and political commentator, Ivins
contributes to various newspapers, including the *Texas
Observer* and the *New York Times*. Her collections of essays
include *Molly Ivins Can't Say That, Can She?* (1991) and
Nothin' but Good Times Ahead (1993).

Henry James (1843–1916)

One of the most celebrated writers of the nineteenth and twentieth centuries, James was born in a wealthy family and grew up in New York City, receiving his education at home with tutors and in private schools at home and abroad. He traveled extensively throughout Europe, where he would ultimately establish himself and write his most famous novels. His numerous titles include *The Portrait of a Lady* (1881), *The Bostonians* (1886), *What Maisie Knew* (1897), *The Wings of the Dove* (1902), and *The Ambassadors* (1903). James's novels and short stories are typically concerned with the uneasy cultural encounters between Americans and Europeans. He died in England.

Erica Jong (Contemporary)

Erica Jong grew up in Manhattan and studied literature and writing at Barnard College; she received her M.A. from Columbia University. She published two books of poetry, *Fruits and Vegetables* (1971) and *Half-Lives* (1973), before the appearance of *Fear of Flying* (1973), a widely acclaimed and enormously popular novel which established her fame and reputation. The frank attitude toward sexuality and the interest in the female experience that mark her first novel continue to dominate Jong's work. Among her many other works are *How to Save Your Own Life* (1977), *Fanny, Being the True History of the Adventures of Fanny Hackabout Jones* (1980), *Ordinary Miracles* (1983), *Parachutes and Kisses* (1984), *Any Woman's Blues* (1990), *Fear of Fifty* (1994) and *Inventing Memory: A Novel of Mothers and Daughters* (1997).

Judith Katz (Contemporary)

Katz was born in Worcester, Massachusetts. She received her B.A. from the University of Massachusetts at Amherst and her M.A. from Smith College. She describes herself as a Jewish Lesbian Feminist and she writes: "My first novel sought to make heroes out of contemporary Jewish lesbian characters." That novel, *Running Fiercely Toward a High Thin Sound*, appeared in 1992. She has worked as an Arts

Administrator in Minneapolis and teaches writing at the Loft, also in Minneapolis, since 1988. She has received an NEA Fellowship.

Bel Kaufman (Contemporary)

The granddaughter of Jewish humorist Sholom Aleichem, Kaufman was born in Germany and emigrated to the United States at the age of twelve. She received her B.A. from Hunter College in New York and her M.A. from Columbia University. Kaufman taught high school in New York City for over thirty years and has taught creative writing at the University of Rochester and the University of Florida. Her best-selling novel *Up the Down Staircase* (1964), from which our passage is excerpted, chronicles the bitter-sweet adventures of a young woman who teaches in an inner-city school. It remained on the best-seller list for sixty-four weeks, was translated into sixteen languages, and was made into a movie starring Sandy Dennis in 1967. She also published the novel *Love, Etc.* in 1979. Despite her novels and her numerous publications in periodicals and newspapers, including *Esquire*, *Ladies' Home Journal*, and the *New York Times*, Kaufman describes herself as a teacher first, and a writer second.

Garrison Keillor (Contemporary)

Keillor was born and raised in Minnesota, a state which has inspired most of his published work. He attended the University of Minnesota and began working in radio in 1963, and his show *Prairie Home Companion*, known for its blend of regional humor, musical guests, and audience participation, airs weekly on National Public Radio. His titles include *Lake Wobegon Days*, *Leaving Home*, *Happy to be Here,* and *We Are Still Married.* Keillor lives in Wisconsin and New York.

Florynce Kennedy (Contemporary)

Florynce Kennedy is a feminist essayist and a lawyer. She is the author of *Color Me Flo*.

Jean Kerr (Contemporary)

Named "one of the funniest women writers of her generation," Kern was born Brigid Jean Collins in Scranton, Pennsylvania. She received her B.A. in 1943 from Marywood College, where she met her future husband, Walter Kerr. The Kerrs collaborated on numerous plays, among which is an adaptation of Franz Werfel's novel *The Song of Bernadette*, in 1945. That same year Kerr received her M.A. from Catholic University. Kerr's first solo effort, *Jenny Kissed Me*, only ran for twenty performances in 1948. The playwright, unfazed by this setback, went on to write ten plays in the next three decades; two of these, *King of Hearts* (1954) and *Mary, Mary* (1961), were made into movies. Kerr also published humorous essays in a number of magazines including *Reader's Digest*, *Ladies' Home Journal*, *Harper's*, and *Saturday Evening Post*. Her collections of essays include *Please Don't Eat the Daisies* (1957), *Penny Candy* (1970), and *How I Got to Be Perfect* (1978). She has received honorary degrees from Fordham and Northwestern University.

James Kincaid (Contemporary)

Kincaid is Aerol Arnold Professor of English at the University of California in Los Angeles, where he teaches Victorian literature and cultural theory. He has written extensively on Dickens and Trollope and edited numerous scholarly collections of literary criticism. His titles include *Child-Loving: The Erotic Child and Victorian Culture* (1992), *Annoying the Victorians* (1995), and *Manufacturing Virtue: The Culture of Child Molesting* (1998).

Alan King (Contemporary)

Alan King has been a prominent figure in American entertainment for decades, as an actor, producer, and comic. He is the author of such works as the autobiography *Name Dropping: The Life and Lies of Alan King* (1996), *Is Salami and Eggs Better Than Sex?: Memoirs of a Happy Eater* (with Mimi Sheraton), *Help! I'm a Prisoner in a Chinese Bakery* (1964) and *Anybody Who Owns His Own Home De-*

serves It. In *Chinese Bakery,* King writes, "If I can laugh at 'the system,' I can always keep it in its proper perspective. Then there may be hope for all of us."

Robert Klane (Contemporary)

A novelist, screenwriter, and movie director, Robert Klane grew up on Long Island and worked in advertising before moving to the West Coast to be a film director. His novel *Where's Poppa?* (1970) was made into a movie starring George Segal and Ruth Gordon. Klane's other credits include the films *Thank God It's Friday* (1978) and *Folks* (1992) as director, and *The Man with One Red Shoe* (1985), as screenwriter.

Tony Kornheiser (Contemporary)

Tony Kornheiser was born and raised in Long Island, New York. He graduated from Harper College with a B.A. in English and Social Sciences and taught grammar school for a year. He began his writing career with features for *New York Newsday* until 1976, when he was hired by the *New York Times* to cover sports. Kornheiser has been a sports columnist for the *Washington Post* since 1979; he also writes a weekly humor column for the *Post* which has been syndicated nationally since 1991. His books include *The Baby Chase* (1993) and *Pumping Irony* (1995).

Fran Lebowitz (Contemporary)

Fran Lebowitz grew up in Morristown, New Jersey, but is generally associated with New York, where she now lives. She is a columnist, critic and essayist whose humor is fused with social commentary. She is perhaps best known for her best-selling works from the 1970s, *Metropolitan Life* and *Social Studies*, reissued in *The Fran Lebowitz Reader* in 1994. She has made numerous talk show appearances—particularly on *Late Night With David Letterman*—and publishes essays in *Vanity Fair* and other magazines. Her next book, *Exterior Signs: Health* is scheduled to appear in 1999.

Sinclair Lewis (1885–1951)

One of the foremost social critics of American letters and the first American writer to win the Nobel Prize, Lewis was born in Sauk Centre, Minnesota, but traveled extensively in America and abroad. His novels deal with issues of race, gender, and class, and are as pertinent today as they were in the 1920s. Lewis's titles include *Main Street* (1920), *Babbitt* (1922), *Arrowsmith* (1925), for which he won the Pulitzer Prize, and *Dodsworth* (1929). He was a member of the American Academy of Arts and Letters and the National Institute of Arts and Letters. Lewis died in Rome.

David Ross Locke (1833–1888)

David Ross Locke was born in the town of Vestal, New York. He didn't have much of a formal education and after an apprenticeship as a printer, he found work at the Toledo *Blade*. Before long, he was the paper's editor, and he became an influential journalist over the next twenty years. He created the persona of "Petroleum Vesuvius Nasby" in his columns and articles as a vehicle for his satire. In addition to his professional duties, he was involved in the Republican Party and met with Abraham Lincoln. He counted Mark Twain among his friends and he wrote novels, plays, poems, and short stories as well as journalism and satirical pieces. He died in Cortland, New York, in 1888.

Anita Loos (1893–1981)

Any biographical information about Anita Loos should be prefaced by a warning: the celebrated novelist, playwright, and screenwriter consistently lied about her age (usually subtracting five years) throughout her life. She performed on stage in San Francisco at the age of ten and sold her first screenplay in 1911. Loos wrote numerous screenplays for D. W. Griffith's company and articles for *Vanity Fair*. In addition to her modern classic *Gentlemen Prefer Blondes* (1925) and its sequel, *But Gentlemen Marry Brunettes* (1928), she wrote the autobiographies *A Girl Like I* (1966), *Kiss Hollywood Goodby* (1974), and *Cast of Thousands* (1977). Her most famous screenplays are *Red-Headed*

Woman (1932), starring Jean Harlow, and *The Women* (1939), directed by George Cukor. Loos also adapted the Colette novels *Gigi* and *Cheri* for Broadway. She continued to write until her death from a heart attack.

"Moms" Mabley (1897–1975)

Born Loretta May Aiken, "Moms" Mabley was an African-American comedian, singer and actress. She performed at the Apollo Theater and the Cotton Club in Harlem at the height of their popularity and appeared in movies such as *Boarding House Blues* (1929), *Emperor Jones* (1939), and *Amazing Grace* (1974). Thirteen of her comedy albums made the top two hundred on the Billboard Charts during the 1960s; among her biggest hits were *At the UN* (1961) and *Young Men Si, Old Men No* (1963). She was known for her fusion of bawdy humor with a female perspective.

Merrill Markoe (Contemporary)

Merrill Markoe taught art at the University of Southern California before she began writing for television and performing as a stand-up comic in Los Angeles. In 1978 she met David Letterman, an alliance that led to a major development in her career: she became the head writer for *The David Letterman Show* and later for *Late Night With David Letterman*, winning several Emmy awards for her work; she was the creator of, among other things, the ever-popular "Stupid Pet Tricks." After leaving the show in 1987, Markoe became a regular contributor to *Not Necessarily the News* (for which she won Writer's Guild and Ace Awards) and appeared in a number of HBO comedy specials. She is the author of *What the Dogs Have Taught Me and Other Amazing Things I've Learned* (1992), *How to Be Hap-Hap-Happy Like Me* (1994), and *Merrill Markoe's Guide to Love* (1997).

Julius "Groucho" Marx (1890–1977)
Adolph-Arthur "Harpo" Marx (1888–1964)
Leonard "Chico" Marx (1886–1961)
Herbert "Zeppo" Marx (1901–1979)

The Marx Brothers were encouraged at a young age by their mother Minnie, herself the daughter of vaudevillians, to pursue show-business careers. The brothers conquered Broadway in 1925 with their play *The Cocoanuts*; this success led to a contract with Paramount in 1929 and a move to Hollywood the following year. They wrote three original films together: *Monkey Business* (1931), *Horse Feathers* (1932), and *Duck Soup* (1933). They began a productive and successful partnership with Irving Thalberg at MGM in 1934; before his early death the legendary producer teamed the Marx Brothers with writers like George S. Kaufman and produced the most successful films in the brothers' careers, *A Night at the Opera* (1935) and *A Day at the Races* (1937). The group eventually split up in 1941. Groucho remained the most visible member with occasional film appearances and a long career in television and radio; he received a special Oscar in 1973.

Jackie Mason (Contemporary)

Jackie Mason grew up on the Lower East Side of Manhattan and was once a rabbi; he went on to become a popular comedian. He won a Tony Award for *The World According To Me*, his highly successful first Broadway show, and an Emmy Award for *Jackie Mason On Broadway*, an HBO special. His Broadway success continued with *Jackie Mason: Brand New* and *Politically Incorrect*. His published works include *How To Talk Jewish* (with Ira Berkov; 1991), *Jackie Mason's America*, *The World According To Me*, and *Jackie Mason and Raoul Felder's Survival Guide to New York City* (1997).

H. L. Mencken (1880–1956)

Henry Louis Mencken, better known as H. L. Mencken, was born in Baltimore; he attended the Baltimore Polytechnic Institute before working in his father's cigar factory from 1896 to 1899. He then began working as reporter or editor for a variety of local papers. From 1914 to 1923, Mencken co-edited *The Smart Set* with drama critic George Jean Nathan; the two co-founded several other publications, among them the influential magazine *American Mercury* (1923–1933). As a literary critic in the 1920s, Mencken's role was extremely important; he helped to establish the careers of such major authors as Theodore Dreiser and Sinclair Lewis, among others. He continued to contribute essays to numerous publications, including the *Chicago Tribune,* the *New York American*, *The Nation*, the *Evening Mail*, and *The Baltimore Sun.* No aspect of American life was safe from Mencken's satire. His work was collected and published in a number of volumes, including *Ventures Into Verse* (1903), *The Philosophy of Nietzsche* (1908), *Damn: A Book of Calumny* (1918), *In Defense of Women* (1918), *The American Language* (1919), *Notes on Democracy* (1926), *Treatise On the Gods* (1930), *Happy Days* (1940) and *Heathen Days* (1943).

Alice Duer Miller (1874–1942)

Unlike most humorists, Miller received a degree in mathematics from Barnard College in 1899. From 1914 to 1917, her column "Are Women People?" ran in the New York *Tribune.* She belonged to the group of radical feminists Heterodoxy which met in Greenwich Village from 1912 to 1940. She was also a member of the Algonquin Round Table and the subject of a *New Yorker* profile in 1927. Although she wrote primarily about the upper classes during her career, some of Miller's earlier work appeared in the socialist magazine *The Masses.* She published regularly in the *Saturday Evening Post* from 1916 to the 1930s. Her novels *The Charm School* (1919) and *Gowns by Roberta* (1933) were adapted for the screen.

Margaret Mitchell (1900–1949)

Born in Atlanta, Georgia, Margaret Mitchell was the daughter of a founder of the Georgia suffrage movement and the president of the Atlanta Historical Society, a pair of influences which certainly manifest themselves in her work. Mitchell's studies at Smith College were cut short by her mother's death, following which she returned home. Her first marriage ended in divorce after two years, and she married John Marsh shortly thereafter. Meanwhile, she had become a journalist, working as a reporter for the Atlanta *Journal* at a time when this was an unconventional occupation for women. She left after three years and began writing *Gone With the Wind*, on which she worked in secret for years; it was published in 1936 and won instant popularity. Movie rights were sold immediately, the book sold over a million copies in the first six months, and Mitchell received the 1937 Pulitzer Prize for the novel that was to become a popular classic. Although she wrote fiction from an early age, *Gone With the Wind* was the only book Mitchell ever published, and her life was cut short at forty-nine when she was hit by a car.

Pat Mora (Contemporary)

Mora was born and raised in El Paso, Texas. She has taught at high school, community college, and university levels. She considers herself Mexican-American and she has written extensively about the life of her family on the Texas-Mexico border. Mora has been called "one of the most significant Chicana poets of our time" by the *New Mexican*. Her titles include *House of Houses*, a family memoir; *Nepantla: Essays from the Land in the Middle*, and *Aunt Carmen's Book of Practical Saints* (1997). Mora is the recipient of numerous awards, including a National Endowment for the Arts Fellowship.

Ogden Nash (1902–1971)

Ogden Nash was raised in Rye, New York, and Savannah, Georgia, and attended Harvard briefly. His career as a writer began with a job writing ad copy in 1925; in the same year he published his first book for children, *The Cricket of Caradon*. He published his first poem in *The New Yorker* in 1930, and joined the magazine's staff in 1930. Elected to the National Institute of Arts and Letters in 1950, Nash published nineteen books of poetry in all. His works include *Hard Lines* (1931), *Good Intentions* (1942), *You Can't Get There From Here* (1957), *Marriage Lines* (1964), and *Bed Riddance* (1972).

Bill Nye (1850–1896)

One of the most important humorists of the late nineteenth century, Nye was born in Maine and raised in Wisconsin. He later moved to Wyoming, where he became a successful writer and edited the *Laramie Boomerang*. Nye moved to New York in 1887 and wrote a humor column for the *New York World*. His genres of choice were the short comic essay and the sketch, but he also wrote two Broadway plays and two books of burlesque history. He traveled extensively throughout Europe from the late 1880s until his death and he used his travels as column material. He died in North Carolina, where he had lived since 1891. His titles include *Bill Nye and Boomerang* (1881), *Hits and Skits* (1884), *Baled Hay* (1884), *Bill Nye's Red Book* (1891), and *Bill Nye's History of the United States* (1894).

Dorothy Parker (1893–1967)

Dorothy Parker was born in New Jersey and attended the Blessed Sacrament Convent School in New York City until she was expelled for claiming that the Immaculate Conception was "spontaneous combustion." One of the most celebrated members of the legendary Algonquin Round Table in the 1920s, Parker was known for her acerbic wit and her epigrammatic style. She published reviews and articles in *The New Yorker* as well as poems and short stories. Her publications include volumes of poetry like *Enough Rope* (1926) and *Death and Taxes* (1931); and the short story collections *Laments for the Living* (1930) and *Here Lies* (1939). Parker was involved with the Communist Party in the 1930s and subsequently blacklisted. From 1925 to 1950 she spent much time in Hollywood where she wrote numerous screenplays, including *A Star Is Born* (1937), for which she received an Academy Award nomination. An edition of her *Complete Stories* appeared in 1995.

Samuel Pickering, Jr. (Contemporary)

The real-life inspiration behind Robin Williams's beloved teacher in the film *Dead Poets Society*, Pickering has been teaching children's literature and the familiar essay at the University of Connecticut since 1978. He has published numerous articles of literary criticism in academic journals, and his scholarly titles include *The Moral Tradition in English Fiction, 1785–1850* (1976). Pickering is most famous for his numerous essay collections, whose titles include *A Continuing Education* (1985), *Still Life* (1990), *Trespassing* (1994), *The Blue Caterpillar* (1997), *Living to Prowl* (1998), and *Deprived of Unhappiness* (1998).

Sylvia Plath (1932–1963)

Plath was born in Boston and published poems and stories as an adolescent in numerous publications. She received a scholarship to attend Smith College, from which she graduated *summa cum laude* with a B.A. in English in 1955. In the summer of 1953, Plath served as a guest editor on *Mademoiselle*, and she would later use this experience as the basis of her only novel, *The Bell Jar* (1963). She attended Cambridge University on a Fulbright Fellowship and received an M.A. Plath lived in England with her husband, the poet Ted Hughes, until 1957 when they moved to the United States and Plath taught freshman English at her alma mater. The couple returned to England in 1959, and during Plath's most intensely creative period she wrote and published *The Colossus and Other Poems* (1960) and *The Bell Jar*, and she composed the poems which would appear posthumously as the collection *Ariel* (1965). Plagued with depression throughout her life, Plath committed suicide in her London flat. Her *Collected Poems* (1981) won the Pulitzer Prize for Poetry in 1982.

Edgar Allan Poe (1809–1849)

Poe was born in Boston and an orphan by the age of two. He attended the University of Virginia and published his first volume of poetry, *Tamerlane and Other Poems*, while still in his teens. He worked as an editor for the *Southern Literary Messenger* in Richmond, Virginia, until he left in 1837 to go to New York, where he wrote *The Narrative of Arthur Gordon Pym*. He then moved to Philadelphia, where he worked as an editor on *Burton's Gentleman's Magazine*. Between 1839 and 1844 Poe composed many of his now famous tales like "The Tell-Tale Heart" and "The Pit and the Pendulum." He published *Tales of the Grotesque and Arabesque* in 1840 and *The Raven and Other Poems* in 1845. He moved back to New York and unsuccessfully edited a literary magazine, *The Broadway Journal*. The *Journal* quickly folded and Poe's wife Virginia died. He returned to Richmond and for a brief period he was feted and celebrated for his literary achievement. He was found dying on the streets of Baltimore, on his way to New York City.

Roger Price (Contemporary)

A novelist, essayist, publisher, comedian, and TV performer, Price was born in West Virginia and has published articles in numerous publications like *Playboy* and the *Saturday Evening Post*. His titles include *In One Head and Out the Other*, *I'm for Me First!*, *The Decline and Fall*, and *The Great Roob Revolution*.

Ishmael Reed (Contemporary)

Reed was born in Chattanooga, Tennessee, and graduated from the State University of New York at Buffalo in 1960. A poet, novelist, actor, dramatist, journalist, and editor, Reed has written numerous plays, novels, and volumes of poetry as well as essays and articles since the publication of his first novel, *The Free-Lance Pallbearers,* in 1967. His work is known for its biting satire and its parody of literary form. He cites among his inspirations Zora Neale Hurston, Claude McKay, Countee Cullen, Langston Hughes, and Frank Chin. Reed's novels include *Yellow Back Radio*

Broke-Down (1969), *Mumbo Jumbo* (1972), for which he received a National Book Award nomination, and *Flight to Canada* (1976). His poetry is collected in the volumes *Conjure* (1972), nominated for a National Book Award, *Points of View* (1988), and *New and Collected Poems* (1989), among others. He has also published collections of articles, including *Writin' Is Fighting* (1988). Ishmael Reed lives in Oakland, California.

Carl Reiner (Contemporary)

Reiner was born in the Bronx and performed in Broadway musicals before he began working with Sid Caesar on *Your Show of Shows*. He went on to receive two Emmys for Best Supporting Actor for his work on another television program, *Caesar's Hour*. In addition to his highly successful collaboration with Mel Brooks on "The 2000 Year Old Man," Reiner in 1961 created the popular *Dick Van Dyke Show*, for which he won seven Emmys in five years. Since 1967, he has worked mostly as a film director and screenwriter. His credits include *Enter Laughing* (1967), *Oh, God!* (1977), and four films starring Steve Martin which include *The Jerk* (1979) and *All of Me* (1984). He is also the author of three autobiographical novels: *Enter Laughing* (1958), *All Kinds of Love* (1993), and *Continue Laughing* (1995).

Agnes Repplier (1855–1950)

Born in Philadelphia and raised in a well-to-do family, Agnes Repplier "learned [her] letters at the cost of infinite tribulation, out of a horrible little book called 'Reading Without Fears' " and attended two schools for girls from which she was expelled for rebellious behavior. She set out to educate herself and started writing stories and sketches for publication after her father's bankruptcy. Repplier contributed essays and stories to the *Catholic World*, among which was "The Good Humor of the Saints": the purpose of the essay, according to her biographer, "was to offer the point of view that a sense of humor is not incompatible with otherworldliness." She fulfilled her ambition to contribute to the prestigious *Atlantic Monthly* in 1886 when the magazine published her essay "Children, Past and Present." The monthly became a regular outlet for her writing. She also began lecturing in 1889 and this pursuit would take her traveling around the country for three decades. Over the next fifty years, Repplier became known for her incisive wit and published more than fifteen books. Her collections of essays and sketches include *Books and Men* (1888), *Points of View* (1891), *In the Dozy Hours* (1894), *Americans and Others* (1912), and *Counter-Currents* (1916). She also wrote biographies of distinguished religious figures, including *Père Marquette* and *Junipero Serra.* One of her last books published was a history of humor from the Middle Ages to the twentieth century entitled *In Pursuit of Laughter* (1936).

Will Rogers (1879–1935)

Will Rogers grew up on an Oklahoma ranch in the Cherokee Nation; there he gained the expertise in the use of the lasso that helped establish his early career in wild west shows and in vaudeville and shaped his popular cowboy image. Known for his folksy brand of humor, Rogers went on to star in seventy-one movies; he was also a radio personality and newspaper columnist. He wrote six books, including *Not a Bathing Suit in Russia, Ether and Me or Just Relax*, and various collections of his essays and addresses.

Helen Rowland (1875–1950)

Born in Washington, D.C., Rowland wrote a satiric dialogue for the *Washington Post* at the age of sixteen. She left for New York City after the death of her father and wrote for the Sunday edition of the New York *World.* Her columns were quickly syndicated; in them she deals with issues of gender inequality, particularly the dependent status of women within marriage. Her collections of columns include *The Digressions of Polly* (1905), *Reflections of a Bachelor Girl* (1909), *The Widow* (1908), *A Guide to Men* (1922), and *This Married Life* (1927).

Rita Rudner (Contemporary)

Rudner grew up in Florida and moved to New York City in 1972 to work as a dancer. She appeared in various Broadway productions during the 1970s, culminating in her role as Lily in the musical *Annie* in 1980. She started working as a stand-up comedian in the 80s; Rudner gained national exposure when she made regular appearances on the CBS *Morning Program* show. In 1989 she starred in her first solo HBO special, *One Night Stand: Rita Rudner*. Other television specials include *Born to Be Mild* (1990) and *Married Without Children* (1995). In 1992 she published her first book, *Naked Beneath My Clothes: Tales of a Revealing Nature*. Rudner published her second book, *Rita Rudner's Guide to Men*, in 1994. She co-wrote, with her husband Martin Bergman, and starred in the dramatic comedy *Peter's Friends* (1992), directed by Kenneth Branagh.

Carl Sandburg (1878–1967)

Born in Galesburg, Illinois, to Swedish immigrant parents, Carl Sandburg's early life was varied: he left school after eighth grade and supported himself at odd jobs, enlisted in the army during the Spanish American War, and worked for the Social Democratic Party from 1907 to 1908. He first gained recognition as a poet with the publication of "Chicago" in *Poetry* in 1914; in 1916 a collection of his poetry was published as *Chicago Poems*. His other collections of poetry include *Cornhuskers* (1918), *Smoke and Steel* (1920), *Good Morning America* (1928), and *Complete Poems* (1950), which won the 1951 Pulitzer Prize. He also published acclaimed biographies of Abraham Lincoln, several children's books, and a number of essays.

Henry Wheeler Shaw "Josh Billings" (1818–1885)

One of the most famous humor writers of the Civil War era, Shaw was born in Massachusetts and attended a preparatory school. He spent one year in college before setting out for the West, where he traveled and worked between 1835 and

1845. Shaw's first volume of sketches using his Josh Billings persona, *Josh Billings, Hiz Sayings*, appeared in 1865 and met with great success. Shaw's blend of aphorisms, puns, misspellings, and malapropisms was in part inspired by the essays of Addison and Steele. He settled in Poughkeepsie, New York, in 1867 and wrote a humor column for the *New York Weekly*. His annual series titled *Josh Billings's Farmer's Allminax*, published between 1869 and 1879, became his most successful literary endeavor. Shaw's titles include *Josh Billings on Ice, and Other Things* (1868) and *Josh Billings's Wit and Humor* (1874). His *Complete Works* (1888) appeared posthumously. Shaw died of apoplexy in Monterey, California, in 1885.

Jean Shepherd (Contemporary)

Jean Shepherd arrived in New York City in the 1950s, and later made his name as a radio personality. His career eventually expanded to include theater, film, and television; he has performed live at Carnegie Hall and many other venues. His short stories have frequently been published in *Playboy* magazine, and have received various awards for fiction. His works include *In God We Trust, All Others Pay Cash* (1966), *Wanda Hickey's Night of Golden Memories and Other Disasters* (1971), *A Ferrari in the Bedroom* (1972), *The Phantom of the Open Hearth* (1978), and *A Fistful of Fig Newtons* (1987).

Allan Sherman (1924–1973)

A television writer, lyricist, and album producer, Sherman attended the University of Illinois where he wrote and produced the annual campus variety show. His specialty was the song parody and he produced three best-selling albums including *My Son, the Folksinger* (1963). His book *The Rape of the A.P.E.*—the American Puritan Ethic—appeared in 1973.

Betty Smith (1896–1972)

Betty Smith was forced to leave school early in order to support her family; nonetheless, she later went on to study at Yale and later to hold a fellowship at the University of North Carolina. She published over seventy novels and plays, including *A Tree Grows in Brooklyn* (1943), *Tomorrow Will Be Better* (1948) and *Joy in the Morning* (1963).

Charles Henry Smith (Bill Arp)
(1826–1903)

Like many of his literary predecessors, Smith practiced law to earn a living. He was born in Georgia and lived there all his life. He created the persona of Bill Arp, a jester for the South, in his first letter published in 1861. Two volumes of letters, *Bill Arp, so Called* (1866) and *Bill Arp's Peace Papers* (1873), followed. He was elected city alderman of Rome, Georgia, and elected to the state Senate in 1865. During the Civil War, Smith was in charge of trying cases of treason against the Confederacy. He contributed occasionally to the *Metropolitan Record* of New York and worked as a professional lecturer in addition to his political duties.

Gloria Steinem (Contemporary)

Gloria Steinem studied political science at Smith College and later attended the University of Delhi and the University of Calcutta, where she became involved in local peace activism. When she returned to the United States she became active in the civil rights movement of the 60s and worked as a freelance writer, co-founding *New York Magazine* in 1968. During this time her political interests increasingly focused on feminist issues, and eventually she found it difficult to publish her work in the mainstream press. This led Steinem to found *Ms. Magazine*, a groundbreaking feminist publication controlled entirely by women, in 1972. Steinem remains a prominent feminist, well known for her activism as well as her writing. Her works include *Outrageous Acts and Everyday Rebellions* (1983), *Marilyn* (1986), *Revolution from Within: A Book of Self-Esteem* (1992) and *Moving Beyond Words* (1994).

Pam Stone (Contemporary)

Pam Stone is an actress and stand-up comic whose credits include the ABC sitcom *Coach*.

Harriet Beecher Stowe (1811–1896)

Harriet Beecher Stowe was born in Connecticut, the daughter of a minister, and married Calvin Ellis Stowe (a biblical scholar) in 1836. In the years that followed she bore seven children; she also became a prolific and controversial writer. Best known for the best-selling abolitionist novel *Uncle Tom's Cabin* (1852), Stowe was the author of a number of other novels in addition to many essays and short stories, frequently dealing with domestic issues, but treating politics and religion as well; the division between public and private roles that characterized her life finds an echo as a theme of much of her writing. Her works include *The Mayflower* (1843), *The Minister's Wooing* (1859), *The Pearl of Orr's Island* (1862), *My Wife and I* (1871), *Pink and White Tyranny* (1871), *Sam Lawson's Oldtown Fireside Stories* (1872), and *We and Our Neighbors* (1873).

Frank Sullivan (1892–1976)

Frank Sullivan, the well-known author of countless newspaper and magazine pieces, was born in Saratoga Springs, New York, where he began contributing to the *Saratogian* at an early age. After graduating from Cornell University, Sullivan was drafted into the army in 1917. After the war he moved to New York and began writing for the *Herald*, the *Evening Sun*, and the *World*; he also became a member of the notorious Algonquin Round Table, a group of writers who gathered at the Hotel Algonquin in the 1920s. The invention of a fictitious old woman he called Aunt Sarah Gallup, while covering the 1924 Democratic Convention, brought him national attention, and from that time on he was no longer a reporter, but a humor columnist. In 1926 he began contributing humorous pieces to *The New Yorker*, embarking on what would be a lifelong affiliation. Moving back to Saratoga Springs in 1935, Sullivan continued to contribute humorous essays to a wide range of publications for the rest of his life. Through the years his essays were collected and published in a number of volumes, among which are *The Life and Times of Martha Hepplethwaite* (1926), *Innocent Bystanding* (1928), *A Rock in Every Snowball* (1946), *The Night the Old Nostalgia Burned Down* (1953), and *Well, There's No Harm in Laughing* (1972).

Robert Sullivan (Contemporary)

Robert Sullivan is an Assistant Managing Editor at *LIFE* magazine and author of several books, including *Flight of the Reindeer: The True Story of Santa Claus and His Christmas Mission* and *Atlantis Found: The True Story of a Submerged Land, Yesterday and Today*. Before joining *LIFE* he was a writer and editor at *Sports Illustrated* focusing on athletic and natural-history topics. His feature writing and humor has appeared in *LIFE*, *Sports Illustrated*, *Time*, The *New York Times*, *Outside*, *New England Monthly* and other places. Sullivan has received a number of awards for his writing. He lives with his wife and daughter in Westchester County and New York City.

Judy Tenuta (Contemporary)

An improv artist and stand-up comic dubbed the "fun feminist of the 90s," Judy Tenuta has appeared on David Letterman's *Late Show* and starred in her own specials on HBO, Lifetime, and Showtime. She was the first stand-up to win the "Best Female Comedian" prize at the American Comedy Awards. An animated version of Tenuta has appeared on the Comedy Central show *Dr. Katz*. A self-proclaimed "Multi-Media Bondage Goddess," Tenuta has produced an album, *Buy This, Pigs*, and published *The Power of Judyism* (1991).

Henry David Thoreau (1817–1862)

Thoreau was raised in Concord, Massachusetts, where he lived for most of his life. Most famous for his second book, *Walden* (1854), a celebrated account of his two-year stay in a cabin on Walden Pond, Thoreau also wrote travel narratives about New England and eastern Canada, and political pamphlets like "Civil Disobedience," "Slavery in Massachusetts," and "A Plea for Captain John Brown." *The Writings of Henry David Thoreau*, in twenty volumes and including his *Journal*, appeared in 1906. Thoreau died of tuberculosis in Concord.

James Thurber (1896–1961)

James Thurber was born in Columbus, Ohio, and is most famous for his classic story "The Secret Life of Walter Mitty," which first appeared in *The New Yorker* and was made into a successful movie. His titles include *My Life and Hard Times*, *The Seal in the Bedroom*, *The Middle-Aged Man on the Flying Trapeze*, *Men, Women and Dogs*, and *My World—and Welcome to It.*

John Trumbull (1750–1831)

A famous satirist in his day and prominent member of the Connecticut Wits, John Trumbull was born in Connecticut and was remarkably precocious. He learned to read at two and passed the Yale entrance exam at the tender age of seven, although he had to wait six years before he was allowed to enter college. Trumbull received his B. A. from Yale in 1767, worked as a tutor on campus, and received a law degree. He passed the bar in 1773 and moved to Boston to work closely with John Adams. Trumbull was a prominent voice for educational reform. He wrote most of his satirical work in the 1770s and 1780s, when he published the poem *The Progress of Dulness*, the mock epic *M'Fingal*, and the *Anarchiad*. He also wrote a series of essays called the *Meddler* (1769–70) and the *Correspondent* (1770–73) with a fellow Connecticut Wit, Timothy Dwight. Trumbull died in Detroit in 1831. His *Satiric Poems* were reprinted in one volume in 1962.

Mark Twain (1835–1910)

The most celebrated American humorist needs little introduction. He was born Samuel Clemens in Missouri and at the age of twelve became a printer's apprentice for the *Missouri Courier.* He published his first piece of writing in a

Boston magazine at the age of sixteen and worked as a steamboat pilot on the Mississippi from 1857 until the outbreak of the Civil War. Clemens was appointed secretary for the Nevada territory during the war and started using the pseudonym Mark Twain for his humor pieces. He lived in California, where he worked as a journalist and lecturer; the letters he wrote for publication during his trip around the Mediterranean and the Holy Land became *The Innocents Abroad* (1869). His most famous books include *The Adventures of Tom Sawyer* (1876), *Life on the Mississippi* (1883), *The Adventures of Huckleberry Finn* (1885), and *Pudd'nhead Wilson* (1894). His *Autobiography* appeared in 1924.

John Updike (Contemporary)

John Updike grew up in Pennsylvania and attended Harvard University on a full scholarship. He graduated *summa cum laude* in 1954 and began his fruitful collaboration with *The New Yorker* in 1955. The magazine regularly publishes Updike's stories, poems, and literary criticism. His major fiction titles include *Rabbit, Run* (1960), *Couples* (1968), *Bech: A Book* (1970), *The Coup* (1978), *Rabbit Is Rich* (1980), *The Witches of Eastwick* (1984), and *Rabbit at Rest* (1990). Updike has also published a memoir, *Self-Consciousness* (1989), and a volume of essays, *Odd Jobs* (1991). He has received many honors for his work, including the National Book Award and the Pulitzer Prize. Updike lives in Massachusetts.

Judith Viorst (Contemporary)

Judith Viorst was raised in suburban New Jersey and received her B.A. from Rutgers University. She moved to Greenwich Village after college and published her first volume of poetry, *The Village Square*, in 1965. She has published numerous collections of verse since, including *It's Hard to Be Hip over Thirty* (1968), *Forever Fifty and Other Negotiations* (1989), and *Sad Underwear and Other Complications* (1995). She has referred to her poetry as "aggravation recollected in tranquility" and is well known for her humorous descriptions of women's anxieties. A popular author of children's books, Viorst also published *Alexander and the Terrible Horrible No Good Very Bad Day* (1972), among others. She works as a columnist for *Redbook* magazine and published a best-selling self-help book, *Necessary Losses*, in 1986. Viorst lives in Washington, D.C.

Jane Wagner (Contemporary)

Jane Wagner was born in Tennessee. She is most famous for her longtime collaboration with actress Lily Tomlin on the play *The Search for Signs of Intelligent Life in the Universe*, for which she received a Tony Award and a New York Drama Critics Circle special citation in 1986. Wagner also received two Emmy Awards, in 1975 and 1982, for comedy-variety specials starring Lily Tomlin. She wrote the screenplay for the movie *Moment by Moment* (1979), starring Tomlin and John Travolta. Their most successful collaboration has been without a doubt *The Search for Signs*; it ran in theaters for two years, was made into a movie, and was also published in book form.

Mae West (1893–1980)

Born in Brooklyn, Mae West began her career as a child star in vaudeville and went on to produce, write, and star in numerous plays, films and musical revues. Her first play, *Sex* (1926), led to her arrest for obscenity and corrupting the morals of youth. Throughout her life, the bawdy humor and frank sexuality that made her popular both as an actress and screenwriter also drew attacks from censors and moralists. Her works include *Diamond Lil* (1928), *The Constant Sinner* (1931), and *Go West Young Man* (1936).

Edith Wharton (1862–1937)

A best-selling author in her time and recognized modern classic in ours, Wharton was born Edith Newbold Jones in one of the oldest New York families. She married Teddy Wharton in 1885; the unhappy union would eventually end in a divorce that scandalized the bride's milieu. Her first story appeared in *Scribner's* in 1891 and she published her first book, *The Decoration of Houses*, in 1897. She suffered a nervous breakdown in 1898 and published her first collection of stories, *The Greater Inclination*, the following year. Wharton left America in 1911 and settled permanently in France. She organized relief efforts during World War I and received a medal from the French government for her relief work. Wharton is most famous for her short stories and her three major novels: the best-seller *The House of Mirth* (1905), *Ethan Frome* (1911), and the Pulitzer prize-winning *The Age of Innocence* (1920). The contrast between American and European customs, the tribal rituals of Old New York families and the inequality of women in a patriarchal society are recurrent themes in her fiction. She published her memoirs, *A Backward Glance*, in 1934.

Frances Miriam Whitcher (1812–1852)

Born Miriam Berry in 1812, this pioneer of women's humor lived for thirty-five years in Whitesboro, Oneida County, New York, in the popular inn run by her family. Her extreme shyness kept her from boarding school but she educated herself with the local circulating library. She also joined the Maeonian Circle, a society of men and women who met for music, reading, and conversation. Whitcher contributed to the circle a literary burlesque read one chapter at a time and serialized in a local newspaper under the title *The Widow Spriggins*, with only the name "Frank" as author. She went on to publish her first sketch with the Widow Bedott persona in the *Saturday Gazette* in 1846, and the vernacular heroine Aunt Maguire first appeared in *Godey's Lady's Book* magazine in 1848; she published most of her work anonymously. She married Benjamin Whitcher, an Episcopalian minister, in 1846 and died of tuberculosis six years later. Her fame spread posthumously with the publication of her major works, *The Widow Bedott Papers*, in 1855. In the words of her biographer, "For more than fifty years, Miriam Whitcher stood alone among women as creator of vernacular humor that mocked not women, per se, but the way women behaved." In the 1870s, David Locke adapted selections from *The Widow Bedott Papers* for the stage; Whitcher's heroine was played by a man in drag, Neil Burgess. Whitcher's humor influenced later female authors like Marietta Holley and Fanny Fern.

E. B. White (1899–1985)

Born Elwyn Brooks White in Mount Vernon, New York, E. B. White is one of the most important humorists and essayists in American literature. After graduating from Cornell University in 1921, White worked as a reporter for the United Press, the American Legion News Service, and later the *Seattle Times*. Upon his return to New York, he began contributing pieces to the then-young *New Yorker*; by 1927, he was working there full time and became one of its most prominent figures. In 1929 he published his first two books, *The Lady Is Cold* and (with James Thurber) *Is Sex Necessary*. As time went on his writing became more political; he treated the issues of the day with irony and skepticism. In 1941 he coedited *A Sub-Treasury of American Humor*, a work influential in broadening and redefining the very concept of American humor. Among White's numerous other works are *Every Day Is Saturday* (1934), *Stuart Little* (1945), *Here Is New York* (1949), *Charlotte's Web* (1952), and *The Points of My Compass* (1962).

N. P. Willis (1806–1867)

A journalist, poet, editor, and dramatist, Nathaniel P. Willis was born in Portland, Maine, and attended Yale University. He was the brother of another celebrated nineteenth-century American writer, Fanny Fern, and Edgar Allan Poe's friend. In his time he was the most famous American man of letters abroad after Washington Irving and James Fenimore Cooper. He contributed regularly to English periodicals and became a correspondent for the *Home Journal* during the Civil War. His essays and letters were collected in the volumes *Pencillings by the Way* (1844), *Rural Letters* (1849), and *Famous Persons and Places* (1854). He also produced short story collections and two plays, *Bianca Visconti* (1839), and *Tortesa, or the Usurer Matched* (1839). He influenced greatly the field of American journalism, and the pallbearers at his funeral included Oliver Wendell Holmes, Henry Dana, Longfellow, and Lowell.

Herman Wouk (Contemporary)

Wouk was born in the Bronx, wrote poetry from the age of eight, and graduated from Columbia University with a B.A. in Philosophy and Comparative Literature in 1934. During college he contributed humorous columns to the *Columbia Spectator*. He worked as a gag writer for radio comedians from 1934 to 1941. He joined the Navy in 1941, served in the Pacific from 1943 to 1945, and spent some of his time aboard the USS *Zane* reading and working on his first novel, *Aurora Dawn* (1947). Wouk went on to publish *The Caine Mutiny* (1951), for which he received the Pulitzer in 1952, *Marjorie Morningstar*, which was made into a movie, and the best-sellers *The Winds of War* and *War and Remembrance*, dramatized as mini-series on ABC. The subject of Wouk's second novel, *City Boy* (1948), from which the passage in this collection is excerpted, is his childhood memories as the son of immigrant Jewish parents in New York City.

Grateful Acknowledgment Is Made to the Following for Permission to Reprint Copyrighted Material

❧❧ ❧❧